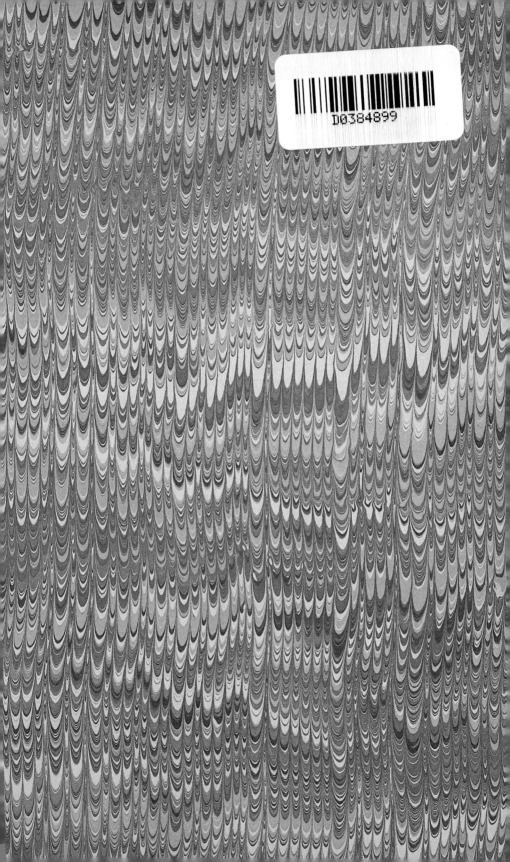

WILLIAM FAULKNER

WILLIAM FAULKNER

THE SOUND AND THE FURY

AS I LAY DYING

SANCTUARY

INTRUDER IN THE DUST

AMARANTH
P·R·E·S·S

The Sound and the Fury first published in the United States in 1929
by Jonathan Cape and Harrison Smith, Inc.
As I Lay Dying first published in the United States in 1930
by Jonathan Cape and Harrison Smith, Inc.
Sanctuary first published in the United States in 1931
by Jonathan Cape and Harrison Smith, Inc.
Intruder in the Dust first published in the United States in 1948
by Random House, Inc.

This edition first published in the United States in 1987
by arrangement with Random House, Inc. by

Octopus Books Limited
59 Grosvenor Street
London W1

Amaranth Press is the exclusive imprint of B. Dalton Booksellers,
Minneapolis, Minesota.

ISBN 0 8081 6313 2

Printed in the United States of America by R.R. Donnelley & Sons

CONTENTS

THE
SOUND AND
THE FURY

April Seventh, 1928

Through the fence, between the curling flower spaces, I could see them hitting. They were coming toward where the flag was and I went along the fence. Luster was hunting in the grass by the flower tree. They took the flag out, and they were hitting. Then they put the flag back and they went to the table, and he hit and the other hit. Then they went on, and I went along the fence. Luster came away from the flower tree and we went along the fence and they stopped and we stopped and I looked through the fence while Luster was hunting in the grass.

'Here, caddie.' He hit. They went away across the pasture. I held to the fence and watched them going away.

'Listen at you, now.' Luster said. 'Ain't you something, thirty-three years old, going on that way. After I done went all the way to town to buy you that cake. Hush up that moaning. Ain't you going to help me find that quarter so I can go to the show tonight.'

They were hitting little, across the pasture. I went back along the fence to where the flag was. It flapped on the bright grass and the trees.

'Come on.' Luster said. 'We done looked there. They ain't no more coming right now. Let's go down to the branch and find that quarter before them niggers finds it.'

It was red, flapping on the pasture. Then there was a bird slanting and tilting on it. Luster threw. The flag flapped on the bright grass and the trees. I held to the fence.

'Shut up that moaning.' Luster said. 'I can't make them come if they ain't coming, can I. If you don't hush up, mammy ain't going to have no birthday for you. If you don't hush, you know what I going to do. I going to eat that cake all up. Eat them candles, too. Eat all them thirty-three candles. Come on, let's go down to the branch. I got to find my quarter. Maybe we can find one of they balls. Here. Here they is. Way over yonder. See.' He came to the fence and pointed his arm. 'See them. They ain't coming back here no more. Come on.'

We went along the fence and came to the garden fence, where our shadows were. My shadow was higher than Luster's on the fence. We came to the broken place and went through it.

'Wait a minute.' Luster said. 'You snagged on that nail again. Can't you never crawl through here without snagging on that nail.'

Caddy uncaught me and we crawled through. Uncle Maury said to not let anybody see us, so we better stoop over, Caddy said. Stoop over, Benjy. Like this, see. We stooped over and crossed the garden, where the flowers rasped and rattled against us. The ground was hard. We climbed the fence, where the pigs were grunting and snuffing. I expect they're sorry because one of them got killed today, Caddy said. The ground was hard, churned and knotted.

Keep your hands in your pockets, Caddy said. Or they'll get froze. You don't want your hands froze on Christmas do you.

'It's too cold out there.' Versh said. 'You don't want to go out doors.'

'What is it now.' Mother said.

'He want to go out doors.' Versh said.

'Let him go.' Uncle Maury said.

'It's too cold.' Mother said. 'He'd better stay in. Benjamin. Stop that, now.'

'It won't hurt him.' Uncle Maury said.

'You, Benjamin.' Mother said. 'If you don't be good, you'll have to go to the kitchen.'

'Mammy say keep him out the kitchen today.' Versh said. 'She say she got all that cooking to get done.'

'Let him go, Caroline.' Uncle Maury said. 'You'll worry yourself sick over him.'

'I know it.' Mother said. 'It's a judgement on me. I sometimes wonder.'

'I know, I know.' Uncle Maury said. 'You must keep your strength up. I'll make you a toddy.'

'It just upsets me that much more.' Mother said. 'Don't you know it does.'

'You'll feel better.' Uncle Maury said. 'Wrap him up good boy, and take him out for a while.'

Uncle Maury went away. Versh went away.

'Please hush.' Mother said. 'We're trying to get you out as fast as we can. I don't want you to get sick.'

Versh put my overshoes and overcoat on and we took my cap and went out. Uncle Maury was putting the bottle away in the sideboard in the dining-room.

'Keep him out about half an hour, boy.' Uncle Maury said. 'Keep him in the yard, now.'

'Yes, sir.' Versh said. 'We don't never let him get off the place.' We went out doors. The sun was cold and bright.

'Where you heading for.' Versh said. 'You don't think you going to town, does you.' We went through the rattling leaves. The gate was cold. 'You better keep them hands in your pockets.' Versh said, 'You get them froze onto that gate, then what you do. Whyn't you wait for them in the house.' He put my hands into my pockets. I could hear him rattling in the leaves. I could smell the cold. The gate was cold.

'Here some hickeynuts. Whooey. Git up that tree. Look here at this squirl, Benjy.'

I couldn't feel the gate at all, but I could smell the bright cold.

'You better put them hands back in your pockets.'

Caddy was walking. Then she was running, her book-satchel swinging and jouncing behind her.

'Hello, Benjy.' Caddy said. She opened the gate and came in and stooped down. Caddy smelled like leaves. 'Did you come to meet me.' she said. 'Did you come to meet Caddy. What did you let him get his hands so cold for, Versh.'

'I told him to keep them in his pockets.' Versh said. 'Holding onto that ahun gate.'

'Did you come to meet Caddy.' she said, rubbing my hands. 'What is it. What are you trying to tell Caddy.' Caddy smelled like trees and like when she says we were asleep.

What are you moaning about, Luster said. You can watch them again when we get to the branch. Here. Here's you a jimson weed. He gave me the flower. We went through the fence, into the lot.

'What is it.' Caddy said. 'What are you trying to tell Caddy. Did they send him out, Versh.'

'Couldn't keep him in.' Versh said. 'He kept on until they let him go and he came right straight down here, looking through the gate.'

'What is it.' Caddy said. 'Did you think it would be Christmas when I came home from school. Is that what you thought. Christmas is the day after tomorrow. Santy Claus, Benjy. Santy Claus. Come on, let's run to the house and get warm.' She took my hand and we ran through the bright rustling leaves. We ran

up the steps and out of the bright cold, into the dark cold. Uncle
Maury was putting the bottle back in the sideboard. He called
Caddy. Caddy said,

'Take him in to the fire, Versh. Go with Versh.' she said. 'I'll
come in a minute.'

We went to the fire. Mother said,

'Is he cold, Versh.'

'Nome.' Versh said.

'Take his overcoat and overshoes off' Mother said. 'How many
times do I have to tell you not to bring him into the house with
his overshoes on.'

'Yessum.' Versh said. 'Hold still, now.' He took my overshoes
off and unbuttoned my coat. Caddy said,

'Wait, Versh. Can't he go out again, Mother. I want him to go
with me.'

'You'd better leave him here.' Uncle Maury said. 'He's been
out enough today.'

'I think you'd both better stay in.' Mother said. 'It's getting
colder, Dilsey says.'

'Oh, Mother.' Caddy said.

'Nonsense.' Uncle Maury said. 'She's been in school all day.
She needs the fresh air. Run along, Candace.'

'Let him go, Mother.' Caddy said. 'Please. You know he'll cry.'

'Then why did you mention it before him.' Mother said. 'Why
did you come in here. To give him some excuse to worry me
again. You've been out enough today. I think you'd better sit
down here and play with him.'

'Let them go, Caroline.' Uncle Maury said. 'A little cold won't
hurt them. Remember, you've got to keep your strength up.'

'I know.' Mother said. 'Nobody knows how I dread Christmas.
Nobody knows. I am not one of those women who can stand
things. I wish for Jason's and the children's sake I was stronger.'

'You must do the best you can and not let them worry you.'
Uncle Maury said. 'Run along, you two. But don't stay out long,
now. Your mother will worry.'

'Yes, sir.' Caddy said. 'Come on, Benjy. We're going out doors
again.' She buttoned my coat and we went towards the door.

'Are you going to take that baby out without his overshoes.'
Mother said. 'Do you want to make him sick, with the house full
of company.'

'I forgot.' Caddy said. 'I thought he had them on.'

We went back. 'You must think.' Mother said. *Hold still now*

Versh said. He put my overshoes on. 'Someday I'll be gone, and you'll have to think for him.' *Now stomp* Versh said. 'Come here and kiss Mother, Benjamin.'

Caddy took me to Mother's chair and Mother took my face in her hands and then she held me against her.

'My poor baby.' she said. She let me go. 'You and Versh take good care of him, honey.'

'Yessum.' Caddy said. We went out. Caddy said,

'You needn't go, Versh. I'll keep him for a while.'

'All right.' Versh said. 'I ain't going out in that cold for no fun.' He went on and we stopped in the hall and Caddy knelt and put her arms around me and her cold bright face against mine. She smelled like trees.

'You're not a poor baby. Are you. You've got your Caddy. Haven't you got your Caddy.'

Can't you shut up that moaning and slobbering, Luster said. Ain't you shamed of yourself, making all this racket. We passed the carriage house, where the carriage was. It had a new wheel.

'Git in, now, and set still until your maw come.' Dilsey said. She shoved me into the carriage. T.P. held the reins. ' 'Clare I don't see how come Jason won't get a new surrey.' Dilsey said. 'This thing going to fall to pieces under you all some day. Look at them wheels.'

Mother came out, pulling her veil down. She had some flowers.

'Where's Roskus.' she said.

'Roskus can't lift his arms, today.' Dilsey said. 'T.P. can drive all right.'

'I'm afraid to.' Mother said. 'It seems to me you all could furnish me with a driver for the carriage once a week. It's little enough I ask, Lord knows.'

'You know just as well as me that Roskus got the rheumatism too bad to do more than he have to, Miss Cahline.' Dilsey said. 'You come on and get in, now. T.P. can drive you just as good as Roskus.'

'I'm afraid to.' Mother said. 'With the baby.'

Dilsey went up the steps. 'You calling that thing a baby,' she said. She took Mother's arm. 'A man big as T.P. Come on, now, if you going.'

'I'm afraid to.' Mother said. They came down the steps and Dilsey helped Mother in. 'Perhaps it'll be the best thing, for all of us.' Mother said.

'Ain't you shamed, talking that way.' Dilsey said. 'Don't you know it'll take more than a eighteen year old nigger to make Queenie run away. She older than him and Benjy put together. And don't you start no projecking with Queenie, you hear me, T.P. If you don't drive to suit Miss Cahline, I going to put Roskus on you. He ain't too tied up to do that.'

'Yessum.' T.P. said.

'I just know something will happen.' Mother said. 'Stop, Benjamin.'

'Give him a flower to hold.' Dilsey said, 'That what he wanting.' She reached her hand in.

'No, no.' Mother said. 'You'll have them all scattered.'

'You hold them.' Dilsey said. 'I'll get him one out.' She gave me a flower and her hand went away.

'Go on now, 'fore Quentin see you and have to go too.' Dilsey said.

'Where is she.' Mother said.

'She down to the house playing with Luster.' Dilsey said. 'Go on, T.P. Drive that surrey like Roskus told you, now.'

'Yessum.' T.P. said. 'Hum up, Queenie.'

'Quentin.' Mother said. 'Don't let.'

'Course I is.' Dilsey said.

The carriage jolted and crunched on the drive. 'I'm afraid to go and leave Quentin.' Mother said. 'I'd better not go. T.P.' We went through the gate, where it didn't jolt any more. T.P. hit Queenie with the whip.

'You, T.P.' Mother said.

'Got to get her going.' T.P. said. 'Keep her wake up till we get back to the barn.'

'Turn around.' Mother said. 'I'm afraid to go and leave Quentin.'

'Can't turn here.' T.P. said. Then it was broader.

'Can't you turn here.' Mother said.

'All right.' T.P. said. We began to turn.

'You, T.P.' Mother said, clutching me.

'I got to turn around somehow.' T.P. said. 'Whoa, Queenie.' We stopped.

'You'll turn us over.' Mother said.

'What you want to do, then.' T.P. said.

'I'm afraid for you to try to turn around.' Mother said.

'Get up, Queenie.' T.P. said. We went on.

'I just know Dilsey will let something happen to Quentin while I'm gone.' Mother said. 'We must hurry back.'

'Hum up, there.' T.P. said. He hit Queenie with the whip.

'You, T.P.' Mother said, clutching me. I could hear Queenie's feet and the bright shapes went smooth and steady on both sides, the shadows of them flowing across Queenie's back. They went on like the bright tops of wheels. Then those on one side stopped at the tall white post where the soldier was. But on the other side they went smoothly and steady, but a little slower.

'What do you want.' Jason said. He had his hands in his pockets and a pencil behind his ear.

'We're going to the cemetery.' Mother said.

'All right.' Jason said. 'I don't aim to stop you, do I. Was that all you wanted with me, just to tell me that.'

'I know you won't come.' Mother said. 'I'd feel safer if you would.'

'Safe from what.' Jason said. 'Father and Quentin can't hurt you.'

Mother put her handkerchief under her veil. 'Stop it, Mother.' Jason said. 'Do you want to get that damn loony to bawling in the middle of the square. Drive on, T.P.'

'Hum up, Queenie.' T.P. said.

'It's a judgement on me.' Mother said. 'But I'll be gone too, soon.'

'Here.' Jason said.

'Whoa.' T.P. said. Jason said,

'Uncle Maury's drawing on you for fifty. What do you want to do about it.'

'Why ask me.' Mother said. 'I don't have any say so. I try not to worry you and Dilsey. I'll be gone soon, and then you.'

'Go on, T.P.' Jason said.

'Hum up, Queenie.' T.P. said. The shapes flowed on. The ones on the other side began again, bright and fast and smooth, like when Caddy says we are going to sleep.

Cry baby, Luster said. Ain't you shamed. We went through the barn. The stalls were all open. You ain't got no spotted pony to ride now, Luster said. The floor was dry and dusty. The roof was falling. The slanting holes were full of spinning yellow. What do you want to go that way for. You want to get your head knocked off with one of them balls.

'Keep your hands in your pockets.' Caddy said, 'Or they'll be froze. You don't want your hands froze on Christmas, do you.'

We went around the barn. The big cow and the little one were standing in the door, and we could hear prince and Queenie and

Fancy stomping inside the barn. 'If it wasn't so cold, we'd ride Fancy.' Caddy said, 'But it's too cold to hold on today.' Then we could see the branch, where the smoke was blowing. 'That's where they are killing the pig.' Caddy said. 'We can come back by there and see them.' We went down the hill.

'You want to carry the letter.' Caddy said. 'You can carry it.' She took the letter out of her pocket and put it in mine. 'It's a Christmas present.' Caddy said. 'Uncle Maury is going to surprise Mrs Patterson with it. We got to give it to her without letting anybody see it. Keep your hands in your pockets good, now.' We came to the branch.

'It's froze.' Caddy said, 'Look.' She broke the top of the water and held a piece of it against my face. 'Ice. That means how cold it is.' She helped me across and we went up the hill. 'We can't even tell Mother and Father. You know what I think it is. I think it's a surprise for Mother and Father and Mr Patterson both, because Mr Patterson sent you some candy. Do you remember when Mr Patterson sent you some candy last summer.'

There was a fence. The vine was dry, and the wind rattled in it.

'Only I don't see why Uncle Maury didn't send Versh.' Caddy said. 'Versh won't tell.' Mrs Patterson was looking out the window. 'You wait here.' Caddy said. 'Wait right here, now. I'll be back in a minute. Give me the letter.' She took the letter out of my pocket. 'Keep your hands in your pockets.' She climbed the fence with the letter in her hand and went through the brown, rattling flowers. Mrs Patterson came to the door and opened it and stood there.

Mr Patterson was chopping in the green flowers. He stopped chopping and looked at me. Mrs Patterson came across the garden, running. When I saw her eyes I began to cry. You idiot, Mrs Patterson said, I told him never to send you alone again. Give it to me. Quick. Mr Patterson came fast, with the hoe. Mrs Patterson leaned across the fence, reaching her hand. She was trying to climb the fence. Give it to me, she said, Give it to me. Mr Patterson climbed the fence. He took the letter. Mrs Patterson's dress was caught on the fence. I saw her eyes again and I ran down the hill.

'They ain't nothing over yonder but houses.' Luster said. 'We going down to the branch.'

They were washing down at the branch. One of them was singing. I could smell the clothes flapping, and the smoke blowing across the branch.

'You stay down here.' Luster said. 'You ain't got no business up yonder. Them folks hit you, sho.'

'What he want to do.'

'He don't know what he want to do.' Luster said. 'He think he want to go up yonder where they knocking that ball. You sit down here and play with your jimson weed. Look at them chillen playing in the branch, if you got to look at something. How come you can't behave yourself like folks.' I sat down on the bank, where they were washing, and the smoke blowing blue.

'Is you all seen anything of a quarter down here.' Luster said.

'What quarter.'

'The one I had here this morning.' Luster said. 'I lost it somewhere. It fell through this here hole in my pocket. If I don't find it I can't go to the show tonight.'

'Where'd you get a quarter, boy. Find it in white folks' pocket while they ain't looking.'

'Got it at the getting place.' Luster said. 'plenty more where that one come from. Only I got to find that one. Is you all found it yet.'

'I ain't studying no quarter. I got my own business to tend to.'

'Come on here.' Luster said. 'Help me look for it.'

'He wouldn't know a quarter if he was to see it, would he.'

'He can help look just the same.' Luster said. 'You all going to the show tonight.'

'Don't talk to me about no show. Time I get done over this here tub I be too tired to lift my hand to do nothing.'

'I bet you be there.' Luster said. 'I bet you was there last night. I bet you all be right there when that tent open.'

'Be enough niggers there without me. Was last night.'

'Nigger's money good as white folks, I reckon.'

'White folks gives nigger money because know first white man comes along with a band going to get it all back, so nigger can go to work for some more.'

'Ain't nobody going make you go to that show.'

'Ain't yet. Ain't thought of it, I reckon.'

'What you got against white folks.'

'Ain't got nothing against them. I goes my way and lets white folks go theirs. I ain't studying that show.'

'Got a man in it can play a tune on a saw. play it like a banjo.'

'You go last night.' Luster said. 'I going tonight. If I can find where I lost that quarter.'

'You going take him with you, I reckon.'

'Me.' Luster said. 'You reckon I be found anywhere with him, time he start bellering.'

'What does you do when he start bellering.'

'I whips him.' Luster said. He sat down and rolled up his overalls. They played in the branch.

'You all found any balls yet.' Luster said.

'Ain't you talking biggity. I bet you better not let your grand-mammy hear you talking like that.'

Luster got into the branch, where they were playing. He hunted in the water, along the bank.

'I had it when we was down here this morning.' Luster said.

'Where 'bouts you lose it.'

'Right out this here hole in my pocket.' Luster said. They hunted in the branch. Then they all stood up quick and stopped, then they splashed and fought in the branch. Luster got it and they squatted in the water, looking up the hill through the bushes.

'Where is they.' Luster said.

'Ain't in sight yet.'

Luster put it in his pocket. They came down the hill.

'Did a ball come down here.'

'It ought to be in the water. Didn't any of you boys see it or hear it.'

'Ain't heard nothing come down here.' Luster said. 'Heard something hit that tree up yonder. Don't know which way it went.'

They looked in the branch.

'Hell. Look along the branch. It came down here. I saw it.'

They looked along the branch. They went back up the hill.

'Have you got that ball.' the boy said.

'What I want with it.' Luster said. 'I ain't seen no ball.'

The boy got in the water. He went on. He turned and looked at Luster again. He went on down the branch.

The man said 'Caddie' up the hill. The boy got out of the water and went up the hill.

'Now, just listen at you.' Luster said. 'Hush up.'

'What he moaning about now.'

'Lawd knows.' Luster said. 'He just starts like that. He been at it all morning. Cause it his birthday, I reckon.'

'How old he.'

'He thirty-three.' Luster said. 'Thirty-three this morning.'

'You mean, he been three years old thirty years.'

'I going by what mammy say.' Luster said. 'I don't know. We

going to have thirty-three candles on a cake, anyway. Little cake. Won't hardly hold them. Hush up. Come on back here.' He came and caught my arm. 'You old loony.' he said.

'You want me to whip you.'

'I bet you will.'

'I is done it. Hush, now.' Luster said. 'Ain't I told you you can't go up there. They'll knock your head clean off with one of them balls. Come on, here.' He pulled me back. 'Sit down.' I sat down and he took off my shoes and rolled up my trousers. 'Now, git in that water and play and see can you stop that slobbering and moaning.'

I hushed and got in the water *and Roskus came and said to come to supper and Caddy said,*

It's not supper time yet. I'm not going.

She was wet. We were playing in the branch and Caddy squatted down and got her dress wet and Versh said,

'Your mommer going to whip you for getting your dress wet.'

'She's not going to do any such thing.' Caddy said.

'How do you know.' Quentin said.

'That's all right how I know.' Caddy said. 'How do you know.'

'She said she was.' Quentin said. 'Besides, I'm older than you.'

'I'm seven years old.' Caddy said, 'I guess I know.'

'I'm older than that.' Quentin said. 'I go to school. Don't I, Versh.'

'I'm going to school next year.' Caddy said, 'When it comes. Ain't I, Versh.'

'You know she whip you when you get your dress wet.' Versh said.

'It's not wet.' Caddy said. She stood up in the water and looked at her dress. 'I'll take it off,' she said. 'Then it'll dry.'

'I bet you won't.' Quentin said.

'I bet I will.' Caddy said.

'I bet you better not.' Quentin said.

Caddy came to Versh and me and turned her back.

'Unbutton it, Versh.' she said.

'Don't you do it, Versh.' Quentin said.

'Tain't none of my dress.' Versh said.

'You unbutton it, Versh.' Caddy said, 'Or I'll tell Dilsey what you did yesterday.' So Versh unbuttoned it.

'You just take your dress off.' Quentin said. Caddy took her dress off and threw it on the bank. Then she didn't have on anything but her bodice and drawers, and Quentin slapped her and she slipped and fell down in the water. When she got up she began to splash water on Quentin, and Quentin splashed water on Caddy. Some of it splashed on Versh and me and Versh picked me up and put me on the bank. He said he was going to tell on Caddy and Quentin, and then Quentin and Caddy began to splash water at Versh. He got behind a bush.

'I'm going to tell mammy on you all.' Versh said.

Quentin climbed up the bank and tried to catch Versh, but Versh ran away and Quentin couldn't. When Quentin came back Versh stopped and hollered that he was going to tell. Caddy told him that if he wouldn't tell, they'd let him come back. So Versh said he wouldn't, and they let him.

'Now I guess you're satisfied.' Quentin said, 'We'll both get whipped now.'

'I don't care.' Caddy said. 'I'll run away.'

'Yes you will.' Quentin said.

'I'll run away and nevercome back.' Caddy said. I began to cry. Caddy turned around and said 'Hush.' So I hushed. Then they played in the branch. Jason was playing too. He was by himself further down the branch. Versh came around the bush and lifted me down into the water again. Caddy was all wet and muddy behind, and I started to cry and she came and squatted in the water.

'Hush now.' she said. 'I'm not going to run away.' So I hushed. Caddy smelled like trees in the rain.

What is the matter with you, Luster said. Can't you get done with that moaning and play in the branch like folks.

Whyn't you take him on home. Didn't they told you not to take him off the place.

He still think they own this pasture, Luster said. Can't nobody see down here from the house, noways.

We can. And folks don't like to look at a loony. Tain't no luck in it.

Roskus came and said to come to supper and Caddy said it wasn't supper time yet.

'Yes 'tis.' Roskus said. 'Dilsey say for you all to come on to the house. Bring them on, Versh.' He went up the hill, where the cow was lowing.

'Maybe we'll be dry by the time we get to the house.' Quentin said.

'It was all your fault.' Caddy said. 'I hope we do get whipped.' She put her dress on and Versh buttoned it.

'They won't know you got wet.' Versh said. 'It don't show on you. Less me and Jason tells.'

'Are you going to tell, Jason.' Caddy said.

'Tell on who.' Jason said.

'He won't tell.' Quentin said. 'Will you, Jason.'

'I bet he does tell.' Caddy said. 'He'll tell Damuddy.'

'He can't tell her.' Quentin said. 'She's sick. If we walk slow it'll be too dark for them to see.'

'I don't care whether they see or not.' Caddy said. 'I'm going to tell, myself. You carry him up the hill, Versh.'

'Jason won't tell.' Quentin said. 'You remember that bow and arrow I made you, Jason.'

'It's broke now.' Jason said.

'Let him tell.' Caddy said. 'I don't give a cuss. Carry Maury up the hill, Versh.' Versh squatted and I got on his back.

See you all at the show tonight, Luster said. Come on, here. We got to find that quarter.

'If we go slow, it'll be dark when we get there.' Quentin said.

'I'm not going slow.' Caddy said. We went up the hill, but Quentin didn't come. He was down at the branch when we got to where we could smell the pigs. They were grunting and snuffing in the trough in the corner. Jason came behind us, with his hands in his pockets. Roskus was milking the cow in the barn door.

The cows came jumping out of the barn.

'Go on.' T.P. said. 'Holler again. I going to holler myself. Whooey.' Quentin kicked T.P. again. He kicked T.P. into the trough where the pigs ate and T.P. lay there. 'Hot dog.' T.P. said, 'Didn't he get me then. You see that white man kick me that time. Whooey.'

I wasn't crying, but I couldn't stop. I wasn't crying, but the ground wasn't still, and then I was crying. The ground kept sloping up and the cows ran up the hill T.P. tried to get up. He fell down again and the cows ran down the hill. Quentin held my arm and we went toward the barn. Then the barn wasn't there and we had to wait until it came back. I didn't see it come back. It came behind us and Quentin set me down in the trough where the cows ate. I held on to it. It was going away too, and I held to it. The cows ran down the hill again, across the door. I couldn't stop. Quentin and T.P. came up the hill, fighting. T.P. was falling down the hill and Quentin dragged him up the hill. Quentin hit T.P. I couldn't stop.

'Stand up.' Quentin said, 'You stay right here. Don't you go away until I get back.'

'Me and Benjy going back to the wedding.' T.P. said. 'Whooey.'

Quentin hit T.P. again. Then he began to thump T.P. against the wall. T.P. was laughing. Every time Quentin thumped him against the wall he tried to say Whooey, but he couldn't say it for laughing. I quit crying, but I couldn't stop. T.P. fell on me and the barn door went away. It went down the hill and T.P. was fighting by himself and he fell down again. He was still laughing, and I couldn't stop, and I tried to get up and fell down, and I couldn't stop. Versh said,

'You sho done it now. I'll declare if you ain't. Shut up that yelling.'

T.P. was still laughing. He flopped on the door and laughed. 'Whooey.' he said, 'Me and Benjy going back to the wedding. Sassprilluh.' T.P. said.

'Hush.' Versh said. 'Where you get it.'

'Out the cellar.' T.P. said. 'Whooey.'

'Hush up.' Versh said, 'Where'bouts in the cellar.'

'Anywhere.' T.P. said. He laughed some more. 'More'n a hundred bottles left. More'n a million. Look out, nigger, I going to holler.'

Quentin said, 'Lift him up.'

Versh lifted me up.

'Drink this, Benjy.' Quentin said. The glass was hot. 'Hush, now.' Quentin said. 'Drink it.'

'Sassprilluh.' T.P. said. 'Lemme drink it, Mr Quentin.'

'You shut your mouth.' Versh said, 'Mr Quentin wear you out.'

'Hold him, Versh.' Quentin said.

They held me. It was hot on my chin and on my shirt. 'Drink.' Quentin said. They held my head. It was hot inside me, and I began again. I was crying now, and something was happening inside me and I cried more, and they held me until it stopped happening. Then I hushed. It was still going around, and then the shapes began. 'Open the crib, Versh.' They were going slow. 'Spread those empty sacks on the floor.' They were going faster, almost fast enough. 'Now. pick up his feet.' They went on, smooth and bright. I could hear T.P. laughing. I went on with them, up the bright hill . . .

At the top of the hill Versh put me down. 'Come on here, Quentin.' he called, looking back down the hill. Quentin was still standing there by the branch. He was chunking into the shadows where the branch was.

'Let the old skizzard stay there.' Caddy said. She took my hand and we went on past the barn and through the gate. There was a frog on the brick walk, squatting in the middle of it. Caddy stepped over it and pulled me on.

'Come on, Maury.' she said. It still squatted there until Jason poked at it with his toe.

'He'll make a wart on you.' Versh said. The frog hopped away.

'Come on, Maury.' Caddy said.

'They got company tonight.' Versh said.

'How do you know.' Caddy said.

'With all them lights on.' Versh said, 'Light in every window.'

'I reckon we can turn all the lights on without company, if we want to.' Caddy said.

'I bet it's company.' Versh said. 'You all better go in the back and slip upstairs.'

'I don't care.' Caddy said. 'I'll walk right in the parlour where they are.'

'I bet your pappy whip you if you do.' Versh said.

'I don't care.' Caddy said. 'I'll walk right in the parlour. I'll walk right in the dining-room and eat supper.'

'Where you sit.' Versh said.

'I'd sit in Damuddy's chair.' Caddy said. 'She eats in bed.'

'I'm hungry.' Jason said. He passed us and ran on up the walk. He had his hands in his pockets and he fell down. Versh went and picked him up.

'If you keep them hands out your pockets, you could stay on your feet.' Versh said. 'You can't never get them out in time to catch yourself, fat as you is.'

Father was standing by the kitchen steps.

'Where's Quentin.' he said.

'He coming up the walk.' Versh said. Quentin was coming slow. His short was a white blur.

'Oh.' Father said. Light fell down the steps, on him.

'Caddy and Quentin threw water on each other.' Jason said. We waited.

'They did.' Father said. Quentin came, and Father said, 'You can eat supper in the kitchen tonight.' He stopped and took me up, and the light came tumbling down the steps on me too, and I could look down at Caddy and Jason and Quentin and Versh.

Father turned toward the steps. 'You must be quiet, though.' he said.

'Why must we be quiet, Father.' Caddy said. 'Have we got company.'

'Yes.' Father said.

'I told you they was company.' Versh said.

'You did not.' Caddy said, 'I was the one that said there was. I said I would'

'Hush.' Father said. They hushed and Father opened the door and we crossed the back porch and went in to the kitchen. Dilsey was there, and Father put me in the chair and closed the apron down and pushed it to the table, where supper was. It was steaming up.

'You mind Dilsey, now.' Father said. 'Don't let them make any more noise than they can help, Dilsey.'

'Yes, sir.' Dilsey said. Father went away.

'Remember to mind Dilsey, now.' he said behind us. I leaned my face over where the supper was. It steamed up on my face.

'Let them mind me tonight, Father.' Caddy said.

'I won't.' Jason said. 'I'm going to mind Dilsey.'

'You'll have to, if Father says so.' Caddy said. 'Let them mind me, Father.'

'I won't.' Jason said, 'I won't mind you.'

'Hush.' Father said. 'You all mind Caddy, then. When they are done, bring them up the back stairs, Dilsey.'

'Yes, sir.' Dilsey said.

'There.' Caddy said, 'Now I guess you'll mind me.'

'You all hush now.' Dilsey said. 'You got to be quiet tonight.'

'Why do we have to be quiet tonight.' Caddy whispered.

'Never you mind.' Dilsey said, 'You'll know in the Lawd's own time.' She brought my bowl. The steam from it came and tickled my face. 'Come here, Versh.' Dilsey said.

'When is the Lawd's own time, Dilsey.' Caddy said.

'It's Sunday.' Quentin said, 'Don't you know anything.'

'Shhhhhh.' Dilsey said. 'Didn't Mr Jason say for you all to be quiet. Eat your supper, now. Here, Versh. Git his spoon.' Versh's hand came with the spoon, into the bowl. The spoon came up to my mouth. The steam tickled into my mouth. Then we quit eating and we looked at each other and we were quiet, and then we heard it again and I began to cry.

'What was that.' Caddy said. She put her hand on my hand.

'That was Mother.' Quentin said. The spoon came up and I ate, then I cried again.

'Hush.' Caddy said. But I didn't hush and she came and put her arms around me. Dilsey went and closed both the doors and then we couldn't hear it.

'Hush, now.' Caddy said. I hushed and ate. Quentin wasn't eating, but Jason was.

'That was Mother.' Quentin said. He got up.

'You set right down.' Dilsey said. 'They got company in there, and you in them muddy clothes. You set down too, Caddy, and get done eating.'

'She was crying.' Quentin said.

'It was somebody singing.' Caddy said. 'Wasn't it, Dilsey.'

'You all eat your supper, now, like Mr Jason said.' Dilsey said. 'You'll know in the Lawd's own time.' Caddy went back to her chair.

'I told you it was a party.' she said.

Versh said, 'He done et all that.'

'Bring his bowl here.' Dilsey said. The bowl went away.

'Dilsey.' Caddy said, 'Quentin's not eating his supper. Hasn't he got to mind me.'

'Eat your supper, Quentin.' Dilsey said, 'You all got to get done and get out of my kitchen.'

'I don't want any more supper.' Quentin said.

'You've got to eat if I say you have.' Caddy said. 'Hasn't he, Dilsey.'

The bowl steamed up to my face, and Versh's hand dipped the spoon in it and the steam tickled into my mouth.

'I don't want any more.' Quentin said. 'How can they have a party when Damuddy's sick.'

'They'll have it downstairs.' Caddy said. 'She can come to the landing and see it. That's what I'm going to do when I get my nightie on.'

'Mother was crying.' Quentin said. 'Wasn't she crying, Dilsey.'

'Don't you come pestering at me, boy.' Dilsey said. 'I got to get supper for all them folks soon as you all get done eating.'

After a while even Jason was through eating, and he began to cry.

'Now you got to tune up.' Dilsey said.

'He does it every night since Damuddy was sick and he can't sleep with her.' Caddy said. 'Cry baby.'

'I'm going to tell on you.' Jason said.

He was crying. 'You've already told.' Caddy said. 'There's not anything else you can tell, now.'

'You all needs to go to bed.' Dilsey said. She came and lifted me down and wiped my face and hands with a warm cloth. 'Versh, can you get them up the back stairs quiet. You, Jason, shut up that crying.'

'It's too early to go to bed now.' Caddy said. 'We don't ever have to go to bed this early.'

'You is tonight.' Dilsey said. 'Your pa say for you to come right on upstairs when you et supper. You heard him.'

'He said to mind me.' Caddy said.

'I'm not going to mind you.' Jason said.

'You have to.' Caddy said. 'Come on, now. You have to do like I say.'

'Make them be quiet, Versh.' Dilsey said. 'You all going to be quiet, ain't you.'

'What do we have to be so quiet for, tonight.' Caddy said.

'Your mommer ain't feeling well.' Dilsey said. 'You all go on with Versh, now.'

'I told you Mother was crying.' Quentin said. Versh took me up and opened the door onto the back porch. We went out and Versh closed the door black. I could smell Versh and feel him. 'You all be quiet, now. We're not going upstairs yet. Mr Jason said for you to come right upstairs. He said to mind me. I'm not going to mind you. But he said for all of us to. Didn't he, Quentin.' I could feel Versh's head. I could hear us. 'Didn't he, Versh. Yes, that's right. Then I say for us to go out doors a while. Come on.' Versh opened the door and we went out.

We went down the steps.

'I expect we'd better go down to Versh's house, so we'll be quiet.' Caddy said. Versh put me down and Caddy took my hand and we went down the brick walk.

'Come on.' Caddy said, 'That frog's gone. He's hopped way over to the garden, by now. Maybe we'll see another one.' Roskus came with the milk buckets. He went on. Quentin wasn't coming with us. He was sitting on the kitchen steps. We went down to Versh's house. I liked to smell Versh's house. *There was a fire in it and T.P. squatting in his shirt tail in front of it, chunking it into a blaze.*

Then I got up and T.P. dressed me and we went to the kitchen and ate. Dilsey was singing and I began to cry and she stopped.

'Keep him away from the house, now.' Dilsey said.

'We can't go that way.' T.P. said.

We played in the branch.

'We can't go around yonder.' T.P. said. 'Don't you know mammy say we can't.'

Dilsey was singing in the kitchen and I began to cry.

'Hush.' T.P. said. 'Come on. Let's go down to the barn.'

Roskus was milking at the barn. He was milking with one hand, and groaning. Some birds sat on the barn door and watched him. One of them came down and ate with the cows. I watched Roskus milk while T.P. was feeding Queenie and Prince. The calf was in the pig pen. It nuzzled at the wire, bawling.

'T.P.' Roskus said. T.P. said Sir, in the barn. Fancy held her head over the door, because T.P. hadn't fed her yet. 'Gid done there.' Roskus said. 'You got to do this milking. I can't use my right hand no more.'

T.P. came and milked.

'Whyn't you get the doctor.' T.P. said.

'Doctor can't do no good.' Roskus said. 'Not on this place.'

'What wrong with this place.' T.P. said.

'Tain't no luck on this place.' Roskus said. 'Turn that calf in if you done.'

Tain't no luck on this place, Roskus said. The fire rose and fell behind him and Versh, sliding on his and Versh's face. Dilsey finished putting me to bed. The bed smelled like T.P. I liked it.

'What you know about it.' Dilsey said. 'What trance you been in.'

'Don't need no trance.' Roskus said. 'Ain't the sign of it laying right there on that bed. Ain't the sign of it been here for folks to see fifteen years now.'

'S'pose it is.' Dilsey said. 'It ain't hurt none of you and yourn, is it. Versh working and Frony married off your hands and T.P. getting big enough to take your place when rheumatism finish getting you.'

'They been two, now,' Roskus said. 'Going to be one more. I seen the sign, and you is too.'

'I heard a squinch owl that night.' T.P. said. 'Dan wouldn't come and get his supper, neither. Wouldn't come no closer than the barn. Begun howling right after dark. Versh heard him.'

'Going to be more than one more.' Dilsey said. 'Show me the man what ain't going to die, bless Jesus.'

'Dying ain't all.' Roskus said.

'I knows what you thinking.' Dilsey said. 'And they ain't going to be no luck in saying that name, lessen you going to set up with him while he cries.'

'They ain't no luck on this place.' Roskus said. 'I seen it at first but when they changed his name I knowed it.'

'Hush your mouth.' Dilsey said. She pulled the covers up. It smelled like T.P. 'You all shut up now, till he get to sleep.'

'I seen the sign.' Roskus said.

'Sign T.P. got to do all your work for you.' Dilsey said. *Take him and Quentin down to the house and let them play with Luster, where Frony can watch them, T.P., and go and help your pa.*

We finished eating. T.P. took Quentin up and we went down to T.P.'s house. Luster was playing in the dirt. T.P. put Quentin down and she played in the dirt too. Luster had some spools and he and Quentin fought and Quentin had the spools. Luster cried and Frony came and gave Luster a tincan to play with, and then I had the spools and Quentin fought me and I cried.

'Hush.' Frony said, 'Ain't you shamed of yourself. Taking a baby's play pretty.' She took the spools from me and gave them back to Quentin.

'Hush, now.' Frony said, 'Hush, I tell you.'

'Hush up.' Frony said. 'You needs whipping, that's what you needs.' She took Luster and Quentin up. 'Come on here.' she said. We went to the barn. T.P. was milking the cow. Roskus was sitting on the box.

'What's the matter with him now.' Roskus said.

'You have to keep him down here.' Frony said. 'He fighting these babies again. Taking they play things. Stay here with T.P. now, and see can you hush a while.'

'Clean that udder good now.' Roskus said. 'You milked that young cow dry last winter. If you milk this one dry, they ain't going to be no more milk.'

Dilsey was singing.

'Not around yonder.' T.P. said. 'Don't you know mammy say you can't go around there.'

They were singing.

'Come on.' T.P. said. 'Let's go play with Quentin and Luster. Come on.'

Quentin and Luster were playing in the dirt in front of T.P.'s house. There was a fire in the house, rising and falling, with Roskus sitting black against it.

'That's three, thank the Lawd.' Roskus said. 'I told you two years ago. They ain't no luck on this place.'

'Whyn't you get out, then.' Dilsey said. She was undressing me. 'Your bad luck talk got them Memphis notions into Versh. That ought to satisfy you.'

'If that all the bad luck Versh have.' Roskus said.

Frony came in.

'You all done.' Dilsey said.

'T.P. finishing up.' Frony said. 'Miss Cahline want you to put Quentin to bed.'

'I'm coming just as fast as I can.' Dilsey said. 'She ought to know by this time I ain't got no wings.'

'That's what I tell you.' Roskus said. 'They ain't no luck going be on no place where one of they own chillens' name ain't never spoke.'

'Hush.' Dilsey said. 'Do you want to get him started.'

'Raising a child not to know its own mammy's name.' Roskus said.

'Don't you bother your head about her.' Dilsey said. 'I raised all of them and I reckon I can raise one more. Hush now. Let him get to sleep if he will.'

'Saying a name.' Frony said. 'He don't know nobody's name.'

'You just say it and see if he don't.' Dilsey said. 'You say it to him while he sleeping and I bet he hear you.'

'He know lot more than folks thinks.' Roskus said. 'He knowed they time was coming, like that pointer done. He could tell you when hisn coming, if he could talk. Or yours. Or mine.'

'You take Luster outen that bed, mammy.' Frony said. 'That boy conjure him.'

'Hush your mouth.' Dilsey said, 'Ain't you got no better sense than that. What you want to listen to Roskus for, anyway. Get in, Benjy.'

Dilsey pushed me and I got in the bed, where Luster already was. He was asleep. Dilsey took a long piece of wood and laid it between Luster and me. 'Stay on your side now.' Dilsey said. 'Luster little, and you don't want to hurt him.'

You can't go yet, T.P. said. Wait.

We looked around the corner of the house and watched the carriages go away.

'Now.' T.P. said. He took Quentin up and we ran down to the corner of the fence and watched them pass. 'There he go,' T.P. said. 'See that one with the glass in it. Look at him. He laying in there. See him.'

Come on, Luster said, I going to take this here ball down home, where

I won't lose it. Naw, sir, you can't have it. If them men sees you with it, they'll say you stole it. Hush up, now. You can't have it. What business you got with it. You can't play no ball.

Frony and T.P. were playing in the dirt by the door. T.P. had lightning bugs in a bottle.

'How did you all get back out.' Frony said.

'We've got company.' Caddy said. 'Father said for us to mind me tonight. I expect you and T.P. will have to mind me too.'

'I'm not going to mind you.' Jason said. 'Frony and T.P. don't have to either.'

'They will if I say so.' Caddy said. 'Maybe I won't say for them to.'

'T.P. don't mind nobody.' Frony said. 'Is they started the funeral yet.'

'What's a funeral.' Jason said.

'Didn't mammy tell you not to tell them.' Versh said.

'Where they moans.' Frony said. 'They moaned two days on Sis Beulah Clay.'

They moaned at Dilsey's house. Dilsey was moaning. When Dilsey moaned Luster said, Hush, and we hushed, and then I began to cry and Blue howled under the kitchen steps. Then Dilsey stopped and we stopped.

'Oh.' Caddy said, 'That's niggers. White folks don't have funerals.'

'Mammy said us not to tell them, Frony.' Versh said.

'Tell them what.' Caddy said.

Dilsey moaned, and when it got to the place I began to cry and Blue howled under the steps. Luster, Frony said in the window, Take them down to the barn. I can't get no cooking done with all that racket. That hound too. Get them outen here.

I ain't going down there, Luster said. I might meet pappy down there. I seen him last night, waving his arms in the barn.

'I like to know why not.' Frony said. 'White folks dies too. Your grandmammy dead as any nigger can get, I reckon.'

'Dogs are dead.' Caddy said, 'And when Nancy fell in the ditch and Roskus shot her and the buzzards came and undressed her.'

The bones rounded out of the ditch, where the dark vines were in the black ditch, into the moonlight, like some of the shapes had stopped. Then they all stopped and it was dark, and when I stopped to start again I could hear Mother, and feet walking fast away, and I could smell it. Then the room came, but my eyes went shut. I didn't stop. I could smell it. T.P. unpinned the bedclothes.

'Hush.' he said, 'Shhhhhh.'

But I could smell it. T.P. pulled me up and he put on my clothes fast.

'Hush, Benjy.' he said. 'We going down to our house. You want to go down to our house, where Frony is. Hush. Shhhhh.'

He laced my shoes and put my cap on and we went out. There was a light in the hall. Across the hall we could hear Mother.

'Shhhhhh, Benjy.' T.P. said, 'We'll be out in a minute.'

A door opened and I could smell it more than ever, and a head came out. It wasn't Father. Father was sick there.

'Can you take him out of the house.'

'That's where we going.' T.P. said. Dilsey came up the stairs.

'Hush.' she said, 'Hush. Take him down home, T.P. Frony fixing him a bed. You all look after him, now. Hush, Benjy. Go on with T.P.'

She went where we could hear Mother.

'Better keep him there.' It wasn't Father. He shut the door, but I could still smell it.

We went downstairs. The stairs went down into the dark and T.P. took my hand, and we went out the door, out of the dark. Dan was sitting in the backyard, howling.

'He smell it.' T.P. said. 'Is that the way you found it out.'

We went down the steps, where our shadows were.

'I forgot your coat.' T.P. said. 'You ought to had it. But I ain't going back.'

Dan howled.

'Hush now.' T.P. said. Our shadows moved, but Dan's shadow didn't move except to howl when he did.

'I can't take you down home, bellering like you is.' T.P. said. 'You was bad enough before you got that bullfrog voice. Come on.'

We went along the brick walk, with our shadows. The pig pen smelled like pigs. The cow stood in the lot, chewing at us. Dan howled.

'You going to wake the whole town up.' T.P. said. 'Can't you hush.'

We saw Fancy, eating by the branch. The moon shone on the water when we got there.

'Naw, sir.' T.P. said, 'This too close. We can't stop here. Come on. Now, just look at you. Got your whole leg wet. Come on, here.' Dan howled.

The ditch came up out of the buzzing grass. The bones rounded out of the black vines.

'Now.' T.P. said. 'Beller your head off if you want to. You got the whole night and a twenty-acre pasture to beller in.'

T.P. lay down in the ditch and I sat down, watching the bones where the buzzards ate Nancy, flapping black and slow and heavy out of the ditch.

I had it when we was down here before, Luster said. I showed it to you. Didn't you see it. I took it out of my pocket right here and showed it to you.

'Do you think buzzards are going to undress Damuddy.' Caddy said. 'You're crazy.'

'You're a skizzard.' Jason said. He began to cry.

'You're a knobnot.' Caddy said. Jason cried. His hands were in his pockets.

'Jason going to be rich man.' Versh said. 'He holding his money all the time.'

Jason cried.

'Now you've got him started.' Caddy said. 'Hush up, Jason. How can buzzards get in where Damuddy is. Father wouldn't let them. Would you let a buzzard undress you. Hush up, now.'

Jason hushed. 'Frony said it was a funeral.' he said.

'Well it's not.' Caddy said. 'It's a party. Frony don't know anything about it. He wants your lightning bugs, T.P. Let him hold it a while.'

T.P. gave me the bottle of lightning bugs.

'I bet if we go around to the parlour window we can see something.' Caddy said. 'Then you'll believe me.'

'I already knows.' Frony said. 'I don't need to see.'

'You better hush your mouth, Frony.' Versh said. 'Mammy going whip you.'

'What is it.' Caddy said.

'I knows what I knows.' Frony said.

'Come on.' Caddy said, 'Let's go around to the front.'

We started to go.

'T.P. wants his lightning bugs.' Frony said.

'Let him hold it a while longer, T.P.' Caddy said. 'We'll bring it back.'

'You all never caught them.' Frony said.

'If I say you and T.P. can come too, will you let him hold it.' Caddy said.

'Ain't nobody said me and T.P. got to mind you.' Frony said.

'If I say you don't have to, will you let him hold it.' Caddy said.

'All right.' Frony said. 'Let him hold it, T.P. We going to watch them moaning.'

'They ain't moaning.' Caddy said. 'I tell you it's a party. Are they moaning, Versh.'

'We ain't going to know what they doing, standing here.' Versh said.

'Come on.' Caddy said. 'Frony and T.P. don't have to mind me. But the rest of us do. You better carry him, Versh. It's getting dark.'

Versh took me up and we went on around the kitchen.

When we looked around the corner we could see the lights coming up the drive. T.P. went back to the cellar door and opened it.

You know what's down there, T.P. said. Soda water. I seen Mr Jason come up with both hands full of them. Wait here a minute.

T.P. went and looked in the kitchen door. Dilsey said, What are you peeping in here for. Where's Benjy.

He out here, T.P. said.

Go on and watch him, Dilsey said. Keep him out the house now.

Yessum, T.P. said. Is they started yet.

You go on and keep that boy out of sight, Dilsey said. I got all I can tend to.

A snake crawled out from under the house. Jason said he wasn't afraid of snakes and Caddy said he was but she wasn't and Versh said they both were and Caddy said to be quiet, like father said.

You ain't got to start bellering now, T.P. said. You want some this sassprilluh.

It tickled my nose and eyes.

If you ain't going to drink it, let me get to it, T.P. said. All right, here 'tis. We better get another bottle while ain't nobody bothering us. You be quiet, now.

We stopped under the tree by the parlour window. Versh set me down in the wet grass. It was cold. There were lights in all the windows.

'That's where Damuddy is.' Caddy said. 'She's sick every day now. When she gets well we're going to have a picnic.'

'I knows what I knows.' Frony said.

The trees were buzzing, and the grass.

'The one next to it is where we have the measles.' Caddy said.

'Where do you and T.P. have the measles, Frony.'

'Has them just wherever we is, I reckon.' Frony said.

'They haven't started yet.' Caddy said.

They getting ready to start, T.P. said. You stand right here now while I get that box so we can see in the window. Here, les finish drinking this here sassprilluh. It make me feel just like a squinch owl inside.

We drank the sassprilluh and T.P. pushed the bottle through the lattice, under the house, and went away. I could hear them in the parlour and I clawed my hands against the wall. T.P. dragged the box. He fell down, and he began to laugh. He lay there, laughing into the grass. He got up and dragged the box under the window, trying not to laugh.

'I skeered I going to holler.' T.P. said. 'Git on the box and see is they started.'

'They haven't started because the band hasn't come yet.' Caddy said.

'They ain't going to have no band.' Frony said.

'How do you know.' Caddy said.

'I knows what I knows.' Frony said.

'You don't know anything.' Caddy said. She went to the tree. 'Push me up, Versh.'

'Your paw told you to stay out that tree.' Versh said.

'That was a long time ago.' Caddy said. 'I expect he's forgotten about it. Besides, he said to mind me tonight. Didn't he say to mind me tonight.'

'I'm not going to mind you.' Jason said. 'Frony and T.P. are not going to either.'

'Push me up, Versh.' Caddy said.

'All right.' Versh said. 'You the one going to get whipped. I ain't.' He went and pushed Caddy up into the tree to the first limb. We watched the muddy bottom of her drawers. Then we couldn't see her. We could hear the tree thrashing.

'Mr Jason said if you break that tree he whip you.' Versh said.

'I'm going to tell on her too.' Jason said.

The tree quit thrashing. We looked up into the still branches.

'What you seeing.' Frony whispered.

I saw them. Then I saw Caddy, with flowers in her hair, and a long veil like shining wind. Caddy. Caddy.

'Hush.' T.P. said. 'They going to hear you. Get down quick.' He pulled me. Caddy. I clawed my hands against the wall Caddy. T.P. pulled me.

'Hush.' he said, 'Hush. Come on here quick.' He pulled me

on. Caddy 'Hush up, Benjy. You want them to hear you. Come on, les drink some more sassprilluh, then we can come back if you hush. We better get one more bottle or we both be hollering. We can say Dan drunk it. Mr Quentin always saying he so smart, we can say he sassprilluh dog, too.'

The moonlight came down the cellar stairs. We drank some more sassprilluh.

'You know what I wish.' T.P. said. 'I wish a bear would walk in that cellar door. You know what I do. I walk right up to him and spit in he eye. Gimme that bottle to stop my mouth before I holler.'

T.P. fell down. He began to laugh, and the cellar door and the moonlight jumped away and something hit me.

'Hush up.' T.P. said, trying not to laugh, 'Lawd, they'll all hear us. Get up.' T.P. said, 'Get up, Benjy quick.' He was thrashing about and laughing and I tried to get up. The cellar steps ran up the hill in the moonlight and T.P. fell up the hill, into the moonlight, and I ran against the fence and T.P. ran behind me saying 'Hush up hush up.' Then he fell into the flowers, and I ran into the box. But when I tried to climb onto it it jumped away and hit me on the back of the head and my throat made a sound. It made the sound again and I stopped trying to get up, and it made the sound again and I began to cry. But my throat kept on making the sound while T.P. was pulling me. It kept on making it and I couldn't tell if I was crying or not, and T.P. fell down on top of me, laughing, and it kept on making the sound and Quentin kicked T.P. and Caddy put her arms around me, and her shining veil, and I couldn't smell trees any more and I began to cry.

Benjy, Caddy said, Benjy. She put her arms around me again, but I went away. 'What is it, Benjy.' she said, 'Is it this hat.' She took her hat off and came again, and I went away.

'Benjy.' she said, 'What is it, Benjy. What has Caddy done.'

'He don't like that prissy dress.' Jason said. 'You think you're grown up, don't you. You think you're better than anybody else, don't you. prissy.'

'You shut your mouth.' Caddy said, 'You dirty little beast. Benjy.'

'Just because you are fourteen, you think you're grown up, don't you.' Jason said. 'You think you're something. Don't you.'

'Hush, Benjy.' Caddy said. 'You'll disturb Mother. Hush.'

But I didn't hush, and when she went away I followed, and she stopped on the stairs and waited and I stopped too.

'What is it, Benjy.' Caddy said, 'Tell Caddy. She'll do it. Try.'

'Candace.' Mother said.

'Yessum.' Caddy said.

'Why are you teasing him.' Mother said. 'Bring him here.'

We went to Mother's room, where she was lying with the sickness on a cloth on her head.

'What is the matter now.' Mother said. 'Benjamin.'

'Benjy.' Caddy said. She came again, but I went away.

'You must have done something to him.' Mother said. 'Why won't you let him alone, so I can have some peace. Give him the box and please go on and let him alone.'

Caddy got the box and set it on the floor and opened it. It was full of stars. When I was still, they were still. When I moved, they glinted and sparkled. I hushed.

Then I heard Caddy walking and I began again.

'Benjamin.' Mother said, 'Come here.' I went to the door. 'You Benjamin.' Mother said.

'What is it now.' Father said, 'Where are you going.'

'Take him downstairs and get someone to watch him, Jason.' Mother said. 'You know I'm ill, yet you'

Father shut the door behind us.

'T.P.' he said.

'Sir.' T.P. said downstairs.

'Benjy's coming down.' Father said. 'Go with T.P.'

I went to the bathroom door. I could hear the water.

'Benjy.' T.P. said downstairs.

I could hear the water. I listened to it.

'Benjy.' T.P. said downstairs.

I listened to the water.

I couldn't hear the water, and Caddy opened the door.

'Why, Benjy.' she said. She looked at me and I went and she put her arms around me. 'Did you find Caddy again.' she said. 'Did you think Caddy had run away.' Caddy smelled like trees.

We went to Caddy's room. She sat down at the mirror. She stopped her hands and looked at me.

'Why, Benjy. What is it.' she said. 'You mustn't cry. Caddy's not going away. See here.' she said. She took up the bottle and took the stopper out and held it to my nose. 'Sweet. Smell. Good.'

I went away and I didn't hush, and she held the bottle in her hand, looking at me.

'Oh.' she said. She put the bottle down and came and put her

THE SOUND AND THE FURY

arms around me. 'So that was it. And you were trying to tell Caddy and you couldn't tell her. You wanted to, but you couldn't, could you. Of course Caddy won't. Of course Caddy won't. Just wait till I dress.'

Caddy dressed and took up the bottle again and we went down to the kitchen.

'Dilsey.' Caddy said, 'Benjy's got a present for you.' She stooped down and put the bottle in my hand. 'Hold it out to Dilsey, now.' Caddy held my hand out and Dilsey took the bottle.

'Well I'll declare.' Dilsey said, 'If my baby ain't give Dilsey a bottle of perfume. Just look here, Roskus.'

Caddy smelled like trees. 'We don't like perfume ourselves.' Caddy said.

She smelled like trees.

'Come on, now.' Dilsey said, 'You too big to sleep with folks. You a big boy now. Thirteen years old. Big enough to sleep by yourself in Uncle Maury's room.' Dilsey said.

Uncle Maury was sick. His eye was sick, and his mouth. Versh took his supper up to him on the tray.

'Maury says he's going to shoot the scoundrel.' Father said. 'I told him he'd better not mention it to Patterson beforehand.' He drank.

'Jason.' Mother said.

'Shoot who, Father.' Quentin said. 'What's Uncle Maury going to shoot him for.'

'Because he couldn't take a little joke.' Father said.

'Jason.' Mother said, 'How can you. You'd sit right there and see Maury shot down in ambush, and laugh.'

'Then Maury'd better stay out of ambush.' Father said.

'Shoot who, Father.' Quentin said, 'Who's Uncle Maury going to shoot.'

'Nobody.' Father said. 'I don't own a pistol.'

Mother began to cry. 'If you begrudge Maury your food, why aren't you man enough to say so to his face. To ridicule him before the children, behind his back.'

'Of course I don't.' Father said, 'I admire Maury. He is invaluable to my own sense of racial superiority. I wouldn't swap Maury for a matched team. And do you know why, Quentin.'

'No, sir.' Quentin said.

'*Et ego in arcadia* I have forgotten the latin for hay.' Father said. 'There, there.' he said, 'I was just joking.' He drank and set the glass down and went and put his hand on Mother's shoulder.

'It's no joke.' Mother said. 'My people are every bit as well born as yours. Just because Maury's health is bad.'

'Of course.' Father said. 'Bad health is the primary reason for all life. Created by disease, within putrefaction, into decay. Versh.'

'Sir.' Versh said behind my chair.

'Take the decanter and fill it.'

'And tell Dilsey to come and take Benjamin up to bed.' Mother said.

'You a big boy.' Dilsey said, 'Caddy tired sleeping with you. Hush now, so you can go to sleep.' The room went away, but I didn't hush, and the room came back and Dilsey came and sat on the bed, looking at me.

'Ain't you going to be a good boy and hush.' Dilsey said. 'You ain't, is you. See you can wait a minute, then.'

She went away. There wasn't anything in the door. Then Caddy was in it.

'Hush.' Caddy said. 'I'm coming.'

I hushed and Dilsey turned back the spread and Caddy got in between the spread and the blanket. She didn't take off her bathrobe.

'Now.' she said, 'Here I am.' Dilsey came with a blanket and spread it over her and tucked it around her.

'He be gone in a minute.' Dilsey said. 'I leave the light on in your room.'

'All right.' Caddy said. She snuggled her head beside mine on the pillow. 'Good night, Dilsey.'

'Good night, honey.' Dilsey said. The room went black. *Caddy smelled like trees.*

We looked up into the tree where she was.

'What she seeing, Versh.' Frony whispered.

'Shhhhhhh.' Caddy said in the tree. Dilsey said,

'You come on here.' She came around the corner of the house. 'Whyn't you all go on upstairs, like your paw said, stead of slipping out behind my back. Where's Caddy and Quentin.'

'I told her not to climb up that tree.' Jason said. 'I'm going to tell on her.'

'Who in what tree.' Dilsey said. She came and looked up into the tree. 'Caddy.' Dilsey said. The branches began to shake again.

'You, Satan.' Dilsey said. 'Come down from there.'

'Hush.' Caddy said, 'Don't you know Father said to be quiet.'

Her legs came in sight and Dilsey reached up and lifted her out of the tree.

'Ain't you got any better sense than to let them come around here.' Dilsey said.

'I couldn't do nothing with her.' Versh said.

'What you all doing here.' Dilsey said. 'Who told you to come up to the house.'

'She did.' Frony said. 'She told us to come.'

'Who told you you got to do what she say.' Dilsey said. 'Get on home, now.' Frony and T.P. went on. We couldn't see them when they were still going away.

'Out here in the middle of the night.' Dilsey said. She took me up and we went to the kitchen.

'Slipping out behind my back.' Dilsey said. 'When you knowed it's past your bedtime.'

'Shhhh, Dilsey.' Caddy said. 'Don't talk so loud. We've got to be quiet.'

'You hush your mouth and get quiet then.' Dilsey said. 'Where's Quentin.'

'Quentin's mad because he had to mind me tonight.' Caddy said. 'He's still got T.P.'s bottle of lightning bugs.'

'I reckon T.P. can get along without it.' Dilsey said. 'You go and find Quentin, Versh. Roskus say he seen him going towards the barn.' Versh went on. We couldn't see him.

'They're not doing anything in there.' Caddy said. 'Just sitting in chairs and looking.'

'They don't need no help from you all to do that.' Dilsey said. We went around the kitchen.

Where you want to go now, Luster said. You going back to watch them knocking ball again. We done looked for it over there. Here. Wait a minute. You wait right here while I go back and get that ball. I done thought of something.

The kitchen was dark. The trees were black on the sky. Dan came waddling out from under the steps and chewed my ankle. I went around the kitchen, where the moon was. Dan came scuffling along, into the moon.

'Benjy.' T.P. said in the house.

The flower tree by the parlour window wasn't dark, but the thick trees were. The grass was buzzing in the moonlight where my shadow walked on the grass.

'You, Benjy.' T.P. said in the house. 'Where you hiding. You slipping off. I knows it.'

*Luster came back. Wait, he said. Here. Don't go over there. Miss
Quentin and her beau in the swing yonder. You come on this way. Come
back here, Benjy.*

It was dark under the trees. Dan wouldn't come. He stayed in
the moonlight. Then I could see the swing and I began to cry.

*Come away from there, Benjy, Luster said. You know Miss Quentin
going to get mad.*

It was two now, and then one in the swing. Caddy came fast,
white in the darkness.

'Benjy.' she said, 'How did you slip out. Where's Versh.'

She put her arms around me and I hushed and held to her
dress and tried to pull her away.

'Why, Benjy.' she said. 'What is it. T.P.' she called.

The one in the swing got up and came, and I cried and pulled
Caddy's dress.

'Benjy.' Caddy said. 'It's just Charlie. Don't you know Charlie.'

'Where's his nigger.' Charlie said. 'What do they let him run
around loose for.'

'Hush, Benjy.' Caddy said. 'Go away, Charlie. He doesn't like
you.' Charlie went away and I hushed. I pulled at Caddy's dress.

'Why, Benjy.' Caddy said. 'Aren't you going to let me stay here
and talk to Charlie a while.'

'Call that nigger.' Charlie said. He came back. I cried louder
and pulled at Caddy's dress.

'Go away, Charlie.' Caddy said. Charlie came and put his hands
on Caddy and I cried more. I cried loud.

'No, no.' Caddy said. 'No. No.'

'He can't talk.' Charlie said. 'Caddy.'

'Are you crazy.' Caddy said. She began to breathe fast. 'He
can see. Don't. Don't.' Caddy fought. They both breathed fast.
'Please. Please.' Caddy whispered.

'Send him away.' Charlie said.

'I will.' Caddy said. 'Let me go.'

'Will you send him away.' Charlie said.

'Yes.' Caddy said. 'Let me go.' Charlie went away. 'Hush.'
Caddy said. 'He's gone.' I hushed. I could hear her and feel her
chest going.

'I'll have to take him to the house.' she said. She took my hand.
'I'm coming.' she whispered.

'Wait.' Charlie said. 'Call the nigger.'

'No.' Caddy said. 'I'll come back. Come on, Benjy.'

'Caddy.' Charlie whispered, loud. We went on. 'You better

come back. Are you coming back.' Caddy and I were running. 'Caddy.' Charlie said. We ran out into the moonlight, toward the kitchen.

'Caddy.' Charlie said.

Caddy and I ran. We ran up the kitchen steps, onto the porch, and Caddy knelt down in the dark and held me. I could hear her and feel her chest. 'I won't.' she said. 'I won't any more, ever. Benjy. Benjy.' Then she was crying, and I cried, and we held each other. 'Hush.' she said. 'Hush. I won't any more.' So I hushed and Caddy got up and we went into the kitchen and turned the light on and Caddy took the kitchen soap and washed her mouth at the sink, hard. Caddy smelled like trees.

I kept a-telling you to stay away from there, Luster said. They sat up in the swing, quick. Quentin had her hands on her hair. He had a red tie.

You old crazy loon, Quentin said. I'm going to tell Dilsey about the way you let him follow everywhere I go. I'm going to make her whip you good.

'I couldn't stop him.' Luster said. 'Come on here, Benjy.'

'Yes you could.' Quentin said. 'You didn't try. You were both snooping around after me. Did Grandmother send you all out here to spy on me.' She jumped out of the swing. 'If you don't take him right away this minute and keep him away, I'm going to make Jason whip you.'

'I can't do nothing with him.' Luster said. 'You try it if you think you can.'

'Shut your mouth.' Quentin said. 'Are you going to get him away.

'Ah, let him stay.' he said. He had a red tie. The sun was red on it. 'Look here, Jack.' He struck a match and put it in his mouth. Then he took the match out of his mouth. It was still burning. 'Want to try it.' he said. I went over there. 'Open your mouth.' he said. I opened my mouth. Quentin hit the match with her hand and it went away.

'Goddamn you.' Quentin said. 'Do you want to get him started. Don't you know he'll beller all day. I'm going to tell Dilsey on you.' She went away running.

'Here, kid.' he said. 'Hey. Come on back. I ain't going to fool with him.'

Quentin ran on to the house. She went around the kitchen.

'You played hell then, Jack.' he said. 'Ain't you.'

'He can't tell what you saying.' Luster said. 'He deaf and dumb.'

'Is.' he said. 'How long's he been that way.'

'Been that way thirty-three years today.' Luster said. 'Born looney. Is you one of them show folks.'

'Why.' he said.

'I don't ricklick seeing you around here before.' Luster said.

'Well, what about it.' he said.

'Nothing.' Luster said. 'I going tonight.'

He looked at me.

'You ain't the one can play a tune on that saw, is you.' Luster said.

'It'll cost you a quarter to find that out.' he said. He looked at me. 'Why don't they lock him up.' he said. 'What'd you bring him out here for.'

'You ain't talking to me.' Luster said. 'I can't do nothing with him. I just come over here looking for a quarter I lost so I can go to the show tonight. Look like now I ain't going to get to go.' Luster looked on the ground. 'You ain't got no extra quarter, is you.' Luster said.

'No.' he said. 'I ain't.'

'I reckon I have just to find that other one, then.' Luster said. He put his hand in his pocket. 'You don't want to buy no golf ball neither, does you.' Luster said.

'What kind of ball.' he said.

'Golf ball.' Luster said. 'I don't want but a quarter.'

'What for.' he said. 'What do I want with it.'

'I didn't think you did.' Luster said. 'Come on here, mulehead.' he said, 'Come on here and watch them knocking that ball. Here. Here something you can play with along with that jimson weed.' Luster picked it up and gave it to me. It was bright.

'Where'd you get that.' he said. His tie was red in the sun, walking.

'Found it under this here bush.' Luster said. 'I thought for a minute it was that quarter I lost.'

He came and took it.

'Hush.' Luster said. 'He going to give it back when he done looking at it.'

'Agnes Mabel Becky.' he said. He looked toward the house.

'Hush.' Luster said. 'He fixing to give it back.'

He gave it to me and I hushed.

'Who come to see her last night.' he said.

'I don't know.' Luster said. 'They comes every night she can climb down that tree. I don't keep no track of them.'

'Damn if one of them didn't leave a track.' he said. He looked at the house. Then he went and lay down in the swing. 'Go away.' he said. 'Don't bother me.'

'Come on here.' Luster said. 'You done played hell now. Time Miss Quentin get done telling on you.'

We went to the fence and looked through the curling flower spaces. Luster hunted in the grass.

'I had it right here.' he said. I saw the flag flapping, and the sun slanting on the broad grass.

'They'll be some along soon.' Luster said. 'There some now, but they going away. Come on and help me look for it.'

We went along the fence.

'Hush.' Luster said. 'How can I make them come over here, if they ain't coming. Wait. They'll be some in a minute. Look yonder. Here they come.'

I went along the fence, to the gate, where the girls passed with their booksatchels. 'You, Benjy.' Luster said. 'Come back here.'

You can't do no good looking through the gate, T.P. said. Miss Caddy done gone long ways away. Done get married and left you. You can't do no good, holding to the gate and crying. She can't hear you.

What is it he wants, T.P. Mother said. Can't you play with him and keep him quiet.

He want to go down yonder and look through the gate, T.P. said.

Well, he cannot do it, Mother said. It's raining. You will just have to play with him and keep him quiet. You, Benjamin.

Ain't nothing going to quiet him, T.P. said. He think if he down to the gate, Miss Caddy come back.

Nonsense, Mother said.

I could hear them talking. I went out the door and I couldn't hear them, and I went down to the gate, where the girls passed with their booksatchels. They looked at me, walking fast, with their heads turned. I tried to say, but they went on, and I went along the fence, trying to say, and they went faster. Then they were running and I came to the corner of the fence and I couldn't go any further, and I held to the fence, looking after them and trying to say.

'You, Benjy.' T.P. said. 'What you doing, slipping out. Don't you know Dilsey whip you.'

'You can't do no good, moaning and slobbering through the fence.' T.P. said. 'You done skeered them chillen. Look at them, walking on the other side of the street.'

How did he get out, Father said. Did you leave the gate unlatched when you came in, Jason.

Of course not, Jason said. Don't you know I've got better sense than to do that. Do you think I wanted anything like this to happen. This family is bad enough, God knows. I could have told you, all the time. I reckon you'll send him to Jackson, now. If Mrs Burgess don't shoot him first.

Hush, Father said.

I could have told you, all the time, Jason said.

It was open when I touched it, and I held to it in the twilight. I wasn't crying, and I tried to stop, watching the girls coming along in the twilight. I wasn't crying.

'There he is.'

They stopped.

'He can't get out. He won't hurt anybody, anyway. Come on.'

'I'm scared to. I'm scared. I'm going to cross the street.'

'He can't get out.'

I wasn't crying.

'Don't be a 'fraid cat, Come on.'

They came on in the twilight. I wasn't crying, and I held to the gate. They came slow.

'I'm scared.'

'He won't hurt you. I pass here every day. He just runs along the fence.'

They came on. I opened the gate and they stopped, turning. I was trying to say, and I caught her, trying to say, and she screamed and I was trying to say and trying and the bright shapes began to stop and I tried to get out. I tried to get off of my face, but the bright shapes were going again. They were going up the hill to where it fell away and I tried to cry. But when I breathed in, I couldn't breathe out again to cry, and I tried to keep from falling off the hill and I fell off the hill into the bright, whirling shapes.

Here, loony, Luster said. Here come some. Hush your slobbering and moaning now.

They came to the flag. He took it out and they hit, then he put the flag back.

'Mister.' Luster said.

He looked around. 'What.' he said.

'Want to buy a golf ball.' Luster said.

'Let's see it.' he said. He came to the fence and Luster reached the ball through.

'Where'd you get it.' he said.

'Found it.' Luster said.

'I know that.' he said. 'Where. In somebody's golf bag.'

'I found it laying over here in the yard.' Luster said. 'I'll take a quarter for it.'

'What makes you think it's yours.' he said.

'I found it.' Luster said.

'Then find yourself another one.' he said. He put it in his pocket and went away.

'I got to go to that show tonight.' Luster said.

'That so.' he said. He went to the table. 'Fore, caddie.' he said. He hit.

'I'll declare.' Luster said. 'You fusses when you don't see them and you fusses when you does. Why can't you hush. Don't you reckon folks gets tired of listening to you all the time. Here. You dropped your jimson weed.' He picked it up and gave it back to me. 'You needs a new one. You 'bout wore that one out.' We stood at the fence and watched them.

'That white man hard to get along with.' Luster said. 'You see him take my ball.' They went on. We went on along the fence. We came to the garden and we couldn't go any further. I held to the fence and looked through the flower spaces. They went away.

'Now you ain't got nothing to moan about.' Luster said. 'Hush up. I the one got something to moan over, you ain't. Here. Whyn't you hold on to that weed. You be bellering about it next.' He gave me the flower. 'Where you heading now.'

Our shadows were on the grass. They got to the trees before we did. Mine got there first. Then we got there, and then the shadows were gone. There was a flower in the bottle. I put the other flower in it.

'Ain't you a grown man, now.' Luster said. 'playing with two weeds in a bottle. You know what they going to do with you when Miss Cahline die. They going to send you to Jackson, where you belong. Mr Jason say so. Where you can hold the bars all day long with the rest of the looneys and slobber. How you like that.'

Luster knocked the flowers over with his hand. 'That's what they'll do to you at Jackson when you starts bellering.'

I tried to pick up the flowers. Luster picked them up, and they went away. I began to cry.

'Beller.' Luster said. 'Beller. You want something to beller about. All right, then. Caddy.' he whispered. 'Caddy. Beller now. Caddy.'

'Luster.' Dilsey said from the kitchen.

The flowers came back.

'Hush.' Luster said. 'Here they is. Look. It's fixed back just like it was at first. Hush now.'

'You, Luster.' Dilsey said.

'Yessum.' Luster said. 'We coming. You done played hell. Get up.' He jerked my arm and I got up. We went out of the trees. Our shadows were gone.

'Hush.' Luster said. 'Look at all them folks watching you. Hush.'

'You bring him on here.' Dilsey said. She came down the steps.

'What you done to him now.' she said.

'Ain't done nothing to him.' Luster said. 'He just started bellering.'

'Yes you is.' Dilsey said. 'You done something to him. Where you been.'

'Over yonder under them cedars.' Luster said.

'Getting Quentin all riled up.' Dilsey said. 'Why can't you keep him away from her. Don't you know she don't like him where she at.'

'Got as much time for him as I is.' Luster said. 'He ain't none of my uncle.'

'Don't you sass me, nigger boy.' Dilsey said.

'I ain't done nothing to him.' Luster said. 'He was playing there, and all of a sudden he started bellering.'

'Is you been projecking with his graveyard.' Dilsey said.

'I ain't touched his graveyard.' Luster said.

'Don't lie to me, boy.' Dilsey said. We went up the steps and into the kitchen. Dilsey opened the fire-door and drew a chair up in front of it and I sat down. I hushed.

What you want to get her started for, Dilsey said. Whyn't you keep him out of there.

He was just looking at the fire, Caddy said. Mother was telling him his new name. We didn't mean to get her started.

I knows you didn't, Dilsey said. Him at one end of the house and her at the other. You let my things alone, now. Don't you touch nothing till I get back.

'Ain't you shamed of yourself.' Dilsey said. 'Teasing him.' She set the cake on the table.

'I ain't been teasing him.' Luster said. 'He was playing with that bottle full of dogfennel and all of a sudden he started up bellering. You heard him.'

'You ain't done nothing to his flowers.' Dilsey said.

'I ain't touched his graveyard.' Luster said. 'What I want with his truck. I was just hunting for that quarter.'

'You lost it, did you.' Dilsey said. She lit the candles on the cake. Some of them were little ones. Some were big ones cut into little pieces. 'I told you to go put it away. Now I reckon you want me to get you another one from Frony.'

'I got to go to that show, Benjy or no Benjy.' Luster said. 'I ain't going to follow him around day and night both.'

'You going to do just what he want you to, nigger boy.' Dilsey said. 'You hear me.'

'Ain't I always done it.' Luster said. 'Don't I always does what he wants. Don't I, Benjy.'

'Then you keep it up.' Dilsey said. 'Bringing him in here, bawling and getting her started too. You all go ahead and eat this cake, now, before Jason come. I don't want him jumping on me about a cake I bought with my own money. Me baking a cake here, with him counting every egg that comes into this kitchen. See can you let him alone now, less you don't want to go to that show tonight.'

Dilsey went away.

'You can't blow out no candles.' Luster said. 'Watch me blow them out.' He leaned down and puffed his face. The candles went away. I began to cry. 'Hush.' Luster said. 'Here. Look at the fire while I cuts this cake.'

I could hear the clock, and I could hear Caddy standing behind me, and I could hear the roof. It's still raining, Caddy said. I hate rain. I hate everything. And then her head came into my lap and she was crying, holding me, and I began to cry. Then I looked at the fire again and the bright, smooth shapes went again. I could hear the clock and the roof and Caddy.

I ate some cake. Luster's hand came and took another piece. I could hear him eating. I looked at the fire.

A long piece of wire came across my shoulder. It went to the door, and then the fire went away. I began to cry.

'What you howling for now.' Luster said. 'Look there.' The fire was there. I hushed. 'Can't you set and look at the fire and be quiet like mammy told you.' Luster said. 'You ought to be ashamed of yourself. Here. Here's you some more cake.'

'What you done to him now.' Dilsey said. 'Can't you never let him alone.'

'I was just trying to get him to hush up and not sturb Miss Cahline.' Luster said. 'Something got him started again.'

'And I know what that something name.' Dilsey said. 'I'm going to get Versh to take a stick to you when he comes home. You just trying yourself. You been doing it all day. Did you take him down to the branch.'

'Nome.' Luster said. 'We been right here in this yard all day, like you said.'

His hand came for another piece of cake. Dilsey hit his hand. 'Reach it again, and I chop it right off with this here butcher knife.' Dilsey said. 'I bet he ain't had one piece of it.'

'Yes he is.' Luster said. 'He already had twice as much as me. Ask him if he ain't.'

'Reach hit one more time.' Dilsey said. 'Just reach it.'

That's right, Dilsey said. I reckon it'll be my time to cry next. Reckon Maury going to let me cry on him a while, too.

His name's Benjy now, Caddy said.

How come it is, Dilsey said. He ain't wore out the name he was born with yet, is he.

Benjamin came out of the Bible, Caddy said. It's a better name for him than Maury was.

How come it is, Dilsey said.

Mother says it is, Caddy said.

Huh, Dilsey said. Name ain't going to help him. Hurt him neither. Folks don't have no luck, changing names. My name been Dilsey since fore I could remember and it be Dilsey when they's long forgot me.

How will they know it's Dilsey, when it's long forgot, Dilsey, Caddy said.

It'll be in the Book, honey, Dilsey said. Writ out.

Can you read it, Caddy said.

Won't have to, Dilsey said. They'll read it for me. All I got to do is say Ise here.

The long wire came across my shoulder, and the fire went away. I began to cry.

Dilsey and Luster fought.

'I seen you.' Dilsey said. 'Oho, I seen you.' She dragged Luster out of the corner, shaking him. 'Wasn't nothing bothering him, was they. You just wait till your pappy come home. I wish I was young like I use to be, I'd tear them years right off your head. I good mind to lock you up in the cellar and not let you go to that show tonight, I sho is.'

'Ow, mammy.' Luster said. 'Ow mammy.'

I put my hand out to where the fire had been.

'Catch him.' Dilsey said. 'Catch him back.'

My hand jerked back and I put it in my mouth and Dilsey caught me. I could still hear the clock between my voice. Dilsey reached back and hit Luster on the head. My voice was going loud every time.

'Get that soda.' Dilsey said. She took my hand out of my mouth. My voice went louder then and my hand tried to go back to my mouth, but Dilsey held it. My voice went loud. She sprinkled soda on my hand.

'Look in the pantry and tear a piece off of that rag hanging on the nail.' she said. 'Hush, now. You don't want to make your ma sick again, does you. Here, look at the fire. Dilsey make your hand stop hurting in just a minute. Look at the fire.' She opened the fire-door. I looked at the fire, but my hand didn't stop and I didn't stop. My hand was trying to go to my mouth, but Dilsey held it.

She wrapped the cloth around it. Mother said,

'What is it now. Can't I even be sick in peace. Do I have to get up out of bed to come down to him, with two grown negroes to take care of him.'

'He all right now.' Dilsey said. 'He going to quit. He just burnt his hand a little.'

'With two grown negroes, you must bring him into the house, bawling,' Mother said. 'You got him started on purpose, because you know I'm sick.' She came and stood by me. 'Hush.' she said. 'Right this minute. Did you give him this cake.'

'I bought it.' Dilsey said. 'It never come out of Jason's pantry. I fixed him some birthday.'

'Do you want to poison him with that cheap store cake.' Mother said. 'Is that what you are trying to do. Am I never to have one minute's peace.'

'You go on back upstairs and lay down.' Dilsey said. 'It'll quit smarting him in a minute now, and he'll hush. Come on, now.'

'And leave him down here for you all to do something else to.' Mother said. 'How can I lie there, with him bawling down here. Benjamin. Hush this minute.'

'They ain't nowhere else to take him.' Dilsey said. 'We ain't got the room we use to have. He can't stay out in the yard, crying where all the neighbours can see him.'

'I know, I know.' Mother said. 'It's all my fault. I'll be gone soon, and you and Jason will both get along better.' She began to cry.

'You hush that, now.' Dilsey said. 'You'll get yourself down again. You come on back upstairs. Luster going to take him to the liberry and play with him till I get his supper done.'

Dilsey and Mother went out.

'Hush up.' Luster said. 'You hush up. You want me to burn your other hand for you. You ain't hurt. Hush up.'

'Here.' Dilsey said. 'Stop crying now.' She gave me the slipper, and I hushed. 'Take him to the liberry,' she said. 'And if I hear him again, I going to whip you myself.'

We went to the library, Luster turned on the light. The windows went black, and the dark tall place on the wall came and I went and touched it. It was like a door, only it wasn't a door.

The fire came behind me and I went to the fire and sat on the floor, holding the slipper. The fire went higher. It went onto the cushion in Mother's chair.

'Hush up.' Luster said. 'Can't you never get done for a while. Here I done built you a fire, and you won't even look at it.'

Your name is Benjy. Caddy said. Do you hear. Benjy. Benjy.

Don't tell him that, Mother said. Bring him here.

Caddy lifted me under the arms.

Get up, Mau – I mean Benjy, she said.

Don't try to carry him, Mother said. Can't you lead him over here. Is that too much for you to think of.

I can carry him, Caddy said. 'Let me carry him up, Dilsey.'

'Go on, Minute.' Dilsey said. 'You ain't big enough to tote a flea. You go on and be quiet, like Mr Jason said.'

There was a light at the top of the stairs. Father was there, in his shirt sleeves. The way he looked said Hush. Caddy whispered, 'Is Mother sick.'

Versh set me down and we went into Mother's room. There was a fire. It was rising and falling on the walls. There was another fire in the mirror. I could smell the sickness. It was a cloth folded on Mother's head. Her hair was on the pillow. The fire didn't reach it, but it shone on her hand, where her rings were jumping.

'Come and tell Mother good night.' Caddy said. We went to the bed. The fire went out of the mirror. Father got up from the bed and lifted me up and Mother put her hand on my head.

'What time is it.' Mother said. Her eyes were closed.

'Ten minutes to seven.' Father said.

'It's too early for him to go to bed.' Mother said. 'He'll wake up at daybreak, and I simply cannot bear another day like today.'

'There, there.' Father said. He touched Mother's face.

'I know I'm nothing but a burden to you.' Mother said. 'But I'll be gone soon. Then you will be rid of my bothering.'

'Hush.' Father said. 'I'll take him downstairs awhile.' He took me up. 'Come on, old fellow. Let's go downstairs awhile. We'll have to be quiet while Quentin is studying, now.'

Caddy went and leaned her face over the bed and Mother's hand came into the firelight. Her rings jumped on Caddy's back.

Mother's sick, Father said. Dilsey will put you to bed. Where's Quentin.

Versh getting him, Dilsey said.

Father stood and watched us go past. We could hear Mother in her room. Caddy said 'Hush.' Jason was still climbing the stairs. He had his hands in his pockets.

'You all must be good tonight.' Father said. 'And be quiet, so you won't disturb Mother.'

'We'll be quiet.' Caddy said. 'You must be quiet now, Jason.' she said. We tiptoed.

We could hear the roof. I could see the fire in the mirror too. Caddy lifted me again.

'Come on, now.' she said. 'Then you can come back to the fire. Hush, now.'

'Candace.' Mother said.

'Hush, Benjy.' Caddy said. 'Mother wants you a minute. Like a good boy. Then you can come back, Benjy.'

Caddy let me down, and I hushed.

'Let him stay here, Mother. When he's through looking at the fire, then you can tell him.'

'Candace.' Mother said. Caddy stooped and lifted me. We staggered. 'Candace.' Mother said.

'Hush.' Caddy said. 'You can still see it. Hush.'

'Bring him here.' Mother said. 'He's too big for you to carry. You must stop trying. You'll injure your back. All of our women have prided themselves on their carriage. Do you want to look like a washer-woman.'

'He's not too heavy.' Caddy said. 'I can carry him.'

'Well, I don't want him carried, then.' Mother said. 'A five year old child. No, no. Not in my lap. Let him stand up.'

'If you'll hold him, he'll stop.' Caddy said. 'Hush.' she said.

'You can go right back. Here. Here's your cushion. See.'

'Don't, Candace,' Mother said.

'Let him look at it and he'll be quiet.' Caddy said. 'Hold up just a minute while I slip it out. There, Benjy. Look.'

I looked at it and hushed.

'You humour him too much.' Mother said. 'You and your father both. You don't realize that I am the one who has to pay for it. Damuddy spoiled Jason that way and it took him two years to outgrow it, and I am not strong enough to go through the same thing with Benjamin.'

'You don't need to bother with him.' Caddy said. 'I like to take care of him. Don't I, Benjy.'

'Candace.' Mother said. 'I told you not to call him that. It was bad enough when your father insisted on calling you by that silly nickname, and I will not have him called by one. Nicknames are vulgar. Only common people use them. Benjamin.' she said.

'Look at me.' Mother said.

'Benjamin.' she said. She took my face in her hands and turned it to hers.

'Benjamin.' she said. 'Take that cushion away, Candace.'

'He'll cry.' Caddy said.

'Take that cushion away, like I told you.' Mother said. 'He must learn to mind.'

The cushion went away.

'Hush, Benjy.' Caddy said.

'You go over there and sit down.' Mother said. 'Benjamin.' She held my face to hers.

'Stop that.' she said. 'Stop it.'

But I didn't stop and Mother caught me in her arms and began to cry, and I cried. Then the cushion came back and Caddy held it above Mother's head. She drew Mother back in the chair and Mother lay crying against the red and yellow cushion.

'Hush, Mother.' Caddy said. 'You go upstairs and lay down, so you can be sick. I'll go get Dilsey.' She led me to the fire and I looked at the bright, smooth shapes. I could hear the fire and the roof.

Father took me up. He smelled like rain.

'Well, Benjy.' he said. 'Have you been a good boy today.'

Caddy and Jason were fighting in the mirror.

'You, Caddy.' Father said.

They fought. Jason began to cry.

'Caddy.' Father said. Jason was crying. He wasn't fighting any more, but we could see Caddy fighting in the mirror and Father put me down and went into the mirror and fought too. He lifted Caddy up. She fought. Jason lay on the floor, crying. He had the scissors in his hand. Father held Caddy.

'He cut up all Benjy's dolls.' Caddy said. 'I'll slit his gizzle.'

'Candace.' Father said.

'I will.' Caddy said. 'I will.' She fought. Father held her. She kicked at Jason. He rolled into the corner, out of the mirror. Father brought Caddy to the fire. They were all out of the mirror. Only the fire was in it. Like the fire was in a door.

'Stop that.' Father said. 'Do you want to make Mother sick in her room.'

Caddy stopped. 'He cut up all the dolls Mau – Benjy and I made.' Caddy said. 'He did it just for meanness.'

'I didn't.' Jason said. He was sitting up, crying. 'I didn't know they were his. I just thought they were some old papers.'

'You couldn't help but know.' Caddy said. 'You did it just.'

'Hush.' Father said. 'Jason.' he said.

'I'll make you some more tomorrow.' Caddy said. 'We'll make a lot of them. Here, you can look at the cushion, too.'

Jason came in.

I kept telling you to hush, Luster said.

What's the matter now, Jason said.

'He just trying hisself.' Luster said. 'That the way he been going on all day.'

'Why don't you let him alone, then.' Jason said. 'If you can't keep him quiet, you'll have to take him out to the kitchen. The rest of us can't shut ourselves up in a room like Mother does.'

'Mammy say keep him out the kitchen till she get supper.' Luster said.

'Then play with him and keep him quiet.' Jason said. 'Do I have to work all day and then come home to a mad house.' He opened the paper and read it.

You can look at the fire and the mirror and the cushion too, Caddy said. You won't have to wait until supper to look at the cushion, now. We could hear the roof. We could hear Jason too, crying loud beyond the wall.

Dilsey said, 'You come, Jason. You letting him alone, is you.'

'Yessum.' Luster said.

'Where Quentin.' Dilsey said. 'Supper near bout ready.'

'I don't know'm.' Luster said. 'I ain't seen her.'

Dilsey went away. 'Quentin.' she said in the hall. 'Quentin. Supper ready.'

We could hear the roof. Quentin smelled like rain, too.

What did Jason do, he said.

He cut up all Benjy's dolls, Caddy said.

Mother said to not call him Benjy, Quentin said. He sat on the rug by us. I wish it wouldn't rain, he said. You can't do anything.

You've been in a fight, Caddy said. Haven't you.

It wasn't much, Quentin said.

You can tell it, Caddy said. Father'll see it.

I don't care, Quentin said. I wish it wouldn't rain.

Quentin said, 'Didn't Dilsey say supper was ready.'

'Yessum.' Luster said. Jason looked at Quentin. Then he read the paper again. Quentin came in. 'She say it bout ready.' Luster said. Quentin jumped down in Mother's chair. Luster said.

'Mr Jason.'

'What.' Jason said.

'Let me have two bits.' Luster said.

'What for.' Jason said.

'To go to the show tonight.' Luster said.

'I thought Dilsey was going to get a quarter from Frony for you.' Jason said.

'She did.' Luster said. 'I lost it. Me and Benjy hunted all day for that quarter. You can ask him.'

'Then borrow one from him.' Jason said. 'I have to work for mine.' He read the paper. Quentin looked at the fire. The fire was in her eyes and on her mouth. Her mouth was red.

'I tried to keep him away from there.' Luster said.

'Shut your mouth.' Quentin said. Jason looked at her.

'What did I tell you I was going to do if I saw you with that show fellow again.' he said. Quentin looked at the fire. 'Did you hear me.' Jason said.

'I heard you.' Quentin said. 'Why don't you do it, then.'

'Don't you worry.' Jason said.

'I'm not.' Quentin said. Jason read the paper again.

I could hear the roof. Father leaned forward and looked at Quentin. Hello, he said. Who won.

'Nobody.' Quentin said. 'They stopped us. Teachers.'

'Who was it.' Father said. 'Will you tell.'

'It was all right.' Quentin said. 'He was as big as me.'

'That's good.' Father said. 'Can you tell what it was about.'

'It wasn't anything.' Quentin said. 'He said he would put a frog in her desk and she wouldn't dare to whip him.'

'Oh.' Father said. 'She. And then what.'

'Yes, sir.' Quentin said. 'And then I kind of hit him.'

We could hear the roof and the fire and a snuffling outside the door.

'Where was he going to get a frog in November.' Father said.

'I don't know, sir.' Quentin said.

We could hear them.

'Jason.' Father said. We could hear Jason.

'Jason.' Father said. 'Come in here and stop that.'

We could hear the roof and the fire and Jason.

'Stop that now.' Father said. 'Do you want me to whip you again.' Father lifted Jason up into the chair by him. Jason snuffled. We could hear the fire and the roof. Jason snuffled a little louder.

'One more time.' Father said. We could hear the fire and the roof.

Dilsey said, All right. You all can come on to supper.

Versh smelled like rain. He smelled like a dog, too. We could hear the fire and the roof.

We could hear Caddy walking fast. Father and Mother looked at the door. Caddy passed it walking fast. She didn't look. She walked fast.

'Candace.' Mother said. Caddy stopped walking.

'Yes, Mother.' she said.

'Hush, Caroline.' Father said.

'Come here.' Mother said.

'Hush, Caroline.' Father said. 'Let her alone.'

Caddy came to the door and stood there looking at Father and Mother. Her eyes flew at me, and away. I began to cry. It went loud and I got up. Caddy came in and stood with her back to the wall, looking at me. I went towards her, crying and she shrank against the wall and I saw her eyes and I cried louder and pulled at her dress. She put her hands out but I pulled at her dress. Her eyes ran.

Versh said, Your name Benjamin now. You know how come your name Benjamin now. They making a bluegum out of you. Mammy say in old time your granpa changed nigger's name, and he turn preacher, and when they look at him, he bluegum too. Didn't use to be bluegum, neither. And when family woman look him in the eye in the full of the moon, chile born bluegum. And one evening, when they was about a dozen them bluegum chillen running round the place, he never come home. Possum hunters found him in the woods, et clean. And you know who et him. Them bluegum chillen did.

We were in the hall. Caddy was still looking at me. Her hand was against her mouth and I saw her eyes and I cried. We went up the stairs. She stopped again, against the wall, looking at me and I cried and she went on and I came on, crying and she shrank against the wall, looking at me. She opened the door to her room, but I pulled at her dress and we went to the bathroom and she stood against the door, looking at me. Then she put her arm across her face and I pushed at her, crying.

What are you doing to him, Jason said. Why can't you let him alone.

I ain't touching him, Luster said. He been doing this way all day long. He needs whipping.

He needs to be sent to Jackson, Quentin said. How can anybody live in a house like this.

If you don't like it, young lady, you'd better get out, Jason said.

I'm going to, Quentin said. Don't you worry.

Versh said, 'You move back some, so I can dry my legs off.' He shoved me back a little. 'Don't you start bellering, now. You can still see it. That's all you have to do. You ain't had to be out in the rain like I is. You's born lucky and don't know it.' He lay on his back before the fire.

'You know how come your name Benjamin now.' Versh said. 'Your mamma too proud for you. What mammy say.'

'You be still there and let me dry my legs off.' Versh said. 'Or you know what I'll do. I'll skin your rinktum.'

We could hear the fire and the roof and Versh.

Versh got up quick and jerked his legs back. Father said, 'All right, Versh.'

'I'll feed him tonight.' Caddy said. 'Sometimes he cries when Versh feeds him.'

'Take this tray up.' Dilsey said. 'And hurry back and feed Benjy.'

'Don't you want Caddy to feed you.' Caddy said.

Has he got to keep that old dirty slipper on the table, Quentin said. Why don't you feed him in the kitchen. It's like eating with a pig.

If you don't like the way we eat, you'd better not come to the table, Jason said.

Steam came off of Roskus. He was sitting in front of the stove. The oven door was open and Roskus had his feet in it. Steam came off the bowl. Caddy put the spoon into my mouth easy. There was a black spot on the inside of the bowl.

Now, now, Dilsey said, He ain't going to bother you no more.

It got down below the mark. Then the bowl was empty. It went away. 'He's hungry tonight.' Caddy said. The bowl came back. I couldn't see the spot. Then I could. 'He's starved, tonight.' Caddy said. 'Look how much he's eaten.'

Yes he will, Quentin said. You all send him out to spy on me. I hate this house. I'm going to run away.

Roskus said, 'It going to rain all night.'

You've been running a long time, not to 've got any further off than mealtime, Jason said.

See if I don't, Quentin said.

'Then I don't know what I going to do.' Dilsey said. 'It caught me in the hip so bad now I can't scarcely move. Climbing them stairs all evening.'

Oh, I wouldn't be surprised, Jason said. I wouldn't be surprised at anything you'd do.

Quentin threw her napkin on the table.

Hush your mouth, Jason, Dilsey said. She went and put her arm around Quentin. Sit down, honey, Dilsey said. He ought to be ashamed of hisself, throwing what ain't your fault up at you.

'She sulling again, is she.' Roskus said.

'Hush your mouth.' Dilsey said.

Quentin pushed Dilsey away. She looked at Jason. Her mouth was red. She picked up her glass of water and swung her arm back, looking at Jason. Dilsey caught her arm. They fought. The glass broke on the table, and the water ran into the table. Quentin was running.

'Mother's sick again.' Caddy said.

'Sho she is.' Dilsey said. 'Weather like this make anybody sick. When you going to get done eating, boy.'

Goddam you, Quentin said. Goddam you. We could hear her running on the stairs. We went to the library.

Caddy gave me the cushion, and I could look at the cushion and the mirror and the fire.

'We must be quiet while Quentin's studying.' Father said. 'What are you doing, Jason.'

'Nothing.' Jason said.

'Suppose you come over here to do it, then.' Father said.

Jason came out of the corner.

'What are you chewing.' Father said.

'Nothing.' Jason said.

'He's chewing paper again.' Caddy said.

'Come here, Jason.' Father said.

Jason threw into the fire. It hissed, uncurled, turning black.

Then it was grey. Then it was gone. Caddy and Father and Jason were in Mother's chair. Jason's eyes were puffed shut and his mouth moved, like tasting. Caddy's head was on Father's shoulder. Her hair was like fire, and little points of fire were in her eyes, and I went and Father lifted me into the chair too, and Caddy held me. She smelled like trees.

She smelled like trees. In the corner it was dark, but I could see the window. I squatted there, holding the slipper. I couldn't see it, but my hands saw it, and I could hear it getting night, and my hands saw the slipper but I couldn't see myself, but my hands could see the slipper, and I squatted there, hearing it getting dark.

Here you is, Luster said. Look what I got. He showed it to me. You know where I got it. Miss Quentin gave it to me. I knowed they couldn't keep me out. What you doing, off in here. I thought you done slipped back out doors. Ain't you done enough moaning and slobbering today, without hiding off in this here empty room, mumbling and taking on. Come on here to bed, so I can get up there before it starts. I can't fool with you all night tonight. Just let them horns toot the first toot and I done gone.

We didn't go to our room.

'This is where we have the measles.' Caddy said. 'Why do we have to sleep in here tonight.'

'What you care where you sleep.' Dilsey said. She shut the door and sat down and began to undress me. Jason began to cry. 'Hush.' Dilsey said.

'I want to sleep with Damuddy.' Jason said.

'She's sick.' Caddy said. 'You can sleep with her when she gets well. Can't he, Dilsey.'

'Hush, now.' Dilsey said. Jason hushed.

'Our nighties are here, and everything.' Caddy said. 'It's like moving.'

'And you better get into them.' Dilsey said. 'You be unbuttoning Jason.'

Caddy unbuttoned Jason. He began to cry.

'You want to get whipped.' Dilsey said. Jason hushed.

Quentin, Mother said in the hall.

What, Quentin said beyond the wall. We heard Mother lock the door. She looked in our door and came in and stooped over the bed and kissed me on the forehead.

When you get him to bed, go and ask Dilsey if she objects to my having a hot water bottle, Mother said. Tell her that if she does, I'll try to get along without it. Tell her I just want to know.

Yessum, Luster said. Come on. Get your pants off.

Quentin and Versh came in. Quentin had his face turned away. 'What are you crying for.' Caddy said.

'Hush.' Dilsey said. 'You all get undressed, now. You can go on home, Versh.'

I got undressed and I looked at myself, and I began to cry. Hush, Luster said. Looking for them ain't going to do no good. They're gone. You keep on like this, and we ain't going have you no more birthday. He put my gown on. I hushed, and then Luster stopped, his head toward the window. Then he went to the window and looked out. He came back and took my arm. Here she come, he said. Be quiet, now. We went to the window and looked out. It came out of Quentin's window and climbed across into the tree. We watched the tree shaking. The shaking went down the tree, then it came out and we watched it go away across the grass. Then we couldn't see it. Come on, Luster said. There now. Hear them horns. You get in that bed while my foots behaves.

There were two beds. Quentin got in the other one. He turned his face to the wall. Dilsey put Jason in with him. Caddy took her dress off.

'Just look at your drawers.' Dilsey said. 'You better be glad your ma ain't seen you.'

'I already told on her.' Jason said.

'I bound you would.' Dilsey said.

'And see what you got by it.' Caddy said. 'Tattletale.'

'What did I get by it.' Jason said.

'Whyn't you get your nightie on.' Dilsey said. She went and helped Caddy take off her bodice and drawers. 'Just look at you.' Dilsey said. She wadded the drawers and scrubbed Caddy behind with them. 'It done soaked clean through onto you.' she said. 'But you won't get no bath this night. Here.' She put Caddy's nightie on her and Caddy climbed into the bed and Dilsey went to the door and stood with her hand on the light. 'You all be quiet now, you hear.' she said.

'All right.' Caddy said. 'Mother's not coming in tonight.' she said. 'So we still have to mind me.'

'Yes.' Dilsey said. 'Go to sleep, now.'

'Mother's sick.' Caddy said. 'She and Damuddy are both sick.'

'Hush.' Dilsey said. 'You go to sleep.'

The room went black, except the door. Then the door went black. Caddy said, 'Hush, Maury,' putting her hand on me. So I stayed hushed. We could hear us. We could hear the dark.

It went away, and Father looked at us. He looked at Quentin

and Jason, then he came and kissed Caddy and put his hand on my head.

'Is Mother very sick.' Caddy said.

'No.' Father said. 'Are you going to take good care of Maury.'

'Yes.' Caddy said.

Father went to the door and looked at us again. Then the dark came back, and he stood black in the door, and then the door turned black again. Caddy held me and I could hear us all, and the darkness, and something I could smell. And then I could see the windows, where the trees were buzzing. Then the dark began to go in smooth, bright shapes, like it always does, even when Caddy says that I have been asleep.

June Second, 1910

When the shadow of the sash appeared on the curtains it was between seven and eight o'clock and then I was in time again, hearing the watch. It was Grandfather's and when Father gave it to me he said, Quentin, I give you the mausoleum of all hope and desire; it's rather excrutiating-ly apt that you will use it to gain the reducto absurdum of all human experience which can fit your individual needs no better than it fitted his or his father's. I give it to you not that you may remember time, but that you might forget it now and then for a moment and not spend all your breath trying to conquer it. Because no battle is ever won he said. They are not even fought. The field only reveals to man his own folly and despair, and victory is an illusion of philosophers and fools.

It was propped against the collar box and I lay listening to it. Hearing it, that is, I don't suppose anybody ever deliberately listens to a watch or a clock. You don't have to. You can be oblivious to the sound for a long while, then in a second of ticking it can create in the mind unbroken the long diminishing parade of time you didn't hear. Like Father said down the long and lonely light-rays you might see Jesus walking, like. And the good

Saint Francis that said Little Sister Death, that never had a sister.

Through the wall I heard Shreve's bed-springs and then his slippers on the floor hishing. I got up and went to the dresser and slid my hand along it and touched the watch and turned it face-down and went back to bed. But the shadow of the sash was still there and I had learned to tell almost to the minute, so I'd have to turn my back to it, feeling the eyes animals used to have in the back of their heads when it was on top, itching. It's always the idle habits you acquire which you will regret. Father said that. That Christ was not crucified: he was worn away by a minute clicking of little wheels. That had no sister.

And so as soon as I knew I couldn't see it, I began to wonder what time it was. Father said that constant speculation regarding the position of mechanical hands on an arbitrary dial which is a symptom of mind-function. Excrement Father said like sweating. And I saying All right. Wonder. Go on and wonder.

If it had been cloudy I could have looked at the window, thinking what he said about idle habits. Thinking it would be nice for them down at New London if the weather held up like this. Why shouldn't it? The month of brides, the voice that breathed *She ran right out of the mirror, out of the banked scent. Roses. Roses. Mr and Mrs Jason Richmond Compson announce the marriage of.* Roses. Not virgins like dogwood, milkweed. I said I have committed incest, Father I said. Roses. Cunning and serene. If you attend Harvard one year, but don't see the boat-race, there should be a refund. Let Jason have it. Give Jason a year at Harvard.

Shreve stood in the door, putting his collar on, his glasses glinting rosily, as though he had washed them with his face. 'You taking a cut this morning?'

'Is it that late?'

He looked at his watch. 'Bell in two minutes.'

'I didn't know it was that late.' He was still looking at the watch, his mouth shaping. 'I'll have to hustle. I can't stand another cut. The dean told me last week –' He put the watch back into his pocket. Then I quit talking.

'You'd better slip on your pants and run,' he said. He went out.

I got up and moved about, listening to him through the wall. He entered the sitting-room, toward the door.

'Aren't you ready yet?'

'Not yet. Run along. I'll make it.'

He went out. The door closed. His feet went down the corridor. Then I could hear the watch again. I quit moving around and went to the window and drew the curtains aside and watched them running for chapel, the same ones fighting the same heaving coat-sleeves, the same books and flapping collars flushing past like debris on a flood, and Spoade. Calling Shreve my husband. Ah let him alone, Shreve said, if he's got better sense than to chase after the little dirty sluts, whose business. In the South you are ashamed of being a virgin. Boys. Men. They lie about it. Because it means less to women, Father said. He said it was men invented virginity not women. Father said it's like death: only a state in which the others are left and I said, But to believe it doesn't matter and he said, That's what's so sad about anything: not only virginity, and I said, Why couldn't it have been me and not her who is unvirgin and he said, That's why that's sad too; nothing is even worth the changing of it, and Shreve said if he's got better sense than to chase after the little dirty sluts and I said Did you ever have a sister? Did you? Did you?

Spoade was in the middle of them like a terrapin in a street full of scuttering dead leaves, his collar about his ears, moving at his customary unhurried walk. He was from South Carolina, a senior. It was his club's boast that he never ran for chapel and had never got there on time and had never been absent in four years and had never made either chapel or first lecture with a shirt on his back and socks on his feet. About ten o'clock he'd come in Thompson's, get two cups of coffee, sit down and take his socks out of his pocket and remove his shoes and put them on while the coffee cooled. About noon you'd see him with a shirt and collar on, like anybody else. The others passed him running, but he never increased his pace at all. After a while the quad was empty.

A sparrow slanted across the sunlight, onto the window ledge, and cocked his head at me. His eye was round and bright. First he'd watch me with one eye, then flick! and it would be the other one, his throat pumping faster than any pulse. The hour began to strike. The sparrow quit swapping eyes and watched me steadily with the same one until the chimes ceased, as if he were listening too. Then he flicked off the ledge and was gone.

It was a while before the last stroke ceased vibrating. It stayed in the air, more felt than heard, for a long time. Like all the bells that ever rang still ringing in the long dying light-rays and Jesus and Saint Francis talking about his sister. Because if it were just to hell; if that were all of it. Finished. If things just finished themselves. Nobody else there but her and me. If we could just have done something so dreadful that they would have fled hell except us. *I have committed incest I said Father it was I it was not Dalton Ames* And when he put Dalton Ames. Dalton Ames. Dalton Ames. When he put the pistol in my hand I didn't. That's why I didn't. He would be there and she would and I would. Dalton Ames. Dalton Ames. Dalton Ames. If we could have just done something so dreadful and Father said That's sad too, people cannot do anything that dreadful they cannot do anything very dreadful at all they cannot even remember tomorrow what seemed dreadful today and I said, You can shirk all things and he said, Ah can you. And I will look down and see my murmuring bones and the deep water like wind, like a roof of wind, and after a long time they cannot distinguish even bones upon the lonely and inviolate sand. Until on the Day when He says Rise only the flat-iron would come floating up. It's not when you realize that nothing can help you – religion, pride, anything – it's when you realize that you don't need any aid. Dalton Ames. Dalton Ames. Dalton Ames. If I could have been his mother lying with open body lifted laughing, holding his father with my hand refraining, seeing, watching him die before he lived. *One minute she was standing in the door.*

I went to the dresser and took up the watch, with the face still down. I tapped the crystal on the corner of the dresser and caught the fragments of glass in my hand and put them into the ashtray and twisted the hands off and put them in the tray. The watch ticked on. I turned the face up, the blank dial with little wheels clicking and clicking behind it, not knowing any better. Jesus walking on Galilee and Washington not telling lies. Father brought back a watch-charm from the Saint Louis Fair to Jason: a tiny opera glass into which you squinted with one eye and saw a skyscraper, a ferris wheel all spidery, Niagara Falls on a pinhead. There was a red smear on the dial. When I saw it my thumb began to smart. I put the watch down and went into Shreve's room and got the iodine and painted the cut. I cleaned the rest of the glass out of the rim with the towel.

I laid out two suits of underwear, with socks, shirts, collars and ties, and packed my trunk. I put in everything except my new suit and an old one and two pairs of shoes and two hats, and my books. I carried the books into the sitting-room and stacked them on the table, the ones I had brought from home and the ones

Father said it used to be a gentleman was known by his books; nowadays he is known by the ones he has not returned and locked the trunk and addressed it. The quarter hour sounded. I stopped and listened to it until the chimes ceased.

I bathed and shaved. The water made my finger smart a little, so I painted it again. I put on my new suit and put my watch on and packed the other suit and the accessories and my razor and brushes in my hand bag, and wrapped the trunk key into a sheet of paper and put it in an envelope and addressed it to Father, and wrote the two notes and sealed them.

The shadow hadn't quite cleared the stoop. I stopped inside the door, watching the shadow move. It moved almost perceptibly, creeping back inside the door, driving the shadow back into the door. *Only she was running already when I heard it. In the mirror she was running before I knew what it was. That quick, her train caught up over her arm she ran out of the mirror like a cloud, her veil swirling in long glints her heels brittle and fast clutching her dress onto her shoulder with the other hand, running out of the mirror the smells roses roses the voice that breathed o'er Eden. Then she was across the porch I couldn't hear her heels then in the moonlight like a cloud, the floating shadow of the veil running across the grass, into the bellowing. She ran out of her dress, clutching her bridal, running into the bellowing where T.P. in the dew Whooey Sassprilluh Benjy under the box bellowing. Father had a V-shaped silver cuirass on his running chest.*

Shreve said, 'Well, you didn't . . . Is it a wedding or a wake?'

'I couldn't make it,' I said.

'Not with all that primping. What's the matter? You think this was Sunday?'

'I reckon the police won't get me for wearing my new suit one time,' I said.

'I was thinking about the Square students. Have you got too proud to attend classes too?'

'I'm going to eat first.' The shadow on the stoop was gone. I stepped into sunlight, finding my shadow again. I walked down the steps just ahead of it. The half-hour went. Then the chimes ceased and died away.

Deacon wasn't at the post office either. I stamped the two envelopes and mailed the one to Father and put Shreve's in my inside pocket, and then I remembered where I had last seen the Deacon. It was on Decoration Day, in a GAR uniform, in the middle of the parade. If you waited long enough on any corner you would see him in whatever parade came along. The one

before was on Columbus' or Garibaldi's or somebody's birthday.
He was in the Street Sweeper's section, in a stovepipe hat, carrying
a two-inch Italian flag, smoking a cigar among the brooms and
scoops. But the last time was the GAR one, because Shreve said:

'There now. just look at what your grandpa did to that poor
old nigger.'

'Yes,' I said, 'Now he can spend day after day marching in
parades. If it hadn't been for my grandfather, he'd have to work
like white folks.'

I didn't see him anywhere. But I never knew even a working
nigger that you could flnd when you wanted him, let alone one
that lived off the fat of the land. A car came along. I went over
to town and went to Parker's and had a good breakfast. While I
was eating I heard a clock strike the hour. But then I suppose it
takes at least one hour to lose time in, who has been longer than
history getting into the mechanical progression of it.

When I finished breakfast I bought a cigar. The girl said a fifty
cent one was the best, so I took one and lit it and went out to
the street. I stood there and took a couple of puffs, then I held
it in my hand and went on toward the corner. I passed a jeweller's
window, but I looked away in time. At the corner two bootblacks
caught me, one on either side, shrill and raucous, like blackbirds.
I gave the cigar to one of them, and the other one a nickel. Then
they let me alone. The one with the cigar was trying to sell it to
the other for the nickel.

There was a clock, high up in the sun, and I thought about
how, when you don't want to do a thing, your body will try to
trick you into doing it, sort of unawares. I could feel the muscles
in the back of my neck, and then I could hear my watch ticking
away in my pocket and after a while I had all the other sounds
shut away, leaving only the watch in my pocket. I turned back
up the street, to the window. He was working at the table behind
the window. He was going bald. There was a glass in his eye – a
metal tube screwed into his face. I went in.

The place was full of ticking, like crickets in September grass,
and I could hear a big clock on the wall above his head. He
looked up, his eye big and blurred and rushing beyond the glass.
I took mine out and handed it to him.

'I broke my watch.'

He flipped it over in his hand. 'I should say you have. You
must have stepped on it.'

'Yes, sir. I knocked it off the dresser and stepped on it in the dark. It's still running though.'

He pried the back open and squinted into it. 'Seems to be all right. I can't tell until I go over it, though. I'll go into it this afternoon.'

'I'll bring it back later.' I said. 'Would you mind telling me if any of those watches in the window are right?'

He held my watch on his palm and looked up at me with his blurred rushing eye.

'I made a bet with a fellow,' I said, 'And I forgot my glasses this morning.'

'Why, all right,' he said. He laid the watch down and half rose on his stool and looked over the barrier. Then he glanced up at the wall. 'It's twen –'

'Don't tell me,' I said, 'please sir. Just tell me if any of them are right.'

He looked at me again. He sat back on the stool and pushed the glass up on his forehead. It left a red circle around his eye and when it was gone his whole face looked naked. 'What're you celebrating today?' he said. 'That boat race ain't until next week, is it?'

'No sir. This is just a private celebration. Birthday. Are any of them right?'

'No. But they haven't been regulated and set yet. If you're thinking of buying one of them –'

'No, sir. I don't need a watch. We have a clock in our sitting-room. I'll have this one fixed when I do.' I reached my hand.

'Better leave it now.'

'I'll bring it back later.' He gave me the watch. I put it in my pocket. I couldn't hear it now, above all the others. 'I'm much obliged to you. I hope I haven't taken up your time.'

'That's all right. Bring it in when you are ready. And you better put off this celebration until after we win that boat race.'

'Yes, sir. I reckon I had.'

I went out, shutting the door upon the ticking. I looked back into the window. He was watching me across the barrier. There were about a dozen watches in the window, a dozen different hours and each with the same assertive and contradictory assurance that mine had, without any hands at all. Contradicting one another. I could hear mine, ticking away inside my pocket, even though nobody could see it, even though it could tell nothing if anyone could.

And so I told myself to take that one. Because Father said clocks slay time. He said time is dead as long as it is being clicked off by little wheels; only when the clock stops does time come to life. The hands were extended, slightly off the horizontal at a faint angle, like a gull tilting into the wind. Holding all I used to be sorry about like the new moon holding water, niggers say. The jeweller was working again, bent over his bench, the tube tunnelled into his face. His hair was parted in the centre. The part ran up into a bald spot, like a drained marsh in December.

I saw the hardware store from across the street. I didn't know you bought flat-irons by the pound.

The clerk said, 'These weigh ten pounds.' Only they were bigger than I thought. So I got two six-pound little ones, because they would look like a pair of shoes wrapped up. They felt heavy enough together, but I thought again how Father had said about the reducto absurdum of human experience, thinking how the only opportunity I seemed to have for the application of Harvard. Maybe by next year; thinking maybe it takes two years in school to learn to do that properly.

But they felt heavy enough in the air. A street car came. I got on. I didn't see the placard on the front. It was full, mostly prosperous looking people reading newspapers. The only vacant seat was beside a nigger. He wore a derby and shined shoes and he was holding a dead cigar stub. I used to think that a Southerner had to be always conscious of niggers. I thought that Northerners would expect him to. When I first came East I kept thinking You've got to remember to think of them as coloured people not niggers, and if it hadn't happened that I wasn't thrown with many of them, I'd have wasted a lot of time and trouble before I learned that the best way to take all people, black or white, is to take them for what they think they are, then leave them alone. That was when I realized that a nigger is not a person so much as a form of behaviour; a sort of obverse reflection of the white people he lives among. But I thought at first that I ought to miss having a lot of them around me because I thought that Northerners thought I did, but I didn't know that I really had missed Roskus and Dilsey and them until that morning in Virginia. The train was stopped when I waked and I raised the shade and looked out. The car was blocking a road crossing, where two white fences came down a hill and then sprayed outward and downward like part of a skeleton of a horn, and there was a nigger on a mule in the middle of the stiff ruts, waiting for the train to move. How long he had been there I didn't know, but he sat straddle of the mule, his head wrapped in a piece of blanket, as if they had been built there with the fence and the road, or with the hill, carved out of the hill itself, like a sign put there saying You are home again. He didn't have a saddle and his feet dangled almost to the ground. The mule looked like a rabbit. I raised the window.

'Hey, Uncle,' I said, 'Is this the way?'

'Suh?' He looked at me, then he loosened the blanket and lifted it away from his ear.

'Christmas gift!' I said.

'Sho comin, boss. You done caught me, ain't you?'

'I'll let you off this time.' I dragged my pants out of the little hammock and got a quarter out. 'But look out next time. I'll be coming back through here two days after New Year, and look out then.' I threw the quarter out the window. 'Buy yourself some Santy Claus.'

'Yes, suh,' he said. He got down and picked up the quarter and rubbed it on his leg. 'Thanky, young marster. Thanky.' Then the train began to move. I leaned out the window, into the cold air, looking back. He stood there beside the gaunt rabbit of a mule, the two of them shabby and motionless and unimpatient. The train swung around the curve, the engine puffing with short, heavy blasts, and they passed smoothly from sight that way, with the quality about them of shabby and timeless patience, of static serenity: that blending of childlike and ready incompetence and paradoxical reliability that tends and protects them it loves out of all reason and robs them steadily and evades responsibility and obligations by means too barefaced to be called subterfuge even and is taken in theft or evasion with only that frank and spontaneous admiration for the victor which the gentleman feels for anyone who beats him in a fair contest, and withal a fond and unflagging tolerance for white folks' vagaries like that of a grandparent for unpredictable and troublesome children, which I had forgotten. And all that day, while the train wound through rushing gaps and along ledges where movement was only a labouring sound of the exhaust and groaning wheels and the eternal mountains stood fading into the thick sky, I thought of home, of the bleak station and the mud and the niggers and country folks thronging slowly about the square, with toy monkeys and wagons and candy in sacks and roman candles sticking out, and my insides would move like they used to do in school when the bell rang.

I wouldn't begin counting until the clock struck three. Then I would begin, counting to sixty and folding down one finger and thinking of the other fourteen fingers waiting to be folded down, or thirteen or twelve or eight or seven, until all of a sudden I'd realize silence and the unwinking minds, and I'd say 'Ma'am?' 'Your name is Quentin, isn't it?' Miss Laura said. Then more silence and the cruel unwinking minds and hands jerking into the silence. 'Tell Quentin who discovered Mississippi River, Henry.' 'DeSoto.' Then the minds would go away, and after a while I'd be afraid I had gotten behind and I'd count fast and fold down another finger, then I'd be afraid I was going too fast and I'd slow up, then I'd get afraid and count fast again. So I never could come out even with the bell, and the released surging of feet moving already, feeling earth in the scuffed floor, and the day like a pane of glass struck a light, sharp blow, and my insides would move, sitting still. *Moving sitting still. One minute she was standing in the door. Benjy. Bellowing. Benjamin the child of mine old age bellowing. Caddy! Caddy!*

I'm going to run away. He began to cry she went and touched him. Hush. I'm not going to. Hush. He hushed. Dilsey.

He smell what you tell him when he want to. Don't have to listen nor talk.

Can he smell that new name they give him? Can he smell bad luck?

What he want to worry about luck for? Luck can't do him no hurt.

What they change his name for then if ain't trying to help his luck?

The street car stopped, started, stopped again. Below the window I watched the crowns of people's heads passing beneath new straw hats not yet unbleached. There were women in the car now, with market baskets, and men in work-clothes were beginning to outnumber the shined shoes and collars.

The nigger touched my knee. 'Pardon me,' he said. I swung my legs out and let him pass. We were going beside a blank wall, the sound clattering back into the car, at the women with market baskets on their knees and a man in a stained hat with a pipe stuck in the band. I could smell water, and in a break in the wall I saw a glint of water and two masts, and a gull motionless in mid-air, like on an invisible wire between the masts, and I raised my hand and through my coat touched the letters I had written. When the car stopped I got off.

The bridge was open to let a schooner through. She was in tow, the tug nudging along under her quarter, trailing smoke, but the ship herself was like she was moving without visible means. A man naked to the waist was coiling down a line on the fo'c'sle head. His body was burned the colour of leaf tobacco. Another man in a straw hat without any crown was at the wheel. The ship went through the bridge, moving under bare poles like a ghost in broad day, with three gulls hovering above the stern like toys on invisible wires.

When it closed I crossed to the other side and leaned on the rail above the boathouses. The float was empty and the doors were closed. The crew just pulled in the late afternoon now, resting up before. The shadow of the bridge, the tiers of railing, my shadow leaning flat upon the water, so easily had I tricked it that would not quit me. At least fifty feet it was, and if I only had something to blot it into the water, holding it until it was drowned, the shadow of the package like two shoes wrapped up lying on the water. Niggers say a drowned man's shadow was watching for him in the water all the time. It twinkled and glinted, like breathing, the float slow like breathing too, and debris half submerged, healing out to the sea, and the caverns and the grottoes of the sea. The displacement of water is equal to the something of something. Reducto absurdum of all human experience, and two six-pound flat-irons weigh more than one tailor's goose. What a sinful waste Dilsey would say. Benjy knew it when Damuddy died. He cried. *He smell hit. He smell hit.*

The tug came back downstream, the water shearing in long rolling cylinders, rocking the float at last with the echo of passage, the float lurching on to the rolling cylinder with a plopping sound and a long jarring noise as the door rolled back and two men emerged, carrying a shell. They set it in the water and a moment later Bland come out, with the sculls. He wore flannels, a grey jacket, and a stiff straw hat. Either he or his mother had read somewhere that Oxford students pulled in flannels and stiff hats, so early one March they bought Gerald a one pair shell and in his flannels and stiff hat he went on the river. The folks at the boathouses threatened to call a policeman, but he went anyway. His mother came down in a hired motor, in a fur suit like an arctic explorer's, and saw him off in a twenty-five mile wind and a steady drove of ice floes like dirty sheep. Ever since then I have believed that God is not only a gentleman and a sport; He is a Kentuckian too. When he sailed away she made a detour and came down to the river again and drove along parallel with him, the car in low gear. They said you couldn't have told they'd ever seen one another before, like a King and Queen, not even looking at one another, just moving side by side across Massachusetts on parallel courses like a couple of planets.

He got in and pulled away. He pulled pretty well now. He ought to. They said his mother tried to make him give rowing up and do something else the rest of his class couldn't or wouldn't do, but for once he was stubborn. If you could call it stubbornness, sitting in his attitudes of princely boredom, with his curly yellow hair and his violet eyes and his eyelashes and his New York clothes, while his mamma was telling us about Gerald's horses and Gerald's niggers and Gerald's women. Husbands and fathers in Kentucky must have been awful glad when she carried Gerald off to Cambridge. She had an apartment over in town, and Gerald had one there too, besides his rooms in college. She approved of Gerald associating with me because I at least revealed a blundering sense of noblesse oblige by getting myself born below Mason and Dixon, and a few others whose geography met the requirements (minimum). Forgave, at least. Or condoned. But since she met Spoade coming out of chapel one He said she couldn't be a lady no lady would be out at that hour of the night she never had been able to forgive him for having five names, including that of a present English ducal house. I'm sure she solaced herself by being convinced that some misfit Maingault or Mortemar had got mixed up with the lodge-keeper's daughter. Which was quite probable, whether she invented it or not. Spoade was the world's champion sitter-a-round, no holds barred and gouging discretionary.

The shell was a speck now, the oars catching the sun in spaced glints, as if the hull were winking itself along. *Did you ever have a sister? No but they're all bitches. Did you ever have a sister? One minute she was. Bitches. Not bitch one minute she stood in the door* Dalton Ames. Dalton Ames. Dalton Shirts. I thought all the time they were khaki, army issue khaki, until I saw they were of heavy Chinese silk or finest flannel because they made his face so brown his eyes so blue. Dalton Ames. It just missed gentility. Theatrical fixture. Just papiermâché, then touch. Oh. Asbestos. Not quite bronze. *But won't see him at the house.*

Caddy's a woman too, remember. She must do things for women's reasons, too.

Why won't you bring him to the house, Caddy? Why must you do like nigger women do in the pasture the ditches the dark woods hot hidden furious in the dark woods.

And after a while I had been hearing my watch for some time

and I could feel the letters crackle through my coat, against the railing, and I leaned on the railing, watching my shadow, how I had tricked it. I moved along the rail, but my suit was dark too and I could wipe my hands, watching my shadow, how I had tricked it. I walked into the shadow of the quay. Then I went east.

Harvard my Harvard boy Harvard harvard That pimple-faced infant she met at the field-meet with coloured ribbons. Skulking along the fence trying to whistle her out like a puppy. Because they couldn't cajole him into the dining-room Mother believed he had some sort of spell he was going to cast on her when he got her alone. Yet any blackguard *He was lying beside the box under the window bellowing* that could drive up in a limousine with a flower in his buttonhole. *Harvard. Quentin this is Herbert. My Harvard boy. Herbert will be a big brother has already promised Jason a position in the bank.*

Hearty, celluloid like a drummer. Face full of teeth white but not smiling. *I've heard of him up there. All* teeth but not smiling. *You going to drive?*

Get in Quentin.

You going to drive.

It's her car aren't you proud of your little sister owns first auto in town Herbert his present. Louis has been giving her lessons every morning didn't you get my letter Mr and Mrs Jason Richmond Compson announce the marriage of their daughter Candace to Mr Sydney Herbert Head on the twenty-fifth of April one thousand nine hundred and ten at Jefferson Mississippi. At home after the first of August number Something Something Avenue South Bend Indiana. Shreve said Aren't you even going to open it? *Three days. Times. Mr and Mrs Jason Richmond Compson* Young Lochinvar rode out of the west a little too soon, didn't he?

I'm from the south. You're funny, aren't you.

O yes I knew it was somewhere in the country.

You're funny, aren't you. You ought to join the circus.

I did. That's how I ruined my eyes watering the elephant's fleas, *Three times* These country girls. You can't even tell about them, can you. Well, anyway Byron never had his wish, thank God. *But not hit a man in glasses.* Aren't you even going to open it? *It lay on the table a candle burning at each corner upon the envelope tied in a soiled pink garter two artificial flowers. Not hit a man in glasses.*

Country people poor things they never saw an auto before lots

of them honk the horn Candace so *She wouldn't look at me* they'll
get out of the way *wouldn't look at me* your father wouldn't like
it if you were to injure one of them I'll declare your father will
simply have to get an auto now I'm almost sorry you brought it
down Herbert I've enjoyed it so much of course there's the
carriage but so often when I'd like to go out Mr Compson has
the darkies doing something it would be worth my head to
interrupt he insists that Roskus is at my call all the time but I
know what that means I know how often people make promises
just to satisfy their consciences are you going to treat my little
baby girl that way Herbert but I know you won't Herbert has
spoiled us all to death Quentin did I write you that he is going
to take Jason into his bank when Jason finishes high school Jason
will make a splendid banker he is the only one of my children
with any practical sense you can thank me for that he takes after
my people the others are all Compson *Jason furnished the flour.*
They made kites on the back porch and sold them for a nickle a piece,
he and the Patterson boy. Jason was treasurer.

There was no nigger in this street car, and the hats unbleached
as yet flowing past under the window. Going to Harvard. We
have sold Benjy's *He lay on the ground under the window, bellowing.*
We have sold Benjy's pasture so that Quentin may go to Harvard a
brother to you. Your little brother.

You should have a car it's done you no end of good don't you
think so Quentin I call him Quentin at once you see I have heard
so much about him from Candace.

Why shouldn't you I want my boys to be more than friends yet
Candace and Quentin more than friends *Father I have committed*
what a pity you had no brother or sister *No sister no sister had no*
sister Don't ask Quentin he and Mr Compson both feel a little
insulted when I am strong enough to come down to the table I
am going on nerve now I'll pay for it after it's all over and you
have taken my little daughter away from me *My little sister had*
no. If I could say Mother. Mother

Unless I do what I am tempted to and take you instead I don't
think Mr Compson could overtake the car.

Ah Herbert Candace do you hear that *She wouldn't look at me*
soft stubborn jaw-angle not back-looking You needn't be jealous
though it's just an old woman he's flattering a grown married
daughter I can't believe it.

Nonsense you look like a girl you are lots younger than Candace
colour in your cheeks like a girl *A face reproachful tearful an odour*

of camphor and of tears a voice weeping steadily and softly beyond the twilit door the twilight-coloured smell of honeysuckle. Bringing empty trunks down the attic stairs they sounded like coffins French Lick. Found not death at the salt lick

Hats not unbleached and not hats. In three years I cannot wear a hat. I could not. Will there be hats then since I was not and not Harvard then. Where the best of thought Father said clings like dead ivy vines upon old dead brick. Not Harvard then. Not to me, anyway. Again. Sadder than was. Again. Saddest of all. Again.

Spoade had a shirt on; then it must be. When I can see my shadow again if not careful that I tricked into the water shall tread again upon my impervious shadow. But no sister. I wouldn't have done it. *I won't have my daughter spied on* I wouldn't have.

How can I control any of them when you have always taught them to have no respect for me and my wishes I know you look down on my people but is that any reason for teaching my children my own children I suffered for to have no respect Trampling my shadow's bones into the concrete with hard heels and then I was hearing the watch, and I touched the letters through my coat.

I will not have my daughter spied on by you or Quentin or anybody no matter what you think she has done

At least you agree there is reason for having her watched

I wouldn't have I wouldn't have. *I know you wouldn't I didn't mean to speak so sharply but women have no respect for each other for themselves*

But why did she The chimes began as I stepped on my shadow, but it was the quarter-hour. The Deacon wasn't in sight anywhere. *think I would have could have*

She didn't mean that that's the way women do things it's because she loves Caddy

The street lamps would go down the hill then rise toward town I walked upon the belly of my shadow. I could extend my hand beyond it. *feeling Father behind me beyond the rasping darkness of summer and August the street lamps* Father and I protect women from one another from themselves our women *Women are like that they don't acquire knowledge of people we are for that they are just born with a practical fertility of suspicion that makes a crop every so often and usually right they have an affinity for evil for supplying whatever the evil lacks in itself for drawing it about them instinctively as you do bed-clothing in slumber fertilizing the mind for it until the evil has served its purpose whether it ever existed or no* He was coming along between a couple of freshmen. He hadn't quite recovered from the parade, for he gave me a salute, a very superior-officerish kind.

'I want to see you a minute,' I said, stopping.

'See me? All right. See you again, fellows,' he said, stopping and turning back; 'glad to have chatted with you.' That was the Deacon, all over. Talk about your natural psychologists. They said he hadn't missed a train at the beginning of school in forty years, and that he could pick out a Southerner with one glance. He never missed, and once he had heard you speak, he could name your state. He had a regular uniform he met trains in, a sort of Uncle Tom's cabin outfit, patches and all.

'Yes, suh. Right dis way, young marster, hyer we is,' taking your bags. 'Hyer, boy, come hyer and git dese grips.' Whereupon a moving mountain of luggage would edge up, revealing a white boy of about fifteen, and the Deacon would hang another bag on him somehow and drive him off. 'Now, den, don't you drap hit. Yes, suh, young marster, jes give de old nigger yo room number, and hit'll be done got cold dar when you arrives.'

From then on until he had you completely subjugated he was always in or out of your room, ubiquitous and garrulous, though his manner gradually moved northward as his raiment improved, until at last when he had bled you until you began to learn better he was calling you Quentin or whatever, and when you saw him next he'd be wearing a cast-off Brooks suit and a hat with a Princeton club I forget which band that someone had given him and which he was pleasantly and unshakably convinced was a part of Abe Lincoln's military sash. Someone spread the story years ago, when he first appeared around college from wherever he came from, that he was a graduate of the divinity school. And when he came to understand what it meant he was so taken with it that he began to retail the story himself, until at last he must come to believe he really had. Anyway he related long pointless anecdotes of his undergraduate days, speaking familiarly of dead and departed professors by their first names, usually incorrect ones. But he had been guide mentor and friend to unnumbered crops of innocent and lonely freshmen, and I suppose that with all his petty chicanery and hypocrisy he stank no higher in heaven's nostrils than any other.

'Haven't seen you in three-four days,' he said, staring at me from his still military aura. 'You been sick?'

'No. I've been all right. Working, I reckon. I've seen you, though.'

'Yes?'

'In the parade the other day.'

'Oh, that. Yes, I was there. I don't care nothing about that sort of thing, you understand, but the boys likes to have me with them, the vet'runs does. Ladies wants all the old vet'runs to turn out, you know. So I has to oblige them.'

'And on that Wop holiday, too,' I said. 'You were obliging the WCTU then, I reckon.'

'That? I was doing that for my son-in-law. He aims to get a job on the city forces. Street cleaner. I tells him all he wants is a broom to sleep on. You saw me, did you?'

'Both times. Yes.'

'I mean, in uniform. How'd I look?'

'You looked fine. You looked better than any of them. They ought to make you a general, Deacon.'

He touched my arm, lightly, his hand that worn, gentle quality of niggers' hands. 'Listen. This ain't for outside talking. I don't mind telling you because you and me's the same folk, come long and short.' He leaned a little to me, speaking rapidly, his eyes not looking at me. 'I've got strings out, right now. Wait till next year. Just wait. Then see where I'm marching. I won't need to tell you how I'm fixing it; I say, just wait and see, my boy.' He looked at me now and clapped me lightly on the shoulder and rocked back on his heels, nodding at me. 'Yes, sir. I didn't turn Democrat three years ago for nothing. My son-in-law on the city; me – Yes, sir. If just turning Democrat'll make that son of a bitch go to work . . . And me: just you stand on that corner yonder a year from two days ago, and see.'

'I hope so. You deserve it, Deacon. And while I think about it –' I took the letter from my pocket. 'Take this around to my room tomorrow and give it to Shreve. He'll have something for you. But not till tomorrow, mind.'

He took the letter and examined it. 'It's sealed up.'

'Yes. And it's written inside, Not good until tomorrow.'

'H'm,' he said. He looked at the envelope, his mouth pursed. 'Something for me, you say?'

'Yes. A present I'm making you.'

He was looking at me now, the envelope white in his black hand, in the sun. His eyes were soft and irisless and brown, and suddenly I saw Roskus watching me from behind all his white folks' claptrap of uniforms and politics and Harvard manner, diffident, secret, inarticulate and sad. 'You ain't playing a joke on the old nigger, is you?'

'You know I'm not. Did any Southerner ever play a joke on you?'

'You're right. They're fine folks. But you can't live with them.'

'Did you ever try?' I said. But Roskus was gone. Once more he was that self he had long since taught himself to wear in the world's eye, pompous, spurious, not quite gross.

'I'll confer to your wishes, my boy.'

'Not until tomorrow, remember.'

'Sure,' he said; 'understand, my boy. Well –'

'I hope –' I said. He looked down at me, benignant, profound. Suddenly I held out my hand and we shook, he gravely, from the pompous height of his municipal and military dream. 'You're a good fellow, Deacon. I hope . . . You've helped a lot of young fellows, here and there.'

'I've tried to treat all folks right,' he said. 'I draw no petty social lines. A man to me is a man, wherever I find him.'

'I hope you'll always find as many friends as you've made.'

'Young fellows. I get along with them. They don't forget me, neither,' he said, waving the envelope. He put it into his pocket and buttoned his coat. 'Yes, sir, he said, 'I've had good friends.'

The chimes began again, the half-hour. I stood in the belly of my shadow and listened to the strokes spaced and tranquil along the sunlight, among the thin, still little leaves. Spaced and peaceful and serene, with that quality of autumn always in bells even in the month of brides. *Lying on the ground under the window bellowing* He took one look at her and knew. Out of the mouths of babes. *The street lamps* The chimes ceased. I went back to the post office, treading my shadow into pavement. *go down the hill then they rise toward town like lanterns hung one above another on a wall.* Father said because she loves Caddy she loves people through their shortcomings. Uncle Maury straddling his legs before the fire must remove one hand long enough to drink Christmas. Jason ran on, his hands in his pockets fell down and lay there like a trussed fowl until Versh set him up. *Whyn't you keep them hands outen your pockets when you running you could stand up then* Rolling his head in the cradle rolling it flat across the back. Caddy told Jason Versh said that the reason Uncle Maury didn't work was that he used to roll his head in the cradle when he was little.

Shreve was coming up the walk, shambling, fatly earnest, his glasses glinting beneath the running leaves like little pools.

'I gave Deacon a note for some things. I may not be in this afternoon, so don't you let him have anything until tomorrow, will you?'

'All right.' He looked at me. 'Say, what're you doing to-day anyhow? All dressed up and mooning around like the prologue to a suttee. Did you go to psychology this morning.'

'I'm not doing anything. Not until tomorrow, now.'

'What's that you got there?'

'Nothing. Pair of shoes I had half-soled. Not until tomorrow, you hear?'

'Sure. All right. Oh, by the way, did you get a letter off the table this morning?'

'No.'

'It's there. From Semiramis. Chauffeur brought it before ten o'clock.'

'All right. I'll get it. Wonder what she wants now.'

'Another band recital, I guess. Tumpty ta ta Gerald blah. "A little louder on the drum, Quentin." God, I'm glad I'm not a gentleman.' He went on, nursing a book, a little shapeless, fatly intent. *The street lamps* do you think so because one of our forefathers was a governor and three were generals and Mother's weren't

any live man is better than any dead man but no live or dead man is very much better than any other live or dead man *Done in Mother's mind though. Finished. Finished. Then we were all poisoned* you are confusing sin and morality women don't do that your Mother is thinking of morality whether it be sin or not has not occurred to her

Jason I must go away you keep the others I'll take Jason and go where nobody knows us so he'll have a chance to grow up and forget all this the others don't love me they have never loved anything with that streak of Compson selfishness and false pride Jason was the only one my heart went out to without dread

nonsense Jason is all right I was thinking that as soon as you feel better you and Caddy might go up to French Lick

and leave Jason here with nobody but you and the darkies

she will forget him then all the talk will die away *found not death at the salt licks*

maybe I could find a husband for her *not death at the salt licks*

The car came up and stopped. The bells were still ringing the half-hour. I got on and it went on again, blotting the half-hour.

No: the three-quarters. Then it would be ten minutes anyway. To leave Harvard your *Mother's dream for sold Benjy's pasture for* what have I done to have been given children like these Benjamin was punishment enough and now for her to have no more regard for me her own mother I've suffered for her dreamed and planned and sacrificed I went down into the valley yet never since she opened her eyes has she given me one unselfish thought at times I look at her I wonder if she can be my child except Jason he has never given me one moment's sorrow since I first held him in my arms I knew then that he was to be my joy and my salvation I thought that Benjamin was punishment enough for any sins I have committed I thought he was my punishment for putting aside my pride and marrying a man who held himself above me I don't complain I loved him above all of them because of it because my duty though Jason pulling at my heart all the while but I see now that I have not suffered enough I see now that I must pay for your sins as well as mine what have you done what sins have your high and mighty people visited upon me but you'll take up for them you always have found excuses for your own blood only Jason can do wrong because he is more Bascomb than Compson while your own daughter my little daughter my baby girl she is she is no better than that when I was a girl I was unfortunate I was only a Bascomb I was taught that there is no half-way ground that a woman is either a lady or not but I never dreamed when I held her in my arms that any daughter of mine could let herself don't you know I can look at her eyes and tell you may think she'd tell you but she doesn't tell things she is secretive you don't know her I know things she's done that I'd die before I'd have you know that's it go on criticize Jason accuse me of setting him to watch her as if it were a crime while your own daughter can I know you don't love him that you wish to believe faults against him you never have yes ridicule him as you always have Maury you cannot hurt me any more than your children already have and then I'll be gone and Jason with no one to love him shield him from this I look at him every day dreading to see this Compson blood beginning to show in him at last with his sister slipping out to see what do you call it then have you ever laid eyes on him will you even let me try to find out who he is it's not for myself I couldn't bear to see him it's for your sake to protect you but who can fight against bad blood you won't let me try we are to sit back with our hands folded while she not only drags your name in the dirt but corrupts the

very air your children breathe Jason you must let me go away I
cannot stand it let me have Jason and you keep the others they're
not my flesh and blood like he is strangers nothing of mine and
I am afraid of them I can take Jason and go where we are not
known I'll go down on my knees and pray for the absolution of
my sins that he may escape this curse to try to forget that the
others ever were

If that was the three-quarters, not over ten minutes now. One
car had just left, and people were already waiting for the next
one. I asked, but he didn't know whether another one would
leave before noon or not because you'd think that interurbans.
So the first one was another trolley. I got on. You can feel noon.
I wonder if even miners in the bowels of the earth. That's why
whistles; because people that sweat, and if just far enough from
sweat you won't hear whistles and in eight minutes you should
be that far from sweat in Boston. Father said a man is the sum
of his misfortunes. One day you'd think misfortune would get
tired, but then time is your misfortune Father said. A gull on an
invisible wire attached through space dragged. You carry the
symbol of your frustration into eternity. Then the wings are
bigger Father said only who can play a harp.

I could hear my watch whenever the car stopped, but not often
they were already eating *Who would play a* Eating the business of
eating inside of you space too space and time confused Stomach
saying noon brain saying eat o'clock All right I wonder what time
it is what of it. People were getting out. The trolley didn't stop
so often now, emptied by eating.

Then it was past. I got off and stood in my shadow and after
a while a car came along and I got on and went back to the
interurban station. There was a car ready to leave, and I found
a seat next the window and it started and I watched it sort of
frazzle out into slack tide flats, and then trees. Now and then I
saw the river and I thought how nice it would be for them down
at New London if the weather and Gerald's shell going solemnly
up the glinting forenoon and I wondered what the old woman
would be wanting now, sending me a note before ten o'clock in
the morning. What picture of Gerald I to be one of the *Dalton
Ames oh asbestos Quentin has shot* background. Something with
girls in it. Women do have *always his voice above the gabble voice
that breathed* an affinity for evil, for believing that no woman is
to be trusted, but that some men are too innocent to protect
themselves. Plain girls. Remote cousins and family friends whom

mere acquaintanceship invested with a sort of blood obligation noblesse oblige. And she sitting there telling us before their faces what a shame it was that Gerald should have all the family looks because a man didn't need it, was better off without it but without it a girl simply lost. Telling us about Gerald's women in a *Quentin has shot Herbert he shot his voice through the floor of Caddy's room* tone of smug approbation. 'When he was seventeen I said to him one day "What a shame that you should have a mouth like that it should be on a girl's face" and can you imagine *the curtains leaning in on the twilight upon the odour of the apple tree her head against the twilight her arms behind her head kimono-winged the voice that breathed o'er eden clothes upon the bed by the nose seen above the apple* what he said? just seventeen, mind. "Mother" he said "it often is." ' And him sitting there in attitudes regal watching two or three of them through his eyelashes. They gushed like swallows swooping his eyelashes. Shreve said he always had *Are you going to look after Benjy and Father*

The less you say about Benjy and Father the better when have you ever considered them Caddy

Promise

You needn't worry about them you're getting out in good shape

Promise I'm sick you'll have to promise wondered who invented that joke but then he always had considered Mrs Bland a remarkably preserved woman he said she was grooming Gerald to seduce a duchess sometime. She called Shreve that fat Canadian youth twice she arranged a new room-mate for me without consulting me at all, once for me to move out, once for

He opened the door in the twilight. His face looked like a pumpkin pie.

'Well, I'll say a fond farewell. Cruel fate may part us, but I will never love another. Never.'

'What are you talking about?'

'I'm talking about cruel fate in eight yards of apricot silk and more metal pound for pound than a galley slave and the sole owner and proprietor of the unchallenged peripatetic john of the late Confederacy.' Then he told me how she had gone to the proctor to have him moved out and how the proctor had revealed enough low stubbornness to insist on consulting Shreve first. Then she suggested that he send for Shreve right off and do it, and he wouldn't do that, so after that she was hardly civil to Shreve. 'I make it a point never to speak harshly of females,' Shreve said, 'but that woman has got more ways like a bitch than any lady in these sovereign states and dominions.' and now Letter on the table by hand, command orchid scented coloured If she knew I had passed almost beneath the window knowing it there without My dear Madam I have not yet had an opportunity of receiving your communication but I beg in advance to be excused today or yesterday and tomorrow or when As I remember that the next one is to be how Gerald throws his nigger downstairs and how the nigger plead to be allowed to matriculate in the divinity school to be near marster marse gerald and How he ran all the way to the station beside the carriage with tears in his eyes when marse gerald rid away I will wait until the day for the one about the sawmill husband came to the kitchen door with a shotgun Gerald went down and bit the gun in two and handed it back and wiped his hands on a silk handkerchief threw the handkerchief in the stove I've only heard that one twice

shot him through the I saw you come in here so I watched my chance and came along thought we might get acquainted have a cigar

Thanks I don't smoke

No things must have changed up there since my day mind if I light up

Help yourself

Thanks I've heard a lot I guess your mother won't mind if I put the match behind the screen will she a lot about you Candace talked about you all the time up there at the Licks. I got pretty jealous I says to myself who is this Quentin anyway I must see what this animal looks like because I was hit pretty hard see soon as I saw the little girl I don't mind telling you it never occurred to me it was her brother she kept talking about she couldn't have talked about you any more if you'd been the only man in the world husband wouldn't have been in it you won't change your mind and have a smoke

I don't smoke

In that case I won't insist even though it is a pretty fair weed cost me twenty-five bucks a hundred wholesale friend in Havana yes I guess there are lots of changes up there I keep promising myself a visit but I never get around to it been hitting the ball now for ten years I can't get away from the bank during school fellow's habits change things that seem important to an under-graduate you know tell me about things up there

I'm not going to tell Father and Mother if that's what you are getting at

Not going to tell not going to oh that that's what you are talking about is it you understand that I don't give a damn whether you tell or not understand that a thing like that unfortunate but no police crime I wasn't the first or the last I was just unlucky you might have been luckier

You lie

Keep your shirt on I'm not trying to make you tell anything you don't want to meant no offence of course a young fellow like you would consider a thing of that sort a lot more serious than you will in five years

I don't know but one way to consider cheating I don't think I'm likely to learn different at Harvard

We're better than a play you must have made the Dramat well you're right no need to tell them we'll let bygones be bygones eh no reason why you and I should let a little thing like that come between us I like you Quentin I like your appearance you don't look like these other hicks I'm glad we're going to hit it off like this I've promised your mother to do something for Jason but I would like to give you a hand too Jason would be just as well off here but there's no future in a hole like this for a young fellow like you

Thanks you'd better stick to Jason he'd suit you better than I would

I'm sorry about that business but a kid like I was then I never had a mother like yours to teach me the finer points it would just hurt her necessarily to know it yes you're right to need to that includes Candace of course

I said Mother and Father

Look here take a look at me how long do you think you'd last with me

I won't have to last long if you learned to fight up at school too try and see how long I would

You damned little what do you think you're getting at

Try and see

My God the cigar what would your mother say if she found a blister on her mantel just in time too look here Quentin we're about to do something we'll both regret I like you liked you as soon as I saw you I says he must be a damned good fellow whoever he is or Candace wouldn't be so keen on him listen I've been out in the world now for ten years things don't matter so much then you'll find that out let's you and I get together on this thing sons of old Harvard and all I guess I wouldn't know the place now

best place for a young fellow in the world I'm going to send my
sons there give them a better chance than I had wait don't go
yet let's discuss this thing a young man gets these ideas and I'm
all for them does him good while he's in school forms his character
good for tradition the school but when he gets out into the world
he'll have to get his the best way he can because he'll find that
everybody else is doing the same thing and be damned to here
let's shake hands and let bygones be bygones for your mother's
sake remember her health come on give me your hand here look
at it it's just out of convent look not a blemish not even been
creased yet see here

To hell with your money

No no come on I belong to the family now see I know how it
is with a young fellow he has lots of private affairs it's always
pretty hard to get the old man to stump up for I know haven't I
been there and not so long ago either but now I'm getting
married and all specially up there come on don't be a fool listen
when we get a chance for a real talk I want to tell you about a
little widow over in town

I've heard that too keep your damned money

Call it a loan then just shut your eyes a minute and you'll be
fifty

Keep your hands off me you'd better get that cigar off the
mantel

Tell and be damned than see what it gets you if you were not
a damned fool you'd have seen that I've got them too tight for
any half-baked Galahad of a brother your mother's told me about
your sort with your head swelled up come in oh come in dear
Quentin and I were just getting acquainted talking about Harvard
did you want me can't stay away from the old man can she

Go out a minute Herbert I want to talk to Quentin

Come in come in let's all have a gabfest and get acquainted I
was just telling Quentin

Go on Herbert go out a while

Well all right than I suppose you and bubber do want to see
one another once more eh

You'd better take that cigar off the mantel

Right as usual my boy then I'll toddle along let them order
you around while they can Quentin after day after tomorrow it'll
be pretty please to the old man won't it dear give us a kiss honey

Oh stop that save that for day after tomorrow

I'll want interest then don't let Quentin do anything he can't finish oh by the way did I tell Quentin the story about the man's parrot and what happened to it a sad story remind me of that think of it yourself ta-ta see you in the funny paper

Well

Well

What are you up to now

Nothing

You're meddling in my business again didn't you get enough of that last summer

Caddy you've got fever *You're sick how are you sick*

I'm just sick. I can't ask.

Shot his voice through the

Not that blackguard Caddy

Now and then the river glinted beyond things in sort of swooping glints, across noon and after. Well after now, though we had passed where he was still pulling upstream majestical in the face of god gods. Better. Gods. God would be canaille too in Boston in Massachusetts. Or maybe just not a husband. The wet oars winking him along in bright winks and female palms. Adulant. Adulant if not a husband he'd ignore God. *That blackguard, Caddy* The river glinted away beyond a swooping curve.

I'm sick you'll have to promise

Sick how are you sick

I'm just sick I can't ask anybody yet promise you will

If they need any looking after it's because of you how are you sick Under the window we could hear the car leaving for the station, the 8:10 train. To bring back cousins. Heads. Increasing himself head by head but not barbers. Manicure girls. We had a blood horse once. In the stable yes, but under leather a cur. *Quentin has shot all of their voices through the floor of Caddy's room*

The car stopped. I got off, into the middle of my shadow. A road crossed the track. There was a wooden marquee with an old man eating something out of a paper bag, and then the car was out of hearing too. The road went into the trees, where it would be shady, but June foliage in New England not much thicker than April at home in Mississippi. I could see a smoke stack. I turned my back to it, tramping my shadow into the dust. *There was something terrible in me sometimes at night I could see it grinning at me I could see it through them grinning at me through their faces it's gone now and I'm sick*

Caddy

Don't touch me just promise

If you're sick you can't
Yes I can after that it'll be all right it won't matter don't let them
send him to Jackson promise
I promise Caddy Caddy
Don't touch me don't touch me
What does it look like Caddy
What
That that grins at you that thing through them
I could still see the smoke stack. That's where the water would
be, heading out to the sea and the peaceful grottoes. Tumbling
peacefully they would, and when He said Rise only the flat irons.
When Versh and I hunted all day we wouldn't take any lunch,
and at twelve o'clock I'd get hungry. I'd stay hungry until about
one, then all of a sudden I'd even forget that I wasn't hungry
any more. *The street lamps go down the hill then heard the car go*
down the hill. The chair-arm flat cool smooth under my forehead
shaping the chair the apple tree leaning on my hair above the eden
clothes by the nose seen You've got fever I felt it yesterday it's like
being near a stove.
Don't touch me.
Caddy you can't do it if you are sick. That blackguard.
I've got to marry somebody. *Then they told me the bone would*
have to be broken again
At last I couldn't see the smoke stack. The road went beside a
wall. Trees leaned over the wall, sprayed with sunlight. The stone
was cool. Walking near it you could feel the coolness. Only our
country was not like this country. There was something about
just walking through it. A kind of still and violent fecundity
that satisfied ever bread-hunger like. Flowing around you, not
brooding and nursing every niggard stone. Like it were put to
makeshift for enough green to go around among the trees and
even the blue of distance not that rich chimaera. *told me the bone*
would have to be broken again and inside me it began to say Ah Ah Ah
and I began to sweat. What do I care I know what a broken leg is all
it is it won't be anything I'll just have to stay in the house a little longer
that's all and my jaw-muscles getting numb and my mouth saying Wait
Wait just a minute through the sweat ah ah ah behind my teeth and
Father damn that horse damn that horse. Wait it's my fault. He came
along the fence every morning with a basket toward the kitchen dragging
a stick along the fence every morning I dragged myself to the window
cast and all and laid for him with a piece of coal Dilsey said you goin
to ruin yoself ain't you got no mo sense than that not fo days since you

bruck hit. Wait I'll get used to it in a minute wait just a minute I'll get

Even sound seemed to fail in this air, like the air was worn out with carrying sounds so long. A dog's voice carries further than a train, in the darkness anyway. And some people's. Niggers. Louis Hatcher never even used his horn carrying it and that old lantern. I said, 'Louis, when was the last time you cleaned that lantern?'

'I cleant hit a little while back. You member when all dat flood-watter wash dem folks away up yonder? I cleant hit dat ve'y day. Old woman and me setting fore de fire dat night and she say "Louis, whut you gwine do ef dat flood git out dis fur?" and I say "Dat's a fack. I reckon I had better clean dat lantun up." So I cleant hit dat night.'

'That flood was way up in Pennsylvania,' I said. 'It couldn't even have got down this far.'

'Dat's whut you says,' Louis said. 'Watter kin git des ez high en wet in Jefferson ez hit kin in Pennsylvaney, I reckon. Hit's de folks dat says de high watter can't git dis fur dat comes floatin out on de ridge-pole, too.'

'Did you and Martha get out that night?'

'We done jest that. I cleant dat lantun and me and her sot de balance of de night on top o dat knoll back de graveyard. En ef I'd knowed of aihy one higher, we'd a been on hit instead.'

'And you haven't cleaned that lantern since then.'

'Whut I want to clean hit when dey ain't no need?'

'You mean, until another flood comes along?'

'Hit kep us outen dat un.'

'Oh, come on, Uncle Louis,' I said.

'Yes, suh. You do you way en I do mine. Ef all I got to do to keep outen de high watter is to clean dis yere lantun, I wont quoil wid no man.'

'Unc' Louis wouldn't ketch nothin wid a light he could see by,' Versh said.

'I wuz huntin possums in dis country when dey was still drowndin nits in yo pappy's head wid coal oil, boy,' Louis said. 'Ketchin um, too.'

'Dat's de troof,' Versh said. 'I reckon Unc' Louis done caught mo possums than aihy man in dis country.'

'Yes, suh,' Louis said, 'I got plenty light fer possums to see, all right. I ain't heard none o dem complainin. Hush, now. Dar he. Whooey. Hum awn, dawg.' And we'd sit in the dry leaves that whispered a little with the slow respiration of our waiting and with the slow breathing of the earth and the windless October, the rank smell of the lantern fouling the brittle air, listening to the dogs and to the echo of Louis' voice dying away. He never raised it, yet on a still night we have heard it from our front porch. When he called the dogs in he sounded just like the horn he carried slung on his shoulder and never used, but clearer, mellower, as though his voice were a part of darkness and silence, coiling out of it, coiling into it again. WhoOoooo. WhoOoooo. WhoOoooooooooooooooo. *Got to marry somebody*

Have there been very many Caddy
I don't know too many will you look after Benjy and Father
You don't know whose it is then does he know
Don't touch me will you look after Benjy and Father

I began to feel the water before I came to the bridge. The bridge was of grey stone, lichened, dappled with slow moisture where the fungus crept. Beneath it the water was clear and still in the shadow, whispering and clucking about the stone in fading swirls of spinning sky. *Caddy that*

I've got to marry somebody Versh told me about a man mutilated himself. He went into the woods and did it with a razor, sitting in a ditch. A broken razor flinging them backward over his shoulder the same motion complete the jerked skein of blood backward not looping. But that's not it. It's not not having them. It's never to have had them then I could say O That That's Chinese I don't know Chinese. And Father said it's because you are a virgin: don't you see? Women are never virgins. Purity is a negative state and therefore contrary to nature. It's nature is hurting you not Caddy and I said That's just words and he said So is virginity and I said you don't know. You can't know and he said Yes. On the instant when we come to realize that tragedy is second-hand.

Where the shadow of the bridge fell I could see down for a long way, but not as far as the bottom. When you leave a leaf in water a long time after awhile the tissue will be gone and the delicate fibres waving slow as the motion of sleep. They don't touch one another, no matter how knotted up they once were, no matter how close they lay once to the bones. And maybe when He says Rise the eyes will come floating up too, out of the deep quiet and the sleep, to look on glory. And after a while the flat irons would come floating up. I hid them under the end of the bridge and went back and leaned on the rail.

I could not see the bottom, but I could see a long way into the motion of the water before the eye gave out, and then I saw a shadow hanging like a fat arrow stemming into the current. Mayflies skimmed in and out of the shadow of the bridge just above the surface. *If it could just be a hell beyond that: the clean flame the two of us more than dead. Then you will have only me then only me then the two of us amid the pointing and the horror beyond the clean flame* The arrow increased without motion, then in a quick swirl the trout lipped a fly beneath the surface with that sort of gigantic delicacy of an elephant picking up a peanut. The fading vortex drifted away down stream and then I saw the arrow again, nose into the current, wavering delicately to the motion of the water above which the Mayflies slanted and poised. *Only you and me then amid the pointing and the horror walled by the clean flame*

The trout hung, delicate and motionless among the wavering shadows. Three boys with fishing poles came on to the bridge and we leaned on the rail and looked down at the trout. They knew the fish. He was a neighbourhood character.

'They've been trying to catch that trout for twenty-five years. There's a store in Boston offers a twenty-five dollar fishing rod to anybody that can catch him.'

'Why don't you all catch him, then? Wouldn't you like to have a twenty-five dollar fishing rod?'

'Yes,' they said. They leaned on the rail, looking down at the trout. 'I sure would,' one said.

'I wouldn't take the rod,' the second said. 'I'd take the money instead.'

'Maybe they wouldn't do that,' the first said. 'I bet he'd make you take the rod.'

'Then I'd sell it.'

'You couldn't get twenty-five dollars for it.'

'I'd take what I could get then. I can catch just as many fish with this pole as I could with a twenty-five dollar one.' Then they talked about what they would do with twenty-five dollars. They all talked at once, their voices insistent and contradictory and impatient, making of unreality a possibility, then a probability, then an incontrovertible fact, as people will when their desires become words.

'I'd buy a horse and wagon,' the second said.

'Yes, you would,' the others said.

'I would. I know where I can buy one for twenty-five dollars. I know the man.'

'Who is it?'

'That's all right who it is. I can buy it for twenty-five dollars.'

'Yah,' the others said, 'He don't know any such thing. He's just talking.'

'Do you think so?' the boy said. They continued to jeer at him, but he said nothing more. He leaned on the rail, looking down at the trout which he had already spent, and suddenly the acrimony, the conflict, was gone from their voices, as if to them too it was as though he had captured the fish and bought his horse and wagon, they too partaking of that adult trait of being convinced of anything by an assumption of silent superiority. I suppose that people using themselves and each other so much by words, are at least consistent in attributing wisdom to a still tongue, and for a while I could feel the other two seeking swiftly for some means by which to cope with him, to rob him of his horse and wagon.

'You couldn't get twenty-five dollars for that pole,' the first said. 'I bet anything you couldn't.'

'He hasn't caught that trout yet,' the third said suddenly, then they both cried:

'Yah, wha'd I tell you? What's the man's name? I dare you to tell. There ain't any such man.'

'Ah, shut up,' the second said. 'Look, Here he comes again.' They leaned on the rail, motionless, identical, their poles slanting slenderly in the sunlight, also identical. The trout rose without haste, a shadow in faint wavering increase; again the little vortex faded slowly downstream. 'Gee,' the first one murmured.

'We don't try to catch him any more,' he said. 'We just watch Boston folks that come out and try.'

'Is he the only fish in this pool?'

'Yes. He ran all the others out. The best place to fish around here is down at the Eddy.'

'No it ain't,' the second said. 'It's better at Bigelow's Mill two to one.' Then they argued for a while about which was the best fishing and then left off all of a sudden to watch the trout rise again and the broken swirl of water suck down a little of the sky. I asked how far it was to the nearest town. They told me.

'But the closest car line is that way,' the second said, pointing back down the road. 'Where are you going?'

'Nowhere. Just walking.'

'You from the college?'

'Yes. Are there any factories in that town?'

'Factories?' They looked at me.

'No,' the second said. 'Not there.' They looked at my clothes. 'You looking for work?'

'How about Bigelow's Mill?' the third said. 'That's a factory.'

'Factory my eye. He means a sure enough factory.'

'One with a whistle,' I said. 'I haven't heard any one o'clock whistles yet.'

'Oh,' the second said. 'There's a clock in the Unitarian steeple. You can find out the time from that. Haven't you got a watch on that chain?'

'I broke it this morning.' I showed them my watch. They examined it gravely.

'It's still running,' the second said. 'What does a watch like that cost?'

'It was a present,' I said. 'My father gave it to me when I graduated from high school.'

'Are you a Canadian?' the third said. He had red hair.

'Canadian?'

'He don't talk like them,' the second said. 'I've heard them talk. He talks like they do in minstrel shows.'

'Say,' the third said, 'Ain't you afraid he'll hit you?'

'Hit me?'

'You said he talks like a coloured man.'

'Ah, dry up,' the second said. 'You can see the steeple when you get over that hill there.'

I thanked them. 'I hope you have good luck. Only don't catch that old fellow down there. He deserves to be let alone.'

'Can't anybody catch that fish,' the first said. They leaned on the rail, looking down into the water, the three poles like three slanting threads of yellow fire in the sun. I walked upon my shadow, tramping it into the dappled shade of trees again. The road curved, mounting away from the water. It crossed the hill, then descended winding, carrying the eye, the mind on ahead beneath a still green tunnel, and the square cupola above the trees and the round eye of the clock but far enough. I sat down at the roadside. The grass was ankle deep, myriad. The shadows on the road were as still as if they had been put there with a stencil, with slanting pencils of sunlight. But it was only a train, and after while it died away beyond the trees, the long sound, and then I could hear my watch and the train dying away, as though it were running through another month or another summer somewhere, rushing away under the poised gull and all things rushing. Except Gerald. He would be sort of grand too, pulling in lonely state across the noon, rowing himself right out of noon, up the long bright air like an apotheosis, mounting into a drowsing infinity where only he and the gull, the one terrifically motionless, the other in a steady and measured pull and recover that partook of inertia itself, the world punily beneath their shadows on the sun. Caddy that blackguard that blackguard Caddy

Their voices came over the hill, and the three slender poles like balanced threads of running fire. They looked at me passing, not slowing.

'Well,' I said, 'I don't see him.'

'We didn't try to catch him,' the first said. 'You can't catch that fish.'

'There's the clock,' the second said, pointing. 'You can tell the time when you get a little closer.'

'Yes,' I said, 'All right.' I got up. 'You all going to town?'

'We're going to the Eddy for chub,' the first said.

'You can't catch anything at the Eddy,' the second said.

'I guess you want to go to the mill, with a lot of fellows splashing and scaring all the fish away.'

'You can't catch any fish at the Eddy.'

'We won't catch none nowhere if we don't go on,' the third said.

'I don't see why you keep on talking about the Eddy,' the second said. 'You can't catch anything there.'

'You don't have to go,' the first said. 'You're not tied to me.'

'Let's go to the mill and go swimming,' the third said.

'I'm going to the Eddy and fish,' the first said. 'You can do as you please.'

'Say, how long has it been since you heard of anybody catching a fish at the Eddy?' the second said to the third.

'Let's go to the mill and go swimming,' the third said. The cupola sank slowly beyond the trees, with the round face of the clock far enough yet. We went on in the dappled shade. We came to an orchard, pink and white. It was full of bees; already we could hear them.

'Let's go to the mill and go swimming,' the third said. A lane turned off beside the orchard. The third boy slowed and halted. The first went on, flecks of sunlight slipping along the pole across his shoulder and down the back of his shirt. 'Come on,' the third said. The second boy stopped too. *Why must you marry somebody Caddy*

Do you want me to say it do you think that if I say it it won't be
'Let's go up to the mill,' he said. 'Come on.'

The first boy went on. His bare feet made no sound, falling softer than leaves in the thin dust. In the orchard the bees sounded like a wind getting up, a sound caught by a spell just under crescendo and sustained. The lane went along the wall, arched over, shattered with bloom, dissolving into trees. Sunlight slanted into it, sparse and eager. Yellow butterflies flickered along the shade like flecks of sun.

'What do you want to go to the Eddy for?' the second boy said. 'You can fish at the mill if you want to.'

'Ah, let him go,' the third said. They looked after the first boy. Sunlight slid patchily across his walking shoulders, glinting along the pole like yellow ants.

'Kenny,' the second said. *Say it to Father will you I will am my fathers Progenitive I invented him created I him Say it to him it will not be for he will say I was not and then you and I since philoprogenitive*

'Ah, come on,' the boy said. 'They're already in.' They looked after the first boy. 'Yah,' they said suddenly, 'go on then, mamma's boy. If he goes swimming he'll get his head wet and then he'll get a licking.' They turned into the lane and went on, the yellow butterflies slanting about them along the shade.

it is because there is nothing else I believe there is something else but there may not be and then I You will find that even injustice is scarcely worthy of what you believe yourself to be. He paid me no attention, his jaw set in profile, his face turned a little away beneath his broken hat.

'Why don't you go swimming with them?' I said. *that blackguard Caddy*

Were you trying to pick a fight with him were you

A liar and a scoundrel Caddy was dropped from his club for cheating at cards got sent to Coventry caught cheating at midterm exams and expelled

Well what about it I'm not going to play cards with

'Do you like fishing better than swimming?' I said. The sound of the bees diminished, sustained yet, as though instead of sinking into silence, silence merely increased between us, as water rises. The road curved again and became a street between shady lawns with white houses. *Caddy that blackguard can you think of Benjy and Father and do it not of me*

What else can I think about what else have I thought about The boy turned from the street. He climbed a picket fence without looking back and crossed the lawn to a tree and laid the pole down and climbed into the fork of the tree and sat there, his back to the road and the dappled sun motionless at last upon his white shirt. *Else have I thought about I can't even cry I died last year I told you I had but I didn't know then what I meant I didn't know what I was saying* Some days in late August at home are like this, the air thin and eager like this, with something in it sad and nostalgic and familiar. Man the sum of his climatic experiences Father said. Man the sum of what have you. A problem in impure properties carried tediously to an unvarying nil: stalemate of dust and desire. *But now I know I'm dead I tell you*

Then why must you listen we can go away you and Benjy and me where nobody knows us where The buggy was drawn by a white horse, his feet clopping in the thin dust; spidery wheels chattering thin and dry, moving uphill beneath a rippling shawl of leaves. Elm. No: ellum. Ellum.

On what on your school money the money they sold the pasture for so you could go to Harvard don't you see you've got to finish now if you don't finish he'll have nothing

Sold the pasture His white shirt was motionless in the fork, in the flickering shade. The wheels were spidery. Beneath the sag of the buggy the hooves neatly rapid like the motions of a lady doing embroidery, diminishing without progress like a figure on a treadmill being drawn rapidly off stage. The street turned again. I could see the white cupola, the round stupid assertion of the clock. *Sold the pasture*

Father will be dead in a year they say if he doesn't stop drinking and he won't stop he can't stop since I since last summer and then they'll send Benjy to Jackson I can't cry I can't even cry one minute she was standing in the door the next minute he was pulling at her dress and bellowing his voice hammered back and forth between the walls in waves and she shrinking against the wall getting smaller and smaller with her white face her eyes like thumbs dug into it until he pushed her out of the room his voice hammering back and forth as though its own momentum would not let it stop as though there were no place for it in silence bellowing

When you opened the door a bell tinkled, but just once, high and clear and small in the neat obscurity above the door, as though it were gauged and tempered to make that single clear small sound so as not to wear the bell out nor to require the expenditure of too much silence in restoring it when the door opened upon the recent warm scent of baking; a little dirty child with eyes like a toy bear's and two patent-leather pig-tails.

'Hello, sister.' Her face was like a cup of milk dashed with coffee in the sweet warm emptiness. 'Anybody here?'

But she merely watched me until a door opened and the lady came. Above the counter where the ranks of crisp shapes behind the glass her neat grey face her hair tight and sparse from her neat grey skull, spectacles in neat grey rims riding approaching like something on a wire, like a cash box in a store. She looked like a librarian. Something among dusty shelves of ordered certitudes long divorced from reality, desiccating peacefully, as if a breath of that air which sees injustice done

'Two of these, please, ma'am.'

From under the counter she produced a square cut from a newspaper and laid it on the counter and lifted the two buns out. The little girl watched them with still and unwinking eyes like two currants floating motionless in a cup of weak coffee Land of the kike home of the wop. Watching the bread, the neat grey hands, a broad gold band on the left forefinger, knuckled there by a blue knuckle.

'Do you do your own baking, ma'am?'

'Sir?' she said. Like that. Sir? Like on the stage. Sir? 'Five cents. Was there anything else?'

'No, ma'am. Not for me. This lady wants something.' She was not tall enough to see over the case, so she went to the end of the counter and looked at the little girl.

'Did you bring her in here?'

'No, ma'am. She was here when I came.'

'You little wretch,' she said. She came out around the counter, but she didn't touch the little girl. 'Have you got anything in your pockets?'

'She hasn't got any pockets,' I said. 'She wasn't doing anything. She was just standing here, waiting for you.'

'Why didn't the bell ring, then?' She glared at me. She just needed a bunch of switches, a blackboard behind her 2 x 2 e 5. 'She'll hide it under her dress and a body'd never know it. You, child. How'd you get in here?'

The little girl said nothing. She looked at the woman, then she gave me a flying black glance and looked at the woman again. 'Them foreigners,' the woman said. 'How'd she get in without the bell ringing?'

'She came in when I opened the door,' I said. 'It rang once for both of us. She couldn't reach anything from here, anyway.

Besides, I don't think she would. Would you, sister?' The little girl looked at me secretive, contemplative. 'What do you want? bread?'

She extended her fist. It uncurled upon a nickel, moist and dirty, moist dirt ridged into her flesh. The coin was damp and warm. I could smell it, faintly metallic.

'Have you got a five cent loaf, please, ma'am?'

From beneath the counter she produced a square cut from a newspaper sheet and laid it on the counter and wrapped a loaf into it. I laid the coin and another one on the counter. 'And another one of those buns, please, ma'am.'

She took another bun from the case. 'Give me that parcel,' she said. I gave it to her and she unwrapped it and put the third bun in and wrapped it and took up the coins and found two coppers in her apron and gave them to me. I handed them to the little girl. Her fingers closed about them, damp and hot, like worms.

'You going to give her that bun?' the woman said.

'Yessum,' I said. 'I expect your cooking smells as good to her as it does to me.'

I took up the two packages and gave the bread to the little girl, the woman all iron-grey behind the counter, watching us with cold certitude. 'You wait a minute,' she said. She went to the rear. The door opened again and closed. The little girl watched me, holding the bread against her dirty dress.

'What's your name?' I said. She quit looking at me, but she was still motionless. She didn't even seem to breathe. The woman returned. She had a funny looking thing in her hand. She carried it sort of like it might have been a dead pet rat.

'Here,' she said. The child looked at her. 'Take it,' the woman said, jabbing it at the little girl. 'It just looks peculiar. I calculate you won't know the difference when you eat it. Here. I can't stand here all day.' The child took it, still watching her. The woman rubbed her hands on her apron. 'I got to have that bell fixed,' she said. She went to the door and jerked it open. The little bell tinkled once, faint and clear and invisible. We moved toward the door and the woman's peering back.

'Thank you for the cake,' I said.

'Them foreigners,' she said, staring up into the obscurity where the bell tinkled. 'Take my advice and stay clear of them, young man.'

'Yessum,' I said. 'Come on, sister.' We went out. 'Thank you, ma'am.'

She swung the door to, then jerked it open again, making the bell give forth its single small note. 'Foreigners,' she said, peering up at the bell.

We went on. 'Well,' I said, 'How about some ice cream?' She was eating the gnarled cake. 'Do you like ice cream?' She gave me a black still look, chewing. 'Come on.'

We came to the drug-store and had some ice cream. She wouldn't put the loaf down. 'Why not put it down so you can eat better?' I said, offering to take it. But she held to it, chewing the ice cream like it was taffy. The bitten cake lay on the table. She ate the ice cream steadily, then she fell to on the cake again, looking about at the showcases. I finished mine and we went out.

'Which way do you live?' I said.

A buggy, the one with the white horse it was. Only Dog peabody is fat. Three hundred pounds. You ride with him on the uphill side, holding on. Children. Walking easier than holding uphill. *Seen the doctor yet have you seen Caddy*

I don't have to I can't ask now afterward it will be all right, it won't matter

Because women so delicate so mysterious Father said. Delicate equilibrium of periodical filth between two moons balanced. Moons he said full and yellow as harvest moons her hips thighs. Outside outside of them always but. Yellow. Feet soles with walking like. Then know that some man that all those mysterious and imperious concealed. With all that inside of them shapes an outward suavity waiting for a touch to. Liquid putrefaction like drowned things floating like pale rubber flabbily filled getting the odour of honeysuckle all mixed up.

'You'd better take your bread on home, hadn't you?'

She looked at me. She chewed quietly and steadily; at regular intervals a small distension passed smoothly down her throat. I opened my package and gave her one of the buns. 'Good-bye,' I said.

I went on. Then I looked back. She was behind me. 'Do you live down this way?' She said nothing. She walked beside me, under my elbow sort of, eating. We went on. It was quiet, hardly anyone about *getting the odour of honeysuckle all mixed She would have told me not to let me sit there on the steps hearing her door twilight slamming hearing Benjy still crying Supper she would have to come down then getting honeysuckle all mixed up in it.* We reached the corner.

'Well, I've got to go down this way,' I said, 'Good-bye.' She stopped too. She swallowed the last of the cake, then she began on the bun, watching me across it. 'Good-bye,' I said. I turned into the street and went on, but I went to the next corner before I stopped.

'Which way do you live?' I said. 'This way?' I pointed down the street. She just looked at me. 'Do you live over that way? I bet you live close to the station, where the trains are. Don't you?' She just looked at me, serene and secret and chewing. The street was empty both ways, with quiet lawns and houses neat among the trees, but no one at all except back there. We turned and went back. Two men sat in chairs in front of a store.

'Do you all know this little girl? She sort of took up with me and I can't find where she lives.'

They quit looking at me and looked at her.

'Must be one of them new Italian families,' one said. He wore a rusty frock coat. 'I've seen her before. What's your name, little girl?' She looked at them blackly for awhile, her jaws moving steadily. She swallowed without ceasing to chew.

'Maybe she can't speak English,' the other said.

'They sent her after bread,' I said. 'She must be able to speak something.'

'What's your pa's name?' the first said. 'Pete? Joe? name John huh?' She took another bite from the bun.

'What must I do with her?' I said. 'She just follows me. I've got to get back to Boston.'

'You from the college?'

'Yes, sir. And I've got to get on back.'

'You might go up the street and turn her over to Anse. He'll be up at the livery stable. The marshall.'

'I reckon that's what I'll have to do,' I said. 'I've got to do something with her. Much obliged. Come on sister.'

We went up the street, on the shady side, where the shadow of the broken façade blotted slowly across the road. We came to the livery stable. The marshall wasn't there. A man sitting in a chair tilted in the broad low door, where a dark cool breeze of ammonia blew among the ranked stalls, said to look at the post office. He didn't know her either.

'Them furriners. I can't tell one from another. You might take her across the tracks where they live, and maybe somebody'll claim her.'

We went to the post office. It was back down the street. The man in the frock coat was opening a newspaper.

'Anse just drove out of town,' he said. 'I guess you'd better go down past the station and walk past them houses by the river. Somebody there'll know her.'

'I guess I'll have to,' I said. 'Come on, sister.' She pushed the last piece of the bun into her mouth and swallowed it. 'Want another?' I said. She looked at me, chewing, her eyes black and unwinking and friendly. I took the other two buns out and gave her one and bit into the other. I asked a man where the station was and he showed me. 'Come on, sister.'

We reached the station and crossed the tracks, where the river was. A bridge crossed it, and a street of jumbled frame houses followed the river, backed on to it. A shabby street, but with an air heterogeneous and vivid too. In the centre of an untrimmed plot enclosed by a fence of gaping and broken pickets stood an ancient lopsided surrey and a weathered house from an upper window of which hung a garment of vivid pink.

'Does that look like your house?' I said. She looked at me over the bun. 'This one?' I said, pointing. She just chewed, but it seemed to me that I discerned something affirmative, acquiescent even if it wasn't eager, in her air. 'This one?' I said. 'Come on, then.' I entered the broken gate. I looked back at her. 'Here?' I said. 'This look like your house?'

She nodded her head rapidly, looking at me, gnawing into the damp half moon of the bread. We went on. A walk of broken random flags, speared by fresh coarse blades of grass, led to the broken stoop. There was no movement about the house at all, and the pink garment hanging in no wind from the upper window. There was a bell pull with a porcelain knob, attached to about six feet of wire when I stopped pulling and knocked. The little girl had the crust edgeways in her chewing mouth.

A woman opened the door. She looked at me, then she spoke rapidly to the little girl in Italian, with a rising inflexion, then a pause, interrogatory. She spoke to her again, the little girl looking at her across the end of the crust, pushing it into her mouth with a dirty hand.

'She says she lives here,' I said. 'I met her downtown. Is this your bread?'

'No spika,' the woman said. She spoke to the little girl again. The little girl just looked at her.

'No live here?' I said. I pointed to the girl, then at her, then at the door. The woman shook her head. She spoke rapidly. She came to the edge of the porch and pointed down the road, speaking.

I nodded violently too. 'You come show?' I said. I took her arm, waving my other hand toward the road. She spoke swiftly, pointing. 'You come show,' I said, trying to lead her down the steps.

'Si, si,' she said, holding back, showing me whatever it was. I nodded again.

'Thanks. Thanks. Thanks.' I went down the steps and walked toward the gate, not running, but pretty fast. I reached the gate and stopped and looked at her for a while. The crust was gone now, and she looked at me with her black friendy stare. The woman stood on the stoop, watching us.

'Come on, then,' I said. 'We'll have to find the right one sooner or later.'

She moved along just under my elbow. We went on. The houses all seemed empty. Not a soul in sight. A sort of breathlessness that empty houses have. Yet they couldn't all be empty. All the different rooms, if you could just slice the walls away all of a sudden Madam, your daughter, if you please. No. Madam, for God's sake, your daughter. She moved along just under my elbow, her shiny pigtails, and then the last house played out and the road curved out of sight beyond a wall, following the river. The woman was emerging from the broken gate, with a shawl over her head and clutched under her chin. The road curved on, empty. I found a coin and gave it to the little girl. A quarter. 'Good-bye sister,' I said. Then I ran.

I ran fast, not looking back. Just before the road curved away I looked back. She stood in the road, a small figure clasping the loaf of bread to her filthy little dress, her eyes still and black and unwinking. I ran on.

A lane turned from the road. I entered it and after a while I slowed to a fast walk. The lane went between back premises – unpainted houses with more of those gay and startling coloured garments on lines, a barn broken-backed, decaying quietly among rank orchard trees, unpruned and weed-choked pink and white and murmurous with sunlight and with bees. I looked back. The entrance to the lane was empty. I slowed still more my shadow pacing me, dragging its head through the weeds that hid the fence.

The lane went back to a barred gate, became defunctive in grass, a mere path scarred quietly into new grass. I climbed the gate into a wood-lot and crossed it and came to another wall and followed that one, my shadow behind me now. There were vines and creepers where at home would be honeysuckle. Coming and coming especially in the dusk when it rained, getting honeysuckle all mixed up in it as though it were not enough without that, not unbearable enough. *What did you let him for kiss kiss*

I didn't let him I made him watching me getting mad What do you think of that? Red print of my hand coming up through her face like turning a light on under your hand her eyes going bright

It's not for kissing I slapped you. Girl's elbows at fifteen Father said you swallow like you had a fishbone in your throat what's the matter with you and Caddy across the table not to look at me. It's for letting it be some darn town squirt I slapped you you will will you now I guess you say calf rope. My red hand coming up out of her face. What do you think of that scouring her head into the. Grass sticks criss-crossed into the flesh tingling scouring her head. Say calf rope say it

I didn't kiss a dirty girl like Natalie anyway The wall went into shadow, and then my shadow, I had tricked it again. I had forgot about the river curving along the road. I climbed the wall. And then she watched me jump down, holding the loaf against her dress.

I stood in the weeds and we looked at one another for a while.

'Why didn't you tell me you lived out this way, sister?' The loaf was wearing slowly out of the paper; already it needed a new one. 'Well, come on then and show me the house.' *not a dirty girl like Natalie. It was raining we could hear it on the roof, sighing through the high sweet emptiness of the barn.*

There? touching her

Not there

There? not raining hard but we couldn't hear anything but the roof and as if it was my blood or her blood

She pushed me down the ladder and ran off and left me Caddy did

Was it there it hurt you when Caddy did ran off was it there

Oh She walked just under my elbow, the top of her patent leather head, the loaf fraying out of the newspaper.

'If you don't get home pretty soon you're going to wear that loaf out. And then what'll your mamma say?' *I bet I can lift you up*

You can't I'm too heavy

Did Caddy go away did she go to the house you can't see the barn from our house did you ever try to see the barn from

It was her fault she pushed me she ran away

I can lift you up see how I can

Oh her blood or my blood Oh We went on in the thin dust, our feet silent as rubber in the thin dust where pencils of sun slanted in the trees. And I could feel water again running swift and peaceful in the secret shade.

'You live a long way, don't you. You're mighty smart to go this far to town by yourself.' *It's like dancing sitting down did you ever dance sitting down? We could hear the rain, a rat in the crib, the empty barn vacant with horses. How do you hold to dance do you hold like this*

Oh

I used to hold like this you thought I wasn't strong enough didn't you Oh Oh Oh Oh

I hold to use like this I mean did you hear what I said I said oh oh oh oh

The road went on, still and empty, the sun slanting more and more. Her stiff little pigtails were bound at the tips with bits of crimson cloth. A corner of the wrapping flapped a little as she walked, the nose of the loaf naked. I stopped.

'Look here. Do you live down this road? We haven't passed a house in a mile, almost.'

She looked at me, black and secret and friendly.

'Where do you live, sister? Don't you live back there in town?'

There was a bird somewhere in the woods, beyond the broken and infrequent slanting of sunlight.

'Your papa's going to be worried about you. Don't you reckon you'll get a whipping for not coming straight home with that bread?'

The bird whistled again, invisible, a sound meaningless and profound, inflexionless, ceasing as though cut off with the blow of a knife, and again, and that sense of water swift and peaceful above secret places, felt, not seen not heard.

'Oh, hell, sister.' About half the paper hung limp. 'That's not doing any good now.' I tore it off and dropped it beside the road. 'Come on. We'll have to go to town. We'll go back along the river.'

We left the road. Among the moss little pale flowers grew, and the sense of water mute and unseen. *I hold to use like this I mean I use to hold She stood in the door looking at us her hands on her hips*

You pushed me it was your fault it hurt me too

We were dancing sitting down I bet Caddy can't dance sitting down Stop that stop that

I was just brushing the trash off the back of your dress

You keep your nasty old hands off of me it was your fault you pushed me down I'm mad at you

I don't care she looked at us stay mad she went away We began to hear the shouts, the splashings; I saw a brown body gleam for an instant.

Stay mad. My shirt was getting wet and my hair. Across the roof hearing the roof loud now I could see Natalie going through the garden among the rain. Get wet I hope you catch pneumonia go on home Cowface. I jumped hard as I could into the hog-wallow the mud yellowed up to my waist stinking I kept on plunging until I fell down and rolled over in it 'Hear them in swimming, sister? I wouldn't mind doing that myself.' If I had time. When I have time. I could hear my watch. *mud was warmer than the rain it smelled awful. She had her back turned I went around in front of her. You know what I was doing? She turned her back I went around in front of her the rain creeping into the mud flatting her bodice through her dress it smelled horrible. I was hugging her that's what I was doing. She turned her back I went around in front of her. I was hugging her I tell you.*

I don't give a damn what you were doing.

You don't you don't I'll make you I'll make you give a damn. She hit my hands away I smeared mud on her with the other hand I couldn't feel the wet smacking of her hand I wiped mud from my legs smeared it on her wet hard turning body hearing her fingers going into my face but I couldn't feel it even when the rain began to taste sweet on my lips

They saw us from the water first, heads and shoulders. They yelled and one rose squatting and sprang among them. They looked like beavers, the water lipping about their chins, yelling.

'Take that girl away! What did you want to bring a girl here for? Go on away!'

'She won't hurt you. We just want to watch you for a while.'

They squatted in the water. Their heads drew into a clump, watching us, then they broke and rushed toward us, hurling water with their hands. We moved quick.

'Look out, boys; she won't hurt you.'

'Go on away, Harvard!' It was the second boy, the one that thought the horse and wagon back there at the bridge. 'Splash them, fellows!'

'Let's get out and throw them in,' another said. 'I ain't afraid of any girl.'

'Splash them! Splash them!' They rushed toward us, hurling water. We moved back. 'Go on away!' they yelled. 'Go on away!'

We went away. They huddled just under the bank, their slick heads in a row against the bright water. We went on. 'That's not for us, is it.' The sun slanted through to the moss here and there, leveller. 'Poor kid, you're just a girl.' Little flowers grew among the moss, littler than I had ever seen. 'You're just a girl. Poor kid.' There was a path, curving along beside the water. Then the water was still again, dark and still and swift. 'Nothing but a girl. Poor sister.' *We lay in the wet grass panting the rain like cold shot on my back. Do you care now do you do you.*

My Lord we sure are in a mess get up. Where the rain touched my forehead it began to smart my hand came red away streaking off pink in the rain. Does it hurt.

Of course it does what do you reckon

I tried to scratch your eyes out my Lord we sure do stink we better try to wash it off in the branch 'There's town again, sister. You'll have to go home now. I've got to get back to school. Look how late it's getting. You'll go home now, won't you?' But she just looked at me with her black, secret, friendly gaze, the half-naked loaf clutched to her breast. 'It's wet. I thought we jumped back in time.' I took my handkerchief and tried to wipe the loaf, but the crust began to come off, so I stopped. 'We'll just have to let it dry itself. Hold it like this.' She held it like that. It looked kind of like rats had been eating it now. *and the water building and building up the squatting back the sloughed mud stinking surfaceward pocking the pattering surface like grease on a hot stove. I told you I'd make you*

I don't give a goddam what you do

Then we heard the running and we stopped and looked back and saw him coming up the path running, the level shadows flicking upon his legs.

'He's in a hurry. We'd –' then I saw another man, an oldish man running heavily, clutching a stick, and a boy naked from the waist up, clutching his pants as he ran.

'There's Julio,' the little girl said, and then I saw his Italian face and his eyes as he sprang upon me. We went down. His hands were jabbing at my face and he was saying something and trying to bite me, I reckon, and then they hauled him off and held him heaving and thrashing and yelling and they held his arms and he tried to kick me until they dragged him back. The little girl was howling, holding the loaf in both arms. The half-naked boy was darting and jumping up and down, clutching his trousers and someone pulled me up in time to see another stark naked figure come around the tranquil bend in the path running and change direction in midstride and leap into the woods, a couple of garments rigid as boards behind it. Julio still struggled. The man who had pulled me up said, 'Whoa now. We got you.' He wore a vest but no coat. Upon it was a metal shield. In his other hand he clutched a knotted, polished stick.

'You're Anse aren't you?' I said. 'I was looking for you. What's the matter?'

'I warn you that anything you say will be used against you,' he said. 'You're under arrest.'

'I killa heem,' Julio said. He struggled. Two men held him. The little girl howled steadily, holding the bread. 'You steala my seester,' Julio said. 'Let go, meesters.'

'Steal his sister?' I said. 'Why, I've been –'

'Shet up,' Anse said. 'You can tell that to Squire.'

'Steal his sister?' I said Julio broke from the men and sprang at me again, but the marshall met him and they struggled until the other two pinioned his arms again. Anse released him, panting.

'You durn furriner,' he said, 'I've a good mind to take you up too, for assault and battery.' He turned to me again. 'Will you come peaceable, or do I handcuff you?'

'I'll come peaceable,' I said. 'Anything, just so I can find someone – do something with – Stole his sister,' I said. 'Stole his –'

'I've warned you,' Anse said, 'He aims to charge you with meditated criminal assault. Here, you, make that gal shut up that noise.'

'Oh,' I said. Then I began to laugh. Two more boys with plastered heads and round eyes came out of the bushes buttoning shirts that had already dampened on to their shoulders and arms, and I tried to stop the laughter, but I couldn't.

'Watch him, Anse, he's crazy, I believe.'

'I'll have to qu-quit,' I said, 'It'll stop in a mu-minute. The other time it said ah ah ah,' I said, laughing. 'Let me sit down a while.' I sat down, they watching me, and the little girl with her streaked face and the gnawed-looking loaf, and the water swift and peaceful below the path. After a while the laughter ran out. But my throat wouldn't quit trying to laugh, like retching after your stomach is empty.

'Whoa, now,' Anse said. 'Get a grip on yourself.'

'Yes,' I said, tightening my throat. There was another yellow butterfly, like one of the sunflecks had come loose. After a while

I didn't have to hold my throat so tight. I got up. 'I'm ready. Which way?'

We followed the path, the two others watching Julio and the little girl and the boys somewhere in the rear. The path went along the river to the bridge. We crossed it and the tracks, people coming to the doors to look at us and more boys materializing from somewhere until when we turned into the main street we had quite a procession. Before the drug-store stood a motor, a big one, but I didn't recognize them until Mrs Bland said:

'Why, Quentin! Quentin Compson!' Then I saw Gerald, and Spoade in the back seat, sitting on the back of his neck. And Shreve. I didn't know the two girls.

'Quentin Compson!' Mrs Bland said.

'Good afternoon,' I said, raising my hat. 'I'm under arrest. I'm sorry I didn't get your note. Did Shreve tell you?'

'Under arrest?' Shreve said. 'Excuse me,' he said. He heaved himself up and climbed over their feet and got out. He had on a pair of my flannel pants, like a glove. I didn't remember forgetting them. I didn't remember how many chins Mrs Bland had, either. The prettiest girl was with Gerald in front, too. They watched me through veils, with a kind of delicate horror. 'Who's under arrest.' Shreve said. 'What's this, mister?'

'Gerald,' Mrs Bland said, 'Send these people away. You get in this car, Quentin.'

Gerald got out. Spoade hadn't moved.

'What's he done, Cap?' he said. 'Robbed a hen house?'

'I warn you,' Anse said. 'Do you know the prisoner?'

'Know him,' Shreve said. 'Look here —'

'Then you can come along to the squire's. You're obstructing justice. Come along.' He shook my arm.

'Well, good afternoon,' I said. 'I'm glad to have seen you all. Sorry I couldn't be with you.'

'You, Gerald,' Mrs Bland said.

'Look here, constable,' Gerald said.

'I warn you you're interfering with an officer of the law,' Anse said. 'If you've anything to say, you can come to the squire's and make cognizance of the prisoner.' We went on. Quite a procession now, Anse and I leading. I could hear them telling them what it was, and Spoade asking questions and then Julio said something violently in Italian and I looked back and saw the little girl standing at the curb, looking at me with her friendly, inscrutable regard.

'Git on home,' Julio shouted at her, 'I beat hell outa you.'

We went down the street and turned into a bit of lawn in which, set back from the street, stood a one-storey building of brick trimmed with white. We went up the rock path to the door, where Anse halted everyone except us and made them remain outside. We entered a bare room smelling of stale tobacco. There was a sheet iron stove in the centre of a wooden frame filled with sand, and a faded map on the wall and the dingy plat of a township. Behind a scarred table a man with a fierce roach of iron grey hair peered at us over steel spectacles.

'Got him, did ye, Anse?' he said.

'Got him, Squire.'

He opened a huge dusty book and drew it to him and dipped a foul pen into an inkwell filled with what looked like coal dust.

'Look here, mister,' Shreve said.

'The prisoner's name,' the Squire said. I told him. He wrote it slowly into the book, the pen scratching with excruciating deliberation.

'Look here, mister,' Shreve said, 'We know this fellow. We –'

'Order in the court,' Anse said.

'Shut up, bud,' Spoade said. 'Let him do it his way. He's going to anyhow.'

'Age,' the squire said. I told him. He wrote that, his mouth moving as he wrote. 'Occupation.' I told him. 'Harvard student, hey?' he said. He looked up at me, bowing his neck a little to see over the spectacles. His eyes were clear and cold, like a goat's. 'What are you up to, coming out here kidnapping children?'

'They're crazy, Squire,' Shreve said. 'Whoever says this boy's kidnapping –'

Julio moved violently. 'Crazy?' he said. 'Don't I catcha heem, eh? Don't I see weetha my own eyes –'

'You're a liar,' Shreve said. 'You never –'

'Order, order,' Anse said, raising his voice.

'You fellers shet up.' the Squire said. 'If they don't stay quiet, turn 'em out, Anse.' They got quiet. The Squire looked at Shreve, then at Spoade, then at Gerald. 'You know this young man?' he said to Spoade.

'Yes, your honour,' Spoade said. 'He's just a country boy in school up there. He don't mean any harm. I think the marshall'll find it's a mistake. His father's a congregational minister.'

'H'm,' the squire said. 'What was you doing, exactly?' I told him, he watched me with his cold, pale eyes. 'How about it, Anse?'

'Might have been,' Anse said. 'Them durn furriners.'

'I American,' Julio said. 'I gotta da pape'.'

'Where's the gal?'

'He sent her home,' Anse said.

'Was she scared or anything?'

'Not till Julio there jumped on the prisoner. They were just walking along the river path, towards town. Some boys swimming told us which way they went.'

'It's a mistake, Squire,' Spoade said. 'Children and dogs are always taking up with him like that. He can't help it.'

'H'm,' the Squire said. He looked out of the window for a while. We watched him. I could hear Julio scratching himself. The Squire looked back.

'Air you satisfied the gal ain't took any hurt, you, there?'

'No hurt now,' Julio said sullenly.

'You quit work to hunt for her?'

'Sure I quit. I run. I run like hell. Looka here, looka there, then man tella me he seen him giva her she eat. She go weetha.'

'H'm,' the squire said. 'Well, son, I calculate you owe Julio something for taking him away from his work.'

'Yes, sir,' I said. 'How much?'

'Dollar, I calculate.'

I gave Julio a dollar.

'Well,' Spoade said, 'If that's all – I reckon he's discharged, your honour?'

The Squire didn't look at him. 'Howfar'd you run him, Anse?'

'Two miles, at least. It was about two hours before we caught him.'

'H'm,' the squire said. He mused a while. We watched him, his stiff crest, the spectacles riding low on his nose. The yellow shape of the window grew slowly across the floor, reaching the wall, climbing. Dust motes whirled and slanted. 'Six dollars.'

'Six dollars?' Shreve said. 'What's that for?'

'Six dollars,' the squire said. He looked at Shreve a moment, then at me again.

'Look here,' Shreve said.

'Shut up,' Spoade said. 'Give it to him, bud, and let's get out of here. The ladies are waiting for us. You got six dollars?'

'Yes,' I said. I gave him six dollars.

'Case dismissed,' he said.

'You get a receipt,' Shreve said. 'You get a signed receipt for that money.'

The squire looked at Shreve mildly. 'Case dismissed,' he said without raising his voice.

'I'll be damned –' Shreve said.

'Come on here,' Spoade said, taking his arm. 'Good afternoon, Judge. Much obliged.' As we passed out the door Julio's voice rose again, violent, then ceased. Spoade was looking at me, his brown eyes quizzical, a little cold. 'Well, bud, I reckon you'll do your girl chasing in Boston after this.'

'You damned fool,' Shreve said, 'What the hell do you mean anyway, straggling off here, fooling with these damn wops?'

'Come on,' Spoade said, 'They must be getting impatient.'

Mrs Bland was talking to them. They were Miss Holmes and Miss Daingerfield and they quit listening to her and looked at me again with that delicate and curious horror, their veils turned back upon their little white noses and their eyes fleeing and mysterious beneath the veils.

'Quentin Compson,' Mrs Bland said, 'What would your mother say? A young man naturally gets into scrapes, but to be arrested on foot by a country policeman. What did they think he'd done, Gerald?'

'Nothing,' Gerald said.

'Nonsense. What was it, you, Spoade?'

'He was trying to kidnap that little dirty girl, but they caught him in time,' Spoade said.

'Nonsense,' Mrs Bland said, but her voice sort of died away and she stared at me for a moment, and the girls drew their breaths in with a soft concerted sound. 'Fiddlesticks,' Mrs Bland said briskly, 'If that isn't just like these ignorant low class Yankees. Get in, Quentin.'

Shreve and I sat on two small collapsible seats. Gerald cranked the car and got in and we started.

'Now, Quentin, you tell me what all this foolishness is about,' Mrs Bland said. I told them, Shreve hunched and furious on his little seat and Spoade sitting again on the back of his neck beside Miss Daingerfield.

'And the joke is, all the time Quentin had us all fooled,' Spoade said. 'All the time we thought he was the model youth that anybody could trust a daughter with, until the police showed him up at his nefarious work.'

'Hush up, Spoade,' Mrs Bland said. We drove down the street

and crossed the bridge and passed the house where the pink garment hung in the window. 'That's what you get for not reading my note. Why didn't you come and get it? Mr MacKenzie says he told you it was there.'

'Yessum. I intended to, but I never went back to the room.'

'You'd have let us sit there waiting I don't know how long, if it hadn't been for Mr MacKenzie. When he said you hadn't come back, that left an extra place, so we asked him to come. We're very glad to have you anyway, Mr MacKenzie.' Shreve said nothing. His arms were folded and he glared straight ahead past Gerald's cap. It was a cap for motoring in England. Mrs Bland said so. We passed that house, and three others, and another yard where the little girl stood by the gate. She didn't have the bread now, and her face looked like it had been streaked with coal-dust. I waved my hand, but she made no reply, only her head turned slowly as the car passed, following us with her unwinking gaze. Then we ran beside the wall, our shadows running along the wall, and after a while we passed a piece of torn newspaper lying beside the road and I began to laugh again. I could feel it in my throat and I looked off into the trees where the afternoon slanted, thinking of afternoon and of the bird and the boys in swimming. But still I couldn't stop it and then I knew that if I tried too hard to stop it I'd be crying and I thought about how I'd thought about I could not be a virgin, with so many of them walking in the shadows and whispering with their soft girl voices lingering in the shadowy places and the words coming out and perfume and eyes you could feel not see, but if it was that simple to do it wouldn't be anything and if it wasn't anything, what was I and then Mrs Bland said, 'Quentin? Is he sick, Mr MacKenzie?' and then Shreve's fat hand touched my knee and Spoade began talking and I quit trying to stop it.

'If that hamper is in his way, Mr MacKenzie, move it over on your side. I brought a hamper of wine because I think young gentlemen should drink wine, although my father, Gerald's grandfather' *ever do that have you ever done that In the grey darkness a little light her hands locked about*

'They do, when they can get it,' Spoade said. 'Hey, Shreve?' *her knees her face looking at the sky the smell of honeysuckle upon her face and throat*

'Beer, too,' Shreve said. His hand touched my knee again. I moved my knee again. *like a thin wash of lilac coloured paint talking about him bringing*

'You're not a gentleman,' Spoade said. *him between us until the shape of her blurred not with dark*

'No. I'm Canadian,' Shreve said. *talking about him the oar blades winking him along winking the Cap made for motoring in England and all time rushing beneath and they two blurred within the other for ever more he had been in the army had killed men*

'I adore Canada,' Miss Daingerfield said. 'I think it's marvellous.'

'Did you ever drink perfume?' Spoade said. *with one hand he could lift her to his shoulder and run with her running Running*

'No,' Shreve said. *running the beast with two backs and she blurred in the winking oars running the swine of Euboeleus running coupled within how many Caddy*

'Neither did I,' Spoade said. *I don't know too many there was something terrible in me terrible in me Father I have committed Have you ever done that we didn't we didn't do that did we do that*

'and Gerald's grandfather always picked his own mint before breakfast, while the dew was still on it. He wouldn't ever let old Wilkie touch it do you remember Gerald but always gathered it himself and made his own julep. He was as crochety about his julep as an old maid, measuring everything by a recipe in his head. There was only one man he ever gave that recipe to; that was' *we did how can you not know it if you'll just wait I'll tell you how it was it was a crime we did a terrible crime it cannot be hid you think it can but wait Poor Quentin you've never done that have you and I'll tell you how it was I'll tell Father then it'll have to be because you love Father then we'll have to go away amid the pointing and the horror the clean flame I'll make you say we did I'm stronger than you I'll make you know we did you thought it was them but it was me listen I fooled you all the time it was me you thought I was in the house where that damn honeysuckle trying not to think the swing the cedars the secret surges the breathing locked drinking the wild breath the yes Yes Yes yes* 'never be got to drink wine himself, but he always said that a hamper what book did you read that in the one where Gerald's rowing suit of wine was a necessary part of any gentleman's picnic basket' *did you love them Caddy did you love them When they touched me I died*

one minute she was standing there the next he was yelling and pulling at her dress they went into the hall and up the stairs yelling and shoving at her up the stairs to the bathroom door and stopped her back against the door and her arm across her face yelling and trying to shove her into the bathroom when she

came in to supper T.P. was feeding him he started just whimpering at first until she touched him then he yelled she stood
there her eyes like cornered rats then I was running in the grey
darkness it smelled of rain and all flower scents the damp warm
air released and crickets sawing away in the grass pacing me with
a small travelling island of silence Fancy watched me across the
fence blotchy like a quilt on a line I thought damn that nigger
he forgot to feed her again I ran down the hill in that vacuum
of crickets like a breath travelling across a mirror she was lying
in the water her head on the sand spit the water flowing about
her hips there was a little more light in the water her skirt half
saturated flopped along her flanks to the water's motion in
heavy ripples going nowhere renewed themselves of their own
movement I stood on the bank I could smell the honeysuckle on
the water gap the air seemed to drizzle with honeysuckle and
with the rasping of crickets a substance you could feel on the
flesh

is Benjy still crying

I don't know yes I dont know

poor Benjy

I sat down on the bank the grass was damp a little then I found
my shoes wet

get out of that water are you crazy

but she didnt move her face was a white blur framed out of
the blur of the sand by her hair

get out now

she sat up then she rose her skirt flopping against her draining
she climbed the bank her clothes flopping sat down

why dont you wring it out do you want to catch cold

yes

the water sucked and gurgled across the sand spit and on in
the dark among the willows across the shallow the water rippled
like a piece of cloth holding still a little light as water does

hes crossed all the oceans all around the world

then she talked about him clasping her wet knees her face tilted
back in the grey light the smell of honeysuckle there was a light
in mothers room and in Benjys where T.P. was putting him to
bed

do you love him

her hand came out I didnt move it fumbled down my arm and
she held my hand flat against her chest her heart thudding

no no

did he make you then he made you do it let him he was stronger than you and he tomorrow Ill kill him I swear I will father neednt know until afterward and then you and I nobody need ever know we can take my school money we can cancel my matriculation Caddy you hate him dont you dont you

she held my hand against her chest her heart thudding I turned and caught her arm

Caddy you hate him dont you

she moved my hand up against her throat her heart was hammering there

poor Quentin

her face looked at the sky it was low so low that all smells and sounds of night seemed to have been crowded down like under a slack tent especially the honeysuckle it had got into my breathing it was on her face and throat like paint her blood pounded against my hand I was leaning on my other arm it began to jerk and jump and I had to pant to get any air at all out of that thick grey honeysuckle

yes I hate him I would die for him Ive already died for him I die for him over and over again every time this goes

when I lifted my hand I could still feel criss-crossed twigs and grass burning into the palm

poor Quentin

she leaned back on her arms her hands locked about her knees

youve never done that have you

what done what

that what I have what I did

yes yes lots of times with lots of girls

then I was crying her hand touched me again and I was crying against her damp blouse then she lying on her back looking past my head into the sky I could see a rim of white under her irises I opened my knife

do you remember the day damuddy died when you sat down in the water in your drawers

yes

I held the point of the knife at her throat

it wont take but a second just a second then I can do mine I can do mine then

all right can you do yours by yourself

yes the blades long enough Benjys in bed by now

yes

it wont take but a second Ill try not to hurt

all right
will you close your eyes
no like this you'll have to push it harder
touch your hand to it
but she didnt move her eyes were wide open looking past my head at the sky
Caddy do you remember how Dilsey fussed at you because your drawers were muddy
dont cry
Im not crying Caddy
push it are you going to
do you want me to
yes push it
touch your hand to it
dont cry poor Quentin
but I couldnt stop she held my head against her damp hard breast I could hear her heart going firm and slow now not hammering and the water gurgling among the willows in the dark and waves of honeysuckle coming up the air my arm and shoulder were twisted under me
what is it what are you doing
her muscles gathered I sat up
its my knife I dropped it
she sat up
what time is it
I dont know
she rose to her feet I fumbled along the ground
Im going let it go
I could feel her standing there I could smell her damp clothes feeling her there
its right here somewhere
let it go you can find it tomorrow come on
wait a minute Ill find it
are you afraid to
here it is it was right here all the time
was it come on
I got up and followed we went up the hill the crickets hushed before us
its funny how you can sit down and drop something and have to hunt all around for it
the grey it was grey with dew slanting up into the grey sky then the trees beyond

damn that honeysuckle I wish it would stop
   you used to like it
   we crossed the crest and went on toward the trees she walked
into me she gave over a little the ditch was a black scar on the
grey grass she walked into me again she looked at me and gave
over we reached the ditch
   lets go this way
   what for
   lets see if you can still see Nancys bones I havent thought to
look in a long time have you
   it was matted with vines and briers dark
   they were right here you cant tell whether you see them or not
can you
   stop Quentin
   come on
   the ditch narrowed closed she turned toward the trees
   stop Quentin
   Caddy
   I got in front of her again
   Caddy
   stop it
   I held her
   Im stronger than you
   she was motionless hard unyielding but still
   I wont fight stop youd better stop
   Caddy dont Caddy
   it wont do any good dont you know it wont let me go
   the honeysuckle drizzled and drizzled I could hear the crickets
watching us in a circle she moved back went around me on toward
the trees
   you go on back to the house you neednt come
   I went on
   why dont you go on back to the house
   damn that honeysuckle
   we reached the fence she crawled through I crawled through
when I rose from stooping he was coming out of the trees into
the grey toward us coming toward us tall and flat and still even
moving like he was still she went to him
   this is Quentin Im wet Im wet all over you dont have to if you
dont want to
   their shadows one shadow her head rose it was above his on
the sky higher their two heads

you dont have to if you dont want to

then not two heads the darkness smelled of rain of damp grass and leaves the grey light drizzling like rain the honeysuckle coming up in damp waves I could see her face a blur against his shoulder he held her in one arm like she was no bigger than a child he extended his hand

glad to know you

we shook hands then we stood there her shadow high against his shadow one shadow

whatre you going to do Quentin

walk a while I think Ill go through the woods to the road and come back through town

I turned away going

good night

Quentin

I stopped

what do you want

in the woods the tree frogs were going smelling rain in the air they sounded like toy music boxes that were hard to turn and the honeysuckle

come here

what do you want

come here Quentin

I went back she touched my shoulder leaning down her shadow the blur of her face leaning down from his high shadow I drew back

look out

you go on home

Im not sleepy Im going to take a walk

wait for me at the branch

Im going for a walk

Ill be there soon wait for me you wait

no Im going through the woods

I didnt look back the tree frogs didnt pay me any mind the grey light like moss in the trees drizzling but still it wouldnt rain after a while I turned went back to the edge of the woods as soon as I got there I began to smell honeysuckle again I could see the lights on the courthouse clock and the glare of town the square on the sky and the dark willows along the branch and the light in mother's windows the light still on in Benjys room and I stooped through the fence and went across the pasture running I ran in the grey grass among the crickets the honeysuckle getting stronger and stronger and the smell of water then I could see the water the colour of grey honeysuckle I lay down on the bank with my face close to the ground so I couldnt smell the honeysuckle I couldnt smell it then and I lay there feeling the earth going through my clothes listening to the water and after a while I wasnt breathing so hard and I lay there thinking that if I didnt move my face I wouldnt have to breathe hard and smell it and then I wasnt thinking about anything at all she came along the bank and stopped I didnt move

its late you go on home

what

you go on home its late

all right

her clothes rustled I didnt move they stopped rustling

are you going in like I told you

I didnt hear anything

Caddy

yes I will if you want me to I will

I sat up she was sitting on the ground her hands clasped about her knee

go on to the house like I told you

yes Ill do anything you want me to anything yes

she didnt even look at me I caught her shoulder and shook her hard

you shut up

I shook her

you shut up you shut up

yes

she lifted her face then I saw she wasnt even looking at me at all I could see that white rim

get up

I pulled her she was limp I lifted her to her feet

go on now

was Benjy still crying when you left

go on

we crossed the branch the roof came in sight then the windows upstairs

hes asleep now

I had to stop and fasten the gate she went on in the grey light the smell of rain and still it wouldnt rain and honeysuckle beginning to come from the garden fence beginning she went into the shadow I could hear her feet then

Caddy

I stopped at the steps I couldnt hear her feet

Caddy

I heard her feet then my hand touched her not warm not cool just still her clothes a little damp still

do you love him now

not breathing except slow like far away breathing

Caddy do you love him now

I dont know

outside the grey light the shadows of things like dead things in stagnant water

I wish you were dead

do you you coming in now

are you thinking about him now

I dont know

tell me what youre thinking about tell me

stop stop Quentin

you shut up you shut up you hear me you shut up are you going to shut up

all right I will stop well make too much noise

Ill kill you do you hear

lets go out to the swing theyll hear you here

Im not crying do you say Im crying

no hush now well wake Benjy up

you go on into the house go on now

I am dont cry Im bad anyway you cant help it

theres a curse on us its not our fault is it our fault

hush come on and go to bed now

you cant make me theres a curse on us

finally I saw him he was just going into the barber-shop he looked out and I went on and waited

Ive been looking for you two or three days

you wanted to see me

Im going to see you

he rolled the cigarette quickly with about two motions he struck the match with his thumb

we cant talk here suppose I meet you somewhere

Ill come to your room are you at the hotel

no thats not so good you know that bridge over the creek in there back of

yes all right

at one oclock right

yes

I turned away

Im obliged to you

look

I stopped looked back

she all right

he looked like he was made out of bronze his khaki shirt

she need me for anything now

Ill be there at one

she heard me tell T.P. to saddle Prince at one oclock she kept watching me not eating much she came too

what are you going to do

nothing cant I go for a ride if I want to

youre going to do something what is it

none of your business whore whore

T.P. had Prince at the side door

I wont want him Im going to walk

I went down the drive and out the gate I turned into the lane then I ran before I reached the bridge I saw him leaning on the rail the horse hitched in the woods he looked over his shoulder then he turned his back he didnt look up until I came on to the bridge and stopped he had a piece of bark in his hands breaking pieces from it and dropping them over the rail into the water.

I came to tell you to leave town

he broke a piece of bark deliberately dropped it carefully into the water watched it float away

I said you must leave town

he looked at me

did she send you to me

I say you must go not my father not anybody I say it

listen save this for a while I want to know if shes all right have they been bothering her up there

thats something you dont need to trouble yourself about

then I heard myself saying Ill give you until sundown to leave town

he broke a piece of bark and dropped it into the water then he laid the bark on the rail and rolled a cigarette with those two swift motions spun the match over the rail

what will you do if I dont leave

Ill kill you dont think that just because I look like a kid to you the smoke flowed in two jets from his nostrils across his face

how old are you

I began to shake my hands were on the rail I thought if I hid them hed know why

Ill give you until tonight

listen buddy whats your name Benjys the natural isnt he you are

Quentin

my mouth said it I didnt say it at all

Ill give you till sundown

Quentin

he raked the cigarette ash carefully off against the rail he did it slowly and carefully like sharpening a pencil my hands had quit shaking

listen no good taking it so hard its not your fault kid it would have been some other fellow

did you ever have a sister did you

no but theyre all bitches

I hit him my open hand beat the impulse to shut it to his face his hand moved as fast as mine the cigarette went over the rail I swung with the other hand he caught it too before the cigarette reached the water he held both my wrists in the same hand his other hand flicked to his arm pit under his coat behind him the sun slanted and a bird singing somewhere beyond the sun we looked at one another while the bird singing he turned my hands loose

look here

he took the bark from the rail and dropped it into the water it bobbed up the current took it floated away his hand lay on the rail holding the pistol loosely we waited

you cant hit it now

no

it floated on it was quite still in the woods I heard the bird again and the water afterward the pistol came up he didnt aim at all the bark disappeared then pieces of it floated up spreading he hit two more of them pieces of bark no bigger than silver dollars

thats enough I guess

he swung the cylinder out and blew into the barrel a thin wisp of smoke dissolved he reloaded the three chambers shut the cylinder he handed it to me butt first

what for I wont try to beat that

youll need it from what you said Im giving you this one because youve seen what itll do to hell with your gun

I hit him I was still trying to hit him long after he was holding my wrists but I still tried then it was like I was looking at him through a piece of coloured glass I could hear my blood and then I could see the sky again and branches against it and the sun slanting through them and he holding me on my feet

did you hit me

I couldnt hear

what

yes how do you feel

all right let go

he let me go I leaned against the rail

do you feel all right

let me alone Im all right

can you make it home all right

go on let me alone

youd better not try to walk take my horse

no you go on

you can hang the reins on the pommel and turn him loose hell go back to the stable

let me alone you go on and let me alone

I leaned on the rail looking at the water I heard him untie the horse and ride off and after a while I couldnt hear anything but the water and then the bird again I left the bridge and sat down with my back against a tree and leaned my head against the tree and shut my eyes a patch of sun came through and fell across my eyes and I moved a little further around the tree I heard the bird again and the water and then everything sort of rolled away and I didnt feel anything at all I felt almost good after all those days and the nights with honeysuckle coming up out of the darkness into my room where I was trying to sleep even when after a while I knew that he hadnt hit me that he had lied about that for her sake too and that I had just passed out like a girl but even that didnt matter any more and I sat there against the tree with little flecks of sunlight brushing across my face like yellow leaves on a twig listening to the water and not thinking about anything at all even when I heard the horse coming fast I sat there with my eyes closed and heard its feet bunch scuttering the hissing sand and feet running and her hard running hands

fool fool are you hurt

I opened my eyes her hands running on my face

I didnt know which way until I heard the pistol I didnt know

where I didnt think he and you running off slipping I didnt think
he would have

she held my face between her hands bumping my head against
the tree

stop stop that

I caught her wrists

quit that quit it

I knew he wouldnt I knew he wouldnt

she tried to bump my head against the tree

I told him never to speak to me again I told him

she tried to break her wrists free

let me go

stop it Im stronger than you stop it now

let me go Ive got to catch him and ask his let me go Quentin
please let me go let me go

all at once she quit her wrists went lax

yes I can tell him I can make him believe any time I can make
him

Caddy

she hadnt hitched Prince he was liable to strike out for home
if the notion took him

any time he will believe me

do you love him Caddy

do I what

she looked at me then everything emptied out of her eyes and
they looked like the eyes in the statues blank and unseeing and
serene

put your hand against my throat

she took my hand and held it flat against her throat

now say his name

Dalton Ames

I felt the first surge of blood there it surged in strong acceler-
ating beats

say it again

her face looked off into the trees where the sun slanted and
where the bird

say it again

Dalton Ames

her blood surged steadily beating and beating against my hand

It kept on running for a long time, but my face felt cold and
sort of dead, and my eye, and the cut place on my finger was
smarting again. I could hear Shreve working the pump, then he

came back with the basin and a round blob of twilight wobbling
in it, with a yellow edge like a fading balloon, then my reflection.
I tried to see my face in it.

'Has it stopped?' Shreve said. 'Give me the rag.' He tried to
take it from my hand.

'Look out,' I said, 'I can do it. Yes, it's about stopped now.' I
dipped the rag again, breaking the balloon. The rag stained the
water. 'I wish I had a clean one.'

'You need a piece of beefsteak for that eye,' Shreve said. 'Damn
if you won't have a shiner tomorrow. The son of a bitch,' he said.

'Did I hurt him any?' I wrung out the handkerchief and tried
to clean the blood off of my vest.

'You can't get that off,' Shreve said. 'You'll have to send it to
the cleaner's. Come on, hold it on your eye, why don't you.

'I can get some of it off,' I said. But I wasn't doing much good.
'What sort of shape is my collar in?'

'I don't know,' Shreve said. 'Hold it against your eye. Here.'

'Look out,' I said. 'I can do it. Did I hurt him any?'

'You may have hit him. I may have looked away just then or
blinked or something. He boxed the hell out of you. He boxed
you all over the place. What did you want to fight him with your
fists for? You goddamn fool. How do you feel?'

'I feel fine,' I said. 'I wonder if I can get something to clean
my vest.'

'Oh, forget your damn clothes. Does your eye hurt?'

'I feel fine,' I said. Everything was sort of violet and still, the
sky green paling into gold beyond the gable of the house and a
plume of smoke rising from the chimney without any wind. I
heard the pump again. A man was filling a pail, watching us
across his pumping shoulder. A woman crossed the door, but she
didn't look out. I could hear a cow lowing somewhere.

'Come on,' Shreve said, 'Let your clothes alone and put that
rag on your eye. I'll send your suit out first thing tomorrow.'

'All right. I'm sorry I didn't bleed on him a little, at least.'

'Son of a bitch,' Shreve said. Spoade came out of the house,
talking to the woman I reckon, and crossed the yard. He looked
at me with his cold, quizzical eyes.

'Well, bud,' he said, looking at me, 'I'll be damned if you don't
go to a lot of trouble to have your fun. Kidnapping, then fighting.
What do you do on your holidays? burn houses?'

'I'm all right,' I said. 'What did Mrs Bland say?'

'She's giving Gerald hell for bloodying you up. She'll give you hell for letting him, when she sees you. She don't object to the fighting, it's the blood that annoys her. I think you lost caste with her a little by not holding your blood better. How do you feel?'

'Sure,' Shreve said, 'If you can't be a Bland, the next best thing is to commit adultery with one or get drunk and fight him, as the case may be.'

'Quite right,' Spoade said. 'But I didn't know Quentin was drunk.'

'He wasn't,' Shreve said. 'Do you have to be drunk to want to hit that son of a bitch?'

'Well, I think I'd have to be pretty drunk to try it, after seeing how Quentin came out. Where'd he learn to box?'

'He's been going to Mike's every day, over in town,' I said.

'He has?' Spoade said. 'Did you know that when you hit him?'

'I don't know,' I said. 'I guess so. Yes.'

'Wet it again,' Shreve said. 'Want some fresh water?'

'This is all right,' I said. I dipped the cloth again and held it to my eye. 'Wish I had something to clean my vest.' Spoade was still watching me.

'Say,' he said, 'What did you hit him for? What was it he said?'

'I don't know. I don't know why I did.'

'The first I knew was when you jumped up all of a sudden and said, "Did you ever have a sister? did you?" and when he said No, you hit him. I noticed you kept on looking at him, but you didn't seem to be paying any attention to what anybody was saying until you jumped up and asked him if he had any sisters.'

'Ah, he was blowing off as usual,' Shreve said, 'about his women. You know: like he does, before girls, so they don't know exactly what he's saying. All his damn innuendo and lying and a lot of stuff that don't make sense even. Telling us about some wench that he made date with to meet at a dance hall in Atlantic City and stood her up and went to the hotel and went to bed and how he lay there being sorry for her waiting on the pier for him, without him there to give her what she wanted. Talking about the body's beauty and the sorry ends thereof and how tough women have it, without anything else they can do except lie on their backs. Leda lurking in the bushes, whimpering and moaning for the swan, see. The son of a bitch. I'd hit him myself. Only I'd grabbed up her damn hamper of wine and done it if it had been me.'

'Oh,' Spoade said, 'the champion of dames. Bud, you excite not only admiration, but horror.'

He looked at me, cold and quizzical. 'Good God,' he said.

'I'm sorry I hit him,' I said. 'Do I look too bad to go back and get it over with?'

'Apologies, hell,' Shreve said, 'Let them go to hell. We're going to town.'

'He ought to go back so they'll know he fights like a gentleman,' Spoade said. 'Gets licked like one, I mean.'

'Like this?' Shreve said, 'With his clothes all over blood?'

'Why, all right,' Spoade said, 'You know best.'

'He can't go around in his undershirt,' Shreve said, 'He's not a senior yet. Come on, let's go to town.'

'You needn't come,' I said. 'You go on back to the picnic.'

'Hell with them,' Shreve said. 'Come on here.'

'What'll I tell them?' Spoade said. 'Tell them you and Quentin had a fight too?'

'Tell them nothing,' Shreve said. 'Tell her her option expired at sunset. Come on, Quentin. I'll ask that woman where the nearest interurban –'

'No,' I said, 'I'm not going back to town.'

Shreve stopped, looking at me. Turning, his glasses looked like small yellow moons.

'What are you going to do?'

'I'm not going back to town yet. You go on back to the picnic. Tell them I wouldn't come back because my clothes were spoiled.'

'Look here,' he said, 'What are you up to?'

'Nothing. I'm all right. You and Spoade go on back. I'll see you tomorrow.' I went on across the yard toward the road.

'Do you know where the station is?' Shreve said.

'I'll find it. I'll see you all tomorrow. Tell Mrs Bland I'm sorry I spoiled her party.' They stood watching me. I went around the house. A rock path went down to the road. Roses grew on both sides of the path. I went through the gate, onto the road. It dropped downhill, toward the woods, and I could make out the motor beside the road. I went up the hill. The light increased as I mounted, and before I reached the top I heard a car. It sounded far away across the twilight and I stopped and listened to it. I couldn't make out the motor any longer, but Shreve was standing in the road before the house, looking up the hill. Behind him the yellow light lay like a wash of paint on the roof of the house. I lifted my hand and went on over the hill, listening to the car. Then the house was gone and I stopped in the green and yellow light and heard the car growing louder and louder and louder, until just as it began to die away it ceased all together. I waited until I heard it start again. Then I went on.

As I descended the light dwindled slowly, yet at the same time without altering its quality, as if I and not light were changing, decreasing, though even when the road ran into trees you could have read a newspaper. Pretty soon I came to a lane. I turned into it. It was closer and darker than the road, but when it came out at the trolley stop – another wooden marquee – the light was still unchanged. After the lane it seemed brighter, as though I had walked through night in the lane and come out into morning again. Pretty soon the car came. I got on it, they turning to look at my eye, and found a seat on the left side.

The lights were on in the car, so while we ran between trees I couldn't see anything except my own face and a woman across the aisle with a hat sitting right on top of her head, with a broken feather in it, but when we ran out of the trees I could see the twilight again, that quality of light as if time really had stopped for a while, with the sun hanging just under the horizon, and then we passed the marquee where the old man had been eating out of the sack, and the road going on under the twilight, into twilight and the sense of water peaceful and swift beyond. Then the car went on, the draught building steadily up in the open door until it was drawing steadily through the car with the odour of summer and darkness except honeysuckle. Honeysuckle was the saddest odour of all, I think. I remember lots of them. Wistaria was one. On the rainy days when Mother wasn't feeling quite bad enough to stay away from the windows we used to play under it. When Mother stayed in bed Dilsey would put old clothes on us and let us go out in the rain because she said rain never hurt young folks. But if Mother was up we always began by playing on the porch until she said we were making too much noise, then we went out and played under the wistaria frame.

This was where I saw the river for the last time this morning, about here. I could feel water beyond the twilight, smell. When it bloomed in the spring and it rained the smell was everywhere you didn't notice it so much as other times but when it rained the smell began to come into the house at twilight either it would rain more at twilight or there was something in the light itself but it always smelled strongest then until I would lie in bed thinking when will it stop when will it stop. The draught in the door smelled of water, a damp steady breath. Sometimes I could put myself to sleep saying that over and over until after the honeysuckle got all mixed up in it the whole thing came to symbolize night and unrest I seemed to be lying neither asleep nor awake looking down a long corridor of grey half-light where all stable things had become shadowy paradoxical all I had done shadows all I had felt suffered taking visible form antic and perverse mocking without relevance inherent themselves with the denial of the significance they should have affirmed thinking I was I was not who was not was not who.

I could smell the curves of the river beyond the dusk and I saw the last light supine and tranquil upon tide-flats like pieces of broken mirror, then beyond them lights began in the pale clear air, trembling a little like butterflies hovering a long way off. Benjamin the child of. How he used to sit before that mirror. Refuge unfailing in which conflict tempered silenced reconciled. Benjamin the child of mine old age held hostage into Egypt. O Benjamin. Dilsey said it was because Mother was too proud for him. They come into white people's lives like that in sudden sharp black trickles that isolate white facts for an instant in unarguable truth like under a microscope; the rest of the time just voices that laugh when you see nothing to laugh at, tears when no reason for tears. They will bet on the odd or even number of mourners at a funeral. A brothel full of them in Memphis went into a religious trance ran naked into the street. It took three policemen to subdue one of them. Yes Jesus O good man Jesus O that good man.

The car stopped. I got out, with them looking at my eye. When the trolley came it was full. I stopped on the back platform.

'Seats up front,' the conductor said. I looked into the car. There were no seats on the left side.

'I'm not going far,' I said. 'I'll just stand here.'

We crossed the river. The bridge, that is, arching slow and high into space, between silence and nothingness where lights – yellow and red and green – trembled in the clear air, repeating themselves.

'Better go up front and get a seat,' the conductor said.

'I get off pretty soon,' I said. 'A couple of blocks.'

I got off before we reached the post office. They'd all be sitting around somewhere by now though, and then I was hearing my watch and I began to listen for the chimes and I touched Shreve's letter through my coat, the bitten shadows of the elms flowing upon my hand. And then as I turned into the quad the chimes did begin and I went on while the notes came up like ripples on a pool and passed me and went on, saying Quarter to what? All right. Quarter to what.

Our windows were dark. The entrance was empty. I walked close to the left wall when I entered, but it was empty: just the stairs curving up into shadows echoes of feet in the sad generations like light dust upon the shadows, my feet waking them like dust, lightly to settle again.

I could see the letter before I turned the light on, propped against a book on the table so I would see it. Calling him my husband. And then Spoade said they were going somewhere, would not be back until late, and Mrs Bland would need another cavalier. But I would have seen him and he cannot get another car for an hour because after six o'clock. I took out my watch and listened to its clicking away, not knowing it couldn't even lie. Then I laid it face up on the table and took Mrs Bland's letter and tore it across and dropped the pieces into the waste basket and took off my coat, vest, collar, tie and shirt. The tie was spoiled too, but then niggers. Maybe a pattern of blood he could call that the one Christ was wearing. I found the gasoline in Shreve's room and spread the vest on the table, where it would be flat, and opened the gasoline.

the first car in town a girl Girl that's what Jason couldn't bear smell of gasoline making him sick then got madder than ever because a girl had no sister but Benjamin Benjamin the child of my sorrowful if I'd just had a mother so I could say Mother Mother It took a lot of gasoline, and then I couldn't tell if it was still the stain or just the gasoline. It had started the cut smarting again so when I went to wash I hung the vest on a chair and lowered the light cord so that the bulb would be drying the splotch. I washed my face and hands, but even then I could smell it within the soap stinging, constricting the nostrils a little. Then I opened the bag and took the shirt and collar and tie out and put the bloody ones in and closed the bag, and dressed. While I was brushing my hair the half-hour went. But there was until the three-quarters anyway except suppose *seeing on the rushing darkness only his own face no broken feather unless two of them but not two like that going to Boston the same night then my face his face for an instant across the crashing when out of darkness two lighted windows in rigid fleeing crash gone his face and mine just I see saw did I see not good-bye the marquee empty of eating the road empty in darkness in silence the bridge arching into silence darkness sleep the water peaceful and swift not good-bye*

I turned out the light and went into my bedroom, out of the

gasoline but I could still smell it. I stood at the window the curtains moved slow out of the darkness touching my face like someone breathing asleep, breathing slow into the darkness again, leaving the touch. *After they had gone upstairs Mother lay back in her chair, the camphor handkerchief to her mouth. Father hadn't moved he still sat beside her holding her hand the bellowing hammering away like no place for it in silence* When I was little there was a picture in one of our books, a dark place into which a single weak ray of light came slanting upon two faces lifted out of the shadow. *You know what I'd do if I were King?* she never was a queen or a fairy she was always a king or a giant or a general *I'd break that place open and drag them out and I'd whip them good* It was torn out, jagged out. I was glad. I'd have to turn back to it until the dungeon was Mother herself she and Father upward into weak light holding hands and us lost somewhere below even them without even a ray of light. Then the honeysuckle got into it. As soon as I turned off the light and tried to go to sleep it would begin to come into the room in waves building and building up until I would have to pant to get any air at all out of it until I would have to get up and feel my way like when I was a little boy *hands can see touching in the mind shaping unseen door Door now nothing hands can see* My nose could see gasoline, the vest on the table, the door. The corridor was still empty of all the feet in sad generations seeking water. *yet the eyes unseeing clenched like teeth not disbelieving doubting even the absence of pain shin ankle knee the lung invisible flowering of the stair-railing where a misstep in the darkness filled with sleeping Mother Father Caddy Jason Maury door I am not afraid only Mother Father Caddy Jason Maury getting so far ahead asleep I will sleep fast when I door Door door* It was empty too, the pipes, the porcelain, the stained quiet walls, the throne of contemplation. I had forgotten the glass, but I could *hands can see cooling fingers invisible swan-throat where less than Moses rod the glass touch tentative not to drumming lean cool throat drumming cooling the metal the glass full overfull cooling the glass the fingers Rushing sleep leaving the taste of dampened sleep in the long silence of the throat* I returned up the corridor, waking the lost feet in whispering battalions in the silence, into the gasoline, the watch telling its furious lie on the dark table. Then the curtains breathing out of the dark upon my face, leaving the breathing upon my face. A quarter-hour yet. And then I'll not be. The peacefullest words. Peacefullest words. *Non fui. Sum. Fui. Non sum.* Somewhere I heard bells once. Mississippi or Massachusetts.

I was. I am not. Massachusetts or Mississippi. Shreve has a bottle in his trunk. *Aren't you even going to open it* Mr and Mrs Jason Richmond Compson announce the *Three Times. Days. Aren't you even going to open it* marriage of their daughter Candace *that liquor teaches you to confuse the means with the end.* I am. Drink. I was not. Let us sell Benjy's pasture so that Quentin may go to Harvard and I may knock my bones together and together. I will be dead in. Was it one year Caddy said. Shreve has a bottle in his trunk. Sir I will not need Shreve's I have sold Benjy's pasture and I can be dead in Harvard Caddy said in the caverns and the grottoes of the sea tumbling peacefully to the wavering tides because Harvard is such a fine sound forty acres is no high price for a fine sound. A fine dead sound we will swap Benjy's pasture for a fine dead sound. It will last him a long time because he cannot hear it unless he can smell it *as soon as she came in the door he began to cry* I thought all the time it was just one of those town squirts that Father was always teasing her about until. I didn't notice him any more than any other stranger drummer or what thought they were army shirts until all of a sudden I knew he wasn't thinking of me at all as a potential source of harm, but was thinking of her when he looked at me was looking at me through her like through a piece of coloured glass why *must you meddle with me don't you know it won't do any good I thought you'd have left that for Mother and Jason*

did Mother set Jason to spy on you I wouldn't have.

Women only use other people's codes of honour it's because she loves Caddy staying downstairs even when she was sick so Father couldn't kid Uncle Maury before Jason Father said Uncle Maury was too poor a classicist to risk the blind immortal boy in person he should have chosen Jason because Jason would have made only the same kind of blunder Uncle Maury himself would have made not one to get him a black eye the Patterson boy was smaller than Jason too they sold the kites for a nickel apiece until the trouble over finances Jason got a new partner still smaller one small enough anyway because T.P. said Jason still treasurer but Father said why should Uncle Maury work if he father could support five or six niggers that did nothing at all but sit with their feet in the oven he certainly could board and lodge Uncle Maury now and then and lend him a little money who kept his Father's belief in the celestial derivation of his own species at such a fine heat then Mother would cry and say that Father believed his people were better than hers that he was ridiculing

Uncle Maury to teach us the same thing she couldn't see that Father was teaching us that all men are just accumulations dolls stuffed with sawdust swept up from the trash heaps where all previous dolls had been thrown away the sawdust flowing from what wound in what side that not for me died not. It used to be I thought of death as a man something like Grandfather a friend of his a kind of private and particular friend like we used to think of Grandfather's desk not to touch it not even to talk loud in the room where it was I always thought of them as being together somewhere all the time waiting for old Colonel Sartoris to come down and sit with them waiting on a high place beyond cedar trees Colonel Sartoris was on a still higher place looking out across at something and they were waiting for him to get done looking at it and come down Grandfather wore his uniform and we could hear the murmur of their voices from beyond the cedars they were always talking and Grandfather was always right.

The three-quarters began. The first note sounded, measured and tranquil, serenely peremptory, emptying the unhurried silence for the next one and that's it if people could only change one another for ever that way merge like a flame swirling up for an instant then blown cleanly out along the cool eternal dark instead of lying there trying not to think of the swing until all cedars came to have that vivid dead smell of perfume that Benjy hated so. Just by imagining the clump it seemed to me that I could hear whispers secret surges smell the beating of hot blood under wild unsecret flesh watching against red eyelids the swine untethered in pairs rushing coupled into the sea and he we must just stay awake and see evil done for a little while its not always and it doesnt have to be even that long for a man of courage and he do you consider hat courage and i yes sir dont you and he every man is the arbiter of his own virtues whether or not you consider it courageous is more important than the act itself than any act otherwise you could not be in earnest and i you dont believe i am serious and he i think you are too serious to give me any cause for alarm you wouldnt have felt driven to the expedient of telling me you have committed incest otherwise and i i wasnt lying i wasnt lying and he you wanted to sublimate a piece of natural human folly into a horror and then exorcize it with truth and i it was to isolate her out of the loud world so that it would have to flee us of necessity and then the sound of it would be as though it had never been and he did you try to make her do it and i i was afraid to i was afraid she might and then it wouldnt

have done any good but if i could tell you we did it would have
been so and then the others wouldnt be so and then the world
would roar away and he and now this other you are not lying
now either but you are still blind to what is in yourself to that
part of general truth the sequence of natural events and their
causes which shadows every mans brow even benjys you are not
thinking of finitude you are contemplating an apotheosis in which
a temporary state of mind will become symmetrical above the
flesh and aware both of itself and of the flesh it will not quite
discard you will not even be dead and i temporary and he you
cannot bear to think that some day it will no longer hurt you like
this now were getting at it you seem to regard it merely as an
experience that will whiten your hair overnight so to speak
without altering your appearance at all you wont do it under
these conditions it will be a gamble and the strange thing is that
man who is conceived by accident and whose every breath his a
fresh cast with dice already loaded against him will not lace that
final main which he knows beforehand he has assuredly to face
without essaying expedients ranging all the way from violence to
petty chicanery that would not deceive a child until some day in
very disgust he risks everything on a single blind turn of a card
no man ever does that under the first fury of despair or remorse
or bereavement he does it only when he has realized that even
the despair or remorse or bereavement is not particularly important to the dark diceman and i temporary and he it is hard
believing to think that a love or a sorrow is a bond purchased
without design and which matures willy-nilly and is recalled
without warning to be replaced by whatever issue the gods happen
to be floating at the time no you will not do that until you come
to believe that even she was not quite worth despair perhaps and
i i will never do that nobody knows what i know and he i think
you'd better go on to cambridge right away you might go up into
maine for a month you can afford it if you are careful it might
be a good thing watching pennies has healed more scars than
jesus and i suppose i realize what you believe i will realize up
there next week or next month and he then you will remember
that for you to go to harvard has been your mothers dream since
you were born and no compson has ever disappointed a lady and
i temporary it will be better for me for all of us and he every
man is the arbiter of his own virtues but let no man prescribe for
another mans well-being and i temporary and he was the saddest
word of all there is nothing else in the world its not despair until

time its not even time until it was

The last note sounded. At last it stopped vibrating and the darkness was still again. I entered the sitting-room and turned on the light. I put my vest on. The gasoline was faint now, barely noticeable, and in the mirror the stain didn't show. Not like my eye did, anyway. I put on my coat. Shreve's letter crackled through the cloth and I took it out and examined the address, and put it in my side pocket. Then I carried the watch into Shreve's room and put it in his drawer and went to my room and got a fresh handkerchief and went to the door and put my hand on the light switch. Then I remembered I hadn't brushed my teeth, so I had to open the bag again. I found my toothbrush and got some of Shreve's paste and went out and brushed my teeth.. I squeezed the brush as dry as I could and put it back in the bag and shut it, and went to the door again. Before I snapped the light out I looked around to see if there was anything else, then I saw that I had forgotten my hat. I'd have to go by the post office and I'd be sure to meet some of them, and they'd think I was a Harvard Square student making like he was a senior. I had forgotten to brush it too, but Shreve had a brush, so I didn't have to open the bag any more.

April Sixth, 1928

Once a bitch always a bitch, what I say. I says you're lucky if her playing out of school is all that worries you. I says she ought to be down there in that kitchen right now, instead of up there in her room, gobbing paint on her face and waiting for six niggers that can't even stand up out of a chair unless they've got a panful of bread and meat to balance them, to fix breakfast for her. And Mother says,

'But to have the school authorities think that I have no control over her, that I can't –'

'Well,' I says, 'You can't, can you? You never have tried to do anything with her,' I says, 'How do you expect to begin this late, when she's seventeen years old?'

She thought about that for a while.

'But to have them think that . . . I didn't even know she had a report card. She told me last fall that they had quit using them this year. And now for Professor Junkin to call me on the telephone and tell me if she's absent one more time, she will have to leave school. How does she do it? Where does she go? You're downtown all day; you ought to see her if she stays on the streets.'

'Yes,' I says, 'If she stayed on the streets. I don't reckon she'd be playing out of school just to do something she could do in public,' I says.

'What do you mean?' she says.

'I don't mean anything,' I says. 'I just answered your question.' Then she begun to cry again talking about how her own flesh and blood rose up to curse her.

'You asked me,' I says.

'I don't mean you,' she says. 'You are the only one of them that isn't a reproach to me.'

'Sure,' I says, 'I never had time to be. I never had time to go to Harvard like Quentin or drink myself into the ground like Father. I had to work. But of course if you want me to follow her around and see what she does, I can quit the store and get a job where I can work at night. Then I can watch her during the day and you can use Ben for the night shift.'

'I know I'm just a trouble and a burden to you,' she says, crying on the pillow.

'I ought to know it,' I says. 'You've been telling me that for thirty years. Even Ben ought to know it now. Do you want me to say anything to her about it?'

'Do you think it will do any good?' she says.

'Not if you come down there interfering just when I get started,' I says. 'If you want me to control her, just say so and keep your hands off. Every time I try to, you come butting in and then she gives both of us the laugh.'

'Remember she's your own flesh and blood,' she says.

'Sure,' I says, 'that's just what I'm thinking of – flesh. And a little blood too, if I had my way. When people act like niggers, no matter who they are the only thing to do is treat them like a nigger.'

'I'm afraid you'll lose your temper with her,' she says.

'Well,' I says, 'You haven't had much luck with your system. You want me to do anything about it, or not? Say one way or the other; I've got to get on to work.'

'I know you have to slave your life away for us,' she says. 'You know if I had my way, you'd have an office of your own to go to, and hours that became a Bascomb. Because you are a Bascomb, despite your name. I know that if your father could have foreseen –'

'Well,' I says, 'I reckon he's entitled to guess wrong now and then, like anybody else, even a Smith or a Jodes.' She begun to cry again.

'To hear you speak bitterly of your dead father,' she says.

'All right,' I says, 'All right. Have it your way. But as I haven't got an office, I'll have to get on to what I have got. Do you want me to say anything to her?'

'I'm afraid you'll lose your temper with her,' she says.

'All right,' I says. 'I won't say anything, then.'

'But something must be done,' she says. 'To have people think I permit her to stay out of school and run about the streets, or that I can't prevent her doing it . . . Jason, Jason,' she says, 'How could you. How could you leave me with these burdens.'

'Now, now,' I says, 'You'll make yourself sick. Why don't you either lock her up all day too, or turn her over to me and quit worrying over her?'

'My own flesh and blood,' she says, crying. So I says,

'All right. I'll tend to her. Quit crying, now.'

'Don't lose your temper,' she says. 'She's just a child, remember.'

'No,' I says, 'I won't.' I went out, closing the door.

'Jason,' she says. I didn't answer. I went down the hall. 'Jason,' she says beyond the door. I went on downstairs. There wasn't anybody in the dining-room, then I heard her in the kitchen. She was trying to make Dilsey let her have another cup of coffee. I went in.

'I reckon that's your school costume, is it?' I says. 'Or maybe today's a holiday?'

'Just a half a cup, Dilsey,' she says. 'please.'

'No, suh,' Dilsey says, 'I ain't gwine do it. You ain't got no business wid mo'n one cup, a seventeen year old gal, let lone whut Miss Cahline say. You go on and git dressed for school, you kin ride to town wid Jason. You fixin to be late again.'

'No she's not,' I says. 'We're going to fix that right now.' She looked at me, the cup in her hand. She brushed her hair back from her face, her kimono slipping off her shoulder. 'You put that cup down and come in here a minute,' I says.

'What for?' she says.

'Come on,' I says, 'put that cup in the sink and come in here.'

'What you up to now, Jason?' Dilsey says.

'You may think you can run over me like you do your grandmother and everybody else,' I says, 'But you'll find out different. I'll give you ten seconds to put that cup down like I told you.'

She quit looking at me. She looked at Dilsey. 'What time is it, Dilsey?' she says. 'When it's ten seconds, you whistle. Just a half a cup. Dilsey, pl –'

I grabbed her by the arm. She dropped the cup. It broke on the floor and she jerked back, looking at me, but I held her arm. Dilsey got up from her chair.

'You, Jason,' she says.

'You turn me loose,' Quentin says, 'I'll slap you.'

'You will, will you?' I says, 'You will, will you?' She slapped at me. I caught that hand too and held her like a wildcat. 'You will, will you?' I says. 'You think you will?'

'You, Jason!' Dilsey says. I dragged her into the dining-room. Her kimono came unfastened, flapping about her, damn near naked. Dilsey came hobbling along. I turned and kicked the door shut in her face.

'You keep out of here,' I says.

Quentin was leaning against the table, fastening her kimono. I looked at her.

'Now,' I says, 'I want to know what you mean, playing out of school and telling your grandmother lies and forging her name on your report and worrying her sick. What do you mean by it?'

She didn't say anything. She was fastening her kimono up under her chin, pulling it tight around her, looking at me. She hadn't got around to painting herself yet and her face looked like she had polished it with a gun rag. I went and grabbed her wrist. 'What do you mean?' I says.

'None of your damn business,' she says. 'You turn me loose.'

Dilsey came in the door. 'You, Jason,' she says.

'You get out of here, like I told you,' I says, not even looking back. 'I want to know where you go when you play out of school,' I says. 'You keep off the streets, or I'd see you. Who do you play out with? Are you hiding out in the woods with one of those damn slick-headed jellybeans? Is that where you go?'

'You – you old goddamn!' she says. She fought, but I held her. 'You damn old goddamn!' she says.

'I'll show you,' I says. 'You may can scare an old woman off, but I'll show you who's got hold of you now.' I held her with one hand, then she quit fighting and watched me, her eyes getting wide and black.

'What are you going to do?' she says.

'You wait until I get this belt out and I'll show you,' I says, pulling my belt out. Then Dilsey grabbed my arm.

'Jason,' she says, 'You, Jason! Ain't you ashamed of yourself.'

'Dilsey,' Quentin says, 'Dilsey.'

'I ain't gwine let him,' Dilsey says, 'Don't you worry, honey.' She held to my arm. Then the belt came out and I jerked loose and flung her away. She stumbled into the table. She was so old she couldn't do any more than move hardly. But that's all right: we need somebody in the kitchen to eat up the grub the young ones can't tote off. She came hobbling between us, trying to hold me again. 'Hit me, den,' she says, 'ef nothin else but hittin somebody won't do you. Hit me,' she says.

'You think I won't?' I says.

'I don't put no devilment beyond you,' she says. Then I heard Mother on the stairs. I might have known she wasn't going to keep out of it. I let go. She stumbled back against the wall holding her kimono shut.

'All right,' I says, 'We'll just put this off a while. But don't think you can run it over me. I'm not an old woman, nor an old half dead nigger, either. You damn little slut,' I says.

'Dilsey,' she says, 'Dilsey, I want my mother.'

Dilsey went to her. 'Now, now,' she says, 'He ain't gwine so much as lay his hand on you while Ise here.' Mother came on down the stairs.

'Jason,' she says, 'Dilsey.'

'Now, now,' Dilsey says, 'I ain't gwine let him tech you.' She put her hand on Quentin. She knocked it down.

'You damn old nigger,' she says. She ran toward the door.

'Dilsey,' Mother says on the stairs. Quentin ran up the stairs, passing her. 'Quentin,' Mother says, 'You, Quentin,' Quentin ran on. I could hear her when she reached the top, then in the hall. Then the door slammed.

Mother had stopped. Then she came on. 'Dilsey,' she says.

'All right,' Dilsey says, 'Ise coming. You go on and git dat car and wait now,' she says, 'so you kin cahy her to school.'

'Don't you worry,' I says. 'I'll take her to school and I'm going to see that she stays there. I've started this thing, and I'm going through with it.'

'Jason,' Mother says on the stairs.

'Go on, now,' Dilsey says, going toward the door. 'You want to git her started too? Ise comin, Miss Cahline.'

I went on out. I could hear them on the steps. 'You go on back to bed now,' Dilsey was saying, 'Don't you know you ain't feeling well enough to git up yet? Go on back, now. I'm gwine to see she gits to school in time.'

I went on out the back to back the car out, then I had to go all the way round to the front before I found them.

'I thought I told you to put that tyre on the back of the car,' I says.

'I ain't had time,' Luster says. 'Ain't nobody to watch him till mammy git done in de kitchen.'

'Yes,' I says, 'I feed a whole damn kitchenful of niggers to follow around after him, but if I want an automobile tyre changed, I have to do it myself.'

'I ain't had nobody to leave him wid,' he says. Then he begun moaning and slobbering.

'Take him on round to the back,' I says. 'What the hell makes you want to keep him around here where people can see him?' I made them go on, before he got started bellowing good. It's bad enough on Sundays, with that damn field full of people that haven't got a side-show and six niggers to feed, knocking a damn oversize mothball around. He's going to keep on running up and down that fence and bellowing every time they come in sight until first thing I know they're going to begin charging me golf dues, then Mother and Dilsey'll have to get a couple of china door knobs and a walking-stick and work it out, unless I play at night with a lantern. Then they'd send us all to Jackson, maybe. God knows, they'd hold Old Home week when that happened.

I went on back to the garage. There was the tyre, leaning against the wall, but be damned if I was going to put it on. I backed out and turned around. She was standing by the drive. I says,

'I know you haven't got any books: I just want to ask you what you did with them, if it's any of my business. Of course I haven't got any right to ask,' I says, 'I'm just the one that paid $11.65 for them last September.'

'Mother buys my books,' she says. 'There's not a cent of your money on me. I'd starve first.'

'Yes?' I says. 'You tell your grandmother that and see what she says. You don't look all the way naked,' I says, 'even if that stuff on your face does hide more of you than anything else you've got on.'

'Do you think your money or hers either paid for a cent of this?' she says.

'Ask your grandmother,' I says. 'Ask her what became of those cheques. You saw her burn one of them, as I remember.' She wasn't even listening, with her face all gummed up with paint and her eyes hard as a fice dog's.

'Do you know what I'd do if I thought your money or hers either bought one cent of this?' she says, putting her hand on her dress.

'What would you do?' I says, 'Wear a barrel?'

'I'd tear it right off and throw it into the street,' she says. 'Don't you believe me?'

'Sure you would,' I says. 'You do it every time.'

'See if I wouldn't,' she says. She grabbed the neck of her dress in both hands and made like she would tear it.

'You tear that dress,' I says, 'And I'll give you a whipping right here that you'll remember all your life.'

'See if I don't,' she says. Then I saw that she really was trying to tear it, to tear it right off of her. By the time I got the car stopped and grabbed her hands there was about a dozen people looking. It made me so mad for a minute it kind of blinded me.

'You do a thing like that again and I'll make you sorry you ever drew breath,' I says.

'I'm sorry now,' she says. She quit, then her eyes turned kind of funny and I says to myself if you cry here in this car, on the street, I'll whip you. I'll wear you out. Lucky for her she didn't, so I turned her wrists loose and drove on. Luckily we were near an alley, where I could turn into the back street and dodge the square. They were already putting the tent up in Beard's lot. Earl had already given me the two passes for our show windows. She sat there with her face turned away, chewing her lip. 'I'm sorry now,' she says. 'I don't see why I was ever born.'

'And I know of at least one other person that don't understand all he knows about that,' I says. I stopped in front of the school house. The bell had rung, and the last of them were just going in. 'You're on time for once, anyway,' I says. 'Are you going in there and stay there, or am I coming with you and make you?' She got out and banged the door. 'Remember what I say,' I says.

'I mean it. Let me hear one more time that you are slipping up and down back alleys with one of those damn squirts.'

She turned back at that. 'I don't slip around,' she says. 'I dare anybody to know everything I do.'

'And they all know it, too,' I says. 'Everybody in this town knows what you are. But I won't have it any more, you hear? I don't care what you do, myself,' I says, 'But I've got a position in this town, and I'm not going to have any member of my family going on like a nigger wench. You hear me?'

'I don't care,' she says, 'I'm bad and I'm going to hell, and I don't care. I'd rather be in hell than anywhere where you are.'

'If I hear one more time that you haven't been to school, you'll wish you were in hell,' I says. She turned and ran on across the yard. 'One more time, remember,' I says. She didn't look back.

I went to the post office and got the mail and drove on to the store and parked. Earl looked at me when I came in. I gave him a chance to say something about my being late, but he just said,

'Those cultivators have come. You'd better help Uncle Job put them up.'

I went on to the back, where old Job was uncrating them, at the rate of about three bolts to the hour.

'You ought to be working for me,' I says. 'Every other no-count nigger in town eats in my kitchen.'

'I works to suit de man whut pays me Sat'dy night,' he says. 'When I does dat, it don't leave me a whole lot of time to please other folks.' He screwed up a nut. 'Ain't nobody works much in dis country cep de boll-weevil, noways,' he says.

'You'd better be glad you're not a boll-weevil waiting on those cultivators,' I says. 'You'd work yourself to death before they'd be ready to prevent you.'

'Dat's de troof,' he says, 'Boll-weevil got tough time. Work ev'y day in de week out in de hot sun, rain er shine. Ain't got no front porch to set on en watch de wattermilyuns growin and Sat'dy don't mean nothin a-tall to him.'

'Saturday wouldn't mean nothing to you, either,' I says, 'if it depended on me to pay you wages. Get those things out of the crates now and drag them inside.'

I opened her letter first and took the cheque out. Just like a woman. Six days late. Yet they try to make men believe that they're capable of conducting a business. How long would a man that thought the first of the month came on the sixth last in business. And like as not, when they sent the bank statement out, she would want to know why I never deposited my salary until the sixth. Things like that never occur to a woman.

'I had no answer to my letter about Quentin's easter dress. Did it arrive all right? I've had no answer to the last two letters I wrote her, though the cheque in the second one was cashed with the other cheque. Is she sick? Let me know at once or I'll come there and see for myself. You promised you would let me know when she needed things. I will expect to hear from you before the 10th. No you'd better wire me at once. You are opening my letters to her. I know that as well as if I were looking at you. You'd better wire me at once about her to this address.'

About that time Earl started yelling at Job, so I put them away and went over to try to put some life into him. What this country needs is white labour. Let these damn trifling niggers starve for a couple of years, then they'd see what a soft thing they have.

Along toward ten o'clock I went up front. There was a drummer there. It was a couple of minutes to ten, and I invited him up the street to get a cocacola. We got to talking about crops.

'There's nothing to it,' I says, 'Cotton is a speculator's crop. They fill the farmer full of hot air and get him to raise a big crop for them to whipsaw on the market, to trim the suckers with. Do you think the farmer gets anything out of it except a red neck and a hump in his back? You think the man that sweats to put it into the ground gets a red cent more than a bare living,' I says. 'Let him make a big crop and it won't be worth picking; let him make a small crop and he won't have enough to gin. And what for? so a bunch of damn eastern jews, I'm not talking about men of the jewish religion,' I says, 'I've known some jews that were fine citizens. You might be one yourself,' I says.

'No,' he says, 'I'm an American.'

'No offence,' I says. 'I give every man his due, regardless of religion or anything else. I have nothing against jews as an individual,' I says. 'It's just the race. You'll admit that they produce nothing. They follow the pioneers into a new country and sell them clothes.'

'You're thinking of Armenians,' he says, 'aren't you. A pioneer wouldn't have any use for new clothes.'

'No offence,' I says. 'I don't hold a man's religion against him.'

'Sure,' he says, 'I'm an American. My folks have some French blood, why I have a nose like this. I'm an American, all right.'

'So am I,' I says. 'Not many of us left. What I'm talking about is the fellows that sit up there in New York and trim the sucker gamblers.'

'That's right,' he says. 'Nothing to gambling, for a poor man. There ought to be a law against it.'

'Don't you think I'm right?' I says.

'Yes,' he says, 'I guess you're right. The farmer catches it coming and going.'

'I know I'm right,' I says. 'It's a sucker game, unless a man gets inside information from somebody that knows what's going on. I happen to be associated with some people who're right there in the ground. They have one of the biggest manipulators in New York for an adviser. Way I do it,' I says, 'I never risk much at a time. It's the fellow that thinks he knows it all and is trying to make a killing with three dollars that they're laying for. That's why they are in the business.'

Then it struck ten. I went up to the telegraph office. It opened up a little, just like they said. I went into the corner and took out the telegram again, just to be sure. While I was looking at it a report came in. It was up two points. They were all buying. I could tell that from what they were saying. Getting aboard. Like they didn't know it could go but one way. Like there was a law or something against doing anything but buying. Well, I reckon those eastern jews have got to live too. But I'll be damned if it hasn't come to a pretty pass when any damn foreigner that can't make a living in the country where God put him, can come to this one and take money right out of an American's pockets. It was up two points more. Four points. But hell, they were right there and knew what was going on. And if I wasn't going to take the advice, what was I paying them ten dollars a month for. I went out, then I remembered and came back and sent the wire. 'All well. Q writing today.'

'Q?' the operator says.

'Yes,' I says. 'Q. Can't you spell Q?'

'I just asked to be sure,' he says.

'You send it like I wrote it and I'll guarantee you to be sure,' I says. 'Send it collect.'

'What are you sending, Jason?' Doc Wright says, looking over my shoulder. 'Is that a code message to buy?'

'That's all right about that,' I says. 'You boys use your own judgement. You know more about it than those New York folks do.'

'Well, I ought to,' Doc says, 'I'd a saved money this year raising it at two cents a pound.'

Another report came in. It was down a point.

'Jason's selling,' Hopkins says. 'Look at his face.'

'That's all right about what I'm doing,' I says. 'You boys follow your own judgement. Those rich New York jews have got to live like everybody else,' I says.

I went on back to the store. Earl was busy up front. I went on back to the desk and read Lorraine's letter. 'Dear daddy wish you were here. No good parties when daddys out of town I miss my sweet daddy.' I reckon she does. Last time I gave her forty dollars. Gave it to her. I never promise a woman anything nor let her know what I'm going to give her. That's the only way to manage them. Always keep them guessing. If you can't think of any other way to surprise them, give them a bust in the jaw.

I tore it up and burned it over the spittoon. I make it a rule never to keep a scrap of paper bearing a woman's hand, and I never write them at all. Lorraine is always after me to write to her but I says anything I forgot to tell you will save till I get to Memphis again but I says I don't mind you writing me now and then in a plain envelope, but if you ever try to call me up on the telephone, Memphis won't hold you I says. I says when I'm up there I'm one of the boys, but I'm not going to have any woman calling me on the telephone. Here I says, giving her the forty dollars. If you ever get drunk and takes a notion to call me on the phone, just remember this and count ten before you do it.

'When'll that be?' she says.

'What?' I says.

'When you're coming back,' she says.

'I'll let you know,' I says. Then she tried to buy a beer, but I wouldn't let her. 'Keep your money,' I says. 'Buy yourself a dress with it.' I gave the maid a five, too. After all, like I say money has no value; it's just the way you spend it. It don't belong to anybody, so why try to hoard it. It just belongs to the man that can get it and keep it. There's a man right here in Jefferson made a lot of money selling rotten goods to niggers, lived in a room over the store about the size of a pig-pen, and did his own cooking. About four or five years ago he was taken sick. Scared the hell out of him so that when he was up again he joined the church and bought himself a Chinese missionary, five thousand dollars a year. I often think how mad he'll be if he was to die and find out there's not any heaven, when he thinks about that five thousand a year. Like I say, he'd better go on and die now and save money.

'When it was burned good I was just about to shove the others into my coat when all of a sudden something told me to open Quentin's before I went home, but about that time Earl started yelling for me up front, so I put them away and went and waited on the damn redneck while he spent fifteen minutes deciding whether he wanted a twenty cent hame string or a thirty-five cent one.

'You'd better take that good one,' I says. 'How do you fellows ever expect to get ahead, trying to work with cheap equipment?'

'If this one ain't any good,' he says, 'why have you got it on sale?'

'I didn't say it wasn't any good,' I says, 'I said it's not as good as that other one.'

'How do you know it's not,' he says. 'You ever use airy one of them?'

'Because they don't ask thirty-five cents for it,' I says. 'That's how I know it's not as good.'

He held the twenty cent one in his hands, drawing it through his fingers. 'I reckon I'll take this hyer one,' he says. I offered to take it and wrap it, but he rolled it up and put it in his overalls. Then he took out a tobacco sack and finally got it untied and shook some coins out. He handed me a quarter. 'That fifteen cents will buy me a snack of dinner,' he says.

'All right,' I says. 'You're the doctor. But don't come complaining to me next year when you have to buy a new outfit.'

'I ain't makin' next year's crop yit,' he says. Finally I got rid of him, but every time I took that letter out something would come up. They were all in town for the show, coming in in droves to give their money to something that brought nothing to the town and wouldn't leave anything except what those grafters in the Mayor's office will split among themselves, and Earl chasing back and forth like a hen in a coop, saying 'Yes, ma'am, Mr Compson will wait on you. Jason, show this lady a churn or a nickel's worth of screen hooks.'

Well, Jason likes work. I says no I never had university advantages because at Harvard they teach you how to go for a swim at night without knowing how to swim and at Sewanee they don't even teach you what water is. I says you might send me to the state University; maybe I'll learn how to stop my clock with a nose spray and then you can send Ben to the Navy I says or to the cavalry anyway, they use geldings in the cavalry. Then when she sent Quentin home for me to feed too I says I guess that's right too, instead of me having to go way up north for a job they sent the job down here to me and then Mother begun to cry and I says it's not that I have any objection to having it here; if it's any satisfaction to you I'll quit work and nurse it myself and let you and Dilsey keep the flour barrel full, or Ben. Rent him out to a sideshow; there must be folks somewhere that would pay a dime to see him then she cried more and kept saying my poor afflicted baby and I says yes he'll be quite a help to you when he gets his growth not being more than one and a half times as high as me now and she says she'd be dead soon and then we'd all be better off and so I says all right, all right, have it your way. It's your grandchild, which is more than any other grandparents it's got can say for certain. Only I says it's only a question of time. If you believe she'll do what she says and not try to see it, you fool yourself because the first time that was that Mother kept on saying thank God you are not a Compson except in name, because you are all I have left now, you and Maury, and I says well I could spare Uncle Maury myself and then they came and said they were ready to start. Mother stopped crying then. She pulled her veil down and we went downstairs. Uncle Maury was coming out of the dining-room, his handkerchief to his mouth. They kind of made a lane and we went out the door just in time to see Dilsey driving Ben and T.P. back around the corner. We went down the steps and got in. Uncle Maury kept saying poor little sister, poor little sister, talking around his mouth and patting Mother's hand. Talking around whatever it was.

'Have you got your band on?' she says. 'Why don't they go on, before Benjamin comes out and makes a spectacle. Poor little boy. He doesn't know. He can't even realize.'

'There, there,' Uncle Maury says, patting her hand, talking around his mouth. 'It's better so. Let him be unaware of bereavement until he has to.'

'Other women have their children to support them in times like this,' Mother says.

'You have Jason and me,' he says.

'It's so terrible to me,' she says, 'Having the two of them like this, in less than two years.'

'There, there,' he says. After a while he kind of sneaked his hand to his mouth and dropped them out of the window. Then I knew what I had been smelling. Clove stems. I reckon he thought that the least he could do at Father's funeral or maybe the sideboard thought it was still Father and tripped him up when he passed. Like I say, if he had to sell something to send Quentin to Harvard we'd all been a damn sight better off if he'd sold that sideboard and bought himself a one-armed strait-jacket with part of the money. I reckon the reason all the Compson gave out before it got to me like Mother says, is that he drank it up. At least I never heard of him offering to sell anything to send me to Harvard.

So he kept on patting her hand and saying 'Poor little sister,' patting her hand with one of the black gloves that we got the bill for four days later because it was the twenty-sixth because it was the same day one month that Father went up there and got it and brought it home and wouldn't tell anything about where she was or anything and Mother crying and saying 'And you didn't even see him? You didn't even try to get him to make any provision for it?' and Father says 'No she shall not touch his money not one cent of it' and Mother says 'He can be forced to by law. He can prove nothing unless — Jason Compson,' she says, 'Were you fool enough to tell —'

'Hush, Caroline,' Father says, then he sent me to help Dilsey get that old cradle out of the attic and I says,

'Well, they brought my job home tonight' because all the time we kept hoping they'd get things straightened out and he'd keep her because Mother kept saying she would at least have enough regard for the family not to jeopardize my chance after she and Quentin had had theirs.

'And whar else do she belong?' Dilsey says, 'Who else gwine raise her cep me? Ain't I raised ev'y one of y'all?'

'And a damn fine job you made of it,' I says. 'Anyway it'll give her something to sure enough worry over now.' So we carried the cradle down and Dilsey started to set it up in her old room. Then Mother started sure enough.

'Hush, Miss Cahline,' Dilsey says, 'You gwine wake her up.'

'In there?' Mother says, 'To be contaminated by that atmosphere? It'll be hard enough as it is, with the heritage she already has.'

'Hush,' Father says, 'Don't be silly.'

'Why ain't she gwine sleep in here,' Dilsey says, 'In the same room whar I put her ma to bed ev'y night of her life since she was big enough to sleep by herself.'

'You don't know,' Mother says, 'To have my own daughter

cast off by her husband. Poor little innocent baby,' she says, looking at Quentin. 'You will never know the suffering you've caused.'

'Hush, Caroline,' Father says.

'What you want to go on like that fo Jason fer?' Dilsey says.

'I've tried to protect him.' Mother says. 'I've always tried to protect him from it. At least I can do my best to shield her.'

'How sleepin in dis room gwine hurt her, I like to know,' Dilsey says.

'I can't help it,' Mother says. 'I know I'm just a troublesome old woman. But I know that people cannot flout God's laws with impunity.'

'Nonsense,' Father said. 'Fix it in Miss Caroline's room then, Dilsey.'

'You can say nonsense,' Mother says. 'But she must never know. She must never even learn that name. Dilsey, I forbid you ever to speak that name in her hearing. If she could grow up never to know that she had a mother, I would thank God.'

'Don't be a fool,' Father says.

'I have never interfered with the way you brought them up,' Mother says, 'But now I cannot stand anymore. We must decide this now, tonight. Either that name is never to be spoken in her hearing, or she must go, or I will go. Take your choice.'

'Hush,' Father says, 'You're just upset. Fix it in here, Dilsey.'

'En you's about sick too,' Dilsey says. 'You looks like a hant. You git in bed and I'll fix you a toddy and see kin you sleep. I bet you ain't had a full night's sleep since you left.'

'No,' Mother says, 'Don't you know what the doctor says? Why must you encourage him to drink? That's what's the matter with him now. Look at me, I suffer too, but I'm not so weak that I must kill myself with whisky.'

'Fiddlesticks,' Father says, 'What do doctors know? They make their livings advising people to do whatever they are not doing at the time, which is the extent of anyone's knowledge of the degenerate ape. You'll have a minister in to hold my hand next.' Then Mother cried, and he went out. Went downstairs, and then I heard the sideboard. I woke up and heard him going down again. Mother had gone to sleep or something, because the house was quiet at last. He was trying to be quiet too, because I couldn't hear him, only the bottom of his nightshirt and his bare legs in front of the sideboard.

Dilsey fixed the cradle and undressed her and put her in it.

She never had waked up since he brought her in the house.

'She pretty near too big fer it,' Dilsey says. 'Dar now. I gwine spread me a pallet right acrost de hall, so you won't need to git up in de night.'

'I won't sleep,' Mother says. 'You go on home. I won't mind. I'll be happy to give the rest of my life to her, if I can just prevent –'

'Hush, now,' Dilsey says. 'We gwine take keer of her. En you go on to bed too,' she says to me, 'You got to go to school tomorrow.'

So I went out, then Mother called me back and cried on me a while.

'You are my only hope,' she says. 'Every night I thank God for you.' While we were waiting there for them to start she says Thank God if he had to be taken too, it is you left me and not Quentin. Thank God you are not a Compson, because all I have left now is you and Maury and I says, Well I could spare Uncle Maury myself. Well, he kept on patting her hand with his black glove, talking away from her. He took them off when his turn with the shovel came. He got up near the first, where they were holding the umbrellas over them, stamping every now and then and trying to kick the mud off their feet and sticking to the shovels so they'd have to knock it off, making a hollow sound when it fell on it, and when I stepped back around the hack I could see him behind a tombstone, taking another one out of a bottle. I thought he never was going to stop because I had on my new suit too, but it happened that there wasn't much mud on the wheels yet, only Mother saw it and says I don't know when you'll ever have another one and Uncle Maury says, 'Now, now. Don't you worry at all. You have me to depend on, always.'

And we have. Always. The fourth letter was from him. But there wasn't any need to open it. I could have written it myself, or recited it to her from memory, adding ten dollars just to be safe. But I had a hunch about that other letter. I just felt that it was about time she was up to some of her tricks again. She got pretty wise after that first time. She found out pretty quick that I was a different breed of cat from Father. When they begun to get it filled up toward the top Mother started crying sure enough, so Uncle Maury got in with her and drove off. He says You can come in with somebody; they'll be glad to give you a lift. I'll have to take your mother on and I thought about saying, Yes you ought to brought two bottles instead of just one only I thought

about where we were so I let them go on. Little they cared how
wet I got, because then Mother could have a whale of a time
being afraid I was taking pneumonia.

Well, I got to thinking about that and watching them throwing
dirt into it, slapping it on anyway like they were making mortar
or something or building a fence, and I began to feel sort of
funny and so I decided to walk around a while. I thought that if
I went toward town they'd catch up and be trying to make me
get in one of them, so I went on back toward the nigger graveyard.
I got under some cedars, where the rain didn't come much, only
dripping now and then, where I could see when they got through
and went away. After a while they were all gone and I waited a
minute and came out.

I had to follow the path to keep out of the wet grass so I didn't
see her until I was pretty near there, standing there in a black
cloak, looking at the flowers, I knew who it was right off, before
she turned and looked at me and lifted up her veil.

'Hello, Jason,' she says, holding out her hand. We shook hands.

'What are you doing here?' I says, 'I thought you promised her
you wouldn't come back here. I thought you had more sense
than that.'

'Yes?' she says. She looked at the flowers again. There must
have been fifty dollars' worth. Somebody had put one bunch on
Quentin's. 'You did?' she says.

'I'm not surprised though,' I says. 'I wouldn't put anything
past you. You don't mind anybody. You don't give a damn about
anybody.'

'Oh,' she says, 'that job.' She looked at the grave. 'I'm sorry
about that, Jason.'

'I bet you are,' I says. 'You'll talk mighty meek now. But you
needn't have come back. There's not anything left. Ask Uncle
Maury, if you don't believe me.'

'I don't want anything,' she says. She looked at the grave. 'Why
didn't they let me know?' she says. 'I just happened to see it in
the paper. On the back page. Just happened to.'

I didn't say anything. We stood there, looking at the grave,
and then I got to thinking about when we were little and one
thing and another and I got to feeling funny again, kind of mad
or something, thinking about now we'd have Uncle Maury around
the house all the time, running things like the way he left me to
come home in the rain by myself. I says,

'A fine lot you care, sneaking in here soon as he's dead. But it

won't do you any good. Don't think that you can take advantage
of this to come sneaking back. If you can't stay on the horse
you've got, you'll have to walk,' I says. 'We don't even know your
name at that house,' I says. 'Do you know that? We don't even
know you with him and Quentin,' I says. 'Do you know that?'

'I know it,' she says, 'Jason,' she says, looking at the grave, 'if
you'll fix it so I can see her a minute I'll give you fifty dollars.'

'You haven't got fifty dollars,' I says.

'Will you?' she says, not looking at me.

'Let's see it,' I says. 'I don't believe you've got fifty dollars.'

I could see where her hands were moving under her cloak,
then she held her hand out. Damn if it wasn't full of money. I
could see two or three yellow ones.

'Does he still give you money?' I says. 'How much does he send
you?'

'I'll give you a hundred,' she says. 'Will you?'

'Just a minute,' I says, 'And just like I say I wouldn't have her
know it for a thousand dollars.'

'Yes,' she says. 'Just like you say do it. Just so I see her a minute.
I won't beg or do anything. I'll go right on away.'

'Give me the money,' I says.

'I'll give it to you afterwards,' she says.

'Don't you trust me?' I says.

'No,' she says. 'I know you. I grew up with you.'

'You're a fine one to talk about trusting people,' I says. 'Well,'
I says, 'I got to get on out of the rain. Good-bye,' I made to go
away.

'Jason,' she says. I stopped.

'Yes?' I says. 'Hurry up. I'm getting wet.'

'All right,' she says. 'Here.' There wasn't anybody in sight. I
went back and took the money. She still held to it. 'You'll do it?'
she says, looking at me from under the veil, 'You promise?'

'Let go,' I says, 'You want somebody to come along and see
us?'

She let go. I put the money in my pocket. 'You'll do it, Jason?'
she says. 'I wouldn't ask you, if there was any other way.'

'You're damn right there's no other way,' I says. 'Sure I'll do
it. I said I would, didn't I? Only you'll have to do just like I say,
now.'

'Yes,' she says, 'I will.' So I told her where to be, and went to
the livery stable. I hurried and got there just as they were
unhitching the hack. I asked if they had paid for it yet and he

said No and I said Mrs Compson forgot something and wanted
it again, so they let me take it. Mink was driving. I bought him
a cigar, so we drove around until it begun to get dark on the
back streets where they wouldn't see him. Then Mink said he'd
have to take the team on back and so I said I'd buy him another
cigar and so we drove into the lane and I went across the yard
to the house. I stopped in the hall until I could hear Mother and
Uncle Maury upstairs, then I went on back to the kitchen. She
and Ben were there with Dilsey. I said Mother wanted her and I
took her into the house. I found Uncle Maury's raincoat and put
it around her and picked her up and went back to the lane and
got in the hack. I told Mink to drive to the depot. He was afraid
to pass the stable, so we had to go the back way and I saw her
standing on the corner under the light and I told Mink to drive
close to the walk and when I said Go on, to give the team a bat.
Then I took the raincoat off of her and held her to the window
and Caddy saw her and sort of jumped forward.

'Hit em Mink!' I says, and Mink gave them a cut and we went
past her like a fire-engine. 'Now get on that train like you
promised,' I says. I could see her running after us through the
back window. 'Hit em again,' I says, 'Let's get on home.' When
we turned the corner she was still running.

And so I counted the money again that night and put it away,
and I didn't feel so bad. I says I reckon that'll show you. I reckon
you'll know now that you can't beat me out of a job and get away
with it. It never occurred to me she wouldn't keep her promise
and take that train. But I didn't know much about them then; I
didn't have any more sense than to believe what they said, because
the next morning damn if she didn't walk right into the store,
only she had sense enough to wear the veil and not speak to
anybody. It was Saturday morning, because I was at the store,
and she came right on back to the desk where I was, walking fast.

'Liar,' she says, 'Liar.'

'Are you crazy?' I says. 'What do you mean? coming in here
like this?' She started in, but I shut her off. I says, 'You already
cost me one job; do you want me to lose this one too? If you've
got anything to say to me, I'll meet you somewhere after dark.
What have you got to say to me?' I says, "Didn't I do everything
I said? I said see her a minute, didn't I? Well, didn't you?' She
just stood there looking at me, shaking like an ague-fit, her hands
clenched and kind of jerking. 'I did just what I said I would,' I
says, 'You're the one that lied. You promised to take that train.

Didn't you Didn't you promise? If you think you can get that money back, just try it,' I says. 'If it'd been a thousand dollars, you'd still owe me after the risk I took. And if I see or hear you're still in town after number 17 runs,' I says, 'I'll tell Mother and Uncle Maury. Then hold your breath until you see her again.' She just stood there, looking at me, twisting her hands together.

'Damn you,' she says, 'Damn you.'

'Sure,' I says, 'That's all right too. Mind what I say, now. After number 17, and I tell them.'

After she was gone I felt better. I says I reckon you'll think twice before you deprive me of a job that was promised me. I was a kid then. I believed folks when they said they'd do things. I've learned better since. Besides, like I say I guess I don't need any man's help to get along I can stand on my own feet like I always have. Then all of a sudden I thought of Dilsey and Uncle Maury. I thought how she'd get around Dilsey and that Uncle Maury would do anything for ten dollars. And there I was, couldn't even get away from the store to protect my own Mother. Like she says, if one of you had to be taken, thank God it was you left me I can depend on you and I says well I don't reckon I'll ever get far enough from the store to get out of your reach. Somebody's got to hold on to what little we have left, I reckon.

So as soon as I got home I fixed Dilsey. I told Dilsey she had leprosy and I got the bible and read where a man's flesh rotted off and I told her that if she ever looked at her or Ben or Quentin they'd catch it too. So I thought I had everything all fixed until that day when I came home and found Ben bellowing. Raising hell and nobody could quiet him. Mother said, Well, get him the slipper then. Dilsey made out she didn't hear. Mother said it again and I says I'd go I couldn't stand that damn noise. Like I say I can stand lots of things I don't expect much from them but if I have to work all day long in a damn store damn if I don't think I deserve a little peace and quiet to eat dinner in. So I says I'd go and Dilsey says quick, 'Jason!'

Well, like a flash I knew what was up, but just to make sure went and got the slipper and brought it back, and just like I thought, when he saw it you'd thought we were killing him. So I made Dilsey own up, then I told Mother. We had to take her up to bed then, and after things got quieted down a little I put the fear of God into Dilsey. As much as you can into a nigger, that is. That's the trouble with nigger servants, when they've

been with you for along time they get so full of self-importance
that they're not worth a damn. Think they run the whole family.

'I like to know whut's de hurt in lettin dat po chile see her own
baby,' Dilsey says. 'If Mr Jason was still her hit ud be different.'

'Only Mr Jason's not here,' I says. 'I know you won't pay me
any mind, but I reckon you'll do what Mother says. You keep on
worrying her like this until you get her into the graveyard too,
then you can fill the whole house full of ragtag and bobtail. But
what did you want to let that damn idiot see her for?'

'You's a cold man, Jason, if man you is,' she says. 'I thank de
Lawd I got mo heart dan dat, even ef hit is black.'

'At least I'm man enough to keep that flour barrel full,' I says.
'And if you do that again, you won't be eating out of it either.'

So the next time I told her that if she tried Dilsey again, Mother
was going to fire Dilsey and send Ben to Jackson and take Quentin
and go away. She looked at me for a while. There wasn't any
street light close and I couldn't see her face much. But I could
feel her looking at me. When we were little when she'd get mad
and couldn't do anything about it her upper lip would begin to
jump. Every time it jumped it would leave a little more of her
teeth showing, and all the time she'd be as still as a post, not a
muscle moving except her lip jerking higher and higher up her
teeth. But she didn't say anything. She just said,

'All right. How much?'

'Well, if one look through a hack window was worth a hundred,'
I says. So after that she behaved pretty well, only one time she
asked to see a statement of the bank account.

'I know they have Mother's endorsement on them,' she says,
'But I want to see the bank statement. I want to see myself where
those cheques go.'

'That's in mother's private business,' I says. 'If you think you
have any right to pry into her private affairs I'll tell her you
believe those cheques are being misappropriated and you want
an audit because you don't trust her.'

She didn't say anything or move. I could hear her whispering
Damn you oh damn you oh damn you.

'Say it out,' I says, 'I don't reckon it's any secret what you and
I think of one another. Maybe you want the money back,' I says.

'Listen, Jason,' she says, 'Don't lie to me now. About her. I
won't ask to see anything. If that isn't enough, I'll send more
each month. Just promise that she'll – that she – You can do that.
Things for her. Be kind to her. Little things that I can't, they

won't let? . . . But you won't. You never had a drop of warm
blood in you. Listen,' she says, 'If you'll get Mother to let me
have her back, I'll give you a thousand dollars.'

'You haven't got a thousand dollars,' I says, 'I know you're
lying now.'

'Yes I have. I will have. I can get it.'

'And I know how you'll get it,' I says, 'You'll get it the same
way you got her. And when she gets big enough –' Then I thought
she really was going to hit at me, and then I didn't know what
she was going to do. She acted for a minute like some kind of a
toy that's wound up too tight and about to burst all to pieces.

'Oh, I'm crazy,' she says, 'I'm insane. I can't take her. Keep
her. What am I thinking of. Jason,' she says, grabbing my arm.
Her hands were hot as fever. 'You'll have to promise to take care
of her, to – She's kin to you; your own flesh and blood. Promise,
Jason. You have Father's name: do you think I'd have to ask him
twice? once, even?'

'That's so,' I says, 'He did leave me something. What do you
want me to do,' I says, 'Buy an apron and a go-cart? I never got
you into this,' I says, 'I run more risk than you do, because you
haven't got anything at stake. So if you expect –'

'No,' she says, then she begun to laugh and to try to hold it
back all at the same time. 'No. I have nothing at stake,' she says,
making that noise, putting her hands to her mouth. 'Nuh-nuh-
nothing,' she says.

'Here,' I says, 'Stop that!'

'I'm tr-trying to,' she says, holding her hands over her mouth.
'Oh God, oh God.'

'I'm going away from here,' I says, 'I can't be seen here.'

'You get on out of town now, you hear?'

'Wait,' she says, catching my arm. 'I've stopped. I won't again.
You promise, Jason?' she says, and me feeling her eyes almost
like they were touching my face, 'You promise? Mother – that
money – if sometimes she needs things – If I send cheques for
her to you, other ones besides those, you'll give them to her? You
won't tell? You'll see that she has things like other girls?'

'Sure,' I says, 'As long as you behave and do like I tell you.'
And so when Earl came up front with his hat on he says, 'I'm
going to step up to Rogers' and get a snack. We won't have time
to go home to dinner, I reckon.'

'What's the matter we won't have time?' I says.

'With this show in town and all,' he says. 'They're going to give an afternoon performance too, and they'll all want to get done trading in time to go to it. So we'd better just run up to Rogers'.'

'All right,' I says, 'It's your stomach. If you want to make a slave of yourself to your business, it's all right with me.'

'I reckon you'll never be a slave to any business,' he says.

'Not unless it's Jason Compson's business,' I says.

So when I went back and opened it the only thing that surprised me was it was a money order not a cheque. Yes, sir. You can't trust a one of them. After all the risk I'd taken, risking Mother finding out about her coming down here once or twice a year sometimes, and me having to tell Mother lies about it. That's gratitude for you. And I wouldn't put it past her to try to notify the post office not to let anyone except her cash it. Giving a kid like that fifty dollars. Why I never saw fifty dollars until I was twenty-one years old, with all the other boys with the afternoon off and all day Saturday and me working in a store. Like I say, how can they expect anybody to control her, with her giving her money behind our backs. She has the same home you had I says, and the same raising. I reckon Mother is a better judge of what she needs than you are, that haven't even got a home. 'If you want to give her money,' I says, 'You send it to Mother, don't be giving it to her. If I've got to run this risk every few months, you'll have to do like I say, or it's out.'

And just about the time I got ready to begin on it because if Earl thought I was going to dash up the street and gobble two bits' worth of indigestion on his account he was bad fooled. I may not be sitting with my feet on a mahogany desk but I am being paid for what I do inside this building and if I can't manage to live a civilized life outside of it I'll go where I can. I can stand on my own feet; I don't need any man's mahogany desk to prop me up. So just about the time I got ready to start. I'd have to drop everything and run to sell some redneck a dime's worth of nails or something, and Earl up there gobbling a sandwich and half-way back already, like as not, and then I found that all the blanks were gone. I remembered then that I had aimed to get some more, but it was too late now, and then I looked up and there Quentin came. In the back door. I heard her asking old Job if I was there. I just had time to stick them in the drawer and close it.

She came around to the desk. I looked at my watch.

'You been to dinner already?' I says. 'It's just twelve; I just heard it strike. You must have flown home and back.'

'I'm not going home to dinner,' she says. 'Did I get a letter today?'

'Were you expecting one?' I says. 'Have you got a sweetie that can write?'

'From Mother,' she says. 'Did I get a letter from Mother?' she says, looking at me.

'Mother got one from her,' I says. 'I haven't opened it. You'll have to wait until she opens it. She'll let you see it, I imagine.'

'Please, Jason,' she says, not paying any attention, 'Did I get one?'

'What's the matter?' I says. 'I never knew you to be this anxious about anybody. You must expect some money from her.'

'She said she –' she says. 'Please, Jason,' she says, 'Did I?'

'You must have been to school today, after all,' I says, 'Some-where where they taught you to say please. Wait a minute, while I wait on that customer.'

I went and waited on him. When I turned to come back she was out of sight behind the desk. I ran. I ran around the desk and caught her as she jerked her hand out of the drawer. I took the letter away from her, beating her knuckles on the desk until she let go.

'You would, would you?' I says.

'Give it to me,' she says, 'You've already opened it. Give it to me. Please, Jason. It's mine. I saw the name.'

'I'll take a hame string to you,' I says. 'That's what I'll give you. Going into my papers.'

'Is there some money in it?' she says, reaching for it. 'She said she would send me some money. She promised she would. Give it to me.'

'What do you want with money?' I says.

'She said she would,' she says, 'Give it to me. Please, Jason. I won't ever ask you anything again if you'll give it to me this time.'

'I'm going to, if you'll give me time,' I says. I took the letter and the money order out and gave her the letter. She reached for the money order, not hardly glancing at the letter. 'You'll have to sign it first,' I says.

'How much is it?' she says.

'Read the letter,' I says. 'I reckon it'll say.'

She read it fast, in about two looks.

'It don't say,' she says, looking up. She dropped the letter to the floor. 'How much is it?'

'It's ten dollars,' I says.

'Ten dollars?' she says, staring at me.

'And you ought to be damn glad to get that,' I says, 'A kid like you. What are you in such a rush for money all of a sudden for?'

'Ten dollars?' she says, like she was talking in her sleep, 'Just ten dollars?' She made a grab at the money order. 'You're lying,' she says. 'Thief!' she says, 'Thief!'

'You would, would you?' I says, holding her off.

'Give it to me!' she says, 'It's mine. She sent it to me. I will see it. I will.'

'You will?' I says, holding her, 'How're you going to do it?'

'Just let me see it, Jason,' she says, 'Please. I won't ask you for anything again.'

'Think I'm lying, do you?' I says. 'Just for that you won't see it.'

'But just ten dollars,' she says, 'She told me she – she told me – Jason, please please please. I've got to have some money. I've just got to. Give it to me, Jason. I'll do anything if you will.'

'Tell me what you've got to have money for,' I says.

'I've got to have it,' she says. She was looking at me. Then all of a sudden she quit looking at me without moving her eyes at all. I knew she was going to lie. 'It's some money I owe,' she says. 'I've got to pay it. I've got to pay it today.'

'Who to?' I says. Her hands were sort of twisting. I could watch her trying to think of a lie to tell 'Have you been charging things at stores again?' I says. 'You needn't bother to tell me that. If you can find anybody in this town that'll charge anything to you after what I told them, I'll eat it.'

'It's a girl,' she says, 'It's a girl. I borrowed some money from a girl. I've got to pay it back. Jason, give it to me. Please. I'll do anything. I've got to have it. Mother will pay you. I'll write to her to pay you and that I won't ever ask her for anything again. You can see the letter. Please, Jason. I've got to have it.'

'Tell me what you want with it, and I'll see about it,' I says. 'Tell me.' She just stood there, with her hands working against her dress. 'All right,' I says, 'If ten dollars is too little for you, I'll just take it home to Mother, and you know what'll happen to it then. Of course, if you're so rich you don't need ten dollars –'

She stood there, looking at the floor, kind of mumbling to herself. 'She said she would send me some money. She said she sends money here and you say she don't send any. She said she's sent a lot of money here. She says it's for me. That it's for me to have some of it. And you say we haven't got any money.'

'You know as much about that as I do,' I says. 'You've seen what happens to those cheques.'

'Yes,' she says, looking at the floor. 'Ten dollars,' she says, 'Ten dollars.'

'And you'd better thank your stars it's ten dollars,' I says. 'Here,' I says. I put the money order face down on the desk, holding my hand on it, 'Sign it.'

'Will you let me see it?' she says. 'I just want to look at it. Whatever it says, I won't ask for but ten dollars. You can have the rest. I just want to see it.'

'Not after the way you've acted,' I says. 'You've got to learn one thing, and that is that when I tell you to do something, you've got it to do. You sign your name on that line.'

She took the pen, but instead of signing it she just stood there with her head bent and the pen shaking in her hand. Just like her mother. 'Oh, God,' she says, 'oh, God.'

'Yes,' I says, 'That's one thing you'll have to learn if you never learn anything else. Sign it now, and get on out of here.'

She signed it. 'Where's the money?' she says. I took the order and blotted it and put it in my pocket. Then I gave her the ten dollars.

'Now you go on back to school this afternoon, you hear?' I says. She didn't answer. She crumpled the bill up in her hand like it was a rag or something and went on out the front door just as Earl came in. A customer came in with him and they stopped up front. I gathered up the things and put on my hat and went up front.

'Been much busy?' Earl says.

'Not much,' I says. He looked out the door.

'That your car over yonder?' he says. 'Better not try to go out home to dinner. We'll likely have another rush just before the show opens. Get you a lunch at Rogers' and put a ticket in the drawer.'

'Much obliged,' I says. 'I can still manage to feed myself, I reckon.'

And right there he'd stay, watching that door like a hawk until I came through it again. Well, he'd just have to watch it for a while; I was doing the best I could. The time before I says that's the last one now; you'll have to remember to get some more right away. But who can remember anything in all this hurrah. And now this damn show had to come here the one day I'd have to hunt all over town for a blank cheque, besides all the other things I had to do to keep the house running, and Earl watching the door like a hawk.

I went to the printing shop and told him I wanted to play a joke on a fellow, but he didn't have anything. Then he told me to have a look in the old opera house, where somebody had stored a lot of papers and junk out of the old Merchants' and Farmers' Bank when it failed, so I dodged up a few more alleys so Earl couldn't see me and finally found old man Simmons and got the key from him and went up there and dug around. At last I found a pad on a Saint Louis bank. And of course she'd pick this one time to look at it close. Well, it would have to do. I couldn't waste any more time now.

I went back to the store. 'Forgot some papers Mother wants to go to the bank,' I says. I went back to the desk and fixed the cheque. Trying to hurry and all, I says to myself it's a good thing her eyes are giving out, with that little whore in the house, a Christian forbearing woman like Mother. I says you know just as well as I do what she's going to grow up into but I says that's your business, if you want to keep her and raise her in your house, just because of Father. Then she would begin to cry and say it was her own flesh and blood so I just says All right. Have it your own way. I can stand it if you can.

I fixed the letter up again and glued it back and went out.

'Try not to be gone any longer than you can help,' Earl says.

'All right,' I says. I went to the telegraph office. The smart boys were all there.

'Any of you boys made your million yet?' I says.

'Who can do anything, with a market like that?' Doc says.

'What's it doing?' I says. I went in and looked. It was three points under the opening. 'You boys are not going to let a little thing like the cotton market beat you, are you?' I says. 'I thought you were too smart for that.'

'Smart, hell,' Doc says. 'It was down twelve points at twelve o'clock. Cleaned me out.'

'Twelve points?' I says. 'Why the hell didn't somebody let me know? Why didn't you let me know?' I says to the operator.

'I take it as it comes in,' he says. 'I'm not running a bucket shop.'

'You're smart, aren't you?' I says. 'Seems to me, with the money I spend with you, you could take time to call me up. Or maybe your damn company's in a conspiracy with those damn eastern sharks.'

He didn't say anything. He made like he was busy.

'You're getting a little too big for your pants,' I says. 'First thing you know you'll be working for a living.'

'What's the matter with you?' Doc says. 'You're still three points to the good.'

'Yes,' I says, 'If I happened to be selling. I haven't mentioned that yet, I think. You boys all cleaned out?'

'I got caught twice,' Doc says. 'I switched just in time.'

'Well,' I.O. Snopes says, 'I've picked hit; I reckon tain't no more than fair fer hit to pick me once in a while.'

So I left them buying and selling among themselves at a nickel a point. I found a nigger and sent him for my car and stood on the corner and waited. I couldn't see Earl looking up and down the street, with one eye on the clock because I couldn't see the door from here. After about a week he got back with it.

'Where the hell have you been?' I says, 'Riding around where the wenches could see you?'

'I come straight as I could,' he says, 'I had to drive clean around the square, wid all dem wagons.'

I never found a nigger yet that didn't have an airtight alibi for whatever he did. But just turn one loose in a car and he's bound to show off. I got in and went on around the square. I caught a glimpse of Earl in the door across the square.

I went straight to the kitchen and told Dilsey to hurry up with dinner.

'Quentin ain't come yit,' she says.

'What of that?' I says. 'You'll be telling me next that Luster's not quite ready to eat yet. Quentin knows when meals are served in this house. Hurry up with it, now.'

Mother was in her room. I gave her the letter. She opened it and took the cheque out and sat holding it in her hand. I went and got the shovel from the corner and gave her a match. 'Come on,' I says, 'Get it over with. You'll be crying in a minute.'

She took the match, but she didn't strike it. She sat there, looking at the cheque. Just like I said it would be.

'I hate to do it,' she says, 'To increase your burden by adding Quentin ... '

'I guess we'll get along,' I says. 'Come on. Get it over with.' But she just sat there, holding the cheque.

'This one is on a different bank,' she says. 'They have been on an Indianapolis bank.'

'Yes,' I says. 'Women are allowed to do that too.'

'Do what?' she says.

'Keep money in two different banks,' I says.

'Oh,' she says. She looked at the cheque a while. 'I'm glad to know she's so . . . she has so much . . . God sees that I am doing right,' she says.

'Come on,' I says, 'Finish it. Get the fun over.'

'Fun?' she says, 'When I think –'

'I thought you were burning this two hundred dollars a month for fun,' I says. 'Come on, now. Want me to strike the match?'

'I could bring myself to accept them,' she says, 'For my children's sake. I have no pride.'

'You'd never be satisfied,' I says, 'You know you wouldn't. You've settled that once, let it stay settled. We can get along.'

'I leave everything to you,' she says. 'But sometimes I become afraid that in doing this I am depriving you all of what is rightfully yours. Perhaps I shall be punished for it. It you want me to, I will smother my pride and accept them.'

'What would be the good in beginning now, when you've been destroying them for fifteen years?' I says. 'If you keep on doing it, you have lost nothing, but if you'd begin to take them now, you'll have lost fifty thousand dollars. We've got along so far, haven't we?' I says. 'I haven't seen you in the poor-house yet.'

'Yes,' she says, 'We Bascombs need nobody's charity. Certainly not that of a fallen woman.'

She struck the match and lit the cheque and put it in the shovel, and then the envelope, and watched them burn.

'You don't know what it is,' she says, 'Thank God you will never know what a mother feels.'

'There are lots of women in this world no better than her,' I says.

'But they are not my daughters,' she says. 'It's not myself,' she says, 'I'd gladly take her back, sins and all, because she is my flesh and blood. It's for Quentin's sake.'

Well, I could have said it wasn't much chance of anybody hurting Quentin much, but like I say I don't expect much but I do want to eat and sleep without a couple of women squabbling and crying in the house.

'And yours,' she says. 'I know how you feel toward her.'

'Let her come back,' I says, 'far as I'm concerned.'

'No,' she says. 'I owe that to your father's memory.'

'When he was trying all the time to persuade you to let her come home when Herbert threw her out?' I says.

'You don't understand,' she says. 'I know you don't intend to make it more difficult for me. But it's my place to suffer for my children,' she says. 'I can bear it.'

'Seems to me you go to a lot of unnecessary trouble doing it,' I says. The paper burned out. I carried it to the grate and put it in. 'It just seems a shame to me to burn up good money,' I says.

'Let me never see the day when my children will have to accept that, the wages of sin,' she says. 'I'd rather see even you dead in your coffin first.'

'Have it your way,' I says. 'Are we going to have dinner soon?' I says, 'Because if we're not, I'll have to go on back. We're pretty busy today.' She got up. 'I've told her once, I says. 'It seems she's waiting on Quentin or Luster or somebody. Here, I'll call her. Wait.' But she went to the head of the stairs and called.

'Quentin ain't come yit,' Dilsey says.

'Well, I'll have to get on back,' I says. 'I can get a sandwich downtown. I don't want to interfere with Dilsey's arrangements,' I says. Well, that got her started again, with Dilsey hobbling and mumbling back and forth, saying,

'All right, all right, Ise puttin hit on fast as I kin.'

'I try to please you all,' Mother says, 'I try to make things as easy for you as I can.'

'I'm not complaining, am I?' I says. 'Have I said a word except I had to go back to work?'

'I know,' she says, 'I know you haven't had the chance the others had, that you've had to bury yourself in a little country store. I wanted you to get ahead. I knew your father would never realize that you were the only one who had any business sense, and then when everything else failed I believed that when she married, and Herbert . . . after his promise . . .'

'Well, he was probably lying too,' I says. 'He may not have even had a bank, And if he had, I don't reckon he'd have to come all the way to Mississippi to get a man for it.'

We ate a while. I could hear Ben in the kitchen, where Luster was feeding him. Like I say, if we've got to feed another mouth and she won't take that money, why not send him down to Jackson. He'll be happier there, with people like him. I says God knows there's little enough room for pride in this family, but it don't take much pride to not like to see a thirty year old man playing around the yard with a nigger boy, running up and down the fence and lowing like a cow whenever they play golf over there. I says if they'd sent him to Jackson at first we'd all be better off today. I says, you've done your duty by him; you've done all anybody can expect of you and more than most folks would do, so why not send him there and get that much benefit out of the taxes we pay. Then she says, 'I'll be gone soon. I know I'm just a burden to you' and I says 'You've been saying that so long that I'm beginning to believe you' only I says you'd better be sure and not let me know you're gone because I'll sure have him on number seventeen that night and I says I think I know a place where they'll take her too and the name of it's not Milk street and Honey avenue either. Then she begun to cry and I says All right all right I have as much pride about my kinfolks as anybody even if I don't always know where they come from.

We ate for a while. Mother sent Dilsey to the front to look for Quentin again.

'I keep telling you she's not coming to dinner,' I says.

'She knows better than that,' Mother says, 'She knows I don't permit her to run about the streets and not come home at meal time. Did you look good, Dilsey?'

'Don't let her, then,' I says.

'What can I do,' she says. 'You have all of you flouted me. Always.'

'If you wouldn't come interfering, I'd make her mind,' I says. 'It wouldn't take me but about one day to straighten her out.'

'You'd be too brutal with her,' she says. 'You have your Uncle Maury's temper.'

That reminded me of the letter. I took it out and handed it to her. 'You won't have to open it,' I says. 'The bank will let you know how much it is this time.'

'It's addressed to you,' she says.

'Go on and open it,' I says. She opened it and read it and handed it to me.

' "My dear young nephew," it says,

'You will be glad to learn that I am now in a position to avail myself of an opportunity regarding which, for reasons which I shall make obvious to you, I shall not go into details until I have an opportunity to divulge it to you in a more secure manner. My business experience has taught me to be chary of committing anything of a confidential nature to any more concrete medium than speech, and my extreme precaution in this instance should give you some inkling of its value. Needless to say, I have just completed a most exhaustive examination of all its phases, and I feel no hesitancy in telling you that it is that sort of golden chance that comes but once in a lifetime, and I now see clearly before me that goal toward which I have long and unflaggingly striven, i.e. the ultimate solidification of my affairs by which I may restore to its rightful position that family of which I have the honour to be the sole remaining male descendant; that family in which I have ever included your lady mother and her children.

'As it so happens, I am not quite in a position to avail myself of this opportunity to the uttermost which it warrants, but rather than go out of the family to do so, I am today drawing upon your Mother's bank for the small sum necessary to complement my own initial investment, for which I herewith enclose, as a matter of formality, my note of hand at eight per cent per annum. Needless to say, this is merely a formality, to secure your Mother in the event of that circumstance of which man is ever the plaything and sport. For naturally I shall employ this sum as though it were my own and so permit your Mother to avail herself of this opportunity which my exhaustive investigation has shown to be a bonanza – if you will permit the vulgarism – of the first water and purest ray serene.

'This is in confidence, you will understand, from one business man to another; we will harvest our own vineyards, eh? And knowing your Mother's delicate health and that timorousness which such delicately nurtured Southern ladies would naturally feel regarding matters of business, and their charming proneness to divulge unwittingly such matters in conversation, I would suggest that you do not mention it to her at all. On second thought, I advise you not to do so. It might be better to simply restore this sum to the bank at some future date, say, in a lump sum with the other small sums for which I am indebted to her, and say nothing about it at all. It is our duty to shield her from the crass material world as much as possible.

'Your affectionate Uncle,
'Maury L. Bascomb'

'What do you want to do about it?' I says, flipping it across the table.

'I know you grudge what I give him,' she says.

'It's your money,' I says, 'If you want to throw it to the birds even, it's your business.'

'He's my own brother,' Mother says. 'He's the last Bascomb. When we are gone there won't be any more of them.'

'That'll be hard on somebody, I guess,' I says. 'All right, all right,' I says. 'It's your money. Do as you please with it. You want me to tell the bank to pay it?'

'I know you begrudge him,' she says. 'I realize the burden on your shoulders. When I'm gone it will be easier on you.'

'I could make it easier right now,' I says, 'All right, all right, I won't mention it again. Move all bedlam in here if you want to.'

'He's your own brother,' she says, 'Even if he is afflicted.'

'I'll take your bank book,' I says, 'I'll draw my cheque today.'

'He kept you waiting six days,' she says. 'Are you sure the business is sound? It seems strange to me that a solvent business cannot pay its employees promptly.'

'He's all right,' I says, 'Safe as a bank. I tell him not to bother about mine until we get done collecting every month. That's why it's late sometimes.'

'I just couldn't bear to have you lose the little I had to invest for you,' she says. 'I've often thought that Earl is not a good business man. I know he doesn't take you into his confidence to the extent that your investment in the business should warrant. I'm going to speak to him.'

'No, you let him alone,' I says. 'It's his business.'

'You have a thousand dollars in it.'

'You let him alone,' I says, 'I'm watching things. I have your power of attorney. It'll be all right.'

'You don't know what a comfort you are to me,' she says. 'You have always been my pride and joy, but when you came to me of your own accord and insisted on banking your salary each month in my name, I thanked God it was you left me if they had to be taken.'

'They were all right,' I says. 'They did the best they could, I reckon.'

'When you talk that way I know you are thinking bitterly of your father's memory,' she says. 'You have a right to. I suppose. But it breaks my heart to hear you.'

I got up. 'If you've got any crying to do,' I says, 'you'll have to do it alone, because I've got to get on back. I'll get the bank book.'

'I'll get it,' she says.

'Keep still,' I says, 'I'll get it.' I went upstairs and got the bank book out of her desk and went back to town. I went to the bank and deposited the cheque and the money order and the other ten, and stopped at the telegraph office. It was one point above the opening. I had already lost thirteen points, all because she had to come helling in there at twelve, worrying me about that letter.

'What time did that report come in?' I says.

'About an hour ago,' he says.

'An hour ago?' I says. 'What are we paying you for?' I says, 'Weekly reports? How do you expect a man to do anything? The whole damn top could blow off and we'd not know it.'

'I don't expect you to do anything,' he says. 'They changed that law making folks play the cotton market.'

'They have?' I says. 'I hadn't heard. They must have sent the news out over the Western Union.'

I went back to the store. Thirteen points. Damn if I believe anybody knows anything about the damn thing except the ones that sit back in those New York offices and watch the country suckers come up and beg them to take their money. Well, a man that just calls shows he has no faith in himself, and like I say if you aren't going to take the advice, what's the use in paying money for it. Besides, these people are right up there on the ground; they know everything that's going on. I could feel the telegram in my pocket. I'd just have to prove that they were using the telegraph company to defraud. That would constitute a bucket shop. And I wouldn't hesitate that long, either. Only be damned if it doesn't look like a company as big and rich as the Western Union could get a market report out on time. Half as quick as they'll get a wire to you saying Your account closed out. But what the hell do they care about the people. They're hand in glove with that New York crowd. Anybody could see that.

When I came in Earl looked at his watch. But he didn't say anything until the customer was gone. Then he says,

'You go home to dinner?'

'I had to go to the dentist,' I says because it's not any of his business where I eat but I've got to be in the store with him all the afternoon. And with his jaw running off after all I've stood. You take a little two by four country storekeeper like I say it takes a man with just five hundred dollars to worry about it fifty thousand dollars' worth.

'You might have told me,' he says, 'I expected you back right away.'

'I'll trade you this tooth and give you ten dollars to boot, any time,' I says. 'Our arrangement was an hour for dinner,' I says, 'and if you don't like the way I do, you know what you can do about it.'

'I've known that some time,' he says. 'If it hadn't been for your mother I'd have done it before now, too. She's a lady I've got a lot of sympathy for, Jason. Too bad some other folks I know can't say as much.'

'Then you can keep it,' I says. 'When we need any sympathy I'll let you know in plenty of time.'

'I've protected you about that business a long time, Jason,' he says.

'Yes?' I says, letting him go on. Listening to what he would say before I shut him up.

'I believe I know more about where that automobile came from than she does.'

'You think so, do you?' I says. 'When are you going to spread the news that I stole it from my mother?'

'I don't say anything,' he says, 'I know you have her power of attorney. And I know she still believes that thousand dollars is in this business.'

'All right,' I says, 'Since you know so much, I'll tell you a little more: go to the bank and ask them whose account I've been depositing a hundred and sixty dollars on the first of every month for twelve years.'

'I don't say anything,' he says, 'I just ask you to be a little more careful after this.'

I never said anything more. It doesn't do any good. I've found that when a man gets into a rut the best thing you can do is let him stay there. And when a man gets it in his head that he's got to tell something on you for your own good, good night. I'm glad I haven't got the sort of conscience I've got to nurse like a sick puppy all the time. If I'd ever be as careful over anything as he is to keep his little shirt tail full of business from making him more than eight per cent. I reckon he thinks they'd get him on the usury law if he netted more than eight per cent. What the hell chance has a man got, tied down in a town like this and to a business like this. Why I could take his business in one year and fix him so he'd never have to work again, only he'd give it all away to the church or something. If there's one thing gets under my skin, it's a damn hypocrite. A man that thinks anything he don't understand all about must be crooked and that first chance he gets he's morally bound to tell the third party what's none of his business to tell. Like I say if I thought every time a man did something I didn't know all about he was bound to be a crook, I reckon I wouldn't have any trouble finding something back there on those books that you wouldn't see any use for running and telling somebody I thought ought to know about it, when for all I knew they might know a damn sight more about it now than I did, and if they didn't it was damn little of my business anyway and he says, 'My books are open to anybody. Anybody that has any claim or believes she has any claim on this business can go back there and welcome.'

'Sure, you won't tell,' I says, 'You couldn't square your conscience with that. You'll just take her back there and let her find it. You won't tell, yourself.'

'I'm not trying to meddle in your business,' he says. 'I know you missed out on some things like Quentin had. But your mother has had a misfortunate life too, and if she was to come in here and ask me why you quit, I'd have to tell her. It ain't that thousand dollars. You know that. It's because a man never gets anywhere if fact and his ledgers don't square. And I'm not going to lie to anybody, for myself or anybody else.'

'Well, then,' I says, 'I reckon that conscience of yours is a more valuable clerk than I am; it don't have to go home at noon to eat. Only don't let it interfere with my appetite,' I says, because how the hell can I do anything right, with that damn family and her not making any effort to control her nor any of them, like that time when she happened to see one of them kissing Caddy and all next day she went around the house in a black dress and a veil and even Father couldn't get her to say a word except crying and saying her little daughter was dead and Caddy about fifteen then only in three years she'd been wearing haircloth or probably sandpaper at that rate. Do you think I can afford to have her running about the streets with every drummer that comes to town, I says, and them telling the new ones up and down the road where to pick up a hot one when they made Jefferson. I haven't got much pride, I can't afford it with a kitchenful of niggers to feed and robbing the state asylum of its star freshman. Blood, I says, governors and generals. It's a damn good thing we never had any kings and presidents; we'd all be down there at Jackson chasing butterflies. I say it'd be bad enough if it was mine; I'd at least be sure it was a bastard to begin with, and now even the Lord doesn't know that for certain probably.

So after a while I heard the band start up, and then they began to clear out. Headed for the show, every one of them. Haggling over a twenty cent hame string to save fifteen cents, so they can give it to a bunch of Yankees that come in and pay maybe ten dollars for the privilege. I went on out to the back.

'Well,' I says, 'If you don't look out, that bolt will grow into your hand. And then I'm going to take an axe and chop it out. What do you reckon the boll-weevils'll eat if you don't get those cultivators in shape to raise them a crop?' I says, 'sage grass?'

'Dem folks sho do play dem horns,' he says. 'Tell me man in dat show kin play a tune on a handsaw. Pick hit like a banjo.'

'Listen,' I says. 'Do you know how much that show'll spend in this town? About ten dollars,' I says. 'The ten dollars Buck Turpin has in his pocket right now.'

'Whut dey give Mr Buck ten dollars fer?' he says.

'For the privilege of showing here,' I says. 'You can put the balance of what they'll spend in your eye.'

'You mean dey pays ten dollars jest to give dey show here?' he says.

'That's all,' I says. 'And how much do you reckon . . .'

'Gret day,' he says, 'You mean to tell me dey chargin um to let um show here? I'd pay ten dollars to see dat man pick dat saw, ef I had to. I figures dat tomorrow mawnin I be still owin um nine dollars and six bits at dat rate.'

And then a Yankee will talk your head off about niggers getting ahead. Get them ahead, what I say. Get them so far ahead you can't find one south of Louisville with a bloodhound. Because when I told him about how they'd pick up Saturday night and carry off at least a thousand dollars out of the county, he says,

'I don't begrudge um. I kin sho afford my two bits.'

'Two bits hell,' I says. 'That don't begin it. How about the dime or fifteen cents you'll spend for a damn two cent box of candy or something. How about the time you're wasting right now, listening to that band.'

'Dat's de troof,' he says. 'Well, ef I lives twell night hit's gwine to be two bits mo dey takin out of town, dat's sho.'

'Then you're a fool,' I says.

'Well,' he says, 'I don't spute dat neither. Ef dat uz a crime, all chain-gangs wouldn't be black.'

Well, just about that time I happened to look up the alley and saw her. When I stepped back and looked at my watch I didn't notice at the time who he was because I was looking at the watch. It was just two thirty, forty-five minutes before anybody but me expected her to be out. So when I looked around the door the first thing I saw was the red tie he had on and I was thinking what the hell kind of a man would wear a red tie. But she was sneaking along the alley, watching the door, so I wasn't thinking anything about him until they had gone past. I was wondering if she'd have so little respect for me that she'd not only play out of school when I told her not to, but would walk right past the store, daring me not to see her. Only she couldn't see into the door because the sun fell straight into it and it was like trying to see through an automobile searchlight, so I stood there and watched her go on past, with her face painted up like a damn clown's and her hair all gummed and twisted and a dress that if a woman had come out doors even on Gayoso or Beale Street when I was a young fellow with no more than that to cover her legs and behind, she'd been thrown in jail. I'll be damned if they don't dress like they were trying to make every man they passed on the street want to reach out and clasp his hand on it. And so I was thinking what kind of a damn man would wear a red tie when all of a sudden I knew he was one of those show folks well as if she'd told me. Well, I can stand a lot; if I couldn't, damn if I wouldn't be in a hell of a fix, so when they turned the corner I jumped down and followed. Me, without any hat, in the middle of the afternoon, having to chase up and down back alleys because of my mother's good name. Like I say you can't do anything with a woman like that, if she's got it in her. If it's in her blood, you can't do anything with her. The only thing you can do is to get rid of her, let her go on and live with her own sort.

I went on to the street, but they were out of sight. And there I was, without any hat, looking like I was crazy too. Like a man would naturally think, one of them is crazy and another one drowned himself and the other one was turned out into the street by her husband, what's the reason the rest of them are not crazy too. All the time I could see them watching me like a hawk, waiting for a chance to say Well I'm not surprised I expected it all the time the whole family's crazy. Selling land to send him to Harvard and paying taxes to support a state University all the time that I never saw except twice at a baseball game and not letting her daughter's name be spoken on the place until after a while Father wouldn't even come downtown any more but just

THE SOUND AND THE FURY

sat there all day with the decanter I could see the bottom of his nightshirt and his bare legs and hear the decanter clinking until finally T.P. had to pour it for him and she says You have no respect for your Father's memory and I says I don't know why not it sure is preserved well enough to last only if I'm crazy too God knows what I'll do about it just to look at water makes me sick and I'd just as soon swallow gasoline as a glass of whisky and Lorraine telling them he may not drink but if you don't believe he's a man I can tell you how to find out she says If I catch you fooling with any of these whores you know what I'll do she says I'll whip her grabbing at her I'll whip her as long as I can find her she says and I says if I don't drink that's my business but have you ever found me short I says I'll buy you enough beer to take a bath in if you want it because I've got every respect for a good honest whore because with Mother's health and the position I try to uphold to have her with no more respect for what I try to do for her than to make her name and my name and my Mother's name a byword in the town.

She had dodged out of sight somewhere. Saw me coming and dodged into another alley, running up and down the alleys with a damn show man in a red tie that everybody would look at and think what kind of a damn man would wear a red tie. Well, the boy kept speaking to me and so I took the telegram without knowing I had taken it. I didn't realize what it was until I was signing for it, and I tore it open without even caring much what it was. I knew all the time what it would be, I reckon. That was the only thing else that could happen, especially holding it up until I had already had the cheque entered on the pass book.

I don't see how a city no bigger than New York can hold enough people to take the money away from us country suckers. Work like hell all day every day, send them your money and get a little piece of paper back, Your account closed at 20.62. Teasing you along, letting you pile up a little paper profit, then bang! Your account closed at 20.62, And if that wasn't enough, paying ten dollars a month to somebody to tell you how to lose it fast, that either don't know anything about it or is in cahoots with the telegraph company. Well, I'm done with them. They've sucked me in for the last time. Any fool except a fellow that hasn't got any more sense than to take a jew's word for anything could tell the market was going up all the time, with the whole damn delta about to be flooded again and the cotton washed right out of the ground like it was last year. Let it wash a man's crop out of the ground year after year, and them up there in Washington spending fifty thousand dollars a day keeping an army in Nicaragua or some place. Of course it'll overflow again, and then cotton'll be worth thirty cents a pound. Well, I just want to hit them one time and get my money back. I don't want a killing; only these small town gamblers are out for that, I just want my money back that these damn jews have got with all their guaranteed inside dope. Then I'm through; they can kiss my foot for every other red cent of mine they get.

I went back to the store. It was half-past three almost. Damn little time to do anything in, but then I am used to that. I never had to go to Harvard to learn that. The band had quit playing. Got them all inside now, and they wouldn't have to waste any more wind. Earl says,

'He found you, did he? He was in here with it a while ago. I thought you were out back somewhere.'

'Yes,' I says, 'I got it. They couldn't keep it away from me all afternoon. The town's too small. I've got to go out home a minute,' I says. 'You can dock me if it'll make you feel any better.'

'Go ahead,' he says, 'I can handle it now. No bad news, I hope.'

'You'll have to go to the telegraph office and find that out,' I says. 'They'll have time to tell you. I haven't.'

'I just asked,' he says. 'Your mother knows she can depend on me.'

'She'll appreciate it,' I says. 'I won't be gone any longer than I have to.'

'Take your time,' he says. 'I can handle it now. You go ahead.'

I got the car and went home. Once this morning, twice at noon, and now again, with her and having to chase all over town and having to beg them to let me eat a little of the food I am paying for. Sometimes I think what's the use of anything. With the precedent I've been set I must be crazy to keep on. And now I reckon I'll get home just in time to take a nice long drive after a basket of tomatoes or something and then have to go back to town smelling like a camphor factory so my head won't explode right on my shoulders. I keep telling her there's not a damn thing in that aspirin except flour and water for imaginary invalids. I says you don't know what a headache is. I says you think I'd fool with that damn car at all if it depended on me. I says I can get along without one I've learned to get along without lots of things but if you want to risk yourself in that old wornout surrey with a half grown nigger boy all right because I says God looks after

Ben's kind, God knows He ought to do something for him, but if you think I'm going to trust a thousand dollars' worth of delicate machinery to a half grown nigger or a grown one either, you'd better buy him one yourself because I says you like to ride in the car and you know you do.

Dilsey said Mother was in the house. I went on into the hall and listened, but I didn't hear anything. I went upstairs, but just as I passed her door she called me.

'I just wanted to know who it was,' she says. 'I'm here alone so much that I hear every sound.'

'You don't have to stay here,' I says. 'You could spend the whole day visiting like other women, if you wanted to.' She came to the door.

'I thought maybe you were sick,' she says. 'Having to hurry through your dinner like you did.'

'Better luck next time,' I says. 'What do you want?'

'Is anything wrong?' she says.

'What could be?' I says. 'Can't I come home in the middle of the afternoon without upsetting the whole house?'

'Have you seen Quentin?' she says.

'She's in school,' I says.

'It's after three,' she says. 'I heard the clock strike at least a half an hour ago. She ought to be home by now.'

'Ought she?' I says. 'When have you ever seen her before dark?'

'She ought to be home,' she says. 'When I was a girl . . .'

'You had somebody to make you behave yourself,' I says.

'She hasn't.'

'I can't do anything with her,' she says. 'I've tried and I've tried.'

'And you won't let me, for some reason,' I says, 'So you ought to be satisfied.' I went on to my room. I turned the key easy and stood there until the knob turned. Then she says,

'Jason.'

'What,' I says.

'I just thought something was wrong.'

'Not in here,' I says. 'You've come to the wrong place.'

'I don't mean to worry you,' she says.

'I'm glad to hear that,' I says. 'I wasn't sure. I thought I might have been mistaken. Do you want anything?'

After a while she says, 'No. Not anything.' Then she went away. I took the box down and counted out the money and hid the box again and unlocked the door and went out. I thought about the camphor, but it would be too late now, anyway. And I'd just have one more round trip. She was at her door, waiting.

'You want anything from town?' I says.

'No,' she says. 'I don't mean to meddle in your affairs. But I don't know what I'd do if anything happened to you, Jason.'

'I'm all right,' I says. 'Just a headache.'

'I wish you'd take some aspirin,' she says. 'I know you're not going to stop using the car.'

'What's the car got to do with it?' I says. 'How can a car give a man a headache?'

'You know gasoline always made you sick,' she says. 'Ever since you were a child. I wish you'd take some aspirin.'

'Keep on wishin it,' I says. 'It won't hurt you.'

I got in the car and started back to town. I had just turned on to the street when I saw a ford coming helling toward me. All of a sudden it stopped. I could hear the wheels sliding and it slewed around and backed and whirled and just as I was thinking what the hell they were up to, I saw that red tie. Then I recognized her face looking back through the window. It whirled into the alley. I saw it turn again, but when I got to the back street it was just disappearing, running like hell.

I saw red. When I recognized that red tie, after all I had told her, I forgot about everything. I never thought about my head even until I came to the first forks and had to stop. Yet we spend money and spend money on roads and damn if it isn't like trying to drive over a sheet of corrugated iron roofing. I'd like to know how a man could be expected to keep up with even a wheelbarrow. I think too much of my car; I'm not going to hammer it to pieces like it was a ford. Chances were they had stolen it, anyway, so why should they give a damn. Like I say blood always tells. If you've got blood like that in you, you'll do anything. I says whatever claim you believe she has on you has already been discharged, I says from now on you have only yourself to blame because you know what any sensible person would do. I says if I've got to spend half my time being a damn detective, at least I'll go where I can get paid for it.

So I had to stop there at the forks. Then I remembered it. It felt like somebody was inside with a hammer, beating on it. I says I've tried to keep you from being worried by her; I says far as I'm concerned, let her go to hell as fast as she pleases and the sooner the better. I says what else do you expect except every drummer and cheap show that comes to town because even these town jellybeans give her the go-by now. You don't know what goes on I says, you don't hear the talk that I hear and you can just bet I shut them up too. I says my people owned slaves here when you all were running little shirt tail country stores and farming land no nigger would look at on shares.

If they ever farmed it. It's a good thing the Lord did something for this country; the folks that live on it never have. Friday afternoon, and from right here I could see three miles of land that hadn't even been broken, and every able-bodied man in the county in town at that show. I might have been a stranger starving to death, and there wasn't a soul in sight to ask which way to town even. And she trying to get me to take aspirin. I says when I eat bread I'll do it at the table. I says you always talking about how much you give up for us when you could buy ten new dresses a year on the money you spend for those damn patent medicines. It's not something to cure it I need it's just an even break not to have to have them but as long as I have to work ten hours a day to support a kitchenful of niggers in the style they're accustomed to and send them to the show with every other nigger in the county, only he was late already. By the time he got there it would be over.

After a while he got up to the car and when I finally got it through his head if two people in a ford had passed him, he said yes. So I went on, and when I came to where the wagon road turned off I could see the tyre tracks. Ab Russell was in his lot, but I didn't bother to ask him and I hadn't got out of sight of his barn hardly when I saw the ford. They had tried to hide it. Done about as well at it as she did at everything else she did. Like I say it's not that I object to so much; maybe she can't help that, it's because she hasn't even got enough consideration for her own family to have any discretion. I'm afraid all the time I'll run into them right in the middle of the street or under a wagon on the square, like a couple of dogs.

I parked and got out. And now I'd have to go way around and cross a ploughed field, the only one I had seen since I left town, with every step like somebody was walking along behind me, hitting me on the head with a club. I kept thinking that when I got across the field at least I'd have something level to walk on, that wouldn't jolt me every step, but when I got into the woods it was full of underbrush and I had to twist around through it, and then I came to a ditch full of briers. I went along it for a while, but it got thicker and thicker, and all the time Earl probably telephoning home about where I was and getting Mother all upset again.

When I finally got through I had had to wind around so much that I had to stop and figure out just where the car would be. I knew they wouldn't be far from it, just under the closest bush, so I turned and worked back toward the road. Then I couldn't tell just how far I was, so I'd have to stop and listen, and then with my legs not using so much blood, it all would go into my head like it would explode any minute, and the sun getting down just to where it could shine straight into my eyes and my ears ringing so I couldn't hear anything. I went on, trying to move quiet, then I heard a dog or something and I knew that when he scented me he'd have to come helling up, then it would be all off.

I had got beggar lice and twigs and stuff all over me, inside my clothes and shoes and all, and then I happened to look around and I had my hand right on a bunch of poison oak. The only thing I couldn't understand was why it was just poison oak and not a snake or something. So I didn't even bother to move it. I just stood there until the dog went away. Then I went on.

I didn't have any idea where the car was now. I couldn't think about anything except my head, and I'd just stand in one place and sort of wonder if I had really seen a ford even, and I didn't even care much whether I had or not. Like I say, let her out all day and all night with everything in town that wears pants, what do I care. I don't owe anything to anybody that has no more consideration for me, that wouldn't be a damn bit above planting that ford there and making me spend a whole afternoon and Earl taking her back there and showing her the books just because he's too damn virtuous for this world. I says you'll have one hell of a time in heaven, without anybody's business to meddle in only don't you ever let me catch you at it I says, I close my eyes to it because of your grandmother, but just you let me catch you doing it one time on this place, where my mother lives. These damn little slick-haired squirts, thinking they are raising so much hell, I'll show them something about hell I says, and you too. I'll make him think that damn red tie is the latch string to hell, if he thinks he can run the woods with my niece.

With the sun and all in my eyes and my blood going so I kept thinking every time my head would go on and burst and get it over with, with briers and things grabbing at me, then I came to on the sand ditch where they had been and I recognized the tree where the car was, and just as I got out of the ditch and started running I heard the car start. It went off fast, blowing the horn. They kept on blowing it, like it was saying Yah. Yah. Yaaahhhhhhhh, going out of sight. I got to the road just in time to see it go out of sight.

By the time I got up to where my car was, they were clean out of sight, the horn still blowing. Well, I never thought anything about it except I was saying Run. Run back to town. Run home and try to convince Mother that I never saw you in that car. Try to make her believe that I don't know who he was. Try to make her believe that I didn't miss ten feet of catching you in that ditch. Try to make her believe you were standing up, too.

It kept on saying Yahhhhh, Yahhhhh, Yaaahhhhhhhhh, getting fainter and fainter. Then it quit, and I could hear a cow lowing up at Russell's barn. And still I never thought. I went up to the door and opened it and raised my foot. I kind of thought then that the car was leaning a little more than the slant of the road would be, but I never found it out until I got in and started off.

Well, I just sat there. It was getting on toward sundown, and town was about five miles. They never even had guts enough to puncture it, to jab a hole in it. They just let the air out. I just stood there for a while, thinking about that kitchenful of niggers and not one of them had time to lift a tyre on to the rack and screw up a couple of bolts. It was kind of funny because even she couldn't have seen far enough ahead to take the pump out on purpose, unless she thought about it while he was letting out the air maybe. But what it probably was, was somebody took it out and gave it to Ben to play with for a squirt gun because they'd take the whole car to pieces if he wanted it and Dilsey says, Ain't nobody teched yo car. What we want to fool with hit fer? and I says You're a nigger. You're lucky, do you know it? I says I'll swap with you any day because it takes a white man not to have any more sense than to worry about what a little slut of a girl does.

I walked up to Russell's. He had a pump. That was just an oversight on their part, I reckon. Only I still couldn't believe she'd have had the nerve to. I kept thinking that. I don't know why it is I can't seem to learn that a woman'll do anything. I kept thinking, Let's forget for a while how I feel toward you and how you feel toward me: I just wouldn't do you this way. I wouldn't do you this way no matter what you had done to me. Because

like I say blood is blood and you can't get around it. It's not
playing a joke that any eight year old boy could have thought of,
it's letting your own uncle be laughed at by a man that would
wear a red tie. They come into town and call us all a bunch of
hicks and think it's too small to hold them. Well he doesn't know
just how right he is. And her too. If that's the way she feels about
it, she'd better keep right on going and a damn good riddance.

I stopped and returned Russell's pump and drove on to town.
I went to the drug store and got a cocacola and then I went to
the telegraph office. It had closed at 12.21, forty points down.
Forty times five dollars; buy something with that if you can, and
she'll say, I've got to have it I've just got to and I'll say that's too
bad you'll have to try somebody else, I haven't got any money;
I've been too busy to make any.

I just looked at him.

'I'll tell you some news,' I says, 'You'll be astonished to learn
that I am interested in the cotton market,' I says. 'That never
occurred to you, did it?'

'I did my best to deliver it,' he says. 'I tried the store twice and
called up your house, but they didn't know where you were,' he
says, digging in the drawer.

'Deliver what?' I says. He handed me a telegram. 'What time
did this come?' I says.

'About half-past three,' he says.

'And now it's ten minutes past five,' I says.

'I tried to deliver it,' he says. 'I couldn't find you.'

'That's not my fault, is it?' I says. I opened it, just to see what
kind of a lie they'd tell me this time. They must be in one hell
of a shape if they've got to come all the way to Mississippi to steal
ten dollars a month. Sell, it says. The market will be unstable,
with a general downward tendency. Do not be alarmed following
government report.

'How much would a message like this cost?' I says. He told me.

'They paid it,' he says.

'Then I owe them that much,' I says. 'I already knew this. Send
this collect,' I says, taking a blank. Buy I wrote, Market just on
point of blowing its head off. Occasional flurries for purpose of
hooking a few more country suckers who haven't got in to the
telegraph office yet. Do not be alarmed. 'Send that collect,' I
says.

He looked at the message, then he looked at the clock. 'Market
closed an hour ago,' he says.

'Well,' I says, 'That's not my fault either. I didn't invent it; I just bought a little of it while under the impression that the telegraph company would keep me informed as to what it was doing.'

'A report is posted whenever it comes in,' he says.

'Yes,' I says, 'And in Memphis they have it on a blackboard every ten seconds,' I says. 'I was within sixty-seven miles of there once this afternoon.'

He looked at the message. 'You want to send this?' he says.

'I still haven't changed my mind,' I says. I wrote the other one out and counted the money. And this one too, if you're sure you can spell b-u-y.'

I went back into the store. I could hear the band from down the street. Prohibition's a fine thing. Used to be they'd come in Saturday with just one pair of shoes in the family and him wearing them, and they'd go down to the express office and get his package; now they all go to the show barefooted, with the merchants in the door like a row of tigers or something in a cage, watching them pass. Earl says,

'I hope it wasn't anything serious.'

'What?' I says. He looked at his watch. Then he went to the door and looked at the courthouse clock. 'You ought to have a dollar watch,' I says. 'It won't cost you so much to believe it's lying each time.'

'What?' he says.

'Nothing,' I says. 'Hope I haven't inconvenienced you.'

'We were not busy much,' he says. 'They all went to the show. It's all right.'

'If it's not all right,' I says, 'You know what you can do about it.'

'I said it was all right,' he says.

'I heard you,' I says. 'And if it's not all right, you know what you can do about it.'

'Do you want to quit?' he says.

'It's not my business,' I says. 'My wishes don't matter. But don't get the idea that you are protecting me by keeping me.'

'You'd be a good business man if you'd let yourself, Jason,' he says.

'At least I can tend to my own business and let other peoples' alone,' I says.

'I don't know why you are trying to make me fire you,' he says.

'You know you could quit any time and there wouldn't be any hard feelings between us.'

'Maybe that's why I don't quit,' I says. 'As long as I tend to my job, that's what you are paying me for.' I went on to the back and got a drink of water and went on out to the back door. Job had the cultivators all set up at last. It was quiet there, and pretty soon my head got a little easier. I could hear them singing now, and then the band played again. Well, let them get every quarter and dime in the county; it was no skin off my back. I've done what I could; a man that can live as long as I have and not know when to quit is a fool. Especially as it's no business of mine. If it was my own daughter now it would be different, because she wouldn't have time to; she'd have to work some to feed a few invalids and idiots and niggers, because how could I have the face to bring anybody there. I've too much respect for anybody to do that. I'm a man, I can stand it, it's my own flesh and blood and I'd like to see the colour of the man's eyes that would speak disrespectful of any woman that was my friend it's these damn good women that do it I'd like to see the good, church-going woman that's half as square as Lorraine, whore or no whore. Like I say if I was to get married you'd go up like a balloon and you know it and she says I want you to be happy to have a family of your own not to slave your life away for us. But I'll be gone soon and then you can take a wife but you'll never find a woman who is worthy of you and I says yes I could. You'd get right up out of your grave you know you would. I say no thank you I have all the women I can take care of now if I married a wife she'd probably turn out to be a hophead or something. That's all we lack in this family, I says.

The sun was down beyond the Methodist church now, and the pigeons were flying back and forth around the steeple, and when the band stopped I could hear them cooing. It hadn't been four months since Christmas, and yet they were almost as thick as ever. I reckon Parson Walthall was getting a bellyful of them now. You'd have thought we were shooting people, with him making speeches and even holding on to a man's gun when they came over. Talking about peace on earth good will toward all and not a sparrow can fall to earth. But what does he care how thick they get, he hasn't got anything to do what does he care what time it is. He pays no taxes, he doesn't have to see his money going every year to have the courthouse clock cleaned to where it'll run. They had to pay a man forty-five dollars to clean it. I counted over a hundred half-hatched pigeons on the ground. You'd think they'd have sense enough to leave town. It's a good thing I don't have any more ties than a pigeon, I'll say that.

The band was playing again, a loud fast tune, like they were breaking up. I reckon they'd be satisfied now. Maybe they'd have enough music to entertain them while they drove fourteen or fifteen miles home and unharnessed in the dark and fed the stock and milked. All they'd have to do would be to whistle the music and tell the jokes to the livestock in the barn, and then they could count up how much they'd made by not taking the stock to the show too. They could figure that if a man had five children and seven mules, he cleared a quarter by taking his family to the show. Just like that. Earl came back with a couple of packages.

'Here's some more stuff going out,' he says. 'Where's Uncle Job?'

'Gone to the show, I imagine,' I says. 'Unless you watched him.'

'He doesn't slip off,' he says. 'I can depend on him.'

'Meaning me by that,' I says.

He went to the door and looked out, listening.

'That's a good band,' he says. 'It's about time they were breaking up, I'd say.'

'Unless they're going to spend the night there,' I says. The swallows had begun, and I could hear the sparrows beginning to swarm in the trees in the courthouse yard. Every once in a while a bunch of them would come swirling around in sight above the roof, then go away. They are as big a nuisance as the pigeons, to my notion. You can't even sit in the courthouse yard for them. First thing you know, bing. Right on your hat. But it would take a millionaire to afford to shoot them at five cents a shot. If they'd just put a little poison out there in the square, they'd get rid of them in a day, because if a merchant can't keep his stock from running around the square, he'd better try to deal in something besides chickens, something that don't eat, like ploughs or onions. And if a man don't keep his dogs up, he either don't want it or he hasn't any business with one. Like I say if all the businesses in a town are run like country businesses, you're going to have a country town.

'It won't do you any good if they have broke up,' I says. 'They'll have to hitch up and take out to get home by midnight as it is.'

'Well,' he says, 'They enjoy it. Let them spend a little money on a show now and then. A hill farmer works pretty hard and gets mighty little for it.'

'There's no law making them farm in the hills,' I says, 'Or anywhere else.'

'Where would you and me be, if it wasn't for the farmers?' he says.

'I'd be home right now,' I says, 'Lying down, with an ice pack on my head.'

'You have these headaches too often,' he says. 'Why don't you have your teeth examined good? Did he go over them all this morning?'

'Did who?' I says.

'You said you went to the dentist this morning.'

'Do you object to my having the headache on your time?' I says. 'Is that it?' They were crossing the alley now, coming up from the show.

'There they come,' he says. 'I reckon I better get up front.' He went on. It's a curious thing how no matter what's wrong with you, a man'll tell you to have your teeth examined and a woman'll tell you to get married. It always takes a man that never made much at anything to tell you how to run your business, though. Like these college professors without a whole pair of socks to their name, telling you how to make a million in ten years, and a woman that couldn't even get a husband can always tell you how to raise a family.

Old man Job came up with the wagon. After a while he got through wrapping the lines around the whip socket.

'Well,' I says, 'Was it a good show?'

'I ain't been yit,' he says. 'But I kin be arrested in dat tent tonight dough.'

'Like hell you haven't,' I says. 'You've been away from here since three o'clock. Mr Earl was just back here looking for you.'

'I been tending to my business,' he says. 'Mr Earl knows whar I been.'

'You may can fool him,' I says. 'I won't tell on you.'

'Den he's de onliest man here I'd try to fool,' he says. 'Whut I want to waste my time foolin a man whut I don't keer whether I sees him Sat'dy night er not? I won't try to fool you,' he says. 'You too smart fer me. Yes, suh,' he says, looking busy as hell, putting five or six little packages into the wagon, 'You's too smart fer me. Ain't a man in dis town kin keep up wid you fer smartness. You fools a man whut so smart he can't even keep up wid hisself,' he says, getting in the wagon and unwrapping the reins.

'Who's that?' I says.

'Dat's Mr Jason Compson,' he says. 'Git up dar, Dan!'

One of the wheels was just about to come off. I watched to see if he'd get out of the alley before it did. Just turn any vehicle over to a nigger, though. I says that old rattletrap's just an eyesore, yet you'll keep it standing there in the carriage house a hundred years just so that boy can ride to the cemetery once a week. I says he's not the first fellow that'll have to do things he doesn't want to. I'd make him ride in that car like a civilized man or stay at home. What does he know about where he goes or what he goes in, and us keeping a carriage and a horse so he can take a ride on Sunday afternoon.

A lot Job cared whether the wheel came off or not, long as he wouldn't have too far to walk back. Like I say the only place for them is in the field, where they'd have to work from sunup to sundown. They can't stand prosperity or an easy job. Let one stay around white people for a while and he's not worth killing. They get so they can outguess you about work before your very eyes, like Roskus the only mistake he ever made was he got careless one day and died. Shirking and stealing and giving you a little more lip and a little more lip until some day you have to lay them out with a scantling or something. Well, it's Earl's business. But I'd hate to have my business advertised over this town by an old doddering nigger and a wagon that you thought every time it turned a corner it would come all to pieces.

The sun was all high up in the air now, and inside it was beginning to get dark. I went up front. The square was empty. Earl was back closing the safe, and then the clock begun to strike.

'You lock the back door,' he says. I went back and locked it and came back. 'I suppose you're going to the show tonight,' he says. 'I gave you those passes yesterday, didn't I?'

'Yes,' I said. 'You want them back?'

'No, no,' he says. 'I just forgot whether I gave them to you or not. No sense in wasting them.'

He locked the door and said Good night and went on. The sparrows were still rattling away in the trees, but the square was empty except for a few cars. There was a ford in front of the drug-store, but I didn't even look at it. I know when I've had enough of anything. I don't mind trying to help her, but I know when I've had enough. I guess I could teach Luster to drive it, then they could chase her all day long if they wanted to, and I could stay home and play with Ben.

I went in and got a couple of cigars. Then I thought I'd have another headache shot for luck, and I stood and talked with them for a while.

'Well,' Mac says, 'I reckon you've got your money on the Yankees this year.'

'What for?' I says.

'The pennant,' he says. 'Not anything in the League can beat them.'

'Like hell there's not,' I says. 'They're shot,' I says. 'You think a team can be that lucky for ever?'

'I don't call it luck,' Mac says.

'I wouldn't bet on any team that fellow Ruth played on,' I says. 'Even if I knew it was going to win.'

'Yes?' Mac says.

'I can name you a dozen men in either League who're more valuable than he is,' I says.

'What have you got against Ruth?' Mac says.

'Nothing,' I says. 'I haven't got anything against him. I don't even like to look at his picture.' I went on out. The lights were coming on, and people going along the streets toward home. Sometimes the sparrows never got still until full dark. The night they turned on the new lights around the courthouse it waked them up and they were flying around and blundering into the lights all night long. They kept it up two or three nights, then one morning they were all gone. Then after two months they all came back again.

I drove on home. There were no lights in the house yet, but they'd all be looking out the windows, and Dilsey jawing away in the kitchen like it was her own food she was having to keep hot until I got there. You'd think to hear her that there wasn't but one supper in the world, and that was the one she had to keep back a few minutes on my account. Well at least I could come home one time without finding Ben and that nigger on the gate like a bear and a monkey in the same cage. Just let it come toward sundown and he'd head for the gate like a cow for the barn, hanging on to it and bobbing his head and sort of moaning to himself. That's a hog for punishment for you. If what had happened to him for fooling with open gates had happened to me, I never would want to see another one. I often wondered what he'd be thinking about, down there at the gate, watching the girls going home from school, trying to want something he couldn't even remember he didn't and couldn't want any longer. And what he'd think when they'd be undressing him and he'd happen to take a look at himself and begin to cry like he'd do. But like I say they never did enough of that. I says I know what you need, you need what they did to Ben then you'd behave. And if you don't know what that was I says, ask Dilsey to tell you.

There was a light in Mother's room. I put the car up and went on into the kitchen. Luster and Ben were there.

'Where's Dilsey?' I says. 'Putting supper on?'

'She upstairs wid Miss Cahline,' Luster says. 'Dey been goin hit. Ever since Miss Quentin come home. Mammy up there keepin um fum fightin. Is dat show come, Mr Jason?'

'Yes,' I says.

'I thought I heard de band,' he says. 'Wish I could go,' he says. 'I could ef I jes had a quarter.'

Dilsey came in. 'You come is you?' she says. 'Whut you been up to dis evenin? You know how much work I got to do; whyn't you git here on time?'

'Maybe I went to the show,' I says. 'Is supper ready?'

'Wish I could go,' Luster said. 'I could ef I jes had a quarter.'

'You ain't got no business at no show,' Dilsey says. 'You go on in de house and set down,' she says. 'Don't you go upstairs and git um started again, now.'

'What's the matter?' I says.

'Quentin come in a while ago and says you been follerin her around all evenin and den Miss Cahline jumped on her. Whyn't you let her alone? Can't you live in de same house wid you own blood niece widout quoilin?'

'I can't quarrel with her,' I says, 'because I haven't seen her since this morning. What does she say I've done now? made her go to school? That's pretty bad,' I says.

'Well, you tend to yo business and let her alone,' Dilsey says, 'I'll take keer of her ef you'n Miss Cahline'll let me. Go on in dar now and behave yoself twell I git supper on.'

'Ef I jes had a quarter,' Luster says, 'I could go to dat show.'

'En ef you had wings you could fly to heaven,' Dilsey says. 'I don't want to hear another word about dat show.'

'That reminds me,' I says, 'I've got a couple of tickets they gave me.' I took them out of my coat.

'You fixin to use um?' Luster says.

'Not me,' I says. 'I wouldn't go to it for ten dollars.'

'Gimme one of um, Mr Jason,' he says.

'I'll sell you one,' I says. 'How about it?'

'I ain't got no money,' he says.

'That's too bad,' I says. I made to go out.

'Gimme one of um, Mr Jason,' he says. 'You ain't gwine need um bofe.'

'Hush yo mouf,' Dilsey says, 'Don't you know he ain't gwine give nothing away?'

'How much you want fer hit?' he says.

'Five cents,' I says.

'I ain't got dat much,' he says.

'How much you got?' I says.

'I ain't got nothing,' he says.

'All right,' I says. I went on.

'Mr Jason,' he says.

'Whyn't you hush up?' Dilsey says. 'He jes teasin you. He fixin to use dem tickets hisself. Go on, Jason, and let him lone.'

'I don't want them,' I says. I came back to the stove. 'I came in here to burn them up. But if you want to buy one for a nickel?' I says, looking at him and opening the stove lid.

'I ain't got dat much,' he says.

'All right,' I says. I dropped one of them in the stove.

'You, Jason,' Dilsey says, 'Ain't you shamed?'

'Mr Jason,' he says, 'Please, suh, I'll fix dem tyres ev'y day fer a mont'.'

'I need the cash,' I says. 'You can have it for a nickel.'

'Hush, Luster,' Dilsey says. She jerked him back. 'Go on,' she says, 'Drop hit in. Go on. Git hit over with.'

'You can have it for a nickel,' I says.

'Go on,' Dilsey says. 'He ain't got no nickel. Go on. Drop hit in.'

'All right,' I says. I dropped it in and Dilsey shut the stove.

'A big growed man like you,' she says. 'Git on outen my kitchen. Hush,' she says to Luster. 'Don't you git Benjy started. I'll git you a quarter fum Frony tonight and youl kin go tomorrow night. Hush up, now.'

I went on into the living-room. I couldn't hear anything from upstairs. I opened the paper. After a while Ben and Luster came in. Ben went to the dark place on the wall where the mirror used to be, rubbing his hands on it and slobbering and moaning. Luster began punching at the fire.

'What're you doing?' I says. 'We don't need any fire tonight.'

'I trying to keep him quiet,' he says. 'Hit always cold Easter,' he says.

'Only this is not Easter,' I says. 'Let it alone.'

He put the poker back and got the cushion out of Mother's chair and gave it to Ben, and he hunkered down in front of the fireplace and got quiet.

I read the paper. There hadn't been a sound from upstairs when Dilsey came in and sent Ben and Luster on to the kitchen and said supper was ready.

'All right,' I says. She went out. I sat there, reading the paper. After a while I heard Dilsey looking in at the door.

'Whyn't you come on and eat?' she says.

'I'm waiting for supper,' I says.

'Hit's on the table,' she says. 'I done told you.'

'Is it?' I says. 'Excuse me. I didn't hear anybody come down.'

'They ain't comin,' she says. 'You come on and eat, so I can take something up to them.'

'Are they sick?' I says. 'What did the doctor say it was? Not smallpox, I hope.'

'Come on here, Jason,' she says, 'So I kin git done.'

'All right,' I says, raising the paper again. 'I'm waiting for supper now.'

I could feel her watching me at the door. I read the paper.

'Whut you want to act like this fer?' she says. 'When you knows how much bother I has anyway.'

'If Mother is any sicker than she was when she came down to dinner, all right,' I says. 'But as long as I am buying food for people younger than I am, they'll have to come down to the table to eat it. Let me know when supper's ready,' I says, reading the paper again. I heard her climbing the stairs, dragging her feet and grunting and groaning like they were straight up and three feet apart. I heard her at Mother's door, then I heard her calling Quentin, like the door was locked, then she went back to Mother's room and then Mother went and talked to Quentin. Then they came downstairs. I read the paper.

Dilsey came back to the door. 'Come on,' she says, 'fo you kin think up some mo devilment. You just trying yoself tonight.'

I went to the dining-room. Quentin was sitting with her head bent. She had painted her face again. Her nose looked like a porcelain insulator.

'I'm glad you feel well enough to come down,' I says to Mother.

'It's little enough I can do for you, to come to the table,' she says. 'No matter how I feel. I realize that when a man works all day he likes to be surrounded by his family at the supper table. I want to please you. I only wish you and Quentin got along better. It would be easier for me.'

'We get along all right,' I says. 'I don't mind her staying locked up in her room all day if she wants to. But I can't have all this whoop-de-do and sulking at meal times. I know that's a lot to ask her, but I'm that way in my own house. Your house, I meant to say.'

'It's yours,' Mother says, 'You are the head of it now.'

Quentin hadn't looked up. I helped the plates and she begun to eat.

'Did you get a good piece of meat?' I says. 'If you didn't, I'll try to find you a better one.'

She didn't say anything.

'I say, did you get a good piece of meat?' I says.

'What?' she says. 'Yes. It's all right.'

'Will you have some more rice?' I says.

'No,' she says.

'Better let me give you some more,' I says.

'I don't want any more,' she says.

'Not at all,' I says, 'You're welcome.'

'Is your headache gone?' Mother says.

'Headache?' I says.

'I was afraid you were developing one,' she says. 'When you came in this afternoon.'

'Oh,' I says. 'No, it didn't show up. We stayed so busy this afternoon I forgot about it.'

'Was that why you were late?' Mother says. I could see Quentin listening. I looked at her. Her knife and fork were still going, but I caught her looking at me, then she looked at her plate again. I says,

'No. I loaned my car to a fellow about three o'clock and I had to wait until he got back with it.' I ate for a while.

'Who was it?' Mother says.

'It was one of those show men,' I says. 'It seems his sister's husband was out riding with some town woman, and he was chasing them.'

Quentin sat perfectly still, chewing.

'You ought not to lend your car to people like that,' Mother says. 'You are too generous with it. That's why I never call on you for it if I can help it.'

'I was beginning to think that myself, for a while,' I says. 'But he got back, all right. He says he found what he was looking for.'

'Who was the woman?' Mother says.

'I'll tell you later,' I says. 'I don't like to talk about such things before Quentin.'

Quentin had quit eating. Every once in a while she'd take a drink of water, then she'd sit there crumbling a biscuit up, her face bent over her plate.

'Yes,' Mother says, 'I suppose women who stay shut up like I do have no idea what goes on in this town.'

'Yes,' I says, 'They don't.'

'My life has been so different from that,' Mother says. 'Thank God I don't know about such wickedness. I don't even want to know about it. I'm not like most people.'

I didn't say any more. Quentin sat there, crumbling the biscuit until I quit eating, then she says,

'Can I go now?' without looking at anybody.

'What?' I says. 'Sure, you can go. Were you waiting on us?'

She looked at me. She had crumbled all the biscuit, but her hands still went on like they were crumbling it yet and her eyes looked like they were cornered or something and then she started biting her mouth like it ought to have poisoned her, with all that red lead.

'Grandmother,' she says, 'Grandmother –'

'Did you want something else to eat?' I says.

'Why does he treat me like this, Grandmother?' she says. 'I never hurt him.'

'I want you all to get along with one another,' Mother says, 'You are all that's left now, and I do want you all to get along better,'

'It's his fault,' she says, 'He won't let me alone, and I have to. If he doesn't want me here, why won't he let me go back to –'

'That's enough,' I says, 'Not another word.'

'Then why won't he let me alone?' she says. 'He – he just –'

'He is the nearest thing to a father you've ever had,' Mother says. 'It's his bread you and I eat. It's only right that he should expect obedience from you.'

'It's his fault,' she says. She jumped up. 'He makes me do it. If he would just –' she looked at us, her eyes cornered, kind of jerking her arms against her sides.

'If I would just what?' I says.

'Whatever I do, it's your fault,' she says. 'If I'm bad, it's because

I had to be. You made me. I wish I was dead. I wish we were all dead.' Then she ran. We heard her run up the stairs. Then a door slammed.

'That's the first sensible thing she ever said,' I says.

'She didn't go to school today,' Mother says.

'How do you know?' I says. 'Were you downtown?'

'I just know,' she says. 'I wish you could be kinder to her.'

'If I did that I'd have to arrange to see her more than once a day,' I says. 'You'll have to make her come to the table every meal. Then I could give her an extra piece of meat every time.'

'There are little things you could do,' she says.

'Like not paying attention when you ask me to see that she goes to school?' I says.

'She didn't go to school today,' she says. 'I just know she didn't. She says she went for a car ride with one of the boys this afternoon and you followed her.'

'How could I,' I says, 'When somebody had my car all afternoon? Whether or not she was in school today is already past,' I says. 'If you've got to worry about it, worry next Monday.'

'I wanted you and she to get along with one another,' she says. 'But she has inherited all of the headstrong traits. Quentin's too. I thought at the time, with the heritage she would already have, to give her that name, too. Sometimes I think she is the judgement of Caddy and Quentin upon me.'

'Good Lord,' I says, 'You've got a fine mind. No wonder you kept yourself sick all the time.'

'What?' she says. 'I don't understand.'

'I hope not,' I says. 'A good woman misses a lot she's better off without knowing.'

'They were both that way,' she says, 'They would make interest with your father against me when I tried to correct them. He was always saying they didn't need controlling, that they already knew what cleanliness and honesty were, which was all that anyone could hope to be taught. And now I hope he's satisfied.'

'You've got Ben to depend on,' I says, 'Cheer up.'

'They deliberately shut me out of their lives,' she says, 'It was always her and Quentin. They were always conspiring against me. Against you, too, though you were too young to realize it. They always looked on you and me as outsiders, like they did your Uncle Maury. I always told your father that they were allowed too much freedom, to be together too much. When Quentin started to school we had to let her go the next year, so she could be with him. She couldn't bear for any of you to do anything she couldn't. It was vanity in her, vanity and false pride. And then when her troubles began I knew that Quentin would feel that he had to do something just as bad. But I didn't believe that he could have been so selfish as to – I didn't dream that he –'

'Maybe he knew it was going to be a girl,' I says, 'And that one more of them would be more than he could stand.'

'He could have controlled her,' she says. 'He seemed to be the only person she had any consideration for. But that is a part of the judgement too, I suppose.'

'Yes,' I says, 'Too bad it wasn't me instead of him. You'd be a lot better off.'

'You say things like that to hurt me,' she says. 'I deserve it though. When they began to sell the land to send Quentin to Harvard I told your father that he must make an equal provision for you. Then when Herbert offered to take you into the bank I said, Jason is provided for now, and when all the expense began to pile up and I was forced to sell our furniture and the rest of the pasture, I wrote her at once because I said she will realize that she and Quentin have had their share and part of Jason's too and that it depends on her now to compensate him. I said she will do that out of respect for her father. I believed that, then. But I'm just a poor old woman; I was raised to believe that people would deny themselves for their own flesh and blood. It's my fault. You were right to reproach me.'

'Do you think I need any man's help to stand on my feet?' I says, 'Let alone a woman that can't name the father of her own child.'

'Jason,' she says.

'All right,' I says. 'I didn't mean that. Of course not.'

'If I believed that were possible, after all my suffering.'

'Of course it's not,' I says. 'I didn't mean it.'

'I hope that at least is spared me,' she says.

'Sure it is,' I says, 'She's too much like both of them to doubt that.'

'I couldn't bear that,' she says.

'Then quit thinking about it,' I says. 'Has she been worrying you any more about getting out at night?'

'No. I made her realize that it was for her own good and that she'd thank me for it some day. She takes her books with her and studies after I lock the door. I see the light on as late as eleven o'clock some nights.'

'How do you know she's studying?' I says.

'I don't know what else she'd do in there alone,' she says. 'She never did read any.'

'No,' I says, 'You wouldn't know. And you can thank your stars for that,' I says. Only what would be the use in saying it aloud. It would just have her crying on me again.

I heard her go upstairs. Then she called Quentin and Quentin says What? through the door. 'Good night,' Mother says. Then I heard the key in the lock, and Mother went back to her room.

When I finished my cigar and went up, the light was still on. I could see the empty keyhole, but I couldn't hear a sound. She studied quiet. Maybe she learned that in school. I told Mother good night and went on to my room and got the box out and counted it again. I could hear the Great American Gelding snoring away like a planing mill. I read somewhere they'd fix men that way to give them women's voices. But maybe he didn't know what they'd done to him. I don't reckon he even knew what he had been trying to do, or why Mr Burgess knocked him out with the fence picket. And if they'd just sent him on to Jackson while he was under the ether, he'd never have known the difference. But that would have been too simple for a Compson to think of. Not half complex enough. Having to wait to do it at all until he broke out and tried to run a little girl down on the street with her own father looking at him. Well, like I say they never started soon enough with their cutting, and they quit too quick. I know at least two more that needed something like that, and one of them not over a mile away, either. But then I don't reckon even that would do any good. Like I say once a bitch always a bitch. And just let me have twenty-four hours without any damn New York jew to advise me what it's going to do. I don't want to make a killing; save that to suck in the smart gamblers with. I just want an even chance to get my money back. And once I've done that they can bring all Beale Street and all bedlam in here and two of them can sleep in my bed and another one can have my place at the table too.

April Eighth, 1928

The day dawned bleak and chill, a moving wall of grey light out of the north-east which, instead of dissolving into moisture, seemed to disintegrate into minute and venomous particles, like dust that, when Dilsey opened the door of the cabin and emerged, needled laterally into her flesh, precipitating not so much a moisture as a substance partaking of the quality of thin, not quite congealed oil. She wore a stiff black straw hat perched upon her turban, and a maroon velvet cape with a border of mangy and anonymous fur above a dress of purple silk, and she stood in the door for a while with her myriad and sunken face lifted to the weather, and one gaunt hand flac-soled as the belly of a fish, then she moved the cape aside and examined the bosom of her gown.

The gown fell gauntly from her shoulders, across her fallen breasts, then tightened upon her paunch and fell again, ballooning a little above the nether garments which she would remove layer by layer as the spring accomplished and the warm days, in colour regal and moribund. She had been a big woman once but now her skeleton rose, draped loosely in unpadded skin that tightened again upon a paunch almost dropsical, as though muscle and tissue had been courage or fortitude which the days or the years had consumed until only the indomitable skeleton was left rising like a ruin or a landmark above the somnolent and impervious guts, and above that the collapsed face that gave the impression of the bones themselves being outside the flesh, lifted into the driving day with an expression at once fatalistic and of a child's astonished disappointment, until she turned and entered the house again and closed the door.

The earth immediately about the door was bare. It had a patina, as though from the soles of bare feet in generations, like old silver or the walls of Mexican houses which have been plastered by hand. Beside the house, shading it in summer, stood three mulberry trees, the fledged leaves that would later be broad and placid as the palms of hands streaming flatly undulant upon the driving air. A pair of jaybirds came up from nowhere, whirled up on the blast like gaudy scraps of cloth or paper and lodged in the mulberries, where they swung in raucous tilt and recover, screaming into the wind that ripped their harsh cries onward and away like scraps of paper or of cloth in turn. Then three more joined them and they swung and tilted in the wrung branches for a time, screaming. The door of the cabin opened and Dilsey emerged once more, this time in a man's felt hat and an army overcoat, beneath the frayed skirts of which her blue gingham dress fell in uneven balloonings, streaming too about her as she crossed the yard and mounted the steps to the kitchen door.

A moment later she emerged, carrying an open umbrella now, which she slanted ahead into the wind, and crossed to the woodpile and laid the umbrella down, still open. Immediately she caught at it and arrested it and held to it for a while, looking about her. Then she closed it and laid it down and stacked stovewood into her crooked arm, against her breast, and picked up the umbrella and got it open at last and returned to the steps and held the wood precariously balanced while she contrived to close the umbrella, which she propped in the corner just within the door. She dumped the wood into the box behind the stove. Then she removed the overcoat and hat and took a soiled apron down from the wall and put it on and built a fire in the stove. While she was doing so, rattling the grate bars and clattering the lids, Mrs Compson began to call her from the head of the stairs.

She wore a dressing gown of quilted black satin, holding it close under her chin. In the other hand she held a red rubber hot water bottle and she stood at the head of the back stairway, calling 'Dilsey' at steady and inflexionless intervals into the quiet stairwell that descended into complete darkness, then opened again where a grey window fell across it. 'Dilsey', she called, without inflexion or emphasis or haste, as though she were not listening for a reply at all. 'Dilsey.'

Dilsey answered and ceased clattering the stove, but before she could cross the kitchen Mrs Compson called her again, and before she crossed the dining-room and brought her head into relief against the grey splash of the window, still again.

'All right,' Dilsey said, 'All right, here I is. I'll fill hit soon ez I git some hot water.' She gathered up her skirts and mounted the stairs, wholly blotting the grey light. 'Put hit down dar en g'awn back to bed.'

'I couldn't understand what was the matter,' Mrs Compson said. 'I've been lying awake for an hour at least, without hearing a sound from the kitchen.'

'You put hit down and g'awn back to bed,' Dilsey said. She toiled painfully up the steps, shapeless, breathing heavily. 'I'll have de fire gwine in a minute, en de water hot in two mo'.'

'I've been lying there for an hour, at least,' Mrs Compson said. 'I thought maybe you were waiting for me to come down and start the fire.'

Dilsey reached the top of the stairs and took the water bottle. 'I'll fix hit in a minute,' she said. 'Luster overslep dis mawnin, up half de night at dat show. I gwine build de fire myself. Go on now, so you won't wake de others twell I ready.'

'If you permit Luster to do things that interfere with his work, you'll have to suffer for it yourself,' Mrs Compson said. 'Jason won't like this if he hears about it. You know he won't.'

'Twusn't none of Jason's money he went on,' Dilsey said. 'Dat's one thing sho.' She went on down the stairs. Mrs Compson returned to her room. As she got into bed again she could hear Dilsey yet descending the stairs with a sort of painful and terrific slowness that would have become maddening had it not presently ceased beyond the flapping diminishment of the pantry door.

She entered the kitchen and built up the fire and began to prepare breakfast. In the midst of this she ceased and went to the window and looked out towards her cabin, then she went to the door and opened it and shouted into the driving weather.

'Luster!' she shouted, standing to listen, tilting her face from the wind, 'You, Luster?' She listened, then as she prepared to shout again Luster appeared around the corner of the kitchen.

'Ma'am?' he said innocently, so innocently that Dilsey looked down at him, for a moment motionless, with something more than mere surprise.

'Whar you at?' she said.

'Nowhere,' he said. 'Jes in de cellar.'

'Whut you doin in de cellar?' she said. 'Don't stand dar in de rain, fool,' she said.

'Ain't doin nothing,' he said. He came up the steps.

'Don't you dare come in dis do' widout a armful of wood,'

she said. 'Here I done had to tote yo wood en build yo fire bofe. Didn't I tole you not to leave dis place last night befo dat woodbox wus ful to de top?'

'I did,' Luster said, 'I filled hit.'

'Whar hit gone to, den?'

'I don't know'm. I ain't teched hit.'

'Well, you git hit full up now,' she said. 'And git on up den en see bout Benjy.'

She shut the door. Luster went to the woodpile. The five jaybirds whirled over the house, screaming, and into the mulberries again. He watched them. He picked up a rock and threw it. 'Whoo,' he said, 'Git on back to hell, whar you belong to. Tain't Monday yit.'

He loaded himself mountainously with stovewood. He could not see over it, and he staggered to the steps and up them and blundered crashing against the door, shedding billets. Then Dilsey came and opened the door for him and he blundered across the kitchen. 'You, Luster!' she shouted, but he had already hurled the wood into the box with a thunderous crash. 'Hah!' he said.

'Is you tryin to wake up de whole house?' Dilsey said. She hit him on the back of his head with the flat of her hand. 'Go on up dar and git Benjy dressed, now.'

'Yessum,' he said. He went towards the outer door.

'Whar you gwine?' Dilsey said.

'I thought I better go round de house en in by de front, so I won't wake up Miss Cahline en dem.'

'You go on up dem back stairs like I tole you en git Benjy's clothes on him,' Dilsey said. 'Go on, now.'

'Yessum,' Luster said. He returned and left by the dining-room door. After a while it ceased to flap. Dilsey prepared to make biscuit. As she ground the sifter steadily above the bread board, she sang, to herself at first, something without particular tune or words, repetitive, mournful and plaintive, austere, as she ground a faint, steady snowing of flour onto the bread board. The stove had begun to heat the room and to fill it with murmurous minors of the fire, and presently she was singing louder, as if her voice too had been thawed out by the growing warmth, and then Mrs Compson called her name again from within the house. Dilsey raised her face as if her eyes could and did penetrate the walls and ceiling and saw the old woman in her quilted dressing gown at the head of the stairs, calling her name with machine-like regularity.

'Oh, Lawd,' Dilsey said. She set the sifter down and swept up the hem of her apron and wiped her hands and caught up the bottle from the chair on which she had laid it and gathered her apron about the handle of the kettle which was now jetting faintly. 'Jes a minute,' she called, 'De water jes dis minute got hot.'

It was not the bottle which Mrs Compson wanted, however, and clutching it by the neck like a dead hen Dilsey went to the foot of the stairs and looked upward.

'Ain't Luster up dar wid him?' she said.

'Luster hasn't been in the house. I've been lying here listening for him. I knew he would be late, but I did hope he'd come in time to keep Benjamin from disturbing Jason on Jason's one day in the week to sleep in the morning.'

'I don't see how you expect anybody to sleep, wid you standin in de hall, holl'in at folks fum de crack of dawn,' Dilsey said. She began to mount the stairs, toiling heavily. 'I sont dat boy up dar half-hour ago.'

Mrs Compson watched her, holding the dressing gown under her chin. 'What are you going to do?' she said.

'Gwine git Benjy dressed en bring him down to de kitchen, whar he won't wake Jason en Quentin,' Dilsey said.

'Haven't you started breakfast yet?'

'I'll tend to dat too,' Dilsey said. 'You better git back in bed twell Luster make yo fire. Hit cold dis mawnin.'

'I know it,' Mrs Compson said. 'My feet are like ice. They were so cold they waked me up.' She watched Dilsey mount the stairs. It took her a long while. 'You know how it frets Jason when breakfast is late,' Mrs Compson said.

'I can't do but one thing at a time,' Dilsey said. 'You git on back to bed, fo I has you on my hands dis mawnin too.'

'If you're going to drop everything to dress Benjamin, I'd better come down and get breakfast. You know as well as I do how Jason acts when it's late.'

'En who gwine eat yo messin?' Dilsey said. 'Tell me dat. Go on now,' she said, toiling upward. Mrs Compson stood watching her as she mounted, steadying herself against the wall with one hand, holding her skirts up with the other.

'Are you going to wake him up just to dress him?' she said.

Dilsey stopped. With her foot lifted to the next step she stood there, her hand against the wall and the grey splash of the window behind her, motionless and shapeless she loomed.

'He ain't awake den?' she said.

'He wasn't when I looked in,' Mrs Compson said. 'But it's past his time. He never does sleep after half-past seven. You know he doesn't.'

Dilsey said nothing. She made no further move, but though she could not see her save as a blobby shape without depth, Mrs Compson knew that she had lowered her face a little and that she stood now like a cow in the rain, as she held the empty water bottle by its neck.

'You're not the one who has to bear it,' Mrs Compson said. 'It's not your responsibility. You can go away. You don't have to bear the brunt of it day in and day out. You owe nothing to them, to Mr Compson's memory. I know you have never had any tenderness for Jason. You've never tried to conceal it.'

Dilsey said nothing. She turned slowly and descended, lowering her body from step to step, as a small child does, her hand against the wall. 'You go on and let him alone,' she said. 'Don't go in dar no mo, now. I'll send Luster up soon as I find him. Let him alone, now.'

She returned to the kitchen. She looked into the stove, then she drew her apron over her head and donned the overcoat and opened the outer door and looked up and down the yard. The weather drove upon her flesh, harsh and minute, but the scene was empty of all else that moved. She descended the steps, gingerly, as if for silence, and went around the corner of the kitchen. As she did so Luster emerged quickly and innocently from the cellar door.

Dilsey stopped. 'Whut you up to?' she said.

'Nothing,' Luster said, 'Mr Jason say fer me to find out whar dat water leak in de cellar fum.'

'En when wus hit he say fer you to do that?' Dilsey said. 'Last New Year's day, wasn't hit?'

'I thought I jes be lookin whiles dey sleep,' Luster said. Dilsey went to the cellar door. He stood aside and she peered down into the obscurity odorous of dank earth and mould and rubber.

'Huh,' Dilsey said. She looked at Luster again. He met her gaze blandly, innocent and open. 'I don't know whut you up to, but you ain't got no business doin hit. You jes tryin me too dis mawnin cause de others is, ain't you? You git on up dar en see to Benjy, you hear?'

'Yessum,' Luster said. He went on toward the kitchen steps, swiftly.

'Here,' Dilsey said, 'You git me another armful of wood while I got you.'

'Yessum,' he said. He passed her on the steps and went to the woodpile. When he blundered again at the door a moment later, again invisible and blind within and beyond his wooden avatar, Dilsey opened the door and guided him across the kitchen with a firm hand.

'Jes thow hit at dat box again,' she said, 'Jes thow hit.'

'I got to,' Luster said, panting, 'I can't put hit down no other way.'

'Den you stand dar en hold hit a while,' Dilsey said. She unloaded him a stick at a time. 'Whut got into you dis mawnin? Here I sont you fer wood en you ain't never brought mo'n six sticks at a time to save yo life twell today. Whut you fixin to ax me kin you do now? Ain't dat show lef town yit?'

'Yessum. Hit done gone.'

She put the last stick into the box. 'Now you go on up dar wid Benjy, like I tole you befo,' she said. 'And I don't want nobody else yellin down dem stairs at me twell I rings de bell. You hear me.'

'Yessum,' Luster said. He vanished through the swing door. Dilsey put some more wood in the stove and returned to the bread board. Presently she began to sing again.

The room grew warmer. Soon Dilsey's skin had taken on a rich, lustrous quality as compared with that as of a faint dusting of wood ashes which both it and Luster's had worn, as she moved about the kitchen, gathering about her the raw materials of food, coordinating the meal. On the wall above the cupboard, invisible save at night, by lamplight and even then evincing an enigmatic profundity because it had but one hand, a cabinet clock ticked, then with a preliminary sound as if it had cleared its throat, struck five times.

'Eight o'clock,' Dilsey said. She ceased and tilted her head upward, listening. But there was no sound save the clock and the fire. She opened the oven and looked at the pan of bread, then stooping she paused while someone descended the stairs. She heard the feet cross the dining-room, then the swing door opened and Luster entered, followed by a big man who appeared to have been shaped of some substance whose particles would not or did not cohere to one another or to the frame which supported it. His skin was dead-looking and hairless; dropsical too, he moved with a shambling gait like a trained bear. His hair was pale and fine. It had been brushed smoothly down upon his brow like that of children in daguerro-types. His eyes were clear, of the pale sweet blue of cornflowers, his thick mouth hung open, drooling a little.

'Is he cold?' Dilsey said. She wiped her hands on her apron and touched his hand.

'Ef he ain't, I is,' Luster said. 'Always cold Easter. Ain't never seen hit fail. Miss Cahline say ef you ain't got time to fix her hot water bottle to never mind about hit.'

'Oh, Lawd,' Dilsey said. She drew a chair into the corner between the woodbox and the stove. The man went obediently and sat in it. 'Look in de dining-room and see whar I laid dat bottle down,' Dilsey said. Luster fetched the bottle from the dining-room and Dilsey filled it and gave it to him. 'Hurry up, now,' she said. 'See ef Jason wake now. Tell em hit's all ready.'

Luster went out. Ben sat beside the stove. He sat loosely, utterly motionless save for his head, which made a continual bobbing sort of movement as he watched Dilsey with his sweet vague gaze as she moved about. Luster returned.

'He up,' he said, 'Miss Cahline say put hit on de table.' He came to the stove and spread his hands palm down above the firebox. 'He up, too,' he said, 'Gwine hit wid bofe feet dis mawnin.'

'Whut's de matter now?' Dilsey said. 'Git away fum dar. How kin I do anything wid you standin over de stove?'

'I cold,' Luster said.

'You ought to thought about dat whiles you wus down dar in dat cellar,' Dilsey said. 'Whut de matter wid Jason?'

'Sayin me en Benjy broke dat winder in his room.'

'Is dey one broke?' Dilsey said.

'Dat's whut he sayin,' Luster said. 'Say I broke hit.'

'How could you, when he keep hit locked all day en night?'

'Say I broke hit chunkin rocks at hit,' Luster said.

'En did you?'

'Nome,' Luster said.

'Don't lie to me, boy,' Dilsey said.

'I never done hit,' Luster said. 'Ask Benjy ef I did. I ain't stud'in dat winder.'

''Who could a broke hit, den?' Dilsey said. 'He jes tryin hisself, to wake Quentin up,' she said, taking the pan of biscuits out of the stove.

'Reckin so,' Luster said. 'Dese is funny folks. Glad I ain't none of em.'

'Ain't none of who?' Dilsey said. 'Lemme tell you somethin, nigger boy, you got jes es much Compson devilment in you es any of em. Is you right sho you never broke dat window?'

'Whut I want to break hit fur?'

'Whut you do any of yo devilment fur?' Dilsey said. 'Watch him now, so he can't burn his hand again twell I git de table set.'

She went to the dining-room, where they heard her moving about, then she returned and set a plate at the kitchen table and set food there. Ben watched her, slobbering, making a faint, eager sound.

'All right, honey,' she said, 'Here yo breakfast. Bring his chair, Luster.' Luster moved the chair up and Ben sat down, whimpering and slobbering. Dilsey tied a cloth about his neck and wiped his mouth with the end of it. 'And see kin you kep fum messin up his clothes one time,' she said, handing Luster a spoon.

Ben ceased whimpering. He watched the spoon as it rose to his mouth. It was as if even eagerness were muscle-bound in him too, and hunger itself inarticulate, not knowing it is hunger. Luster fed him with skill and detachment. Now and then his attention would return long enough to enable him to feint the spoon and cause Ben to close his mouth upon the empty air, but it was apparent that Luster's mind was elsewhere. His other hand lay on the back of the chair and upon that dead surface it moved tentatively, delicately, as if he were picking an inaudible tune out of the dead void, and once he even forgot to tease Ben with the spoon while his fingers teased out of the slain wood a soundless and involved arpeggio until Ben recalled him by whimpering again.

In the dining-room Dilsey moved back and forth. Presently she rang a small clear bell, then in the kitchen Luster heard Mrs Compson and Jason descending, and Jason's voice, and he rolled his eyes whitely with listening.

'Sure, I know they didn't break it,' Jason said. 'Sure, I know that. Maybe the change of weather broke it.'

'I don't see how it could have,' Mrs Compson said. 'Your room stays locked all day long, just as you leave it when you go to town. None of us ever go in there except Sunday, to clean it. I don't want you to think that I would go where I'm not wanted, or that I would permit anyone else to.'

'I never said you broke it, did I?' Jason said.

'I don't want to go in your room,' Mrs Compson said. 'I respect anybody's private affairs. I wouldn't put my foot over the threshold, even if I had a key.'

'Yes,' Jason said, 'I know your keys won't fit. That's why I had the lock changed. What I want to know is, how that window got broken.'

'Luster say he didn't do hit,' Dilsey said.

'I knew that without asking him,' Jason said. 'Where's Quentin?' he said.

'Where she is ev'y Sunday mawnin,' Dilsey said. 'Whut got into you de last few days, anyhow?'

'Well, we're going to change all that,' Jason said. 'Go up and tell her breakfast is ready.'

'You leave her alone now, Jason,' Dilsey said. 'She gits up fer breakfast ev'y week mawnin, en Cahline lets her stay in bed ev'y Sunday. You knows dat.'

'I can't keep a kitchenful of niggers to wait on her pleasure, much as I'd like to,' Jason said. 'Go and tell her to come down to breakfast.'

'Ain't nobody have to wait on her,' Dilsey said. 'I puts her breakfast in de warmer en she –'

'Did you hear me?' Jason said.

'I hears you,' Dilsey said. 'All I been hearin, when you in de house. Ef hit ain't Quentin er yo maw, hit's Luster en Benjy. Whut you let him go on dat way fer, Miss Cahline?'

'You'd better do as he says,' Mrs Compson said, 'He's head of the house now. It's his right to require us to respect his wishes. I try to do it, and if I can, you can too.'

'Tain't no sense in him being so bad tempered he got to make Quentin git up jes to suit him,' Dilsey said. 'Maybe you think she broke dat window.'

'She would, if she happened to think of it,' Jason said. 'You go and do what I told you.'

'En I wouldn't blame her none ef she did,' Dilsey said, going toward the stairs. 'Wid you naggin at her all de blessed time you in de house.'

'Hush, Dilsey,' Mrs Compson said, 'It's neither your place nor mine to tell Jason what to do. Sometimes I think he is wrong, but I try to obey his wishes for you alls' sakes. If I'm strong enough to come to the table, Quentin can, too.'

Dilsey went out. They heard her mounting the stairs. They heard her a long while on the stairs.

'You've got a prize set of servants,' Jason said. He helped his mother and himself to food. 'Did you ever have one that was worth killing? You must have had some before I was big enough to remember.'

'I have to humour them,' Mrs Compson said. 'I have to depend on them so completely. It's not as if I were strong. I wish I were. I wish I could do all the housework myself. I could at least take that much off your shoulders.'

'And a fine pigsty we'd live in, too,' Jason said. 'Hurry up, Dilsey,' he shouted.

'I know you blame me,' Mrs Compson said, 'for letting them off to go to church today.'

'Go where?' Jason said. 'Hasn't that damn show left yet?'

'To church,' Mrs Compson said. 'The darkies are having a special Easter service. I promised Dilsey two weeks ago that they could get off.'

'Which means we'll eat cold dinner,' Jason said, 'or none at all.'

'I know it's my fault,' Mrs Compson said. 'I know you blame me.'

'For what?' Jason said. 'You never resurrected Christ, did you?'

They heard Dilsey mount the final stair, then her slow feet overhead.

'Quentin,' she said. When she called the first time Jason laid his knife and fork down and he and his mother appeared to wait across the table from one another, in identical attitudes; the one cold and shrewd, with close-thatched brown hair curled into two stubborn hooks, one on either side of his forehead like a bartender in caricature, and hazel eyes with black-ringed irises like marbles, the other cold and querulous, with perfectly white hair and eyes pouched and baffled and so dark as to appear to be all pupil or all iris.

'Quentin,' Dilsey said, 'Get up, honey. Dey waitin breakfast on you.'

'I can't understand how that window got broken,' Mrs Compson said. 'Are you sure it was done yesterday? It could have been like that a long time, with the warm weather. The upper sash, behind the shade like that.'

'I've told you for the last time it happened yesterday,' Jason said. 'Don't you reckon I know the room I live in? Do you reckon I could have lived in it a week with a hole in the window you could stick your hand –' his voice ceased, ebbed, left him staring at his mother with eyes that for an instant were quite empty of anything. It was as though his eyes were holding their breath, while his mother looked at him, her face flaccid and querulous, interminable, clairvoyant yet obtuse. As they sat so Dilsey said,

'Quentin. Don't play wid me, honey. Come on to breakfast, honey. Dey waitin fer you.'

'I can't understand it,' Mrs Compson said, 'It's just as if somebody had tried to break into the house –' Jason sprang up. His chair crashed over backward. 'What –' Mrs Compson said, staring at him as he ran past her and went jumping up the stairs, where he met Dilsey. His face was now in shadow, and Dilsey said,

'She sullin. Yo ma ain't unlocked –' But Jason ran on past her and along the corridor to a door. He didn't call. He grasped the knob and tried it, then he stood with the knob in his hand and his head bent a little, as if he were listening to something much further away than the dimensioned room beyond the door, and which he already heard. His attitude was that of one who goes through the motions of listening in order to deceive himself as to what he already hears. Behind him Mrs Compson mounted the stairs, calling his name. Then she saw Dilsey and she quit calling him and began to call Dilsey instead.

'I told you she ain't unlocked dat do' yit,' Dilsey said.

When she spoke he turned and ran toward her, but his voice was quiet, matter of fact. 'She carry the key with her?' he said. 'Has she got it now, I mean, or will she have –'

'Dilsey,' Mrs Compson said on the stairs.

'Is which?' Dilsey said. 'Whyn't you let –'

'The key,' Jason said, 'To that room. Does she carry it with her all the time. Mother.' Then he saw Mrs Compson and he went down the stairs and met her. 'Give me the key,' he said. He fell to pawing at the pockets of the rusty black dressing sacque she wore. She resisted.

'Jason,' she said, 'Jason! Are you and Dilsey trying to put me to bed again?' she said, trying to fend him off, 'Can't you even let me have Sunday in peace?'

'The key,' Jason said, pawing at her, 'Give it here.' He looked
back at the door, as if he expected it to fly open before he could
get back to it with the key he did not yet have.

'You, Dilsey!' Mrs Compson said, clutching her sacque about
her

'Give me the key, you old fool!' Jason cried suddenly. From
her pocket he tugged a huge bunch of rusted keys on an iron
ring like a medieval jailer's and ran back up the hall with the
two women behind him.

'You, Jason!' Mrs Compson said. 'He will never find the right
one,' she said, 'You know I never let anyone take my keys,
Dilsey,' she said. She began to wail.

'Hush,' Dilsey said, 'He ain't gwine to do nothin to her. I
ain't gwine let him.'

'But on Sunday morning, in my own house,' Mrs Compson
said, 'When I've tried so hard to raise them Christians. Let me
find the right key, Jason,' she said. She put her hand on his
arm. Then she began to struggle with him, but he flung her
aside with a motion of his elbow and looked around at her for
a moment, his eyes cold and harried, then he turned to the
door again and the unwieldy keys.

'Hush,' Dilsey said, 'You, Jason!'

'Something terrible has happened,' Mrs Compson said, wailing
again, 'I know it has. You, Jason,' she said, grasping at him
again. 'He won't even let me find the key to a room in my own
house!'

'Now, now,' Dilsey said, 'Whut kin happen? I right here. I
ain't gwine let him hurt her. Quentin,' she said, raising her
voice, 'don't you be skeered, honey, Ise right here.'

The door opened, swung inward. He stood in it for a moment,
hiding the room, then he stepped aside. 'Go in,' he said in a
thick, light voice. They went in. It was not a girl's room. It was
not anybody's room, and the faint scent of cheap cosmetics and
the few feminine objects and the other evidence of crude and
hopeless efforts to feminize it but added to its anonymity, giving
it that dead and stereotyped transience of rooms in assignation
houses. The bed had not been disturbed. On the floor lay a
soiled undergarment of cheap silk a little too pink; from a half
open bureau drawer dangled a single stocking. The window was
open. A pear tree grew there, close against the house. It was in
bloom and the branches scraped and rasped against the house
and the myriad air, driving in the window, brought into the

room the forlorn scent of the blossoms.

'Dar now,' Dilsey said, 'Didn't I told you she all right?'

'All right?' Mrs Compson said. Dilsey followed her into the room and touched her.

'You come on and lay down, now,' she said. 'I find her in ten minutes.'

Mrs Compson shook her off. 'Find the note,' she said. 'Quentin left a note when he did it.'

'All right,' Dilsey said, 'I'll find hit. You come on to yo room, now.

'I knew the minute they named her Quentin this would happen,' Mrs Compson said. She went to the bureau and began to turn over the scattered objects there – scent bottles, a box of powder, a chewed pencil, a pair of scissors with one broken blade lying upon a darned scarf dusted with powder and stained with rouge. 'Find the note,' she said.

'I is,' Dilsey said. 'You come on, now. Me and Jason'll find hit. You come on to yo room.'

'Jason,' Mrs Compson said, 'Where is he?' She went to the door. Dilsey followed her on down the hall, to another door. It was closed. 'Jason,' she called through the door. There was no answer. She tried the knob, then she called him again. But there was still no answer, for he was hurling things backward out of the closet: garments, shoes, a suitcase. Then he emerged carrying a sawn section of tongue-and-groove planking and laid it down and entered the closet again and emerged with a metal box. He set it on the bed and stood looking at the broken lock while he dug a key ring from his pocket and selected a key, and for a time longer he stood with the selected key in his hand, looking at the broken lock, then he put the keys back in his pocket and carefully tilted the contents of the box out upon the bed. Still carefully he sorted the papers, taking them up one at a time and shaking them. Then he upended the box and shook it too and slowly replaced the papers and stood again, looking at the broken lock, with the box in his hands and his head bent. Outside the window he heard some jaybirds swirl shrieking past, and away, their cries whipping away along the wind, and an automobile passed somewhere and died away also. His mother spoke his name again beyond the door, but he didn't move. He heard Dilsey lead her away up the hall, and then a door closed. Then he replaced the box in the closet and flung the garments back into it and went downstairs to the telephone. While he stood there with the receiver to his ear, waiting, Dilsey came down the stairs. She looked at him, without stopping, and went on.

The wire opened. 'This is Jason Compson,' he said, his voice so harsh and thick that he had to repeat himself. 'Jason Compson,' he said, controlling his voice. 'Have a car ready, with a deputy, if you can't go, in ten minutes. I'll be there – What? – Robbery. My house. I know who it – Robbery, I say. Have a car read – What? Aren't you a paid law enforcement – Yes, I'll be there in five minutes. Have that car ready to leave at once. If you don't, I'll report it to the governor.'

He clapped the receiver back and crossed the dining-room, where the scarce-broken meal now lay cold on the table, and entered the kitchen. Dilsey was filling the hot water bottle. Ben sat, tranquil and empty. Beside him Luster looked like a fice dog, brightly watchful. He was eating something. Jason went on across the kitchen.

'Ain't you going to eat no breakfast?' Dilsey said. He paid her no attention. 'Go on and eat yo breakfast, Jason.' He went on. The outer door banged behind him. Luster rose and went to the window and looked out.

'Whoo,' he said, 'Whut happenin up dar? He been beatin' Miss Quentin?'

'You hush yo mouf,' Dilsey said. 'You git Benjy started now en I beat yo head off. You keep him quiet es you kin twell I get back, now.' She screwed the cap on the bottle and went out. They heard her go up the stairs, then they heard Jason pass the house in his car. Then there was no sound in the kitchen save the simmering murmur of the kettle and the clock.

'You know whut I bet?' Luster said. 'I bet he beat her. I bet he knock her in de head en now he gone fer de doctor. Dat's whut I bet.' The clock tick-tocked, solemn and profound. It might have been the dry pulse of the decaying house itself; after a while it whirred and cleared its throat and struck six times. Ben looked up at it, then he looked at the bullet-like silhouette of Luster's head in the window and he begun to bob his head again, drooling. He whimpered.

'Hush up, loony,' Luster said without turning. 'Look like we ain't gwine git to go to no church today.' But Ben sat in the chair, his big soft hands dangling between his knees, moaning faintly. Suddenly he wept, a slow bellowing sound, meaningless and sustained. 'Hush,' Luster said. He turned and lifted his hand. 'You want me to whup you?' But Ben looked at him, bellowing slowly with each expiration. Luster came and shook him. 'You hush dis minute!' he shouted. 'Here,' he said. He hauled Ben out of the chair and dragged the chair around facing the stove and opened the door to the firebox and shoved Ben into the chair. They looked like a tug nudging at a clumsy tanker in a narrow dock. Ben sat down again facing the rosy door. He hushed. Then they heard the clock again, and Dilsey slow on the stairs. When she entered he began to whimper again. Then he lifted his voice.

'Whut you done to him?' Dilsey said. 'Why can't you let him lone dis mawnin, of all times?'

'I ain't doin nothin to him,' Luster said. 'Mr Jason skeered him, dat's whut hit is. He ain't kilt Miss Quentin, is he?'

'Hush, Benjy,' Dilsey said. He hushed. She went to the window and looked out. 'Is it quit raining?' she said.

'Yessum,' Luster said. 'Quit long time ago.'

'Den y'all go out do's a while,' she said. 'I jes got Miss Cahline quiet now?'

'Is we gwine to church?' Luster said.

'I let you know bout dat when de time come. You keep him away fum de house twell I calls you.'

'Kin we go to de pastuh?' Luster said.

'All right. Only you keep him away fum de house. I done stood all I kin.'

'Yessum,' Luster said. 'Whar Mr Jason gone, mammy?'

'Dat's some mo of yo business, ain't it?' Dilsey said. She began to clear the table. 'Hush, Benjy. Luster gwine take you out to play.'

'Whut he done to Miss Quentin, mammy?' Luster said.

'Ain't done nothin to her. You all git on outen here?'

'I bet she ain't here,' Luster said.

Dilsey looked at him. 'How you know she ain't here?'

'Me and Benjy seed her clamb out de window last night. Didn't us, Benjy?'

'You did?' Dilsey said, looking at him.

'We sees her doin hit ev'y night,' Luster said, 'Clamb right down dat pear tree.'

'Don't you lie to me, nigger boy,' Dilsey said.

'I ain't lying. Ask Benjy ef I is.'

'Whyn't you say somethin about it, den?'

'Twarn't none o my business,' Luster said. 'I ain't gwine git mixed up in white folks' business. Come on here, Benjy, les go out do's.'

They went out. Dilsey stood for a while at the table, then she went and cleared the breakfast things from the dining-room and ate her breakfast and cleaned up the kitchen. Then she removed her apron and hung it up and went to the foot of the stairs and listened for a moment. There was no sound. She donned the overcoat and the hat and went across to her cabin.

The rain had stopped. The air now drove out of the south-east, broken overhead into blue patches. Upon the crest of a hill beyond the trees and roofs and spires of town sunlight lay like a pale scrap of cloth, was blotted away. Upon the air a bell came, then as if at a signal, other bells took up the sound and repeated it.

The cabin door opened and Dilsey emerged, again in the maroon cape and the purple gown, and wearing soiled white elbow-length gloves and minus her headcloth now. She came into the yard and called Luster. She waited a while, then she went to the house and around it to the cellar door, moving close to the wall, and looked into the door. Ben sat on the steps. Before him Luster squatted on the damp floor. He held a saw in his left hand, the blade sprung a little by pressure of his hand, and he was in the act of striking the blade with the worn wooden mallet with which she had been making beaten biscuit for more than thirty years. The saw gave forth a single sluggish twang that ceased with lifeless alacrity, leaving the blade in a thin clean curve between Luster's hand and the floor. Still, inscrutable, it bellied.

'Dat's de way he done hit,' Luster said. 'I jes ain't foun de right thing to hit it wid.'

'Dat's whut you doin, is it?' Dilsey said. 'Bring me dat mallet,' she said.

'I ain't hurt hit,' Luster said.

'Bring hit here,' Dilsey said. 'Put dat saw whar you got hit first.'

He put the saw away and brought the mallet to her. Then Ben wailed again, hopeless and prolonged. It was nothing. Just sound. It might have been all time and injustice and sorrow become vocal for an instant by a conjunction of planets.

'Listen at him,' Luster said, 'He been gwine on dat way ev'y since you sont us outen de house. I don't know whut got into him dis mawnin.'

'Bring him here,' Dilsey said.

'Come on, Benjy,' Luster said. He went back down the steps and took Ben's arm. He came obediently, wailing, that slow hoarse sound that ships make, that seems to begin before the sound itself has started, seems to cease before the sound itself has stopped.

'Run and git his cap,' Dilsey said. 'Don't make no noise Miss Cahline kin hear. Hurry, now. We already late.'

'She gwine hear him anyhow, ef you don't stop him.' Luster said.

'He stop when we git off de place,' Dilsey said. 'He smellin hit. Dat's whut hit is.'

'Smell whut, mammy?' Luster said.

'You go git dat cap,' Dilsey said. Luster went on. They stood in the cellar door, Ben one step below her. The sky was broken now into scudding patches that dragged their swift shadows up out of the shabby garden, over the broken fence and across the yard. Dilsey stroked Ben's head, slowly and steadily, smoothing the bang upon his brow. He wailed quietly, unhurriedly. 'Hush,' Dilsey said, 'Hush, now. We be gone in a minute. Hush, now.' He wailed quietly and steadily.

Luster returned, wearing a stiff new straw hat with a coloured band and carrying a cloth cap. The hat seemed to isolate Luster's skull, in the beholder's eyes as a spotlight would, in all its individual planes and angles. So peculiarly individual was its shape that at first glance the hat appeared to be on the head of someone standing immediately behind Luster. Dilsey looked at the hat.

'Whyn't you wear yo old hat?' she said.

'Couldn't find hit,' Luster said.

'I bet you couldn't. I bet you fixed hit last night so you couldn't find hit. You fixin to ruin dat un.'

'Aw, mammy,' Luster said. 'Hit ain't gwine rain.'

'How you know? You go git dat old hat en put dat new un away.'

'Aw, mammy.'

'Den you go git de umbreller.'

'Aw, mammy.'

'Take yo choice,' Dilsey said. 'Git yo old hat, er de umbreller. I don't keer which.'

Luster went to the cabin. Ben wailed quietly.

'Come on,' Dilsey said, 'Dey kin ketch up wid us. We gwine

to hear de singin.' They went around the house, toward the gate. 'Hush,' Dilsey said from time to time as they went down the drive. They reached the gate. Dilsey opened it. Luster was coming down the drive behind them, carrying the umbrella. A woman was with him. 'Here dey come,' Dilsey said. They passed out the gate. 'Now den,' she said. Ben ceased. Luster and his mother overtook them. Frony wore a dress of bright blue silk and a flowered hat. She was a thin woman, with a flat, pleasant face.

'You got six weeks' work right dar on yo back,' Dilsey said. 'Whut you gwine do ef hit rain?'

'Git wet, I reckon,' Frony said. 'I ain't never stopped no rain yit.'

'Mammy always talkin bout hit gwine rain,' Luster said.

'Ef I don't worry bout y'all, I don't know who is,' Dilsey said. 'Come on, we already late.'

'Rev'un Shegog gwine preach today,' Frony said.

'Is?' Dilsey said. 'Who him?'

'He fum Saint Looey,' Frony said. 'Dat big preacher.'

'Huh,' Dilsey said, 'Whut dey needs is a man kin put de fear of God into dese here triflin young niggers.'

'Rev'un Shegog gwine preach today,' Frony said. 'So dey tells.'

They went on along the street. Along its quiet length white people in bright clumps moved churchward, under the windy bells, walking now and then in the random and tentative sun. The wind was gusty, out of the south-east, chill and raw after the warm days.

'I wish you wouldn't keep on bringin him to Church, mammy,' Frony said. 'Folks talkin.'

'Whut folks?' Dilsey said.

'I hears em,' Frony said.

'And I know whut kind of folks,' Dilsey said, 'Trash white folks. Dat's who it is. Thinks he ain't good enough fer white church, but nigger church ain't good enough fer him.'

'Dey talks, jes de same,' Frony said.

'Den you send um to me,' Dilsey said. 'Tell um de good Lawd don't keer whether he smart er not. Don't nobody but white trash keer dat.'

A street turned off at right angles, descending, and became a dirt road. On either hand the land dropped more sharply; a broad flat dotted with small cabins whose weathered roofs were on a level with the crown of the road. They were set in small grassless plots littered with broken things, bricks, planks, crockery, things of a once utilitarian value. What growth there was consisted of rank weeds and the trees were mulberries and locusts and sycamores – trees that partook also of the foul desiccation which surrounded the houses; trees whose very burgeoning seemed to be the sad and stubborn remnant of September, as if even spring had passed them by, leaving them to feed upon the rich and unmistakable smell of negroes in which they grew.

From the doors negroes spoke to them as they passed, to Dilsey usually:

'Sis' Gibson! How you dis mawnin?'

'I'm well. Is you well?'

'I'm right well, I thank you.'

They emerged from the cabins and struggled up the shading levee to the road – men in staid, hard brown or black, with gold watch chains and now and then a stick; young men in cheap violent blues or stripes and swaggering hats; women a little stiffly sibilant, and children in garments bought second hand of white people, who looked at Ben with the covertness of nocturnal animals:

'I bet you won't go up en tech him.'

'How come I won't?'

'I bet you won't. I bet you skeered to.'

'He won't hurt folks. He des a loony.'

'How come a loony won't hurt folks?'

'Dat un won't. I teched him.'

'I bet you won't now.'

'Case Miss Dilsey lookin.'

'You won't noways.'

'He don't hurt folks. He des a loony.'

And steadily the older people speaking to Dilsey, though, unless they were quite old, Dilsey permitted Frony to respond.

'Mammy ain't feeling well dis mawnin.'

'Dat's too bad. But Rev'un Shegog'll cure dat. He'll give her de comfort en de unburdenin.'

The road rose again, to a scene like a painted backdrop. Notched into a cut of red clay crowned with oaks the road appeared to stop short off like a cut ribbon. Beside it a weathered church lifted its crazy steeple like a painted church, and the whole scene was as flat and without perspective as a painted cardboard set upon the ultimate edge of the flat earth, against

the windy sunlight of space and April and a midmorning filled
with bells. Toward the church they thronged with slow sabbath
deliberation. The women and children went on in, the men
stopped outside and talked in quiet groups until the bell ceased
ringing. Then they too entered.

The church had been decorated, with sparse flowers from
kitchen gardens and hedgerows, and with streamers of coloured
crepe paper. Above the pulpit hung a battered Christmas bell,
the accordion sort that collapses. The pulpit was empty, though
the choir was already in place, fanning themselves although it
was not warm.

Most of the women were gathered on one side of the room.
They were talking. Then the bell struck one time and they
dispersed to their seats and the congregation sat for an instant,
expectant. The bell struck again one time. The choir rose and
began to sing and the congregation turned its head as one, as
six small children – four girls with tight pigtails bound with
small scraps of cloth like butterflies, and two boys with close
napped heads, – entered and marched up the aisle, strung
together in a harness of white ribbons and flowers, and followed
by two men in single file. The second man was huge, of a light
coffee colour, imposing in a frock coat and white tie. His head
was magisterial and profound, his neck rolled above his collar
in rich folds. But he was familiar to them, and so the heads
were still reverted when he had passed, and it was not until the
choir ceased singing that they realized that the visiting clergyman
had already entered, and when they saw the man who had
preceded their minister enter the pulpit still ahead of him an
indescribable sound went up, a sigh, a sound of astonishment
and disappointment.

The visitor was undersized, in a shabby alpaca coat. He had
a wizened black face like a small, aged monkey. And all the
while that the choir sang again and while the six children rose
and sang in thin, frightened, tuneless whispers, they watched
the insignificant looking man sitting dwarfed and countrified by
the minister's imposing bulk, with something like consternation.
They were still looking at him with consternation and unbelief
when the minister rose and introduced him in rich, rolling tones
whose very unction served to increase the visitor's insignificance.

'En dey brung dat all de way fum Saint Looey,' Frony
whispered.

'I've knowed de Lawd to use cuiser tools dan dat,' Dilsey said.

'Hush, now,' she said to Ben, 'Dey fixin to sing again in a minute.'

When the visitor rose to speak he sounded like a white man. His voice was level and cold. It sounded too big to have come from him and they listened at first through curiosity, as they would have to a monkey talking. They began to watch him as they would a man on a tight rope. They even forgot his insignificant appearance in the virtuosity with which he ran and poised and swooped upon the cold inflexioniess wire of his voice, so that at last, when with a sort of swooping glide he came to rest again beside the reading desk with one arm resting upon it at shoulder height and his monkey body as reft of all motion as a mummy or an emptied vessel, the congregation sighed as if it waked from a collective dream and moved a little in its seats. Behind the pulpit the choir fanned steadily. Dilsey whispered. 'Hush, now. Dey fixin to sing in a minute.'

Then a voice said, 'Brethren.'

The preacher had not moved. His arm lay yet across the desk, and he still held that pose while the voice died in sonorous echoes between the walls. It was as different as day and dark from his former tone, with a sad, timbrous quality like an alto horn, sinking into their hearts and speaking there again when it had ceased in fading and cumulate echoes.

'Brethren and sisteren,' it said again. The preacher removed his arm and he began to walk back and forth before the desk, his hands clasped behind him, a meagre figure, hunched over upon itself like that of one long immured in striving with the implacable earth, 'I got the recollection and the blood of the Lamb!' He tramped steadily back and forth beneath the twisted paper and the Christmas bell, hunched, his hands clasped behind him. He was like a worn small rock whelmed by the successive waves of his voice. With this body he seemed to feed the voice that, succubus like, has fleshed its teeth in him. And the congregation seemed to watch with its own eyes while the voice consumed him, until he was nothing and they were nothing and there was not even a voice but instead their hearts were speaking to one another in chanting measures beyond the need for words, so that when he came to rest against the reading desk, his monkey face lifted and his whole attitude that of a serene, tortured crucifix that transcended its shabbiness and insignificance and made it of no moment, a long moaning expulsion of breath rose from them, and a woman's single soprano: 'Yes, Jesus!'

As the scudding day passed overhead the dingy windows glowed and faded in ghostly retrograde. A car passed along the road outside, labouring in the sand, died away. Dilsey sat bolt upright, her hand on Ben's knee. Two tears slid down her fallen cheeks, in and out of the myriad coruscations of immolation and abnegation and time.

'Brethren,' the minister said in a harsh whisper, without moving.

'Yes, Jesus!' the woman's voice said, hushed yet.

'Breddren en sistuhn!' His voice rang again, with the horns. He removed his arm and stood erect and raised his hands. 'I got de ricklickshun en de blood of de Lamb!' They did not mark just when his intonation, his pronunciation, became negroid, they just sat swaying a little in their seats as the voice took them into itself.

'When de long, cold – Oh, I tells you, breddren, when de long, cold – I sees de light en I sees de word, po sinner! Dey passed away in Egypt, de swingin chariots; de generations passed away. Wus a rich man: whar he now, O breddren? Wus a po man: whar he now, O sistuhn? Oh I tells you, ef you ain't got de milk en de dew of de old salvation when de long, cold years rolls away!'

'Yes, Jesus!'

'I tells you, breddren, en I tells you, sistuhn, dey'll come a time. Po sinner sayin Let me lay down wid de Lawd, lemme lay down my load. Den whut Jesus gwine say, O breddren? O sistuhn? Is you got de ricklickshun en de blood of de Lamb? Case I ain't gwine load down heaven!'

He fumbled in his coat and took out a handkerchief and mopped his face. A low concerted sound rose from the congregation: 'Mmmmmmmmmmmmm!' The woman's voice said, 'Yes, Jesus! Jesus!'

'Breddren! Look at dem little chillen settin dar. Jesus wus like dat once. He mammy suffered de glory en de pangs. Sometime maybe she helt him at de nightfall, whilst de angels singin him to sleep; maybe she look out de do' en see de Roman po-lice passin.' He tramped back and forth, mopping his face. 'Listen, breddren! I sees de day. Ma'y settin in de do' wid Jesus on her lap, de little Jesus. Like dem chillen dar, de little Jesus. I hears de angels singing de peaceful songs en de glory; I sees de closin

eyes; sees Mary jump up, sees de sojer face: We gwine to kill!
We gwine to kill! We gwine to kill yo little Jesus! I hears de
weepin en de lamentation of de po mammy widout de salvation
en de word of God!'

'Mmmmmmmmmmmmmmmmm! Jesus! Little Jesus!' and
another voice, rising:

'I sees, O Jesus! Oh I sees!' and still another, without words,
like bubbles rising in water.

'I sees hit, breddren! I sees hit! Sees de blastin, blindin sight!
I sees Calvary, wid de sacred trees, sees de thief en de murderer
en de least of dese; I hears de boastin en de braggin: Ef you be
Jesus, lif up yo tree en walk! I hears de wailing of women en de
evenin lamentations; I hears de weepin en de crying en de turnt-
away face of God: dey done kilt Jesus; dey done kilt my Son!'

'Mmmmmmmmmmmmm! Jesus! I sees, O Jesus!'

'O blind sinner! Breddren, I tells you; sistuhn, I says to you,
when de Lawd did turn His Mighty face, say, Ain't gwine
overload heaven! I can see de widowed God shet His do'; I sees
de whelmin flood roll between; I sees de darkness en de death
everlastin upon de generations. Den, lo! Breddren! Yes, breddren!
Whut I see? Whut I see, O sinner? I sees de resurrection en de
light; sees de meek Jesus sayin Dey kilt Me dat ye shall live
again; I died dat dem whut sees en believes shall never die.
Breddren, O breddren! I sees de doom crack en hears de golden
horns shoutin down de glory, en de arisen dead whut got de
blood en de ricklickshun fo de Lamb!'

In the midst of the voices and the hands Ben sat, rapt in his
sweet blue gaze. Dilsey sat bolt upright beside, crying rigidly
and quietly in the annealment and the blood of the remembered
Lamb.

As they walked through the bright noon, up the sandy road
with the dispersing congregation talking easily again group to
group, she continued to weep, unmindful of the talk.

'He sho a preacher, mon! He didn't look like much at first
but hush!'

'He seed de power en de glory.'

'Yes, suh. He seed hit. Face to face he seed hit.'

Dilsey made no sound, her face did not quiver as the tears
took their sunken and devious courses, walking with her head
up, making no effort to dry them away even.

'Whyn't you quit dat, mammy?' Frony said. 'Wid all dese
people lookin. We be passin white folks soon.'

'I've seed de first en de last,' Dilsey said. 'Never you mind me.'

'First en last whut?' Frony said.

'Never you mind,' Dilsey said. 'I seed de beginnin, en now I sees de endin.'

Before they reached the street, though, she stopped and lifted her skirt and dried her eyes on the hem of her topmost underskirt. Then they went on. Ben shambled along beside Dilsey, watching Luster who anticked along ahead, the umbrella in his hand and his new straw hat slanted viciously in the sunlight, like a big foolish dog watching a small clever one. They reached the gate and entered. Immediately Ben began to whimper again, and for a while all of them looked up the drive at the square, paintless house with its rotting portico.

'Whut's gwine on up dar today!' Frony said. 'Something is.'

'Nothin,' Dilsey said. 'You tend to yo business en let de white folks tend to deir'n.'

'Somethin is,' Frony said. I heard him first thing dis mawnin. Tain't none of my business, dough.'

'En I knows whut, too,' Luster said.

'You knows mo dan you got any use fer,' Dilsey said. 'Ain't you jes heard Frony say hit ain't none of yo business? You take Benjy on to de back and keep him quiet twell I put dinner on.'

'I knows whar Miss Quentin is,' Luster said.

'Den jes keep hit,' Dilsey said. 'Soon es Quentin need any of you egvice, I'll let you know. Y'all g'awn en play in de back, now.'

'You know whut gwine happen soon es dey start playing dat ball over yonder,' Luster said.

'Dey won't start fer a while yit. By dat time T.P. be here to take him ridin. Here, you gimme dat new hat.'

Luster gave her the hat and he and Ben went on across the back yard. Ben was still whimpering, though not loud. Dilsey and Frony went to the cabin. After a while Dilsey emerged, again in the faded calico dress, and went to the kitchen. The fire had died down. There was no sound in the house. She put on the apron and went upstairs. There was no sound anywhere. Quentin's room was as they had left it. She entered and picked up the undergarment and put the stocking back in the drawer and closed it. Mrs Compson's door was closed. Dilsey stood beside it for a moment, listening. Then she opened it and entered, entered a pervading reek of camphor. The shades were drawn, the room in half-light, and the bed, so that at first she thought Mrs Compson was asleep and was about to close the door when the other spoke.

'Well?' she said, 'What is it?'

'Hit's me,' Dilsey said. 'You want anything?'

Mrs Compson didn't answer. After a while, without moving her head at all, she said: 'Where's Jason?'

'He ain't come back yit,' Dilsey said. 'Whut you want?'

Mrs Compson said nothing. Like so many cold, weak people, when faced at last by the incontrovertible disaster she exhumed from somewhere a sort of fortitude, strength. In her case it was an unshakable conviction regarding the yet unplumbed event. 'Well,' she said presently, 'Did you find it?'

'Find whut? Whut you talkin about?'

'The note. At least she would have enough consideration to leave a note. Even Quentin did that.'

'Whut you talkin about?' Dilsey said, 'Don't you know she all right? I bet she be walkin right in dis do' befo dark.'

'Fiddlesticks,' Mrs Compson said, 'It's in the blood. Like uncle, like niece. Or mother. I don't know which would be worse. I don't seem to care.'

'Whut you keep on talking that way fur?' Dilsey said. 'Whut she want to do anything like that fur?'

'I don't know. What reason did Quentin have? Under God's heaven what reason did he have? It can't be simply to flout and hurt me. Whoever God is, He would not permit that. I'm a lady. You might not believe that from my offspring, but I am.'

'You des wait en see,' Dilsey said. 'She be here by night, right dar in her bed.' Mrs Compson said nothing. The camphor-soaked cloth lay upon her brow. The black robe lay across the foot of the bed. Dilsey stood with her hand on the door knob.

'Well,' Mrs Compson said. 'What do you want? Are you going to fix some dinner for Jason and Benjamin, or not?'

'Jason ain't come yit,' Dilsey said. 'I gwine fix somethin. You sho you don't want nothing? Yo bottle still hot enough?'

'You might hand me my Bible.'

'I give hit to you dis mawnin, befo I left.'

'You laid it on the edge of the bed. How long did you expect it to stay there?'

Dilsey crossed to the bed and groped among the shadows beneath the edge of it and found the Bible, face down. She smoothed the bent pages and laid the book on the bed again.

Mrs Compson didn't open her eyes. Her hair and the pillow were the same colour, beneath the wimple of the medicated cloth she looked like an old nun praying. 'Don't put it there again,' she said, without opening her eyes. 'That's where you put it before. Do you want me to have to get out of bed to pick it up?'

Dilsey reached the book across her and laid it on the broad side of the bed. 'You can't see to read, noways,' she said. 'You want me to raise de shade a little?'

'No. Let them alone. Go on and fix Jason something to eat.'

Dilsey went out. She closed the door and returned to the kitchen. The stove was almost cold. While she stood there the clock above the cupboard struck ten times. 'One o'clock,' she said aloud, 'Jason ain't comin home. Ise seed de first en de last,' she said, looking at the cold stove, 'I seed de first en de last.' She set out some cold food on a table. As she moved back and forth she sang a hymn. She sang the first two lines over and over to the complete tune. She arranged the meal and went to the door and called Luster, and after a time Luster and Ben entered. Ben was still moaning a little, as to himself.

'He ain't never quit,' Luster said.

'Y'all come on en eat,' Dilsey said. 'Jason ain't coming to dinner.' They sat down at the table. Ben could manage solid food pretty well for himself, though even now, with cold food before him, Dilsey tied a cloth about his neck. He and Luster ate. Dilsey moved about the kitchen, singing the two lines of the hymn which she remembered. 'Y'all kin g'awn en eat,' she said, 'Jason ain't comin home.'

He was twenty miles away at that time. When he left the house he drove rapidly to town, overreaching the slow sabbath groups and the peremptory bells along the broken air. He crossed the empty square and turned into a narrow street that was abruptly quieter even yet, and stopped before a frame house and went up the flower-bordered walk to the porch.

Beyond the screen door people were talking. As he lifted his hand to knock he heard steps, so he withheld his hand until a big man in black broadcloth trousers and a stiff-bosomed white shirt without collar opened the door. He had vigorous untidy iron-grey hair and his grey eyes were round and shiny like a little boy's. He took Jason's hand and drew him into the house, still shaking it.

'Come right in,' he said, 'Come right in.'

'You ready to go now?' Jason said.

'Walk right in,' the other said, propelling him by the elbow into a room where a man and a woman sat. 'You know Myrtle's husband, don't you? Jason Compson, Vernon.'

'Yes,' Jason said. He did not even look at the man, and as the sheriff drew a chair across the room the man said,

'We'll go out so you can talk. Come on, Myrtle.'

'No, no,' the sheriff said, 'You folks keep your seat. I reckon it ain't that serious, Jason? Have a seat.'

'I'll tell you as we go along,' Jason said. 'Get your hat and coat.'

'We'll go out,' the man said, rising.

'Keep your seat,' the sheriff said. 'Me and Jason will go out on the porch.'

'You get your hat and coat,' Jason said. 'They've already got a twelve hour start.' The sheriff led the way back to the porch. A man and a woman passing spoke to him. He responded with a hearty florid gesture. Bells were still ringing, from the direction of the section known as Nigger Hollow. 'Get your hat, Sheriff,' Jason said. The sheriff drew up two chairs.

'Have a seat and tell me what the trouble is.'

'I told you over the phone,' Jason said, standing. 'I did that to save time. Am I going to have to go to law to compel you to do your sworn duty?'

'You sit down and tell me about it,' the sheriff said. 'I'll take care of you all right.'

'Care, hell,' Jason said. 'Is this what you call taking care of me?'

'You're the one that's holding us up,' the sheriff said. 'You sit down and tell me about it.'

Jason told him, his sense of injury and impotence feeding upon its own sound, so that after a time he forgot his haste in the violent cumulation of his self justification and his outrage. The sheriff watched him steady with his cold shiny eyes.

'But you don't know they done it,' he said. 'You just think so.'

'Don't know?' Jason said. 'When I spent two damn days chasing her through alleys, trying to keep her away from him, after I told her what I'd do to her if I ever caught her with him, and you say I don't know that that little b –'

'Now, then,' the sheriff said, 'That'll do. That's enough of that.' He looked out across the street, his hands in his pockets.

'And when I come to you, a commissioned officer of the law,' Jason said.

'That show's in Mottson this week,' the sheriff said.

'Yes,' Jason said, 'And if I could find a law officer that gave a solitary damn about protecting the people that elected him to office, I'd be there too by now.' He repeated his story, harshly recapitulant, seeming to get an actual pleasure out of his outrage and impotence. The sheriff did not appear to be listening at all.

'Jason,' he said, 'What were you doing with three thousand dollars hid in the house?'

'What?' Jason said. 'That's my business where I keep my money. Your business is to help me get it back.'

'Did your mother know you had that much on the place?'

'Look here,' Jason said, 'My house has been robbed. I know who did it and I know where they are. I come to you as the commissioned officer of the law, and I ask you once more, are you going to make any effort to recover my property, or not?'

'What do you aim to do with that girl, if you catch them?'

'Nothing,' Jason said, 'Not anything. I wouldn't lay my hand on her. The bitch that cost me a job, the one chance I ever had to get ahead, that killed my father and is shortening my mother's life every day and made my name a laughing stock in the town. I won't do anything to her,' he said. 'Not anything.'

'You drove that girl into running off, Jason,' the sheriff said.

'How I conduct my family is no business of yours,' Jason said. 'Are you going to help me or not?'

'You drove her away from home,' the sheriff said. 'And I have some suspicions about who that money belongs to that I don't reckon I'll ever know for certain.'

Jason stood, slowly wringing the brim of his hat in his hands. He said quietly: 'You're not going to make any effort to catch them for me?'

'That's not any of my business, Jason. If you had any actual proof, I'd have to act. But without that I don't figger it's any of my business.'

'That's your answer, is it?' Jason said. 'Think well, now.'

'That's it, Jason.'

'All right,' Jason said. He put his hat on. 'You'll regret this. I won't be helpless. This is not Russia, where just because he wears a little metal badge, a man is immune to law.' He went down the steps and got in his car and started the engine. The sheriff watched him drive away, turn, and rush past the house toward town.

The bells were ringing again, high in the scudding sunlight in bright disorderly tatters of sound. He stopped at a filling station and had his tyres examined and the tank filled.

'Gwine on a trip, is you?' the negro asked him. He didn't answer. 'Look like hit gwine fair off, after all,' the negro said.

'Fair off, hell,' Jason said, 'It'll be raining like hell by twelve o'clock.' He looked at the sky, thinking about rain, about the slick clay roads, himself stalled somewhere miles from town. He thought about it with a sort of triumph, of the fact that he was going to miss dinner, that by starting now and so serving his compulsion of haste, he would be at the greatest possible distance from both towns when noon came. It seemed to him that, in this, circumstance was giving him a break, so he said to the negro:

'What the hell are you doing? Has somebody paid you to keep this car standing here as long as you can?'

'Dis here ty' ain't got no air a-tall in hit,' the negro said.

'Then get the hell away from there and let me have that tube,' Jason said.

'Hit up now,' the negro said, rising. 'You kin ride now.'

Jason got in and started the engine and drove off. He went into second gear, the engine spluttering and gasping, and he raced the engine, jamming the throttle down and snapping the choker in and out savagely. 'It's goin to rain,' he said, 'Get me half-way there, and rain like hell.' And he drove on out of the bells and out of town, thinking of himself slogging through the mud, hunting a team. 'And every damn one of them will be at church.' He thought of how he'd find a church at last and take a team and of the owner coming out, shouting at him and of himself striking the man down. 'I'm Jason Compson. See if you can stop me. See if you can elect a man to office that can stop me,' he said, thinking of himself entering the courthouse with a file of soldiers and dragging the sheriff out. 'Thinks he can sit with his hands folded and see me lose my job. I'll show him about jobs.' Of his niece he did not think at all, nor of the arbitrary valuation of the money. Neither of them had had entity or individuality for him for ten years; together they merely symbolized the job in the bank of which he had been deprived before he ever got it.

The air brightened, the running shadow patches were not the

obverse, and it seemed to him that the fact that the day was clearing was another cunning stroke on the part of the foe, the fresh battle toward which he was carrying ancient wounds. From time to time he passed churches, unpainted frame buildings with sheet iron steeples, surrounded by tethered teams and shabby motor-cars, and it seemed to him that each of them was a picket-post where the rear guards of Circumstance peeped fleetingly back at him. 'And damn You, too,' he said, 'See if You can stop me,' thinking of himself, his file of soldiers with the manacled sheriff in the rear, dragging Omnipotence down from His throne, if necessary; of the embattled legions of both hell and heaven through which he tore his way and put his hands at last on his fleeing niece.

The wind was out of the south-east. It blew steadily upon his cheek. It seemed that he could feel the prolonged blow of it sinking through his skull, and suddenly with an old premonition he clapped the brakes on and stopped and sat perfectly still. Then he lifted his hand to his neck and began to curse, and sat there, cursing in a harsh whisper. When it was necessary for him to drive for any length of time he fortified himself with a handkerchief soaked in camphor, which he would tie about his throat when clear of town, thus inhaling the fumes, and he got out and lifted the seat cushion on the chance that there might be a forgotten one there. He looked beneath both seats and stood again for a while, cursing, seeing himself mocked by his own triumphing. He closed his eyes, leaning on the door. He could return and get the forgotten camphor, or he could go on. In either case, his head would be splitting, but at home he could be sure of finding camphor on Sunday, while if he went on he could not be sure. But if he went back, he would be an hour and a half later in reaching Mottson. 'Maybe I can drive slow,' he said. 'Maybe I can drive slow, thinking of something else –'

He got in and started. 'I'll think of something else,' he said, so he thought about Lorraine. He imagined himself in bed with her, only he was just lying beside her, pleading with her to help him, then he thought of the money again, and that he had been outwitted by a woman, a girl. If he could just believe it was the man who had robbed him. But to have been robbed of that which was to have compensated him for the lost job, which he had acquired through so much effort and risk, by the very symbol of the lost job itself, and worst of all, by a bitch of a

girl. He drove on, shielding his face from the steady wind with
the corner of his coat.

He could see the opposed forces of his destiny and his will
drawing swiftly together now, toward a junction that would be
irrevocable; he became cunning. I can't make a blunder, he
told himself. There would be just one right thing, without
alternatives: he must do that. He believed that both of them
would know him on sight, while he'd have to trust to seeing her
first, unless the man still wore the red tie. And the fact that he
must depend on that red tie seemed to be the sum of the
impending disaster; he could almost smell it, feel it above the
throbbing of his head.

He crested the final hill. Smoke lay in the valley, and roofs,
a spire or two above trees. He drove down the hill and into the
town, slowing, telling himself again of the need for caution, to
find where the tent was located first. He could not see very well
now, and he knew that it was the disaster which kept telling
him to go directly and get something for his head. At a filling
station they told him that the tent was not up yet, but that the
show cars were on a siding at the station. He drove there.

Two gaudily painted pullman cars stood on the track. He
reconnoitred them before he got out. He was trying to breathe
shallowly, so that the blood would not beat so in his skull. He
got out and went along the station wall, watching the cars. A
few garments hung out of the windows, limp and crinkled, as
though they had been recently laundered. On the earth beside
the steps of one sat three canvas chairs. But he saw no sign of
life at all until a man in a dirty apron came to the door and
emptied a pan of dishwater with a broad gesture, the sunlight
glinting on the metal belly of the pan, then entered the car
again.

Now I'll have to take him by surprise, before he can warn
them, he thought. It never occurred to him that they might not
be there, in the car. That they should not be there, that the
whole result should not hinge on whether he saw them first or
they saw him first, would be opposed to all nature and contrary
to the whole rhythm of events. And more than that: he must
see them first, get the money back, then what they did would
be of no importance to him, while otherwise the whole world
would know that he, Jason Compson, had been robbed by
Quentin, his niece, a bitch.

He reconnoitred again. Then he went to the car and mounted

the steps, swiftly and quietly, and paused at the door. The galley was dark, rank with stale food. The man was a white blur, singing in a cracked, shaky tenor. An old man, he thought, and not as big as I am. He entered the car as the man looked up.

'Hey?' the man said, stopping his song.

'Where are they?' Jason said. 'Quick. In the sleeping car?'

'Where's who?' the man said.

'Don't lie to me,' Jason said. He blundered on in the cluttered obscurity.

'What's that?' the other said, 'Who you calling a liar?' And when Jason grasped his shoulder he exclaimed, 'Look out, fellow!'

'Don't lie,' Jason said, 'Where are they?'

'Why, you bastard,' the man said. His arm was frail and thin in Jason's grasp. He tried to wrench free, then he turned and fell to scrabbling on the littered table behind him.

'Come on,' Jason said, 'Where are they?'

'I'll tell you where they are', the man shrieked, 'Lemme find my butcher knife.'

'Here,' Jason said, trying to hold the other, 'I'm just asking you a question.'

'You bastard,' the other shrieked, scrabbling at the table. Jason tried to grasp him in both arms, trying to prison the puny fury of him. The man's body felt so old, so frail, yet so fatally single-purposed that for the first time Jason saw clear and unshadowed the disaster toward which he rushed.

'Quit it!' he said, 'Here! Here! I'll get out. Give me time, and I'll get out.'

'Call me a liar,' the other wailed, 'Lemme go. Lemme go just one minute. I'll show you.'

Jason glared wildly about, holding the other. Outside it was now bright and sunny, swift and bright and empty, and he thought of the people soon to be going quietly home to Sunday dinner, decorously festive, and of himself trying to hold the fatal, furious little old man whom he dared not release long enough to turn his back and run.

'Will you quit long enough for me to get out?' he said, 'Will you?' But the other still struggled, and Jason freed one hand and struck him on the head. A clumsy, hurried blow, and not hard, but the other slumped immediately and slid clattering among pans and buckets to the floor. Jason stood above him, panting, listening. Then he turned and ran from the car. At the door he restrained himself and descended more slowly and stood there again. His breath made a hah hah hah sound and he stood there trying to repress it, darting his gaze this way and that, when at a scuffling sound behind him he turned in time to see the little old man leaping awkwardly and furiously from the vestibule, a rusty hatchet high in his hand.

He grasped at the hatchet, feeling no shock but knowing that he was falling, thinking So this is how it'll end, and he believed that he was about to die and when something crashed against the back of his head he thought How did he hit me there? Only maybe he hit me a long time ago, he thought. And I just now felt it, and he thought Hurry. Hurry. Get it over with, and then a furious desire not to die seized him and he struggled, hearing the old man wailing and cursing in his cracked voice.

He still struggled when they hauled him to his feet, but they held him and he ceased.

'Am I bleeding much?' he said, 'The back of my head. Am I bleeding?' He was still saying that while he felt himself being propelled rapidly away, heard the old man's thin furious voice dying away behind him. 'Look at my head,' he said, 'Wait, I –'

'Wait, hell,' the man who held him said, 'That damn little wasp'll kill you. Keep going. You ain't hurt.'

'He hit me,' Jason said. 'Am I bleeding?'

'Keep going,' the other said. He led Jason on around the corner of the station, to the empty platform where an express truck stood, where grass grew rigidly in a plot bordered with

rigid flowers and a sign in electric lights: Keep your

on Mottson, the gap filled by a human eye with an electric pupil. The man released him.

'Now,' he said, 'You get on out of here and stay out. What were you trying to do? Commit suicide?'

'I was looking for two people,' Jason said. 'I just asked him where they were.'

'Who you looking for?'

'It's a girl,' Jason said. 'And a man. He had on a red tie in Jefferson yesterday. With this show. They robbed me.'

'Oh,' the man said. 'You're the one, are you. Well, they ain't here.'

'I reckon so,' Jason said. He leaned against the wall and put his hand to the back of his head and looked at his palm. 'I thought I was bleeding,' he said, 'I thought he hit me with that hatchet.'

'You hit your head on the rail,' the man said. 'You better go on. They ain't here.'

'Yes. He said they were not here. I thought he was lying.'

'Do you think I'm lying?' the man said.

'No,' Jason said. 'I know they're not here.'

'I told him to get the hell out of there, both of them,' the man said. 'I won't have nothing like that in my show. I run a respectable show, with a respectable troupe.'

'Yes,' Jason said. 'You don't know where they went?'

'No. And I don't want to know. No member of my show can pull a stunt like that. You her – brother?'

'No,' Jason said. 'It don't matter. I just wanted to see them. You sure he didn't hit me? No blood, I mean.'

'There would have been blood if I hadn't got there when I did. You stay away from here, now. That little bastard'll kill you. That your car yonder?'

'Yes.'

'Well, you get in it and go back to Jefferson. If you find them, it won't be in my show. I run a respectable show. You say they robbed you?'

'No,' Jason said, 'It don't make any difference.' He went to the car and got in. What is it I must do? he thought. Then he remembered. He started the engine and drove slowly up the street until he found a drug-store. The door was locked. He stood for a while with his hand on the knob and his head bent a little. Then he turned away and when a man came along after a while he asked if there was a drug-store open anywhere, but there was not. Then he asked when the northbound train ran, and the man told him at two-thirty. He crossed the pavement and got in the car again and sat there. After a while two negro lads passed. He called to them.

'Can either of you boys drive a car?'

'Yes, suh.'

'What'll you charge to drive me to Jefferson right away?' They looked at one another, murmuring.

'I'll pay a dollar,' Jason said.

They murmured again. 'Couldn't go fer dat,' one said.

'What will you go for?'

'Kin you go?' one said.

'I can't git off,' the other said. 'Whyn't you drive him up dar? You ain't got nothin to do.'

'Yes, I is.'

'Whut you got to do?'

They murmured again, laughing.

'I'll give you two dollars,' Jason said. 'Either of you.'

'I can't git away neither,' the first said.

'All right,' Jason said. 'Go on.'

He sat there for some time. He heard a clock strike the half-hour, then people began to pass, in Sunday and Easter clothes. Some looked at him as they passed, at the man sitting quietly behind the wheel of a small car, with his invisible life ravelled out about him like a wornout sock. After a while a negro in overalls came up.

'Is you de one wants to go to Jefferson?' he said.

'Yes,' Jason said. 'What'll you charge me?'

'Fo dollars.'

'Give you two.'

'Can't go fer no less'n fo.' The man in the car sat quietly. He wasn't even looking at him. The negro said, 'You want me er not?'

'All right,' Jason said, 'Get in.'

He moved over and the negro took the wheel. Jason closed his eyes. I can get something for it at Jefferson, he told himself, easing himself to the jolting, I can get something there. They drove on, along the streets where people were turning peacefully into houses and Sunday dinners, and on out of town. He thought that. He wasn't thinking of home, where Ben and Luster were eating cold dinner at the kitchen table. Something – the absence of disaster, threat, in any constant evil – permitted him to forget Jefferson as any place which he had ever seen before, where his life must resume itself.

When Ben and Luster were done Dilsey sent them out doors. 'And see kin you keep let him alone twell fo o'clock. T.P. be here den.'

'Yessum,' Luster said. They went out. Dilsey ate her dinner and cleared up the kitchen. Then she went to the foot of the stairs and listened, but there was no sound. She returned through the kitchen and out the outer door and stopped on the steps. Ben and Luster were not in sight, but while she stood there she heard another sluggish twang from the direction of the cellar door and she went to the door and looked down upon a repetition of the morning's scene.

'He done it jes dat way,' Luster said. He contemplated the motionless saw with a kind of hopeful dejection. 'I ain't got de right thing to hit it wid yit,' he said.

'En you ain't gwine find hit down here, neither,' Dilsey said. 'You take him on out in de sun. You bofe get pneumonia down here on dis wet flo.'

She waited and watched them cross the yard toward a clump of cedar trees near the fence. Then she went on to her cabin.

'Now, don't you git started,' Luster said, 'I had enough trouble wid you to-day.' There was a hammock made of barrel staves slatted into woven wires. Luster lay down in the swing, but Ben went on vaguely and purposelessly. He began to whimper again. 'Hush, now,' Luster said, 'I fixin to whup you.' He lay back in the swing. Ben had stopped moving but Luster could hear him whimpering. 'Is you gwine hush, er ain't you?' Luster said. He got up and followed and came upon Ben squatting before a small mound of earth. At either end of it an empty bottle of blue glass that once contained poison was fixed in the ground. In one was a withered stalk of jimson weed. Ben squatted before it, moaning, a slow, inarticulate sound. Still moaning he sought vaguely about and found a twig and put it in the other bottle 'Whyn't you hush?' Luster said, 'You want me to give you somethin' to sho nough moan about? Sposin I does dis.' He knelt and swept the bottle suddenly up and behind him. Ben ceased moaning. He squatted, looking at the small depression where the bottle had sat, then as he drew his lungs full Luster brought the bottle back into view. 'Hush!' he hissed, 'Don't you dast to beller! Don't you. Dar hit is. See? Here. You fixin to start ef you stays here. Come on, les go see ef dey started knockin ball yit.' He took Ben's arm and drew him up and they went to the fence and stood side by side there, peering between the matted honeysuckle not yet in bloom.

'Dar,' Luster said, 'Dar come some. See um?'

They watched the foursome play on to the green and out, and move to the tee and drive. Ben watched, whimpering, slobbering. When the foursome went on he followed along the fence, bobbing and moaning. One said,

'Here, caddie. Bring the bag.'

'Hush, Benjy,' Luster said, but Ben went on at his shambling trot, clinging to the fence, wailing in his hoarse, hopeless voice. The man played and went on, Ben keeping pace with him until the fence turned at right angles, and he clung to the fence, watching the people move on and away.

'Will you hush now?' Luster said, 'Will you hush now?' He shook Ben's arm. Ben clung to the fence, wailing steadily and hoarsely. 'Ain't you gwine stop?' Luster said, 'Or is you?' Ben gazed through the fence. 'All right, den,' Luster said, 'You want somethin to beller about?' He looked over his shoulder, toward the house. Then he whispered: 'Caddy! Beller now. Caddy! Caddy! Caddy!'

A moment later, in the slow intervals of Ben's voice, Luster heard Dilsey calling. He took Ben by the arm and they crossed the yard toward her.

'I tole you he warn't gwine stay quiet,' Luster said.

'You vilyun!' Dilsey said, 'Whut you done to him?'

'I ain't done nothin. I tole you when dem folks start playin, he git started up.'

'You come on here,' Dilsey said. 'Hush, Benjy. Hush, now.' But he wouldn't hush. They crossed the yard quickly and went to the cabin and entered. 'Run git dat shoe,' Dilsey said. 'Don't you sturb Miss Cahline, now. Ef she say anything, tell her I got him. Go on, now; you kin sho do dat right, I reckon.' Luster went out. Dilsey led Ben to the bed and drew him down beside her and she held him, rocking back and forth, wiping his drooling mouth upon the hem of her skirt. 'Hush, now,' she said, stroking his head, 'Hush. Dilsey got you.' But he bellowed slowly, abjectly, without tears; the grave hopeless sound of all voiceless misery under the sun. Luster returned, carrying a white satin slipper. It was yellow now, and cracked and soiled, and when they placed it into Ben's hand he hushed for a while. But he still whimpered, and soon he lifted his voice again.

'You reckon you kin find T.P.?' Dilsey said.

'He say yistiddy he gwine out to St John's today. Say he be back at fo.'

Dilsey rocked back and forth, stroking Ben's head.

'Dis long time, O Jesus,' she said, 'Dis long time.'

'I kin drive dat surrey, mammy,' Luster said.

'You kill bofe y'all,' Dilsey said, 'You do hit fer devilment. I knows you got plenty sense to. But I can't trust you. Hush, now,' she said. 'Hush. Hush.'

'Nome I won't,' Luster said. 'I drives wid T.P.' Dilsey rocked back and forth, holding Ben. 'Miss Cahline say ef you can't quiet him, she gwine git up en come down en do hit.

'Hush, honey,' Dilsey said, stroking Ben's head. 'Luster, honey,' she said, 'Will you think about yo ole mammy en drive dat surrey right?'

'Yessum,' Luster said. 'I drive hit jes like T.P.'

Dilsey stroked Ben's head, rocking back and forth. 'I does de bes I kin,' she said. 'Lawd knows dat. Go git it, den,' she said, rising. Luster scuttled out. Ben held the slipper, crying. 'Hush, now. Luster gone to git de surrey en take you to de graveyard. We ain't gwine risk gittin yo cap,' she said. She went to a closet contrived of a calico curtain hung across a corner of the room and got the felt hat she had worn. 'We's down to worse'n dis, ef folks jes knowed,' she said. 'You's de Lawd's chile, anyway. En I be His'n too, fo long, praise Jesus. Here.' She put the hat on his head and buttoned his coat. He wailed steadily. She took the slipper from him and put it away and they went out. Luster came up, with an ancient white horse in a battered and lopsided surrey.

'You gwine be careful, Luster?' she said.

'Yessum,' Luster said. She helped Ben into the back seat. He had ceased crying, but now he began to whimper again.

'Hit's his flower,' Luster said, 'Wait, I'll git him one.'

'You set right dar,' Dilsey said. She went and took the cheekstrap. 'Now, hurry en git him one.' Luster ran around the house, toward the garden. He came back with a single narcissus.

'Dat un broke,' Dilsey said, 'Whyn't you git him a good un?'

'Hit de onliest one I could find,' Luster said. 'Y'all took all of um Friday to dec'rate de church. Wait, I'll fix hit.' So while Dilsey held the horse Luster put a splint on the flower stalk with a twig and two bits of string and gave it to Ben. Then he mounted and took the reins. Dilsey still held the bridle.

'You knows de way now?' she said, 'Up de street, round de square, to de graveyard, den straight back home.'

'Yessum,' Luster said, 'Hum up, Queenie.'

'You gwine be careful, now?'

'Yessum.' Dilsey released the bridle.

'Hum up, Queenie,' Luster said.

'Here,' Dilsey said, 'You han me dat whup.'

'Aw, mammy,' Luster said.

'Give hit here,' Dilsey said, approaching the wheel. Luster gave it to her reluctantly.

'I won't never git Queenie started now.'

'Never you mind about dat,' Dilsey said. 'Queenie know mo

bout whar she gwine dan you does. All you got to do is set dar en hold dem reins. You knows de way, now?'

'Yessum. Same way T.P. goes ev'y Sunday.'

'Den you do de same thing dis Sunday.'

'Cose I is. Ain't I drove fer T.P. mo'n a hund'ed times?'

'Den do hit again,' Dilsey said. 'G'awn, now. En ef you hurts Benjy, nigger boy, I don't know whut I do. You bound fer de chain-gang, but I'll send you dar fo even chain-gang ready fer you.'

'Yessum,' Luster said. 'Hum up, Queenie.'

He flapped the lines on Queenie's broad back and the surrey lurched into motion.

'You, Luster!' Dilsey said.

'Hum up, dar!' Luster said. He flapped the lines again. With subterranean rumblings Queenie jogged slowly down the drive and turned into the street, where Luster exhorted her into a gait resembling a prolonged and suspended fall in a forward direction.

Ben quit whimpering. He sat in the middle of the seat, holding the repaired flower upright in his fist, his eyes serene and ineffable. Directly before him Luster's bullet head turned backward continually until the house passed from view, then he pulled to the side of the street and while Ben watched him he descended and broke a switch from a hedge. Queenie lowered her head and fell to cropping the grass until Luster mounted and hauled her head up and harried her into motion again, then he squared his elbows and with the switch and the reins held high he assumed a swaggering attitude out of all proportion to the sedate clopping of Queenie's hoofs and the organlike basso of her internal accompaniment. Motors passed them, and pedestrians; once a group of half grown negroes:

'Dar Luster. Whar you gwine, Luster? To de boneyard?'

'Hi,' Luster said, 'Ain't de same boneyard y'all headed fer. Hum up, elefump.'

They approached the square, where the Confederate soldier gazed with empty eyes beneath his marble hand into wind and weather. Luster took still another notch in himself and gave the impervious Queenie a cut with the switch, casting his glance about the square. 'Dar Mr Jason's car,' he said then he spied another group of negroes. 'Les show dem niggers how quality does, Benjy,' he said, 'Whut you say?' He looked back. Ben sat, holding the flower in his fist, his gaze empty and untroubled.

Luster hit Queenie again and swung her to the left at the monument.

For an instant Ben sat in an utter hiatus. Then he bellowed. Bellow on bellow, his voice mounted, with scarce interval for breath. There was more than astonishment in it, it was horror; shock; agony eyeless, tongueless; just sound, and Luster's eyes backrolling for a white instant. 'Gret God,' he said, 'Hush! Hush! Gret God!' He whirled again and struck Queenie with the switch. It broke and he cast it away and with Ben's voice mounting toward its unbelievable crescendo Luster caught up the end of the reins and leaned forward as Jason came jumping across the square and on to the step.

With a backhanded blow he hurled Luster aside and caught the reins and sawed Queenie about and doubled the reins back and slashed her across the hips. He cut her again and again, into a plunging gallop, while Ben's hoarse agony roared about them, and swung her about to the right of the monument. Then he struck Luster over the head with his fist.

'Don't you know any better than to take him to the left?' he said. He reached back and struck Ben, breaking the flower stalk again. 'Shut up!' he said, 'Shut up!' He jerked Queenie back and jumped down. 'Get to hell on home with him. If you ever cross that gate with him again, I'll kill you!'

'Yes, suh!' Luster said. He took the reins and hit Queenie with the end of them. 'Git up! Git up, dar! Benjy, fer God's sake!'

Ben's voice roared. Queenie moved again, her feet began to clop-clop steadily again, and at once Ben hushed. Luster looked quickly back over his shoulder, then he drove on. The broken flower drooped over Ben's fist and his eyes were empty and blue and serene again as cornice and facade flowed smoothly once more from left to right; post and tree, window and doorway, and signboard, each in its ordered place.

APPENDIX
COMPSON: 1699–1945

IKKEMOTUBBE. A dispossessed American king. Called 'l'Homme' (and sometimes 'de l'homme') by his foster-brother, a Chevalier of France, who had he not been born too late could have been among the brightest in that glittering galaxy of knightly blackguards who were Napoleon's marshals, who thus translated the Chickasaw title meaning 'The Man'; which translation Ikkemotubbe, himself a man of wit and imagination as well as a shrewd judge of character, including his own, carried one step further and anglicized it to 'Doom'. Who granted out of his vast lost domain a solid square mile of virgin North Mississippi dirt as truly angled as the four corners of a cardtable top (forested then because these were the old days before 1833 when the stars fell and Jefferson Mississippi was one long rambling one-storey mud chinked log building housing the Chickasaw Agent and his trading-post store) to the grandson of a Scottish refugee who had lost his own birthright by casting his lot with a king who himself had been dispossessed. This in partial return for the right to proceed in peace, by whatever means he and his people saw fit, afoot or ahorse provided they were Chickasaw horses, to the wild western land presently to be called Oklahoma: not knowing then about the oil.

JACKSON. A Great White Father with a sword. (An old duellist, a brawling lean fierce mangy durable imperishable old lion who set the well-being of the nation above the White House and the health of his new political party above either and above them all set not his wife's honour but the principle that honour must be defended whether it was or not because defended it was whether or not.) Who patented sealed and countersigned the grant with his own hand in his old tepee in Wassi Town, not knowing about the oil either: so that one day the homeless descendants of the dispossessed would ride supine with drink and splendidly comatose above the dusty allotted harbourage of their bones in specially built scarlet-painted hearses and fire-engines.

These were Compsons:

QUENTIN MACLACHAN. Son of a Glasgow printer, orphaned and raised by his mother's people in the Perth highlands. Fled to Carolina from Culloden Moor with a claymore and the tartan he wore by day and slept under by night, and little else. At eighty, having fought once against an English king and lost, he would not make that mistake twice and so fled again one night in 1779, with his infant grandson and the tartan (the claymore had vanished, along with his son, the grandson's father, from one of Tarleton's regiments on a Georgia battlefield about a year ago) into Kentucky, where a neighbour named Boon or Boone had already established a settlement.

CHARLES STUART. Attained and proscribed by name and grade in his British regiment. Left for dead in a Georgia swamp by his own retreating army and then by the advancing American one, both of which were wrong. He still had the claymore even when on his home-made wooden leg he finally overtook his father and son four years later at Harrodsburg, Kentucky, just in time to bury the father and enter upon a long period of being a split personality while still trying to be the schoolteacher which he believed he wanted to be, until he gave up at last and became the gambler he actually was and which no Compson seemed to realize they all were provided the gambit was desperate and the odds long enough. Succeeded at last in risking not only his neck but the security of his family and the very integrity of the name he would leave behind him, by joining the confederation headed by an acquaintance named Wilkinson (a man of considerable talent and influence and intellect and power) in a plot to secede the whole Mississippi Valley from the United States and join it to Spain. Fled in his turn when the bubble burst (as anyone except a Compson schoolteacher should have known it would), himself unique in being the only one of the plotters who had to flee the country: this not from the vengeance and retribution of the government which he had attempted to dismember, but from the furious revulsion of his late confederates now frantic for their own safety. He was not expelled from the United States, he talked himself countryless, his expulsion due not to the treason but to his having been so vocal and vociferant in the conduct of it, burning each bridge vocally behind him before he had even reached the place to build the next one: so that it was no provost marshal nor even a civic agency but his late co-plotters themselves who put afoot the movement to evict him from Kentucky and the United States and, if they had caught him, probably from the world too. Fled by night, running true to family tradition, with his son and the old claymore and the tartan.

JASON LYCURGUS. Who, driven perhaps by the compulsion of the flamboyant name given him by the sardonic embittered woodenlegged indomitable father who perhaps still believed with his heart that what he wanted to be was a classicist schoolteacher, rode up the Natchez Trace one day in 1811 with a pair of fine pistols and one meagre saddlebag on a small lightwaisted but stronghocked mare which could do the first two furlongs in definitely under the halfminute and the next two in not appreci-ably more, though that was all. But it was enough: who reached the Chickasaw Agency at Okatoba (which in 1860 was still called Old Jefferson) and went no further. Who within six months was the Agent's clerk and within twelve his partner, officially still the clerk though actually halfowner of what was now a considerable store stocked with the mare's winnings in races against the horses of Ikkemotubbe's young men which he, Compson, was always careful to limit to a quarter or at most three furlongs; and in the next year it was Ikkemotubbe who owned the little mare and Compson owned the solid square mile of land which someday would be almost in the centre of the town of Jefferson, forested then and still forested twenty years later though rather a park than a forest by that time, with its slavequarters and stables and kitchen-gardens and the formal lawns and promenades and pavilions laid out by the same architect who built the columned porticoed house furnished by steamboat from France and New Orleans, and still the square intact mile in 1840 (with not only the little white village called Jefferson beginning to enclose it but an entire white county about to surround it because in a few years now Ikkemotubbe's descendants and people would be gone, those remaining living not as warriors and hunters but as white

men – as shiftless farmers or, here and there, the masters of what
they too called plantations and the owners of shiftless slaves, a
little dirtier than the white man, a little lazier, a little crueller –
until ar last even the wild blood itself would have vanished, to
be seen only occasionally in the noseshape of a Negro on a
cottonwagon or a white sawmill hand or crapper or locomotive
fireman), known as the Compson Domain then, since now it was
fit to breed princes, statesmen and generals and bishops, to
avenge the dispossessed Compson from Culloden and Carolina
and Kentucky, then known as the Governor's house because sure
enough in time it did produce or at least spawn a governor –
Quentin MacLachan again, after the Culloden grandfather – and
still known as the Old Governor's even after it had spawned (1861)
a general - (called so by predetermined accord and agreement by
the whole town and county, as though they knew even then and
beforehand that the old governor was the last Compson who
would not fail at everything he touched save longevity or suicide)
– the Brigadier Jason Lycurgus II who failed at Shiloh in '62 and
failed again though not so badly at Resaca in '64, who put the
first mortgage on the still intact square mile to a New England
carpetbagger in '66, after the old town had been burned by the
Federal General Smith and the new little town, in time to be
populated mainly by the descendants not of Compsons but of
Snopeses, had begun to encroach and then nibble at and into it
as the failed brigadier spent the next forty years selling fragments
of it off to keep up the mortgage on the remainder: until one
day in 1900 he died quietly on an army cot in the hunting and
fishing camp in the Tallahatchie River bottom where he passed
most of the end of his days.

    And even the old governor was forgotten now; what was left
of the old square mile was now known merely as the Compson
place – the weed-choked traces of the old ruined lawns and
promenades, the house which had needed painting too long
already, the scaling columns of the portico where Jason III (bred
for a lawyer and indeed he kept an office upstairs above the
Square, where entombed in dusty filingcases some of the oldest
names in the county – Holston and Sutpen, Grenier and Beauchamp and Coldfield – faded year by year among the bottomless
labyrinths of chancery: and who knows what dream in the perennial heart of his father, now completing the third of his three
avatars – the one as son of a brilliant and gallant statesman, the
second as battle-leader of brave and gallant men, the child as a

sort of privileged pseudo-Daniel Boone-Robinson Crusoe, who had not returned to juvenility because actually he had never left it – that the lawyer's office might again be the ante-room to the governor's mansion and the old splendour) sat all day long with a decanter of whisky and a litter of dogeared Horaces and Livys and Catulluses, composing (it was said) caustic and satiric eulogies on both his dead and his living fellow-townsmen, who sold the last of the property, except that fragment containing the house and the kitchen-garden and the collapsing stables and one servant's cabin in which Dilsey's family lived, to a golfclub for the ready money with which his daughter Candace could have her fine wedding in April and his son Quentin could finish one year at Harvard and commit suicide in the following June of 1910; already known as the Old Compson place even while Compsons were still living in it on that spring dusk in 1928 when the old governor's doomed lost nameless seventeen-year-old great-great-grandaughter robbed her last remaining sane male relative (her uncle Jason IV) of his secret hoard of money and climbed down a rainpipe and ran off with a pitchman in a travelling streetshow, and still known as the Old Compson place long after all traces of Compsons were gone from it: after the widowed mother died and Jason IV, no longer needing to fear Dilsey now, committed his idiot brother, Benjamin, to the State Asylum in Jackson and sold the house to a countryman who operated it as a boarding-house for juries and horse-and mule-traders, and still known as the Old Compson place even after the boardinghouse (and presently the golfcourse too) had vanished and the old square mile was even intact again in row after row of small crowded jerrybuilt individually-owned demi-urban bungalows.

And these:
QUENTIN III. Who loved not his sister's body but some concept of Compson honour precariously and (he knew well) only temporarily supported by the minute fragile membrane of her maidenhead as a miniature replica of all the whole vast globy earth may be poised on the nose of a trained seal. Who loved not the idea of the incest which he would not commit, but some presbyterian concept of its eternal punishment: he, not God, could by that means cast himself and his sister both into hell, where he could guard her forever and keep her forevermore intact amid the eternal fires. But who loved death above all, who loved only

death, loved and lived in a deliberate and almost perverted anticipation of death as a lover loves and deliberately refrains from the waiting willing friendly tender incredible body of his beloved, until he can no longer bear not the refraining but the restraint and so flings, hurls himself, relinquishing, drowning. Committed suicide in Cambridge, Massachusetts, June 1910, two months after his sister's wedding, waiting first to complete the current academic year and so get the full value of his paid-in-advance tuition, not because he had his old Culloden and Carolina and Kentucky grandfathers in him but because the remaining piece of the old Compson mile which had been sold to pay for his sister's wedding and his year at Harvard had been the one thing, excepting that same sister and the sight of an open fire, which his youngest brother, born an idiot, had loved.

CANDACE (CADDY). Doomed and knew it, accepted the doom without either seeking or fleeing it. Loved her brother despite him, loved not only him but loved in him that bitter prophet and inflexible corruptless judge of what he considered the family's honour and its doom, as he thought he loved but really hated in her what he considered the frail doomed vessel of its pride and the foul instrument of its disgrace; not only this, she loved him not only in spite of but because of the fact that he himself was incapable of love, accepting the fact that he must value above all not her but the virginity of which she was custodian and on which she placed no value whatever: the frail physical stricture which to her was no more than a hangnail would have been. Knew the brother loved death best of all and was not jealous, would (and perhaps in the calculation and deliberation of her marriage did) have handed him the hypothetical hemlock. Was two months pregnant with another man's child which regardless of what its sex would be she had already named Quentin after the brother whom they both (she and the brother) knew was already the same as dead, when she married (1910) an extremely eligible young Indianian she and her mother had met while vacationing at French Lick the summer before. Divorced by him 1911. Married 1920 to a minor moving-picture magnate, Hollywood California. Divorced by mutual agreement, Mexico 1925. Vanished in Paris with the German occupation, 1940, still beautiful and probably still wealthy too since she did not look within fifteen years of her actual forty-eight, and was not heard of again. Except there was

a woman in Jefferson, the county librarian, a mouse-sized and -
coloured woman who had never married, who had passed through
the city schools in the same class with Candace Compson and
then spent the rest of her life trying to keep *Forever Amber* in its
orderly overlapping avatars and *Jurgen* and *Tom Jones* out of the
hands of the highschool juniors and seniors who could reach
them down without even having to tiptoe from the back shelves
where she herself would have to stand on a box to hide them.
One day in 1943, after a week of a distraction bordering on
disintegration almost, during which those entering the library
would find her always in the act of hurriedly closing her desk
drawer and turning the key in it (so that the matrons, wives of
the bankers and doctors and lawyers, some of whom had also
been in that old highschool class, who came and went in the
afternoons with the copies of the *Forever Ambers*, and the volumes
of Thorne Smith carefully wrapped from view in sheets of Memphis and Jackson newspapers, believed she was on the verge of
illness or perhaps even loss of mind), she closed and locked the
library in the middle of the afternoon and with her handbag
clasped tightly under her arm and two feverish spots of determi-
nation in her ordinary colourless cheeks, she entered the farmers'
supply store where Jason IV had started as a clerk and where he
now owned his own business as a buyer of and dealer in cotton,
striding on through that gloomy cavern which only men ever
entered – a cavern cluttered and walled and stalagmite-hung with
ploughs and discs and loops of trace-chain and singletrees and
mule-collars and sidemeat and cheap shoes and horse-linament
and flour and molasses, gloomy because the goods it contained
were not shown but hidden rather since those who supplied
Mississippi farmers or at least Negro Mississippi farmers for a
share of the crop did not wish, until that crop was made and its
value approximately computable, to show them what they could
learn to want but only to supply them on specific demand with
what they could not help but need – and strode on back to Jason's
particular domain in the rear: a railed enclosure cluttered with
shelves and pigeonholes bearing spiked dust-and-lint-gathering
gin receipts and ledgers and money and sunlight – a Cannebiere
backdrop smell of cheese and kerosene and harness oil and the
tremendous iron stove against which chewed tobacco had been
spat for almost a hundred years, and up to the long high sloping
counter behind which Jason stood and, not looking again at the
overalled men who had quietly stopped talking and even chewing

when she entered, with a kind of fainting desperation she opened
the handbag and fumbled something out of it and laid it open
on the counter and stood trembling and breathing rapidly while
Jason looked down at it – a picture, a photograph in colour
clipped obviously from a slick magazine – a picture filled with
luxury and money and sunlight – a Cannebire backdrop of
mountains and palms and cypresses and the sea, an open powerful
expensive chromium-trimmed sports car, the woman's face hatless between a rich scarf and a seal coat, ageless and beautiful,
cold serene and damned; beside her a handsome lean man of
middle-age in the ribbons and tabs of a German staffgeneral – and
the mouse-sized mouse-coloured spinster trembling and aghast at
her own temerity, staring across it at the childless bachelor in
whom ended that long line of men who had had something in
them of decency and pride even after they had begun to fail at
the integrity and the pride had become mostly vanity and selfpity:
from the expatriate who had to flee his native land with little else
except his life yet who still refused to accept defeat, though the
man who gambled his life and his good name twice and lost twice
and declined to accept that either, and the one who with only a
clever small quarterhorse for tool avenged his dispossessed father
and grandfather and gained a principality, and the brilliant and
gallant governor and the general who though he failed at leading
in battle brave and gallant men at least risked his own life too in
the failing, to the cultured dipsomaniac who sold the last of his
patrimony not to buy drink but to give one of his descendants at
least the best chance in life he could think of.

'It's Caddy!' the libarian whispered. 'He must save her!'

'It's Cad, all right,' Jason said. Then he began to laugh. He
stood there laughing above the picture, above the cold beautiful
face now creased and dogeared from its week's sojourn in the
desk drawer and the handbag. And the librarian knew why he
was laughing, who had not called him anything but Mr Compson
for thirty-two years now, ever since the day in 1911 when Candace, cast off by her husband, had brought her infant daughter
home and left the child and departed by the next train, to return
no more, and not only the Negro cook, Dilsey, but the librarian
too divined by simple instinct that Jason was somehow using the
child's life and its illegitimacy both to blackmail the mother not
only into staying away from Jefferson for the rest of her life but
into appointing them sole unchallengable trustee of the money
she would send for the child's maintenance, and had refused to

speak to him at all since that day in 1928 when the daughter
climbed down the rainpipe and ran away with the pitchman.

'Jason!' she cried. 'We must save her! Jason! Jason! – and still
crying it even when he took up the picture between thumb and
finger and threw it back across the counter towards her.

'That Candace?' he said. 'Don't make me laugh. This bitch
ain't thirty yet. The other one's fifty now.'

And the library was still locked all the next day too when
at three o'clock in the afternoon, footsore and spent yet still
unflagging and still clasping the handbag tightly under her arm,
she turned into a neat small yard in the Negro residence section
of Memphis and mounted the steps of the neat small house and
rang the bell and the door opened and a black woman of about
her own age looked quietly out at her. 'It's Frony, isn't it?' the
librarian said. 'Don't you remember me – Melissa Meck, from
Jefferson –'

'Yes,' the Negress said. 'Come in. You want to see Mama.' And
she entered the room, the neat yet cluttered bedroom of an old
Negro, rank with the smell of old people, old women, old
Negroes, where the old woman herself sat in a rocker beside the
hearth where even though it was June a fire smouldered – a big
woman once, in faded clean calico and an immaculate turban
wound round her head above the bleared and now apparently
almost sightless eyes – and put the dogeared clipping into the
black hands which, like the women of her race, were still as
supple and delicately shaped as they had been when she was thirty
or twenty or even seventeen.

'It's Caddy!' the librarian said. 'It is! Dilsey! Dilsey!'

'What did he say?' the old Negress said. And the librarian knew
whom she meant by 'he', nor did the librarian marvel, not only
that the old Negress would know that she (the librarian) would
know whom she meant by the 'he', but that the old Negress
would know at once that she had already shown the picture to
Jason.

'Don't you know what he said?' she cried. 'When he realized
she was in danger, he said it was her, even if I hadn't even had
a picture to show him. But as soon as he realized that somebody,
anybody, even just me, wanted to save her, would try to save her,
he said it wasn't. But it is! Look at it!'

'Look at my eyes,' the old Negress said. 'How can I see that
picture?'

'Call Frony!' the librarian cried. 'She will know her!' But already the old Negress was folding the clipping carefully back into its old creases, handing it back.

'My eyes ain't good any more,' she said. 'I can't see it.'

And that was all. At six o'clock she fought her way through the crowded bus terminal, the bag clutched under one arm and the return half of her roundtrip ticket in the other hand, and was swept out onto the roaring platform on the diurnal tide of a few middle-aged civilians but mostly soldiers and sailors enroute either to leave or to death and the homeless young women, their companions, who for two years now had lived from day to day in pullmans and hotels when they were lucky and in day-coaches and buses and stations and lobbies and public restrooms when not, pausing only long enough to drop their foals in charity wards or police stations and then move on again, and fought her way into the bus, smaller than any other there so that her feet touched the floor only occasionally until a shape (a man in khaki; she couldn't see him at all because she was already crying) rose and picked her up bodily and set her into a seat next the window, where still crying quietly she could look out upon the fleeing city as it streaked past and then was behind and presently now she would be home again, safe in Jefferson where life lived too with all its incomprehensible passion and turmoil and grief and fury and despair, but here at six o'clock you could close the covers on it and even the weightless hand of a child could put it back among its unfeatured kindred on the quiet eternal shelves and turn the key upon it for the whole and dreamless night. *Yes* she thought, crying quietly *that was it she didn't want to see it know whether it was Caddy or not because she knows Caddy doesn't want to be saved hasn't anything anymore worth being saved for nothing worth being lost that she can lose.*

JASON IV. The first sane Compson since before Culloden and (a childless bachelor) hence the last. Logical rational contained and even a philosopher in the old stoic tradition: thinking nothing whatever of God one way or the other and simply considering the police and so fearing and respecting only the Negro woman, his sworn enemy since his birth and his mortal one since that day in 1911 when she too divined by simple clairvoyance that he was somehow using his infant niece's illegitimacy to blackmail its mother, who cooked the food he ate. Who not only fended off and held his own with Compsons but competed and held his own

with the Snopeses who took over the little town following the
turn of the century as the Compsons and Sartorises and their ilk
faded from it (no Snopes, but Jason Compson himself who as
soon as his mother died – the niece had already climbed down
the rainpipe and vanished so Dilsey no longer had either of these
clubs to hold over him – committed his idiot younger brother to
the state and vacated the old house, first chopping up the vast
once-splendid rooms into what he called apartments and selling
the whole thing to a countryman who opened a boardinghouse
in it), though this was not difficult since to him all the rest of the
town and the world and the human race too except himself were
Compsons, inexplicable yet quite predictable in that they were
in no sense whatever to be trusted. Who, all the money from the
sale of the pasture having gone for his sister's wedding and his
brother's course at Harvard, used his own niggard savings out of
his meagre wages as a storeclerk to send himself to a Memphis
school where he learned to class and grade cotton, and so established his own business with which, following his dipsomaniac
father's death, he assumed the entire burden of the rotting family
in the rotting house, supporting his idiot brother because of their
mother, sacrificing what pleasures might have been the right and
just due and even the necessity of a thirty-year-old bachelor, so
that his mother's life might continue as nearly as possible to what
it had been; this not because he loved her but (a sane man always)
simply because he was afraid of the Negro cook whom he could
not even force to leave, even when he tried to stop paying her
weekly wages; and who despite all this, still managed to save
almost three thousand dollars ($2840.50) as he reported it on
the night his niece stole it; in niggard and agonized dimes and
quarters and halfdollars, which hoard he kept in no bank because
to him a banker too was just one more Compson, but hid in a
locked bureau drawer in his bedroom whose bed he made and
changed himself since he kept the bedroom door locked all the
time save when he was passing through it. Who, following a
fumbling abortive attempt by his idiot brother on a passing female
child, had himself appointed the idiot's guardian without letting
their mother know and so was able to have the creature castrated
before the mother even knew it was out of the house, and who
following the mother's death in 1933 was able to free himself
forever not only from the idiot brother and the house but from
the Negro woman too, moving into a pair of offices up a flight
of stairs above the supplystore containing his cotton ledgers and

samples, which he had converted into a bedroom-kitchen-bath, in and out of which on weekends there would be seen a big plain friendly brazenhaired pleasantfaced woman no longer very young, in round picture hats and (in its season) an imitation fur coat, the two of them, the middle-aged cottonbuyer and the woman whom the town called, simply, his friend from Memphis, seen at the local picture show on Saturday night and on Sunday morning mounting the apartment stairs with paper bags from the grocers containing loaves and eggs and oranges and cans of soup, domestic, uxorious, connubial, until the late afternoon bus carried her back to Memphis. He was emancipated now. He was free. 'In 1865,' he would say, 'Abe Lincoln freed the niggers from the Compsons. In 1933, Jason Compson freed the Compsons from the niggers.'

BENJAMIN. Born Maury, after his Mother's only brother: a handsome flashing swaggering workless bachelor who borrowed money from almost anyone, even Dilsey although she was a Negro, explained to her as he withdrew his hand from his pocket that she was not only in his eyes the same as a member of his sister's family, she would be considered a born lady anywhere in any eyes. Who, when at last even his mother realized what he was and insisted weeping that his name must be changed, was rechristened Benjamin by his brother Quentin (Benjamin, our lastborn, sold into Egypt). Who loved three things: the pasture which was sold to pay for Candace's wedding and to send Quentin to Harvard, his sister Candace, firelight. Who lost none of them because he could not remember his sister but only the loss of her, and firelight was the same bright shape as going to sleep, and the pasture was even better sold than before because now he and T.P. could not only follow timeless along the fence the motions which it did not even matter to him were human-beings swinging golfsticks, T.P. could lead them to clumps of grass or weeds where there would appear suddenly at T.P.'s hand small white spherules which competed with and even conquered what he did not even know was gravity and all the immutable laws when released from the hand towards plank floor or smokehouse wall or concrete sidewalk. Gelded 1913. Committed to the State Asylum, Jackson 1933. Lost nothing then either because, as with his sister, he remembered not the pasture but, only its loss, and firelight was still the same bright shape of sleep.

QUENTIN. The last. Candace's daughter. Fatherless nine months before her birth, nameless at birth and already doomed to be unwed from the instant the dividing egg determined its sex. Who at seventeen, on the one thousand eight hundred ninetyfifth anniversary of the day before the resurrection of Our Lord, swung herself by a rainpipe from the window of the room in which her uncle had locked her at noon, to the locked window of his own locked and empty bedroom and broke a pane and entered the window and with the uncle's firepoker burst open the locked bureau drawer and took the money (it was not $2840.50 either, it was almost seven thousand dollars and this was Jason's rage, the red unbearable fury which on that night and at intervals recurring with little or no diminishment for the next five years, made him seriously believe would at some unwarned instant destroy him, kill him as instantaneously dead as a bullet or a lightning-bolt: that although he had been robbed not of a mere petty three thousand dollars but of almost seven thousand he couldn't even tell anybody; because he had been robbed of seven thousand dollars instead of just three he could not only never receive justification – he did not want sympathy – from other men unlucky enough to have one bitch for a sister and another for a niece, he couldn't even go to the police; because he had lost four thousand dollars which did not belong to him he couldn't even recover the three thousand which did since those first four thousand dollars were not only the legal property of his niece as a part of the money supplied for her support and maintenance by her mother over the last sixteen years, they did not exist at all, having been officially recorded as expended and consumed in the annual reports he submitted to the district Chancellor, as required of him as guardian and trustee by his bondsmen: so that he had been robbed not only of his thievings but his savings too, and by his own victim; he had been robbed not only of the four thousand dollars which he had risked jail to acquire but of the three thousand which he had hoarded at the price of sacrifice and denial, almost a nickel and a dime at a time, over a period of almost twenty years: and this not only by his own victim but by a child who did it at one blow, without premeditation or plan, not even knowing or even caring how much she would find when she broke the drawer open; and now he couldn't even go to the police for help: he who had considered the police always, never given them any trouble, had paid the taxes for years which supported them in parasitic and sadistic idleness; not only that, he didn't dare pursue the girl himself because he might catch her and she would talk, so that his only recourse was a vain dream which kept him tossing and sweating on nights two and three and even four years after the event, when he should have forgotten about it: of catching her without warning, springing on her out of the dark, before she had spent all the money, and murder her before she had time to open her mouth) and climbed down the same rainpipe in the dusk and ran away with the pitchman who was already under sentence for bigamy. And so vanished; whatever occupation overtook her would have arrived in no chromium Mercedes; whatever snapshot would have contained no general staff.

And that was all. These others were not Compson. They were black:

T.P. Who wore on Memphis's Beale Street the fine bright cheap intransigent clothes manufactured specifically for him by the owners of Chicago and New York sweatshops.

FRONY. Who married a pullman porter and went to St Louis to live and later moved back to Memphis to make a home for her mother since Dilsey refused to go further than that.

LUSTER. A man, aged fourteen. Who was not only capable of the complete care and security of an idiot twice his age and three times his size, but could keep him entertained.

DILSEY.
They endured.

AS I LAY DYING

Darl

Jewel and I come up from the field, following the path in single file. Although I am fifteen feet ahead of him, anyone watching us from the cotton-house can see Jewel's frayed and broken straw hat a full head above my own.

The path runs straight as a plumb-line, worn smooth by feet and baked brick hard by July, between the green rows of laid-by cotton, to the cotton-house in the centre of the field, where it turns and circles the cotton-house at four soft right angles and goes on across the field again, worn so by feet in fading precision.

The cotton-house is of rough logs, from between which the chinking has long fallen. Square, with a broken roof set at a single pitch, it leans in empty and shimmering dilapidation in the sunlight, a single broad window in two opposite walls giving on to the approaches of the path. When we reach it I turn and follow the path which circles the house. Jewel, fifteen feet behind me, looking straight ahead, steps in a single stride through the window. Still staring straight ahead, his pale eyes like wood set into his wooden face, he crosses the floor in four strides with the rigid gravity of a cigar-store Indian dressed in patched overalls and endued with life from the hips down, and steps in a single stride through the opposite window and into the path again just as I come around the corner. In single file and five feet apart and Jewel now in front, we go on up the path toward the foot of the bluff.

Tull's wagon stands beside the spring, hitched to the rail, the reins wrapped about the seat stanchion. In the wagon-bed are two chairs. Jewel stops at the spring and takes the gourd from the willow branch and drinks. I pass him and mount the path, beginning to hear Cash's saw.

When I reach the top he has quit sawing. Standing in a litter of chips, he is fitting two of the boards together. Between the shadow spaces they are yellow as gold, like soft gold, bearing on

their flanks in smooth undulations the marks of the adze
blade: a good carpenter, Cash is. He holds the two planks on the
trestle, fitted along the edges in a quarter of the finished box.
He kneels and squints along the edge of them, then he lowers
them and takes up the adze. A good carpenter. Addie Bundren
could not want a better box to lie in. It will give her confidence
and comfort. I go on to the house, followed by the Chuck Chuck
Chuck of the adze.

Cora

So I saved out the eggs and baked yesterday. The cakes turned
out right well. We depend a lot on our chickens. They are good
layers, what few we have left after the possums and such. Snakes,
too, in the summer. A snake will break up a hen-house quicker
than anything. So after they were going to cost so much more
than Mr Tull thought, and after I promised that the difference
in the number of eggs would make it up, I had to be more careful
than ever because it was on my final say-so we took them. We
could have stocked cheaper chickens, but I gave my promise as
Miss Lawington said when she advised me to get a good breed,
because Mr Tull himself admits that a good breed of cows or
hogs pays in the long run. So when we lost so many of them we
couldn't afford to use the eggs ourselves, because I could not
have had Mr Tull chide me when it was on my say-so we took
them. So when Miss Lawington told me about the cakes I thought
that I could bake them and earn enough at one time to increase
the net value of the flock the equivalent of two head. And that
by saving the eggs out one at a time, even the eggs wouldn't be
costing anything. And that week they laid so well that I not only
saved out enough eggs above what we had engaged to sell, to
bake the cakes with, I had saved enough so that the flour and
the sugar and the stove wood would not be costing anything. So
I baked yesterday, more careful than ever I baked in my life, and
the cakes turned out right well. But when we got to town this

morning Miss Lawington told me the lady had changed her mind and was not going to have the party after all.

'She ought to taken those cakes anyway,' Kate says.

'Well,' I say,'I reckon she never had no use for them now.'

'She ought to taken them,' Kate says. 'But those rich town ladies can change their minds. Poor folks can't.'

Riches is nothing in the face of the Lord, for He can see into the heart. 'Maybe I can sell them at the bazaar Saturday,' I say. They turned out real well.

'You can't get two dollars a piece for them,' Kate says.

'Well, it isn't like they cost me anything,' I say. I saved them out and swapped a dozen of them for the sugar and flour. It isn't like the cakes cost me anything, as Mr Tull himself realizes that the eggs I saved were over and beyond what we had engaged to sell, so it was like we had found the eggs or they had been given to us.

'She ought to taken those cakes when she same as gave you her word,' Kate says. The Lord can see into the heart. If it is His will that some folks has different ideas of honesty from other folks, it is not my place to question His decree.

'I reckon she never had any use for them,' I say. They turned out real well, too.

The quilt is drawn up to her chin, hot as it is, with only her two hands and her face outside. She is propped on the pillow, with her head raised so she can see out the window, and we can hear him every time he takes up the adze or the saw. If we were deaf we could almost watch her face and hear him, see him. Her face is wasted away so that the bones draw just under the skin in white lines. Her eyes are like two candles when you watch them gutter down into the sockets of iron candle-sticks. But the eternal and the everlasting salvation and grace is not upon her.

'They turned out real nice,' I say. 'But not like the cakes Addie used to bake.' You can see that girl's washing and ironing in the pillow-slip, if ironed it ever was. Maybe it will reveal her blindness to her, laying there at the mercy and the ministration of four men and a tom-boy girl. 'There's not a woman in this section could ever bake with Addie Bundren,' I say. 'First thing we know she'll be up and baking again, and then we won't have any sale for ours at all.' Under the quilt she makes no more of a hump than a rail would, and the only way you can tell she is breathing is by the sound of the mattress shucks. Even the hair at her cheek does not move, even with that girl standing right over her, fanning her with the fan. While we watch she swaps the fan to the other hand without stopping it.

'Is she sleeping?' Kate whispers.

'She just can't watch Cash yonder,' the girl says. We can hear the saw in the board. It sounds like snoring. Eula turns on the trunk and looks out the window. Her necklace looks real nice with her red hat. You wouldn't think it only cost twenty-five cents.

'She ought to taken those cakes,' Kate says.

I could have used the money real well. But it's not like they cost me anything except the baking. I can tell him that anybody is likely to make a miscue, but it's not all of them that can get out of it without loss, I can tell him. It's not everybody can eat their mistakes, I can tell him.

Someone comes through the hall. It is Darl. He does not look in as he passes the door. Eula watches him as he goes on and passes from sight again toward the back. Her hand rises and touches her beads lightly, and then her hair. When she finds me watching her, her eyes go blank.

Darl

Pa and Vernon are sitting on the back porch. Pa is tilting snuff from the lid of his snuff-box into his lower lip, holding the lip outdrawn between thumb and finger. They look around as I cross the porch and dip the gourd into the water bucket and drink.

'Where's Jewel?' pa says. When I was a boy I first learned how much better water tastes when it has set a while in a cedar bucket. Warmish-cool, with a faint taste like the hot July wind in cedar trees smells. It has to set at least six hours, and be drunk from a gourd. Water should never be drunk from metal.

And at night it is better still. I used to lie on the pallet in the hall, waiting until I could hear them all asleep, so I could get up and go back to the bucket. It would be black, the shelf black, the still surface of the water a round orifice in nothingness, where before I stirred it awake with the dipper I could see maybe a star or two in the bucket, and maybe in the dipper a star or two before I drank. After that I was bigger, older. Then I would wait until they all went to sleep so I could lie with my shirt-tail up, hearing them asleep, feeling myself without touching myself, feeling the cool silence blowing upon my parts and wondering if Cash was yonder in the darkness doing it too, had been doing it perhaps for the last two years before I could have wanted to or could have.

Pa's feet are badly splayed, his toes cramped and bent and warped, with no toenail at all on his little toes, from working so hard in the wet in home-made shoes when he was a boy. Beside his chair his brogans sit. They look as though they had been hacked with a blunt axe out of pig-iron. Vernon has been to town. I have never seen him go to town in overalls. His wife, they say. She taught school too, once.

I fling the dipper dregs to the ground and wipe my mouth on my sleeve. It is going to rain before morning. Maybe before dark. 'Down to the barn,' I say. 'Harnessing the team.'

Down there fooling with that horse. He will go on through the barn, into the pasture. The horse will not be in sight: he is up there among the pine seedlings, in the cool. Jewel whistles, once and shrill. The horse snorts, then Jewel sees him, glinting for a gaudy instant among the blue shadows. Jewel whistles again; the horse comes dropping down the slope, stiff-legged, his ears cocking and flicking, his mis-matched eyes rolling, and fetches up twenty feet away, broadside on, watching Jewel over his shoulder in an attitude kittenish and alert.

'Come here, sir,' Jewel says. He moves. Moving that quick his coat, bunching, tongues swirling like so many flames. With tossing mane and tail and rolling eye the horse makes another short curveting rush and stops again, feet bunched, watching Jewel. Jewel walks steadily toward him, his hands at his sides. Save for Jewel's legs they are like two figures carved for a tableau savage in the sun.

When Jewel can almost touch him, the horse stands on his hind legs and slashes down at Jewel. Then Jewel is enclosed by a glittering maze of hooves as by an illusion of wings; among them, beneath the upreared chest, he moves with the flashing limberness of a snake. For an instant before the jerk comes on to his arms he sees his whole body earth-free, horizontal, whipping snake-limber, until he finds the horse's nostrils and touches earth again. Then they are rigid, motionless, terrific, the horse back-thrust on stiffened, quivering legs, with lowered head; Jewel with dug heels, shutting off the horse's wind with one hand, with the other patting the horse's neck in short strokes myriad and caressing, cursing the horse with obscene ferocity.

They stand in rigid terrific hiatus, the horse trembling and groaning. Then Jewel is on the horse's back. He flows upward in a stooping swirl like the lash of a whip, his body in mid-air shaped to the horse. For another moment the horse stands spraddled, with lowered head, before it bursts into motion. They descend the hill in a series of spine jolting jumps, Jewel high, leech-like on the withers, to the fence where the horse bunches to a scuttering halt again.

'Well,' Jewel says, 'you can quit now, if you got a-plenty.'

Inside the barn Jewel slides running to the ground before the horse stops. The horse enters the stall, Jewel following. Without looking back the horse kicks at him, slamming a single hoof into the wall with a pistol-like report. Jewel kicks him in the stomach; the horse arches his neck back, crop-toothed; Jewel strikes him across the face with his fist and slides on to the trough and mounts upon it. Clinging to the hay-rack he lowers his head and peers out across the stall tops and through the doorway. The path is empty; from here he cannot even hear Cash sawing. He reaches up and drags down hay in hurried armfuls and crams it into the rack.

'Eat,' he says. 'Get the goddamn stuff out of sight while you got a chance, you pussel-gutted bastard. You sweet son of a bitch,' he says.

Jewel

It's because he stays out there, right under the window, hammering and sawing on that goddamn box. Where she's got to see him. Where every breath she draws is full of his knocking and sawing where she can see him saying See. See what a good one I am making for you. I told him to go somewhere else. I said Good God do you want to see her in it. It's like when he was a little boy and she says if she had some fertilizer she would try to raise some flowers and he taken the bread-pan and brought it back from the barn full of dung.

And now them others sitting there, like buzzards. Waiting, fanning themselves. Because I said If you wouldn't keep on sawing and nailing at it until a man can't sleep even and her hands laying on the quilt like two of them roots dug up and tried to wash and you couldn't get them clean. I can see the fan and Dewey Dell's arm. I said if you'd just let her alone. Sawing and knocking, and keeping the air always moving so fast on her face that when you're tired you can't breathe it, and that goddamn adze going One lick less. One lick less. One lick less until everybody that passes in the road will have to stop and see it and say what a fine carpenter he is. If it had just been me when Cash fell off of that church and if it had just been me when pa laid sick with that load of wood fell on him, it would not be happening with every bastard in the county coming in to stare at her because if there is a God what the hell is He for. It would just be me and her on a high hill and me rolling the rocks down the hill at their faces, picking them up and throwing them down the hill, faces and teeth and all by God until she was quiet and not that goddamn adze going One lick less. One lick less and we could be quiet.

Darl

We watch him come around the corner and mount the steps. He does not look at us. 'You ready?' he says.

'If you're hitched up,' I say. I say 'Wait.' He stops, looking at pa. Vernon spits, without moving. He spits with decorous and deliberate precision into the pocked dust below the porch. Pa rubs his hands slowly on his knees. He is gazing out beyond the crest of the bluff, out across the land. Jewel watches him a moment, then he goes on to the pail and drinks again.

'I mislike undecision as much as ere a man,' pa says.

'It means three dollars,' I say. The shirt across pa's hump is faded lighter than the rest of it. There is no sweat-stain on his shirt. I have never seen a seat-stain on his shirt. He was sick once from working in the sun when he was twenty-two years old, and he tells people that, if he ever sweats, he will die. I suppose he believes it.

'But if she don't last until you get back,' he says. 'She will be disappointed.'

Vernon spits into the dust. But it will rain before morning.

'She's counted on it,' pa says. 'She'll want to start right away. I know her. I promised her I'd keep the team here and ready, and she's counting on it.'

'We'll need that three dollars then, sure,' I say. He gazes out over the land, rubbing his hands on his knees. Since he lost his teeth his mouth collapses in slow repetition when he dips. The stubble gives his lower face that appearance that old dogs have. 'You'd better make up your mind soon, so we can get there and get a load on before dark,' I say.

'Ma ain't that sick,' Jewel says. 'Shut up, Darl.'

'That's right,' Vernon says. 'She seems more like herself today than she has in a week. Time you and Jewel get back, she'll be setting up.'

'You ought to know,' Jewel says. 'You been here often enough looking at her. You or your folks.' Vernon looks at him. Jewel's eyes look like pale wood in his high-blooded face. He is a head taller than any of the rest of us, always was. I told them that's why ma always whipped him and petted him more. Because he was peakling around the house more. That's why she named him Jewel I told them.

'Shut up, Jewel,' pa says, but as though he is not listening much. He gazes out across the land, rubbing his knees.

'You could borrow the loan of Vernon's team and we could catch up with you,' I say. 'If she didn't wait for us.'

'Ah, shut your goddamn mouth,' Jewel says.

'She'll want to go in ourn,' pa says. He rubs his knees. 'Don't ere a man mislike it more.'

'It's laying there, watching Cash whittle on that damn . . .' Jewel says. He says it harshly, savagely, but he does not say the word. Like a little boy in the dark to flail his courage and suddenly aghast into silence by his own noise.

'She wanted that like she wants to go in our own wagon,' pa says. 'She'll rest easier for knowing it's a good one, and private. She was ever a private woman. You know it well.'

'Then let it be private,' Jewel says. 'But how the hell can you expect it to be –' He looks at the back of pa's head, his eyes like pale wooden eyes.

'Sho,' Vernon says, 'she'll hold on till it's finished. She'll hold on till everything's ready, till her own good time. And with the roads like they are now, it won't take you no time to get her to town.'

'It's fixing up to rain,' pa says. 'I am a luckless man. I have ever been.' He rubs his hands on his knees. 'It's that durn doctor, liable to come at any time. I couldn't get word to him till so late. If he was to come tomorrow and tell her the time was nigh, she wouldn't wait. I know her. Wagon or no wagon, she wouldn't wait. Then she'd be upset, and I wouldn't upset her for the living world. With that family burying-ground in Jefferson and them of her blood waiting for her there, she'll be impatient. I promised my word me and the boys would get her there quick as mules could walk it, so she could rest quiet.' He rubs his hands on his knees. 'No man ever misliked it more.'

'If everybody wasn't burning hell to get her there,' Jewel says in that harsh, savage voice. 'With Cash all day long right under the window, hammering and sawing at that –'

'It was her wish,' pa says. 'You got no affection nor gentleness for her. You never had. We would be beholden to no man,' he says, 'me and her. We have never yet been, and she will rest quieter for knowing it and that it was her own blood sawed out the boards and drove the nails. She was ever one to clean up after herself.'

'It means three dollars,' I say. 'Do you want us to go, or not?' Pa rubs his knees. 'We'll be back by tomorrow, sundown.'

'Well . . .' pa says. He looks out over the land, awry-haired, mouthing the snuff slowly against his gums.

'Come on,' Jewel says. He goes down the steps. Vernon spits neatly into the dust.

'By sundown, now,' pa says. 'I would not keep her waiting.'

Jewel glances back, then he goes on around the house. I enter the hall, hearing the voices before I reach the door. Tilting a little down the hill, as our house does, a breeze draws through the hall all the time, upslanting. A feather dropped near the front door will rise and brush along the ceiling, slanting backward, until it reaches the down-turning current at the back door: so with voices. As you enter the hall, they sound as though they were speaking out of the air about your head.

Cora

It was the sweetest thing I ever saw. It was like he knew he would never see her again, that Anse Bundren was driving him from his mother's death-bed, never to see her in this world again. I always said Darl was different from those others. I always said he was the only one of them that had his mother's nature, had any natural affection. Not that Jewel, the one she laboured so to bear and coddled and petted so and him flinging into tantrums or sulking spells, inventing devilment to devil her till I would have frailed him time and time. Not him to come and tell her good-bye. Not him to miss a chance to make that extra three dollars at the price of his mother's good-bye kiss. A Bundren through and through, loving nobody, caring for nothing except how to get something with the least amount of work. Mr Tull says Darl asked them to wait. He said Darl almost begged them on his knees not to force him to leave her in her condition. But nothing would do but Anse and Jewel must make that three dollars. Nobody that knows Anse could have expected different, but to think of that boy, that Jewel, selling all those years of self-denial and down-right partiality – they couldn't fool me: Mr Tull says Mrs Bundren liked Jewel the least of all, but I knew better. I knew she was partial to him, to the same quality in him that let her put up with Anse Bundren when Mr Tull said she ought to poisoned him – for three dollars, denying his dying mother the good-bye kiss.

Why, for the last three weeks I have been coming over every time I could, coming sometimes when I shouldn't have, neglecting my own family and duties so that somebody would be with her in her last moments and she would not have to face the Great Unknown without one familiar face to give her courage. Not that I deserve credit for it: I will expect the same for myself. But thank God it will be the faces of my loved kin, my blood and flesh, for in my husband and children I have been more blessed than most, trials though they have been at times.

She lived, a lonely woman, lonely with her pride, trying to make folks believe different, hiding the fact that they just suffered her, because she was not cold in the coffin before they were carting her forty miles away to bury her, flouting the will of God to do it. Refusing to let her lie in the same earth with those Bundrens.

'But she wanted to go,' Mr Tull said. 'It was her own wish to lie among her own people.'

'Then why didn't she go alive?' I said. 'Not one of them would have stopped her, with even that little one almost old enough now to be selfish and stone-hearted like the rest of them.'

'It was her own wish,' Mr Tull said. 'I heard Anse say it was.'

'And you would believe Anse, of course,' I said. 'A man like you would. Don't tell me.'

'I'd believe him about something he couldn't expect to make anything off of me by not telling,' Mr Tull said.

'Don't tell me,' I said. 'A woman's place is with her husband and children, alive or dead. Would you expect me to want to go back to Alabama and leave you and the girls when my time comes, that I left of my own will to cast my lot with yours for better and worse, until death and after?'

'Well, folks are different,' he said.

'I should hope so. I have tried to live right in the sight of God and man, for the honour and comfort of my Christian husband and the love and respect of my Christian children. So that when I lay me down in the consciousness of my duty and reward I will be surrounded by loving faces, carrying the farewell kiss of each of my loved ones into my reward. Not like Addie Bundren dying alone, hiding her pride and her broken heart. Glad to go: Lying there with her head propped up so she could watch Cash building the coffin, having to watch him so he would not skimp it, like as not, with those other men not worrying about anything except if there was time to earn another three dollars before the rain came and the river got too high to get across it. Like as not, if they hadn't decided to make that last load, they would have loaded her into the wagon on a quilt and crossed the river first and then stopped and give her time to die what Christian death they would let her.

Except Darl. It was the sweetest thing I ever saw. Sometimes I lose faith in human nature for a time; I am assailed by doubt. But always the Lord restores my faith and reveals to me His bounteous love for His creatures. Not Jewel, the one she had always cherished, not him. He was after that three extra dollars. It was Darl, the one that folks says is queer, lazy, pottering about the place no better than Anse, with Cash a good carpenter and always more building than he can get around to, and Jewel always doing something that made him some money or got him talked about, and that near-naked girl always standing over Addie with a fan so that every time a body tried to talk to her and cheer her up, would answer for her right quick, like she was trying to keep anybody from coming near her at all.

It was Darl. He come to the door and stood there, looking at his dying mother. He just looked at her, and I felt the bounteous love of the Lord again and His mercy. I saw that with Jewel she had just been pretending, but that it was between her and Darl that the understanding and the true love was. He just looked at her, not even coming in where she could see him and get upset, knowing that Anse was driving him away and he would never see her again. He said nothing, just looking at her.

'What you want, Darl?' Dewey Dell said, not stopping the fan, speaking up quick, keeping even him from her. He didn't answer. He just stood and looked at his dying mother, his heart too full for words.

Dewey Dell

The first time me and Lafe picked on down the row. Pa dassent sweat because he will catch his death from the sickness so everybody that comes to help us. And Jewel don't care about anything he is not kin to us in caring, not care-kin. And Cash like sawing the long hot sad yellow days up into planks and nailing them to something. And pa thinks because neighbours will always treat one another that way because he has always been too busy letting neighbours do for him to find out. And I did not think that Darl would, that sits at the supper table with his eyes gone further than the food and the lamp, full of the land dug out of his skull and the holes filled with distance beyond the land.

We picked on down the row, the woods getting closer and closer and the secret shade, picking on into the secret shade with my sack and Lafe's sack. Because I said will I or won't I when the sack was half-full because I said if the sack is full when we get to the woods it won't be me. I said if it don't mean for me to do it the sack will not be full and I will turn up the next row but if the sack is full, I cannot help it. It will be that I had to do it all the time and I cannot help it. And we picked on toward the secret shade and our eyes would drown together touching on his hands and my hands and I didn't say anything. I said, 'What are you doing?' and he said 'I am picking into your sack.' And so it was full when we came to the end of the row and I could not help it.

And so it was because I could not help it. It was then, and then I saw Darl and he knew. He said he knew without the words like he told me that ma is going to die without words, and I knew he knew because if he had said he knew with the words I would not have believed that he had been there and saw us. But he said he did not know and I said 'Are you going to tell pa are you going to kill him?' without the words I said it and he said 'Why?' without the words. And that's why I can talk to him with knowing with hating because he knows.

He stands in the door, looking at her.

'What you want, Darl?' I say.

'She is going to die,' he says. And old turkey-buzzard Tull is coming to watch her die but I can fool them.

'When is she going to die?' I say.

'Before we get back,' he says.

'Then why are you taking Jewel?' I say.

'I want him to help me load,' he says.

Tull

Anse keeps on rubbing his knees. His overalls are faded; on one knee a serge patch cut out of a pair of Sunday pants, worn iron-slick. 'No man mislikes it more than me,' he says.

'A fellow's got to guess ahead now and then,' I say. 'But, come long and short, it won't be no harm done either way.'

'She'll want to get started right off,' he says. 'It's far enough to Jefferson at best.'

'But the roads is good now,' I say. It's fixing to rain to-night, too. His folks buries at New Hope, too, not three miles away. But it's just like him to marry a woman born a day's hard ride away and have her die on him.

He looks out over the land, rubbing his knees. 'No man so mislikes it,' he says.

'They'll get back in plenty of time,' I say. 'I wouldn't worry none.'

'It means three dollars,' he says.

'Might be it won't be no need for them to rush back, noways,' I say. 'I hope it.'

'She's a-going,' he says. 'Her mind is set on it.' It's a hard life on women, for a fact. Some women. I mind my mammy lived to be seventy and more. Worked every day, rain or shine; never a sick day since her last chap was born until one day she kind of looked around her and then she went and taken that lace-trimmed nightgown she had had forty-five years and never wore out of the chest and put it on and laid down on the bed and pulled the covers up and shut her eyes. 'You all will have to look out for pa the best you can,' she said. 'I'm tired.'

Anse rubs his hands on his knees. 'The Lord giveth,' he says. We can hear Cash a-hammering and sawing beyond the corner.

It's true, Never a truer breath was ever breathed. 'The Lord giveth,' I say.

That boy comes up the hill. He is carrying a fish nigh long as he is. He slings it to the ground and grunts 'Hah' and spits over his shoulder like a man. Durn nigh long as he is.

'What's that?' I say. 'A hog? Where'd you get it?'

'Down to the bridge,' he says. He turns it over, the underside caked over with dust where it is wet, the eye coated over, humped under the dirt.

'Are you aiming to leave it laying there?' Anse says.

'I aim to show it to ma,' Vardaman says. He looks toward the door. We can hear the talking, coming out on the draught. Cash, too, knocking and hammering at the boards. 'There's company in there,' he says.

'Just my folks,' I say. 'They'd enjoy to see it, too.'

He says nothing, watching the door. Then he looks down at the fish laying in the dust. He turns it over with his foot and prods at the eye-bump with his toe, gouging at it. Anse is looking out over the land. Vardaman looks at Anse's face, then at the door. He turns, going toward the corner of the house, when Anse calls him without looking around.

'You clean that fish,' Anse says.

Vardaman stops. 'Why can't Dewey Dell clean it?' he says.

'You clean that fish,' Anse says.

'Aw, pa,' Vardaman says.

'You clean it,' Anse says. He don't look around. Vardaman comes back and picks up the fish. It slides out of his hands, smearing the wet dirt on to him, and flops down, dirtying itself again, gap-mouthed, goggle-eyed, hiding into the dust like it was ashamed of being dead, like it was in a hurry to get back hid again. Vardaman cusses it. He cusses it like a grown man, standing a-straddle of it. Anse don't look around. Vardaman picks it up again. He goes on around the house, toting it in both arms like an armful of wood, it overlapping him on both ends, head and tail. Durn nigh as big as he is.

Anse's wrists dangle out of his sleeves: I never see him with a shirt on that looked like it was his in all my life. They all looked like Jewel might have given him his old ones. Not Jewel, though. He's long-armed, even if he is spindling. Except for the lack of sweat. You could tell they ain't been nobody else's but Anse's that way without no mistake. His eyes look like pieces of burnt-out cinder fixed in his face, looking out over the land.

When the shadow touches the steps he says 'It's five o'clock.'

Just as I get up Cora comes to the door and says it's time to get on. Anse reaches for his shoes. 'Now, Mr Bundren,' Cora says, 'don't you get up now.' He puts his shoes on, stomping into them, like he does everything, like he is hoping all the time he really can't do it and can quit trying to. When we go up the hall we can hear them clumping on the floor like they was iron shoes. He comes toward the door where she is, blinking his eyes, kind of looking ahead of hisself before he sees, like he is hoping to find her setting up, in a chair maybe or maybe sweeping, and looks into the door in that surprised way he looks in and finds her still in bed every time and Dewey Dell still a-fanning her with the fan. He stands there, like he don't aim to move again nor nothing else.

'Well, I reckon we better get on,' Cora says. 'I got to feed the chickens. It's fixing to rain, too. Clouds like that don't lie, and the cotton making every day the Lord sends. That'll be something else for him. Cash is still trimming at the boards. 'If there's ere a thing we can do,' Cora says.

'Anse'll let us know,' I say.

Anse don't look at us. He looks around, blinking, in that surprised way, like he had wore hisself down being surprised and was even surprised at that. If Cash just works that careful on my barn.

'I told Anse it likely won't be no need,' I say. 'I so hope it.'

'Her mind is set on it,' he says. 'I reckon she's bound to go.'

'It comes to all of us,' Cora says. 'Let the Lord comfort you.'

'About that corn,' I say. I tell him again I will help him out if he gets into a tight, with her sick and all. Like most folks around here, I done holp him so much already I can't quit now.

'I aimed to get to it today,' he says. 'Seems like I can't get my mind on nothing.'

'Maybe she'll hold out till you are laid by,' I say.

'If God wills it,' he says.

'Let Him comfort you,' Cora says.

If Cash just works that careful on my barn. He looks up when we pass. 'Don't reckon I'll get to you this week,' he says.

' 'Tain't no rush,' I say. 'Whenever you get around to it.' We get into the wagon. Cora sets the cake-box on her lap.

It's fixing to rain, sho.

'I don't know what he'll do,' Cora says. 'I just don't know.'

'Poor Anse,' I say. 'She kept him at work for thirty-odd years. I reckon she is tired.'

'And I reckon she'll be behind him for thirty years more,' Kate says. 'Or if it ain't her, he'll get another one before cotton-picking.'

'I reckon Cash and Darl can get married now,' Bula says.

'That poor boy,' Cora says. 'The poor little tyke.'

'What about Jewel?' Kate says.

'He can, too,' Eula says.

'Humph,' Kate says. 'I reckon he will. I reckon so. I reckon there's more gals than one around here that don't want to see Jewel tied down. Well, they needn't to worry.'

'Why, Kate!' Cora says. The wagon begins to rattle. 'The poor little tyke,' Cora says.

It's fixing to rain this night. Yes, sir. A rattling wagon is mighty dry weather, for a Birdsell. But that'll be cured. It will for a fact.

'She ought to taken them cakes after she said she would,' Kate says.

Anse

Durn that road. And it fixing to rain, too. I can stand here and same as see it with second-sight, a-shutting down behind them like a wall, shutting down betwixt them and my given promise. I do the best I can, much as I can get my mind on anything, but durn them boys.

A-laying there, right up to my door, where every bad luck that comes and goes is bound to find it. I told Addie it wasn't any luck living on a road when it come by here, and she said, for the world like a woman, 'Get up and move, then.' But I told her it wasn't no luck in it, because the Lord put roads for travelling: why He laid them down flat on the earth. When He aims for something to be always a moving, He makes it long ways, like a road or a horse or a wagon, but when He aims for something to stay put, He makes it up-and-down ways, like a tree or a man. And so He never aimed for folks to live on a road, because which gets there first, I says, the road or the house? Did you ever know Him to set a road down by a house? I says. No you Never, I says, because it's always men can't rest till they gets the house set where everybody that passes in a wagon can spit in the doorway, keeping the folks restless and wanting to get up and go somewheres else when He aimed for them to stay put like a tree or a stand of corn. Because if He'd a aimed for man to be always a-moving and going somewheres else, wouldn't He a put him longways on his belly, like a snake? It stands to reason He would.

Putting it where every bad luck prowling can find it and come straight to my door, charging me taxes on top of it. Making me pay for Cash having to get them carpenter notions when if it hadn't been no road come there, he wouldn't a got them; falling off of churches and lifting no hand in six months and me and Addie slaving and a-slaving, when there's plenty of sawing on this place he could do if he's got to saw.

And Darl, too. Talking me out of him, durn them. It ain't that I am afraid of work; I always have fed me and mine and kept a roof above us: it's that they would short-hand me just because he tends to his own business, just because he's got his eyes full of the land all the time. I says to them, he was all right at first, with his eyes full of the land, because the land laid up-and-down ways then; it wasn't till that ere road come and switched the land around longways and his eyes still full of the land, that they begun to threaten me out of him, trying to short-hand me with the law.

Making me pay for it. She was well and hale as ere a woman ever were, except for that road. Just laying down, resting herself in her own bed, asking naught of none. 'Are you sick, Addie?' I said.

'I am not sick,' she said.

'You lay you down and rest you,' I said. 'I knowed you are not sick. You're just tired. You lay you down and rest.'

'I am not sick,' she said. 'I will get up.'

'Lay still and rest,' I said. 'You are just tired. You can get up tomorrow.' And she was laying there, well and hale as ere a woman ever were, except for that road.

'I never sent for you,' I said. 'I take you to witness I never sent for you.'

'I know you didn't,' Peabody said. 'I bound that. Where is she?'

'She's a-laying down,' I said. 'She's just a little tired, but she'll –'

'Get outen here, Anse,' he said. 'Go set on the porch a while.'

And now I got to pay for it, me without a tooth in my head, hoping to get ahead enough so I could get my mouth fixed where I could eat God's own victuals as a man should, and her hale and well as ere a woman in the land until that day. Got to pay for being put to the need of that three dollars. Got to pay for the way for them boys to have to go away to earn it. And now I can see same as second sight the rain shutting down betwixt us, a-coming up that road like a durn man, like it wasn't ere a other house to rain on in all the living land.

I have heard men cuss their luck, and right, for they were sinful men. But I do not say it's a curse on me, because I have done no wrong to be cussed by. I am not religious, I reckon. But peace is my heart: I know it is. I have done things but neither better nor worse than them that pretend otherlike, and I know that Old Marster will care for me as for ere a sparrow that falls. But it seems hard that a man in his need could be so flouted by a road.

Vardaman comes around the house, bloody as a hog to his knees, and that ere fish chopped up with the axe like as not, or maybe throwed away for him to lie about the dogs et it. Well, I reckon I ain't no call to expect no more of him than of his man-growed brothers. He comes along, watching the house, quiet, and sits on the steps. 'Whew,' he says, 'I'm pure tired.'

'Go wash them hands,' I say. But couldn't no woman strove harder than Addie to make them right, man and boy: I'll say that for her.

'It was full of blood and guts as a hog,' he says. But I just can't seem to get no heart into anything, with this here weather sapping me, too. 'Pa,' he says, 'is ma sick some more?'

'Go wash them hands,' I say. But I just can't seem to get no heart into it.

Darl

He has been to town this week: the back of his neck trimmed close, with a white line between hair and sunburn like a joint of white bone. He has not once looked back.

'Jewel,' I say. Back running, tunnelled between the two sets of bobbing mule ears, the road vanishes beneath the wagon as though it were a ribbon and the front axle were a spool. 'Do you know she is going to die, Jewel?'

It takes two people to make you, and one people to die. That's how the world is going to end.

I say to Dewey Dell: 'You want her to die so you can get to town: is that it?' She wouldn't say what we both knew. 'The reason you will not say it is, when you say it, even to yourself, you will know it is true: is that it? But you know it is true now. I can almost tell you the day when you knew it is true. Why won't you say it, even to yourself?' She will not say it. She just keeps on saying Are you going to tell pa? Are you going to kill him? 'You cannot believe it is true because you cannot believe that Dewey Dell, Dewey Dell Bundren, could have such bad luck: is that it?'

The sun, an hour above the horizon, is poised like a bloody egg upon the crest of thunderheads; the light has turned copper: in the eye portentous, in the nose sulphurous, smelling of lightning. When Peabody comes, they will have to use the rope. He has pussel-gutted himself eating cold greens. With the rope they will haul him up the path, balloon-like up the sulphurous air.

'Jewel,' I say, 'do you know that Addie Bundren is going to die? Addie Bundren is going to die?'

Peabody

When Anse finally sent for me of his own accord, I said 'He has wore her out at last.' And I said a damn good thing and at first I would not go because there might be something I could do and I would have to haul her back, by God. I thought maybe they have the same sort of fool ethics in heaven they have in the Medical College and that it was maybe Vernon Tull sending for me again, getting me there in the nick of time, as Vernon always does things, getting the most for Anse's money like he does for his own. But when it got far enough into the day for me to read weather sign I knew it couldn't have been anybody but Anse that sent. I knew that nobody but a luckless man could ever need a doctor in the face of a cyclone. And I knew that if it had finally occurred to Anse himself that he needed one, it was already too late.

When I reach the spring and get down and hitch the team, the sun has gone down behind a bank of black cloud like a top-heavy mountain range, like a load of cinders dumped over there, and there is no wind. I could hear Cash sawing for a mile before I got there. Anse is standing at the top of the bluff above the path.

'Where's the horse?' I say.

'Jewel's taken and gone,' he says. 'Can't nobody else ketch hit. You'll have to walk up, I reckon.'

'Me, walk up, weighing two hundred and twenty-five pounds?' I say. 'Walk up that burn wall?' He stands there beside a tree. Too bad the Lord made the mistake of giving trees roots and giving the Anse Bundrens He makes feet and legs. If He'd just swapped them, there wouldn't ever be a worry about this country being deforested some day. Or any other country. 'What do you aim for me to do?' I say. 'Stay here and get blowed clean out of the county when that cloud breaks?' Even with the horse it would take me fifteen minutes to ride up across the pasture to the top of the ridge and reach the house. The path looks like a crooked limb blown against the bluff. Anse has not been in town in twelve years. And how his mother ever got up there to bear him, he being his mother's son.

'Vardaman's gittin' the rope,' he says.

After a while Vardaman appears with the ploughline. He gives the end of it to Anse and comes down the path, uncoiling it.

'You hold it tight,' I say. 'I done already wrote this visit on to my books, so I'm going to charge you just the same, whether I get there or not.'

'I got hit,' Anse says. 'You kin come on up.'

I'll be damned if I can see why I don't quit. A man seventy years old, weighing two hundred and odd pounds, being hauled up and down a damn mountain on a rope. I reckon it's because I must reach the fifty-thousand dollar mark of dead accounts on my books before I can quit. 'What the hell does your wife mean,' I say, 'taking sick on top of a durn mountain?'

'I'm right sorry,' he says. He let the rope go, just dropped it, and he has turned toward the house. There is a little daylight up here still, of the colour of sulphur matches. The boards look like strips of sulphur. Cash does not look back. Vernon Tull says he brings each board up to the window for her to see it and say it is all right. The boy overtakes us. Anse looks back at him. 'Where's the rope?' he says.

'It's where you left it,' I say. 'But never you mind that rope. I got to get back down that bluff. I don't aim for that storm to catch me up here. I'd blow too durn far once I got started.'

The girl is standing by the bed, fanning her. When we enter she turns her head and looks at us. She has been dead these ten days. I suppose it's having been a part of Anse for so long that she cannot even make that change, if change it be. I can remember how when I was young I believed death to be a phenomenon of the body; now I know it to be merely a function of the mind – and that of the minds of the ones who suffer the bereavement. The nihilists say it is the end; the fundamentalists, the beginning; when in reality it is no more than a single tenant or family moving out of a tenement or a town.

She looks at us. Only her eyes seem to move. It's like they touch us, not with sight or sense, but like the stream from a hose touches you, the stream at the instant of impact as dissociated from the nozzle as though it had never been there. She does not look at Anse at all. She looks at me, then at the boy. Beneath the quilt she is no more than a bundle of rotten sticks.

'Well, Miss Addie,' I say. The girl does not stop the fan. 'How are you, sister?' I say. Her head lies gaunt on the pillow, looking at the boy. 'You picked out a fine time to get me out here and bring up a storm.' Then I send Anse and the boy out. She watches the boy as he leaves the room. She has not moved save her eyes.

He and Anse are on the porch when I come out, the boy sitting on the steps, Anse standing by a post, not even leaning against it, his arms dangling, the hair pushed and matted up on his head like a dipped rooster. He turns his head, blinking at me.

'Why didn't you send for me sooner?' I say.

'Hit was jest one thing and then another,' he says. 'That ere corn me and the boys was aimin' to git up with, and Dewey Dell a-takin' good keer of her, and folks comin' in, a-offerin' to help and sich, till I jest thought . . .'

'Damn the money,' I say. 'Did you ever hear of me worrying a fellow before he was ready to pay?'

'Hit ain't begrudgin' the money,' he says. 'I just kept a-thinkin' . . . She's goin', is she?' The durn little tyke is sitting on the top step, looking smaller than ever in the sulphur-coloured light. That's the one trouble with this country: everything, weather, all, hangs on too long. Like our rivers, our land: opaque, slow, violent; shaping and creating the life of man in its implacable and brooding image. 'I knowed hit,' Anse says. 'All the while I made sho. Her mind is sot on hit.'

'And a damn good thing, too,' I say. 'With a trifling –' He sits on the top step, small, motionless in faded overalls. When I came out he looked up at me, then at Anse. But now he has stopped looking at us. He just sits there.

'Have you told her yit?' Anse says.

'What for?' I say. 'What the devil for?'

'She'll know hit. I knowed that when she see you she would know hit, same as writing. You wouldn't need to tell her. Her mind –'

Behind us the girl says, 'Paw.' I look at her, at her face.

'You better go quick,' I say.

When we enter the room she is watching the door. She looks at me. Her eyes look like lamps blaring up just before the oil is gone. 'She wants you to go out,' the girl says.

'Now, Addie,' Anse says, 'when he come all the way from Jefferson to git you well?' She watches me: I can feel her eyes. It's like she was shoving at me with them. I have seen it before in women. Seen them drive from the room them coming with sympathy and pity, with actual help, and clinging to some trifling animal to whom they never were more than pack-horses. That's what they mean by the love that passeth understanding: that pride, that furious desire to hide that abject nakedness which we bring here with us, carry with us into operating-rooms, carry stubbornly and furiously with us into the earth again. I leave the room. Beyond the porch Cash's saw snores steadily into the board. A minute later she calls his name, her voice harsh and strong.

'Cash,' she says; 'you, Cash!'

Darl

Pa stands beside the bed. From behind his leg Vardaman peers, with his round head and his eyes round and his mouth beginning to open. She looks at pa; all her failing life appears to drain into her eyes, urgent, irremediable. 'It's Jewel she wants,' Dewey Dell says.

'Why, Addie,' pa says, 'him and Darl went to make one more load. They thought there was time. That you would wait for them, and that three dollars and all . . .' He stoops, laying his hand on hers. For a while yet she looks at him, without reproach, without anything at all, as if her eyes alone are listening to the irrevocable cessation of his voice. Then she raises herself, who has not moved in ten days. Dewey Dell leans down, trying to press her back.

'Ma,' she says; 'ma.'

She is looking out the window, at Cash stooping steadily at the board in the failing light, labouring on toward darkness and into it as though the stroking of the saw illumined its own motion, board and saw engendered.

'You, Cash,' she shouts, her voice harsh, strong, and unimpaired. 'You, Cash!'

He looks up at the gaunt face framed by the window in the twilight. It is a composite picture of all time since he was a child. He drops the saw and lifts the board for her to see, watching the window in which the face has not moved. He drags a second plank into position and slants the two of them into their final juxtaposition, gesturing toward the ones yet on the ground, shaping with his empty hand in pantomime the finished box. For a while still she looks down at him from the composite picture, neither with censure nor approbation. Then the face disappears.

She lies back and turns her head without so much as glancing at pa. She looks at Vardaman; her eyes, the life in them, rushing suddenly upon them; the two flames glare up for a steady instant. Then they go out as though someone had leaned down and blown upon them.

'Ma,' Dewey Dell says; 'ma!' Leaning above the bed, her hands lifted a little, the fan still moving like it has for ten days, she begins to keen. Her voice is strong, young, tremulous, and clear, rapt with its own timbre and volume, the fan still moving steadily up and down, whispering the useless air. Then she flings herself across Addie Bundren's knees, clutching her, shaking her with the furious strength of the young before sprawling suddenly across the handful of rotten bones that Addie Bundren left, jarring the whole bed into a chattering sibilance of mattress shucks, her arms outflung and the fan in one hand still beating with expiring breath into the quilt.

From behind pa's leg Vardaman peers, his mouth full open and all colour draining from his face into his mouth, as though he has by some means fleshed his own teeth in himself, sucking. He begins to move slowly backward from the bed, his eyes round, his pale face fading into the dusk like a piece of paper pasted on a failing wall, and so out of the door.

Pa leans above the bed in the twilight, his humped silhouette partaking of that owl-like quality of awry-feathered, disgruntled outrage within which lurks a wisdom too profound or too inert for even thought.

'Durn them boys,' he says.

Jewel, I say. Overhead the day drives level and grey, hiding the sun by a flight of grey spears. In the rain the mules smoke a little, splashed yellow with mud, the off one clinging in sliding lunges to the side of the road above the ditch. The tilted lumber gleams dull yellow, water-soaked and heavy as lead, tilted at a steep angle into the ditch above the broken wheel, about the shattered spokes and about Jewel's ankles a runnel of yellow neither water nor earth swirls, curving with the yellow road neither of earth nor water, down the hill dissolving into a streaming mass of dark green neither of earth nor sky. Jewel, I say.

Cash comes to the door, carrying the saw. Pa stands beside the bed, humped, his arms dangling. He turns his head, his shabby profile, his chin collapsing slowly as he works the snuff against his gums.

'She's gone,' Cash says.

'She's taken and left us,' pa says. Cash does not look at him. 'How nigh are you done?' pa says. Cash does not answer. He enters, carrying the saw. 'I reckon you better get at it,' pa says. 'You'll have to do the best you can, with them boys gone off that-a-way.' Cash looks down at her face. He is not listening to pa at all. He does not approach the bed. He stops in the middle of the floor, the saw against his leg, his sweating arms powdered lightly with sawdust, his face composed. 'If you get in a tight, maybe some of them'll get here tomorrow and help you,' pa says. 'Vernon could.' Cash is not listening. He is looking down at her peaceful, rigid face fading into the dusk as though darkness were a precursor of the ultimate earth, until at last the face seems to float detached upon it, lightly as the reflection of a dead leaf. 'There is Christians enough to help you,' pa says. Cash is not listening. After a while he turns without looking at pa and leaves the room. Then the saw begins to snore again. 'They will help us in our sorrow,' pa says.

The sound of the saw is steady, competent, unhurried, stirring the dying light so that at each stroke her face seems to wake a little into an expression of listening and of waiting, as though she were counting the strokes. Pa looks down at the face, at the black sprawl of Dewey Dell's hair, the outflung arms, the clutched fan now motionless on the fading quilt. 'I reckon you better get supper on,' he says.

Dewey Dell does not move.

'Git up, now, and put supper on,' pa says. 'We got to keep our strength up. I reckon Doctor Peabody's right hungry, coming all this way. And Cash'll need to eat quick and get back to work so he can finish it in time.'

Dewey Dell rises, heaving to her feet. She looks down at the face. It is like a casting of fading bronze upon the pillow, the hands alone still with any semblance of life: a curled, gnarled inertness; a spent yet alert quality from which weariness, exhaustion, travail has not yet departed, as though they doubted even yet the actuality of rest, guarding with horned and penurious alertness the cessation which they know cannot last.

Dewey Dell stoops and slides the quilt from beneath them and draws it up over them to the chin, smoothing it down, drawing it smooth. Then without looking at pa she goes around the bed and leaves the room.

She will go out where Peabody is, where she can stand in the twilight and look at his back with such an expression that, feeling her eyes and turning, he will say: I would not let it grieve me, now. She was old, and sick too. Suffering more than we knew. She couldn't have got well. Vardaman's getting big now, and with you to take good care of them all. I would try not to let it grieve me. I expect you'd better go and get some supper ready. It don't have to be much. But they'll need to eat, and she looking at him, saying You could do so much for me if you just would. If you just knew. I am I and you are you and I know it and you don't know it and you could do so much for me if you just would and if you just would then I could tell you and then nobody would have to know it except you and me and Darl.

Pa stands over the bed, dangle-armed, humped, motionless. He raises his hand to his head, scouring his hair, listening to the saw. He comes nearer and rubs his hand, palm and back, on his thigh and lays it on her face and then on the hump of quilt where her hands are. He touches the quilt as he saw Dewey Dell do, trying to smooth it up to the chin, but disarranging it instead. He tries to smooth it again, clumsily, his hand awkward as a claw, smoothing at the wrinkles which he made and which continue to emerge beneath his hand with perverse ubiquity, so that at last he desists, his hand falling to his side and stroking itself again, palm and back, on his thigh. The sound of the saw snores steadily into the room. Pa breathes with a quiet, rasping sound, mouthing the snuff against his gums. 'God's will be done,' he says. 'Now I can get them teeth.'

Jewel's hat droops limp about his neck, channelling water on to the soaked tow-sack tied about his shoulders as, ankle-deep in the running ditch, he pries with a slipping two-by-four, with a piece of rotting log for fulcrum, at the axle. Jewel, I say, she is dead, Jewel. Addie Bundren is dead.

Vardaman

Then I begin to run. I run toward the back and come to the edge of the porch and stop. Then I begin to cry. I can feel where the fish was in the dust. It is cut up into pieces of not-fish now, not-blood on my hands and overalls. Then it wasn't so. It hadn't happened then. And now she is getting so far ahead I cannot catch her.

The trees look like chickens when they ruffle out into the cool dust on the hot days. If I jump off the porch I will be where the fish was, and it all cut up into not-fish now. I can hear the bed and her face and them and I can feel the floor shake when he walks on it that came and did it. That came and did it when she was all right but he came and did it.

'The fat son of a bitch.'

I jump from the porch, running. The top of the barn comes swooping up out of the twilight. If I jump I can go through it like the pink lady in the circus, into the warm smelling, without having to wait. My hands grab at the bushes; beneath my feet the rocks and dirt go rubbling down.

Then I can breathe again, in the warm smelling. I enter the stall, trying to touch him, and then I can cry then I vomit the crying. As soon as he gets through kicking I can and then I can cry, the crying can.

'He kilt her. He kilt her.'

The life in him runs under the skin, under my hand, running through the splotches, smelling up into my nose where the sickness is beginning to cry, vomiting the crying, and then I can breathe, vomiting it. It makes a lot of noise. I can smell the life running up from under my hands, up my arms, and then I can leave the stall.

I cannot find it. In the dark, along the dust, the walls I cannot find it. The crying makes a lot of noise. I wish it wouldn't make so much noise. Then I find it in the wagon-shed, in the dust, and

I run across the lot and into the road, the stick jouncing on my shoulder.

They watch me as I run up, beginning to jerk back, their eyes rolling, snorting, jerking back on the hitch rein. I strike. I can hear the stick striking; I can see it hitting their heads, the breast-yoke, missing altogether sometimes as they rear and plunge, but I am glad.

'You kilt my maw!'

The stick breaks, they rearing and snorting, their feet popping loud on the ground; loud because it is going to rain and the air is empty for the rain. But it is still long enough. I run this way and that as they rear and jerk at the hitch-rein, striking.

'You kilt her!'

I strike at them, striking, they wheeling in a long lunge, the buggy wheeling on to two wheels and motionless like it is nailed to the ground and the horses motionless like they are nailed by the hind feet to the centre of a whirling-plate.

I run in the dust. I cannot see, running in the sucking dust where the buggy vanishes tilted on two wheels. I strike, the stick hitting into the ground, bouncing, striking into the dust and then into the air again and the dust sucking on down the road faster than if a car was in it. And then I can cry, looking at the stick. It is broken down to my hand, not longer than stove wood that was a long stick. I throw it away and I can cry. It does not make so much noise now.

The cow is standing in the barn door, chewing. When she sees me come into the lot she lows, her mouth full of flopping green, her tongue flopping.

'I ain't a-goin' to milk you. I ain't a-goin' to do nothing for them.'

I hear her turn when I pass. When I turn she is just behind me with her sweet, hot, hard breath.

'Didn't I tell you I wouldn't?'

She nudges me, snuffing. She moans deep inside, her mouth closed. I jerk my hand, cursing her like Jewel does.

'Git, now.'

I stoop my hand to the ground and run at her. She jumps back and whirls away and stops, watching me. She moans. She goes on to the path and stands there, looking up the path.

It is dark in the barn, warm, smelling, silent. I can cry quietly, watching the top of the hill.

Cash comes to the hill, limping where he fell off the church.

He looks down at the spring, then up the road and back toward the barn. He comes down the path stiffly and looks at the broken hitch-rein and at the dust in the road and then up the road, where the dust is gone.

'I hope they've got clean past Tull's by now. I so hope hit.'

Cash turns and limps up the path.

'Durn him. I showed him. Durn him.'

I am not crying now. I am not anything. Dewey Dell comes to the hill and calls me. 'Vardaman.' I am not anything. I am quiet. 'You, Vardaman.' I can cry quiet now, feeling and hearing my tears.

'Then hit want. Hit hadn't happened then. Hit was a-layin' right there on the ground. And now she's gittin' ready to cook hit.'

It is dark. I can hear wood, silence: I know them. But not living sounds, not even him. It is as though the dark were resolving him out of his integrity, into an unrelated scattering of components – snuffings and stampings; smells of cooling flesh and ammoniac hair; an illusion of a coordinated whole of splotched hide and strong bones within which, detached and secret and familiar, an *is* different from my *is*. I see him dissolve – legs, a rolling eye, a gaudy splotching like cold flames – and float upon the dark in fading solution; all one yet neither; all either yet none. I can see hearing coil toward him, caressing, shaping his hard shape – fetlock, hip, shoulder, and head; smell and sound. I am not afraid.

'Cooked and et. Cooked and et.'

Dewey Dell

He could do so much for me if he just would. He could do everything for me. It's like everything in the world for me is inside a tub full of guts, so that you wonder how there can be any room in it for anything else very important. He is a big tub of guts and I am a little tub of guts and if there is not any room for anything else important in a big tub of guts, how can it be room in a little tub of guts. But I know it is there because God gave women a sign when something has happened bad.

It's because I am alone. If I could just feel it, it would be different, because I would not be alone. But if I were not alone, everybody would know it. And he could do so much for me, and then I would not be alone. Then I could be all right alone.

I would let him come in between me and Lafe, like Darl came in between me and Lafe, and so Lafe is alone too. He is Lafe and I am Dewey Dell, and when mother died I had to go beyond and outside of me and Lafe and Darl to grieve because he could do so much for me and he don't know it. He don't even know it.

From the back porch I cannot see the barn. Then the sound of Cash's sawing comes in from that way. It is like a dog outside the house, going back and forth around the house to whatever door you come to, waiting to come in. He said I worry more than you do and I said You don't know what worry is so I can't worry. I try to but I can't think long enough to worry.

I light the kitchen lamp. The fish, cut into jagged pieces, bleeds quietly in the pan. I put it into the cupboard quick, listening into the hall, hearing. It took her ten days to die; maybe she don't know it is yet. Maybe she won't go until Cash. Or maybe until Jewel. I take the dish of greens from the cupboard and the bread-pan from the cold stove, and I stop, watching the door.

'Where's Vardaman?' Cash says. In the lamp his sawdusted arms look like sand.

'I don't know. I ain't seen him.'

'Peabody's team run away. See if you can find Vardaman. The horse will let him catch him.'

'Well. Tell them to come to supper.'

I cannot see the barn. I said, I don't know how to worry. I don't know how to cry. I tried, but I can't. After a while the sound of the saw comes around, coming dark along the ground in the dust-dark. Then I can see him, going up and down above the plank.

'You come in to supper,' I say. 'Tell him.' He could do everything for me. And he don't know it. He is his guts and I am my guts. And I am Lafe's guts. That's it. I don't see why he didn't stay in town. We are country people not as good as town people. I don't see why he didn't. Then I can see the top of the barn. The cow stands at the foot of the path, lowing. When I turn back, Cash is gone.

I carry the buttermilk in. Pa and Cash and he are at the table.

'Where's that big fish Bud caught, sister?' he says.

I set the milk on the table. 'I never had no time to cook it.'

'Plain turnip greens is mighty spindling eating for a man my size,' he says. Cash is eating. About his head the print of his hat sweated into his hair. His shirt is blotched with sweat. He has not washed his hands and arms.

'You ought to took time,' pa says. 'Where's Vardaman?'

I go toward the door. 'I can't find him.'

'Here, sister,' he says; 'never mind about the fish. It'll save, I reckon. Come on and sit down.'

'I ain't minding it,' I say. 'I'm going to milk before it sets in to rain.'

Pa helps himself and pushes the dish on. But he does not begin to eat. His hands are half-closed on either side of his plate, his head bowed a little, his awry hair standing into the lamplight. He looks like right after the maul hits the steer and it no longer alive and don't yet know that it is dead.

But Cash is eating, and he is too. 'You better eat something,' he says. He is looking at pa. 'Like Cash and me. You'll need it.'

'Ay,' pa says. He rouses up, like a steer that's been kneeling in a pond and you run at it. 'She would not begrudge me it.'

When I am out sight of the house, I go fast. The cow lows at the foot of the bluff. She nuzzles at me, snuffing, blowing her breath in a sweet, hot blast, through my dress, against my hot nakedness, moaning. 'You got to wait a little while. Then I'll tend you.' She follows me into the barn where I set the bucket down. She breathes into the bucket, moaning. 'I told you. You just got to wait, now. I got more to do than I can tend to.' The barn is dark. When I pass, he kicks the wall a single blow. I go on. The broken plank is like a pale plank standing on end. Then I can see the slope, feel the air moving on my face again, slow, pale, with lesser dark and with empty seeing, the pine clumps blotched up the tilted slopes, secret and waiting.

The cow in silhouette against the door nuzzles at the silhouette of the bucket, moaning.

When I pass the stall. I have almost passed it. I listen to it saying for a long time before it can say the word and the listening part is afraid that there may not be time to say it. I feel my body, my bones and flesh beginning to part and open upon the alone, and the process of coming unalone is terrible. Lafe, Lafe. 'Lafe' Lafe. Lafe. I lean a little forward, one foot advanced with dead walking. I feel the darkness rushing past my breast, past the cow;

I begin to rush upon the darkness but the cow stops me and the darkness rushes on upon the sweet blast of her moaning breath, filled with wood and with silence.

'Vardaman. You, Vardaman.'

He comes out of the stall. 'You durn little sneak. You durn little sneak!'

He does not resist; the last of rushing darkness flees whistling away. 'What? I ain't done nothing.'

'You durn little sneak!' My hands shake him, hard. Maybe I couldn't stop them. I didn't know they could shake so hard. They shake both of us, shaking.

'I never done it,' he says. 'I never touched them.'

My hands stop shaking him, but I still hold him. 'What are you doing here? Why didn't you answer when I called you?'

'I ain't doing nothing.'

'You go on to the house and get your supper.'

He draws back. I hold him. 'You quit now. You leave me be.'

'What were you doing down here? You didn't come down here to sneak after me?'

'I never. I never. You quit, now. I didn't even know you was down here. You leave me be.'

I hold him, leaning down to see his face, feel it with my eyes. He is about to cry. 'Go on, now. I done put supper on and I'll be there soon as I milk. You better go on before he eats everything up. I hope that team runs clean back to Jefferson.'

'He kilt her,' he says. He begins to cry.

'Hush.'

'She never hurt him and he come and kilt her.'

'Hush.' He struggles. I hold him. 'Hush.'

'He kilt her.' The cow comes up behind us, moaning. I shake him again.

'You stop it, now. Right this minute. You're fixing to make yourself sick and then you can't go to town. You go on to the house and eat your supper.'

'I don't want no supper. I don't want to go to town.'

'We'll leave you here, then. Lessen you behave, we will leave you. Go on, now, before that old green-eating tub of guts eats everything up from you.' He goes on, disappearing slowly into the hill. The crest, the trees, the roof of the house stand against the sky. The cow nuzzles at me, moaning. 'You'll just have to wait. What you got in you ain't nothing to what I got in me, even if you are a woman too.' She follows me, moaning. Then the dead, hot, pale air breathes on my face again. He could fix it all right, if he just would. And he don't even know it. He could do everything for me if he just knowed it. The cow breathes upon my hips and back, her breath warm, sweet, stertorous, moaning. The sky lies flat down the slope, upon the secret clumps. Beyond the hill sheet-lightning stains upwards and fades. The dead air shapes the dead earth in the dead darkness, farther away than seeing shapes the dead earth. It lies dead and warm upon me, touching me naked through my clothes. I said You don't know what worry is. I don't know what it is. I don't know whether I am worrying or not. Whether I can or not. I don't know whether I can cry or not. I don't know whether I have tried to or not. I feel like a wet seed wild in the hot blind earth.

Vardaman

When they get it finished they are going to put her in it and then for a long time I couldn't say it. I saw the dark stand up and go whirling away and I said 'Are you going to nail her up in it, Cash? Cash? Cash?' I got shut up in the crib and the new door it was too heavy for me it went shut I couldn't breathe because the rat was breathing up all the air. I said 'Are you going to nail it shut, Cash? Nail it? *Nail* it?'

Pa walks around. His shadow walks around, over Cash going up and down above the saw, at the bleeding plank.

Dewey Dell said we will get some bananas. The train is behind the glass, red on the track. When it runs the track shines on and off. Pa said flour and sugar and coffee costs so much. Because I am a country boy because boys in town. Bicycles. Why do flour and sugar and coffee cost so much when he is a country boy. 'Wouldn't you ruther have some bananas instead?' Bananas are gone, eaten. Gone. When it runs on the track shines again. 'Why ain't I a town boy, pa?' I said God made me. I did not said to God to made me in the country. If He can make the train, why can't He make them all in the town because flour and sugar and coffee. 'Wouldn't you ruther have bananas?'

He walks around. His shadow walks around.

It was not her. I was there, looking. I saw. I thought it was her, but it was not. It was not my mother. She went away when the other one laid down in her bed and drew the quilt up, She went away. 'Did she go as far as town?' 'She went farther than town.' 'Did all those rabbits and possums go farther than town?' God made the rabbits and possums. He made the train. Why must He make a different place for them to go if she is just like the rabbit.

Pa walks around. His shadow does. The saw sounds like it is asleep.

And so if Cash nails the box up, she is not a rabbit. And so if she is not a rabbit I couldn't breathe in the crib and Cash is going to nail it up. And so if she lets him it is not her. I know. I was there. I saw when it did not be her. I saw. They think it is and Cash is going to nail it up.

It was not her because it was laying right yonder in the dirt. And now it's all chopped up. I chopped it up. It's laying in the kitchen in the bleeding pan, waiting to be cooked and et. Then it wasn't and she was, and now it is and she wasn't. And tomorrow it will be cooked and et and she will be him and pa and Cash and Dewey Dell and there won't be anything in the box and so she can breathe. It was laying right yonder on the ground. I can get Vernon. He was there and he seen it and with both of us it will be and then it will not be.

Tull

It was nigh to midnight and it had set in to rain when he woke us. It had been a misdoubtful night, with the storm making; a night when a fellow looks for most anything to happen before he can get the stock fed and himself to the house an supper et and in bed with the rain starting, and when Peabody's team come up, lathered, with the broke harness dragging and the neck-yoke betwixt the off critter's legs, Cora says, 'It's Addie Bundren. She's gone at last.'

'Peabody mought have been to ere a one of a dozen houses hereabouts,' I says. 'Besides, how do you know it's Peabody's team?'

'Well, ain't it?' she says. 'You hitch up, now.'

'What for?' I says. 'If she is gone, we can't do nothing till morning. And it fixing to storm too.'

'It's my duty,' she says. 'You put the team in.'

But I wouldn't do it. 'It stands to reason they'd send for us if they needed us. You don't even know she's gone yet.'

'Why, don't you know that's Peabody's team? Do you claim it ain't? Well, then.' But I wouldn't go. When folks wants a fellow, it's best to wait till they sends for him, I've found. 'It's my Christian duty,' Cora says. 'Will you stand between me and my Christian duty?'

'You can stay there all day tomorrow, if you want,' I says.

So when Cora waked me it had set in to rain. Even while I was going to the door with the lamp and it shining on the glass so he could see I am coming, it kept on knocking. Not loud, but steady, like he might have gone to sleep thumping, but I never noticed how low down on the door the knocking was till I opened it and never seen nothing. I held the lamp up, with the rain sparkling across it and Cora back in the hall saying 'Who is it, Vernon?' but I couldn't see nobody a-tall at first until I looked down and around the door, lowering the lamp.

He looked like a drowned puppy, in them overalls, without no hats, splashed up to his knees where he had walked them four miles in the mud. 'Well, I'll be durned,' I says.

'Who is it, Vernon?' Cora says.

He looked at me, his eyes round and black in the middle like when you throw a light in a owl's face. 'You mind that ere fish,' he says.

'Come in the house,' I says. 'What is it? Is your maw –'

'Vernon,' Cora says.

He stood kind of around behind the door, in the dark. The rain was blowing on to the lamp, hissing on it so I am scared every minute it'll break. 'You was there,' he says. 'You seen it.'

Then Cora come to the door. 'You come right in outen the rain,' she says, pulling him in and him watching me. He looked just like a drowned puppy. 'I told you,' Cora says. 'I told you it was a-happening. You go and hitch.'

'But he ain't said –' I says.

He looked at me, dripping on to the floor. 'He's a-ruining the rug,' Cora says. 'You go get the team while I take him to the kitchen.'

But he hung back, dripping, watching me with them eyes. 'You was there. You seen it laying there. Cash is fixing to nail her up, and it was a-laying right there on the ground. You seen it. You seen the mark in the dirt. The rain never come up till after I was a-coming here. So we can get back in time.'

I be durn if it didn't give me the creeps, even when I didn't know yet. But Cora did. 'You get that team as quick as you can,' she says. 'He's outen his head with grief and worry.'

I be durn if it didn't give me the creeps. Now and then a fellow gets to thinking. About all the sorrow and afflictions in this world; how it's liable to strike anywhere, like lightning. I reckon it does take a powerful trust in the Lord to guard a fellow, though sometimes I think that Cora's a mite over-cautious, like she was trying to crowd the other folks away and get in closer than anybody else. But then, when something like this happens, I reckon she is right and you got to keep after it and I reckon I am blessed in having a wife that ever strives for sanctity and well-doing like she says I am.

Now and then a fellow gets to thinking about it. Not often, though. Which is a good thing. For the Lord aimed for him to do and not to spend too much time thinking, because his brain it's like a piece of machinery: it won't stand a whole lot of racking. It's best when it all runs along the same, doing the day's work and not no one part used no more than needful. I have said and I say again, that's ever living thing the matter with Darl: he just thinks by himself too much. Cora's right when she says all he needs is a wife to straighten him out. And when I think about that, I think that if nothing but being married will help a man, he's durn nigh hopeless. But I reckon Cora's right when she says the reason the Lord had to create women is because man don't know his own good when he sees it.

When I come back to the house with the team, they was in the kitchen. She was dressed on top of her nightgown with a shawl over her head and her umbrella and her Bible wrapped up in the oilcloth, and him sitting on a up-turned bucket on the stove-zinc where she had put him, dripping on to the floor. 'I can't get nothing outen him except about a fish,' she says. 'It's a judgement on them. I see the hand of the Lord upon this boy for Anse

Bundren's judgement and warning.'

'The rain never come up till after I left,' he says. 'I had done left. I was on the way. And so it was there in the dust. You seen it. Cash is fixing to nail her, but you seen it.'

When we got there it was raining hard, and him sitting on the seat between us, wrapped up in Cora's shawl. He hadn't said nothing else, just sitting there with Cora holding the umbrella over him. Now and then Cora would stop singing long enough to say 'It's a judgement on Anse Bundren. May it show him the path of sin he is a-trodding.' Then she would sing again, and him sitting there between us, leaning forward a little like the mules couldn't go fast enough to suit him.

'It was laying right yonder,' he says, 'but the rain come up after I taken and left. So I can go and open the windows, because Cash ain't nailed her yet.'

It was long a-past midnight when we drove the last nail, and almost dust-dawn when I got back home and taken the team out and got back in bed, with Cora's nightcap laying on the other pillow. And be durned if even then it wasn't like I could still hear Cora singing and feel that boy leaning forward between us like he was ahead of the mules, and still see Cash going up and down with that saw, and Anse standing there like a scarecrow, like he was a steer standing knee-deep in a pond and somebody come by and set the pond up on edge and he ain't missed it yet.

It was nigh toward daybreak when we drove the last nail and toted it into the house, where she was laying on the bed with the window open and the rain blowing on her again. Twice he did it, and him so dead for sleep that Cora says his face looked like one of these here Christmas masts that had done been buried a while and then dug up, until at last they put her into it and nailed it down so he couldn't open the window on her no more. And the next morning they found him in his shirt-tail laying asleep on the floor like a felled steer, and the top of the box bored clean full of holes and Cash's new auger broke off in the last one. When they had taken the lid off they found that two of them had bored on into her face.

If it's a judgement, it ain't right. Because the Lord's got more to do than that. He's bound to have. Because the only burden Anse Bundren's ever had is himself. And when folks talks him low, I think to myself he ain't that less of a man or he couldn't a bore himself this long.

It ain't right. I be durn if it is. Because He said Suffer little children to come unto Me don't make it right, neither. Cora said, 'I have bore you what the Lord God sent me. I faced it without fear nor terror because my faith was strong in the Lord, a-bolstering and sustaining me. If you have no son, it's because the Lord has decreed otherwise in His wisdom. And my life is and has ever been a open book to ere a man or woman among His creatures because I trust in my God and my reward.'

I reckon she's right. I reckon if there's ere a man or woman anywhere that He could turn it all over to and go away with His mind at rest, it would be Cora. And I reckon she would make a few changes, no matter how He was running it. And I reckon they would be for man's good. Leastways, we would have to like them. Leastways, we might as well go on and make like we did.

Darl

The lantern sits on a stump. Rusted, grease-fouled, its cracked chimney smeared on one side with a soaring smudge of soot, it sheds a feeble and sultry glare upon the trestles and the boards and the adjacent earth. Upon the dark ground the chips look like random smears of soft pale paint on a black canvas. The boards look like long smooth tatters torn from the flat darkness and turned backside out.

Cash labours about the trestles, moving back and forth, lifting and placing the planks with long clattering reverberations in the dead air as though he were lifting and dropping them at the bottom of an invisible well, the sounds ceasing without departing, as if any movement might dislodge them from the immediate air in reverberant repetition. He saws again, his elbow flashing slowly, a thin thread of fire running along the edge of the saw, lost and recovered at the top and bottom of each stroke in unbroken elongation, so that the saw appears to be six feet long, into and out of pa's shabby and aimless silhouette. 'Give me that plank,' Cash says. 'No; the other one.' He puts the saw down and comes and picks up the plank he wants, sweeping pa away with the long swinging gleam of the balanced board.

The air smells like sulphur. Upon the impalpable plane of it their shadows form as upon a wall, as though like sound they had not gone very far away in falling but had merely congealed for a moment, immediate and musing. Cash works on, half turned into the feeble light, one thigh and one pole thin arm braced, his face sloped into the light with a rapt, dynamic immobility above his tireless elbow. Below the sky sheet-lightning slumbers lightly; against it the trees, motionless, are ruffled out to the last twig, swollen, increased as though quick with young.

It begins to rain. The first harsh, sparse, swift drops rush through the leaves and across the ground in a long sigh, as though of relief from intolerable suspense. They are big as buckshot, warm as though fired from a gun; they sweep across the lantern in a vicious hissing. Pa lifts his face, slack-mouthed, the wet black rim of snuff plastered close along the base of his gums; from behind his slack-faced astonishment he muses, as though from beyond time, upon the ultimate outrage. Cash looks once at the sky, then at the lantern. The saw has not faltered, the running gleam of its pistoning edge unbroken. 'Get something to cover the lantern,' he says.

Pa goes to the house. The rain rushes suddenly down, without thunder, without warning of any sort; he is swept on to the porch upon the edge of it and in an instant Cash is wet to the skin. Yet the motion of the saw has not faltered, as though it and the arms functioned in a tranquil conviction that rain was an illusion of the mind. Then he puts down the saw and goes and crouches above the lantern, shielding it with his body, his back shaped lean and scrawny by his wet shirt as though he had been abruptly turned wrong-side out, shirt and all.

Pa returns. He is wearing Jewel's raincoat and carrying Dewey Dell's. Squatting over the lantern, Cash reaches back and picks up four sticks and drives them into the earth and takes Dewey Dell's raincoat from pa and spreads it over the sticks, forming a roof above the lantern. Pa watches him. 'I don't know what you'll do,' he says. 'Darl taken his coat with him.'

'Get wet,' Cash says. He takes up the saw again; again it moves up and down, in and out of that unhurried imperviousness as a piston moves in the oil; soaked, scrawny, tireless, with the lean light body of a boy or an old man. Pa watches him, blinking, his face streaming; again he looks up at the sky with that expression of dumb and brooding outrage and yet of vindication, as though he had expected no less; now and then he stirs, moves, gaunt and streaming, picking up a board or a tool and then laying it down. Vernon Tull is there now, and Cash is wearing Mrs Tull's raincoat and he and Vernon are hunting the saw. After a while they find it in pa's hand.

'Why don't you go on to the house, out of the rain?' Cash says. Pa looks at him, his face streaming slowly. It is as though upon a face carved by a savage caricaturist a monstrous burlesque of all bereavement flowed. 'You go on in,' Cash says. 'Me and Vernon can finish it.'

Pa looks at them. The sleeves of Jewel's coat are too short for him. Upon his face the rain streams, slow as cold glycerine. 'I don't begrudge her the wetting,' he says. He moves again and falls to shifting the planks, picking them up, laying them down again carefully, as though they are glass. He goes to the lantern and pulls at the propped raincoat until he knocks it down and Cash comes and fixes it back.

'You get on to the house,' Cash says. He leads pa to the house and returns with the raincoat and folds it and places it beneath the shelter where the lantern sits. Vernon has not stopped. He looks up, still sawing.

'You ought to done that at first,' he says. 'You knowed it was fixing to rain.'

'It's his fever,' Cash says. He looks at the board.

'Ay,' Vernon says. 'He'd a come, anyway.'

Cash squints at the board. On the long flank of it the rain crashes steadily, myriad, fluctuant. 'I'm going to bevel it,' he says.

'It'll take more time,' Vernon says. Cash sets the plank on edge; a moment longer Vernon watches him, then he hands him the plane.

Vernon holds the board steady while Cash bevels the edge of it with the tedious and minute care of a jeweller. Mrs Tull comes to the edge of the porch and calls Vernon 'How near are you done?' she says.

Vernon does not look up. 'Not long. Some, yet.'

She watches Cash stooping at the plank, the turgid savage gleam of the lantern slicing on the raincoat as he moves. 'You go down and get some planks off the barn and finish it and come in out of the rain,' she says, 'You'll both catch your death.' Vernon does not move. 'Vernon,' she says.

'We won't be long,' he says. 'We'll be done after a spell.' Mrs Tull watches them a while, Then she re-enters the house.

'If we get in a tight, we could take some of them planks,' Vernon says. 'I'll help you put them back.'

Cash ceases the plane and squints along the plank, wiping it with his palm. 'Give me the next one,' he says.

Some time toward dawn the rain ceases. But it is not yet day when Cash drives the last nail and stands stiffly up and looks down at the finished coffin, the others watching him. In the lantern-light his face is calm, musing; slowly he strokes his hands on his raincoated thighs in a gesture deliberate, final, and composed. Then the four of them – Cash and pa and Vernon and Peabody – raise the coffin to their shoulders and turn toward the house. It is light, yet they move slowly; empty, yet they carry it carefully; lifeless, yet they move with hushed precautionary words to one another, speaking of it as though, complete, it now slumbered lightly alive, waiting to come awake. On the dark floor their feet clump awkwardly, as though for a long time they have not walked on floors.

They set it down by the bed. Peabody says quietly: 'Let's eat a snack. It's almost daylight. Where's Cash?'

He has returned to the trestles, stooped again in the lantern's feeble glare as he gathers up his tools and wipes them on a cloth carefully and puts them into the box with its leather sling to gover the shoulder. Then he takes up box, lantern, and raincoat, and returns to the house, mounting the steps into faint silhouette against the paling east.

In a strange room you must empty yourself for sleep. And before you are emptied for sleep, what are you. And when you are emptied for sleep, you are not. And when you are filled with sleep, you never were. I don't know what I am. I don't know if I am or not. Jewel knows he is, because he does not know that he does not know whether he is or not. He cannot empty himself for sleep because he is not what he is and he is what he is not. Beyond the unlamped wall I can hear the rain shaping the wagon that is ours, the load that is no longer theirs that felled and sawed it nor yet theirs that bought it and which is not ours either, lie on our wagon though it does, since only the wind and the rain shape it only to Jewel and me, that are not asleep. And since sleep is is-not and rain and wind are *was*, it is not. Yet the wagon *is*, because when the wagon is *was*, Addie Bundren will not be. And Jewel *is*, so Addie Bundren must be. And then I must be, or I could not empty myself for sleep in a strange room. And so if I am not emptied yet, I am *is*.

How often have I lain beneath rain on a strange roof, thinking of home.

Cash

I made it on the bevel.

1. There is more surface for the nails to grip.
2. There is twice the gripping-surface to each seam.
3. The water will have to seep into it on a slant. Water moves easiest up and down or straight across.
4. In a house people are upright two-thirds of the time. So the seams and joints are made up-and-down. Because the stress is up-and-down.
5. In a bed where people lie down all the time, the joints and seams are made sideways, because the stress is sideways.
6. Except.
7. A body is not square like a cross-tie.
8. Animal magnetism.
9. The animal magnetism of a dead body makes the stress come slanting, so the seams and joints of a coffin are made on the bevel.
10. You can see by an old grave that the earth sinks down on the bevel.
11. While in a natural hole it sinks by the centre, the stress being up-and-down.
12. So I made it on the bevel.
13. It makes a neater job.

Vardaman

My mother is a fish.

Tull

It was ten o'clock when I got back, with Peabody's team hitched on to the back of the wagon. They had already dragged the buckboard back from where Quick found it up side down straddle of the ditch about a mile from the spring. It was pulled out of the road at the spring, and about a dozen wagons was already there. It was Quick found it. He said the river was up and still rising. He said it had already covered the highest water-mark on the bridge-piling he had ever seen. 'That bridge won't stand a whole lot of water,' I said. 'Has somebody told Anse about it?'

'I told him,' Quick said. 'He says he reckons them boys has heard and unloaded and are on the way back by now. He says they can load up and get across.'

'He better go on and bury her at New Hope,' Armstid said. 'That bridge is old. I wouldn't monkey with it.'

'His mind is set on taking her to Jefferson,' Quick said.

'Then he better get at it soon as he can,' Armstid said.

Anse meets us at the door. He has shaved, but not good. There is a long cut on his jaw, and he is wearing his Sunday pants and a white shirt with the neckband buttoned. It is drawn smooth over his hump, making it look bigger than ever, like a white shirt will, and his face is different too. He looks folks in the eye now,

dignified, his face tragic and composed, shaking us by the hand
as we walk up on to the porch and scrape our shoes, a little stiff
in our Sunday clothes, our Sunday clothes rustling, not looking
full at him as he meets us.

'The Lord giveth,' we say.

'The Lord giveth.'

That boy is not there. Peabody told about how he come into
the kitchen, hollering, swarming, and clawing at Cora when he
found her cooking that fish, and how Dewey Dell taken him down
to the barn. 'My team all right?' Peabody says.

'All right,' I tell him. 'I give them a bait this morning. Your
buggy seems all right too. It ain't hurt.'

'And no fault of somebody's,' he says. 'I'd give a nickel to know
where that boy was when that team broke away.'

'If it's broke anywhere, I'll fix it,' I say.

The women folks go on into the house. We can hear them,
talking and fanning. The fans go whish, whish, whish and them
talking, the talking sounding kind of like bees murmuring in a
water-bucket. The men stop on the porch, talking some, not
looking at one another.

'Howdy, Vernon,' they say. 'Howdy, Tull.'

'Looks like more rain.'

'It does for a fact.'

'Yes, sir. It will rain some more.'

'It come up quick.'

'And going away slow. It don't fail.'

I go around to the back. Cash is filling up the holes he bored
in the top of it. He is trimming out plugs for them, one at a time,
the wood wet and hard to work. He could cut up a tin can
and hide the holes and nobody wouldn't know the difference.
Wouldn't mind, anyway. I have seen him spend a hour trimming
out a wedge like it was glass he was working, when he could have
reached around and picked up a dozen sticks and drove them
into the joint and made it do.

When we finished I go back to the front. The men have gone
a little piece from the house, sitting on the ends of the boards
and on the saw-horses where we made it last night, some sitting
and some squatting. Whitfield ain't come yet.

They looked up at me, their eyes asking.

'It's about,' I say. 'He's ready to nail.'

While they are getting up Anse comes to the door and looks
at us and we return to the porch. We scrape our shoes again,

careful, walting for one another to go in first, milling a little at
the door. Anse stands inside the door, dignified, composed. He
waves us in and leads the way into the room.

They had laid her in it reversed. Cash made it clock-shaped
like this with every joint and seam bevelled and
scrubbed with the plane, tight as a drum and neat
as a sewing basket, and they had laid her in it head to foot so it
wouldn't crush her dress. It was her wedding-dress and it had a
flare-out bottom, and they had laid her head to foot in it so the
dress could be spread out, and they had made her a veil out of a
mosquito bar so the auger holes in her face wouldn't show.

When we are going out, Whitfield comes. He is wet and muddy
to the waist, coming in. 'The Lord comfort this house,' he says.
'I was late because the bridge has gone. I went down to the old
ford and swum my horse over, the Lord protecting me. His grace
be upon this house.'

We go back to the trestles and plank-ends and sit or squat.

'I knowed it would go,' Armstid says.

'It's been there a long time, that ere bridge,' Quick says.

'The Lord has kept it there, you mean,' Uncle Billy says.

'I don't know ere a man that's touched hammer to it in twenty-
five years.'

'How long has it been there, Uncle Billy?' Quick says.

'It was built in . . . let me see . . . It was in the year 1888,' Uncle
Billy says. 'I mind it because the first man to cross it was Peabody
coming to my house when Jody was born.'

'If I'd a crossed it every time your wife littered since, it'd a
been wore out long before this, Billy,' Peabody says.

We laugh, suddenly loud, then suddenly quiet again. We look
a little aside at one another.

'Lots of folks has crossed it that won't cross no more bridges,'
Houston says.

'It's a fact,' Littlejohn says. 'It's so.'

'One more ain't, no ways,' Armstid says. 'It'd taken them two-
three days to got her to town in the wagon. They'd be gone a
week, getting her to Jefferson and back.'

'What's Anse so itching to take her to Jefferson for, anyway?'
Houston says.

'He promised her,' I say. 'She wanted it. She come from there.
Her mind was set on it.'

'And Anse is set on it, too,' Quick says.

'Ay,' Uncle Billy says. 'It's like a man that's let everything slide all his life to get set on something that will make the most trouble for everybody he knows.'

'Well, it'll take the Lord to get her over that river now,' Peabody says. 'Anse can't do it.'

'And I reckon He will,' Quick says. 'He's took care of Anse a long time, now.'

'It's a fact,' Littlejohn says.

'Too long to quit now,' Armstid says.

'I reckon He's like everybody else around here,' Uncle Billy says. 'He's done it so long now He can't quit.'

Cash comes out. He has put on a clean shirt; his hair, wet, is combed smooth down on his brow, smooth and black as if he had painted it on to his head. He squats stiffly among us, we watching him.

'You feeling this weather, ain't you?' Armstid says.

Cash says nothing.

'A broke bone always feels it,' Little John says. 'A fellow with a broke bone can tell it a-coming.'

'Lucky Cash got off with just a broke leg,' Armstid says. 'He might have hurt himself bed-rid. How far'd you fall, Cash?'

'Twenty-eight foot, four and a half inches, about,' Cash says. I move over beside him.

'A fellow can sho slip quick on wet planks,' Quick says.

'It's too bad,' I say. 'But you couldn't a holp it.'

'It's them durn women,' he says. 'I made it to balance with her. I made it to her measure and weight.'

If it takes wet boards for folks to fall, it's fixing to be lots of falling before this spell is done.

'You couldn't have holp it,' I say.

I don't mind the folks falling. It's the cotton and corn I mind.

Neither does Peabody mind the folks falling. How'bout it, Dot?

It's a fact. Washed clean outen the ground it will be. Seems like something is always happening to it.

'Course it does. That's why it's worth anything. If nothing didn't happen and everybody made a big crop, do you reckon it would be worth the raising?

Well, I be durn if I like to see my work washed outen the ground, work I sweat over.

It's a fact. A fellow wouldn't mind seeing it washed up if he could just turn on the rain himself.

Who is that man can do that? Where is the colour of his eyes?

Ay. The Lord made it to grow. It's Hisn to wash up if He sees it fitten so.

'You couldn't have holp it,' I say.

'It's them durn women,' he says.

In the house the women begin to sing. We hear the first line commence, beginning to swell as they take hold, and we rise and move toward the door, taking off our hats and throwing our chews away, We do not go in. We stop at the steps, clumped, holding our hats between our lax hands in front or behind, standing with one foot advanced and our heads lowered, looking aside, down at our hats in our hands and at the earth or now and then at the sky and at one another's grave, composed face.

The song ends; the voices quaver away with a rich and dying fall. Whitfield begins. His voice is bigger than him. It's like they are not the same. It's like he is one, and his voice is one, swimming on two horses side by side across the ford and coming into the house, the mud-splashed one and the one that never even got wet, triumphant and sad. Somebody in the house begins to cry. It sounds like her eyes and her voice were turned back inside her, listening; we move, shifting to the other leg, meeting one another's eye and making like they hadn't touched.

Whitfield stops at last. The women sing again. In the thick air it's like their voices come out of the air, flowing together and on in the sad, comforting tunes. When they cease it's like they hadn't gone away. It's like they had just disappeared into the air and when we moved we would loose them again out of the air around us, sad and comforting. Then they finish and we put on our hats, our movements stiff, like we hadn't never wore hats before.

On the way home Cora is still singing. 'I am bounding toward my God and my reward,' she sings, sitting on the wagon, the shawl around her shoulders and the umbrella open over her, though it is not raining.

'She has hern,' I say. 'Wherever she went, she has her reward in being free of Anse Bundren.' *She laid there three days in that box, waiting for Darl and Jewel to come clean back home and get a new wheel and go back to where the wagon was in the ditch. Take my team, Anse, I said.*

We'll wait for ourn, he said. She'll want it so. She was ever a particular woman.

On the third day they got back and they loaded her into the wagon and started and it already too late. You'll have to go all the way round by Samson's bridge. It'll take you a day to get there. Then you'll be forty miles from Jefferson. Take my team, Anse.

We'll wait for ourn. She'll want it so.

It was about a mile from the house we saw him, sitting on the edge of the slough. It hadn't had a fish in it never that I knowed. He looked around at us, his eyes round and calm, his face dirty, the pole across his knees. Cora was still singing.

'This ain't no good day to fish,' I said. 'You come on home with us and me and you'll go down to the river fist thing in the morning and catch some fish.'

'It's one in here,' he said. 'Dewey Dell seen it.'

'You come on with us. The river's the best place.'

'It's in here,' he said. 'Dewey Dell seen it.'

'I'm bounding toward my God and my reward,' Cora sung.

Darl

'It's not your horse that's dead, Jewel,' I say. He sits erect on the seat, leaning a little forward, wooden-backed. The brim of his hat has soaked free of the crown in two places, drooping across his wooden face so that, head lowered, he looks through it like through the visor of a helmet, looking long across the valley to where the barn leans against the bluff, shaping the invisible horse. 'See then?' I say. High above the house, against the quick thick sky, they hang in narrowing circles. From here they are no more than specks, implacable, patient, portentous. 'But it's not your horse that's dead.'

'Goddamn you,' he says. 'Goddamn you.'

I cannot love my mother because I have no mother. Jewel's mother is a horse.

Motionless, the tall buzzards hang in soaring circles, the clouds giving them an illusion of retrograde.

Motionless, wooden-backed, wooden-faced, he shapes the horse in a rigid stoop like a hawk, hook-winged. They are waiting for us, ready for the moving of it, waiting for him. He enters the stall and waits until it kicks at him so that he can slip past and mount on to the trough and pause, peering out across the intervening stall-tops toward the empty path, before he reaches into the loft.

'Goddamn him. Goddamn him.'

Cash

'It won't balance. If you want it to tote and ride on a balance, we will have –'

'Pick up. Goddamn you, pick up.'

'I'm telling you it won't tote and it won't ride on a balance unless –'

'Pick up! Pick up, goddamm your thick-nosed soul to hell, pick up!'

It won't balance. If they want it to tote and ride on a balance, they will have –

Darl

He stoops among us above it, two of the eight hands. In his face the blood goes in waves. In between them his flesh is greenish looking, about that smooth, thick, pale green of cow's cud; his face suffocated, furious, his lip lifted upon his teeth. 'Pick up!' he says. 'Pick up, goddamn your thick-nosed soul!'

He heaves, lifting one whole side so suddenly that we all spring into the lift to catch and balance it before he hurls it completely over. For an instant it resists, as though volitional, as though within it her pole-thin body clings furiously, even though dead, to a sort of modesty, as she would have tried to conceal a soiled garment that she could not prevent her body soiling. Then it breaks free, rising suddenly as though the emaciation of her body had added buoyancy to the planks or as though, seeing that the garment was about to be torn from her, she rushes suddenly after it in a passionate reversal that flouts its own desire and need. Jewel's face goes completely green and I can hear teeth in his breath.

We carry it down the hall, our feet harsh and clumsy on the floor, moving with shuffling steps, and through the door.

'Steady it a minute, now,' pa says, letting go. He turns back to shut and lock the door, but Jewel will not wait.

'Come on,' he says in that suffocating voice. 'Come on.'

We lower it carefully down the steps. We move, balancing it as though it were something infinitely precious, our faces averted, breathing through our teeth to keep our nostrils closed. We go down the path, toward the slope.

'We better wait,' Cash says. 'I tell you it ain't balanced now. We'll need another hand on that hill.'

'Then turn loose,' Jewel says. He will not stop. Cash begins to fall behind, hobbling to keep up, breathing harshly; then he is distanced and Jewel carries the entire front end alone, so that, tilting as the path begins to slant, it begins to rush away from me and slip down the air like a sled upon invisible snow, smoothly evacuating atmosphere in which the sense of it is still shaped.

'Wait, Jewel,' I say. But he will not wait. He is almost running now and Cash is left behind. It seems to me that the end which I now carry alone has no weight, as though it coasts like a rushing straw upon the furious tide of Jewel's despair. I am not even touching it when, turning, he lets it overshoot him, swinging, and stops it and sloughs it into the wagon-bed in the same motion and looks back at me, his face suffused with fury and despair.

'Goddamn you. Goddamn you.'

Vardaman

We are going to town. Dewey Dell says it won't be sold because it belongs to Santa Claus and he has taken it back with him until next Christmas. Then it will be behind the glass again, shining with waiting.

Pa and Cash are coming down the hill, but Jewel is going to the barn. 'Jewel,' pa says. Jewel does not stop. 'Where you going?' pa says. But Jewel does not stop. 'You leave that horse here,' pa says. Jewel stops and looks at pa. Jewel's eyes look like marbles. 'You leave that horse here,' pa says. 'We'll all go in the wagon with ma, like she wanted.'

But my mother is a fish. Vernon seen it. He was there.

'Jewel's mother is a horse,' Darl said.

'Then mine can be a fish, can't it, Darl?' I said.

Jewel is my brother.

'Then mine will have to be a horse, too,' I said.

'Why?' Darl said. 'If pa is your pa, why does your ma have to be a horse just because Jewel's is?'

'Why does it?' I said. 'Why does it, Darl?'

Darl is my brother.

'Then what is your ma, Darl?' I said.

'I haven't got ere one,' Darl said. 'Because if I had one, it is *was*. And if it is was, it can't be is. Can it?'

'No,' I said.

'Then I am not,' Darl said. 'Am I?'

'No,' I said.

I am. Darl is my brother.

'But you *are*, Darl,' I said.

'I know it,' Darl said. 'That's why I am not *is*. *Are* is too many for one woman to foal.'

Cash is carrying his tool-box. Pa looks at him. 'I'll stop at Tull's on the way back,' Cash says. 'Get on that barn roof.'

'It ain't respectful,' pa says. 'It's a deliberate flouting of her and of me.'

'Do you want him to come all the way back here and carry them up to Tull's afoot?' Darl says. Pa looks at Darl, his mouth chewing. Pa shaves every day now because my mother is a fish.

'It ain't right,' pa says.

Dewey Dell has the package in her hand. She has the basket with our dinner too.

'What's that?' pa says.

'Mrs Tull's cakes,' Dewey Dell says, getting into the wagon. 'I'm taking them to town for her.'

'It ain't right,' pa says. 'It's a flouting of the dead.'

It'll be there. It'll be there come Christmas, she says, shining on the track. She says he won't sell it to no town boys.

Darl

He goes on toward the barn, entering the lot, wooden-backed.

Dewey Dell carries the basket on one arm, in the other hand something wrapped square in a newspaper. Her face is calm and sullen, her eyes brooding and alert; within them I can see Peabody's back like two round peas in two thimbles: perhaps in Peabody's back two of those worms which work surreptitious and steady through you and out the other side and you waking suddenly from sleep or from waking, with on your face an expression sudden, intent, and concerned. She sets the basket into the wagon and climbs in, her leg coming long from beneath her tightening dress: that lever which moves the world; one of that caliper which measures the length and breadth of life. She sits on the seat beside Vardaman and sets the parcel on her lap.

Then he enters the barn. He has not looked back.

'It ain't right,' pa says. 'It's little enough for him to do for her.'

'Go on,' Cash says. 'Leave him stay if he wants to. He'll be all right here. Maybe he'll go up to Tull's and stay.'

'He'll catch us,' I say. 'He'll cut across and meet us at Tull's lane.'

'He would have rid that horse, too,' pa says, 'if I hadn't a stopped him. A durn spotted critter wilder than a catty-mount. A deliberate flouting of her and of me.'

The wagon moves; the mules' ears begin to bob. Behind us, above the house, motionless in tall and soaring circles, they diminish and disappear.

Anse

I told him not to bring that horse out of respect for his dead ma, because it wouldn't look right, him prancing along on a durn circus animal and her wanting us all to be in the wagon with her that sprung from her flesh and blood, but we hadn't no more than passed Tull's lane when Darl begun to laugh. Setting back there on the plank seat with Cash, with his dead ma lying in her coffin at his feet, laughing. How many times I told him it's doing such things as that that makes folks talk about him, I don't know. I says I got some regard for what folks says about my flesh and blood even if you haven't, even if I have raised such a durn passel of boys, and when you fixes it so folks can say such about you, it's a reflection on your ma, I says, not me: I am a man and I can stand it; it's on your womenfolks, your ma and sister that you should care for, and I turned and looked back at him setting there, laughing.

'I don't expect you to have no respect for me,' I says. 'But with your own ma not cold in her coffin yet.'

'Yonder,' Cash says, jerking his head toward the lane. The horse is still a right smart piece away, coming up at a good pace, but I don't have to be told who it is. I just looked back at Darl, setting there laughing.

'I done my best,' I says. 'I tried to do as she would wish it. The Lord will pardon me and excuse the conduct of them He sent me.' And Darl setting on the plank seat right above her where she was laying, laughing.

Darl

He comes up the lane fast, yet we are three hundred yards beyond the mouth of it when he turns into the road, the mud flying beneath the flickering drive of the hooves. Then he slows a little, light and erect in the saddle, the horse mincing through the mud.

Tull is in his lot. He looks at us, lifts his hand. We go on, the wagon creaking, the mud whispering on the wheels. Vernon still stands there. He watches Jewel as he passes, the horse moving with a light, high-kneed driving gait, three hundred yards back. We go on, with a motion so soporific, so dreamlike as to be uninferant of progress, as though time and not space were decreasing between us and it.

It turns off at right angles, the wheel-marks of last Sunday healed away now: a smooth, red scoriation curving away into the pines; a white signboard with faded lettering: New Hope Church. 3 mi. It wheels up like a motionless hand lifted above the profound desolation of the ocean; beyond it the red road lies like a spoke of which Addie Bundren is the rim. It wheels past, empty, unscarred, the white signboard turns away its fading and tranquil assertion. Cash looks up the road quietly, his head turning as we pass it like an owl's head, his face composed. Pa looks straight ahead, humped. Dewey Dell looks at the road too, then she looks back at me, her eyes watchful and repudiant, not like that question which was in those of Cash, for a smouldering while. The signboard passes; the unscarred road wheels on. Then Dewey Dell turns her head. The wagon creaks on.

Cash spits over the wheel. 'In a couple of days now it'll be smelling,' he says.

'You might tell Jewel that,' I say.

He is motionless now, sitting the horse at the junction, upright, watching us, no less still than the signboard that lifts its fading capitulation opposite him.

'It ain't balanced right for no long ride,' Cash says.

'Tell him that, too,' I say. The wagon creaks on.

A mile farther along he passes us, the horse, arch-necked, reined back to a swift single-foot. He sits lightly, poised, upright, wooden-faced in the saddle, the broken hat raked at a swaggering angle. He passes us swiftly, without looking at us, the horse driving, its hooves hissing in the mud. A gout of mud, back-flung, plops on to the box. Cash leans forward and takes a tool from his box and removes it carefully. When the road crosses White-leaf, the willows leaning near enough, he breaks off a branch and scours at the stain with the wet leaves.

Anse

It's a hard country on man; it's hard. Eight miles of the sweat of his body washed up outen the Lord's earth, where the Lord Himself told him to put it. Nowhere in this sinful world can a honest, hard-working man profit. It takes them that runs the stores in the towns, doing no sweating, living off of them that sweats. It ain't the hard-working man, the farmer. Sometimes I wonder why we keep at it. It's because there is a reward for us above, where they can't take their motors and such. Every man will be equal there and it will be taken from them that have and give to them that have not by the Lord.

But it's a long wait, seems like. It's bad that a fellow must earn the reward of his right-doing by flouting hisself and his dead. We drove all the rest of the day and got to Samson's at dust-dark and then that bridge was gone, too. They hadn't never seen the river so high, and it's not done raining yet. There was old men that hadn't never seen nor heard of it being so in the memory of man. I am the chosen of the Lord, for who He loveth, so doeth He chastiseth. But I be durn if He don't take some curious ways to show it, seems like.

But now I can get them teeth. That will be a comfort. It will.

Samson

It was just before sundown. We were sitting on the porch when the wagon came up the road with the five of them in it and the other one on the horse behind. One of them raised his hand, but they was going on past the store without stopping.

'Who's that?' MacCallum says: I can't think of his name: Rafe's twin; that one it was.

'It's Bundren, from down beyond New Hope,' Quick says. 'There's one of them Snopes horses Jewel's riding.'

'I didn't know there was ere a one of them horses left,' MacCallum says. 'I thought you folks down there finally contrived to give them all away.'

'Try and get that one,' Quick says. The wagon went on.

'I bet old man Lon never gave it to him,' I says.

'No,' Quick says. 'He bought it from pappy.' The wagon went on. 'They must not a heard about the bridge,' he says.

'What're they doing up here, anyway?' MacCallum says.

'Taking a holiday since he got his wife buried, I reckon,' Quick says. 'Heading for town, I reckon, with Tull's bridge gone too. I wonder if they ain't heard about the bridge.'

'They'll have to fly, then,' I says. 'I don't reckon there's ere a bridge between here and Mouth of Ishatawa.'

They had something in the wagon. But Quick had been to the funeral three days ago and we naturally never thought anything about it except that they were heading away from home mighty late and that they hadn't heard about the bridge. 'You better holler at them,' MacCallum says. Durn it, the name is right on the tip of my tongue. So Quick hollered and they stopped and he went to the wagon and told them.

He come back with them. 'They're going to Jefferson,' he says. 'The bridge at Tull's is gone, too.' Like we didn't know it, and his face looked funny, around the nostrils, but they just sat there,

Bundren and the girl and the chap on seat, and Cash and the second one, the one folks talks about, on a plank across the tailgate, and the other one on that spotted horse. But I reckon they was used to it by then because when I said to Cash that they'd have to pass by New Hope again and what they'd better do, he just says,

'I reckon we can get there.'

I ain't much for meddling. Let every man run his own business to suit himself, I say. But after I talked to Rachel about them not having a regular man to fix her and it being July and all, I went back down to the barn and tried to talk to Bundren about it.

'I give her my promise,' he says. 'Her mind was set on it.'

I notice how it takes a lazy man, a man that hates moving, to get set on moving once he does get started off, the same as he was set on staying still, like it ain't the moving he hates so much as the starting and the stopping. And like he would be kind of proud of whatever come up to make the moving or the setting still look hard. He set there on the wagon, hunched up, blinking, listening to us tell about how quick the bridge went and how high the water was, and I be durn if he didn't act like he was proud of it, like he had made the river rise himself.

'You say it's higher than you ever see it before?' he says. 'God's will be done,' he says. 'I reckon it won't go down much by morning, neither,' he says.

'You better stay here tonight,' I says, 'and get a early start for New Hope tomorrow morning.' I was just sorry for them bone-gaunted mules. I told Rachel, I says, 'Well, would you have had me turn them away at dark, eight miles from home? What else could I do,' I says. 'It won't be but one night, and they'll keep it in the barn, and they'll sholy get started by daylight.' And so I says, 'You stay here tonight and early tomorrow you can go back to New Hope. I got tools enough, and the boys can go on right after supper and have it dug and ready if they want,' and then I found that girl watching me. If her eyes had a been pistols, I wouldn't be talking now. I be dog if they didn't blaze at me. And so when I went down to the barn I come on them, her talking so she never noticed when I come up.

'You promised her,' she says. 'She wouldn't go until you promised. She thought she could depend on you. If you don't do it, it will be a curse on you.'

'Can't no man say I don't aim to keep my word,' Bundren says. 'My heart is open to ere a man.'

'I don't care what your heart is,' she says. She was whispering, kind of, talking fast. 'You promised her. You've got to. You –' Then she seen me and quit, standing there. If they'd been pistols, I wouldn't be talking now. So when I talked to him about it, he says,

'I give her my promise. Her mind is set on it.'

'But seems to me she'd rather have her ma buried close by, so she could –'

'It's Addie I give the promise to,' he says. 'Her mind is set on it.

So I told them to drive it into the barn because it was threatening rain again, and that supper was about ready. Only they didn't want to come in.

'I thank you,' Bundren says. 'We couldn't discommode you. We got a little something in the basket. We can make out.'

'Well,' I says, 'since you are so particular about your womenfolks, I am too. And when folks stops with us at meal-time and won't come to the table, my wife takes it as a insult.'

So the girl went on to the kitchen to help Rachel. And then Jewel come to me.

'Sho,' I says. 'Help yourself outen the loft. Feed him when you bait the mules.'

'I rather pay you for him,' he says.

'What for?' I says. 'I wouldn't begrudge no man a bait for his horse.'

'I rather pay you,' he says; I thought he said extra.

'Extra for what?' I says. 'Won't he eat hay and corn?'

'Extra feed,' he says. 'I feed him a little extra and I don't want him beholden to no man.'

'You can't buy no feed from me, boy,' I says. 'And if he can eat that loft clean, I'll help you load the barn on to the wagon in the morning.'

'He ain't never been beholden to no man,' he says. 'I rather pay you for it.'

And if I had my rathers, you wouldn't be here a-tall, I wanted to say. But I just says, 'Then it's high time he commenced. You can't buy no feed from me.'

When Rachel put supper on, her and the girl went and fixed some beds. But wouldn't any of them come in. 'She's been dead long enough to get over that sort of foolishness,' I says. Because I got just as much respect for the dead as ere a man, but you've got to respect the dead themselves, and a woman that's been dead in a box four days, the best way to respect her is to get her into the ground as quick as you can. But they wouldn't do it.

'It wouldn't be right,' Bundren says. 'Course, if the boys wants to go to bed, I reckon I can set up with her. I don't begrudge her it.'

So when I went back down there they were squatting on the ground around the wagon, all of them. 'Let that chap come to the house and get some sleep, anyway,' I says. 'And you better come too,' I says to the girl. I wasn't aiming to interfere with them. And I sholy hadn't done nothing to her that I knowed.

'He's done already asleep,' Bundren says. They had done put him to bed in the trough in a empty stall.

'Well, you come on, then,' I says to her. But still she never said nothing. They just squatted there. You couldn't hardly see them. 'How about you boys?' I says. 'You got a full day tomorrow.' After a while Cash says,

'I thank you. We can make out.'

'We wouldn't be beholden,' Bundren says. 'I thank you kindly.'

So I left them squatting there. I reckon after four days they was used to it. But Rachel wasn't.

'It's a outrage,' she says. 'A outrage.'

'What could he 'a' done?' I says. 'He give her his promised word.'

'Who's talking about him?' she says. 'Who cares about him?' she says, crying. 'I just wish that you and him and all the men in the world that torture us alive and flout us dead, dragging us up and down the country –'

'Now, now,' I says. 'You're upset.'

'Don't you touch me!' she says. 'Don't you touch me!'

A man can't tell nothing about them. I lived with the same one fifteen years and I be durn if I can. And I imagined a lot of things coming up between us, but I be durn if I ever thought it would be a body four days dead and that a woman. But they make life hard on them not taking it as it comes up, like a man does.

So I laid there, hearing it commence to rain, thinking about them down there, squatting around the wagon and the rain on the roof, and thinking about Rachel crying there until after a while it was like I could still hear her crying even after she was asleep, and smelling it even when I knowed I couldn't. I couldn't decide even then whether I could or not, or if it wasn't just knowing it was what it was.

So next morning I never went down there. I heard them

hitching up and then when I knowed they must be about ready to take out, I went out the front and went down the road toward the bridge until I heard the wagon come out of the lot and go back toward New Hope. And then when I come back to the house, Rachel jumped on me because I wasn't there to make them come in to breakfast. You can't tell about them. Just about when you decide they mean one thing, I be durn if you not only haven't got to change your mind, like as not you got to take a raw-hiding for thinking they meant it.

But it was still like I could smell it. And so I decided then that it wasn't smelling it, but it was just knowing it was there, like you will get fooled now and then. But when I went to the barn I knew different. When I walked into the hallway I saw something. It kind of hunkered up when I come in and I thought at first it was one of them got left, then I saw what it was. It was a buzzard. It looked around and saw me and went on down the hall, straddle-legged, with its wings kind of hunkered out, watching me first over one shoulder and then over the other, like a old bald-headed man. When it got outdoors it begun to fly. It had to fly a long time before it ever got up into the air, with it thick and heavy and full of rain like it was.

If they was bent on going to Jefferson, I reckon they could have gone around up by Mount Vernon, like MacCallum did. He'll get home about day after tomorrow, horse-back. Then they'd be just eighteen miles from town. But maybe this bridge being gone too has learned him the Lord's sense and judgement.

That MacCallum. He's been trading with me off and on for twelve years. I have known him from a boy up; know his name as well as I do my own. But be durn if I can say it.

Dewey Dell

The signboard comes in sight. It is looking out at the road now, because it can wait. New Hope. 3 mi. it will say. New Hope. 3 mi. New Hope. 3 mi. And then the road will begin, curving away into the trees, empty with waiting, saying New Hope three miles.

I heard that my mother is dead. I wish I had time to let her die. I wish I had time to wish I had. It is because in the wild and outraged earth too soon too soon too soon. It's not that I wouldn't and will not it's that it is too soon too soon too soon.

Now it begins to say it. Hew Hope three miles. New Hope three miles. *That's what they mean by the womb of time: the agony and the despair of spreading bones, the hard girdle in which lie the outraged entrails of events.* Cash's head turns slowly as we approach, his pale, empty, sad, composed and questioning face following the red and empty curve; beside the back wheels Jewel sits the horse, gazing straight ahead.

The land runs out of Darl's eyes; they swim to pin-points. They begin at my feet and rise along my body to my face, and then my dress is gone: I sit naked on the seat above the unhurrying mules, above the travail. *Suppose I tell him to turn. He will do what I say. Don't you know he will do what I say?* Once I waked with a black void rushing under me. I could not see. I saw Vardaman rise and go to the window and strike the knife into the fish, the blood gushing, hissing like steam but I could not see. *He'll do as I say. He always does. I can persuade him to anything. You know I can. Suppose I say Turn here.* That was when I died that time. *Suppose I do. We'll go to New Hope. We won't have to go to town.* I rose and took the knife from the streaming fish still hissing and I killed Darl.

When I used to sleep with Vardaman I had a nightmare once I thought I was awake but I couldn't see and couldn't feel I couldn't feel the bed under me and I couldn't think what I was I couldn't think of my name I couldn't even think I am a girl I couldn't even think I nor

even think I want to wake up nor remember what was opposite to awake
so I could do that I knew that something was passing but I couldn't
even think of time then all of a sudden I knew that something was it
was wind blowing over me it was like the wind came and blew me back
from where it was I was not blowing the room and Vardaman asleep
and all of them back under me again and going on like a piece of cool
silk dragging across my naked legs.

It blows cool out of the pines, a sad steady sound. New Hope.
Was 3 mi. Was 3 mi. I believe in God I believe in God.

'Why didn't we go to New Hope, pa?' Vardaman says. 'Mr
Samson said we was, but we done passed the road.'

Darl says, 'Look, Jewel.' But he is not looking at me. He is
looking at the sky. The buzzard is as still as if he were nailed to
it.

We turn into Tull's lane. We pass the barn and go on, the
wheels whispering in the mud, passing the green rows of cotton
in the wild earth, and Vernon little across the field behind the
plough. He lifts his hand as we pass and stands there looking
after us for a long while.

'Look, Jewel,' Darl says. Jewel sits on his horse like they were
both made out of wood, looking straight ahead.

I believe in God, God. God, I believe in God.

Tull

After they passed I taken the mule out and looped up the trace
chains and followed. They were setting in the wagon at the end
of the levee. Anse was setting there, looking at the bridge where
it was swagged down into the river with just the two ends in sight.
He was looking at it like he had believed all the time that folks
had been lying to him about it being gone, but like he was hoping
all the time it really was. Kind of pleased astonishment he looked,
setting on the wagon in his Sunday pants, mumbling his mouth.
Looking like a uncurried horse dressed up: I don't know.

The boy was watching the bridge where it was midsunk and

logs and such drifted up over it and it swagging and shivering like the whole thing would go any minute, big-eyed he was watching it, like he was to a circus. And the gal, too. When I come up she looked around at me, her eyes kind of blaring up and going hard like I had made to touch her. Then she looked at Anse again and then back at the water again.

It was nigh up to the levee on both sides, the earth hid except for the tongue of it we was on going out to the bridge and then down into the water, and except for knowing how the road and the bridge used to look, a fellow couldn't tell where was the river and where the land. It was just a tangle of yellow and the levee not less wider than a knife-back kind of, with us setting in the wagon and on the horse and the mule.

Darl was looking at me, and then Cash turned and looked at me with that look in his eyes like when he was figuring on whether the planks would fit her that night, like he was measuring them inside of him and not asking you to say what you thought and not even letting on he was listening if you did say it, but listening all right. Jewel hadn't moved.

He sat there on the horse, leaning a little forward, with that same look on his face when him and Darl passed the house yesterday, coming back to get her.

'If it was just up, we could drive across,' Anse says. 'We could drive right on across it.'

Sometimes a log would get shoved over the jam and float on, rolling and turning, and we could watch it go on to where the ford used to be. It would slow up and whirl crossways and hang out of water for a minute, and you could tell by that that the ford used to be there.

'But that don't show nothing,' I say. 'It could be a bar of quicksand built up there.' We watch the log. Then the gal is looking at me again.

'Mr Whitfield crossed it,' she says.

'He was a horse-back,' I say. 'And three days ago. It's riz five foot since.'

'If the bridge was just up,' Anse says.

The log bobs up and goes on again. There is a lot of trash and foam, and you can hear the water.

'But it's down,' Anse says.

Cash says, 'A careful fellow could walk across yonder on the planks and logs.'

'But you couldn't tote nothing,' I say. 'Likely time you set foot on that mess, it'll all go, too. What you think, Darl?'

He is looking at me. He don't say nothing; just looks at me with them queer eyes of hisn that makes folks talk. I always say it ain't never been what he done so much or said or anything so much as how he looks at you. It's like he had got into the inside of you, someway. Like somehow you was looking at yourself and your doings outen his eyes. Then I can feel that gal watching me like I had made to touch her. She says something to Anse. '. . . Mr Whitfield . . .' she says.

'I give her my promised word in the presence of the Lord,' Anse says. 'I reckon it ain't no need to worry.'

But still he does not start the mules. We set there above the water. Another log bobs up over the jam and goes on; we watch it check up and swing slow for a minute where the ford used to be. Then it goes on.

'It might start falling tonight,' I say. 'You could lay over one more day.'

Then Jewel turns sideways on the horse. He has not moved until then, and he turns and looks at me. His face is kind of green, then it would go red and then green again. 'Get to hell on back to your damn ploughing,' he says. 'Who the hell asked you to follow us here?'

'I never meant no harm,' I say.

'Shut up, Jewel,' Cash says. Jewel looks back at the water, his face gritted, going red and green and then red. 'Well,' Cash says after a while, 'what you want to do?'

Anse don't say nothing. He sets humped up, mumbling his mouth. 'If it was just up, we could drive across it,' he says.

'Come on,' Jewel says, moving the horse.

'Wait,' Cash says. He looks at the bridge. We look at him, except Anse and the gal. They are looking at the water. 'Dewey Dell and Vardaman and pa better walk across on the bridge,' Cash says.

'Vernon can help them,' Jewel says. 'And we can hitch his mule ahead of ourn.'

'You ain't going to take my mule into that water,' I say.

Jewel looks at me. His eyes look like pieces of a broken plate. 'I'll pay for your damn mule. I'll buy it from you right now.'

'My mule ain't going into that water,' I say.

'Jewel's going to use his horse,' Darl says. 'Why won't you risk your mule, Vernon?'

'Shut up, Darl,' Cash says. 'You and Jewel both.'

'My mule ain't going into that water,' I say.

Darl

He sits the horse, glaring at Vernon, his lean face suffused up to and beyond the pale rigidity of his eyes. The summer when he was fifteen, he took a spell of sleeping. One morning when I went to feed the mules the cows were still in the tie-up and then I heard pa go back to the house and call him. When we came on back to the house for breakfast he passed us, carrying the milk buckets, stumbling along like he was drunk, and he was milking when we put the mules in and went on to the field without him. We had been there an hour and still he never showed up. When Dewey Dell came with our lunch, pa sent her back to find Jewel. They found him in the tie-up, sitting on the stool, asleep.

After that, every morning pa would go in and wake him. He would go to sleep at the supper-table and soon as supper was finished he would go to bed, and when I came in to bed he would be lying there like a dead man. Yet still pa would have to wake him in the morning. He would get up, but he wouldn't hardly have half sense: he would stand for pa's jawing and complaining without a word and take the milk buckets and go to the barn, and once I found him asleep at the cow, the bucket in place and half-full and his hands up to the wrists in the milk and his head against the cow's flank.

After that Dewey Dell had to do the milking. He still got up when pa waked him, going about what we told him to do in that dazed way. It was like he was trying hard to do them; that he was as puzzled as anyone else.

'Are you sick?' ma said. 'Don't you feel all right?'

'Yes,' Jewel said. 'I feel all right.'

'He's just lazy, trying me,' pa said, and Jewel standing there, asleep on his feet like as not. 'Ain't you?' he said, waking Jewel up again to answer.

'No,' Jewel said.

'You take off and stay in the house today,' ma said.

'With that whole bottom piece to be busted out?' pa said. 'If you ain't sick, what's the matter with you?'

'Nothing,' Jewel said. 'I'm all right.'

'All right?' pa said. 'You're asleep on your feet this minute.'

'No,' Jewel said. 'I'm all right.'

'I want him to stay at home today,' ma said.

'I'll need him,' pa said. 'It's tight enough, with all of us to do it.'

'You'll just have to do the best you can with Cash and Darl,' ma said. 'I want him to stay in today.'

But he wouldn't do it. 'I'm all right,' he said, going on. But he wasn't all right. Anybody could see it. He was losing flesh, and I have seen him go to sleep chopping; watched the hoe going slower and slower up and down, with less and less of an arc, until it stopped and he leaning on it motionless in the hot shimmer of the sun.

Ma wanted to get the doctor, but pa didn't want to spend the money without it was needful, and Jewel did seem all right except for his thinness and his way of dropping off to sleep at any moment. He ate hearty enough, except for his way of going to sleep in his plate, with a piece of bread halfway to his mouth and his jaws still chewing. But he swore he was all right.

It was ma that got Dewey Dell to do his milking, paid her somehow, and the other jobs around the house that Jewel had been doing before supper she found some way for Dewey Dell and Vardaman to do them. And doing them herself when pa wasn't there. She would fix him special things to eat and hide them for him. And that may have been when I first found it out, that Addie Bundren should be hiding anything she did, who had tried to teach us that deceit was such that, in a world where it was, nothing else could be very bad or very important, not even poverty. And at times when I went in to go to bed she would be sitting in the dark by Jewel where he was asleep. And I knew that she was hating herself for that deceit and hating Jewel because she had to love him so that she had to act the deceit.

One night she was taken sick and when I went to the barn to put the team in and drive to Tull's, I couldn't find the lantern. I remembered noticing it on the nail the night before, but it wasn't there now at midnight. So I hitched in the dark and went on and came back with Mrs Tull just after daylight. And there the lantern was, hanging on the nail where I remembered it and couldn't find it before. And then one morning while Dewey Dell was milking just before sun-up, Jewel came into the barn from the back, through the hole in the back wall, with the lantern in his hand.

I told Cash, and Cash and I looked at one another.

'Rutting,' Cash said.

'Yes,' I said. 'But why the lantern. And every night, too. No wonder he's losing flesh. Are you going to say anything to him?'

'Won't do any good,' Cash said.

'What he's doing now won't do any good, either.'

'I know. But he'll have to learn that himself. Give him time to realize that it'll save, that there'll be just as much more tomorrow, and he'll be all right. I wouldn't tell anybody, I reckon.'

'No,' I said. 'I told Dewey Dell not to. Not ma, anyway.'

'No. Not ma.'

After that I thought it was right comical: he acting so bewildered and willing and dead for sleep and gaunt as a bean-pole, and thinking he was so smart with it. And I wondered who the girl was. I thought of all I knew that it might be, but I couldn't say for sure.

' 'Taint any girl,' Cash said. 'It's a married woman somewhere. Ain't any young girl got that much daring and staying power. That's what I don't like about it.'

'Why?' I said. 'She'll be safer for him than a girl would. More judgement.'

He looked at me, his eyes fumbling, the words fumbling at what he was trying to say. 'It ain't always the safe things in this world that a fellow . . .'

'You mean, the safe things are not always the best things?'

'Ay; best,' he said, fumbling again. 'It ain't the best things, the things that are good for him . . . A young boy. A fellow kind of hates to see . . . wallowing in somebody else's mire . . .' That's what he was trying to say. When something is new and hard and bright, there ought to be something a little better for it than just being safe, since the safe things are just the things that folks have been doing so long they have worn the edges off and there's nothing to the doing of them that leaves a man to say, That was not done before and it cannot be done again.

So we didn't tell, not even when after a while he'd appear suddenly in the field beside us and go to work, without having had time to get home and make out he had been in bed all night. He would tell ma that he hadn't been hungry at breakfast or that he had eaten a piece of bread while he was hitching up the team. But Cash and I knew that he hadn't been home at all on those nights and he had come up out of the woods when we got to the field. But we didn't tell. Summer was almost over then; we knew that when the nights began to get cool, she would be done if he wasn't.

But when fall came and the nights began to get longer, the only difference was that he would always be in bed for pa to wake him, getting him up at last in that first state of semi-idiocy like when it first started, worse than when he had stayed out all night.

'She's sure a stayer,' I told Cash. 'I used to admire her, but I downright respect her now.'

'It ain't a woman,' he said.

'You know,' I said. But he was watching me. 'What is it, then?'

'That's what I aim to find out,' he said.

'You can trail him through the woods all night if you want to,' I said. 'I'm not.'

'I ain't trailing him,' he said.

'What do you call it, then?'

'I ain't trailing him,' he said. 'I don't mean it that way.'

And so a few nights later I heard Jewel get up and climb out the window, and then I heard Cash get up and follow him. The next morning when I went to the barn, Cash was already there, the mules fed, and he was helping Dewey Dell milk. And when I saw him I knew that he knew what it was. Now and then I would catch him watching Jewel with a queer look, like having found out where Jewel went and what he was doing had given him something to really think about at last. But it was not a worried look; it was the kind of look I would see on him when I would find him doing some of Jewel's work around the house, work that pa still thought Jewel was doing and that ma thought Dewey Dell was doing. So I said nothing to him, believing that when he got done digesting it in his mind, he would tell me. But he never did.

One morning – it was November then, five months since it started – Jewel was not in bed and he didn't join us in the field. That was the first time ma learned anything about what had been going on. She sent Vardaman down to find where Jewel was, and after a while she came down too. It was as though, so long as the deceit ran along quiet and monotonous, all of us let ourselves be deceived, abetting it unawares or maybe through cowardice, since all people are cowards and naturally prefer any kind of treachery

because it has a bland outside. But now it was like we had all –
and by a kind of telepathic agreement of admitted fear – flung
the whole thing back like covers on the bed and we all sitting
bolt upright in our nakedness, staring at one another and saying
'Now is the truth. He hasn't come home. Something has happened
to him. We let something happen to him.'

Then we saw him. He came up along the ditch and then turned
straight across the field, riding the horse. Its mane and tail were
going, as though in motion they were carrying out the splotchy
pattern of its coat; he looked like he was riding on a big pinwheel,
barebacked, with a rope bridle, and no hat on his head. It was a
descendant of those Texas ponies Flem Snopes brought here
twenty-five years ago and auctioned off for two dollars a head
and nobody but old Lon Quick ever caught his and still owned
some of the blood because he could never give it away.

He galloped up and stopped, his heels in the horse's ribs and
it dancing and swirling like the shape of its mane and tail and
the splotches of its coat had nothing whatever to do with the
flesh-and-bone horse inside them, and he sat there, looking at
us.

'Where did you get that horse?' pa said.

'Bought it,' Jewel said. 'From Mr Quick.'

'Bought it?' pa said. 'With what? Did you buy that thing on my
word?'

'It was my money,' Jewel said. 'I earned it. You won't need to
worry about it.'

'Jewel,' ma said; 'Jewel.'

'It's all right,' Cash said. 'He earned the money. He cleaned
up that forty acres of new ground Quick laid out last spring. He
did it single-handed, working at night by lantern. I saw him. So
I don't reckon that horse cost anybody anything except Jewel. I
don't reckon we need worry.'

'Jewel,' ma said. 'Jewel –' Then she said: 'You come right to
the house and go to bed.'

'Not yet,' Jewel said. 'I ain't got time. I got to get me a saddle
and bridle. Mr Quick says he –'

'Jewel,' ma said, looking at him. 'I'll give – I'll give give –'
Then she began to cry. She cried hard, not hiding her face,
standing there in her faded wrapper, looking at him and him on
the horse, looking down at her, his face growing cold and a little
sick looking until he looked away quick and Cash came and
touched her.

'You go on to the house,' Cash said. 'This here ground is too wet for you. You go on, now.' She put her hands to her face then and after a while she went on, stumbling a little on the plough-marks. But pretty soon she straightened up and went on. She didn't look back. When she reached the ditch she stopped and called Vardaman. He was looking at the horse, kind of dancing up and down by it.

'Let me ride, Jewel,' he said. 'Let me ride, Jewel.'

Jewel looked at him, then he looked away again, holding the horse reined back. Pa watched him, mumbling his lip.

'So you bought a horse,' he said. 'You went behind my back and bought a horse. You never consulted me; you know how tight it is for us to make by, yet you bought a horse for me to feed. Taken the work from your flesh and blood and bought a horse with it.'

Jewel looked at pa, his eyes paler than ever.

'He won't never eat a mouthful of yours,' he said. 'Not a mouthful. I'll kill him first. Don't you never think it. Don't you never.'

'Let me ride, Jewel,' Vardaman said. 'Let me ride, Jewel.' He sounded like a cricket in the grass, a little one. 'Let me ride, Jewel.'

That night I found ma sitting beside the bed where he was sleeping, in the dark. She cried hard, maybe because she had to cry so quiet; maybe because she felt the same way about tears she did about deceit, hating herself for doing it, hating him because she had to. And then I knew that I knew. I knew that as plain on that day as I knew about Dewey Dell on that day.

Tull

So they finally got Anse to say what he wanted to do, and him and the gal and the boy got out of the wagon. But even when we were on the bridge Anse kept on looking back, like he thought maybe, once he was outen the wagon, the whole thing would kind of blow up and he would find himself back yonder in the field again and her laying up there in the house, waiting to die and it to do all over again.

'You ought to let them taken your mule,' he says, and the bridge shaking and swaying under us, going down into the moiling water like it went clean through to the other side of the earth, and the other end coming up outen the water like it wasn't the same bridge a-tall and that them that would walk up outen the water on that side must come from the bottom of the earth. But it was still whole; you could tell that by the way when this end swagged, it didn't look like the other end swagged at all: just like the other trees and the bank yonder were swinging back and forth slow like on a big clock. And them logs scraping and bumping at the sunk part and tilting end-up and shooting clean outen the water and tumbling on toward the ford and the walting, slick, whirling, and foamy.

'What good would that 'a' done?' I says. 'If your team can't find the ford and haul it across, what good would three mules or even ten mules do?'

'I ain't asking it of you,' he says. 'I can always do for me and mine. I ain't asking you to risk your mule. It 'ain't your dead; I am not blaming you.'

'They ought to went back and laid over until tomorrow,' I says. The water was cold. It was thick, like slush ice. Only it kind of lived. One part of you knowed it was just water, the same thing that had been running under this same bridge for a long time, yet when them logs would come spewing up outen it, you were not surprised, like they was a part of the water, of the waiting and the threat.

It was like when we was across, up out of the water again and the hard earth under us, that I was surprised. It was like we hadn't expected the bridge to end on the other bank, on something tame like the hard earth again that we had tromped on before this and knowed well. Like it couldn't be me here, because I'd have had better sense than to done what I just done. And when I looked back and saw the other bank and saw my mule standing there where I used to be and knew that I'd have to get back there some way, I knew it couldn't be, because I just couldn't think of anything that could make me cross that bridge ever even once. Yet here I was, and the fellow that could make himself cross it twice, couldn't be me, not even if Cora told him to.

It was that boy. I said 'Here; you better take a holt of my hand,' and he waited and held to me. I be durn if it wasn't like he come back and got me; like he was saying They won't nothing hurt you. Like he was saying about a fine place he knowed where Christmas come twice with Thanksgiving and lasts on through the winter and the spring and the summer, and if I just stayed with him I'd be all right too.

When I looked back at my mule it was like he was one of these here spy-glasses and I could look at him standing there and see all the broad land and my house sweated outen it like it was the more the sweat, the broader the land; the more the sweat, the tighter the house because it would take a tight house for Cora, to hold Cora like a jar of milk in the spring: you've got to have a tight jar or you'll need a powerful spring, so if you have a big spring, why then you have the incentive to have tight, well-made jars, because it is your milk, sour or not, because you would rather have milk that will sour than to have milk that won't, because you are a man.

And him holding to my hand, his hand that hot and confident, so that I was like to say: Look-a-here. Can't you see that mule yonder? He never had no business over here, so he never come, not being nothing but a mule. Because a fellow can see ever now and then that children have more sense than him. But he don't like to admit it to them until they have beards. After they have a beard, they are too busy because they don't know if they'll ever quite make it back to where they were in sense before they was haired, so you don't mind admitting then to folks that are worrying about the same thing that ain't worth the worry that you are yourself.

Then we was over and we stood there, looking at Cash turning the wagon around. We watched them drive back down the road to where the trail turned off into the bottom. After a while the wagon was out of sight.

'We better get on down to the ford and git ready to help,' I said.

'I give her my word,' Anse says. 'It is sacred on me. I know you begrudge it, but she will bless you in heaven.'

'Well, they got to finish circumventing the land before they can dare the water,' I said. 'Come on.'

'It's the turning back,' he said. 'It ain't no luck in turning back.'

He was standing there, humped, mournful, looking at the empty road beyond the swagging and swaying bridge. And that gal, too, with the lunch-basket on one arm and that package under the other. Just going to town. Bent on it. They would risk the fire and the earth and the water and all just to eat a sack of bananas. 'You ought to laid over a day,' I said.' It would 'a' fell some by morning. It mought not 'a' rained tonight. And it can't get no higher.'

'I give my promise,' he says. 'She is counting on it.'

Darl

Before us the thick dark current runs. It talks up to us in a murmur become ceaseless and myriad, the yellow surface dimpled monstrously into fading swirls travelling along the surface for an instant, silent, impermanent, and profoundly significant, as though just beneath the surface something huge and alive waked for a moment of lazy alertness out of and into light slumber again.

It clucks and murmurs among the spokes and about the mules' knees, yellow, skummed with flotsam and with thick soiled gouts of foam as though it had sweat, lathering, like a driven horse. Through the undergrowth it goes with a plaintive sound, a musing sound; in it the unwinded cane and saplings lean as before a little gale, swaying without reflections as though suspended on invisible wires from the branches overhead. Above the ceaseless surface they stand – trees, cane, vines – rootless, severed from the earth, spectral above a scene of immense yet circumscribed desolation filled with the voice of the waste and mournful water.

Cash and I sit in the wagon; Jewel sits the horse at the off rear-wheel. The horse is trembling, its eye rolling wild and baby-blue in its long pink face, its breathing stertorous like groaning. He sits erect, poised, looking quietly and steadily and quickly this way and that, his face calm, a little pale, alert. Cash's face is also gravely composed; he and I look at one another with long probing looks, looks that plunge unimpeded through one another's eyes and into the ultimate secret place where for an instant Cash and Darl crouch flagrant and unabashed in all the old terror and the old foreboding, alert and secret and without shame. When we speak our voices are quiet, detached.

'I reckon we're still in the road, all right.'

'Tull taken and cut them two big whiteoaks. I heard tell how at high water in the old days they used to line up the ford by them trees.'

'I reckon he did that two years ago when he was logging down here. I reckon he never thought that anybody would ever use this ford again.'

'I reckon not. Yes, it must have been then. He cut a sight of timber outen here then. Payed off that mortgage with it, I hear tell.'

'Yes. Yes, I reckon so. I reckon Vernon could have done that.'

'That's a fact. Most folks that logs in this here country, they need a durn good farm to support the sawmill. Or maybe a store. But I reckon Vernon could.'

'I reckon so. He's a sight.'

'Ay. Vernon is. Yes, it must still be here. He never would have got that timber out of here if he hadn't cleaned out that old road. I reckon we are still on it.' He looks about quietly, at the position of the trees, leaning this way and that, looking back along the floorless road shaped vaguely high in air by the position of the lopped and felled bees, as if the road too had been soaked free of earth and floated upward, to leave in its spectral tracing a monument to a still more profound desolation than this above which we now sit, talking quietly of old security and old trivial things. Jewel looks at him, then at me, then his face turns in in that quiet, constant questing about the scene, the horse trembling quietly and steadily between his knees.

'He could go on ahead slow and sort of feel it out,' I say.

'Yes,' Cash says, not looking at me. His face is in profile as he looks forward where Jewel has moved on ahead.

'He can't miss the river,' I say. 'He couldn't miss seeing it fifty yards ahead.'

Cash does not look at me, his face in profile. 'If I'd just suspicioned it, I could 'a' come down last week and taken a sight on it.'

'The bridge was up then,' I say. He does not look at me. 'Whitfield crossed it a-horse-back.'

Jewel looks at us again, his expression sober and alert and subdued. His voice is quiet. 'What you want me to do?'

'I ought to come down last week and taken a sight on it,' Cash says.

'We couldn't have known,' I say. 'There wasn't any way for us to know.'

'I'll ride on ahead,' Jewel says. 'You can follow where I am.' He lifts the horse. It shrinks, bowed; he leans to it, speaking to it, lifting it forward almost bodily, it setting its feet down with gingerly splashings, trembling, breathing harshly. He speaks to it, murmurs to it. 'Go on,' he says. 'I ain't going to let nothing hurt you. Go on, now.'

'Jewel,' Cash says. Jewel does not look back. He lifts the horse on.

'He can swim,' I say. 'If he'll just give the horse time, anyhow . . .' When he was born, he had a bad time of it. Ma would sit in the lamplight, holding him on a pillow on her lap. We would wake and find her so. There would be no sound from them.

'That pillow was longer than him,' Cash says. He is leaning a little forward. 'I ought to come down last week and sighted. I ought to done it.'

'That's right,' I say. 'Neither his feet nor his head would reach the end of it. You couldn't have known,' I say.

'I ought to done it,' he says. He lifts the reins. The mules move, into the traces; the wheels murmur alive in the water. He looks back and down at Addie. 'It ain't on a balance,' he says.

At last the trees open; against the open river Jewel sits the horse, half turned, it belly-deep now. Across the river we can see Vernon and pa and Vardaman and Dewey Dell. Vernon is waving at us, waving us farther downstream.

'We are too high up,' Cash says. Vernon is shouting too, but we cannot make out what he says for the noise of the water. It runs steady and deep now, unbroken, without sense of motion until a log comes along, turning slowly. 'Watch it,' Cash says. We watch it and see it falter and hang for a moment, the current building up behind it in a thick wave, submerging it for an instant before it shoots up and tumbles on.

'There it is,' I say.

'Ay,' Cash says. 'It's there.' We look at Vernon again. He is now flapping his arms up and down. We move on downstream, slowly and carefully, watching Vernon. He drops his hands. 'This is the place,' Cash says.

'Well, goddamn it, let's get across, then,' Jewel says. He moves the horse on.

'You wait,' Cash says. Jewel stops again.

'Well, by God –' he says. Cash looks at the water, then he looks back at Addie. 'It ain't on a balance,' he says.

'Then go on back to the goddamn bridge and walk across,' Jewel says. 'You and Darl both. Let me on that wagon.'

Cash does not pay him any attention. 'It ain't on a balance,' he says. 'Yes, sir. We got to watch it.'

'Watch it, hell,' Jewel says. 'You get out of that wagon and let me have it. By God, if you're afraid to drive it over . . .' His eyes are pale as two bleached chips in his face. Cash is looking at him.

'We'll get it over,' he says. 'I'll tell you what you do. You ride on back and walk across the bridge and come down the other bank and meet us with the rope. Vernon'll take your horse home with him and keep it till we get back.'

'You go to hell,' Jewel says.

'You take the rope and come down the bank and be ready with it,' Cash says. 'Three can't do no more than two can – one to drive and one to steady it.'

'Goddamn you,' Jewel says.

'Let Jewel take the end of the rope and cross upstream of us and brace it,' I say. 'Will you do that, Jewel?'

Jewel watches me, hard. He looks quick at Cash, then back at me, his eyes alert and hard. 'I don't give a damn. Just so we do something. Setting here, not lifting a goddamn hand . . .'

'Let's do that, Cash,' I say.

'I reckon we'll have to,' Cash says.

The river itself is not a hundred yards across, and pa and Vernon and Vardaman and Dewey Dell are the only things in sight not of that single monotony of desolation leaning with that terrific quality a little from right to left, as though we had reached the place where the motion of the wasted world accelerates just before the final precipice. Yet they appear dwarfed. It is as though the space between us were time: an irrevocable quality. It is as though time, no longer running straight before us in a diminishing line, now runs parallel between us like a looping string, the distance being the doubling accretion of the thread and not the interval between. The mules stand, their forequarters already sloped a little, their rumps high. They too are breathing now with a deep groaning sound; looking back once, their gaze sweeps across us with in their eyes a wild, sad, profound, and despairing quality as though they had already seen in the thick water the shape of the disaster which they could not speak and we could not see.

Cash turns back into the wagon. He lays his hands flat on Addie, rocking her a little. His face is calm, down-sloped, calculant, concerned. He lifts his box of tools and wedges it forward under the seat; together we shove Addie forward, wedging her between the tools and the wagon-bed. Then he looks at me.

'No,' I say. 'I reckon I'll stay. Might take both of us.'

From the tool-box he takes his coiled rope and carries the end twice around the seat stanchion and passes the end to me without tying it. The other end he pays out to Jewel, who takes a turn about his saddle-horn.

He must force the horse down into the current. It moves, high-kneed, arch-necked, boring and chafing. Jewel sits lightly forward, his knees lifted a little; again his swift alert calm gaze sweeps upon us and on. He lowers the horse into the stream, speaking to it in a soothing murmur. The horse slips, goes under to the saddle, surges to its feet again, the current building up against Jewel's thighs.

'Watch yourself,' Cash says.

'I'm on it now,' Jewel says. 'You can come ahead now.'

Cash takes the reins and lowers the team carefully and skilfully into the stream.

I felt the current take us and I knew we were on the ford by that reason, since it was only by means of that slipping contact that we could tell that we were in motion at all. What had once been a flat surface was now a succession of troughs and hillocks lifting and falling about us, shoving at us, teasing at us with light lazy touches in the vain instants of solidity underfoot. Cash looked back at me, and then I knew that we were gone. But I did not realize the reason for the rope until I saw the log. It surged up out of the water and stood for an instant upright upon that surging and heaving desolation like Christ. Get out and let the current take you down to the bend, Cash said. You can make it all right. No, I said, I'd get just as wet that way as this.

The log appears suddenly between two hills, as if it had rocketed suddenly from the bottom of the river. Upon the end of it a long gout of foam hangs like the beard of an old man or a goat. When Cash speaks to me I know that he has been watching it all the time, watching it and watching Jewel ten feet ahead of us. 'Let the rope go,' he says. With his other hand he reaches down and reeves the two turns from the stanchion. 'Ride on, Jewel,' he says; 'see if you can pull us ahead of the log.'

Jewel shouts at the horse; again he appears to lift it bodily between his knees. He is just above the top of the ford and the horse has a purchase of some sort for it surges forward, shining wetly half out of water, crashing on in a succession of lunges. It moves unbelievably fast; by that token Jewel realizes at last that the rope is free, for I can see him sawing back on the reins, his head turned, as the log rears in a long sluggish lunge between us, bearing down upon the team. They see it too: for a moment they also shine black out of water. Then the downstream one vanishes, dragging the other with him; the wagon sheers cross-wise, poised on the crest of the ford as the log strikes it, tilting it up and on. Cash is half turned, the reins running taut from his hand and disappearing into the water, the other hand reached back upon Addie, holding her jammed over against the high side of the wagon. 'Jump clear,' he says quietly. 'Stay away from the team and don't try to fight it. It'll swing you into the bend all right.'

'You come too,' I say. Vernon and Vardaman are running along the bank, pa and Dewey Dell stand watching us, Dewey Dell with the basket and the package in her arms. Jewel is trying to fight the horse back. The head of one mule appears, its eyes wide; it looks back at us for an instant, making a sound almost human. The head vanishes again.

'Back, Jewel,' Cash shouts. 'Back, Jewel.' For another instant I see him leaning to the tilting wagon, his arm braced back against Addie and his tools; I see the bearded head of the rearing log strike up again, and beyond it Jewel holding the horse upreared, its head wrenched around, hammering its head with his fist. I jump from the wagon on the down-stream side. Between two hills I see the mules once more. They roll up out of the water in succession, turning completely over, their legs stiffly extended as when they had lost contact with the earth.

Vardaman

Cash tried but she fell off and Darl jumped going under he went under and Cash hollering to catch her and I hollering running and hollering and Dewey Dell hollering at me Vardaman you vardaman you vardaman and Vernon passed me because he was seeing her come up and she jumped into the water again and Darl hadn't caught her yet.

He came up to see and I hollering catch her Darl catch her and he didn't come back because she was too heavy he had to go on catching at her and I hollering catch her darl catch her darl because in the water she could go faster than a man and Darl had to grabble for her so I knew he could catch her because he is the best grabbler even with the mules in the way again they dived up rolling their feet stiff rolling down again and their backs up now and Darl had to again because in the water she could go faster than a man or a woman and I passed Vernon and he wouldn't get in the water and help Darl he would grabble for her with Darl he knew but he wouldn't help.

The mules dived up again diving their legs stiff their stiff legs rolling slow and then Darl again and I hollering catch her darl catch her head her into the bank darl and Vernon wouldn't help and then Darl dodged past the mules where he could he had her under the water coming in to the bank coming in slow because in the water she fought to stay under the water but Darl is strong and he was coming in slow and so I knew he had her because he came slow and I ran down into the water to help and I couldn't stop hollering because Darl was strong and steady holding her under the water even if she did fight he would not let her go he was seeing me and he would hold her and it was all right now it was all right now it was all right.

Then he comes up out of the water. He comes a long way up slow before his hands do but he's got to have her got to so I can bear it. Then his hands come up and all of him above the water. I can't stop. I have not got time to try. I will try to when I can but his hands came empty out of the water emptying the water emptying away.

'Where is ma, Darl?' I said. 'You never got her. You knew she is a fish but you let her get away. You never got her. Darl. Darl. Darl.' I began to run along the bank, watching the mules dive up slow again and then down again.

Tull

When I told Cora how Darl jumped out of the wagon and left Cash sitting there trying to save it and the wagon turning over, and Jewel that was almost to the bank fighting that horse back where it had more sense than to go, she says 'And you're one of the folks that says Darl is the queer one, the one that ain't bright, and him the only one of them that had sense enough to get off that wagon. I notice Anse was too smart to been on it a-tall.'

'He couldn't 'a' done no good, if he'd been there,' I said. 'They was going about it right and they would have made it if it hadn't a-been for that log.'

'Log, fiddlesticks,' Cora said. 'It was the hand of God.'

'Then how can you say it was foolish?' I said. 'Nobody can't guard against the hand of God. It would be sacrilege to try to.'

'Then why dare it?' Cora says. 'Tell me that.'

'Anse didn't,' I said. 'That's just what you faulted him for.'

'His place was there,' Cora said. 'If he had been a man, he would 'a' been there instead of making his sons do what he dursn't.'

'I don't know what you want, then,' I said. 'One breath you say they was daring the hand of God to try it, and the next breath you jump on Anse because he wasn't with them.' Then she begun to sing again, working at the wash-tub, with that singing look in her face like she had done give up folks and all their foolishness and had done went on ahead of them, marching up the sky, singing.

The wagon hung for a long time while the current built up under it, shoving it off the ford, and Cash leaning more and more, trying to keep the coffin braced so it wouldn't slip down and finish tilting the wagon over. Soon as the wagon got tilted good, to where the current could finish it, the log went on. It headed around the wagon and went on good as a swimming man could have done. It was like it had been sent there to do a job and done it and went on.

When the mules finally kicked loose, it looked for a minute like maybe Cash would get the wagon back. It looked like him and the wagon wasn't moving at all, and just Jewel fighting that horse back to the wagon. Then that boy passed me, running and hollering at Darl and the gal trying to catch him, and then I see the mules come rolling slow up out of the water, their legs spraddled stiff like they had balked upside down, and roll on into the water again.

Then the wagon tilted over and then it and Jewel and the horse was all mixed up together. Cash went outen sight, still holding the coffin braced, and then I couldn't tell anything for the horse lunging and splashing. I thought that Cash had given up then and was swimming for it and I was yelling at Jewel to come on back and then all of a sudden him and the horse went under too and I thought they was all going. I knew that the horse had got dragged off the ford too, and with that wild drowning horse and that wagon and that loose box, it was going to be pretty bad, and there I was, standing knee deep in the water, yelling at Anse behind me: 'See what you done now? See what you done now?'

The horse come up again. It was headed for the bank now, throwing its head up, and then I saw one of them holding to the saddle on the downstream side, so I started running along the bank, trying to catch sight of Cash because he couldn't swim, yelling at Jewel where Cash was like a durn fool, bad as that boy that was on down the bank still hollering at Darl.

So I went down into the water so I could still keep some kind of grip in the mud, when I saw Jewel. He was middle deep, so I knew he was on the ford, anyway, leaning hard upstream, and then I see the rope, and then I see the water building up where he was holding the wagon snubbed just below the ford.

So it was Cash holding to the horse when it come splashing and scrambling up the bank, moaning and groaning like a natural man. When I come to it it was just kicking Cash loose from his holt on the saddle. His face turned up a second when he was sliding back into the water. It was grey, with his eyes closed and a long swipe of mud across his face. Then he let go and turned over in the water. He looked just like an old bundle of clothes kind of washing up and down against the bank. He looked like he was laying there in the water on his face, rocking up and down a little, looking at something on the bottom.

We could watch the rope cutting down into the water, and we could feel the weight of the wagon kind of blump and lunge lazy like, like it just as soon as not, and that rope cutting down into the water hard as a iron bar. We could hear the water hissing on it like it was red hot. Like it was a straight iron bar stuck into the bottom and us holding the end of it, and the wagon lazing up and down, kind of pushing and prodding at us like it had come around and got behind us, lazy like, like it just as soon as not when it made up its mind. There was a shoat come by, blowed up like a balloon: one of them spotted shoats of Lon Quick's. It bumped against the rope like it was a iron bar and bumped off and went on, and us watching that rope slanting down into the water. We watched it.

Darl

Cash lies on his back on the earth, his head raised on a rolled garment. His eyes are closed, his face is grey, his hair plastered in a smooth smear across his forehead as though done with a paint-brush. His face appears sunken a little, sagging from the bony ridges of eye-sockets, nose, gums, as though the wetting had slacked the firmness which had held the skin full; his teeth, set in pale gums, are parted a little as if he had been laughing quietly. He lies pole-thin in his wet clothes, a little pool of vomit at his head and a thread of it running from the corner of his mouth and down his cheek where he couldn't turn his head quick or far enough, until Dewey Dell stoops and wipes it away with the hem of her dress.

Jewel approaches. He has the plane. 'Vernon just found the square,' he says. He looks down at Cash, dripping too. 'Ain't he talked none yet?'

'He had his saw and hammer and chalk-line and rule,' I say. 'I know that.'

Jewel lays the square down. Pa watches him. 'They can't be far away,' pa says. 'It all went together. Was there ere a such misfortunate man.'

Jewel does not look at pa. 'You better call Vardaman back here,' he says. He looks at Cash. Then he turns and goes away. 'Get him to talk as soon as he can,' he says, 'so he can tell us what else there was.'

We return to the river. The wagon is hauled clear, the wheels chocked (carefully: we all helped; it is as though upon the shabby, familiar, inert shape of the wagon there lingered somehow, latent yet still immediate, that violence which had slain the mules that drew it not an hour since) above the edge of the flood. In the wagon bed it lies profoundly, the long pale planks hushed a little with wetting yet still yellow, like gold seen through water, save for two long muddy smears. We pass it and go on to the bank.

One end of the rope is made fast to a tree. At the edge of the stream, knee-deep, Vardaman stands, bent forward a little, watching Vernon with rapt absorption. He has stopped yelling and he is wet to the armpits. Vernon is at the other end of the rope, shoulder-deep in the river, looking back at Vardaman. 'Farther back than that,' he says, 'You git back by the tree and hold the rope for me, so it can't slip.'

Vardaman backs along the rope, to the tree, moving blindly, watching Vernon. When we come up he looks at us once, his eyes round and a little dazed. Then he looks at Vernon again in that posture of rapt alertness.

'I got the hammer too,' Vernon says. 'Looks like we ought to done already got that chalk-line. It ought to floated.'

'Floated clean away,' Jewel says. 'We won't get it. We ought to find the saw, though.'

'I reckon so,' Vernon says. He looks at the water. 'That chalk-line, too. What else did he have?'

'He ain't talked yet,' Jewel says, entering the water. He looks back at me. 'You go back and get him roused up to talk,' he says.

'Pa's there,' I say. I follow Jewel into the water, along the rope. It feels alive in my hand, bellied faintly in a prolonged and resonant arc. Vernon is watching me.

'You better go,' he says. 'You better be there.'

'Let's see what else we can get before it washes on down,' I say.

We hold to the rope, the current curling and dimpling about our shoulders. But beneath that false blandness the true force of it leans against us lazily. I had not thought that water in July could be so cold. It is like hands moulding and prodding at the very bones. Vernon is still looking back toward the bank.

'Reckon it'll hold us all?' he says. We too look back, following the rigid bar of the rope as it rises from the water to the tree and Vardaman crouched a little beside it, watching us. 'Wish my mule wouldn't strike out for home,' Vernon says.

'Come on,' Jewel says. 'Let's get outen here.'

We submerge in turn, holding to the rope, being clutched by one another while the cold wall of the water sucks the slanting mud backward and upstream from beneath our feet and we are suspended so, groping along the cold bottom. Even the mud there is not still. It has a chill, scouring quality, as though the earth under us were in motion too. We touch and fumble at one another's extended arms, letting ourselves go cautiously against the rope; or, erect in turn, watch the water suck and boil where one of the other two gropes beneath the surface. Pa has come down to the shore, watching us.

Vernon comes up, streaming, his face sloped down into his pursed blowing mouth. His mouth is bluish, like a circle of weathered rubber. He has the rule.

'He'll be glad of that,' I say. 'It's right new. He bought it just last month out of the catalogue.'

'If we just knowed for sho what else,' Vernon says, looking over his shoulder and then turning to face where Jewel had disappeared. 'Didn't he go down 'fore me?' Vernon says.

'I don't know,' I say. 'I think so. Yes. Yes, he did.'

We watch the thick curling surface, streaming away from us in slow whorls.

'Give him a pull on the rope,' Vernon says.

'He's on your end of it,' I say.

'Ain't nobody on my end of it,' he says.

'Pull it in,' I say. But he has already done that, holding the end above the water; and then we see Jewel. He is ten yards away; he comes up, blowing, and looks at us, tossing his long hair back with a jerk of his head, then he looks toward the bank; we can see him filling his lungs.

'Jewel,' Vernon says, not loud, but his voice going full and clear along the water, peremptory yet tactful. 'It'll be back here. Better come back.'

Jewel dives again. We stand there, leaning back against the current, watching the water where he disappeared, holding the dead rope between us like two men holding the nozzle of a fire-hose, waiting for the water. Suddenly Dewey Dell is behind us in the water. 'You make him come back,' she says. 'Jewell' she says. He comes up again, tossing his hair back from his eyes. He is swimming now, toward the bank, the current sweeping him downstream quartering. 'You, Jewel!' Dewey Dell says. We stand holding the rope and see him gain the bank and climb out. As he rises from the water, he stoops and picks up something. He comes back along the bank. He has found the chalk-line. He comes opposite us and stands there, looking about as if he were seeking something. Pa goes on down the bank. He is going back to look at the mules again where their round bodies float and rub quietly together in the slack water within the bend.

'What did you do with the hammer, Vernon?' Jewel says.

'I give it to him,' Vernon says, jerking his head at Vardaman. Vardaman is looking after pa. Then he looks at Jewel. 'With the square.' Vernon is watching Jewel. He moves toward the bank, passing Dewey Dell and me.

'You get on out of here,' I say. She says nothing, looking at Jewel and Vernon.

'Where's the hammer?' Jewel says. Vardaman scuttles up the bank and fetches it.

'It's heavier than the saw,' Vernon says. Jewel is tying the end of the chalk-line about the hammer shaft.

'Hammer's got the most wood in it,' Jewel says. He and Vernon face one another, watching Jewel's hands.

'And flatter, too,' Vernon says. 'It'd float three to one, almost. Try the plane.'

Jewel looks at Vernon. Vernon is tall, too; long and lean, eye to eye they stand in their close wet clothes. Lon Quick could look even at a cloudy sky and tell the time to ten minutes. Big Lon I mean, not little Lon.

'Why don't you get out of the water?' I say.

'It won't float like a saw,' Jewel says.

'It'll float nigher to a saw than a hammer will,' Vernon says.

'Bet you,' Jewel says.

'I won't bet,' Vernon says.

They stand there, watching Jewel's still hands.

'Hell,' Jewel says. 'Get the plane, then.'

So they get the plane and tie it to the chalk-line and enter the water again. Pa comes back along the bank. He stops for a while and looks at us, hunched, mournful, like a failing steer or an old tall bird.

Vernon and Jewel return, leaning against the current. 'Get out of the way,' Jewel says to Dewey Dell. 'Get out of the water.'

She crowds against me a little so they can pass, Jewel holding the plane high as though it were perishable, the blue string trailing back over his shoulder. They pass us and stop; they fall to arguing quietly about just where the wagon went over.

'Darl ought to know,' Vernon says. They look at me.

'I don't know,' I says. 'I wasn't there that long.'

'Hell,' Jewel says. They move on, gingerly, leaning against the current, reading the ford with their feet.

'Have you got a holt of the rope?' Vernon says. Jewel does not answer. He glances back at the shore, calculant, then at the water. He flings the plane outward, letting the string run through his fingers, his fingers turning blue where it runs over them. When the line stops, he hands it back to Vernon.

'Better let me go this time,' Vernon says. Again Jewel does not answer; we watch him duck beneath the surface.

'Jewel,' Dewey Dell whimpers.

'It ain't so deep there,' Vernon says. He does not look back. He is watching the water where Jewel went under.

When Jewel comes up he has the saw.

When we pass the wagon pa is standing beside it, scrubbing at the two mud smears with a handful of leaves. Against the jungle Jewel's horse looks like a patchwork quilt hung on a line.

Cash has not moved. We stand above him, holding the plane, the saw, the hammer, the square, the rule, the chalkline, while Dewey Dell squats and lifts Cash's head. 'Cash,' she says; 'Cash.'

He opens his eyes, staring profoundly up at our inverted faces.

'If ever was such a misfortunate man,' pa says.

'Look, Cash,' we say, holding the tools up so he can see; 'what else did you have?'

He tries to speak, rolling his head, shutting his eyes.

'Cash,' we say; 'Cash.'

It is to vomit he is turning his head. Dewey Dell wipes his mouth on the wet hem of her dress; then he can speak.

'It's his saw-set,' Jewel says. 'The new one he bought when he bought the rule.' He moves, turning away. Vernon looks up after him, still squatting. Then he rises and follows Jewel down to the water.

'If ever was such a misfortunate man,' pa says. He looms tall above us as we squat; he looks like a figure carved clumsily from tough wood by a drunken caricaturist. 'It's a trial,' he says. 'But I don't begrudge her it. No man can say I begrudge her it.' Dewey Dell has laid Cash's head back on the folded coat, twisting his head a little to avoid the vomit. Beside him his tools lie. 'A fellow might call it lucky it was the same leg he broke when he fell offen that church,' pa says. 'But I don't begrudge her it.'

Jewel and Vernon are in the river again. From here they do not appear to violate the surface at all; it is as though it had severed them both at a single blow, the two torsos moving with infinitesimal and ludicrous care upon the surface. It looks peaceful, like machinery does after you have watched it and listened to it for a long time. As though the clotting which is you had dissolved into the myriad original motion, and seeing and hearing in themselves blind and deaf; fury in itself quiet with stagnation. Squatting, Dewey Dell's wet dress shapes for the dead eyes of three blind men those mammalian ludicrosities which are the horizons and the valleys of the earth.

Cash

It wasn't on a balance. I told them that if they wanted it to tote and ride on a balance, they would have to –

Cora

One day we were talking. She had never been pure religious, not even after that summer at the camp meeting when Brother Whitfield wrestled with her spirit, singled her out, and strove with the vanity in her mortal heart, and I said to her many a time, 'God gave you children to comfort your hard human lot and for a token of His own suffering and love, for in love you conceived and bore them.' I said that because she took God's love and her duty to Him too much as a matter of course, and such conduct is not pleasing to Him. I said. 'He gave us the gift to raise our voices in His undying praise' because I said there is more rejoicing in heaven over one sinner than over a hundred that never sinned. And she said 'My daily life is an acknowledgement and expiation of my sin' and I said 'Who are you, to say what is sin and what is not sin? It is the Lord's part to judge; ours to praise His mercy and His holy name in the hearing of our fellow mortals, because He alone can see into the heart, and just because a woman's life is right in the sight of man, she can't know if there is no sin in her heart without she opens her heart to the Lord and receives His grace. I said, 'Just because you have been a faithful wife is no sign that there is no sin in your heart, and just because your life is hard is no sign that the Lord's grace is absolving you.' And she said, 'I know my own sin. I know that I deserve my punishment. I do not begrudge it.' And I said, 'It is out of your vanity that you would judge sin and salvation in the Lord's place. It is our mortal lot to suffer and to raise our voices in praise of Him who judges the sin and offers the salvation through our trials and tribulations time out of mind amen. Not even after Brother Whitfield, a godly man if ever one breathed God's breath, prayed for you and strove as never a man could except him,' I said.

Because it is not us that can judge our sins or know what is sin in the Lord's eyes. She has had a hard life, but so does every

woman. But you'd think from the way she talked that she knew
more about sin and salvation than the Lord God Himself, than
them who have strove and laboured with the sin in this human
world. When the only sin she ever committed was being partial
to Jewel that never loved her and was its own punishment, in
preference to Darl that was touched by God Himself and considered queer by us mortals and that did love her. I said, 'There
is your sin. And your punishment too. Jewel is your punishment.
But where is your salvation? And life is short enough,' I said, 'to
win eternal grace in. And God is a jealous God. It is His to judge
and to mete; not yours.'

'I know,' she said. 'I —' Then she stopped, and I said,

'Know what?'

'Nothing,' she said. 'He is my cross and he will be my salvation.
He will save me from the water and from the fire. Even though
I have laid down my life, he will save me.'

'How do you know, without you open your heart to Him and
lift your voice in His praise?' I said. Then I realized that she did
not mean God. I realized that out of the vanity of her heart she
had spoken sacrilege. And I went down on my knees right there.
I begged her to kneel and open her heart and cast from it the
devil of vanity and cast herself upon the mercy of the Lord. But
she wouldn't. She just sat there, lost in her vanity and her pride,
that had closed her heart to God and set that selfish mortal boy
in His place. Kneeling there I prayed for her. I prayed for that
poor blind woman as I had never prayed for me and mine.

Addie

In the afternoon when school was out and the last one had left
with his little dirty snuffling nose, instead of going home I would
go down the hill to the spring where I could be quiet and hate
them. It would be quiet there then, with the water bubbling up
and away and the sun slanting quiet in the trees and the quiet
smelling of damp and rotting leaves and new earth; especially in

the early spring, for it was worst then.

I could just remember how my father used to say that the reason for living was to get ready to stay dead a long time. And when I would have to look at them day after day, each with his and her secret and selfish thought, and blood strange to each other blood and strange to mine, and think that this seemed to be the only way I could get ready to stay dead, I would hate my father for having ever planted me. I would look forward to the times when they faulted, so I could whip them. When the switch fell I could feel it upon my flesh; when it welted and ridged it was my blood that ran, and I would think with each blow of the switch: Now you are aware of me! Now I am something in your secret and selfish life, who have marked your blood with my own for ever and ever.

And so I took Anse. I saw him pass the school-house three or four times before I learned that he was driving four miles out of his way to do it. I noticed then how he was beginning to hump – a tall man and young – so that he looked already like a tall bird hunched in the cold weather, on the wagon seat. He would pass the school-house, the wagon creaking slow, his head turning slow to watch the door of the school-house as the wagon passed, until he went on around the curve and out of sight. One day I went to the door and stood there when he passed. When he saw me he looked quickly away and did not look back again.

In the early spring it was worst. Sometimes I thought that I could not bear it, lying in bed at night, with the wild geese going north and their honking coming faint and high and wild out of the wild darkness, and during the day it would seem as though I couldn't wait for the last one to go so I could go down to the spring. And so when I looked up that day and saw Anse standing there in his Sunday clothes, turning his hat round and round in his hands, I said:

'If you've got any womenfolks, why in the world don't they make you get your hair cut?'

'I ain't got none,' he said. Then he said suddenly, driving his eyes at me like two hounds in a strange yard: 'That's what I come to see you about.'

'And make you hold your shoulders up,' I said. 'You haven't got any? But you've got a house. They tell me you've got a house and a good farm. And you live there alone, doing for yourself, do you?' He just looked at me, turning the hat in his hands. 'A new house,' I said. 'Are you going to get married?'

And he said again, holding his eyes to mine: 'That's what I come to see you about.'

Later he told me, 'I ain't got no people. So that won't be no worry to you. I don't reckon you can say the same.'

'No. I have people. In Jefferson.'

His face fell a little. 'Well, I got a little property. I'm forehanded; I got a good honest name. I know how town folks are, but maybe when they talk to me . . .'

'They might listen,' I said. 'But they'll be hard to talk to.' He was watching my face. 'They're in the cemetery.'

'But your living kin,' he said. 'They'll be different.'

'Will they?' I said. 'I don't know. I never had any other kind.'

So I took Anse. And when I knew that I had Cash, I knew that living was terrible and that this was the answer to it. That was when I learned that words are no good; that words don't ever fit even what they are trying to say at. When he was born I knew that motherhood was invented by someone who had to have a word for it because the ones that had the children didn't care whether there was a word for it or not. I knew that fear was invented by someone that had never had the fear; pride, who never had the pride. I knew that it had been, not that they had dirty noses, but that we had had to use one another by words like spiders dangling by their mouths from a beam, swinging and twisting and never touching, and that only through the blows of the switch could my blood and their blood flow as one stream. I knew that it had been, not that my aloneness had to be violated over and over each day, but that it had never been violated until Cash came. Not even by Anse in the nights.

He had a word, too. Love, he called it. But I had been used to words for a long time. I knew that that word was like the others: just a shape to fill a lack; that when the right time came, you wouldn't need a word for that any more than for pride or fear. Cash did not need to say it to me nor I to him, and I would say, Let Anse use it, if he wants to. So that it was Anse or love; love or Anse: it didn't matter.

I would think that even while I lay with him in the dark and Cash asleep in the cradle within the swing of my hand. I would think that if he were to wake and cry, I would suckle him, too. Anse or love: it didn't matter. My aloneness had been violated and then made whole again by the violation: time, Anse, love, what you will, outside the circle.

Then I found that I had Darl. At first I would not believe it.

Then I believed that I would kill Anse. It was as though he had tricked me, hidden within a word like within a paper screen and struck me in the back through it. But then I realized that I had been tricked by words older than Anse or love, and that the same word had tricked Anse too, and that my revenge would be that he would never know I was taking revenge. And when Darl was born I asked Anse to promise to take me back to Jefferson when I died, because I knew that father had been right, even when he couldn't have known he was right any more than I could have known I was wrong.

'Nonsense,' Anse said; 'you and me ain't nigh done chapping yet, with just two.'

He did not know that he was dead, then. Sometimes I would lie by him in the dark, hearing the land that was now of my blood and flesh, and I would think: Anse. Why Anse. Why are you Anse. I would think about his name until after a while I could see the word as a shape, a vessel, and I would watch him liquefy and flow into it like cold molasses flowing out of the darkness into the vessel, until the jar stood full and motionless: a significant shape profoundly without life like an empty door frame; and then I would find that I had forgotten the name of the jar. I would think: The shape of my body where I used to be a virgin is in the shape of a   and I couldn't think *Anse*, couldn't remember *Anse*. It was not that I could think of myself as no longer unvirgin, because I was three now. And when I would think *Cash* and *Darl* that way until their names would die and solidify into a shape and then fade away, I would say, All right. It doesn't matter. It doesn't matter what they call them.

And so when Cora Tull would tell me I was not a true mother, I would think how words go straight up in a thin line, quick and harmless, and how terribly doing goes along the earth, clinging to it, so that after a while the two lines are too far apart for the same person to straddle from one to the other; and that sin and love and fear are just sounds that people who never sinned nor loved nor feared have for what they never had and cannot have until they forget the words. Like Cora, who could never even cook.

She would tell me what I owed to my children and to Anse and to God. I gave Anse the children. I did not ask for them. I did not even ask him for what he could have given me: not-Anse. That was my duty to him, to not ask that, and that duty I fulfilled. I would be I; I would let him be the shape and echo of his word.

That was more than he asked, because he could not have asked for that and been Anse, using himself so with a word.

And then he died. He did not know he was dead. I would lie by him in the dark, hearing the dark land talking of God's love and His beauty and His sin; hearing the dark voicelessness in which the words are the deeds, and the other words that are not deeds, that are just the gaps in people's lacks, coming down like the cries of the geese out of the wild darkness in the old terrible nights, fumbling at the deeds like orphans to whom are pointed out in a crowd two faces and told, That is your father, your mother.

I believed that I had found it. I believed that the reason was the duty to the alive, to the terrible blood, the red bitter blood boiling through the land. I would think of sin as I would think of the clothes we both wore in the world's face, of the circumspection necessary because he was he and I was I; the sin the more utter and terrible since he was the instrument ordained by God who created the sin, to sanctify that sin He had created. While I waited for him in the woods, waiting for him before he saw me, I would think of him dressed in sin. I would think of him as thinking of me dressed also in sin, he the more beautiful since the garment which he had exchanged for sin was sanctified. I would think of the sin as garments which we would remove in order to shape and coerce the terrible blood to the forlorn echo of the dead word high in the air. Then I would lay with Anse again – I did not lie to him: I just refused, just as I refused my breast to Cash and Darl after their time was up – hearing the dark land talking the voiceless speech.

I hid nothing. I tried to deceive no one. I would not have cared. I merely took the precautions that he thought necessary for his sake, not for my safety, but just as I wore clothes in the world's face. And I would think then when Cora talked to me, of how the high dead words in time seemed to lose even the significance of their dead sound.

Then it was over. Over in the sense that he was gone and I knew that, see him again though I would, I would never again see him coming swift and secret to me in the woods dressed in sin like a gallant garment already blowing aside with the speed of his secret coming.

But for me it was not over. I mean, over in the sense of beginning and ending, because to me there was no beginning nor ending to anything then. I even held Anse refraining still, not that I was holding him recessional, but as though nothing else had ever been. My children were of me alone, of the wild blood boiling along the earth, of me and of all that lived; of none and of all. Then I found that I had Jewel. When I waked to remember to discover it, he was two months gone.

My father said that the reason for living is getting ready to stay dead. I knew at last what he meant and that he could not have known what he meant himself, because a man cannot know anything about cleaning up the house afterward. And so I have cleaned my house. With Jewel – I lay by the lamp, holding up my own head, watching him cap and suture it before he breathed – the wild blood boiled away and the sound of it ceased. Then there was only the milk, warm and calm, and I lying calm in the slow silence, getting ready to clean my house.

I gave Anse Dewey Dell to negative Jewel. Then I gave him Vardaman to replace the child I had robbed him of. And now he has three children that are his and not mine. And then I could get ready to die.

One day I was talking to Cora. She prayed for me because she believed I was blind to sin, wanting me to kneel and pray too, because people to whom sin is just a matter of words, to them salvation is just words too.

Whitfield

When they told me she was dying, all that night I wrestled with Satan, and I emerged victorious. I woke to the enormity of my sin; I saw the true light at last, and I fell on my knees and confessed to God and asked his guidance and received it. 'Rise,' He said; 'repair to that home in which you have put a living lie, among those people with whom you have outraged My Word; confess your sin aloud. It is for them, for that deceived husband, to forgive you: not I.'

So I went. I heard that Tull's bridge was gone; I said 'Thanks, O Lord, A Mighty Ruler of all'; for by those dangers and difficulties which I should have to surmount I saw that He had not abandoned me; that my reception again into His holy peace and love would be the sweeter for it. 'Just let me not perish before I have begged the forgiveness of the man whom I betrayed,' I prayed; 'let me not be too late; let not the tale of mine and her transgression come from her lips instead of mine. She had sworn then that she would never tell it, but eternity is a fearsome thing to face: have I not wrestled thigh to thigh with Satan myself? let me not have also the sin of her broken vow upon my soul. Let not the waters of Thy mighty wrath encompass me until I have cleansed my soul in the presence of them whom I injured.'

It was His hand that bore me safely above the flood, that fended from me the dangers of the waters. My horse was frightened, and my own heart failed me as the logs and the uprooted trees bore down upon my littleness. But not my soul: time after time I saw them averted at destruction's final instant, and I lifted my voice above the noise of the flood: 'Praise to thee, O Mighty Lord and King. By this token shall I cleanse my soul and gain again into the fold of Thy undying love.'

I knew then that forgiveness was mine. The flood, the danger, behind, and as I rode on across the firm earth again and the scene of my Gethsemane drew closer and closer, I framed the words which I should use. I would enter the house; I would stop her before she had spoken; I would say to her husband: 'Anse, I have sinned. Do with me as you will.'

It was already as though it were done. My soul felt freer, quieter than it had in years; already I seemed to dwell in abiding peace again as I rode on. To either side I saw His hand; in my heart I could hear His voice: 'Courage. I am with thee.'

Then I reached Tull's house. His youngest girl came out and called to me as I was passing. She told me that she was already dead.

I have sinned, O Lord. Thou knowest the extent of my remorse and the will of my spirit. But He is merciful; He will accept the will for the deed, Who knew that when I framed the words of my confession it was to Anse I spoke them, even though he was not there. It was He in His infinite wisdom that restrained the tale from her dying lips as she lay surrounded by those who loved and trusted her; mine the travail by water which I sustained by the strength of His hand. Praise to Thee in Thy bounteous and omnipotent love; O praise.

I entered the house of bereavement, the lowly dwelling where another erring mortal lay while her soul faced the awful and irrevocable judgement, peace to her ashes.

'God's grace upon this house,' I said.

Darl

On the horse he rode up to Armstid's and *came back on the horse,* leading Armstid's team. We hitched up and laid Cash on top of Addie. When we laid him down he vomited again, but he got his head over the wagon bed in time.

'He taken a lick in the stomach too,' Vernon said.

'The horse may have kicked him in the stomach too,' I said. 'Did he kick you in the stomach, Cash?'

He tried to say something. Dewey Dell wiped his mouth again.

'What's he say?' Vernon asked.

'What is it, Cash?' Dewey Dell said. She leaned down. 'His tools,' she said. Vernon got them and put them into the wagon. Dewey Dell lifted Cash's head so he could see. We drove on, Dewey Dell and I sitting beside Cash to steady him *and he riding on ahead on the horse.* Vernon stood watching us for a while. Then he turned and went back toward the bridge. He walked gingerly, beginning to flap the wet sleeves of his shirt as though he had just got wet.

He was sitting the horse before the gate. Armstid was waiting at the gate. We stopped *and he got down* and we lifted Cash down and carried him into the house, where Mrs Armstid had the bed ready. We left her and Dewey Dell undressing him.

We followed pa out to the wagon. He went back and got into the wagon and drove on, we following on foot, into the lot. The wetting had helped, because Armstid said, 'You welcome to the house. You can put it there.' *He followed, leading the horse, and stood beside the wagon, the reins in his hand.*

'I thank you,' pa said. 'We'll use in the shed yonder. I know it's a imposition on you.'

'You're welcome to the house,' Armstid said. *He had that wooden look on his face again; that bold, surly, high, coloured rigid look like his face and eyes were two colours of wood, the wrong one pale and the wrong one dark. His shirt was beginning to dry, but it still clung close upon him when he moved.*

'She would appreciate it,' pa said.

We took the team out and rolled the wagon back under the shed. One side of the shed was open.

'It won't rain under,' Armstid said. 'But if you'd rather . . .'

Back of the barn was some rusted sheets of tin roofing. We took two of them and propped them against the open side.

'You're welcome to the house,' Armstid said.

'I thank you,' pa said. 'I'd take it right kind if you'd give them a little snack.'

'Sho,' Armstid said. 'Lula'll have supper ready soon as she gets Cash comfortable.' *He had gone back to the horse and he was taking the saddle off, his damp shirt lapping flat to him when he moved.*

Pa wouldn't come in the house.

'Come in and eat,' Armstid said. 'It's nigh ready.'

'I wouldn't crave nothing,' pa said. 'I thank you.'

'You come in and dry and eat,' Armstid said. 'It'll be all right here.'

'It's for her,' pa said. 'It's for her sake I am taking the food. I got no team, no nothing. But she will be grateful to ere a one of you.'

'Sho,' Armstid said. 'You folks come in and dry.'

But after Armstid gave pa a drink, he felt better, and when we went in to see about Cash *he hadn't come in with us. When I looked back he was leading the horse into the barn* he was already talking about getting another team, and by supper time he had good as bought it. *He is down there in the barn, sliding fluidly past the gaudy lunging swirl, into the stall with it. He climbs on to the manger and drags the hay down and leaves the stall and seeks and finds the curry-comb. Then he returns and slips quickly past the single crashing thump and up against the horse, where it cannot over-reach. He applies the curry-comb, holding himself within the horse's striking radius with the agility of an acrobat, cursing the horse in a whisper of obscene caress. Its head flashes back, tooth-cropped; its eyes roll in the dusk like marbles on a gaudy velvet cloth as he strikes it upon the face with the back of the curry-comb.*

Armstid

But time I give him another sup of whisky and supper was about
ready, he had done already bought a team from somebody, on a
credit. Picking and choosing he were by then, saying how he
didn't like this span and wouldn't put his money in nothing so-
and-so owned, not even a hen coop.

'You might try Snopes,' I said. 'He's got three-four spans.
Maybe one of them would suit you.'

Then he begun to mumble his mouth, looking at me like it was
me that owned the only span of mules in the country and wouldn't
sell them to him, when I knew that like as not it would be my
team that would ever get them out of the lot at all. Only I don't
know what they would do with them, if they had a team. Littlejohn
had told me that the levee through Haley bottom had done gone
for two miles and that the only way to get to Jefferson would be
to go around by Mottson. But that was Anse's business.

'He's a close man to trade with,' he says, mumbling his mouth.
But when I give him another sup after supper, he cheered up
some. He was aiming to go back to the barn and set up with her.
Maybe he thought that if he just stayed down there ready to take
out, Santa Claus would maybe bring him a span of mules. 'But I
reckon I can talk him around,' he says. 'A man'll always help a
fellow in a tight, if he's got ere a drop of Christian blood in him.'

'Of course you're welcome to the use of mine,' I said, me
knowing how much he believed that was the reason.

'I thank you,' he said. 'She'll want to go in ourn,' and him
knowing how much I believed that was the reason.

After supper Jewel rode over to the Bend to get Peabody. I
heard he was to be there today at Varner's. Jewel come back
about midnight. Peabody had gone down below Inverness somewhere, but Uncle Billy come back with him, with his satchel of
horse-physic. Like he says, a man ain't so different from a horse
or a mule, come long come short, except a mule or a horse has

got a little more sense. 'What you been into now, boy?' he says,
looking at Cash. 'Get me a mattress and a chair and a glass of
whisky,' he says.

He made Cash drink the whisky, then he run Anse out of the
room. 'Lucky it was the same leg he broke last summer,' Anse
says, mournful, mumbling and blinking. 'That's something.'

We folded the mattress across Cash's legs and set the chair on
the mattress and me and Jewel set on the chair and the gal held
the lamp and Uncle Billy taken a chew of tobacco and went to
work. Cash fought pretty hard for a while, until he fainted. Then
he laid still, with big balls of sweat standing on his face like they
had started to roll down and then stopped to wait for him.

When he waked up, Uncle Billy had done packed up and left.
He kept on trying to say something until the gal leaned down
and wiped his mouth. 'It's his tools,' she said.

'I brought them in,' Darl said. 'I got them.'

He tried to talk again; she leaned down. 'He wants to see them,'
she said. So Darl brought them in where he could see them. They
shoved them under the side of the bed, where he could reach his
hand and touch them when he felt better. Next morning Anse
taken that horse and rode over to the Bend to see Snopes. Him
and Jewel stood in the lot talking a while, then Anse got on the
horse and rode off. I reckon that was the first time Jewel ever
let anybody ride that horse, and until Anse come back he hung
around in that swole-up way, watching the road like he was half
a mind to take out after Anse and get the horse back.

Along toward nine o'clock it begun to get hot. That was when
I see the first buzzard. Because of the wetting, I reckon. Anyway
it wasn't until well into the day that I see them. Lucky the breeze
was setting away from the house, so it wasn't until well into the
morning. But soon as I see them it was like I could smell it in the
field a mile away from just watching them, and them circling and
circling for everybody in the county to see what was in my barn.

I was still a good half a mile from the house when I heard that
boy yelling. I thought maybe he might have fell into the well or
something, so I whipped up and come into the lot on the lope.

There must have been a dozen of them setting along the ridge-
pole of the barn, and that boy was chasing another one around
the lot like it was a turkey and it just lifting enough to dodge him
and go flopping back to the roof of the shed again where he had
found it setting on the coffin. It had got hot then, right, and the
breeze had dropped or changed or something, so I went and

found Jewel, but Lula came out.

'You got to do something,' she said. 'It's a outrage.'

'That's what I aim to do,' I said.

'It's a outrage,' she said. 'He should be lawed for treating her so.'

'He's getting her into the ground the best he can,' I said. So I found Jewel and asked him if he didn't want to take one of the mules and go over to the Bend and see about Anse. He didn't say nothing. He just looked at me with his jaws going bone-white and them bone-white eyes of hisn, then he went and begun to call Darl.

'What you fixing to do?' I said.

He didn't answer. Darl came out. 'Come on,' Jewel said.

'What you aim to do?' Darl said.

'Going to move the wagon,' Jewel said over his shoulder.

'Don't be a fool,' I said. 'I never meant nothing. You couldn't help it.' And Darl hung back too, but nothing wouldn't suit Jewel.

'Shut your goddamn mouth,' he says.

'It's got to be somewhere,' Darl said. 'We'll take out soon as pa gets back.'

'You won't help me?' Jewel says, them white eyes of hisn kind of blaring and his face shaking like he had a aguer.

'No,' Darl said. 'I won't. Wait till pa gets back.'

So I stood in the door and watched him push and haul at that wagon. I was on a downhill, and once I thought he was fixing to beat out the back end of the shed. Then the dinnerbell rung. I called him, but he didn't look round. 'Come on to dinner,' I said. 'Tell that boy.' But he didn't answer, so I went on to dinner. The gal went down to get that boy, but she come back without him. About half through dinner we heard him yelling again, running that buzzard out.

'It's a outrage,' Lula said; 'a outrage.'

'He's doing the best he can,' I said. 'A fellow don't trade with Snopes in thirty minutes. They'll set in the shade all afternoon to dicker.'

'Do?' she says. 'Do? He's done too much, already.'

And I reckon he had. Trouble is, his quitting was just about to start our doing. He couldn't buy no team from nobody, let alone Snopes, withouten he had something to mortgage he didn't know would mortgage yet. And so when I went back to the field I looked at my mules and same as told them good-bye for a spell. And when I come back that evening and the sun shining all day on that shed I wasn't so sho I would regret it.

He come riding up just as I went out to the porch, where they all was. He looked kind of funny: kind of more hangdog than common, and kind of proud too. Like he had done something he thought was cute but wasn't so sho now how other folks would take it.

'I got a team,' he said.

'You bought a team from Snopes?' I said.

'I reckon Snopes ain't the only man in this country that can drive a trade,' he said.

'Sho,' I said. He was looking at Jewel, with that funny look, but Jewel had done got down from the porch and was going toward the horse. To see what Anse had done to it, I reckon.

'Jewel,' Anse says. Jewel looked back. 'Come here,' Anse says. Jewel come back a little and stopped again.

'What you want?' he said.

'So you got a team from Snopes,' I said. 'He'll send them over tonight, I reckon? You'll want a early start tomorrow, long as you'll have to go by Mottson.'

Then he quit looking like he had been for a while. He got that badgered look like he used to have, mumbling his mouth.

'I do the best I can,' he said. "Fore God, if there were ere a man in the living world suffered the trials and floutings I have suffered.'

'A fellow that just beat Snopes in a trade ought to feel pretty good,' I said. 'What did you give him, Anse?'

He didn't look at me. 'I give a chattel mortgage on my cultivator and seeder,' he said.

'But they ain't worth forty dollars. How far do you aim to get with a forty-dollar team?'.

They were all watching him now, quiet and steady. Jewel was stopped, half-way back, waiting to go on to the horse. 'I give other things,' Anse said. He begun to mumble his mouth again, standing there like he was waiting for somebody to hit him and him with his mind already made up not to do nothing about it.

'What other things?' Darl said.

'Hell,' I said. 'You take my team. You can bring them back. I'll get along some way.'

'So that's what you were doing in Cash's clothes last night,' Darl said. He said it just like he was reading it outen the paper. Like he never give a durn himself one way or the other. Jewel had come back now, standing there, looking at Anse with them marble eyes of hisn. 'Cash aimed to buy that talking machine from Suratt with that money,' Darl said.

Anse stood there, mumbling his mouth. Jewel watched him. He ain't never blinked yet.

'But that's just eight dollars more,' Darl said, in that voice like he was just listening and never give a durn himself. 'That still won't buy a team.'

Anse looked at Jewel quick, kind of sliding his eye that way, then he looked down again. 'God knows, if they were ere a man,' he says. Still they didn't say nothing. They just watched him, waiting, and him sliding his eyes towards their feet and up their legs but no higher. 'And the horse,' he says.

'What horse?' Jewel said. Anse just stood there. I be durn, if a man can't keep the upper hand of his sons, he ought to run them away from home, no matter how big they are. And if he can't do that, I be durn if he oughtn't to leave himself. I be durn if I wouldn't. 'You mean you tried to swap my horse?' Jewel says.

Anse stands there, dangle-armed. 'For fifteen years I ain't had a tooth in my head,' he says. 'God knows it. He knows in fifteen years I ain't et the victuals He aimed for man to eat to keep his strength up, and me saving a nickel here and a nickel there so my family wouldn't suffer, to buy them teeth so I could eat God's appointed food. I give that money. I thought that if I could do without eating, my sons could do without riding. God knows I did.'

Jewel stands with his hands on his hips, looking at Anse. Then he looks away. He looked out across the field, his face still as a rock, like it was somebody else talking about somebody else's horse and him not even listening. Then he spit, slow, and said 'Hell' and he turned and went on to the gate and unhitched the horse and got on it. It was moving when he come into the saddle and by the time he was on it they was tearing down the road like the Law might have been behind them. They went out of sight that way, the two of them looking like some kind of a spotted cyclone.

'Well,' I says. 'You take my team,' I said. But he wouldn't do it. And they wouldn't even stay, and that boy chasing them buzzards all day in the hot sun until he was nigh as crazy as the rest of them. 'Leave Cash here, anyway,' I said. But they wouldn't do that. They made a pallet for him with quilts on top of the coffin and laid him on it and set his tools by him, and we put my team in and hauled the wagon about a mile down the road.

'If we'll bother you here,' Anse says, 'just say so.'

'Sho,' I said. 'It'll be fine here. Safe, too. Now let's go back and eat supper.'

'I thank you,' Anse said. 'We got a little something in the basket. We can make out.'

'Where'd you get it?' I said.

'We brought it from home.'

'But it'll be stale now,' I said. 'Come and get some hot victuals.'

But they wouldn't come. 'I reckon we can make out,' Anse said. So I went home and et, and taken a basket back to them and tried again to make them come back to the house.

'I thank you,' he said. 'I reckon we can make out.' So I left them there, squatting around a little fire, waiting; God knows what for.

I come on home. I kept thinking about them there, and about that fellow tearing away on that horse. And that would be the last they would see of him. And I be durn if I could blame him. Not for wanting to not give up his horse, but for getting shut of such a durn fool as Anse.

Or that's what I thought then. Because be durn if there ain't something about a durn fellow like Anse that seems to make a man have to help him, even when he knows he'll be wanting to kick himself next minute. Because about a hour after breakfast next morning Eustace Grimm that works Snopes's place come up with a span of mules, hunting Anse.

'I thought him and Anse never traded,' I said.

'Sho,' Eustace said. 'All they liked was the horse. Like I said to Mr Snopes, he was letting this team go for fifty dollars, because if his uncle Flem had a just kept them Texan horses when he owned them, Anse wouldn't a never.

'The horse?' I said. 'Anse's boy taken that horse and cleared out last night, probably half-way to Texas by now, and Anse –'

'I didn't know who brung it,' Eustace said. 'I never see them. I just found the horse in the barn this morning when I went to feed, and I told Mr Snopes and he said to bring the team on over here.'

Well, that'll be the last they'll ever see of him now, sho enough. Come Christmas time they'll maybe get a postal card from him in Texas, I reckon. And if it hadn't a been Jewel, I reckon it'd a been me; I owe him that much, myself. I be durn if Anse don't conjure a man, some way. I be durn if he ain't a sight.

Vardaman

Now there are seven of them, in little black circles.

'Look, Darl,' I say; 'see?'

He looks up. We watch them in little tall black circles of not-moving.

'Yesterday there were just four,' I say.

There were more than four on the barn.

'Do you know what I would do if he tries to light on the wagon again?' I say.

'What would you do?' Darl says.

'I wouldn't let him light on her,' I say. 'I wouldn't let him light on Cash, either.'

Cash is sick. He is sick on the box. But my mother is a fish.

'We got to get some medicine in Mottson,' pa says. 'I reckon we'll just have to.'

'How do you feel, Cash?' Darl says.

'It don't bother none,' Cash says.

'Do you want it propped a little higher?' Darl says.

Cash has a broken leg. He has had two broken legs. He lies on the box with a quilt rolled under his head and a piece of wood under his knee.

'I reckon we ought to left him at Armstid's,' pa says.

I haven't got a broken leg and pa hasn't and Darl hasn't and 'It's just the bumps,' Cash says. 'It kind of grinds together a little on a bump. I don't bother none.' Jewel *has gone away. He and his horse went away one supper time.*

'It's because she wouldn't have us beholden,' pa says. ''Fore God, I do the best that ere a man.' *Is it because Jewel's mother is a horse, Darl? I said.*

'Maybe I can draw the ropes a little tighter,' Darl says. *That's why Jewel and I were both in the shed and she was in the wagon because the horse lives in the barn and I had to keep on running the buzzard away from*

'If you just would,' Cash says. And Dewey Dell hasn't got a broken leg and I haven't. Cash is my brother.

We stop. When Darl loosens the rope Cash begins to sweat again. His teeth look out.

'Hurt?' Darl says.

'I reckon you better put it back,' Cash says.

Darl puts the rope back, pulling hard. Cash's teeth look out.

'Hurt?' Darl says.

'It don't bother none,' Cash says.

'Do you want pa to drive slower?' Darl says.

'No,' Cash says. 'Ain't no time to hang back. It don't bother none.'

'We'll have to get some medicine at Mottson,' pa says. 'I reckon we'll have to.'

'Tell him to go on,' Cash says. We go on. Dewey Dell leans back and wipes Cash's face. Cash is my brother. *But Jewel's mother is a horse. My mother is a fish. Darl says that when we come to the water again I might see her and Dewey Dell said, She's in the box; how could she have got out? She got out through the holes I bored, into the water I said, and when we come to the water again I am going to see her. My mother is not in the box. My mother does not smell like that. My mother is a fish.*

'Those cakes will be in fine shape by the time we get to Jefferson,' Darl says.

Dewey Dell does not look around.

'You better try to sell them in Mottson,' Darl says.

'When will we get to Mottson, Darl?' I say.

'Tomorrow,' Darl says. 'If this team don't rack to pieces. Snopes must have fed them on sawdust.'

'Why did he feed them on sawdust Darl?' I say.

'Look,' Darl says. 'See?'

Now there are nine of them, tall in little tall black circles.

When we come to the foot of the hill pa stops and Darl and Dewey Dell and I get out. Cash can't walk because he has a broken leg. 'Come up, mules,' pa says. The mules walk hard; the wagon creaks. Darl and Dewey Dell and I walk behind the wagon, up the hill. When we come to the top of the hill pa stops and we get back into the wagon.

Now there are ten of them, tall in little tall black circles on the sky.

Moseley

I happened to look up, and saw her outside the window, looking in. Not close to the glass, and not looking at anything in particular; just standing there with her head turned this way and her eyes full on me and kind of blank too, like she was waiting for a sign. When I looked up again she was moving toward the door.

She kind of bumbled at the screen door a minute, like they do, and came in. She had on a stiff-brimmed straw hat setting on the top of her head and she was carrying a package wrapped in newspaper: I thought that she had a quarter or a dollar at the most, and that after she stood around awhile she would maybe buy a cheap comb or a bottle of nigger toilet water, so I never disturbed her for a minute or so except to notice that she was pretty in a kind of sullen, awkward way, and that she looked a sight better in her gingham dress and her own complexion than she would after she bought whatever she would finally decide on. Or tell that she wanted. I knew that she had already decided before she came in. But you have to let them take their time. So I went on with what I was doing, figuring to let Albert wait on her when he caught up at the fountain, when he came back to me.

'That woman,' he said. 'You better see what she wants.'

'What does she want?' I said.

'I don't know. I can't get anything out of her. You better wait on her.'

So I went around the counter. I saw that she was barefooted, standing with her feet flat and easy on the floor, like she was used to it. She was looking at me, hard, holding the package; I saw she had about as black a pair of eyes as ever I saw, and she was a stranger. I never remembered seeing her in Mottson before. 'What can I do for you?' I said.

Still she didn't say anything. She stared at me without winking. Then she looked back at the folks at the fountain. Then she looked past me, toward the back of the store.

'Do you want to look at some toilet things?' I said. 'Or is it medicine you want?'

'That's it,' she said. She looked quick back at the fountain again. So I thought maybe her ma or somebody had sent her in for some of this female dope and she was ashamed to ask for it. I knew she couldn't have a complexion like hers and use it herself, let alone not being much more than old enough to barely know what it was for. It's a shame, the way they poison themselves with it. But a man's got to stock it or go out of business in this country.

'Oh,' I said. 'What do you use? We have –' She looked at me again, almost like she had said hush, and looked toward the back of the store again.

'I'd liefer go back there,' she said.

'All right,' I said. You have to humour them. You save time by it. I followed her to the back. She put her hand on the gate. 'There's nothing back there but the prescription case,' I said. 'What do you want?' She stopped and looked at me. It was like she had taken some kind of a lid off her face, her eyes. It was her eyes: kind of dum and hopeful and sullenly willing to be disappointed all at the same time. But she was in trouble of some sort; I could see that. 'What's your trouble?' I said. 'Tell me what it is you want. I'm pretty busy.' I wasn't meaning to hurry her, but a man just hasn't got the time they have out there.

'It's the female trouble,' she said.

'Oh,' I said. 'Is that all?' I thought maybe she was younger than she looked, and her first one had scared her, or maybe one had been a little abnormal as it will in young women. 'Where's your ma?' I said. 'Haven't you got one?'

'She's out yonder in the wagon,' she said.

'Why not talk to her about it before you take any medicine,' I said. 'Any woman would have told you about it.' She looked at me, and I looked at her again and said, 'How old are you?'

'Seventeen,' she said.

'Oh,' I said. 'I thought maybe you were . . .' She was watching me. But then, in the eyes all of them look like they had no age and knew everything in the world, anyhow. 'Are you too regular, or not regular enough?'

She quit looking at me but she didn't move. 'Yes,' she said. 'I reckon so. Yes.'

'Well, which?' I said. 'Don't you know?' It's a crime and a shame; but after all, they'll buy it from somebody. She stood there, not looking at me. 'You want something to stop it?' I said. 'Is that it?'

'No,' she said. 'That's it. It's already stopped.'

'Well, what –' Her face was lowered a little, still, like they do in all their dealings with a man so he don't ever know just where the lightning will strike next. 'You are not married, are you?' I said.

'No.'

'Oh,' I said. 'And how long has it been since it stopped? about five months maybe?'

'It ain't been but two,' she said.

'Well, I haven't got anything in my store you want to buy,' I said, 'unless it's a nipple. And I'd advise you to buy that and go back home and tell your pa, if you have one, and let him make somebody buy you a wedding licence. Was that all you wanted?'

But she just stood there, not looking at me.

'I got the money to pay you,' she said.

'Is it your own, or did he act enough of a man to give you the money?'

'He give it to me. Ten dollars. He said that would be enough.'

'A thousand dollars wouldn't be enough in my store and ten cents wouldn't be enough,' I said. 'You take my advice and go home and tell your pa or your brothers if you have any or the first man you come to in the road.'

But she didn't move. 'Lafe said I could get it at the drugstore. He said to tell you me and him wouldn't never tell nobody you sold it to us.'

'And I just wish your precious Lafe had come for it himself; that's what I wish. I don't know: I'd have had a little respect for him then. And you can go back and tell him I said so – if he ain't half-way to Texas by now, which I don't doubt. Me, a respectable druggist, that's kept store and raised a family and been a church-member for fifty-six years in this town. I'm a good mind to tell your folks myself, if I can just find who they are.'

She looked at me now, her eyes and face kind of blank again like when I first saw her through the window. 'I didn't know,' she said. 'He told me I could get something at the drug-store. He said they might not want to sell it to me, but if I had ten dollars and told them I wouldn't never tell nobody . . .'

'He never said this drug-store,' I said. 'If he did or mentioned my name, I defy him to prove it. I defy him to repeat it or I'll prosecute him to the full extent of the law, and you can tell him so.'

'But maybe another drug-store would,' she said.

'Then I don't want to know it. Me, that's –' Then I looked at her. But it's a hard life they have; sometimes a man . . . if there can ever be any excuse for sin, which it can't be. And then, life wasn't made to be easy on folks: they wouldn't ever have any reason to be good and die. 'Look here,' I said. 'You get that notion out of your head. The Lord gave you what you have, even if He did use the devil to do it; you let Him take it away from you if it's His will to do so. You go on back to Lafe and you and him take that ten dollars and get married with it.'

'Lafe said I could get something at the drug-store,' she said.

'Then go and get it,' I said. 'You won't get it here.'

She went out, carrying the package, her feet making a little hissing on the floor. She bumbled again at the door and went out. I could see her through the glass going on down the street.

It was Albert told me about the rest of it. He said the wagon was stopped in front of Grummet's hardware store, with the ladies all scattering up and down the street with handkerchiefs to their noses, and a crowd of hard-nosed men and boys standing around the wagon, listening to the marshal arguing with the man. He was a kind of tall, gaunted man sitting on the wagon, saying it was a public street and he reckoned he had as much right there as anybody, and the marshal telling him he would have to move on; folks couldn't stand it. It had been dead eight days, Albert said. They came from some place out in Yoknapatawpha county, trying to get to Jefferson with it. It must have been like a piece of rotten cheese coming into an ant-hill, in that ramshackle wagon that Albert said folks were scared would fall all to pieces before they could get it out of town, with that home-made box and another fellow with a broken leg lying on a quilt on top of it, and the father and a little boy sitting on the seat and the marshal trying to make them get out of town.

'It's a public street,' the man says. 'I reckon we can stop to buy something same as airy other man. We got the money to pay for hit, and hit ain't airy law that says a man can't spend his money where he wants.'

They had stopped to buy some cement. The other son was in Grummet's, trying to make Grummet break a sack and let him have ten cents' worth, and finally Grummet broke the sack to get him out. They wanted the cement to fix the fellow's broken leg, someway.

'Why, you'll kill him,' the marshal said. 'You'll cause him to lose his leg. You take him on to a doctor, and you get this thing buried soon as you can. Don't you know you're liable to jail for endangering the public health?'

'We're doing the best we can,' the father said. Then he told a long tale about how they had to wait for the wagon to come back and how the bridge was washed away and how they went eight miles to another bridge and it was gone too so they came back and swum the ford and the mules got drowned and how they got another team and found that the road was washed out and they had to come clean around by Mottson, and then the one with the cement came back and told him to shut up.

'We'll be gone in a minute,' he told the marshal.

'We never aimed to bother nobody,' the father said.

'You take that fellow to a doctor,' the marshal told the one with the cement.

'I reckon he's all right,' he said.

'It ain't that we're hard-hearted,' the marshal said. 'But I reckon you can tell yourself how it is.'

'Sho,' the other said. 'We'll take out as soon as Dewey Dell comes back. She went to deliver a package.'

So they stood there with the folks backed off with handkerchiefs to their faces, until in a minute the girl came up with that newspaper package.

'Come on,' the one with the cement said, 'we've lost too much time.' So they got in the wagon and went on. And when I went to supper it still seemed like I could smell it. And the next day the marshal and I began to sniff and said,

'Smell anything?'

'I reckon they're in Jefferson by now,' he said.

'Or in jail. Well, thank the Lord it's not our jail.'

'That's a fact,' he said.

Darl

'Here's the place,' pa says. He pulls the team up and sits looking at the house. 'We could get some water over yonder.'

'All right,' I say. 'You'll have to borrow a bucket from them, Dewey Dell.'

'God knows,' pa says. 'I wouldn't be beholden, God knows.'

'If you see a good-sized can, you might bring it,' I say. Dewey Dell gets down from the wagon, carrying the package. 'You had more trouble than you expected, selling those cakes in Mottson,' I say. How do our lives ravel out into the no-wind, no-sound, the weary gestures wearily recapitulant; echoes of old compulsions with no-hand on no-strings: in sunset we fall into furious attitudes, dead gestures of dolls. Cash broke his leg and now the sawdust is running out. He is bleeding to death is Cash.

'I wouldn't be beholden,' pa says. 'God knows.'

'Then make some water yourself,' I say. 'We can use Cash's hat.'

When Dewey Dell comes back the man comes with her. Then he stops and she comes on and he stands there and after a while he goes back to the house and stands on the porch, watching us.

'We better not try to lift him down,' pa says. 'We can fix it here.'

'Do you want to be lifted down, Cash?' I say.

'Won't we get to Jefferson tomorrow?' he says. He is watching us, his eyes interrogatory, intent, and sad. 'I can last it out.'

'It'll be easier on you,' pa says. 'It'll keep it from rubbing together.'

'I can last it,' Cash says. 'We'll lose time stopping.'

'We done bought the cement, now,' pa says.

'I could last it,' Cash says. 'It ain't but one more day. It don't bother none to speak of.' He looks at us, his eyes wide in his thin grey face, questioning. 'It sets up so,' he says.

'We done bought it now,' pa says.

I mix the cement in the can, stirring the slow water into the pale-green thick coils. I bring the can to the wagon where Cash can see. He lies on his back, his thin profile in silhouette, ascetic and profound against the sky. 'Does that look about right?' I say.

'You don't want too much water, or it won't work right,' he says.

'Is this too much?'

'Maybe if you could get a little sand,' he says. 'It ain't but one more day,' he says. 'It don't bother me none.'

Vardaman goes back down the road to where we crossed the branch and returns with sand. He pours it slowly into the thick coiling in the can. I go to the wagon again.

'Does that look all right?'

'Yes,' Cash says. 'I could have lasted. It don't bother me none.'

We loosen the splints and pour the cement over his leg, slow.

'Watch out for it,' Cash says. 'Don't get none on it if you can help.'

'Yes,' I say. Dewey Dell tears a piece of paper from the package and wipes the cement from the top of it as it drips from Cash's leg.

'How does that feel?'

'It feels fine,' he says. 'It's cold. It feels fine.'

'If it'll just help you,' pa says. 'I asks your forgiveness. I never foreseen it no more than you.'

'It feels fine,' Cash says.

If you could just ravel out into time. That would be nice. It would be nice if you could just ravel out into time.

We replace the splints, the cords, drawing them tight, the cement in thick pale green slow surges among the cords, Cash watching us quietly with that profound questioning look.

'That'll steady it,' I say.

'Ay,' said Cash. 'I'm obliged.'

Then we all turn on the wagon and watch him. He is coming up the road behind us, wooden-backed, wooden-faced, moving only from his hips down. He comes up without a word, with his pale rigid eyes in his high sullen face, and gets into the wagon.

'Here's a hill,' pa says. 'I reckon you'll have to get out and walk.'

Vardaman

Darl and Jewel and Dewey Dell and I are walking up the hill
behind the wagon. Jewel came back. He came up the road and
got into the wagon. He was walking. Jewel hasn't got a horse any
more. Jewel is my brother. Cash is my brother. Cash has a broken
leg. We fixed Cash's leg so it doesn't hurt. Cash is my brother.
Jewel is my brother too, but he hasn't got a broken leg.

Now there are five of them, tall in little tall black circles.

'Where do they stay at night, Darl?' I say. 'When we stop at
night in the barn, where do they stay?'

The hill goes off into the sky. Then the sun comes up from
behind the hill and the mules and the wagon and pa walk on the
sun. You cannot watch them, walking slow on the sun. In Jefferson
it is red on the track behind the glass. The track goes shining
round and round. Dewey Dell says so.

Tonight I am going to see where they stay while we are in the
barn.

Darl

'Jewel,' I say, 'whose son are you?'

The breeze was setting up from the barn, so we put her under
the apple tree, where the moonlight can dapple the apple tree
upon the long slumbering flanks within which now and then she
talks in little trickling bursts of secret and murmurous bubble. I
took Vardaman to listen. When we came up the cat leaped down

from it and flicked away with silver claw and silver eye into the shadow.

'Your mother was a horse, but who was your father, Jewel?'

'You goddamn lying son of a bitch.'

'Don't call me that,' I say.

'You goddamn lying son of a bitch.'

'Don't you call me that, Jewel.' In the tall moonlight his eyes look like spots of white paper pasted on a high small football.

After supper Cash began to sweat a little. 'It's getting a little hot,' he said. 'It was the sun shining on it all day, I reckon.'

'You want some water poured on it?' we say. 'Maybe that will ease it some.'

'I'd be obliged,' Cash said. 'It was the sun shining on it, I reckon. I ought to thought and kept it covered.'

'We ought to thought,' we said. 'You couldn't have suspicioned.'

'I never noticed it getting hot,' Cash said. 'I ought to minded it.'

So we poured the water over it. His leg and foot below the cement looked like they had been boiled. 'Does that feel better?' we said.

'I'm obliged,' Cash said. 'It feels fine.'

Dewey Dell wipes his face with the hem of her dress.

'See if you can get some sleep,' we say.

'Sho,' Cash says. 'I'm right obliged. It feels fine now.'

Jewel, I say, Who was your father, Jewel?

Goddamn you. Goddamn you.

Vardaman

She was under the apple tree and Darl and I go across the moon and the cat jumps down and runs and we can hear her inside the wood.

'Hear?' Darl says. 'Put you ear close.'

I put my ear close and I can hear her. Only I can't tell what she is saying.

'What is she saying, Darl?' I say. 'Who is she talking to?'

'She's talking to God,' Darl says. 'She is calling on Him to help her.'

'What does she want Him to do?' I say.

'She wants Him to hide her away from the sight of man,' Darl says.

'Why does she want Him to hide her away from the sight of man, Darl?'

'So she can lay down her life,' Darl says.

'Why does she want to lay down her life, Darl?'

'Listen,' Darl says. We hear her. We hear her turn over on her side. 'Listen,' Darl says.

'She's turned over,' I say. 'She's looking at me through the wood.'

'Yes,' Darl says.

'How can she see through the wood, Darl?'

'Come,' Darl says. 'We must let her be quiet. Come.'

'She can't see out there, because the holes are in the top,' I say. 'How can she see, Darl?'

'Let's go see about Cash,' Darl says.

And I saw something Dewey Dell told me not to tell nobody.

Cash is sick in his leg. We fixed his leg this afternoon, but he is sick in it again, lying on the bed. We pour water on his leg and then he feels fine.

'I feel fine,' Cash says. 'I'm obliged to you.'

'Try to get some sleep,' we say.

'I feel fine,' Cash says. 'I'm obliged to you.'

And I saw something Dewey Dell told me not to tell nobody. It is not about pa and it is not about Cash and it is not about Jewel and it is not about Dewey Dell and it is not about me.

Dewey Dell and I are going to sleep on the pallet. It is on the back porch, where we can see the barn, and the moon shines on half of the pallet and we will lie half in the white and half in the black, with the moonlight on our legs. And then I am going to see where they stay at night while we are in the barn. We are not in the barn tonight but I can see the barn and so I am going to find where they stay at night.

We lie on the pallet, with our legs in the moon.

'Look,' I say, 'my legs look black. Your legs look black, too.'

'Go to sleep,' Dewey Dell says.

Jefferson is a far piece.

'Dewey Dell.'

'If it's not Christmas now, how will it be there?'

It goes round and round on the shining track. Then the track goes shining round and round.

'Will what be there?'

'That train. In the window.'

'You go to sleep. You can see tomorrow if it's there.'

Maybe Santa Claus won't know they are town boys.

'Dewey Dell.'

'You go to sleep. He ain't going to let none of them town boys have it.'

It was behind the window, red on the track, and the track shining round and round. It made my heart hurt. And then it was pa and Jewel and Darl and Mr Gillespie's boy. Mr Gillespie's boy's legs come down under his nightshirt. When he goes into the moon, his legs fuzz. They go on around the house toward the apple tree.

'What are they going to do, Dewey Dell?'

They went around the house toward the apple tree.

'I can smell her,' I say. 'Can you smell her, too?'

'Hush,' Dewey Dell says. 'The wind's changed. Go to sleep.'

And so I am going to know where they stay at night soon. They come around the house, going across the yard in the moon, carrying her on their shoulders. They carry her down to the barn, the moon shining flat and quiet on her. Then they come back and go into the house again. While they were in the moon, Mr Gillespie's boy's legs fuzzed. And then I waited and I said Dewey Dell? and then I waited and then I went to find where they stay at night and I saw something that Dewey Dell told me not to tell nobody.

Darl

Against the dark doorway he seems to materialize out of darkness, lean as a racehorse in his underclothes in the beginning of the glare. He leaps to the ground with on his face an expression of furious unbelief. He has seen me without even turning his head or his eyes in which the glare swims like two small torches. 'Come on,' he says, leaping down the slope toward the barn.

For an instant longer he runs silver in the moonlight, then he springs out like a flat figure cut cleanly from tin against an abrupt and soundless explosion as the whole loft of the barn takes fire at once, as though it had been stuffed with powder. The front, the conical façade with the square orifice of doorway broken only by the square squat shape of the coffin on the saw-horses like a cubistic bug, comes into relief. Behind me pa and Gillespie and Mack and Dewey Dell and Vardaman emerge from the house.

He pauses at the coffin, stooping, looking at me, his face furious. Overhead the flames sound like thunder; across us rushes a cool draught: there is no heat in it at all yet, and a handful of chaff lifts suddenly and sucks swiftly along the stalls where a horse is screaming. 'Quick,' I say; 'the horses.'

He glares a moment longer at me, then at the roof overhead, then he leaps toward the stall where the horse screams. It plunges and kicks, the sound of the crashing blows sucking up into the sound of the flames. They sound like an interminable train crossing an endless trestle. Gillespie and Mack pass me, in knee-length nightshirts, shouting, their voices thin and high and meaningless and at the same time profoundly wild and sad: '. . . cow . . . stall . . .' Gillespie's nightshirt rushes ahead of him on the draught, ballooning about his hairy thighs.

The stall door has swung shut. Jewel thrusts it back with his buttocks and he appears, his back arched, the muscles ridged through his garments as he drags the horse out by its head. In the glare its eyes roll with soft, fleet, wild opaline fire; its muscles bunch and run as it flings its head about, lifting Jewel clear of the ground. He drags it on, slowly, terrifically; again he gives me across his shoulder a single glare furious and brief. Even when they are clear of the barn the horse continues to fight and lash backward toward the doorway until Gillespie passes me, stark naked, his nightshirt wrapped about the mule's head, and beats the maddened horse on out of the door.

Jewel returns, running; again he looks down at the coffin. But he comes on. 'Where's cow?' he cries, passing me. I follow him. In the stall Mack is struggling with the other mule. When its head turns into the glare I can see the wild rolling of its eye too, but it makes no sound. It just stands there, watching Mack over its shoulder, swinging its hindquarters toward him whenever he approaches. He looks back at us, his eyes and mouth three round holes in his face on which the freckles look like English peas on a plate. His voice is thin, high, far away.

'I can't do nothing . . .' It is as though the sound had been swept from his lips and up and away, speaking back to us from an immense distance of exhaustion. Jewel slides past us; the mule whirls and lashes out, but he has already gained its head. I lean to Mack's ear:

'Nightshirt. Around his head.'

Mack stares at me. Then he rips the nightshirt off and flings it over the mule's head, and it becomes docile at once. Jewel is yelling at him: 'Cow? Cow?'

'Back,' Mack cries. 'Last stall.'

The cow watches us as we enter. She is backed into the corner, head lowered, still chewing though rapidly. But she makes no move. Jewel has paused, looking up, and suddenly we watch the entire floor to the loft dissolve. It just turns to fire; a faint litter of sparks rains down. He glances about. Back under the trough is a three-legged milking stool. He catches it up and swings it into the planking of the rear wall. He splinters a plank, then another, a third; we tear the fragments away. While we are stooping at the opening something charges into us from behind. It is the cow; with a single whistling breath she rushes between us and through the gap and into the outer glare, her tail erect and rigid as a broom nailed upright to the end of her spine.

Jewel turns back into the barn. 'Here,' I say; 'Jewel!' I grasp at him; he strikes my hand down. 'You fool,' I say, 'don't you see you can't make it back yonder?' The hall-way looks like a searchlight turned into rain. 'Come on,' I say, 'around this way.'

When we are through the gap he begins to run. 'Jewel,' I say, running. He darts around the corner. When I reach it he has almost reached the next one, running against the glare like that figure cut from tin. Pa and Gillespie and Mack are some distance away, watching the barn, pink against the darkness where for the time the moonlight has been vanquished. 'Catch him!' I cry; 'stop him!'

When I reach the front, he is struggling with Gillespie; the one lean in underclothes, the other stark naked. They are like two figures in a Greek frieze, isolated out of all reality by the red glare. Before I can reach them he has struck Gillespie to the ground and turned and run back into the barn.

The sound of it has become quite peaceful now, like the sound of the river did. We watch through the dissolving proscenium of the doorway as Jewel runs crouching to the far end of the coffin and stoops to it. For an instant he looks up and out at us through the rain of burning hay like a portière of flaming beads, and I can see his mouth shape as he calls my name.

'Jewel!' Dewey Dell cries; 'Jewel!' It seems to me that I now hear the accumulation of her voice through the last five minutes, and I hear her scuffling and struggling as pa and Mack hold her, screaming, 'Jewel! Jewel!' But he is no longer looking at us. We see his shoulders strain as he up-ends the coffin and slides it single-handed from the sawhorses. It looms unbelievably tall, hiding him: I would not have believed that Addie Bundren would have needed that much room to lie comfortable in; for another instant it stands upright while the sparks rain on it in scattering bursts as though they engendered other sparks from the contact. Then it topples forward, gaining momentum, revealing Jewel and the sparks raining on him too in engendering gusts, so that he appears to be enclosed in a thin nimbus of fire. Without stopping it over-ends and rears again, pauses, then crashes slowly forward and through the curtain. This time Jewel is riding upon it, clinging to it, until it crashes down and flings him forward and clear and Mack leaps forward into a thin smell of scorching meat and slaps at widening crimson-edged holes that bloom like flowers in his undershirt.

Vardaman

When I went to find where they stay at night, I saw something. They said, 'Where is Darl? Where did Darl go?'

They carried her back under the apple tree.

The barn was still red, but it wasn't a barn now. It was sunk down, and the red went swirling up. The barn went swirling up in little red pieces, against the sky and the stars so that the stars moved backward.

And then Cash was still awake. He turned his head from side to side, with sweat on his face.

'Do you want some more water on it, Cash?' Dewey Dell said.

Cash's leg and foot turned black. We held the lamp and looked at Cash's foot and leg where it was black.

'Your foot looks like a nigger's foot, Cash,' I said.

'I reckon we'll have to bust it off,' pa said.

'What in the tarnation you put it on there for?' Mr Gillespie said.

'I thought it would steady it some,' pa said. 'I just aimed to help him.'

They got the flat iron and the hammer. Dewey Dell held the lamp. They had to hit it hard. And then Cash went to sleep.

'He's asleep now,' I said. 'It can't hurt him while he's asleep.'

It just cracked. It wouldn't come off.

'It'll take the hide, too,' Mr Gillespie said. 'Why in the tarnation you put it on there? Didn't none of you think to grease his leg first?'

'I just aimed to help him,' pa said. 'It was Darl put it on.'

'Where is Darl?' they said.

'Didn't none of you have more sense than that?' Mr Gillespie said. 'I'd 'a' thought he would, anyway.'

Jewel was lying on his face. His back was red. Dewey Dell put the medicine on it. The medicine was made out of butter and soot, to draw out the fire. Then his back was black.

'Does it hurt, Jewel?' I said. 'Your back looks like a nigger's, Jewel,' I said. Cash's foot and leg looked like a nigger's. Then they broke it off. Cash's leg bled.

'You go on back and lay down,' Dewey Dell said. 'You ought to be asleep.'

'Where is Darl?' they said.

He is out there under the apple tree with her, lying on her. He is there so the cat won't come back. I said, 'Are you going to keep the cat away, Darl?'

The moonlight dappled on him too. On her it was still, but on Darl it dappled up and down.

'You needn't to cry,' I said. 'Jewel got her out. You needn't to cry, Darl.'

The barn is still red. It used to be redder than this. Then it went swirling, making the stars run backward without falling. It hurt my heart like the train did.

When I went to find where they stay at night. I saw something that Dewey Dell says I mustn't never tell nobody.

Darl

We have been passing the signs for some time now: the drugstores, the clothing stores, the patent medicine, and the garages and cafés, and the mile-boards diminishing, becoming more starkly re-accruent: 3 mi. 2 mi. From the crest of a hill, as we get into the wagon again, we can see the smoke low and flat, seemingly unmoving in the unwinded afternoon.

'Is that it, Darl?' Vardaman says. 'Is that Jefferson?' He too has lost flesh; like ours, his face has an expression strained, dreamy, and gaunt.

'Yes,' I say. He lifts his head and looks at the sky. High against it they hang in narrowing circles, like the smoke, with an outward semblance of form and purpose, but with no inference of motion, progress, or retrograde. We mount the wagon again where Cash lies on the box, the jagged shards of cement cracked about his leg. The shabby mules droop rattling and clanking down the hill.

'We'll have to take him to the doctor,' pa says. 'I reckon it ain't no way around it.' The back of Jewel's shirt, where it touches him, stains slow and black with grease. Life was created in the valleys. It blew up on to the hills on the old terrors, the old lusts, the old despairs. That's why you must walk up on the hills so you can ride down.

Dewey Dell sits on the seat, the newspaper package on her lap. When we reach the foot of the hill where the road flattens between close walls of trees, she begins to look about quietly from one side of the road to the other. At last she says,

'I got to stop.'

Pa looks at her, his shabby profile that of anticipant and disgruntled annoyance. He does not check the team. 'What for?'

'I got to go to the bushes,' Dewey Dell says.

Pa does not check the team. 'Can't you wait till we get to town? It ain't over a mile now.'

'Stop,' Dewey Dell says. 'I got to go to the bushes.'

Pa stops in the middle of the road and we watch Dewey Dell descend, carrying the package. She does not look back.

'Why not leave your cakes here?' I say. 'We'll watch them.'

She descends steadily, not looking at us.

'How would she know where to go to if she waited till we get to town?' Vardaman says. 'Where would you go to do it in town, Dewey Dell?'

She lifts the package down and turns and disappears among the trees and undergrowth.

'Don't be no longer than you can help,' pa says. 'We ain't got no time to waste.' She does not answer. After a while we cannot hear her even. 'We ought to done like Armstid and Gillespie said and sent word to town and had it dug and ready,' he said.

'Why didn't you?' I say. 'You could have telephoned.'

'What for?' Jewel says. 'Who the hell can't dig a hole in the ground?'

A car comes over the hill. It begins to sound the horn, slowing. It runs along the roadside in low gear, the outside wheels in the ditch, and passes us and goes on. Vardaman watches it until it is out of sight.

'How far is it now, Darl?' he says.

'Not far,' I say.

'We ought to done it,' pa says. 'I just never wanted to be beholden to none except her flesh and blood.'

'Who the hell can't dig a damn hole in the ground?' Jewel says.

'It ain't respectful, talking that way about her grave,' pa says. 'You all don't know what it is. You never pure loved her, none of you.' Jewel does not answer. He sits a little stiffly erect, his body arched away from his shirt. His high-coloured jaw juts.

Dewey Dell returns. We watch her emerge from the bushes, carrying the package, and climb into the wagon. She now wears her Sunday dress, her beads, her shoes and stockings.

'I thought I told you to leave them clothes to home,' pa says. She does not answer, does not look at us. She sits the package in the wagon and gets in. The wagon moves on.

'How many more hills now, Darl?' Vardaman says.

'Just one,' I say. 'The next one goes right up into town.'

This hill is red sand, bordered on either hand by Negro cabins; against the sky ahead the massed telephone lines run, and the clock on the court-house lifts among the trees. In the sand the wheels whisper, as though the very earth would hush our entry. We descend as the hill commences to rise.

We follow the wagon, the whispering wheels, passing the cabins where faces come suddenly to the doors, white-eyed. We hear sudden voices, ejaculant. Jewel has been looking from side to side; now his head turns forward and I can see his ears taking on a still deeper tone of furious red. Three Negroes walk beside the road ahead of us; ten feet ahead of them a white man walks. When we pass the Negroes their heads turn suddenly with that expression of shock and instinctive outrage. 'Great God,' one says; 'what they got in that wagon?'

Jewel whirls. 'Son of a bitch,' he says. As he does so he is abreast of the white man, who has paused. It is as though Jewel had gone blind for the moment, for it is the white man toward whom he whirls.

'Darl!' Cash says from the wagon. I grasp at Jewel. The white man has fallen back a pace, his face still slack jawed; then his jaw tightens, claps to. Jewel leans above him, his jaw muscles gone white.

'What did you say?' he says.

'Here,' I say. 'He don't mean anything, mister. Jewel,' I say. When I touch him he swings at the man. I grasp his arm; we struggle. Jewel has never looked at me. He is trying to free his arm. When I see the man again he has an open knife in his hand.

'Hold up, mister,' I say; 'I've got him. Jewel,' I say.

'Thinks because he's a goddamn town fellow,' Jewel says,

panting, wrenching at me. 'Son of a bitch,' he says.

The man moves. He begins to edge around me, watching Jewel, the knife low against his flank. 'Can't no man call me that,' he says. Pa has got down, and Dewey Dell is holding Jewel, pushing at him. I release him and face the man.

'Wait,' I say. 'He don't mean nothing. He's sick; got burned in a fire last night, and he ain't himself.'

'Fire or no fire,' the man says, 'can't no man call me that.'

'He thought you said something to him,' I say.

'I never said nothing to him. I never see him before.'

' 'Fore God,' pa says; ' 'fore God.'

'I know,' I say. 'He never meant anything. He'll take it back.'

'Let him take it back, then.'

'Put up your knife, and he will.'

The man looks at me. He looks at Jewel. Jewel is quiet now.

'Put up your knife,' I say.

The man shuts the knife.

' 'Fore God,' pa says. ' 'Fore God.'

'Tell him you didn't mean anything, Jewel,' I say.

'I thought he said something,' Jewel says. 'Just because he's –'

'Hush,' I say. 'Tell him you didn't mean it.'

'I didn't mean it,' Jewel says.

'He better not,' the man says. 'Calling me a –'

'Do you think he's afraid to call you that?' I say.

The man looks at me. 'I never said that,' he said.

'Don't think it, neither,' Jewel says.

'Shut up,' I say. 'Come on. Drive on, pa.'

The wagon moves. The man stands watching us. Jewel does not look back. 'Jewel would 'a' whipped him,' Vardaman says.

We approach the crest, where the street runs, where cars go back and forth; the mules haul the wagon up and on to the crest and the street. Pa stops them. The street runs on ahead, where the square opens and the monument stands before the court-house. We mount again while the heads turn with that expression which we know; save Jewel. He does not get on, even though the wagon has started again. 'Get in, Jewel,' I say. 'Come on. Let's get away from here.' But he does not get in. Instead he sets his foot on the turning hub of the rear wheel, one hand grasping the stanchion, and with the hub turning smoothly under his sole he lifts the other foot and squats there, staring straight ahead, motionless, lean, wooden-backed, as though carved squatting out of the lean wood.

Cash

It wasn't nothing else to do. It was either send him to Jackson, or have Gillespie sue us, because he knowed some way that Darl set fire to it. I don't know how he knowed, but he did. Vardaman see him do it, but he swore he never told nobody but Dewey Dell and that she told him not to tell nobody. But Gillespie knowed it. But he would 'a' suspicioned it sooner or later. He could have done it that night just watching the way Darl acted.

And so pa said, 'I reckon there ain't nothing else to do,' and Jewel said,

'You want to fix him now?'

'Fix him?' pa said.

'Catch him and tie him up,' Jewel said. 'Goddamn it, do you want to wait until he sets fire to the goddamn team and wagon?'

But there wasn't no use in that. 'There ain't no use in that,' I said. 'We can wait till she is underground.' A fellow that's going to spend the rest of his life locked up, he ought to be let to have what pleasure he can have before he goes.

'I reckon he ought to be there,' pa says. 'God knows, it's a trial on me. Seems like it ain't no end to bad luck when once it starts.

Sometimes I ain't so sho who's got ere a right to say when a man is crazy and when he ain't. Sometimes I think it ain't none of us pure crazy and ain't none of us pure sane until the balance of us talks him that-a-way. It's like it ain't so much what a fellow does, but it's the way the majority of folks is looking at him when he does it.

Because Jewel is too hard on him. Of course it was Jewel's horse was traded to get her that nigh to town, and in a sense it was the value of his horse Darl tried to burn up. But I thought more than once before we crossed the river and after, how it would be God's blessing if He did take her outen our hands and get shut of her in some clean way, and it seemed to me that when Jewel worked so to get her outen the river, he was going against

God in a way, and when Darl seen that it looked like one of us would have to do something, I can almost believe he done right in a way. But I don't reckon nothing excuses setting fire to a man's barn and endangering his stock and destroying his property. That's how I reckon a man is crazy. That's how he can't see eye to eye with other folks. And I reckon they ain't nothing else to do with him but what the most folks says is right.

But it's a shame, in a way. Folks seems to get away from the olden right teaching that says to drive the nails down and trim the edges well always like it was for your own use and comfort you were making it. It's like some folks has the smooth, pretty boards to build a court-house with and others don't have no more than rough lumber fitten to build a chicken coop. But it's better to build a tight chicken coop than a shoddy court-house, and when they both build shoddy or build well, neither because it's one or tother is going to make a man feel the better nor the worse.

So we went up the street, toward the square, and he said, 'We better take Cash to the doctor first. We can leave him there and come back for him.' That's it. It's because me and him was born close together, and it nigh ten years before Jewel and Dewey Dell and Vardaman begun to come along. I feel kin to them, all right, but I don't know. And me being the oldest, and thinking already the very thing that he done: I don't know.

Pa was looking at me, then at him, mumbling his mouth.

'Go on,' I said. 'We'll get it done first.'

'She would want us all there,' pa says.

'Let's take Cash to the doctor first,' Darl said. 'She'll wait. She's already waited nine days.'

'You all don't know,' pa says. 'The somebody you was young with and you growed old in her and she growed old in you, seeing the old coming on and it was the one somebody you could hear say it don't matter and know it was the truth outen the hard world and all a man's grief and trials. You all don't know.'

'We got the digging to do, too,' I said.

'Armstid and Gillespie both told you to send word ahead,' Darl said. 'Don't you want to go to Peabody's now, Cash?'

'Go on,' I said. 'It feels right easy now. It's best to get things done in the right place.'

'If it was just dug,' pa says. 'We forgot our spade, too.'

'Yes,' Darl said. 'I'll go to the hardware store. We'll have to buy one.'

'It'll cost money,' pa says.

'Do you begrudge her it?' Darl says.

'Go on and get a spade,' Jewel said. 'Here, give me the money.'

But pa didn't stop. 'I reckon we can get a spade,' he said. 'I reckon there are Christians here.' So Darl set still and we went on, with Jewel squatting on the tail gate, watching the back of Darl's head. He looked like one of these bulldogs, one of these dogs that don't bark none, squatting against the rope, watching the thing he was waiting to jump at.

He set that way all the time we was in front of Mrs Bundren's house, hearing the music, watching the back of Darl's head with them hard white eyes of hisn.

The music was playing in the house. It was one of them graphophones. It was natural as a music-band.

'Do you want to go to Peabody's?' Darl said. 'They can wait here and tell pa, and I'll drive you to Peabody's and come back for them.'

'No,' I said. It was better to get her underground, now we was this close, just waiting until pa borrowed the shovel. He drove along the street until we could hear the music.

'Maybe they got one here,' he said. He pulled up at Mrs Bundren's. It was like he knowed. Sometimes I think that if a working man could see work as far ahead as a lazy man can see laziness. So he stopped there like he knowed, before that little new house, where the music was. We waited there, hearing it. I believe I could have dickered Suratt down to five dollars on that one of his. It's a comfortable thing, music is. 'Maybe they got one here,' pa says.

'You want Jewel to go,' Darl says, 'or do you reckon I better?'

'I reckon I better,' pa says. He got down and went up the path and around the house to the back. The music stopped, then it started again.

'He'll get it, too,' Darl said.

'Ay,' I said. It was just like he knowed, like he could see through the walls and into the next ten minutes.

Only it was more than ten minutes. The music stopped and never commenced again for a good spell, where her and pa was talking at the back. We waited in the wagon.

'You let me take you back to Peabody's,' Darl said.

'No,' I said. 'We'll get her underground.'

'If he ever gets back,' Jewel said. He began to cuss. He started to get down from the wagon. 'I'm going,' he said.

Then we saw pa coming back. He had two spades, coming around the house. He laid them in the wagon and got in and we went on. The music never started again. Pa was looking back at the house. He kind of lifted his hand a little and I saw the shade pulled back a little at the window and her face in it.

But the curiousest thing was Dewey Dell. It surprised me. I see all the while how folks could say he was queer, but that was the very reason couldn't nobody hold it personal. It was like he was outside of it too, same as you, and getting mad as it would be kind of like getting mad at a mud-puddle that splashed you when you stepped in it. And then I always kind of had a idea that him and Dewey Dell kind of knowed things betwixt them. If I'd 'a' said it was ere a one of us she liked better than ere a other, I'd 'a' said it was Darl. But when we got it filled and covered and drove out the gate and turned into the lane where them fellows was waiting, when they come out and come on him and he jerked back, it was Dewey Dell that was on him before even Jewel could get at him. And then I believed I knowed how Gillespie knowed about how his barn taken fire.

She hadn't said a word, hadn't even looked at him, but when them fellows told him what they wanted and that they had come to get him and he throwed back, she jumped on him like a wild cat so that one of the fellows had to quit and hold her and her scratching and clawing at him like a wild cat, while the other one and pa and Jewel throwed Darl down and held him lying on his back, looking up at me.

'I thought you would have told me,' he said. 'I never thought you wouldn't have.'

'Darl,' I said. But he fought again, him and Jewel and the fellow, and the other one holding Dewey Dell and Vardaman yelling and Jewel saying,

'Kill him. Kill the son of a bitch.'

It was bad so. It was bad. A fellow can't get away from a shoddy job. He can't do it. I tried to tell him, but he just said, 'I thought you'd 'a' told me. It's not that I,' he said, then he began to laugh. The other fellow pulled Jewel off of him and he sat there on the ground, laughing.

I tried to tell him. If I could have just moved, even set up. But I tried to tell him and he quit laughing, looking up at me.

'Do you want me to go?' he said.

'It'll be better for you,' I said. 'Down there it'll be quiet, with none of the bothering and such. It'll be better for you, Darl,' I said.

'Better,' he said. He began to laugh again. 'Better,' he said. He couldn't hardly say it for laughing. He sat on the ground and us watching him, laughing and laughing. It was bad. It was bad so. I be durn if I could see anything to laugh at. Because there just ain't nothing justifies the deliberate destruction of what a man has built with his own sweat and stored the fruit of his sweat into.

But I ain't so sho that ere a man has the right to say what is crazy and what ain't. It's like there was a fellow in every man that's done a-past the sanity or the insanity, that watches the sane and the insane doings of that man with the same horror and the same astonishment.

Peabody

I said, 'I reckon a man in a tight might let Bill Varner patch him up like a damn mule, but I be damned if the man that'd let Anse Bundren treat him with raw cement ain't got more spare legs than I have.'

'They just aimed to ease hit some,' he said.

'Aimed, hell,' I said. 'What in hell did Armstid mean by even letting them put you on that wagon again?'

'Hit was gittin' right noticeable,' he said. 'We never had time to wait.' I just looked at him. 'Hit never bothered me none,' he said.

'Don't you lie there and try to tell me you rode six days on a wagon without springs, with a broken leg and it never bothered you.'

'I never bothered me much,' he said.

'You mean, it never bothered Anse much,' I said. 'No more than it bothered him to throw that poor devil down in the public street and handcuff him like a damn murderer. Don't tell me. And don't tell me it ain't going to bother you to lose sixty-odd square inches of skin to get that concrete off. And don't tell me

it ain't going to bother you to have to limp around on one short
leg for the balance of your life – if you walk at all again. Concrete,'
I said. 'God Amighty, why didn't Anse carry you to the nearest
sawmill and stick your leg in the saw? That would have cured it.
Then you all could have stuck his head into the saw and cured a
whole family . . . Where is Anse, anyway? What's he up to now?'

'He's takin' back them spades he borrowed,' he said.

'That's right,' I said. 'Of course he'd have to borrow a spade
to bury his wife with. Unless he could borrow a hole in the
ground. Too bad you all didn't put him in it too . . . Does that
hurt?'

'Not to speak of,' he said, and the sweat big as marbles running
down his face and his face about the colour of blotting-paper.

'Course not,' I said. 'About next summer you can hobble
around fine on this leg. Then it won't bother you, not to speak
of . . . If you had anything you could call luck, you might say it
was lucky this is the same leg you broke before,' I said.

'Hit's what paw says,' he said.

MacGowan

It happened I am back of the prescription case, pouring up some
chocolate sauce, when Jody comes back and says, 'Say, Skeet,
there's a woman up front that wants to see the doctor and when
I said What doctor you want to see, she said she want to see the
doctor that works here and when I said There ain't any doctor
works here, she just stood there, looking back this way.'

'What kind of a woman is it?' I says. 'Tell her to go upstairs to
Alford's office.'

'Country woman,' he says.

'Send her to the court-house,' I says. 'Tell her all the doctors
have gone to Memphis to a Barbers' Convention.'

'All right,' he says, going away. 'She looks pretty good for a
country girl,' he says.

'Wait,' I says. He waited and I went and peeped through the

crack. But I couldn't tell nothing except she had a good leg against the light. 'Is she young, you say?' I says.

'She looks like a pretty hot mamma, for a country girl,' he says.

'Take this,' I says, giving him the chocolate. I took off my apron and went up there. She looked pretty good. One of them black-eyed ones that look like she'd as soon put a knife in you as not if you two-timed her. She looked pretty good. There wasn't nobody else in the store; it was dinner-time.

'What can I do for you?' I says.

'Are you the doctor?' she says.

'Sure,' I says. She quit looking at me and was kind of looking around.

'Can we go back yonder?' she says.

It was just a quarter past twelve, but I went and told Jody to kind of watch out and whistle if the old man come in sight, because he never got back before one.

'You better lay off of that,' Jody says. 'He'll fire your stern out of here so quick you can't wink.'

'He don't never get back before one,' I says. 'You can see him go into the post office. You keep your eye peeled, now, and give me a whistle.'

'What you going to do?' he says.

'You keep your eye out. I'll tell you later.'

'Ain't you going to give me no seconds on it?' he says.

'What the hell do you think this is?' I says; 'a stud-farm? You watch out for him. I'm going into conference.'

So I go on to the back. I stopped at the glass and smoothed my hair, then I went behind the prescription case, where she was waiting. She is looking at the medicine cabinet, then she looks at me.

'Now, madam,' I says; 'what is your trouble?'

'It's the female trouble,' she says, watching me. 'I got the money,' she says.

'Ah,' I says. 'Have you got female troubles or do you want female troubles? If so, you come to the right doctor.' Them country people. Half the time they don't know what they want, and the balance of the time they can't tell it to you. The clock said twenty past twelve.

'No,' she says.

'No which?' I says.

'I ain't had it,' she says. 'That's it.' She looked at me. 'I got the money,' she says.

So I knew what she was talking about.

'Oh,' I says. 'You got something in your belly you wish you didn't have.' She looks at me. 'You wish you had a little more or a little less, huh?'

'I got the money,' she says. 'He said I could git something at the drug-store for hit.'

'Who said so?' I says.

'He did,' she says, looking at me.

'You don't want to call no names,' I says. 'The one that put the acorn in your belly? He the one that told you?' She don't say nothing. 'You ain't married, are you?' I says. I never saw no ring. But like as not, they ain't heard yet out there that they use rings.

'I got the money,' she says. She showed it to me, tied up in her handkerchief: a ten spot.

'I'll swear you have,' I says. 'He give it to you?'

'Yes,' she says.

'Which one?' I says. She looks at me. 'Which one of them give it to you?'

'It ain't but one,' she says. She looks at me.

'Go on,' I says. She don't say nothing. The trouble about the cellar is, it ain't but one way out and that's back up the inside stairs. The clock says twenty-five to one. 'A pretty girl like you,' I says.

She looks at me. She begins to tie the money back up in the handkerchief. 'Excuse me a minute,' I says. I go around the prescription case. 'Did you hear about that fellow sprained his ear?' I says. 'After that he couldn't even hear a belch.'

'You better get her out from back there before the old man comes,' Jody says.

'If you'll stay up there in front where he pays you to stay, he won't catch nobody but me,' I says.

He goes on, slow, toward the front. 'What you doing to her, Skeet?' he says.

'I can't tell you,' I says. 'It wouldn't be ethical. You go on up there and watch.'

'Say, Skeet,' he says.

'Ah, go on,' I says. 'I ain't doing nothing but filling a prescription.'

'He may not do nothing about that woman back there, but if he finds you monkeying with that prescription case, he'll kick your stern clean down them cellar stairs.'

'My stern has been kicked by bigger bastards than him,' I says.

'Go back and watch out for him, now.'

So I come back. The clock said fifteen to one. She is tying the money in the handkerchief. 'You ain't the doctor,' she says.

'Sure I am,' I says. She watches me. 'Is it because I look too young, or am I too handsome?' I says. 'We used to have a bunch of old water-jointed doctors here,' I says; 'Jefferson used to be a kind of Old Doctors' Home for them. But business started falling off and folks stayed so well until one day they found out that the women wouldn't never get sick at all. So they run all the old doctors out and got us young good-looking ones that the women would like and then the women begun to get sick again and so business picked up. They're doing that all over the country. Hadn't you heard about it? Maybe it's because you ain't never needed a doctor.'

'I need one now,' she says.

'And you come to the right one,' I says. 'I already told you that.'

'Have you got something for it?' she says. 'I got the money.'

'Well,' I says, 'of course a doctor has to learn all sorts of things while he's learning to roll calomel; he can't help himself. But I don't know about your trouble.'

'He told me I could get something. He told me I could get it at the drug-store.'

'Did he tell you the name of it?' I says. 'You better go back and ask him.'

She quit looking at me, kind of turning the handkerchief in her hands. 'I got to do something,' she says.

'How bad do you want to do something?' I says. She looks at me. 'Of course, a doctor learns all sorts of things folk don't think he knows. But he ain't supposed to tell all he knows. It's against the law.'

Up front Jody says, 'Skeet.'

'Excuse me a minute,' I says. I went up front. 'Do you see him?' I says.

'Ain't you done yet?' he says. 'Maybe you better come up here and watch and let me do that consulting.'

'Maybe you'll lay a egg,' I says. I come back. She is looking at me. 'Of course you realize that I could be put in the penitentiary for doing what you want,' I says. 'I would lose my licence and then I'd have to go to work. You realize that?'

'I ain't got but ten dollars,' she says. 'I could bring the rest next month, maybe.'

'Pooh,' I says, 'ten dollars? You see, I can't put no price on my knowledge and skill. Certainly not for no little paltry sawbuck.'

She looks at me. She don't even blink. 'What you want, then?'

The clock said four to one. So I decided I better get her out. 'You guess three times and then I'll show you,' I says.

She don't even blink her eyes. 'I got to do something,' she says. She looks behind her and around, then she looks toward the front. 'Gimme the medicine first,' she says.

'You mean, you're ready to right now?' I says. 'Here?'

'Gimme the medicine first,' she says.

So I took a graduated glass and kind of turned my back to her and picked out a bottle that looked all right, because a man that would keep poison setting around in a unlabelled bottle ought to be in jail, anyway. It smelled like turpentine. I poured some into the glass and give it to her. She smelled it, looking at me across the glass.

'Hit smells like turpentine,' she says.

'Sure,' I says. 'That's the beginning of the treatment. You come back at ten o'clock tonight and I'll give you the rest of it and perform the operation.'

'Operation?' she says.

'It won't hurt you. You've had the same operation before. Ever hear about the hair of the dog?'

She looks at me. 'Will it work?' she says.

'Sure it'll work. If you come back and get it.'

So she drunk whatever it was without batting a eye, and went out. I went up front.

'Didn't you get it?' Jody says.

'Get what?' I says.

'Ah, come on,' he says. 'I ain't going to try to beat your time.'

'Oh, her,' I says. 'She just wanted a little medicine. She's got a bad case of dysentery and she's a little ashamed about mentioning it with a stranger there.'

It was my night, anyway, so I helped the old bastard check up and I got his hat on him and got him out of the store by eight-thirty. I went as far as the corner with him and watched him until he passed under two street lamps and went on out of sight. Then I come back to the store and waited until nine-thirty and turned out the front lights and locked the door and left just one light burning at the back, and I went back and put some talcum powder into six capsules and kind of cleared up the cellar and then I was all ready.

She come in just at ten, before the clock had done striking. I let her in and she come in, walking fast. I looked out the door, but there wasn't nobody but a boy in overalls sitting on the kerb. 'You want something?' I says. He never said nothing, just looking at me. I locked the door and turned off the light and went on back. She was waiting. She didn't look at me now.

'Where is it?' she said.

I gave her the box of capsules. She held the box in her hand, looking at the capsules.

'Are you sure it'll work?' she says.

'Sure,' I says. 'When you take the rest of the treatment.'

'Where do I take it?' she says.

'Down in the cellar,' I says.

Vardaman

Now it is wider and lighter, but the stores are dark because they have all gone home. The stores are dark, but the lights pass on the windows when we pass. The lights are in the trees around the court-house. They roost in the trees, but the court-house is dark. The clock on it looks four ways, because it is not dark. The moon is not dark too. Not very dark. *Darl he went to Jackson is my brother Darl is my brother* Only it was over that way, shining on the track.

'Let's go that way, Dewey Dell,' I say.

'What for?' Dewey Dell says. The track went shining around the window, it red on the track But she said he would not sell it to the town boys. 'But it will be there Christmas,' Dewey Dell says. 'You'll have to wait till then, when he brings it back.'

Darl went to Jackson. Lots of people didn't go to Jackson. Darl is my brother. My brother is going to Jackson

While we walk the lights go around, roosting in the trees. On all sides it is the same. They go around the court-house and then you cannot see them. But you can see them in the black windows beyond. They have all gone home to bed except me and Dewey Dell.

Going on the train to Jackson. My brother

There is a light on in the store, far back. In the window are two big glasses of soda-water, red and green. Two men could not drink them. Two mules could not. Two cows could not. *Darl*

A man comes to the door. He looks at Dewey Dell.

'You wait out here,' Dewey Dell says.

'Why can't I come in?' I say. 'I want to come in, too.'

'You wait out here,' she says.

'All right,' I say.

Dewey Dell goes in.

Darl is my brother. Darl went crazy

The walk is harder than sitting on the ground. He is in the open door. He looks at me. 'You want something?' he says. His head is slick. Jewel's head is slick sometimes. Cash's head is not slick. *Darl he went to Jackson my brother Darl* In the street he ate a banana. *Wouldn't you rather have bananas? Dewey Dell said. You wait till Christmas. It'll be there then. Then you can see it. So we are going to have some bananas. We are going to have a bag full, me and Dewey Dell.* He locks the door. Dewey Dell is inside. Then the light winks out.

He went to Jackson. He went crazy and went to Jackson both. Lots of people didn't go crazy. Pa and Cash and Jewel and Dewey Dell and me didn't go crazy. We never did go crazy. We didn't go to Jackson either. Darl

I hear the cow a long time, clopping   on the street. Then she comes into the square. She goes across the square, her head down   clopping   . She lows. There was nothing in the square before she lowed, but it wasn't empty. Now it is empty after she lowed. She goes on, clopping   . She lows. *My brother is Darl. He went to Jackson on the train. He didn't go on the train to go crazy. He went crazy in our wagon. Darl* She has been in there a long time. And the cow is gone too. A long time. She has been in there longer than the cow was. But not as long as empty. *Darl is my brother. My brother Darl*

Dewey Dell comes out. She looks at me.

'Let's go around that way now,' I say.

She looks at me. 'It ain't going to work,' she says. 'That son of a bitch.'

'What ain't going to work, Dewey Dell?'

'I just know it won't,' she says. She is not looking at anything. 'I just know it.'

'Let's go that way,' I say.

'We got to go back to the hotel. It's late. We got to slip back in.'

'Can't we go by and see, anyway?'

'Hadn't you rather have bananas? Hadn't you rather?'

'All right.' *My brother he went crazy and he went to Jackson too. Jackson is farther away than crazy*

'It won't work,' Dewey Dell says. 'I just know it won't.'

'What won't work?' I say. *He had to get on the train to go to Jackson. I have not been on the train, but Darl has been on the train. Darl. Darl is my brother. Darl. Darl*

Darl

Darl has gone to Jackson. They put him on the train, laughing, down the long car laughing, the heads turning like the heads of owls when he passed. 'What are you laughing at?' I said.

'Yes yes yes yes yes.'

Two men put him on the train. They wore mis-matched coats, bulging behind over their right hip pockets. Their necks were shaved to a hair-line, as though the recent and simultaneous barbers had had a chalk-line like Cash's. 'Is it the pistols you're laughing at?' I said. 'Why do you laugh?' I said. 'Is it because you hate the sound of laughing?'

They pulled two seats together so Darl could sit by the window to laugh. One of them sat beside him, the other sat on the seat facing him, riding backward. One of them had to ride backward because the state's money had a face to each backside and a backside to each face, and they are riding on the state's money which is incest. A nickel has a woman on one side and a buffalo on the other; two faces and no back. I don't know what that is. Darl had a little spy-glass he got in France at the war. In it it had a woman and a pig with two backs and no face. I know what that is. 'Is that why you are laughing, Darl?'

'Yes yes yes yes yes yes.'

The wagon stands on the square, hitched, the mules motionless, the reins wrapped about the seat-spring, the back of the wagon toward the court-house. It looks no different from a hundred other wagons there; Jewel standing beside it and looking up the street like any other man in town that day, yet there is something different, distinctive. There is about it that unmistakable air of definite and imminent departure that trains have, perhaps due to the fact that Dewey Dell and Vardaman on the seat and Cash on a pallet in the wagon bed are eating bananas from a paper bag. 'Is that why you are laughing, Darl?'

Darl is our brother, our brother Darl. Our brother Darl in a cage in Jackson where, his grimed hands lying light in the quiet interstices, looking out he foams.

'Yes yes yes yes yes yes yes yes.'

Dewey Dell

When he saw the money I said, 'It's not my money, it doesn't belong to me.'

'Whose is it, then?'

'It's Cora Tull's money. It's Mrs Tull's. I sold the cakes for it.'

'Ten dollars for two cakes?'

'Don't you touch it. It's not mine.'

'You never had them cakes. It's a lie. It was them Sunday clothes you had in that package.'

'Don't you touch it! If you take it you are a thief.'

'My own daughter accuses me of being a thief. My own daughter.'

'Pa. Pa.'

'I have fed you and sheltered you. I give you love and care, yet my own daughter, the daughter of my dead wife, calls me a thief over her mother's grave.'

'It's not mine, I tell you. If it was, God knows you could have
it.'

'Where did you get ten dollars?'

'Pa. Pa.'

'You won't tell me. Did you come by it so shameful you dare
not?'

'It's not mine, I tell you. Can't you understand it's not mine?'

'It's not like I wouldn't pay it back. But she calls her own father
a thief.'

'I can't, I tell you. I tell you it's not my money. God knows you
could have it.'

'I wouldn't take it. My own born daughter that has et my food
for seventeen years begrudges me the loan of ten dollars.'

'It's not mine. I can't.'

'Whose is it, then?'

'It was give to me. To buy something with.'

'To buy what with?'

'Pa. Pa.'

'It's just a loan. God knows, I hate for my blooden children to
reproach me. But I give them what was mine without stint.
Cheerful I give them without stint. And now they deny me.
Addie. It was lucky for you you died, Addie.'

'Pa. Pa.'

'God knows it is.'

He took the money and went out.

Cash

So when we stopped there to borrow the shovels we heard the
graphophone playing in the house, and so when we got done
with the shovels pa says, 'I reckon I better take them back.'

So we went back to the house. 'We better take Cash on to
Peabody's,' Jewel said.

'It won't take but a minute,' pa said. He got down from the
wagon. The music was not playing now.

'Let Vardaman do it,' Jewel said. 'He can do it in half the time you can. Or here, you let me –'

'I reckon I better do it,' pa says. 'Long as it was me that borrowed them.'

So we set in the wagon, but the music wasn't playing now. I reckon it's a good thing we ain't got ere a one of them. I reckon I wouldn't never get no work done a-tall for listening to it. I don't know if a little music ain't about the nicest thing a fellow can have. Seems like when he comes in tired of a night, it ain't nothing could rest him like having a little music played and him resting. I have seen them that shuts up like a hand-grip, with a handle and all, so a fellow can carry it with him wherever he wants.

'What you reckon he's doing?' Jewel says. 'I could a toted them shovels back and forth ten times by now.'

'Let him take his time,' I said. 'He ain't as spry as you, remember.'

'Why didn't you let me take them back, then? We got to get your leg fixed up so we can start home tomorrow.'

'We got plenty of time,' I said. 'I wonder what them machines costs on the instalment.'

'Instalment of what?' Jewel said. 'What you got to buy it with?'

'A fellow can't tell,' I said. 'I could 'a' bought that one from Suratt for five dollars, I believe.'

And so pa come back and we went to Peabody's. While we was there pa said he was going to the barber-shop to get a shave. And so that night he said he had some business to tend to, kind of looking away from us while he said it, with his hair combed wet and slick and smelling sweet with perfume, but I said leave him be; I wouldn't mind hearing a little more of that music myself.

And so next morning he was gone again, then he come back and told us get hitched up and ready to take out and he would meet us and when they was gone he said,

'I don't reckon you got no more money.'

'Peabody just give me enough to pay the hotel with,' I said. 'We don't need nothing else, do we?'

'No,' pa said; 'no. We don't need nothing.' He stood there, not looking at me.

'If it is something we got to have, I reckon maybe Peabody,' I said.

'No,' he said; 'it ain't nothing else. You all wait for me at the corner.'

So Jewel got the team and come for me and they fixed me a
pallet in the wagon and we drove across the square to the corner
where pa said, and we was waiting there in the wagon, with
Dewey Dell and Vardaman eating bananas, when we see them
coming up the street. Pa was coming along with that kind of
daresome and hangdog look all at once like when he has been
up to something he knows ma ain't going to like, carrying a grip
in his hand, and Jewel says,

'Who's that?'

Then we see it wasn't the grip that made him look different;
it was his face, and Jewel says, 'He got them teeth.'

It was a fact. It made him look a foot taller, kind of holding
his head up, hangdog and proud too, and then we see her behind
him, carrying the other grip – a kind of duck-shaped woman all
dressed up, with them kind of hard-looking pop eyes like she was
daring ere a man to say nothing. And there we sat watching
them, with Dewey Dell's and Vardaman's mouth half open and
half-et bananas in their hands and her coming around from
behind pa, looking at us like she dared ere a man. And then
I see that the grip she was carrying was one of them little
graphophones. It was for a fact, all shut up as pretty as a picture,
and every time a new record would come from the mail order
and us setting in the house in the winter, listening to it, I would
think what a shame Darl couldn't be to enjoy it too. But it is
better so for him. This world is not his world; this life his life.

'It's Cash and Jewel and Vardaman and Dewey Dell,' pa says,
kind of hangdog and proud too, with his teeth and all, even if he
wouldn't look at us. 'Meet Mrs Bundren,' he says.

SANCTUARY

Chapter One

From beyond the screen of bushes which surrounded the spring, Popeye watched the man drinking. A faint path led from the road to the spring. Popeye watched the man – a tall, thin man, hatless, in worn grey flannel trousers and carrying a tweed coat over his arm – emerge from the path and kneel to drink from the spring.

The spring welled up at the root of a beech tree and flowed away upon a bottom of whorled and waved sand. It was surrounded by a thick growth of cane and brier, of cypress and gum in which broken sunlight lay sourceless. Somewhere, hidden and secret yet nearby, a bird sang three notes and ceased.

In the spring the drinking man leaned his face to the broken and myriad reflection of his own drinking. When he rose up he saw among them the shattered reflection of Popeye's straw hat, though he had heard no sound.

He saw, facing him across the spring, a man of under size, his hands in his coat pockets, a cigarette slanted from his chin. His suit was black, with a tight, high-waisted coat. His trousers were rolled once and caked with mud above mudcaked shoes. His face had a queer, bloodless colour, as though seen by electric light; against the sunny silence, in his slanted straw hat and his slightly akimbo arms, he had that vicious depthless quality of stamped tin.

Behind him the bird sang again, three bars in monotonous repetition: a sound meaningless and profound out of a suspirant and peaceful following silence which seemed to isolate the spot, and out of which a moment later came the sound of an automobile passing along a road and dying away.

The drinking man knelt beside the spring. 'You've got a pistol in that pocket, I suppose,' he said.

Across the spring Popeye appeared to contemplate him with

two knobs of soft black rubber. 'I'm asking you,' Popeye said. 'What's that in your pocket?'

The other man's coat was still across his arm. He lifted his other hand towards the coat, out of one pocket of which protruded a crushed felt hat, from the other a book. 'Which pocket?' he said.

'Don't show me,' Popeye said. 'Tell me.'

The other man stopped his hand. 'It's a book.'

'What book?' Popeye said.

'Just a book. The kind that people read. Some people do.'

'Do you read books?' Popeye said.

The other man's hand was frozen above the coat. Across the spring they looked at one another. The cigarette wreathed its faint plume across Popeye's face, one side of his face squinted against the smoke like a mask carved into two simultaneous expressions.

From his hip pocket Popeye took a soiled handkerchief and spread it upon his heels. Then he squatted, facing the man across the spring. That was about four o'clock on an afternoon in May. They squatted so, facing one another across the spring, for two hours. Now and then the bird sang back in the swamp, as though it were worked by a clock; twice more invisible automobiles passed along the highroad and died away. Again the bird sang.

'And of course you don't know the name of it,' the man across the spring said. 'I don't suppose you'd know a bird at all, without it was singing in a cage in a hotel lounge, or cost four dollars on a plate.' Popeye said nothing. He squatted in his tight black suit, his right-hand coat pocket sagging compactly against his flank, twisting and pinching cigarettes in his little, doll-like hands, spitting into the spring. His skin had a dead, dark pallor. His nose was faintly aquiline, and he had no chin at all. His face just went away, like the face of a wax doll set too near a hot fire and forgotten. Across his vest ran a platinum chain like a spider web. 'Look here,' the other man said. 'My name is Horace Benbow. I'm a lawyer in Kinston. I used to live in Jefferson yonder; I'm on my way there now. Anybody in this county can tell you I am harmless. If it's whisky, I don't care how much you all make or sell or buy. I just stopped here for a drink of water. All I want to do is get to town, to Jefferson.'

Popeye's eyes looked like rubber knobs, like they'd give to the touch and then recover with the whorled smudge of the thumb on them.

'I want to reach Jefferson before dark,' Benbow said. 'You can't keep me here like this.'

Without removing the cigarette Popeye spat past it into the spring.

'You can't stop me like this,' Benbow said. 'Suppose I break and run.'

Popeye put his eyes on Benbow, like rubber. 'Do you want to run?'

'No,' Benbow said.

Popeye removed his eyes. 'Well, don't, then.'

Benbow heard the bird again, trying to recall the local name for it. On the invisible highroad another car passed, died away. Between them and the sound of it the sun was almost gone. From his trousers pocket Popeye took a dollar watch and looked at it and put it back in his pocket, loose like a coin.

Where the path from the spring joined the sandy by-road a tree had been recently felled, blocking the road. They climbed over the tree and went on, the highroad now behind them. In the sand were two shallow parallel depressions, but no mark of hoof. Where the branch from the spring seeped across it Benbow saw the prints of automobile tyres. Ahead of him Popeye walked, his tight suit and stiff hat all angles, like a modernistic lampstand.

The sand ceased. The road rose, curving, out of the jungle. It was almost dark. Popeye looked, briefly over his shoulder. 'Step out, Jack,' he said.

'Why didn't we cut straight across up the hill?' Benbow said.

'Through all them trees?' Popeye said. His hat jerked in a dull, vicious gleam in the twilight as he looked down the hill where the jungle already lay like a lake of ink. 'Jesus Christ.'

It was almost dark. Popeye's gait had slowed. He walked now beside Benbow, and Benbow could see the continuous jerking of the hat from side to side as Popeye looked about with a sort of vicious cringing. The hat just reached Benbow's chin.

Then something, a shadow shaped with speed, stooped at them and on, leaving a rush of air upon their very faces, on a soundless feathering of taut wings, and Benbow felt Popeye's whole body spring against him and his hand clawing at his coat. 'It's just an owl,' Benbow said. 'It's nothing but an owl.' Then he said: 'They call that Carolina wren a fishing-bird. That's what it is. What I couldn't think of back there,' with Popeye crouching against him, clawing at his pocket and hissing through his teeth like a cat. He smells black, Benbow thought; he smells like that black stuff that ran out of Bovary's mouth and down upon her bridal veil when they raised her head.

A moment later, above a black, jagged mass of trees, the house lifted its stark square bulk against the failing sky.

The house was a gutted ruin rising gaunt and stark out of a grove of unpruned cedar trees. It was a landmark, known as the Old Frenchman place, built before the Civil War; a plantation house set in the middle of a tract of land; of cottonfields and gardens and lawns long since gone back to jungle, which the people of the neighbourhood had been pulling down piecemeal for firewood for fifty years or digging with secret and sporadic optimism for the gold which the builder was reputed to have buried somewhere about the place when Grant came through the county on his Vicksburg campaign.

Three men were sitting in chairs on one end of the porch. In the depths of the open hall a faint light showed. The hall went straight back through the house. Popeye mounted the steps, the three men looking at him and his companion. 'Here's the professor,' he said, without stopping. He entered the house, the hall. He went on and crossed the back porch and turned and entered the room where the light was. It was the kitchen. A woman stood at the stove. She wore a faded calico dress. About her naked ankles a worn pair of man's brogans, unlaced, flapped when she moved. She looked back at Popeye, then to the stove again, where a pan of meat hissed.

Popeye stood in the door. His hat was slanted across his face. He took a cigarette from his pocket, without producing the pack, and pinched and fretted it and put it into his mouth and snapped a match on his thumb-nail. 'There's a bird out front,' he said.

The woman did not look around. She turned the meat. 'Why tell me?' she said. 'I don't serve Lee's customers.'

'It's a professor,' Popeye said.

The woman turned, an iron fork suspended in her hand. Behind the stove, in shadow, was a wooden box. 'A what?'

'Professor,' Popeye said. 'He's got a book with him.'

'What's he doing here?'

'I don't know. I never thought to ask. Maybe to read the book.'

'He came here?'

'I found him at the spring.'

'Was he trying to find this house?'

'I don't know,' Popeye said. 'I never thought to ask.' The

woman was still looking at him. 'I'll send him on to Jefferson on
the truck,' Popeye said. 'He said he wants to go there.'

'Why tell me about it?' the woman said.

'You cook. He'll want to eat.'

'Yes,' the woman said. She turned back to the stove. 'I cook. I
cook for crimps and spungs and feebs. Yes, I cook.'

In the door Popeye watched her, the cigarette curling across
his face. His hands were in his pockets. 'You can quit. I'll take
you back to Memphis Sunday. You can go to hustling again.' He
watched her back. 'You're getting fat here. Laying off in the
country. I won't tell them on Manuel Street.'

The woman turned, the fork in her hand. 'You bastard,' she
said.

'Sure,' Popeye said. 'I won't tell them that Ruby Lamar is down
in the country, wearing a pair of Lee Goodwin's throwed-away
shoes, chopping her own firewood. No, I'll tell them Lee Goodwin
is big rich.'

'You bastard,' the woman said. 'You bastard.'

'Sure,' Popeye said. Then he turned his head. There was a
shuffling sound across the porch, then a man entered. He was
stooped, in overalls. He was barefoot; it was his bare feet which
they had heard. He had a sunburned thatch of hair, matted and
foul. He had pale furious eyes, a short soft beard like dirty gold
in colour.

'I be dawg if he ain't a case, now,' he said.

'What do you want?' the woman said. The man in overalls
didn't answer. In passing, he looked at Popeye with a glance at
once secret and alert, as though he were ready to laugh at a joke,
waiting for the time to laugh. He crossed the kitchen with a
shambling, bear-like gait, and still with that air of alert and gleeful
secrecy, though in plain sight of them, he removed a loose board
in the floor and took out a gallon jug. Popeye watched him, his
forefingers in his vest, the cigarette (he had smoked it down
without once touching it with his hand) curling across his face.
His expression was savage, perhaps baleful; contemplative, watching the man in overalls recross the floor with a kind of alert
diffidence, the jug clumsily concealed below his flank; he was
watching Popeye, with that expression alert and ready for mirth,
until he left the room. Again they heard his bare feet on the
porch.

'Sure,' Popeye said. 'I won't tell them on Manuel Street that
Ruby Lamar is cooking for a dummy and a feeb too.'

'You bastard,' the woman said. 'You bastard.'

Chapter Two

When the woman entered the dining-room, carrying a platter of meat, Popeye and the man who had fetched the jug from the kitchen and the stranger were already at a table made by nailing three rough planks to two trestles. Coming into the light of the lamp which sat on the table, her face was sullen, not old; her eyes were cold. Watching her, Benbow did not see her look once at him as she set the platter on the table and stood for a moment with that veiled look with which women make a final survey of a table, and went and stooped above an open packing case in a corner of the room and took from it another plate and knife and fork, which she brought to the table and set before Benbow with a kind of abrupt yet unhurried finality, her sleeve brushing his shoulder.

As she was doing that, Goodwin entered. He wore muddy overalls. He had a lean, weathered face, the jaws covered by a black stubble; his hair was grey at the temples. He was leading by the arm an old man with a long white beard stained about the mouth. Benbow watched Goodwin seat the old man in a chair, where he sat obediently with that tentative and abject eagerness of a man who has but one pleasure left and whom the world can reach only through one sense, for he was both blind and deaf: a short man with a bald skull and a round, full-fleshed, rosy face in which his cataracted eyes looked like two clots of phlegm. Benbow watched him take a filthy rag from his pocket and regurgitate into the rag an almost colourless wad of what had once been chewing tobacco, and fold the rag up and put it into his pocket. The woman served his plate from the dish. The others were already eating, silently and steadily, but the old man sat there, his head bent over his plate, his beard working faintly. He fumbled at the plate with a diffident, shaking hand and found a small piece of meat and began to suck at it until the woman returned and rapped his knuckles. He put the meat back on the plate then and Benbow watched her cut up the food on the plate, meat, bread and all, and then pour sorghum over it. Then Benbow quit looking. When the meal was over, Goodwin led the old man out again. Benbow watched the two of them pass out the door and heard them go up the hall.

The men returned to the porch. The woman cleared the table and carried the dishes to the kitchen. She set them on the table and she went to the box behind the stove and she stood over it for a time. Then she returned and put her own supper on a plate and sat down to the table and ate and lit a cigarette from the lamp and washed the dishes and put them away. Then she went back up the hall. She did not go out on to the porch. She stood just inside the door listening to them talking, listening to the stranger talking and to the thick, soft sound of the jug as they passed it among themselves. 'That fool,' the woman said. 'What does he want? . . .' She listened to the stranger's voice; a quick, faintly outlandish voice, the voice of a man given to much talk and not much else. 'Not to drinking anyway,' the woman said, quiet inside the door. 'He better get on to where he's going, where his women folks can take care of him.'

She listened to him. 'From my window I could see the grape arbour, and in the winter I could see the hammock too. But in the winter it was just the hammock. That's why we know nature is a she; because of that conspiracy between female flesh and female season. So each spring I could watch the reaffirmation of the old ferment hiding the hammock; the green-snared promise of unease. What blossoms grapes have, this is. It's not much: a wild and waxlike bleeding less of bloom than leaf, hiding and hiding the hammock, until along in late May, in the twilight, her – Little Belle's – voice would be like the murmur of the wild grape itself. She never would say, "Horace, this is Louis or Paul or Whoever" but "It's just Horace." Just, you see; in a little white dress in the twilight, the two of them all demure and quite alert and a little impatient. And I couldn't have felt any more foreign to her flesh if I had begot it myself.

'So this morning – no; that was four days ago; it was Thursday she got home from school and this is Tuesday – I said, "Honey, if you found him on the train, he probably belongs to the railroad company. You can't take him from the railroad company; that's against the law, like the insulators on the poles."

' "He's as good as you are. He goes to Tulane."

' "But on a train, honey," I said.

' "I've found them in worse places than on the train."

' "I know," I said. "So have I. But you don't bring them home, you know. You just step over them and go on. You don't soil your slippers, you know."

'We were in the living-room then; it was just before dinner; just the two of us in the house then. Belle had gone down town.

' "What business is it of yours who comes to see me? You're not my father. You're just – just –"

' "What?" I said. "Just what?"

' "Tell Mother, then! Tell her. That's what you're going to do. Tell her!"

' "But on the train, honey," I said. "If he'd walked into your room in a hotel, I'd just kill him. But on the train, I'm disgusted. Let's send him along and start all over again."

' "You're a fine one to talk about finding things on the train! You're a fine one! Shrimp! Shrimp!" '

'He's crazy,' the woman said, motionless inside the door. The stranger's voice went on, tumbling over itself, rapid and diffuse.

'Then she was saying "No! No!" and me holding her and she clinging to me. "I didn't mean that! Horace, Horace!" And I was smelling the slain flowers, the delicate dead flowers and tears, and then I saw her face in the mirror. There was a mirror behind her and another behind me, and she was watching herself in the one behind me, forgetting about the other one in which I could see her face, see her watching the back of my head with pure dissimulation. That's why nature is "she" and Progress is "he"; nature made the grape arbour, but Progress invented the mirror.'

'He's crazy,' the woman said inside the door, listening.

'But that wasn't quite it. I thought that maybe the spring, or maybe being forty-three years old, had upset me. I thought that maybe I would be all right if I just had a hill to lie on for a while – It was that country. Flat and rich and foul, so that the very winds seem to engender money out of it. Like you wouldn't be surprised to find that you could turn in the leaves off the trees into the banks for cash. That Delta. Five thousand square miles, without any hill save the bumps of dirt the Indians made to stand on when the River overflowed.

'So I thought it was just a hill I wanted; it wasn't Little Belle that set me off. Do you know what it was?'

'He is,' the woman said inside the door. 'Lee ought not to let –'

Benbow had not waited for any answer. 'It was a rag with rouge on it. I knew I would find it before I went into Belle's room. And there it was, stuffed behind the mirror: a handkerchief where she had wiped off the surplus paint when she dressed and stuck it behind the mantel. I put it into the clothes-bag and took my hat and walked out. I had got a lift on a truck before I found that I had no money with me. That was part of it too, you see; I couldn't cash a cheque. I couldn't get off the truck and go back to town and get some money. I couldn't do that. So I have been walking and bumming rides ever since. I slept one night in a sawdust pile at a mill, one night at a negro cabin, one night in a freight car on a siding. I just wanted a hill to lie on, you see. Then I would be all right. When you marry your own wife, you start off from scratch . . . maybe scratching. When you marry somebody else's wife, you start off maybe ten years behind, from somebody else's scratch and scratching. I just wanted a hill to lie on for a while.'

'The fool,' the woman said. 'The poor fool.' She stood inside the door. Popeye came through the hall from the back. He passed her without a word, and went on to the porch.

'Come on,' he said. 'Let's get it loaded.' She heard the three of them go away. She stood there. Then she heard the stranger get unsteadily out of his chair and cross the porch. Then she saw him, in faint silhouette against the sky, the lesser darkness: a thin man in shapeless clothes; a head of thinning and ill-kempt hair; and quite drunk. 'They don't make him eat right,' the woman said.

She was motionless, leaning lightly against the wall, he facing her. 'Do you like living like this?' he said. 'Why do you do it? You are young yet; you could go back to the cities and better yourself without lifting more than an eyelid.' She didn't move, leaning lightly against the wall, her arms folded. 'The poor, scared fool,' she said.

'You see,' he said, 'I lack courage: that was left out of me. The machinery is all here, but it won't run.' His hand fumbled across her cheek. 'You are young yet.' She didn't move, feeling his hand upon her face, touching her flesh as though he were trying to learn the shape and position of her bones and the texture of the flesh. 'You have your whole life before you, practically. How old are you? You're not past thirty yet.' His voice was not loud, almost a whisper.

When she spoke she did not lower her voice at all. She had not moved, her arms still folded across her breast. 'Why did you leave your wife?' she said.

'Because she ate shrimp,' he said. 'I couldn't – You see, it was Friday, and I thought how at noon I'd go to the station and get the box of shrimp off the train and walk home with it, counting a hundred steps and changing hands with it, and it –'

'Did you do that every day?' the woman said.

'No. Just Friday. But I have done it for ten years, since we were married. And I still don't like to smell shrimp. But I wouldn't mind the carrying it home so much. I could stand that. It's because the package drips. All the way home it drips and drips, until after a while I follow myself to the station and stand aside and watch Horace Benbow take that box off the train and start home with it, changing hands every hundred steps, and I following him, thinking Here lies Horace Benbow in a fading series of small stinking spots on a Mississippi sidewalk.'

'Oh,' the woman said. She breathed quietly, her arms folded. She moved; he gave back and followed her down the hall. They entered the kitchen where a lamp burned. 'You'll have to excuse the way I look,' the woman said. She went to the box behind the stove and drew it out and stood above it, her hands hidden in the front of her garment. Benbow stood in the middle of the room. 'I have to keep him in the box so the rats can't get to him,' she said.

'What?' Benbow said. 'What is it?' He approached, where he could see into the box. It contained a sleeping child, not a year old. He looked down at the pinched face quietly.

'Oh,' he said. 'You have a son.' They looked down at the pinched, sleeping face of the child. There came a noise outside; feet came on to the back porch. The woman shoved the box back into the corner with her knee as Goodwin entered.

'All right,' Goodwin said. 'Tommy'll show you the way to the truck.' He went away, on into the house.

Benbow looked at the woman. Her hands were still wrapped into her dress. 'Thank you for the supper,' he said. 'Some day, maybe . . .' He looked at her; she was watching him, her face not sullen so much, as cold, still. 'Maybe I can do something for you in Jefferson. Send you something you need . . .'

She removed her hands from the fold of the dress in a turning, flicking motion; jerked them hidden again. 'With all this dish-water and washing . . . You might send me an orange stick,' she said.

Walking in single file, Tommy and Benbow descended the hill from the house, following the abandoned road. Benbow looked back. The gaunt ruin of the house rose against the sky, above the massed and matted cedars, lightless, desolate, and profound. The road was an eroded scar too deep to be a road and too straight to be a ditch, gutted by winter freshets and choked with fern and rotten leaves and branches. Following Tommy, Benbow walked in a faint path where feet had worn the rotting vegetation down to the clay. Overhead an arching hedgerow of trees thinned against the sky.

The descent increased, curving. 'It was about here that we saw the owl,' Benbow said.

Ahead of him Tommy guffawed. 'It skeered him too, I'll be bound,' he said.

'Yes,' Benbow said. He followed Tommy's vague shape, trying to walk carefully, to talk carefully, with that tedious concern of drunkenness.

'I be a dog if he ain't the skeeriest durn *white* man I ever see,' Tommy said. 'Here he was comin' up the path to the porch and that ere dog come out from under the house and went up and sniffed his heels, like ere a dog will, and I be dog if he didn't flinch off like it was a moccasin and him barefoot, and whupped out that little artermatic pistol and shot it dead as a door-nail. I be durn if he didn't.'

'Whose dog was it?' Horace said.

'Hit was mine,' Tommy said. He chortled. 'An old dog that wouldn't hurt a flea if hit could.'

The road descended and flattened; Benbow's feet whispered into sand, walking carefully. Against the pale sand he could now see Tommy, moving at a shuffling shamble like a mule walks in sand, without seeming effort, his bare feet hissing, flicking the sand back in faint spouting gusts from each inward flick of his toes.

The bulky shadow of the felled tree blobbed across the road. Tommy climbed over it and Benbow followed, still carefully, gingerly, hauling himself through a mass of foliage not yet withered, smelling still green. 'Some more of –' Tommy said. He turned. 'Can you make it?'

'I'm all right,' Horace said. He got his balance again. Tommy went on.

'Some more of Popeye's doin's,' Tommy said. ''Twarn't no

use, blocking this road like that. Just fixed it so we'd have to walk a mile to the trucks. I told him folks been coming out here to buy from Lee for four years now, and ain't nobody bothered Lee yet. Besides gettin' that car of hisn outen here again, big as it is. But 'twarn't no stoppin' him. I be dog if he ain't skeered of his own shadow.'

'I'd be scared of it too,' Benbow said. 'If his shadow was mine.'

Tommy guffawed, in undertone. The road was now a black tunnel floored with that impalpable defunctive glare of the sand. 'It was about here that the path turned off to the spring,' Benbow thought, trying to discern where the path notched into the jungle wall. They went on.

'Who drives the truck?' Benbow said. 'Some more Memphis fellows?'

'Sho,' Tommy said. 'Hit's Popeye's truck.'

'Why can't those Memphis folks stay in Memphis and let you all make your liquor in peace?'

'That's where the money is,' Tommy said. 'Ain't no money in these here pidlin little quarts and half-a-gallons. Lee just does that for a-commodation, to pick up a extry dollar or two. It's in making a run and getting shut of it quick, where the money is.'

'Oh,' Benbow said. 'Well, I think I'd rather starve than have that man around me.'

Tommy guffawed. 'Popeye's all right. He's just a little curious.' He walked on, shapeless against the hushed glare of the road, the sandy road. 'I be dog if he ain't a case, now. Ain't he?'

'Yes,' Benbow said. 'He's all of that.'

The truck was waiting where the road, clay again, began to mount towards the gravel highway. Two men sat on the fender, smoking cigarettes; overhead the trees thinned against the stars of more than midnight.

'You took your time,' one of the men said. 'Didn't you? I aimed to be half-way to town by now. I got a woman waiting for me.'

'Sure,' the other man said. 'Waiting on her back.' The first man cursed him.

'We come as fast as we could,' Tommy said. 'Whyn't you fellows hang out a lantern? If me and him had a been the Law, we'd had you, sho.'

'Ah, go climb a tree, you mat-faced bastard,' the first man said. They snapped their cigarettes away and got into the truck. Tommy guffawed, in undertone. Benbow turned and extended his hand.

'Good-bye,' he said. 'And much obliged, Mister –'

'My name's Tawmmy,' the other said. His limp, calloused hand fumbled into Benbow's and pumped it solemnly once and fumbled away. He stood there, a squat, shapeless figure against the faint glare of the road, while Benbow lifted his foot for the step. He stumbled, catching himself.

'Watch yourself, Doc,' a voice from the cab of the truck said. Benbow got in. The second man was laying a shotgun along the back of the seat. The truck got into motion and ground terrifically up the gutted slope and into the gravelled highroad and turned towards Jefferson and Memphis.

Chapter Three

On the next afternoon Benbow was at his sister's home. It was in the country, four miles from Jefferson; the home of her husband's people. She was a widow, with a boy ten years old, living in a big house with her son and the great-aunt of her husband: a woman of ninety, who lived in a wheel-chair, who was known as Miss Jenny. She and Benbow were at the window, watching his sister and a young man walking in the garden. His sister had been a widow for ten years.

'Why hasn't she ever married again?' Benbow said.

'I ask you,' Miss Jenny said. 'A young woman needs a man.'

'But not that one,' Benbow said. He looked at the two people. The man wore flannels and a blue coat; a broad, plumpish young man with a swaggering air, vaguely collegiate. 'She seems to like children. Maybe because she has one of her own now. Which one is that? Is that the same one she had last fall?'

'Gowan Stevens,' Miss Jenny said. 'You ought to remember Gowan.'

'Yes,' Benbow said. 'I do now. I remember last October.' At that time he had passed through Jefferson on his way home, and he had stopped overnight at his sister's. Through the same window he and Miss Jenny had watched the same two people walking in the same garden, where at that time the late, bright, dusty-odoured flowers of October bloomed. At that time Stevens wore brown, and at that time he was new to Horace.

'He's only been coming out since he got home from Virginia last spring,' Miss Jenny said. 'The one then was that Jones boy; Herschell. Yes. Herschell.'

'Ah,' Benbow said. 'An F.F.V.', or just an unfortunate sojourner there?'

'At the school, the University. He went there. You don't remember him because he was still in diapers when you left Jefferson.'

'Don't let Belle hear you say that,' Benbow said. He watched the two people. They approached the house and disappeared beyond it. A moment later they came up the stairs and into the room. Stevens came in, with his sleek head, his plump, assured face. Miss Jenny gave him her hand and he bent fatly and kissed it.

'Getting younger and prettier every day,' he said. 'I was just telling Narcissa that if you'd just get up out of that chair and be my girl, she wouldn't have a chance.'

'I'm going to tomorrow,' Miss Jenny said. 'Narcissa –'

Narcissa was a big woman, with dark hair, a broad, stupid, serene face. She was in her customary white dress. 'Horace, this is Gowan Stevens,' she said. 'My brother, Gowan.'

'How do you do, sir,' Stevens said. He gave Benbow's hand a quick, hard, high, close grip. At that moment the boy, Benbow Sartoris, Benbow's nephew, came in. 'I've heard of you,' Stevens said.

'Gowan went to Virginia,' the boy said.

'Ah,' Benbow said. 'I've heard of it.'

'Thanks,' Stevens said. 'But everybody can't go to Harvard.'

'Thank you,' Benbow said. 'It was Oxford.'

'Horace is always telling folks he went to Oxford so they'll think he means the State university, and he can tell them different,' Miss Jenny said.

'Gowan goes to Oxford a lot,' the boy said. 'He's got a jelly there. He takes her to the dances. Don't you, Gowan?'

'Right, bud,' Stevens said. 'A red-headed one.'

'Hush, Bory,' Narcissa said. She looked at her brother. 'How are Belle and Little Belle?' She almost said something else, then she ceased. Yet she looked at her brother, her gaze grave and intent.

'If you keep on expecting him to run off from Belle, he will do it,' Miss Jenny said. 'He'll do it some day. But Narcissa wouldn't be satisfied, even then,' she said. 'Some women won't want a man to marry a certain woman. But all the women will be mad if he ups and leaves her.'

'You hush now,' Narcissa said.

'Yes, sir,' Miss Jenny said. 'Horace has been bucking at the halter for some time now. But you better not run against it too hard, Horace; it might not be fastened at the other end.'

Across the hall a small bell rang. Stevens and Benbow both moved towards the handle of Miss Jenny's chair. 'Will you forbear, sir?' Benbow said. 'Since I seem to be the guest.'

'Why, Horace,' Miss Jenny said. 'Narcissa, will you send up to the chest in the attic and get the duelling pistols?' She turned to the boy. 'And you go on ahead and tell them to strike up the music, and to have two roses ready.'

'Strike up what music?' the boy said.

'There are roses on the table,' Narcissa said. 'Gowan sent them. Come on to supper.'

Through the window Benbow and Miss Jenny watched the two people, Narcissa still in white, Stevens in flannels and a blue coat, walking in the garden. 'The Virginia gentleman one, who told us at supper that night about how they had taught him to drink like a gentleman. Put a beetle in alcohol, and you have a scarab; put a Mississippian in alcohol, and you have a gentleman –'

'Gowan Stevens,' Miss Jenny said. They watched the two people disappear beyond the house. It was some time before he heard the two people come down the hall. When they entered, it was the boy instead of Stevens.

'He wouldn't stay,' Narcissa said. 'He's going to Oxford. There is to be a dance at the University Friday night. He has an engagement with a young lady.'

'He should find ample field for gentlemanly drinking there,' Horace said. 'Gentlemanly anything else. I suppose that's why he is going down ahead of time.'

'Taking an old girl to a dance,' the boy said. 'He's going to Starkville Saturday, to the baseball game. He said he'd take me, but you won't let me go.'

Chapter Four

Townspeople taking after-supper drives through the college grounds or an oblivious and bemused faculty-member or a candidate for a master's degree on his way to the library would see Temple, a snatched coat under her arm, and her long legs blonde with running, in speeding silhouette against the lighted windows of the Coop, as the women's dormitory was known, vanishing into the shadow beside the library wall, and perhaps a final squatting swirl of knickers or whatnot as she sprang into the car waiting there with engine running on that particular night. The cars belonged to town boys. Students in the University were not permitted to keep cars, and the men – hatless, in knickers and bright pullovers – looked down upon the town boys who wore hats cupped rigidly upon pomaded heads, and coats a little too tight and trousers a little too full, with superiority and rage.

This was on week nights. On alternate Saturday evenings, at the Letter Club dances, or on the occasion of the three formal yearly balls, the town boys, lounging in attitudes of belligerent casualness, with their identical hats and upturned collars, watched her enter the gymnasium upon black collegiate arms and vanish in a swirling glitter upon a glittering swirl of music, with her high delicate head and her bold painted mouth and soft chin, her eyes blankly right and left looking, cool, predatory and discreet.

Later, the music wailing beyond the glass, they would watch her through the windows as she passed in swift rotation from one pair of black sleeves to the next, her waist shaped slender and urgent in the interval, her feet filling the rhythmic gap with music. Stooping they would drink from flasks and light cigarettes, then erect again, motionless against the light, the upturned collars, the hatted heads, would be like a row of hatted and muffled busts cut from black tin and nailed to the window-sills.

There would always be three or four of them there when the band played 'Home, Sweet Home', lounging near the exit, their

faces cold, bellicose, a little drawn with sleeplessness, watching
the couples emerge in a wan aftermath of motion and noise.
Three of them watched Temple and Gowan Stevens come out,
into the chill presage of spring dawn. Her face was quite pale,
dusted over with recent powder, her hair in spent red curls. Her
eyes, all pupil now, rested upon them for a blank moment. Then
she lifted her hand in a wan gesture, whether at them or not,
none could have said. They did not respond, no flicker in their
cold eyes. They watched Gowan slip his arm into hers, and the
fleet revelation of flank and thigh as she got into his car. It was
a long, low roadster, with a jack-light.

'Who's that son bitch?' one said.

'My father's a judge,' the second said in a bitter, lilting falsetto.

'Hell. Let's go to town.'

They went on. Once they yelled at a car, but it did not stop.
On the bridge across the railroad cutting they stopped and drank
from a bottle. The last made to fling it over the railing. The
second caught his arm.

'Let me have it,' he said. He broke the bottle carefully and
spread the fragments across the road. They watched him.

'You're not good enough to go to a college dance,' the first
said. 'You poor bastard.'

'My father's a judge,' the other said, propping the jagged
shards upright in the road.

'Here comes a car,' the third said.

It had three headlights. They leaned against the railing,
slanting their hats against the light, and watched Temple and
Gowan pass. Temple's head was low and close. The car moved
slowly.

'You poor bastard,' the first said.

'Am I?' the second said. He took something from his pocket
and flipped it out, whipping the sheer, faintly scented web across
their faces. 'Am I?'

'That's what you say.'

'Doc got that step-in in Memphis,' the third said. 'Off a damn
whore.'

'You're a lying bastard,' Doc said.

They watched the fan of light, the diminishing ruby tail-lamp,
come to a stop at the Coop. The lights went off. After a while
the car door slammed. The lights came on; the car moved away.
It approached again. They leaned against the rail in a row, their
hats slanted against the glare. The broken glass glinted in random

sparks. The car drew up and stopped opposite them.

'You gentlemen going to town?' Gowan said, opening the door. They leaned against the rail, then the first said 'Much obliged' gruffly and they got in, the two others in the rumble seat, the first beside Gowan.

'Pull over this way,' he said. 'Somebody broke a bottle there.'

'Thanks,' Gowan said. The car moved on. 'You gentlemen going to Starkville tomorrow to the game?'

The ones in the rumble seat said nothing.

'I don't know,' the first said. 'I don't reckon so.'

'I'm a stranger here,' Gowan said. 'I ran out of liquor tonight, and I've got a date early in the morning. Can you gentlemen tell me where I could get a quart?'

'It's mighty late,' the first said. He turned to the others. 'You know anybody he can find this time of night, Doc?'

'Luke might,' the third said.

'Where does he live?' Gowan said.

'Go on,' the first said. 'I'll show you.' They crossed the square and drove out of town about a half-mile.

'This is the road to Taylor, isn't it?' Gowan said.

'Yes,' the first said.

'I've got to drive down there early in the morning,' Gowan said. 'Got to get there before the special does. You gentlemen not going to the game, you say.'

'I reckon not,' the first said. 'Stop here.' A steep slope rose, crested by stunted blackjacks. 'You wait here,' the first said. Gowan switched off the lights. They could hear the other scrambling the slope.

'Does Luke have good liquor?' Gowan said.

'Pretty good. Good as any, I reckon,' the third said.

'If you don't like it, you don't have to drink it,' Doc said. Gowan turned fatly and looked at him.

'It's as good as that you had tonight,' the third said.

'You didn't have to drink that, neither,' Doc said.

'They can't seem to make good liquor down here like they do up at school,' Gowan said.

'Where you from?' the third said.

'Virgin – oh, Jefferson. I went to school at Virginia. Teach you how to drink, there.'

The other two said nothing. The first returned, preceded by a minute shaling of earth down the slope. He had a fruit jar. Gowan lifted it against the sky. It was pale, innocent-looking. He removed the cap and extended it.

'Drink.'

The first took it and extended it to them in the rumble.

'Drink.'

The third drank, but Doc refused. Gowan drank.

'Good God,' he said, 'how do you fellows drink this stuff?'

'We don't drink rotgut at Virginia,' Doc said. Gowan turned in the seat and looked at him.

'Shut up, Doc,' the third said. 'Don't mind him,' he said. 'He's had a bellyache all night.'

'Son bitch,' Doc said.

'Did you call me that?' Gowan said.

'Course he didn't,' the third said. 'Doc's all right. Come on, Doc. Take a drink.'

'I don't give a damn,' Doc said. 'Hand it here.'

They returned to town. 'The shack'll be open,' the first said. 'At the depot.'

It was a confectionery-lunchroom. It was empty save for a man in a soiled apron. They went to the rear and entered an alcove with a table and four chairs. The man brought four glasses and coca-colas. 'Can I have some sugar and water and a lemon, Cap?' Gowan said. The man brought them. The others watched Gowan make a whisky sour. 'They taught me to drink it this way,' he said. They watched him drink. 'Hasn't got much kick, to me,' he said, filling his glass from the jar. He drank that.

'You sure do drink it,' the third said.

'I learned in a good school.' There was a high window. Beyond it the sky was paler, fresher. 'Have another, gentlemen,' he said, filling his glass again. The others helped themselves moderately. 'Up at school they consider it better to go down than to hedge,' he said. They watched him drink that one. They saw his nostrils bead suddenly with sweat.

'That's all for him, too,' Doc said.

'Who says so?' Gowan said. He poured an inch into the glass. 'If we just had some decent liquor. I know a man in my county named Goodwin that makes –'

'That's what they call a drink up at school,' Doc said.

Gowan looked at him. 'Do you think so? Watch this.' He poured into the glass. They watched the liquor rise.

'Look out, fellow,' the third said. Gowan filled the glass level full and lifted it and emptied it steadily. He remembered setting the glass down carefully, then he became aware simultaneously

of open air, of a chill grey freshness, and an engine panting on
a siding at the head of a dark string of cars, and that he was trying
to tell someone that he had learned to drink like a gentleman. He
was still trying to tell them, in a cramped dark place smelling of
ammonia and creosote, vomiting into a receptacle, trying to tell
them that he must be at Taylor at six-thirty, when the special
arrived. The paroxysm passed; he felt extreme lassitude, weak-
ness, a desire to lie down which was forcibly restrained, and in
the flare of a match he leaned against the wall, his eyes focusing
slowly upon a name written there in pencil. He shut one eye,
propped against the wall, swaying and drooling, and read the
name. Then he looked at them, wagging his head.

'Girl name ... Name girl I know. Good girl. Good sport. Got
date take her to Stark ... Starkville. No chap'rone, see?' Leaning
there, drooling, mumbling, he went to sleep.

At once he began to fight himself out of sleep. It seemed to
him that it was immediately, yet he was aware of time passing all
the while, and that time was a factor in his need to wake; that
otherwise he would be sorry. For a long while he knew that his
eyes were open, waiting for vision to return. Then he was seeing
again, without knowing at once that he was awake.

He lay quite still. It seemed to him that, by breaking out of
sleep, he had accomplished the purpose that he had waked himself
for. He was lying in a cramped position under a low canopy,
looking at the front of an unfamiliar building above which small
clouds rosy with sunlight drove, quite empty of any sense. Then
his abdominal muscles completed the retch upon which he had
lost consciousness and he heaved himself up and sprawled into
the foot of the car, banging his head on the door. The blow
fetched him completely to and he opened the door and half fell
to the ground and dragged himself up and turned towards the
station at a stumbling run. He fell. On hands and knees he looked
at the empty siding and up at the sun-filled sky with unbelief and
despair. He rose and ran on, in his stained dinner-jacket, his
burst collar and broken hair. I passed out, he thought in a kind
of rage, I passed out. *I passed out.*

The platform was deserted save for a negro with a broom.
'Gret Gawd, white folks,' he said.

'The train,' Gowan said, 'the special. The one that was on that
track.'

'Hit done lef. But five minutes ago.' With the broom still in
the arrested gesture of sweeping he watched Gowan turn and

run back to the car and tumble into it.

The jar lay on the floor. He kicked it aside and started the engine. He knew that he needed something on his stomach, but there wasn't time. He looked down at the jar. His inside coiled coldly, but he raised the jar and drank, guzzling, choking the stuff down, clapping a cigarette into his mouth to restrain the paroxysm. Almost at once he felt better.

He crossed the square at forty miles an hour. It was six-fifteen. He took the Taylor road, increasing speed. He drank again from the jar without slowing down. When he reached Taylor the train was just pulling out of the station. He slammed in between two wagons as the last car passed. The vestibule opened; Temple sprang down and ran for a few steps beside the car while an official leaned down and shook his fist at her.

Gowan had got out. She turned and came towards him, walking swiftly. Then she paused, stopped, came on again, staring at his wild face and hair, at his ruined collar and shirt.

'You're drunk,' she said. 'You pig. You filthy pig.'

'Had a big night. You don't know the half of it.'

She looked about, at the bleak yellow station, the overalled men chewing slowly and watching her, down the track at the diminishing train, at the four puffs of vapour that had almost died away when the sound of the whistle came back. 'You filthy pig,' she said. 'You can't go anywhere like this. You haven't even changed clothes.' At the car she stopped again. 'What's that behind you?'

'My canteen,' Gowan said. 'Get in.'

She looked at him, her mouth boldly scarlet, her eyes watchful and cold beneath her brimless hat, a curled spill of red hair. She looked back at the station again, stark and ugly in the fresh morning. She sprang in, tucking her legs under her. 'Let's get away from here.' He started the car and turned it. 'You'd better take me back to Oxford,' she said. She looked back at the station. It now lay in shadow, in the shadow of a high scudding cloud. 'You'd better,' she said.

At two o'clock that afternoon, running at good speed through a high murmurous desolation of pines, Gowan swung the car from the gravel into a narrow road between eroded banks, descending towards a bottom of cypress and gum. He wore a cheap blue workshirt beneath his dinner-jacket. His eyes were bloodshot, puffed, his jowls covered by blue stubble, and looking at him, braced and clinging as the car leaped and bounced in the worn ruts, Temple thought, His whiskers have grown since we left Dumfries. It was hair-oil he drank. He bought a bottle of hair-oil at Dumfries and drank it.

He looked at her, feeling her eyes. 'Don't get your back up, now. It won't take a minute to run up to Goodwin's and get a bottle. It won't take ten minutes. I said I'd get you to Starkville before the train does, and I will. Don't you believe me?'

She said nothing, thinking of the pennant-draped train already in Starkville; of the colourful stands; the band, the yawning glitter of the bass horn; the green diamond dotted with players, crouching, uttering short, yelping cries like marsh-fowl disturbed by an alligator, not certain of where the danger is, motionless, poised, encouraging one another with short meaningless cries, plaintive, wary, and forlorn.

'Trying to come over me with your innocent ways. Don't think I spent last night with a couple of your barber-shop jellies for nothing. Don't think I fed them my liquor just because I'm big-hearted. You're pretty good, aren't you? Think you can play around all week with any badger-trimmed hick that owns a Ford, and fool me on Saturday, don't you? Don't think I didn't see your name where it's written on that lavatory wall. Don't you believe me?'

She said nothing, bracing herself as the car lurched from one bank to the other of the cut, going too fast. He was still watching her, making no effort to steer it.

'By God, I want to see the woman that can –' The road flattened into sand, arched completely over, walled completely by a jungle of cane and brier. The car lurched from side to side in the loose ruts.

She saw the tree blocking the road, but she only braced herself anew. It seemed to her to be the logical and disastrous end to the train of circumstance in which she had become involved. She sat and watched rigidly and quietly as Gowan, apparently looking straight ahead, drove into the tree at twenty miles an hour. The car struck, bounded back, then drove into the tree again and turned on to its side.

She felt herself flying through the air, carrying a numbing shock upon her shoulder and a picture of two men peering from the fringe of cane at the roadside. She scrambled to her feet, her head reverted, and saw them step into the road, the one in a suit of tight black and a straw hat, smoking a cigarette, the other bare-headed, in overalls, carrying a shotgun, his bearded face gaped in slow astonishment. Still running her bones turned to water and she fell flat on her face, still running.

Without stopping she whirled and sat up, her mouth open upon a soundless wail behind her lost breath. The man in overalls was still looking at her, his mouth open in innocent astonishment within a short soft beard. The other man was leaning over the upturned car, his tight coat ridged across his shoulders. Then the engine ceased, though the lifted front wheel continued to spin idly, slowing.

Chapter Five

The man in overalls was barefoot also. He walked ahead of Temple and Gowan, the shotgun swinging in his hand, his splay-feet apparently effortless in the sand into which Temple sank almost to the ankle at each step. From time to time he looked over his shoulder at them, at Gowan's bloody face and splotched clothes, at Temple struggling and lurching on her high heels.

'Putty hard walkin, ain't it?' he said. 'Ef she'll take off them high heel shoes, she'll git along better.'

'Will I?' Temple said. She stopped and stood on alternate legs, holding to Gowan, and removed her slippers. The man watched her, looking at the slippers.

'Durn ef I could git ere two of my fingers into one of them things,' he said. 'Kin I look at 'em?' She gave him one. He turned it slowly in his hand. 'Durn my hide,' he said. He looked at Temple again with his pale, empty gaze. His hair grew innocent and straw-like, bleached on the crown, darkening about his ears and neck in untidy curls. 'She's a right tall gal, too,' he said. 'With them skinny legs of hern. How much she weigh?' Temple extended her hand. He returned the slipper slowly, looking at her, at her belly and loins. 'He ain't laid no crop by yit, has he?'

'Come on,' Gowan said, 'let's get going. We've got to get a car and get back to Jefferson by night.'

When the sand ceased Temple sat down and put her slippers

on. She found the man watching her lifted thigh and she jerked her skirt down and sprang up. 'Well,' she said, 'go on. Don't you know the way?'

The house came into sight, above the cedar grove beyond whose black interstices an apple orchard flaunted in the sunny afternoon. It was set in a ruined lawn, surrounded by abandoned grounds and fallen outbuildings. But nowhere was any sign of husbandry – plough or tool; in no direction was a planted field in sight – only a gaunt weather-stained ruin in a sombre grove through which the breeze drew with a sad, murmurous sound. Temple stopped.

'I don't want to go there,' she said. 'You go on and get the car,' she told the man. 'We'll wait here.'

'He said fer y'all to come on to the house,' the man said.

'Who did?' Temple said. 'Does that black man think he can tell me what to do?'

'Ah, come on,' Gowan said. 'Let's see Goodwin and get a car. It's getting late. Mrs Goodwin's here, isn't she?'

'Hit's likely,' the man said.

'Come on,' Gowan said. They went on to the house. The man mounted to the porch and set the shotgun just inside the door.

'She's around somewhere,' he said. He looked at Temple again. 'Hit ain't no cause fer yo wife to fret,' he said. 'Lee'll git you to town, I reckon.'

Temple looked at him. They looked at one another soberly, like two children or two dogs. 'What's your name?'

'My name's Tawmmy,' he said. 'Hit ain't no need to fret.'

The hall was open through the house. She entered.

'Where you going?' Gowan said. 'Why don't you wait out here?' She didn't answer. She went on down the hall. Behind her she could hear Gowan's and the man's voices. The back porch lay in sunlight, a segment of sunlight framed by the door. Beyond, she could see a weed-choked slope and a huge barn, broken-backed, tranquil in sunny desolation. To the right of the door she could see the corner either of a detached building or of a wing of the house. But she could hear no sound save the voices from the front.

She went on, slowly. Then she stopped. On the square of sunlight framed by the door lay the shadow of a man's head, and she half spun, poised with running. But the shadow wore no hat, so she turned and on tiptoe she went to the door and peered around it. A man sat in a splint-bottom chair, in the sunlight, the back of his bald, white-fringed head towards her, his hands crossed on the head of a rough stick. She emerged on to the back porch.

'Good afternoon,' she said. The man did not move. She advanced again, then she glanced quickly over her shoulder. With the tail of her eye she thought she had seen a thread of smoke drift out of the door in the detached room where the porch made an L, but it was gone. From a line between two posts in front of this door three square cloths hung damp and limp, as though recently washed, and a woman's under-garment of faded pink silk. It had been washed until the lace resembled a ragged, fibre-like fraying of the cloth itself. It bore a patch of pale calico, neatly sewn. Temple looked at the old man again.

For an instant she thought that his eyes were closed, then she believed that he had no eyes at all, for between the lids two objects like dirty yellowish clay marbles were fixed. 'Gowan,' she whispered, then she wailed 'Gowan' and turned running, her head reverted, just as a voice spoke beyond the door where she had thought to have seen smoke:

'He can't hear you. What do you want?'

She whirled again and without a break in her stride and still watching the old man, she ran right off the porch and fetched up on hands and knees in a litter of ashes and tin cans and bleached bones, and saw Popeye watching her from the corner of the house, his hands in his pockets and a slanted cigarette curling across his face. Still without stopping she scrambled on to the porch and sprang into the kitchen, where a woman sat at a table, a burning cigarette in her hand, watching the door.

Chapter Six

Popeye went on around the house. Gowan was leaning over the edge of the porch, dabbing gingerly at his bloody nose. The barefooted man squatted on his heels against the wall.

'For Christ's sake,' Popeye said, 'why can't you take him out back and wash him off? Do you want him sitting around here all day looking like a damn hog with its throat cut?' He snapped the cigarette into the weeds and sat on the top step and began to scrape his muddy shoes with a platinum penknife on the end of his watch-chain.

The barefoot man rose.

'You said something about –' Gowan said.

'Pssst!' the other said. He began to wink and frown at Gowan, jerking his head at Popeye's back.

'And then you get on back down that road,' Popeye said. 'You hear?'

'I thought you was fixin' to watch down ther,' the man said.

'Don't think,' Popeye said, scraping at his trouser-cuffs. 'You've got along forty years without it. You do what I told you.'

When they reached the back porch the barefoot man said: 'He jest cain't stand fer nobody – Ain't he a cur'us feller, now? I be dawg ef he ain't better'n a circus to – He won't stand fer nobody drinkin hyer cep Lee. Won't drink none hisself, and jest let me take one sup and I be dawg ef hit don't look like he'll have a catfit.'

'He said you were forty years old,' Gowan said.

''Tain't that much,' the other said.

'How old are you? Thirty?'

'I don't know. 'Tain't as much as he said, though.' The old man sat in the chair, in the sun. 'Hit's jest Pap,' the man said. The azure shadow of the cedars had reached the old man's feet. It was almost up to his knees. His hand came out and fumbled about his knees dabbling into the shadow, and became still, wrist-deep in shadow. Then he rose and grasped the chair and, tapping ahead with the stick, he bore directly down upon them in a shuffling rush, so that they had to step quickly aside. He dragged the chair into the full sunlight and sat down again, his face lifted into the sun, his hands crossed on the head of the stick. 'That's Pap,' the man said. 'Blind and deef both. I be dawg ef I wouldn't hate to be in a fix wher I couldn't tell and wouldn't even keer whut I was eatin'.'

On a plank fixed between two posts sat a galvanized pail, a tin basin, a cracked dish containing a lump of yellow soap. 'To hell with water,' Gowan said. 'How about that drink?'

'Seems to me like you done already had too much. I be dawg ef you didn't drive that ere car straight into that tree.'

'Come on. Haven't you got some hid out somewhere?'

'Mought be a little in the barn. But don't let him hyear us, er he'll find hit and po hit out.' He went back to the door and peered up the hall. Then they left the porch and went towards the barn, crossing what had once been a kitchen garden choked now with cedar and blackjack saplings. Twice the man looked back over his shoulder. The second time he said:

'Yon's yo wife wantin' somethin'.'

Temple stood in the kitchen door. 'Gowan,' she called.

'Wave yo hand er somethin',' the man said. 'Ef she don't hush, he's goin to hyear us.' Gowan flapped his hand. They went on and entered the barn. Beside the entrance a crude ladder mounted. 'Better wait twell I git up,' the man said. 'Hit's putty rotten; mought not hold us both.'

'Why don't you fix it, then? Don't you use it every day?'

'Hit's helt all right, so fur,' the other said. He mounted. Then Gowan followed, through the trap, into yellow-barred gloom where the level sun fell through the broken walls and roof. 'Walk wher I do,' the man said. 'You'll tromp on a loose boa'd and find yoself downstairs befo you know hit.' He picked his way across the floor and dug an earthenware jug from a pile of rotting hay in the corner. 'One place he won't look fer hit,' he said. 'Skeered of sp'ilin them gal's hands of hisn.'

They drank. 'I've seen you out hyer befo,' the man said. 'Cain't call yo name, though.'

'My name's Stevens. I've been buying liquor from Lee for three years. When'll he be back? We've got to get on to town.'

'He'll be hyer soon. I've seen you befo. Nother feller fum Jefferson out hyer three-fo nights ago. I can't call his name neither. He sho was a talker, now. Kep on tellin how he up and quit his wife. Have some mo,' he said; then he ceased and squatted slowly, the jug in his lifted hands, his head bent with listening. After a moment the voice spoke again, from the hallway beneath.

'Jack.'

The man looked at Gowan. His jaw dropped into an expression of imbecile glee. What teeth he had were stained and ragged within his soft, tawny beard.

'You, Jack, up there,' the voice said.

'Hyear him?' the man whispered, shaking with silent glee. 'Callin me Jack. My name's Tawmmy.'

'Come on,' the voice said. 'I know you're there.'

'I reckon we better,' Tommy said. 'He jest lief take a shot up through the flo as not.'

'For Christ's sake,' Gowan said, 'why didn't you — Here,' he shouted, 'here we come!'

Popeye stood in the door, his forefinger in his vest. The sun had set. When they descended and appeared in the door Temple stepped from the back porch. She paused, watching them, then she came down the hill. She began to run.

'Didn't I tell you to get on down that road?' Popeye said.

'Me an' him jest stepped down hyer a minute,' Tommy said.

'Did I tell you to get on down that road, or didn't I?'

'Yeuh,' Tommy said. 'You told me.' Popeye turned without so much as a glance at Gowan. Tommy followed. His back still shook with secret glee. Temple met Popeye halfway to the house. Without ceasing to run she appeared to pause. Even her flapping coat did not overtake her, yet for an appreciable instant she faced Popeye with a grimace of taut, toothed coquetry. He did not stop; the finicking swagger of his narrow back did not falter. Temple ran again. She passed Tommy and clutched Gowan's arm.

'Gowan, I'm scared. She said for me to — You've been drinking again; you haven't even washed the blood — She says for us to go away from here . . .' Her eyes were quite black, her face small and wan in the dusk. She looked towards the house. Popeye was just turning the corner. 'She has to walk all the way to a spring for water; she — They've got the cutest little baby in a box behind the stove. Gowan, she said for me not to be here after dark. She said to ask him. He's got a car. She said she didn't think he —'

'Ask who?' Gowan said. Tommy was looking back at them. Then he went on.

'That black man. She said she didn't think he would, but he might. Come on.' They went towards the house. A path led around it to the front. The car was parked between the path and the house, in the tall weeds. Temple faced Gowan again, her hand lying upon the door of the car. 'It won't take him any time, in this. I know a boy at home has one. It will run eighty. All he would have to do is just drive us to a town, because she said if we were married and I had to say we were. Just to a railroad. Maybe there's one closer than Jefferson,' she whispered, staring at him, stroking her hand along the edge of the door.

'Oh,' Gowan said, 'I'm to do the asking. Is that it? You're all nuts. Do you think that ape will? I'd rather stay here a week than go anywhere with him.'

'She said to. She said for me not to stay here.'

'You're crazy as a loon. Come on here.'

'You won't ask him? You won't do it?'

'No. Wait till Lee comes, I tell you. He'll get us a car.'

They went on in the path. Popeye was leaning against a post, lighting a cigarette. Temple ran on up the broken steps. 'Say,' she said, 'don't you want to drive us to town?'

He turned his head, the cigarette in his mouth, the match cupped between his hands. Temple's mouth was fixed in that cringing grimace. Popeye leaned the cigarette to the match. 'No,' he said.

'Come on,' Temple said. 'Be a sport. It won't take you any time in that Packard. How about it? We'll pay you.'

Popeye inhaled. He snapped the match into the weeds. He said, in his soft, cold voice: 'Make your whore lay off of me, Jack.'

Gowan moved thickly, like a clumsy, good-tempered horse goaded suddenly. 'Look here, now,' he said. Popeye exhaled, the smoke jetting downwards in two thin spurts. ' I don't like that,' Gowan said. 'Do you know who you're talking to?' He continued that thick movement, like he could neither stop it nor complete it. 'I don't like that.' Popeye turned his head and looked at Gowan. Then he quit looking at him and Temple said suddenly:

'What river did you fall in with that suit on? Do you have to shave it off at night?' Then she was moving towards the door with Gowan's hand in the small of her back, her head reverted, her heels clattering. Popeye leaned motionless against the post, his head turned over his shoulder in profile.

'Do you want' – Gowan hissed.

'You mean old thing!' Temple cried. 'You mean old thing!'

Gowan shoved her into the house. 'Do you want him to slam your damn head off?' he said.

'You're scared of him!' Temple said. 'You're scared!'

'Shut your mouth!' Gowan said. He began to shake her. Their feet scraped on the bare floor as though they were performing a clumsy dance, and clinging together they lurched into the wall. 'Look out,' he said, 'you're getting all that stuff stirred up in me again.' She broke free, running. He leaned against the wall and watched her in silhouette run out the back door.

She ran into the kitchen. It was dark save for a crack of light about the fire-door of the stove. She whirled and ran out the door and saw Gowan going down the hill towards the barn. He's going to drink some more, she thought; he's getting drunk again. That makes three times today. Still more dusk had grown in the hall. She stood on tiptoe, listening, thinking I'm hungry. I haven't eaten all day; thinking of the school, the lighted windows, the slow couples strolling towards the sound of the supper bell, and of her father sitting on the porch at home, his feet on the rail, watching a negro mow the lawn. She moved quietly on tiptoe. In the corner beside the door the shotgun leaned and she crowded into the corner beside it and began to cry.

Immediately she stopped and ceased breathing. Something was moving beyond the wall against which she leaned. It crossed the room with minute, blundering sounds, preceded by a dry tapping. It emerged into the hall and she screamed, feeling her lungs emptying long after all the air was expelled, and her diaphragm labouring long after her chest was empty, and watched the old man go down the hall at a wide-legged shuffling trot, the stick in one hand and the other elbow cocked at an acute angle from his middle. Running, she passed him – a dim, spraddled figure standing at the edge of the porch – and ran on into the kitchen and darted into the corner behind the stove. Crouching, she drew the box out and drew it before her. Her hand touched the child's face, then she flung her arms around the box, clutching it, staring across it at the pale door and trying to pray. But she could not think of a single designation for the heavenly father, so she began to say 'My father's a judge; my father's a judge' over and over until Goodwin ran lightly into the room. He struck a match and held it overhead and looked down at her until the flame reached his fingers.

'Hah,' he said. She heard his light, swift feet twice, then his hand touched her cheek and he lifted her from behind the box by the scruff of the neck, like a kitten. 'What are you doing in my house?' he said.

Chapter Seven

From somewhere beyond the lamplit hall she could hear the voices – a word; now and then a laugh: the harsh, derisive laugh of a man easily brought to mirth by youth or by age, cutting across the spluttering of frying meat on the stove where the woman stood. Once she heard two of them come down the hall in their heavy shoes, and a moment later the clatter of the dipper in the galvanized pail and the voice that had laughed, cursing. Holding her coat close she peered around the door with the wide, abashed curiosity of a child, and saw Gowan and a second man in khaki breeches. He's getting drunk again, she thought. He's got drunk four times since we left Taylor.

'Is he your brother?' she said.

'Who?' the woman said. 'My what?' She turned the meat on the hissing skillet.

'I thought maybe your young brother was here.'

'God,' the woman said. She turned the meat with a wire fork. 'I hope not.'

'Where is your brother?' Temple said, peering around the door. 'I've got four brothers. Two are lawyers and one's a newspaper man. The other's still in school. At Yale. My father's a judge. Judge Drake of Jackson.' She thought of her father sitting on the veranda, in a linen suit, a palm-leaf fan in his hand, watching the negro mow the lawn.

The woman opened the oven and looked in. 'Nobody asked you to come out here. I didn't ask you to stay. I told you to go while it was daylight.'

'How could I? I asked him. Gowan wouldn't, so I had to ask him.'

The woman closed the oven and turned and looked at Temple, her back to the light. 'How could you? Do you know how I get my water? I walk after it. A mile. Six times a day. Add that up. Not because I am somewhere I am afraid to stay.' She went to the table and took up a pack of cigarettes and shook one out.

'May I have one?' Temple said. The woman flipped the pack along the table. She removed the chimney from the lamp and lit hers at the wick. Temple took up the pack and stood listening to Gowan and the other man go back into the house. 'There are so many of them,' she said in a wailing tone, watching the cigarette crush slowly in her fingers. 'But maybe, with so many of them . . .' The woman had gone back to the stove. She turned the meat. 'Gowan kept on getting drunk again. He got drunk three times today. He was drunk when I got off the train at Taylor and I am on probation and I told him what would happen and I tried to get him to throw the jar away and when we stopped at that little country store to buy a shirt he got drunk again. And so we hadn't eaten and we stopped at Dumfries and he went into the restaurant but I was too worried to eat and I couldn't find him and then he came up another street and I felt the bottle in his pocket before he knocked my hand away. He kept on saying I had his lighter and then when he lost it and I told him he had, he swore he never owned one in his life.'

The meat hissed and spluttered in the skillet. 'He got drunk three separate times,' Temple said. 'Three separate times in one day. Buddy – that's Hubert, my youngest brother – said that if he ever caught me with a drunk man, he'd beat hell out of me. And now I'm with one that gets drunk three times in one day.' Leaning her hip against the table, her hand crushing the cigarette, she began to laugh. 'Don't you think that's funny?' she said. Then she quit laughing by holding her breath, and she could hear the faint guttering the lamp made, and the meat in the skillet and the hissing of the kettle on the stove, and the voices, the harsh, abrupt, meaningless masculine sounds from the house. 'And you have to cook for all of them every night. All those men eating here, the house full of them at night, in the dark . . .' She dropped the crushed cigarette. 'May I hold the baby? I know how; I'll hold him good.' She ran to the box, stooping, and lifted the sleeping child. It opened its eyes, whimpering. 'Now, now; Temple's got it.' She rocked it, held high and awkward in her thin arms. 'Listen,' she said, looking at the woman's back, 'will you ask him? your husband, I mean. He can get a car and take me somewhere. Will you? Will you ask him?' The child had stopped whimpering. Its lead-coloured eyelids showed a thin line of eyeball. 'I'm not afraid,' Temple said. 'Things like that don't happen. Do they? They're just like other people. You're just like other people. With a little baby. And besides, my father's a ju-judge. The gu-governor comes to our house to e-eat – what a cute little bu-ba-a-by,' she wailed, lifting the child to her face; 'if bad man hurts Temple, us'll tell the governor's soldiers, won't us?'

'Like what people?' the woman said, turning the meat. 'Do you think Lee hasn't anything better to do than chase after every one of you cheap little –' She opened the fire-door and threw her cigarette in and slammed the door. In nuzzling at the child Temple had pushed her hat on to the back of her head at a precarious dissolute angle above her clotted curls. 'Why did you come here?'

'It was Gowan. I begged him. We had already missed the ball game, but I begged him if he'd just get me to Starkville before the special started back, they wouldn't know I wasn't on it, because the ones that saw me get off wouldn't tell. But he wouldn't. He said we'd stop here just a minute and get some more whisky and he was already drunk then. He had gotten drunk again since we left Taylor and I'm on probation and Daddy would just die. But he wouldn't do it. He got drunk again while I was begging him to take me to a town anywhere and let me out.'

'On probation?' the woman said.

'For slipping out at night. Because only town boys can have cars, and when you had a date with a town boy on Friday or Saturday or Sunday, the boys in school wouldn't have a date with you, because they can't have cars. So I had to slip out. And a girl that didn't like me told the Dean, because I had a date with a boy she liked and he never asked her for another date. So I had to.'

'If you didn't slip out, you wouldn't get to go riding,' the woman said. 'Is that it? And now when you slipped out once too often, you're squealing.'

'Gowan's not a town boy. He's from Jefferson. He went to Virginia. He kept on saying how they had taught him to drink like a gentleman, and I begged him just to let me out anywhere and lend me enough money for a ticket because I only had two dollars, but he –'

'Oh, I know your sort,' the woman said. 'Honest women. Too good to have anything to do with common people. You'll slip out at night with the kids, but just let a man come along.' She turned the meat. 'Take all you can get, and give nothing. "I'm a pure girl; I don't do that." You'll slip out with the kids and burn their gasoline and eat their food, but just let a man so much as look at you and you faint away because your father the judge and your four brothers might not like it. But just let you get into a jam, then who do you come crying to? to us, the ones that are not good enough to lace the judge's almighty shoes.' Across the child Temple gazed at the woman's back, her face like a small pale mask beneath the precarious hat.

'My brother said he would kill Frank. He didn't say he would give me a whipping if he caught me with him; he said he would kill the goddam son of a bitch in his yellow buggy and my father cursed my brother and said he could run his family a while longer and he drove me into the house and locked me in and went down to the bridge to wait for Frank. But I wasn't a coward. I climbed down the gutter and headed Frank off and told him. I begged him to go away, but he said we'd both go. When we got back in the buggy I knew it had been the last time. I knew it, and I begged him again to go away, but he said he'd drive me home to get my suitcase and we'd tell father. He wasn't a coward either. My father was sitting on the porch. He said "Get out of that buggy" and I got out and I begged Frank to go on, but he got out too and we came up the path and father reached around inside the door and got the shotgun. I got in front of Frank and father said "Do you want it too?" and I tried to stay in front but Frank shoved me behind him and held me and father shot him and said "Get down there and sup your dirt, you whore."'

'I have been called that,' Temple whispered, holding the sleeping child in her high thin arms, gazing at the woman's back.

'But you good women. Cheap sports. Giving nothing, then when you're caught . . . Do you know what you've got into now?' She looked across her shoulder, the fork in her hand. 'Do you think you're meeting kids now? kids that give a damn whether you like it or not? Let me tell you whose house you've come into without being asked or wanted; who you're expecting to drop everything and carry you back where you had no business ever leaving. When he was a soldier in the Philippines he killed another soldier over one of those nigger women and they sent him to Leavenworth. Then the war came and they let him out to go to it. He got two medals, and when it was over they put him back in Leavenworth until the lawyer got a congressman to get him out. Then I could quit jazzing again –'

'Jazzing?' Temple whispered, holding the child, looking herself no more than an elongated and leggy infant in her scant dress and uptilted hat.

'Yes, putty-face!' the woman said. 'How do you suppose I paid that lawyer? And that's the sort of man you think will care that much' – with the fork in her hand she came and snapped her fingers softly and viciously in Temple's face 'what happens to you. And you, you little doll-faced slut, that think you can't come into a room where a man is without him . . .' Beneath the faded garment her breast moved deep and full. With her hands on her hips she looked at Temple with cold, blazing eyes. 'Man? You've never seen a real man. You don't know what it is to be wanted by a real man. And thank your stars you haven't and never will, for then you'd find just what that little putty face is worth, and all the rest of it you think you are jealous of when you're just scared of. And if he is just man enough to call you whore, you'll say Yes Yes and you'll crawl naked in the dirt and the mire for him to call you that . . . Give me that baby.' Temple held the child, gazing at the woman, her mouth moving as if she were saying Yes Yes Yes. The woman threw the fork on to the table. 'Turn loose,' she said, lifting the child. It opened its eyes and wailed. The woman drew a chair out and sat down, the child upon her lap. 'Will you hand me one of those diapers on the line yonder?' she said. Temple stood in the door, her lips still moving. 'You're scared to go out there, aren't you?' the woman said. She rose.

'No,' Temple said. 'I'll get –'

'I'll get it.' The unlaced brogans scuffed across the kitchen. She returned and drew another chair up to the stove and spread the two remaining cloths and the undergarment on it, and sat again and laid the child across her lap. It wailed. 'Hush,' she said, 'hush, now,' her face in the lamp-light taking a serene, brooding quality. She changed the child and laid it in the box. Then she took a platter down from a cupboard curtained by a split towsack and took up the fork and came and looked into Temple's face again.

'Listen. If I get a car for you, will you get out of here?' she said. Staring at her Temple moved her mouth as though she were experimenting with words, tasting them. 'Will you go out the back and get into it and go away and never come back here?'

'Yes,' Temple whispered, 'anywhere. Anything.'

Without seeming to move her cold eyes at all the woman looked Temple up and down. Temple could feel all her muscles shrinking like severed vines in the noon sun. 'You poor little gutless fool,' the woman said in her cold undertone. 'Playing at it.'

'I didn't. I didn't.'

'You'll have something to tell them now, when you get back. Won't you?' Face to face, their voices were like shadows upon two close blank walls. 'Playing at it.'

'Anything. Just so I get away. Anywhere.'

'It's not Lee I'm afraid of. Do you think he plays the dog after every hot little bitch that comes along? It's you.'

'Yes. I'll go anywhere.'

'I know your sort. I've seen them. All running, but not too fast. Not so fast you can't tell a real man when you see him. Do you think you've got the only one in the world?'

'Gowan,' Temple whispered, 'Gowan.'

'I have slaved for that man,' the woman whispered, her lips scarce moving, in her still, dispassionate voice. It was as though she was reciting a formula for bread. 'I worked night shift as a waitress so I could see him Sundays at the prison. I lived two years in a single room, cooking over a gas-jet, because I promised him. I lied to him and made money to get him out of prison, and when I told him how I made it, he beat me. And now you must come here where you're not wanted. Nobody asked you to come here. Nobody cares whether you are afraid or not. Afraid? You haven't the guts to be really afraid, any more than you have to be in love.'

'I'll pay you,' Temple whispered. 'Anything you say. My father will give it to me.' The woman watched her, her face motionless, as rigid as when she had been speaking. 'I'll send you clothes. I have a new fur coat. I just wore it since Christmas. It's as good as new.'

The woman laughed. Her mouth laughed, with no sound, no movement of her face. 'Clothes? I had three fur coats once. I gave one of them to a woman in an alley by a saloon. Clothes? God.' She turned suddenly. 'I'll get a car. You get away from here and don't you ever come back. Do you hear?'

'Yes,' Temple whispered. Motionless, pale, like a sleepwalker she watched the woman transfer the meat to the platter and pour the gravy over it. From the oven she took a pan of biscuits and put them on a plate. 'Can I help you?' Temple whispered. The woman said nothing. She took up the two plates and went out.

Temple went to the table and took a cigarette from the pack and stood staring stupidly at the lamp. One side of the chimney was blackened. Across it a crack ran in a thin silver curve. The lamp was of tin, coated about the neck with dirty grease. She lit hers at the lamp, someway, Temple thought, holding the cigarette in her hand, staring at the uneven flame. The woman returned. She caught up the corner of her skirt and lifted the smutty coffee-pot from the stove.

'Can I take that?' Temple said.

'No. Come on and get your supper.' She went out.

Temple stood at the table, the cigarette in her hand. The shadow of the stove fell upon the box where the child lay. Upon the lumpy wad of bedding it could be distinguished only by a series of pale shadows in soft small curves, and she went and stood over the box and looked down at its putty-coloured face and bluish eyelids. A thin whisper of shadow cupped its head and lay moist upon its brow; one thin arm, up-flung, lay curl-palmed beside its cheek. Temple stooped above the box.

'He's going to die,' Temple whispered. Bending, her shadow loomed high upon the wall, her coat shapeless, her hat tilted monstrously above a monstrous escaping of hair. 'Poor little baby,' she whispered, 'poor little baby.' The men's voices grew louder. She heard a trampling of feet in the hall, a rasping of chairs, the voice of the man who had laughed above them, laughing again. She turned, motionless again, watching the door. The woman entered.

'Go and eat your supper,' she said.

'The car,' Temple said. 'I could go now, while they're eating.'

'What car?' the woman said. 'Go on and eat. Nobody's going to hurt you.'

'I'm not hungry. I haven't eaten today. I'm not hungry at all.'

'Go and eat your supper,' she said.

'I'll wait and eat when you do.'

'Go and eat your supper. I've got to get done here some time tonight.'

Chapter Eight

Temple entered the dining-room from the kitchen, her face fixed in a cringing, placative expression; she was quite blind when she entered, holding her coat about her, her hat thrust upward and back at that dissolute angle. After a moment she saw Tommy. She went straight towards him, as if she had been looking for him all the while. Something intervened: a hard forearm; she attempted to evade it, looking at Tommy.

'Here,' Gowan said across the table, his chair rasping back, 'you come around here.'

'Outside, brother,' the one who had stopped her said, whom she recognized then as the one who had laughed so often; 'you're drunk. Come here, kid.' His hard forearm came across her middle. She thrust against it, grinning rigidly at Tommy. 'Move down, Tommy,' the man said. 'Ain't you got no manners, you mat-faced bastard?' Tommy guffawed, scraping his chair along the floor. The man drew her towards him by the wrist. Across the table Gowan stood up, propping himself on the table. She began to resist, grinning at Tommy, picking at the man's fingers.

'Quit that, Van,' Goodwin said.

'Right on my lap here,' Van said.

'Let her go,' Goodwin said.

'Who'll make me?' Van said. 'Who's big enough?'

'Let her go,' Goodwin said. Then she was free. She began to back slowly away. Behind her the woman, entering with a dish, stepped aside. Still smiling her aching, rigid grimace Temple backed from the room. In the hall she whirled and ran. She ran right off the porch, into the weeds, and sped on. She ran to the road and down it for fifty yards in the darkness, then without a break she whirled and ran back to the house and sprang on to the porch and crouched against the door just as someone came up the hall. It was Tommy.

'Oh, hyer you are,' he said. He thrust something awkwardly at her. 'Hyer,' he said.

'What is it?' she whispered.

'Little bite of victuals. I bet you ain't et since mawnin.'

'No. Not then, even,' she whispered.

'You eat a little mite and you'll feel better,' he said, poking the plate at her. 'You set down hyer and eat a little bite wher won't nobody bother you. Durn them fellers.'

Temple leaned around the door, past his dim shape, her face wan as a small ghost in the refracted light from the dining-room. 'Mrs – Mrs . . .' she whispered.

'She's in the kitchen. Want me to go back there with you?' In the dining-room a chair scraped. Between blinks Tommy saw Temple in the path, her body slender and motionless for a moment as though waiting for some laggard part to catch up. Then she was gone like a shadow around the corner of the house. He stood in the door, the plate of food in his hand. Then he turned his head and looked down the hall just in time to see her flit across the darkness towards the kitchen. 'Durn them fellers.'

He was standing there when the others returned to the porch.

'He's got a plate of grub,' Van said. 'He's trying to get his with a plate full of ham.'

'Git my whut?' Tommy said.

'Look here,' Gowan said.

Van struck the plate from Tommy's hand. He turned to Gowan. 'Don't you like it?'

'No,' Gowan said, 'I don't.'

'What are you going to do about it?' Van said.

'Van,' Goodwin said.

'Do you think you're big enough to not like it?' Van said.

'I am,' Goodwin said.

When Van went back to the kitchen Tommy followed him. He stopped at the door and heard Van in the kitchen.

'Come for a walk, little bit,' Van said.

'Get out of here, Van,' the woman said.

'Come for a little walk,' Van said. 'I'm a good guy. Ruby'll tell you.'

'Get out of here, now,' the woman said. 'Do you want me to call Lee?' Van stood against the light, in a khaki shirt and breeches, a cigarette behind his ear against the smooth sweep of his blond hair. Beyond him Temple stood behind the chair in which the woman sat at the table, her mouth open a little, her eyes quite black.

When Tommy went back to the porch with the jug he said to Goodwin: 'Why don't them fellers quit pesterin' that gal?'

'Who's pestering her?'

'Van is. She's skeered. Whyn't they leave her be?'

'It's none of your business. You keep out of it. You hear?'

'Them fellers ought to quit pesterin' her,' Tommy said. He squatted against the wall. They were drinking, passing the jug back and forth, talking. With the top of his mind he listened to them, to Van's gross and stupid tales of city life with rapt interest, guffawing now and then, drinking in his turn. Van and Gowan were doing the talking, and Tommy listened to them. 'Them two's fixin' to have hit out with one another,' he whispered to Goodwin in a chair beside him. 'Hyear 'em?' They were talking quite loud; Goodwin moved swiftly and lightly from his chair, his feet striking the floor with light thuds: Tommy saw Van standing and Gowan holding himself erect by the back of his chair.

'I never meant –' Van said.

'Don't say it, then,' Goodwin said.

Gowan said something. That durn feller, Tommy thought. Can't even talk no more.

'Shut up, you,' Goodwin said.

'Think talk 'bout my –' Gowan said. He moved, swayed against the chair. It fell over. Gowan blundered into the wall.

'By God, I'll –' Van said.

'– ginia gentleman; I don't give a –' Gowan said. Goodwin flung him aside with a backhanded blow of his arm, and grasped Van. Gowan fell against the wall.

'When I say sit down, I mean it,' Goodwin said.

After that they were quiet for a while. Goodwin returned to his chair. They began to talk again, passing the jug, and Tommy listened. But soon he began to think about Temple again. He would feel his feet scouring on the floor and his whole body writhing in acute discomfort. 'They ought to let that gal alone,' he whispered to Goodwin. 'They ought to quit pesterin' her.'

'It's none of your business,' Goodwin said. 'Let every damned one of them . . .'

'They ought to quit pesterin' her.'

Popeye came out the door. He lit a cigarette. Tommy watched his face flare out between his hands, his cheeks sucking; he followed with his eyes the small comet of the match into the weeds. Him too, he said. Two of 'em; his body writhing slowly. Pore little crittur. I be dawg ef I ain't a mind to go down to the barn and stay there, I be dawg ef I ain't. He rose, his feet making no sound on the porch. He stepped down into the path and went around the house. There was a light in the window there. Don't nobody never use in there, he said, stopping. Then he said, That's where she'll be stayin', and he went to the window and looked in. The sash was down. Across a missing pane a sheet of rusted tin was nailed.

Temple was sitting on the bed, her legs tucked under her, erect, her hands lying in her lap, her hat tilted on the back of her head. She looked quite small, her very attitude an outrage to muscle and tissue of more than seventeen and more compatible with eight or ten, her elbows close to her sides, her face turned towards the door against which a chair was wedged. There was nothing in the room save the bed, with its faded patchwork quilt, and the chair. The walls had been plastered once, but the plaster had cracked and fallen in places, exposing the lathing and moulded shreds of cloth. On the wall hung a raincoat and a khaki-covered canteen.

Temple's head began to move. It turned slowly, as if she were following the passage of someone beyond the walls. It turned on to an excruciating degree, though no other muscle moved, like one of those papier-mâché Easter toys filled with candy, and became motionless in that reverted position. Then it turned back, slowly, as though pacing invisible feet beyond the wall, back to the chair against the door and became motionless there for a moment. Then she faced forward and Tommy watched her take a tiny watch from the top of her stocking and look at it. With the watch in her hand she lifted her head and looked directly at him, her eyes calm and empty as two holes. After a while she looked down at the watch again and returned it to her stocking.

She rose from the bed and removed her coat and stood motionless, arrowlike in her scant dress, her head bent, her hands clasped before her. She sat on the bed again. She sat with her legs close together, her head bent. She raised her head and looked about the room. Tommy could hear the voices from the dark porch. They rose again, then sank to the steady murmur.

Temple sprang to her feet. She unfastened her dress, her arms arched thin and high, her shadow anticking her movements. In a single motion she was out of it, crouching a little, match-thin in her scant undergarments. Her head emerged facing the chair against the door. She hurled the dress away, her hand reaching for the coat. She scrabbled it up and swept it about her, pawing at the sleeves. Then, the coat clutched to her breast, she whirled and looked straight into Tommy's eyes and whirled and ran and flung herself upon the chair. 'Durn them fellers,' Tommy whispered, 'durn them fellers.' He could hear them on the front porch and his body began again to writhe slowly in an acute unhappiness. 'Durn them fellers.'

When he looked into the room again Temple was moving towards him, holding the coat about her. She took the raincoat from the nail and put it on over her own coat and fastened it. She lifted the canteen down and returned to the bed. She laid the canteen on the bed and picked her dress up from the floor and brushed it with her hand and folded it carefully and laid it on the bed. Then she turned back the quilt, exposing the mattress. There was no linen, no pillow, and when she touched the mattress it gave forth a faint dry whisper of shucks.

She removed her slippers and set them on the bed and got in beneath the quilt. Tommy could hear the mattress crackle. She didn't lie down at once. She sat upright, quite still, the hat tilted rakishly upon the back of her head. Then she moved the canteen, the dress and the slippers beside her head and drew the raincoat about her legs and lay down, drawing the quilt up, then she sat up and removed the hat and shook her hair out and laid the hat with the other garments and prepared to lie down again. Again she paused. She opened the raincoat and produced a compact from somewhere and, watching her emotions in the tiny mirror, she spread and fluffed her hair with her fingers and powdered her face and replaced the compact and looked at the watch again and fastened the raincoat. She moved the garments one by one under the quilt and lay down and drew the quilt to her chin. The voices had got quiet for a moment and in the silence Tommy could hear a faint, steady chatter of the shucks inside the mattress where Temple lay, her hands crossed on her breast and her legs straight and close and decorous, like an effigy on an ancient tomb.

The voices were still; he had completely forgotten them until he heard Goodwin say 'Stop it. Stop that!' A chair crashed over; he heard Goodwin's light thudding feet; the chair clattered along the porch as though it had been kicked aside, and crouching, his elbows out a little in squat, bear-like alertness, Tommy heard dry, light sounds like billiard balls. 'Tommy,' Goodwin said.

When necessary he could move with that quick, lightning-like celerity of badgers or coons. He was around the house and on the porch in time to see Gowan slam into the wall and slump along it and plunge full length off the porch into the weeds, and Popeye in the door, his head thrust forward. 'Grab him there!' Goodwin said. Tommy sprang upon Popeye in a sidling rush.

'I got – hah!' he said, as Popeye slashed savagely at his face; 'you would, would you? Hole up hyer.'

Popeye ceased. 'Jesus Christ. You let them sit around here all night, swilling that goddam stuff; I told you. Jesus Christ.'

Goodwin and Van were a single shadow, locked and hushed and furious. 'Let go!' Van shouted. 'I'll kill . . .' Tommy sprang to them. They jammed Van against the wall and held him motionless.

'Got him?' Goodwin said.

'Yeuh. I got him. Hole up hyer. You done whupped him.'

'By God, I'll –'

'Now, now; whut you want to kill him fer? You cain't eat him, kin you? You want Mr Popeye to start guttin' us all with that ere artermatic?'

Then it was over, gone like a furious gust of black wind, leaving a peaceful vacuum in which they moved quietly about, lifting Gowan out of the weeds with low-spoken, amicable directions to one another. They carried him into the hall, where the woman stood, and to the door of the room where Temple was.

'She's locked it,' Van said. He struck the door, high. 'Open the door,' he shouted. 'We're bringing you a customer.'

'Hush,' Goodwin said. 'There's no lock on it. Push it.'

'Sure,' Van said, 'I'll push it.' He kicked it. The chair buckled and sprang into the room. Van banged the door open and they entered, carrying Gowan's legs. Van kicked the chair across the room. Then he saw Temple standing in the corner behind the bed. His hair was broken about his face, long as a girl's. He flung it back with a toss of his head. His chin was bloody and he deliberately spat blood on to the floor.

'Go on,' Goodwin said, carrying Gowan's shoulders, 'put him on the bed.' They swung Gowan on to the bed. His bloody head lolled over the edge. Van jerked him over and slammed him into the mattress. He groaned, lifting his hand. Van struck him across the face with his palm.

'Lie still, you –'

'Let be,' Goodwin said. He caught Van's hand. For an instant they glared at one another.

'I said, Let be,' Goodwin said. 'Get out of here.'

'Got proteck . . .' Gowan muttered '. . . girl. 'Ginia gem . . . gemman got proteck . . .'

'Get out of here, now,' Goodwin said.

The woman stood in the door beside Tommy, her back against the door frame. Beneath a cheap coat her nightdress dropped to her feet.

Van lifted Temple's dress from the bed. 'Van,' Goodwin said. 'I said get out.'

'I heard you,' Van said. He shook the dress out. Then he looked at Temple in the corner, her arms crossed, her hands clutching her shoulders. Goodwin moved towards Van. He dropped the dress and went around the bed. Popeye came in the door, a cigarette in his fingers. Beside the woman Tommy drew his breath hissing through his ragged teeth.

He saw Van take hold of the raincoat upon Temple's breast and rip it open. Then Goodwin sprang between them; he saw Van duck, whirling, and Temple fumbling at the torn raincoat. Van and Goodwin were now in the middle of the floor, swinging at one another, then he was watching Popeye walking towards Temple. With the corner of his eye he saw Van lying on the floor and Goodwin standing over him, stooped a little, watching Popeye's back.

'Popeye,' Goodwin said. Popeye went on, the cigarette trailing back over his shoulder, his head turned a little as though he were not looking where he was going, the cigarette slanted as though his mouth were somewhere under the turn of his jaw. 'Don't touch her,' Goodwin said.

Popeye stopped before Temple, his face turned a little aside. His right hand lay in his coat pocket. Beneath the raincoat on Temple's breast Tommy could see the movement of the other hand, communicating a shadow of movement to the coat.

'Take your hand away,' Goodwin said. 'Move it.'

Popeye moved his hand. He turned, his hands in his coat pockets, looking at Goodwin. He crossed the room, watching Goodwin. Then he turned his back on him and went out the door.

'Here, Tommy,' Goodwin said quietly, 'grab hold of this.' They lifted Van and carried him out. The woman stepped aside. She leaned against the wall, holding her coat together. Across the room Temple stood crouched into the corner, fumbling at the torn raincoat. Gowan began to snore.

Goodwin returned. 'You'd better go back to bed,' he said. The woman didn't move. He put his hand on her shoulder. 'Ruby.'

'While you finish the trick Van started and you wouldn't let him finish? You poor fool. You poor fool.'

'Come on, now,' he said, his hand on her shoulder. 'Go back to bed.'

'But don't come back. Don't bother to come back. I won't be there. You owe me nothing. Don't think you do.'

Goodwin took her wrists and drew them steadily apart. Slowly and steadily he carried her hands around behind her and held them in one of his. With the other hand he opened the coat. The nightdress was of faded pink crêpe, lace-trimmed, laundered and laundered until, like the garment on the wire, the lace was a fibrous mass.

'Hah,' he said. 'Dressed for company.'

'Whose fault is it if this is the only one I have? Whose fault is it? Not mine. I've given them away to nigger maids after one night. But do you think any nigger would take this and not laugh in my face?'

He let the coat fall to. He released her hands and she drew the coat together. With his hand on her shoulder he began to push her towards the door. 'Go on,' he said. Her shoulder gave. It alone moved, her body turning on her hips, her face reverted, watching him. 'Go on,' he said. But her torso alone turned, her hips and head still touching the wall. He turned and crossed the room and went swiftly around the bed and caught Temple by the front of the raincoat with one hand. He began to shake her. Holding her up by the gathered wad of coat he shook her, her small body clattering soundlessly inside the loose garment, her shoulders and thighs thumping against the wall. 'You little fool.' he said. 'You little fool!' Her eyes were quite wide, almost black, the lamplight on her face and two tiny reflections of his face in her pupils like peas in two inkwells.

He released her. She began to sink to the floor, the raincoat rustling about her. He caught her up and began to shake her again, looking over his shoulder at the woman. 'Get the lamp,' he said. The woman did not move. Her head was bent a little; she appeared to muse upon them. Goodwin swept his other arm under Temple's knees. She felt herself swooping, then she was lying on the bed beside Gowan, on her back, jouncing to the dying chatter of the shucks. She watched him cross the room and lift the lamp from the mantel. The woman had turned her head, following him also, her face sharpening out of the approaching lamp in profile. 'Go on,' he said. She turned, her face turning into shadow, the lamp now on her back and on his hand on her shoulder. His shadow blotted the room completely; his arm in silhouette back-reaching, drew to the door. Gowan snored, each respiration choking to a huddle fall, as though he would never breathe again.

Tommy was outside the door, in the hall.

'They gone down to the truck yet?' Goodwin said.

'Not yit,' Tommy said.

'Better go and see about it,' Goodwin said. They went on. Tommy watched them enter another door. Then he went to the kitchen, silent on his bare feet, his neck craned a little with listening. In the kitchen Popeye sat, straddling a chair, smoking. Van stood at the table, before a fragment of mirror, combing his hair with a pocket comb. Upon the table lay a damp, blood-stained cloth and a burning cigarette. Tommy squatted outside the door, in the darkness.

He was there when Goodwin came out with the raincoat. Goodwin entered the kitchen without seeing him. 'Where's Tommy?' he said. Tommy heard Popeye say something, then Goodwin emerged with Van following him, the raincoat on his arm now. 'Come on, now,' Goodwin said. 'Let's get that stuff out of here.'

Tommy's pale eyes began to glow faintly, like those of a cat. The woman could see them in the darkness when he crept into the room after Popeye, and while Popeye stood over the bed where Temple lay. They glowed suddenly out of the darkness at her, then they went away and she could hear him breathing beside her; again they glowed up at her with a quality furious and questioning and sad and went away again and he crept behind Popeye from the room.

He saw Popeye return to the kitchen, but he did not follow at once. He stopped at the hall door and squatted there. His body began to writhe again in shocked indecision, his bare feet whispering on the floor with a faint, rocking movement as he swayed from side to side, his hands wringing slowly against his flanks. And Lee too, he said, And Lee too. Durn them fellers. Durn them fellers. Twice he stole along the porch until he could see the shadow of Popeye's hat on the kitchen floor, then returned to the hall and the door beyond which Temple lay and where Gowan snored. The third time he smelled Popeye's cigarette. Ef he'll jest keep that up, he said. And Lee too, he said, rocking from side to side in a dull, excruciating agony, And Lee too.

When Goodwin came up the slope and on to the back porch Tommy was squatting just outside the door again. 'What in hell . . .' Goodwin said. 'Why didn't you come on? I've been looking for you for ten minutes.' He glared at Tommy, then he looked into the kitchen. 'You ready?' he said. Popeye came to the door. Goodwin looked at Tommy again. 'What have you been doing?'

Popeye looked at Tommy. Tommy stood now, rubbing his instep with the other foot, looking at Popeye.

'What're you doing here?' Popeye said.

'Ain't doin' nothin',' Tommy said.

'Are you following me around?'

'I ain't trailin' nobody,' Tommy said sullenly.

'Well, don't, then,' Popeye said.

'Come on,' Goodwin said. 'Van's waiting.' They went on. Tommy followed them. Once he looked back at the house, then he shambled on behind them. From time to time he would feel that acute surge go over him, like his blood was too hot all of a sudden, dying away into that warm unhappy feeling that fiddle music gave him. Durn them fellers, he whispered, Durn them fellers.

Chapter Nine

The room was dark. The woman stood inside the door, against the wall, in the cheap coat, the lace-trimmed crêpe nightgown, just inside the lockless door. She could hear Gowan snoring in the bed, and the other men moving about, on the porch and in the hall and in the kitchen, talking, their voices indistinguishable through the door. After a while they got quiet. Then she could hear nothing at all save Gowan as he choked and snored and moaned through his battered nose and face.

She heard the door open. The man came in, without trying to be silent. He entered, passing within a foot of her. She knew it was Goodwin before he spoke. He went to the bed. 'I want the raincoat,' he said. 'Sit up and take it off.' The woman could hear the shucks in the mattress as Temple sat up and Goodwin took the raincoat off of her. He returned across the floor and went out.

She stood just inside the door. She could tell all of them by the way they breathed. Then, without having heard, felt, the door open, she began to smell something: the brilliantine which Popeye used on his hair. She did not see Popeye at all when he entered and passed her; she did not know he had entered yet; she was waiting for him; until Tommy entered, following Popeye. Tommy crept into the room, also soundless; she would have been no more aware of his entrance than of Popeye's, if it hadn't been for his eyes. They glowed, breast-high, with a profound interrogation, then they disappeared and the woman could then feel him, squatting beside her; she knew that he too was looking towards the bed over which Popeye stood in the darkness, upon which Temple and Gowan lay, with Gowan snoring and choking and snoring. The woman stood just inside the door.

She could hear no sound from the shucks, so she remained motionless beside the door, with Tommy squatting beside her, his face towards the invisible bed. Then she smelled the brilliantine again. Or rather, she felt Tommy move from beside her, without a sound, as though the stealthy evacuation of his position blew soft and cold upon her in the black silence; without seeing or hearing him, she knew that he had crept again from the room, following Popeye. She heard them go down the hall; the last sound died out of the house.

She went to the bed. Temple did not move until the woman touched her. Then she began to struggle. The woman found Temple's mouth and put her hand over it, though Temple had not attempted to scream. She lay on the shuck mattress, turning and thrashing her body from side to side, rolling her head, holding the coat together across her breast but making no sound.

'You fool!' the woman said in a thin, fierce whisper. 'It's me. It's just me.'

Temple ceased to roll her head, but she still thrashed from side to side beneath the woman's hand. 'I'll tell my father!' she said. 'I'll tell my father!'

The woman held her. 'Get up,' she said. Temple ceased to struggle. She lay still, rigid. The woman could hear her wild breathing. 'Will you get up and walk quiet?' the woman said.

'Yes!' Temple said. 'Will you get me out of here? Will you? Will you?'

'Yes,' the woman said. 'Get up.' Temple got up, the shucks whispering. In the further darkness Gowan snored, savage and profound. At first Temple couldn't stand alone. The woman held her up. 'Stop it,' the woman said. 'You've got to stop it. You've got to be quiet.'

'I want my clothes,' Temple whispered. 'I haven't got anything on but . . .'

'Do you want your clothes,' the woman said, 'or do you want to get out of here?'

'Yes,' Temple said. 'Anything. If you'll just get me out of here.'

On their bare feet they moved like ghosts. They left the house and crossed the porch and went on towards the barn. When they were about fifty yards from the house the woman stopped and turned and jerked Temple up to her, and gripping her by the shoulders, their faces close together, she cursed Temple in a whisper, a sound no louder than a sigh and filled with fury. Then she flung her away and they went on. They entered the hallway. It was pitch dark. Temple heard the woman fumbling at the wall. A door creaked open; the woman took her arm and guided her up a single step into a floored room where she could feel walls and smell a faint, dusty odour of grain, and closed the door behind them. As she did so something rushed invisibly near by in a scurrying scrabble, a dying whisper of fairy feet. Temple whirled, treading on something that rolled under her foot, and sprang towards the woman.

'It's just a rat,' the woman said, but Temple hurled herself upon the other, flinging her arms about her, trying to snatch both feet from the floor.

'A rat?' she wailed, 'a rat? Open the door! Quick!'

'Stop it! Stop it!' the woman hissed. She held Temple until she ceased. Then they knelt side by side against the wall. After a while the woman whispered: 'There's some cottonseed-hulls over there. You can lie down.' Temple didn't answer. She crouched against the woman, shaking slowly, and they squatted there in the black darkness, against the wall.

Chapter Ten

While the woman was cooking breakfast, the child still – or already – asleep in the box behind the stove, she heard a blundering sound approaching across the porch and stop at the door. When she looked around she saw the wild and battered and bloody apparition which she recognized as Gowan. His face, beneath a two days' stubble, was marked, his lip was cut. One eye was closed and the front of his shirt and coat were blood-stained to the waist. Through his swollen and stiffened lips he was trying to say something. At first the woman could not understand a word. 'Go and bathe your face,' she said. 'Wait. Come in here and sit down. I'll get the basin.'

He looked at her, trying to talk. 'Oh,' the woman said. 'She's all right. She's down there in the crib, asleep.' She had to repeat it three or four times, patiently. 'In the crib. Asleep. I stayed with her until daylight. Go wash your face, now.'

Gowan got a little calmer then. He began to talk about getting a car.

'The nearest one is at Tull's, two miles away,' the woman said. 'Wash your face and eat some breakfast.'

Gowan entered the kitchen, talking about getting the car. 'I'll get it and take her on back to school. One of the other girls will slip her in. It'll be all right then. Don't you think it'll be all right then?' He came to the table and took a cigarette from the pack and tried to light it with his shaking hands. He had trouble putting it into his mouth, and he could not light it at all until the woman came and held the match. But he took but one draw, then he stood, holding the cigarette in his hand, looking at it with his one good eye in a kind of dull amazement. He threw the cigarette away and turned towards the door, staggering and catching himself. 'Go get car,' he said.

'Get something to eat first,' the woman said. 'Maybe a cup of coffee will help you.'

'Go get car,' Gowan said. When he crossed the porch he paused long enough to splash some water upon his face, without helping his appearance much.

When he left the house he was still groggy and he thought that he was still drunk. He could remember only vaguely what had happened. He had got Van and the wreck confused and he did not know that he had been knocked out twice. He only remembered that he had passed out some time early in the night, and he thought that he was still drunk. But when he reached the wrecked car and saw the path and followed it to the spring and drank of the cold water, he found that it was a drink he wanted, and he knelt there, bathing his face in the cold water and trying to examine his reflection in the broken surface, whispering Jesus Christ to himself in a kind of despair. He thought about returning to the house for a drink, then he thought of having to face Temple, the men; of Temple there among them.

When he reached the highroad the sun was well up, warm. I'll get cleaned up some, he said. And coming back with a car, I'll decide what to say to her on the way to town; thinking of Temple returning among people who knew him, who might know him. I passed out twice, he said. I passed out twice. Jesus Christ, Jesus Christ he whispered, his body writhing inside his disreputable and bloody clothes in an agony of rage and shame.

His head began to clear with air and motion, but as he began to feel better physically the blackness of the future increased. Town, the world, began to appear as a black cul-de-sac; a place in which he must walk forever more, his whole body cringing and flinching from whispering eyes when he had passed, and when in mid morning he reached the house he sought, the prospect of facing Temple again was more than he could bear. So he engaged the car and directed the man and paid him and went on. A little later a car going in the opposite direction stopped and picked him up.

Chapter Eleven

Temple waked lying in a tight ball, with narrow bars of sunlight falling across her face like the tines of a golden fork, and while the stiffened blood trickled and tingled through her cramped muscles she lay gazing quietly up at the ceiling. Like the walls, it was of rough planks crudely laid, each plank separated from the next by a thin line of blackness; in the corner a square opening above a ladder gave into a gloomy loft shot with thin pencils of sun also. From nails in the walls broken bits of desiccated harness hung, and she lay plucking tentatively at the substance in which she lay. She gathered a handful of it and lifted her head, and saw within her fallen coat naked flesh between brassiere and knickers and knickers and stockings. Then she remembered the rat and scrambled up and sprang to the door, clawing at it, still clutching the fist full of cottonseed-hulls, her face puffed with the hard slumber of seventeen.

She had expected the door to be locked and for a time she could not pull it open, her numb hands scoring at the undressed planks until she could hear her finger-nails. It swung back and she sprang out. At once she sprang back into the crib and banged the door to. The blind man was coming down the slope at a scuffling trot, tapping ahead with the stick, the other hand at his waist, clutching a wad of his trousers. He passed the crib with his braces dangling about his hips, his gymnasium shoes scuffing in the dry chaff of the hallway, and passed from view, the stick rattling lightly along the rank of empty stalls.

Temple crouched against the door, clutching her coat about her. She could hear him back there in one of the stalls. She opened the door and peered out, at the house in the bright May sunshine, the sabbath peace, and she thought about the girls and men leaving the dormitories in their new Spring clothes, strolling along the shaded streets towards the cool, unhurried sound of bells. She lifted her foot and examined the soiled sole of her stocking, brushing at it with her palm, then at the other one.

The blind man's stick clattered again. She jerked her head back and closed the door to a crack and watched him pass, slower now, hunching his braces on to his shoulders. He mounted the slope and entered the house. Then she opened the door and stepped gingerly down.

She walked swiftly to the house, her stockinged feet flinching and cringing from the rough earth, watching the house. She mounted to the porch and entered the kitchen and stopped, listening into the silence. The stove was cold. Upon it the blackened coffee-pot sat, and a soiled skillet; upon the table soiled dishes were piled at random. I haven't eaten since ... since ... Yesterday was one day, she thought, but I didn't eat then. I haven't eaten since ... and that night was the dance, and I didn't eat any supper. I haven't eaten since dinner Friday, she thought. And now it's Sunday, thinking about the bells in cool steeples against the blue, and pigeons crooning about the belfries like echoes of the organ's bass. She returned to the door and peered out. Then she emerged, clutching the coat about her.

She entered the house and sped up the hall. The sun lay now on the front porch and she ran with a craning motion of her head, watching the patch of sun framed in the door. It was empty. She reached the door to the right of the entrance and opened it and sprang into the room and shut the door and leaned her back against it. The bed was empty. A faded patchwork quilt was wadded across it. A khaki-covered canteen and one slipper lay on the bed. On the floor her dress and hat lay.

She picked up the dress and hat and tried to brush them with her hand and with the corner of her coat. Then she sought the other slipper, moving the quilt, stooping to look under the bed. At last she found it in the fireplace, in a litter of wood ashes between an iron fire-dog and an overturned stack of bricks, lying on its side, half full of ashes, as though it had been flung or kicked there. She emptied it and wiped it on her coat and laid it on the bed and took the canteen and hung it on a nail in the wall. It bore the letters U S and a blurred number in black stencil. Then she removed the coat and dressed.

Long-legged, thin-armed, with high small buttocks – a small childish figure no longer quite a child, not yet quite a woman – she moved swiftly, smoothing her stockings and writhing into her scant, narrow dress. Now I can stand anything, she thought quietly, with a kind of dull, spent astonishment; I can stand just anything. From the top of one stocking she removed a watch on a broken black ribbon. Nine o'clock. With her fingers she combed her matted curls, combing out three or four cottonseed-hulls. She took up the coat and hat and listened again at the door.

She returned to the back porch. In the basin was a residue of dirty water. She rinsed it and filled it and bathed her face. A soiled towel hung from a nail. She used it gingerly, then she took a compact from her coat and was using it when she found the woman watching her in the kitchen door.

'Good morning,' Temple said. The woman held the child on her hip. It was asleep. 'Hello, baby,' Temple said, stooping; 'you wan s'eep all day? Look at Temple.' They entered the kitchen. The woman poured coffee into a cup.

'It's cold, I expect,' she said. 'Unless you want to make up the fire.' From the oven she took a pan of bread.

'No,' Temple said, sipping the lukewarm coffee, feeling her insides move in small, tickling clots, like loose shot. 'I'm not hungry. I haven't eaten in two days, but I'm not hungry. Isn't that funny? I haven't eaten in . . .' She looked at the woman's back with a fixed placative grimace. 'You haven't got a bathroom, have you?'

'What?' the woman said. She looked at Temple across her shoulder while Temple stared at her with that grimace of cringing and placative assurance. From a shelf the woman took a mail-order catalogue and tore out a few leaves and handed them to Temple. 'You'll have to go to the barn, like we do.'

'Will I?' Temple said, holding the paper. 'The barn.'

'They're all gone,' the woman said. 'They won't be back this morning.'

'Yes,' Temple said. 'The barn.'

'Yes; the barn,' the woman said. 'Unless you're too pure to have to.'

'Yes,' Temple said. She looked out the door, across the weed-choked clearing. Between the sombre spacing of the cedars the orchard lay bright in the sunlight. She donned the coat and hat and went towards the barn, the torn leaves in her hand, splotched over with small cuts of clothes-pins and patent wringers and washing-powder, and entered the hallway. She stopped, folding and folding the sheets, then she went on, with swift, cringing glances at the empty stalls. She walked right through the barn. It was open at the back, upon a mass of jimson weed in savage white-and-lavender bloom. She walked on into the sunlight again, into the weeds. Then she began to run, snatching her feet up almost before they touched the earth, the weeds slashing at her with huge, moist, malodorous blossoms. She stooped and twisted through a fence of sagging rusty wire and ran downhill among trees.

At the bottom of the hill a narrow scar of sand divided the two slopes of a small valley, winding in a series of dazzling splotches where the sun found it. Temple stood in the sand, listening to the birds among the sunshot leaves, listening, looking about. She followed the dry runlet to where a jutting shoulder formed a nook matted with briers. Among the new green last year's dead leaves from the branches overhead clung, not yet fallen to earth. She stood here for a while, folding and folding the sheets in her fingers, in a kind of despair. When she rose she saw, upon the glittering mass of leaves along the crest of the ditch, the squatting outline of a man.

For an instant she stood and watched herself run out of her body, out of one slipper. She watched her legs twinkle against the sand, through the flecks of sunlight for several yards, then whirl and run back and snatch up the slipper and whirl and run again.

When she caught a glimpse of the house she was opposite the front porch. The blind man sat in a chair, his face lifted into the sun. At the edge of the woods she stopped and put on the slipper. She crossed the ruined lawn and sprang on to the porch and ran down the hall. When she reached the back porch she saw a man in the door of the barn, looking towards the house. She crossed the porch in two strides and entered the kitchen, where the woman sat at the table, smoking, the child on her lap.

'He was watching me!' Temple said. 'He was watching me all the time.' She leaned beside the door, peering out, then she came to the woman, her face small and pale, her eyes like holes burned with a cigar, and laid her hand on the cold stove.

'Who was?' the woman said.

'Yes,' Temple said. 'He was there in the bushes, watching me all the time.' She looked towards the door, then back at the woman, and saw her hand lying on the stove. She snatched it up with a wailing shriek, clapping it against her mouth, and turned and ran towards the door. The woman caught her arm, still carrying the child on the other, and Temple sprang back into the kitchen. Goodwin was coming towards the house. He looked once at them and went on into the hall.

Temple began to struggle. 'Let go,' she whispered, 'let go! Let go!' She surged and plunged, grinding the woman's hand against the door jamb until she was free. She sprang from the porch and ran towards the barn and into the hallway and climbed the ladder and scrambled through the trap and to her feet again, running towards the pile of rotting hay.

Then suddenly she ran upside-down in a rushing interval; she could see her legs still running in space, and she struck lightly and solidly on her back and lay still, staring up at an oblong yawn that closed with a clattering vibration of loose planks. Faint dust sifted down across the bars of sunlight.

Her hand moved in the substance in which she lay, then she remembered the rat a second time. Her whole body surged in an involuted spurning movement that brought her to her feet in the loose hulls, so that she flung her hands out and caught herself upright, a hand on either angle of the corner, her face not twelve inches from the cross-beam on which the rat crouched. For an instant they stared eye to eye, then its eyes glowed suddenly like two tiny electric bulbs and it leaped at her head just as she sprang backward, treading again on something that rolled under her foot.

She fell towards the opposite corner, on her face in the hulls and a few scattered corn-cobs gnawed bone-clean. Something thudded against the wall and struck her hand in ricochet. The rat was in that corner now, on the floor. Again their faces were not twelve inches apart, the rat's eyes glowing and fading as though worked by lungs. Then it stood erect, its back to the corner, its forepaws curled against its chest, and began to squeak at her in tiny plaintive gasps. She backed away on hands and knees, watching it. Then she got to her feet and sprang at the door, hammering at it, watching the rat over her shoulder, her body arched against the door, rasping at the planks with her bare hands.

Chapter Twelve

The woman stood in the kitchen door, holding the child, until Goodwin emerged from the house. The lobes of his nostrils were quite white against his brown face, and she said: 'God, are you drunk too?' He came along the porch. 'She's not here,' the woman said. 'You can't find her.' He brushed past her, trailing a reek of whisky. She turned, watching him. He looked swiftly about the kitchen, then he turned and looked at her standing in the door, blocking it. 'You won't find her,' she said. 'She's gone.' He came towards her, lifting his hand. 'Don't put your hand on me,' she said. He gripped her arm, slowly. His eyes were a little bloodshot. The lobes of his nostrils looked like wax.

'Take your hand off me,' she said. 'Take it off.' Slowly he drew her out of the door. She began to curse him. 'Do you think you can? Do you think I'll let you? Or any other little slut?' Motionless, facing one another like the first position of a dance, they stood in a mounting terrific muscular hiatus.

With scarce any movement at all he flung her aside in a complete revolution that fetched her up against the table, her arm flung back for balance, her body bent and her hand fumbling behind her among the soiled dishes, watching him across the inert body of the child. He walked towards her. 'Stand back,' she said, lifting her hand slightly, bringing the butcher knife into view. 'Stand back.' He came steadily towards her, then she struck at him with the knife.

He caught her wrist. She began to struggle. He plucked the child from her and laid it on the table and caught her other hand as it flicked at his face, and holding both wrists in one hand, he slapped her. It made a dry, flat sound. He slapped her again, first on one cheek, then the other, rocking her head from side to side. 'That's what I do to them,' he said, slapping her. 'See?' He released her. She stumbled backwards against the table and caught up the child and half crouched between the table and the wall, watching him as he turned and left the room.

She knelt in the corner, holding the child. It had not stirred.
She laid her palm first on one cheek, then on the other. She rose
and laid the child in the box and took a sunbonnet from a nail
and put it on. From another nail she took a coat trimmed with
what had once been white fur, and took up the child and left the
room.

Tommy was standing in the barn, beside the crib, looking
towards the house. The old man sat on the front porch, in the
sun. She went down the steps and followed the path to the road
and went on without looking back. When she came to the tree
and the wrecked car she turned from the road, into a path. After
a hundred yards or so she reached the spring and sat down beside
it, the child on her lap and the hem of her skirt turned back over
its sleeping face.

Popeye came out of the bushes, walking gingerly in his muddy
shoes, and stood looking down at her across the spring. His hand
flicked to his coat and he fretted and twisted a cigarette and put
it into his mouth and snapped a match with his thumb. 'Jesus
Christ,' he said, 'I told him about letting them sit around all
night, swilling that goddam stuff. There ought to be a law.' He
looked away in the direction in which the house lay. Then he
looked at the woman, at the top of her sunbonnet. 'Goofy house,'
he said. 'That's what it is. It's not four days ago I find a bastard
squatting here, asking me if I read books. Like he would jump
me with a book or something. Take me for a ride with the
telephone directory.' Again he looked off towards the house,
jerking his neck forth as if his collar were too tight. He looked
down at the top of the sunbonnet. 'I'm going to town, see?' he
said. 'I'm clearing out. I've got enough of this.' She did not look
up. She adjusted the hem of the skirt above the child's face.
Popeye went on, with light, finicking sounds in the underbrush.
Then they ceased. Somewhere in the swamp a bird sang.

Before he reached the house Popeye left the road and followed
a wooded slope. When he emerged he saw Goodwin standing
behind a tree in the orchard, looking towards the barn. Popeye
stopped at the edge of the wood and looked at Goodwin's back.
He put another cigarette into his mouth and thrust his fingers
into his vest. He went on across the orchard, walking gingerly.
Goodwin heard him and looked over his shoulder. Popeye took
a match from his vest, flicked it into flame and lit the cigarette.

Goodwin looked towards the barn again and Popeye stood at his shoulder, looking towards the barn.

'Who's down there?' he said. Goodwin said nothing. Popeye jetted smoke from his nostrils. 'I'm clearing out,' he said. Goodwin said nothing, watching the barn. 'I said, I'm getting out of here,' Popeye said. Without turning his head Goodwin cursed him. Popeye smoked quietly, the cigarette wreathing across his still, soft, black gaze. Then he turned and went towards the house. The old man sat in the sun. Popeye did not enter the house. Instead he went on across the lawn and into the cedars until he was hidden from the house. Then he turned and crossed the garden and the weed-choked lot and entered the barn from the rear.

Tommy squatted on his heels beside the crib door, looking towards the house. Popeye looked at him a while, smoking. Then he snapped the cigarette away and entered a stall quietly. Above the manger was a wooden rack for hay, just under an opening in the loft floor. Popeye climbed into the rack and drew himself silently into the loft, his tight coat strained into thin ridges across his narrow shoulders and back.

Chapter Thirteen

Tommy was standing in the hallway of the barn when Temple at last got the door of the crib open. When she recognized him she was half spun, leaping back, then she whirled and ran towards him and sprang down, clutching his arm. Then she saw Goodwin standing in the back door of the house and she whirled and leaped back into the crib and leaned her head around the door, her voice making a thin eeeeeeeeeeeeee sound like bubbles in a bottle. She leaned there, scrabbling her hands on the door, trying to pull it to, hearing Tommy's voice.

'. . . Lee says hit won't hurt you none. All you got to do is lay down . . .' It was a dry sort of sound, not in her consciousness at all, nor his pale eyes beneath the shaggy thatch. She leaned in

the door, wailing, trying to shut it. Then she felt his hand clumsily
on her thigh. '. . . says hit won't hurt you none. All you got to do
is . . .'

She looked at him, his diffident, hard hand on her hip. 'Yes,'
she said, 'all right. Don't you let him in here.'

'You mean fer me not to let none of them in hyer?'

'All right. I'm not scared of rats. You stay there and don't let
him in.'

'All right. I'll fix hit so cain't nobody git to you. I'll be right
hyer.'

'All right. Shut the door. Don't let him in here.'

'All right.' He shut the door. She leaned in it, looking towards
the house. He pushed her back so he could close the door. 'Hit
ain't goin to hurt you none, Lee says. All you got to do is lay
down.'

'All right. I will. Don't you let him in here.' The door closed.
She heard him drive the hasp to. Then he shook the door.

'Hit's fastened,' he said. 'Cain't nobody git to you now. I'll be
right hyer.'

He squatted on his heels in the chaff, looking at the house.
After a while he saw Goodwin come to the back door and look
towards him, and squatting, clasping his knees, Tommy's eyes
glowed again, the pale irises appearing for an instant to spin on
the pupils like tiny wheels. He squatted there, his lip lifted a
little, until Goodwin went back into the house. Then he sighed,
expelling his breath, and he looked at the blank door of the crib
and again his eyes glowed with a diffident, groping, hungry fire
and he began to rub his hands slowly on his shanks, rocking a
little from side to side. Then he ceased, became rigid, and
watched Goodwin move swiftly across the corner of the house
and into the cedars. He squatted rigid, his lip lifted a little upon
his ragged teeth.

Sitting in the cottonseed-hulls, in the litter of gnawed corn-
cobs, Temple lifted her head suddenly towards the trap at the
top of the ladder. She heard Popeye cross the floor of the
loft, then his foot appeared, groping gingerly for the step. He
descended, watching her over his shoulder.

She sat quite motionless, her mouth open a little. He stood
looking at her. He began to thrust his chin out in a series of
jerks, as though his collar were too tight. He lifted his elbows
and brushed them with his palm, and the skirt of his coat, then
he crossed her field of vision, moving without a sound, his hand

in his coat pocket. He tried the door. Then he shook it.

'Open the door,' he said.

There was no sound. Then Tommy whispered: 'Who's that?'

'Open the door,' Popeye said. The door opened. Tommy looked at Popeye. He blinked.

'I didn't know you was in hyer,' he said. He made to look past Popeye, into the crib. Popeye laid his hand flat on Tommy's face and thrust him back and leaned past him and looked up at the house. Then he looked at Tommy.

'Didn't I tell you about following me?'

'I wasn't following you,' Tommy said. 'I was watching him,' jerking his head towards the house.

'Watch him, then,' Popeye said. Tommy turned his head and looked towards the house and Popeye drew his hand from his coat pocket.

To Temple, sitting in the cottonseed-hulls and the corncobs, the sound was no louder than the striking of a match: a short, minor sound shutting down upon the scene, the instant, with a profound finality, completely isolating it, and she sat there, her legs straight before her, her hands limp and palm-up on her lap, looking at Popeye's tight back and the ridges of his coat across the shoulders as he leaned out the door, the pistol behind him, against his flank, wisping thinly along his leg.

He turned and looked at her. He waggled the pistol slightly and put it back in his coat, then he walked towards her. Moving, he made no sound at all; the released door yawned and clapped against the jamb, but it made no sound either; it was as though sound and silence had become inverted. She could hear silence in a thick rustling as he moved towards her through it, thrusting it aside, and she began to say Something is going to happen to me. She was saying it to the old man with the yellow clots for eyes. 'Something is happening to me!' she screamed at him, sitting in his chair in the sunlight, his hands crossed on the top of the stick. 'I told you it was!' she screamed, voiding the words like hot silent bubbles into the bright silence about them until he turned his head and the two phlegm-clots above her where she lay tossing and thrashing on the rough, sunny boards. 'I told you! I told you all the time!'

Chapter Fourteen

While she was sitting beside the spring, with the sleeping child upon her knees, the woman discovered that she had forgot its bottle. She sat there for about an hour after Popeye left her. Then she returned to the road and turned back towards the house. When she was about half-way back to the house, carrying the child in her arms, Popeye's car passed her. She heard it coming and she got out of the road and stood there and watched it come dropping down the hill. Temple and Popeye were in it. Popeye did not make any sign, though Temple looked full at the woman. From beneath her hat Temple looked the woman full in the face, without any sign of recognition whatever. The face did not turn, the eyes did not wake; to the woman beside the road it was like a small, dead-coloured mask drawn past her on a string and then away. The car went on, lurching and jolting in the ruts. The woman went on to the house.

The blind man was sitting on the front porch, in the sun. When she entered the hall, she was walking fast. She was not aware of the child's thin weight. She found Goodwin in their bedroom. He was in the act of putting on a frayed tie; looking at him, she saw that he had just shaved.

'Yes,' she said. 'What is it? What is it?'

'I've got to walk up to Tull's and telephone for the sheriff,' he said.

'The sheriff,' she said. 'Yes. All right.' She came to the bed and laid the child carefully down. 'To Tull's,' she said. 'Yes. He's got a phone.'

'You'll have to cook,' Goodwin said. 'There's Pap.'

'You can give him some cold bread. He won't mind. There's some left in the stove. He won't mind.'

'I'll go,' Goodwin said. 'You stay here.'

'To Tull's,' she said. 'All right.' Tull was the man at whose house Gowan had found a car. It was two miles away. Tull's family was at dinner. They asked her to stop. 'I just want to use the telephone,' she said. The telephone was in the dining-room, where they were eating. She called, with them sitting about the table. She didn't know the number. 'The Sheriff,' she said patiently into the mouthpiece. Then she got the sheriff, with Tull's family sitting about the table, about the Sunday dinner. 'A dead man. You pass Mr Tull's about a mile and turn off to the right . . . Yes, the Old Frenchman place. Yes. This is Mrs Goodwin talking . . . Goodwin. Yes.'

Chapter Fifteen

Benbow reached his sister's home in the middle of the afternoon. It was four miles from town, Jefferson. He and his sister were born in Jefferson, seven years apart, in a house which they still owned, though his sister had wanted to sell the house when Benbow married the divorced wife of a man named Mitchell and moved to Kinston. Benbow would not agree to sell, though he had built a new bungalow in Kinston on borrowed money upon which he was still paying interest.

When he arrived, there was no one about. He entered the house and he was sitting in the dim parlour behind the closed blinds, when he heard his sister come down the stairs, still unaware of his arrival. He made no sound. She had almost crossed the parlour door and vanished when she paused and looked full at him, without outward surpnse, with that serene and stupid impregnability of heroic statuary; she was in white. 'Oh, Horace,' she said.

He did not rise. He sat with something of the air of a guilty small boy. 'How did you –' he said. 'Did Belle –'

'Of course. She wired me Saturday. That you had left, and if you came here, to tell you that she had gone back home to Kentucky and had sent for Little Belle.'

'Ah, damnation,' Benbow said.

'Why?' his sister said. 'You want to leave home yourself, but you don't want her to leave.'

He stayed at his sister's two days. She had never been given to talking, living a life of serene vegetation like perpetual corn or wheat in a sheltered garden instead of a field, and during those two days she came and went about the house with an air of tranquil and faintly ludicrous tragic disapproval.

After supper they sat in Miss Jenny's room, where Narcissa would read the Memphis paper before taking the boy off to bed. When she went out of the room, Miss Jenny looked at Benbow.

'Go back home, Horace,' she said.

'Not to Kinston,' Benbow said. 'I hadn't intended to stay here, anyway. It wasn't Narcissa I was running to. I haven't quit one woman to run to the skirts of another.'

'If you keep on telling yourself that you may believe it, some day,' Miss Jenny said. 'Then what'll you do?'

'You're right,' Benbow said. 'Then I'd have to stay at home.'

His sister returned. She entered the room with a definite air. 'Now for it,' Benbow said. His sister had not spoken directly to him all day.

'What are you going to do, Horace?' she said. 'You must have business of some sort there in Kinston that should be attended to.'

'Even Horace must have,' Miss Jenny said. 'What I want to know is, why he left. Did you find a man under the bed, Horace?'

'No such luck,' Benbow said. 'It was Friday, and all of a sudden I knew that I could not go to the station and get that box of shrimp and –'

'But you have been doing that for ten years,' his sister said.

'I know. That's how I know that I will never learn to like smelling shrimp.'

'Was that why you left Belle?' Miss Jenny said. She looked at him. 'It took you a long time to learn that, if a woman don't make a very good wife for one man, she ain't likely to for another, didn't it?'

'But to walk out just like a nigger,' Narcissa said. 'And to mix yourself up with moonshiners and street-walkers.'

'Well, he's gone and left the street-walker too,' Miss Jenny said. 'Unless you're going to walk the streets with that orange-stick in your pocket until she comes to town.'

'Yes,' Benbow said. He told again about the three of them, himself and Goodwin and Tommy sitting on the porch, drinking from the jug and talking, and Popeye lurking about the house, coming out from time to time to ask Tommy to light a lantern and go down to the barn with him and Tommy wouldn't do it and Popeye would curse him, and Tommy sitting on the floor, scouring his bare feet on the boards with a faint, hissing noise, chortling: 'Ain't he a sight, now?'

'You could feel the pistol on him just like you knew he had a navel,' Benbow said. 'He wouldn't drink, because he said it made him sick to his stomach like a dog; he wouldn't stay and talk with us, he wouldn't do anything: just lurking about, smoking his cigarettes, like a sullen and sick child.

'Goodwin and I were both talking. He had been a cavalry sergeant in the Philippines and on the Border, and in an infantry regiment in France; he never told me why he changed, transferred to infantry and lost his rank. He might have killed someone, might have deserted. He was talking about Manila and Mexican girls, and that halfwit chortling and glugging at the jug and shoving it at me: "Take some mo"; and then I knew that the woman was just behind the door, listening to us. They are not married. I know that just like I know that that little black man had that flat little pistol in his coat pocket. But she's out there, doing a nigger's work, that's owned diamonds and automobiles too in her day, and bought them with a harder currency than cash. And that blind man, that old man sitting there at the table, waiting for somebody to feed him, with that immobility of blind people, like it was the backs of their eyeballs you looked at while they were hearing music you couldn't hear; that Goodwin led out of the room and completely off the earth, as far as I know. I never saw him again. I never knew who he was, who he was kin to. Maybe not to anybody. Maybe that old Frenchman that built the house a hundred years ago didn't want him either and just left him there when he died or moved away.'

The next morning Benbow got the key to the house from his sister, and went into town. The house was on a side street, unoccupied now for ten years. He opened the house, drawing the nails from the windows. The furniture had not been moved. In a pair of new overalls, with mops and pails, he scoured the floors. At noon he went down town and bought bedding and some tinned food. He was still at work at six o'clock when his sister drove up in her car.

'Come on home, Horace,' she said. 'Don't you see you can't do this?'

'I found that out right after I started,' Benbow said. 'Until this morning I thought that anybody with one arm and a pail of water could wash a floor.'

'Horace,' she said.

'I'm the older, remember,' he said. 'I'm going to stay here. I have some covers.' He went to the hotel for supper. When he returned, his sister's car was again in the drive. The negro driver had brought a bundle of bedclothing.

'Miss Narcissa say for you to use them,' the negro said. Benbow put the bundle into a closet and made a bed with the ones which he had bought.

Next day at noon, eating his cold food at the kitchen table, he saw through the window a wagon stop in the street. Three women got down and standing on the kerb they made unabashed toilets, smoothing skirts and stockings, brushing one another's back, opening parcels and donning various finery. The wagon had gone on. They followed, on foot, and he remembered that it was Saturday. He removed the overalls and dressed and left the house.

The street opened into a broader one. To the left it went on to the square, the opening between two buildings black with a slow, continuous throng, like two streams of ants, above which the cupola of the court-house rose from a clump of oaks and locusts covered with ragged snow. He went on towards the square. Empty wagons still passed him and he passed still more women on foot, black and white, unmistakable by the unease of their garments as well as by their method of walking, believing that town dwellers would take them for town dwellers too, not even fooling one another.

The adjacent alleys were choked with tethered wagons, the teams reversed and nuzzling gnawed corn-ears over the tail-boards. The square was lined two-deep with ranked cars, while the owners of them and of the wagons thronged in slow overalls and khaki, in mail-order scarves and parasols, in and out of the stores, soiling the pavement with fruit- and peanut-hulls. Slow as sheep they moved, tranquil, impassable, filling the passages, contemplating the fretful hurrying of those in urban shirts and collars with the large, mild inscrutability of cattle or of gods, functioning outside of time, having left time lying upon the slow and imponderable land green with corn and cotton in the yellow afternoon.

Horace moved among them, swept here and there by the deliberate current, without impatience. Some of them he knew; most of the merchants and professional men remembered him as a boy, a youth, a brother lawyer – beyond a foamy screen of locust branches he could see the dingy second-storey windows where he and his father had practised, the glass still innocent of water and soap as then – and he stopped now and then and talked with them in unhurried backwaters.

The sunny air was filled with competitive radios and phonographs in the doors of drug- and music-stores. Before these doors a throng stood all day, listening. The pieces which moved them were ballads simple in melody and theme, of bereavement and retribution and repentance metallically sung, blurred, emphasized by static or needle – disembodied voices blaring from imitation wood cabinets or pebble-grain horn-mouths above the rapt faces, the gnarled slow hands long shaped to the imperious earth, lugubrious, harsh, and sad.

That was Saturday, in May: no time to leave the land. Yet on Monday they were back again, most of them, in clumps about the court-house and the square, and trading a little in the stores since they were here, in their khaki and overalls and collarless shirts. All day long a knot of them stood about the door to the undertaker's parlour, and boys and youths with and without school-books leaned with flattened noses against the glass, and the bolder ones and the younger men of the town entered in twos and threes to look at the man called Tommy. He lay on a wooden table, barefoot, in overalls, the sun-bleached curls on the back of his head matted with dried blood and singed with powder, while the coroner sat over him, trying to ascertain his last name. But none knew it, not even those who had known him for fifteen years about the countryside, nor the merchants who on infrequent Saturdays had seen him in town, barefoot, hatless, with his rapt, empty gaze and his cheeks bulged innocently by a peppermint jawbreaker. For all general knowledge, he had none.

Chapter Sixteen

On the day when the sheriff brought Goodwin to town, there was a negro murderer in the jail, who had killed his wife; slashed her throat with a razor so that, her whole head tossing further and further backwards from the bloody regurgitation of her bubbling throat, she ran out the cabin door and for six or seven steps up the quiet moonlit lane. He would lean in the window in the evening and sing. After supper a few negroes gathered along the fence below – natty, shoddy suits and sweat-stained overalls shoulder to shoulder – and in chorus with the murderer, they sang spirituals while white people slowed and stopped in the leafed darkness that was almost summer, to listen to those who were sure to die and him who was already dead singing about heaven and being tired; or perhaps in the interval between songs a rich, sourceless voice coming out of the high darkness where the ragged shadow of the heaven-tree which snooded the street lamp at the corner fretted and mourned: 'Fo days mo! Den dey ghy stroy de bes ba'ytone singer in nawth Mississippi!'

Sometimes during the day he would lean there, singing alone then, though after a while one or two ragamuffin boys or negroes with delivery baskets like as not, would halt at the fence, and the white men sitting in tilted chairs along the oil-foul wall of the garage across the street would listen above their steady jaws. 'One day mo! Den Ise a gawn po sonnen bitch. Say, Ain't no place fer you in heavum! Say, Ain't no place fer you in hell? Say, Ain't no place fer you in jail!'

'Damn that fellow,' Goodwin said, jerking up his black head, his gaunt, brown, faintly harried face. 'I ain't in any position to wish any man that sort of luck, but I'll be damned . . .' He wouldn't talk. 'I didn't do it. You know that yourself. You know I wouldn't have. I ain't going say what I think. I didn't do it. They've got to hang it on me first. Let them do that. I'm clear. But if I talk, if I say what I think or believe, I won't be clear.'

He was sitting on the cot in his cell. He looked up at the windows: two orifices not much larger than sabre slashes.

'Is he that good a shot?' Benbow said. 'To hit a man through one of those windows?'

Goodwin looked at him. 'Who?'

'Popeye,' Benbow said.

'Did Popeye do it?' Goodwin said.

'Didn't he?' Benbow said.

'I've told all I'm going to tell. I don't have to clear myself; it's up to them to hang it on me.'

'Then what do you want with a lawyer?' Benbow said. 'What do you want me to do?'

Goodwin was not looking at him. 'If you'll just promise to get the kid a good newspaper grift when he's big enough to make change,' he said. 'Ruby'll be all right. Won't you, old gal?' He put his hand on the woman's head scouring her hair with his hand. She sat on the cot beside him, holding the child on her lap. It lay in a sort of drugged immobility, like the children which beggars on Paris streets carry, its pinched face slick with faint moisture, its hair a damp whisper of shadow across its gaunt, veined skull, a thin crescent of white showing beneath its lead-coloured eyelids.

The woman wore a dress of grey crêpe, neatly brushed and skilfully darned by hand. Parallel with each seam was that faint, narrow, glazed imprint which another woman would recognize at a hundred yards with one glance. On the shoulder was a purple ornament of the sort that may be bought in ten-cent stores or by mail order; on the cot beside her lay a grey hat with a neatly darned veil; looking at it, Benbow could not remember when he had seen one before, when women ceased to wear veils.

He took the woman to his house. They walked, she carrying the child while Benbow carried a bottle of milk and a few groceries, food in tin cans. The child still slept. 'Maybe you hold it too much,' he said. 'Suppose we get a nurse for it.'

He left her at the house and returned to town, to a telephone, and he telephoned out to his sister's, for the car. The car came for him. He told his sister and Miss Jenny about the case over the supper table.

'You're just meddling!' his sister said, her serene face, her voice, furious. 'When you took another man's wife and child away from him I thought it was dreadful, but I said At least he will not have the face to ever come back here again. And when you just walked out of the house like a nigger and left her I thought that was dreadful too, but I would not let myself believe you meant to leave her for good. And then when you insisted without any reason at all on leaving here and opening the house, scrubbing it yourself and all the town looking on and living there like a tramp, refusing to stay here where everybody would expect you to stay and think it funny when you wouldn't; and now to deliberately mix yourself up with a woman you said yourself was a street-walker, a murderer's woman.'

'I can't help it. She has nothing, no one. In a made-over dress all neatly about five years out of mode, and that child that never has been more than half alive, wrapped in a piece of blanket scrubbed almost cotton-white. Asking nothing of anyone except to be let alone, trying to make something out of her life when all you sheltered chaste women –'

'Do you mean to say a moonshiner hasn't got the money to hire the best lawyer in the country?' Miss Jenny said.

'It's not that,' Horace said. 'I'm sure he could get a better lawyer. It's that –'

'Horace,' his sister said. She had been watching him. 'Where is that woman?' Miss Jenny was watching him too, sitting a little forward in the wheel-chair. 'Did you take that woman into my house?'

'It's my house too, honey.' She did not know that for ten years he had been lying to his wife in order to pay interest on a mortgage on the stucco house he had built for her in Kinston, so that his sister might not rent to strangers that other house in Jefferson which his wife did not know he still owned any share in. 'As long as it's vacant, and with that child –'

'The house where my father and mother and your father and mother, the house where I – I won't have it. I won't have it.'

'Just for one night, then. I'll take her to the hotel in the morning. Think of her, alone, with that baby . . . Suppose it were you and Bory, and your husband accused of a murder you knew he didn't –'

'I don't want to think about her. I wish I had never heard of the whole thing. To think that my brother – Don't you see that you are always having to clean up after yourself? It's not that there's a litter left; it's that you – that – But to bring a street-walker, a murderess, into the house where I was born.'

'Fiddlesticks,' Miss Jenny said. 'But, Horace, ain't that what the lawyers call collusion? connivance?' Horace looked at her. 'It seems to me you've already had a little more to do with these folks than the lawyer in the case should have. You were out there where it happened yourself not long ago. Folks might begin to think you know more than you've told.'

'That's so,' Horace said, 'Mrs Blackstone. And sometimes I have wondered why I haven't got rich at the law. Maybe I will, when I get old enough to attend the same law school you did.'

'If I were you,' Miss Jenny said, 'I'd drive back to town now and take her to the hotel and get her settled. It's not late.'

'And go on back to Kinston until the whole thing is over,' Narcissa said. 'These people are not your people. Why must you do such things?'

'I cannot stand idly by and see injustice –'

'You won't ever catch up with injustice, Horace,' Miss Jenny said.

'Well, that irony which lurks in events, then.'

'Hmmph,' Miss Jenny said. 'It must be because she is one woman you know that don't know anything about that shrimp.'

'Anyway, I've talked too much, as usual,' Horace said. 'So I'll have to trust you all –'

'Fiddlesticks,' Miss Jenny said. 'Do you think Narcissa'd want anybody to know that any of her folks could know people that would do anything as natural as make love or rob or steal?' There was that quality about his sister. During all the four days between Kinston and Jefferson he had counted on that imperviousness. He hadn't expected her – any woman? – to bother very much over a man she had neither married nor borne when she had one she did bear to cherish and fret over. But he had expected that imperviousness, since she had had it thirty-six years.

When he reached the house in town a light burned in one room. He entered, crossing floors which he had scrubbed himself, revealing at the time no more skill with a mop than he had expected, than he had with the lost hammer with which he nailed the windows down and the shutters to ten years ago, who could not even learn to drive a motor-car. But that was ten years ago, the hammer replaced by the new one with which he had drawn the clumsy nails, the windows open upon scrubbed floor spaces still as dead pools within the ghostly embrace of hooded furniture.

The woman was still up, dressed save for the hat. It lay on the bed where the child slept. Lying together there, they lent to the room a quality of transience more unmistakable than the makeshift light, the smug paradox of the made bed in a room otherwise redolent of long unoccupation. It was as though femininity were a current running through a wire along which a certain number of identical bulbs were hung.

'I've got some things in the kitchen,' she said. 'I won't be but a minute.'

The child lay on the bed, beneath the unshaded light, and he wondered why women, in quitting a house, will remove all the lamp-shades even though they touch nothing else; looking down at the child, at its bluish eyelids showing a faint crescent of bluish white against its lead-coloured cheeks, the moist shadow of hair capping its skull, its hands uplifted, curl-palmed, sweating too, thinking Good God. Good God.

He was thinking of the first time he had seen it, lying in a wooden box behind the stove in that ruined house twelve miles from town; of Popeye's black presence lying upon the house like the shadow of something no larger than a match falling monstrous and portentous upon something else otherwise familiar and everyday and twenty times its size; of the two of them – himself and the woman – in the kitchen lighted by a cracked and smutty lamp on a table of clean, spartan dishes and Goodwin and Popeye somewhere in the outer darkness peaceful with insects and frogs yet filled too with Popeye's presence in black and nameless threat. The woman drew the box out from behind the stove and stood above it, her hands still hidden in her shapeless garment. 'I have to keep him in this so the rats can't get to him,' she said.

'Oh,' Horace said, 'you have a son.' Then she showed him her hands, flung them out in a gesture at once spontaneous and diffident and self-conscious and proud, and told him he might bring her an orange-stick.

She returned, with something wrapped discreetly in a piece of newspaper. He knew that it was a diaper, freshly washed, even before she said: 'I made a fire in the stove. I guess I over-stepped.'

'Of course not,' he said. 'It's merely a matter of legal precaution, you see,' he said. 'Better to put everybody to a little temporary discomfort than to jeopardize our case.' She did not appear to be listening. She spread the blanket on the bed and lifted the child on to it. 'You understand how it is,' Horace said. 'If the judge suspected that I knew more about it than the facts would warrant – I mean, we must try to give everybody the idea that holding Lee for that killing is just –'

'Do you live in Jefferson?' she said, wrapping the blanket about the child.

'No. I live in Kinston. I used to – I have practised here, though.'

'You have kinfolks here, though. Women. That used to live in this house.' She lifted the child, tucking the blanket about it. Then she looked at him. 'It's all right. I know how it is. You've been kind.'

'Damn it,' he said, 'do you think – Come on. Let's go on to the hotel. You get a good night's rest, and I'll be in early in the morning. Let me take it.'

'I've got him,' she said. She started to say something else, looking at him quietly for a moment, but she went on. He turned out the light and followed and locked the door. She was already in the car. He got in.

'Hotel, Isom,' he said. 'I never did learn to drive one,' he said. 'Sometimes when I think of all the time I have spent not learning to do things . . .'

The street was narrow, quiet. It was paved now, though he could remember when, after a rain, it had been a canal of blackish substance half earth, half water, with murmuring gutters in which he and Narcissa paddled and splashed with tucked-up garments and muddy bottoms, after the crudest of whittled boats, or made loblollies by treading and treading in one spot with the intense oblivion of alchemists. He could remember when, innocent of concrete, the street was bordered on either side by paths of red brick tediously and unevenly laid and worn in rich, random maroon mosaic into the black earth which the noon sun never reached; at that moment, pressed into the concrete near the entrance of the drive, were the prints of his and his sister's naked feet in the artificial stone.

The infrequent lamps mounted to crescendo beneath the arcade of a filling-station at the corner. The woman leaned suddenly forward. 'Stop here, please, boy,' she said. Isom put on the brakes. 'I'll get out here and walk,' she said.

'You'll do nothing of the kind,' Horace said. 'Go on, Isom.'

'No; wait,' the woman said. 'We'll be passing people that know you. And then the square.'

'Nonsense,' Horace said. 'Go on, Isom.'

'You get out and wait, then,' she said. 'He can come straight back.'

'You'll do no such thing,' Horace said. 'By heaven, I – Drive on, Isom!'

'You'd better,' the woman said. She sat back in the seat. Then she leaned forward again. 'Listen. You've been kind. You mean all right, but –'

'You don't think I am lawyer enough, you mean?'

'I guess I've got just what was coming to me. There's no use fighting it.'

'Certainly not, if you feel that way about it. But you don't. Or you'd have told Isom to drive you to the railroad station. Wouldn't you?' She was looking down at the child, fretting the blanket about its face. 'You get a good night's rest and I'll be in early tomorrow.' They passed the jail – a square building slashed harshly by pale slits of light. Only the central window was wide enough to be called a window, criss-crossed by slender bars. In it the negro murderer leaned; below along the fence a row of heads hatted and bare above work-thickened shoulders, and the blended voices swelled rich and sad into the soft, depthless evening, singing of heaven and being tired. 'Don't you worry at all, now. Everybody knows Lee didn't do it.'

They drew up to the hotel, where the drummers sat in chairs along the kerb, listening to the singing. 'I must –' the woman said. Horace got down and held the door open. She didn't move. 'Listen, I've got to tell –'

'Yes,' Horace said, extending his hand. 'I know. I'll be in early tomorrow.' He helped her down. They entered the hotel, the drummers turning to watch her legs, and went to the desk. The singing followed them, dimmed by the walls, the lights.

The woman stood quietly near by, holding the child, until Horace had done.

'Listen,' she said. The porter went on with the key, towards the stairs. Horace touched her arm, turning her that way. 'I've got to tell you,' she said.

'In the morning,' he said. 'I'll be in early,' he said, guiding her towards the stairs. Still she hung back, looking at him; then she freed her arm by turning to face him.

'All right, then,' she said. She said, in a low, level tone, her face bent a little towards the child: 'We haven't got any money. I'll tell you now. That last batch Popeye didn't –'

'Yes, yes,' Horace said; 'first thing in the morning. I'll be in by the time you finish breakfast. Good night.' He returned to the car, into the sound of the singing. 'Home, Isom,' he said. They turned and passed the jail again and the leaning shape beyond the bars and the heads along the fence. Upon the barred and slitted wall the splotched shadow of the heaven-tree shuddered and pulsed monstrously in scarce any wind; rich and sad, the singing fell behind. The car went on, smooth and swift, passing the narrow street. 'Here,' Horace said, 'where are you –' Isom clapped on the brakes.

'Miss Narcissa say to bring you back out home,' he said.

'Oh, she did?' Horace said. 'That was kind of her. You can tell her I changed her mind.'

Isom backed and turned into the narrow street and then into the cedar drive, the lights lifting and boring ahead into the unpruned tunnel as though into the most profound blackness of the sea, as though among straying rigid shapes to which not even light could give colour. The car stopped at the door and Horace got out. 'You might tell her it was not to her I ran,' he said. 'Can you remember that?'

Chapter Seventeen

The last trumpet-shaped bloom had fallen from the heaven-tree at the corner of the jail yard. They lay thick, viscid underfoot, sweet and oversweet in the nostrils with a sweetness surfeitive and moribund, and at night now the ragged shadow of full-fledged leaves pulsed upon the barred window in shabby rise and fall. The window was in the general room, the white-washed walls of which were stained with dirty hands, scribbled and scratched over with names and dates and blasphemous and obscene doggerel in pencil or nail or knife-blade. Nightly the negro murderer leaned there, his face checkered by the shadow of the grating in the restless interstices of leaves, singing in chorus with those along the fence below.

Sometimes during the day he sang also, alone then save for the slowing passer-by and ragamuffin boys and the garage men across the way. 'One day mo! Ain't no place fer you in heavum! Ain't no place fer you in hell! Ain't no place fer you in white folks' jail! Nigger, whar you gwine to? Whar you gwine to, nigger?'

Each morning Isom fetched in a bottle of milk, which Horace

delivered to the woman at the hotel, for the child. On Sunday afternoon he went out to his sister's. He left the woman sitting on the cot in Goodwin's cell, the child on her lap. Heretofore it had lain in that drugged apathy, its eyelids closed to thin crescents, but today it moved now and then in frail, galvanic jerks, whimpering.

Horace went up to Miss Jenny's room. His sister had not appeared. 'He won't talk,' Horace said. 'He just says they will have to prove he did it. He said they had nothing on him, no more than on the child. He wouldn't even consider bond, if he could have got it. He says he is better off in the jail. And I suppose he is. His business out there is finished now, even if the sheriff hadn't found his kettles and destroyed –'

'Kettles?'

'His still. After he surrendered, they hunted around until they found the still. They knew what he was doing, but they waited until he was down. Then they all jumped on him. The good customers, that had been buying whisky from him and drinking all that he would give them free and maybe trying to make love to his wife behind his back. You should hear them down town. This morning the Baptist minister took him for a text. Not only as a murderer, but as an adulterer; a polluter of the free Democratico-protestant atmosphere of Yoknapatawpha county. I gathered that his idea was that Goodwin and the woman should both be burned as a sole example to that child; the child to be reared and taught the English language for the sole end of being taught that it was begot in sin by two people who suffered by fire for having begot it. Good God, can a man, a civilized man, seriously . . .'

'They're just Baptists,' Miss Jenny said. 'What about the money?'

'He had a little, almost a hundred and sixty dollars. It was buried in a can in the barn. They let him dig that up. "That'll keep her", he says, "until it's over. Then we'll clear out. We've been intending to for a good while. If I'd listened to her, we'd have been gone already. You've been a good girl" he says. She was sitting on the cot beside him, holding the baby, and he took her chin in his hand and shook her head a little.'

'It's a good thing Narcissa ain't going to be on that jury,' Miss Jenny said.

'Yes. But the fool won't even let me mention that that gorilla was ever on the place. He said "They can't prove anything on me. I've been in a jam before. Everybody that knows anything about me knows that I wouldn't hurt a feeb." But that wasn't the reason he doesn't want it told about that thug. And he knew I knew it wasn't, because he kept on talking, sitting there in his overalls, rolling his cigarettes with the sack hanging in his teeth. "I'll just stay here until it blows over. I'll be better off here; can't do anything outside, anyway. And this will keep her, with maybe something for you until you're better paid."

'But I knew what he was thinking. "I didn't know you were a coward" I said.

' "You do like I say," he said. "I'll be all right here." But he doesn't . . .' He sat forward, rubbing his hands slowly. He doesn't realize '. . . Dammit, say what you want to, but there's a corruption about even looking upon evil, even by accident; you cannot haggle, traffic, with putrefaction — You've seen how Narcissa, just hearing about it, how it's made her restless and suspicious. I thought I had come back here of my own accord, but now I see that — Do you suppose she thought I was bringing that woman into the house at night, or something like that?'

'I did too, at first,' Miss Jenny said. 'But I reckon now she's learned that you'll work harder for whatever reason you think you have, than for anything anybody could offer you or give you.'

'You mean, she'd let me think they never had any money, when she —'

'Why not? Ain't you doing all right without it?'

Narcissa entered.

'We were just talking about murder and crime,' Miss Jenny said.

'I hope you're through, then,' Narcissa said. She did not sit down.

'Narcissa has her sorrows too,' Miss Jenny said. 'Don't you, Narcissa?'

'What now?' Horace said. 'She hasn't caught Bory with alcohol on his breath, has she?'

'She's been jilted. Her beau's gone and left her.'

'You're such a fool,' Narcissa said.

'Yes, sir,' Miss Jenny said, 'Gowan Stevens has thrown her down. He didn't even come back from that Oxford dance to say good-bye. He just wrote her a letter.' She began to search about her in the chair. 'And now I flinch every time the door-bell rings, thinking that his mother —'

'Miss Jenny,' Narcissa said, 'you give me my letter.'

'Wait,' Miss Jenny said, 'here it is. Now, what do you think of that for a delicate operation on the human heart without anaesthetic? I'm beginning to believe all this I hear, about how young folks learn all the things in order to get married, that we had to get married in order to learn.'

Horace took the single sheet.

Narcissa my dear,

This has no heading. I wish it could have no date. But if my heart was as blank as this page, this would not be necessary at all. I will not see you again. I cannot write it, for I have gone through with an experience which I cannot face. I have but one rift in the darkness, that is that I have injured no one save myself by my folly, and that the extent of that folly you will never learn. I need not say that the hope that you never learn it is the sole reason why I will not see you again. Think as well of me as you can. I wish I had the right to say, if you learn of my folly think not the less of me.

G.

Horace read the note, the single sheet. He held it between his hands. He did not say anything for a while.

'Good Lord,' Horace said. 'Someone mistook him for a Mississippi man on the dance floor.'

'I think, if I were you –' Narcissa said. After a moment she said: 'How much longer is this going to last, Horace?'

'Not any longer than I can help. If you know of any way in which I can get him out of that jail by tomorrow . . .'

'There's only one way,' she said. She looked at him a moment. Then she turned towards the door. 'Which way did Bory go? Dinner'll be ready soon.' She went out.

'And you know what that way is,' Miss Jenny said. 'If you ain't got any backbone.'

'I'll know whether or not I have any backbone when you tell me what the other way is.'

'Go back to Belle,' Miss Jenny said. 'Go back home.'

The negro murderer was to be hung on a Saturday without pomp, buried without circumstance: one night he would be singing at the barred window and yelling down out of the soft myriad darkness of a May night; the next night he would be gone, leaving the window for Goodwin. Goodwin had been bound over for the June term of court, without bail. But still he would not agree to let Horace divulge Popeye's presence at the scene of the murder.

'I tell you, they've got nothing on me,' Goodwin said.

'How do you know they haven't?' Horace said.

'Well, no matter what they think they have on me, I stand a chance in court. But just let it get to Memphis that I said he was anywhere around there, what chance do you think I'd have to get back to this cell after I testified?'

'You've got the law, justice, civilization.'

'Sure, if I spend the rest of my life squatting in that corner yonder. Come here.' He led Horace to the window. 'There are five windows in that hotel yonder that look into this one. And I've seen him light matches with a pistol at twenty feet. Why, damn it all, I'd never get back here from the court-room the day I testified that.'

'But there's such a thing as obstruct —'

'Obstructing damnation. Let them prove I did it. Tommy was found in the barn, shot from behind. Let them find the pistol. I was there, waiting. I didn't try to run. I could have, but I didn't. It was me notified the sheriff. Of course my being there alone except for her and Pap looked bad. If it was a stall, don't common sense tell you I'd have invented a better one?'

'You're not being tried by common sense,' Horace said. 'You're being tried by a jury.'

'Then let them make the best of it. That's all they'll get. The dead man is in the barn, hadn't been touched; me and my wife and child and Pap in the house; nothing in the house touched; me the one that sent for the sheriff. No, no; I know I run a chance this way, but let me just open my head about that fellow, and there's no chance to it. I know what I'll get.'

'But you heard the shot,' Horace paid. 'You have already told that.'

'No,' he said, 'I didn't. I didn't hear anything. I don't know anything about it . . . Do you mind waiting outside a minute while I talk to Ruby?'

It was five minutes before she joined him. He said:

'There's something about this that I don't know yet; that you and Lee haven't told me. Something he just warned you not to tell me. Isn't there?' She walked beside him, carrying the child. It was still whimpering now and then, tossing its thin body in sudden jerks. She tried to soothe it, crooning to it, rocking it in her arms. 'Maybe you carry it too much,' Horace said; 'maybe if you could leave it at the hotel . . .'

'I guess Lee knows what to do,' she said.

'But the lawyer should know all the facts, everything. He is the one to decide what to tell and what not to tell. Else, why have one? That's like paying a dentist to fix your teeth and then refusing to let him look into your mouth, don't you see? You wouldn't treat a dentist or a doctor this way.' She said nothing, her head bent over the child. It wailed.

'Hush,' she said, 'hush, now.'

'And worse than that, there's such a thing called obstructing justice. Suppose he swears there was nobody else there. Suppose he is about to be cleared – which is not likely – and somebody turns up who saw Popeye about the place, or saw his car leaving. Then they'll say, if Lee didn't tell the truth about an unimportant thing, why should we believe him when his neck's in danger?'

They reached the hotel. He opened the door for her. She did not look at him. 'I guess Lee knows best,' she said, going in. The child wailed, a thin, whimpering, distressful cry. 'Hush,' she said. 'Shhhhhhhhhhhh.'

Isom had been to fetch Narcissa from a party; it was late when the car stopped at the corner and picked him up. A few of the lights were beginning to come on, and men were already drifting back towards the square after supper, but it was still too early for the negro murderer to begin to sing. 'And he'd better sing fast, too,' Horace said. 'He's only got two days more.' But he was not there yet. The jail faced west; a last faint copper-coloured light lay upon the dingy grating and upon the small, pale blob of a hand, and in scarce any wind a blue wisp of tobacco floated out and dissolved raggedly away. 'If it wasn't bad enough to have her husband there, without that poor brute counting his remaining breaths at the top of his voice . . .'

'Maybe they'll wait and hang them both together,' Narcissa said. 'They do that sometimes, don't they?'

That night Horace built a small fire in the grate. It was not cool. He was using only one room now, taking his meals at the hotel; the rest of the house was locked again. He tried to read, then he gave up and undressed and went to bed, watching the fire die in the grate. He heard the town clock strike twelve. 'When this is over, I think I'll go to Europe,' he said. 'I need a change. Either I, or Mississippi, one.'

Maybe a few of them would still be gathered along the fence, since this would be his last night; the thick, small-headed shape of him would be clinging to the bars, gorilla-like, singing, while upon his shadow, upon the checkered orifice of the window, the ragged grief of the heaven-tree would pulse and change, the last bloom fallen now in viscid smears upon the sidewalk. Horace turned again in the bed. 'They ought to clean that damn mess off the sidewalk,' he said. 'Damn. Damn. Damn.'

He was sleeping late the next morning; he had seen daylight. He was wakened by someone knocking at the door. It was half-past six. He went to the door. The negro porter of the hotel stood there.

'What?' Horace said. 'Is it Mrs Goodwin?'

'She say for you to come when you up,' the negro said.

'Tell her I'll be there in ten minutes.'

As he entered the hotel he passed a young man with a small black bag, such as doctors carry. Horace went on up. The woman was standing in the half-open door, looking down the hall.

'I finally got the doctor,' she said. 'But I wanted anyway . . .' The child lay on the bed, its eyes shut, flushed and sweating, its curled hands above its head in the attitude of one crucified, breathing in short, whistling gasps. 'He was sick all last night. I went and got some medicine and I tried to keep him quiet until daylight. At last I got the doctor.' She stood beside the bed, looking down at the child. 'There was a woman there,' she said. 'A young girl.'

'A –' Horace said. 'Oh,' he said. 'Yes. You'd better tell me about it.'

Chapter Eighteen

Popeye drove swiftly but without any quality of haste or of flight, down the clay road and into the sand. Temple was beside him. Her hat was jammed on to the back of her head, her hair escaping beneath the crumpled brim in matted clots. Her face looked like a sleep-walker's as she swayed limply to the lurching of the car. She lurched against Popeye, lifting her hand in limp reflex. Without releasing the wheel he thrust her back with his elbow. 'Brace yourself,' he said. 'Come on, now.'

Before they came to the tree they passed the woman. She stood beside the road, carrying the child, the hem of her dress folded back over its face, and she looked at them quietly from beneath the faded sun-bonnet, flicking swiftly in and out of Temple's vision without any motion, any sign.

When they reached the tree Popeye swung the car out of the road and drove it crashing into the undergrowth and through the prone tree-top and back into the road again in a running popping of cane-stalks like musketry along a trench, without any diminution of speed. Beside the tree Gowan's car lay on its side. Temple looked vaguely and stupidly at it as it too shot behind.

Popeye swung back into the sandy ruts. Yet there was no flight in the action: he performed it with a certain vicious petulance, that was all. It was a powerful car. Even in the sand it held forty miles an hour, and up the narrow gulch to the highroad, where he turned north. Sitting beside him, braced against jolts that had already given way to a smooth increasing hiss of gravel, Temple gazed dully forward as the road she had traversed yesterday began to flee backwards under the wheels as on to a spool, feeling her blood seeping slowly inside her loins. She sat limp in the corner of the seat, watching the steady backward rush of the land pines in opening vistas splashed with fading dogwood; sedge; fields green with new cotton and empty of any movement, peaceful, as though Sunday were a quality of atmosphere, of light

and shade – sitting with her legs close together, listening to the
hot minute seeping of her blood, saying dully to herself, I'm still
bleeding. I'm still bleeding.

It was a bright, soft day, a wanton morning filled with that
unbelievable soft radiance of May, rife with a promise of noon
and of heat, with high fat clouds like gobs of whipped cream
floating lightly as reflections in a mirror, their shadows scudding
sedately across the road. It had been a lavender spring. The fruit
trees, the white ones, had been in small leaf when the blooms
matured; they had never attained that brilliant whiteness of last
spring, and the dogwood had come into full bloom after the leaf
also, in green retrograde before crescendo. But lilac and wistaria
and redbud, even the shabby heaven-trees, had never been finer,
fulgent, with a burning scent blowing for a hundred yards along
the vagrant air of April and May. The bougainvillea against
the veranda would be large as basketballs and lightly poised as
balloons, and looking vacantly and stupidly at the rushing roadside Temple began to scream.

It started as a wail, raising, cut suddenly off by Popeye's hand.
With her hands lying on her lap, sitting erect, she screamed,
tasting the gritty acridity of his fingers while the car slewed
squealing in the gravel, feeling her secret blood. Then he gripped
her by the back of the neck and she sat motionless, her mouth
round and open like a small empty cave. He shook her head.

'Shut it,' he said, 'shut it'; gripping her silent. 'Look at yourself.
Here.' With the other hand he swung the mirror on the wind-
shield around and she looked at her image, at the uptilted hat
and her matted hair and her round mouth. She began to fumble
at her coat pockets, looking at her reflection. He released her
and she produced the compact and opened it and peered into
the mirror, whimpering a little. She powdered her face and
rouged her mouth and straightened her hat, whimpering into
the tiny mirror on her lap while Popeye watched her. He lit a
cigarette. 'Ain't you ashamed of yourself?' he said.

'It's still running,' she whimpered. 'I can feel it.' With the
lipstick poised she looked at him and opened her mouth again.
He gripped her by the back of the neck.

'Stop it now. You going to shut it?'

'Yes,' she whimpered.

'See you do, then. Come on. Get yourself fixed.'

She put the compact away. He started the car again.

The road began to thicken with pleasure cars Sunday-bent –

small, clay-crusted Fords and Chevrolets; an occasional larger car moving swiftly, with swathed women, and dust-covered hampers; trucks filled with wooden-faced country people in garments like a coloured wood meticulously carved; now and then a wagon or a buggy. Before a weathered frame church on a hill the grove was full of tethered teams and battered cars and trucks. The woods gave way to fields; houses became more frequent. Low above the skyline, above roofs and a spire or two, smoke hung. The gravel became asphalt and they entered Dumfries.

Temple began to look about, like one waking from sleep. 'Not here!' she said. 'I can't –'

'Hush it, now,' Popeye said.

'I can't – I might –' she whimpered. 'I'm hungry,' she said. 'I haven't eaten since . . .'

'Ah, you ain't hungry. Wait till we get to town.'

She looked about with dazed, glassy eyes. 'There might be people here . . .' He swung in towards a filling station. 'I can't get out,' she whimpered. 'It's still running, I tell you!'

'Who told you to get out?' He descended and looked at her across the wheel. 'Don't you move.' She watched him go up the street and enter a door. It was a dingy confectionery. He bought a pack of cigarettes and put one in his mouth. 'Gimme a couple of bars of candy,' he said.

'What kind?'

'Candy,' he said. Under a glass bell on the counter a plate of sandwiches sat. He took one and flipped a dollar on the counter and turned towards the door.

'Here's your change,' the clerk said.

'Keep it,' he said. 'You'll get rich faster.'

When he saw the car it was empty. He stopped ten feet away and changed the sandwich to his left hand, the unlighted cigarette slanted beneath his chin. The mechanic, hanging the hose up, saw him and jerked his thumb towards the corner of the building.

Beyond the corner the wall made an offset. In the niche was a greasy barrel half full of scraps of metal and rubber. Between the barrel and the wall Temple crouched. 'He nearly saw me!' she whispered. 'He was almost looking right at me!'

'Who?' Popeye said. He looked back up the street. 'Who saw you?'

'He was coming right towards me! A boy. At school. He was looking right towards –'

'Come on. Come out of it.'

'He was look —' Popeye took her by the arm. She crouched in the corner, jerking at the arm he held, her wan face craned around the corner.

'Come on now.' Then his hand was at the back of her neck, gripping it.

'Oh,' she wailed in a choked voice. It was as though he were lifting her slowly erect by that one hand. Excepting that, there was no movement between them. Side by side, almost of a height, they appeared as decorous as two acquaintances stopped to pass the time of day before entering church.

'Are you coming?' he said. 'Are you?'

'I can't. It's down to my stocking now. Look.' She lifted her skirt away in a shrinking gesture, then she dropped the skirt and rose again, her torso arching backwards, her soundless mouth open as he gripped her. He released her.

'Will you come now?'

She came out from behind the barrel. He took her arm.

'It's all over the back of my coat,' she whimpered. 'Look and see.'

'You're all right. I'll get you another coat tomorrow. Come on.'

They returned to the car. At the corner she hung back again. 'You want some more of it, do you?' he whispered, not touching her. 'Do you?' She went on and got into the car quietly. He took the wheel. 'Here, I got you a sandwich.' He took it from his pocket and put it in her hand. 'Come on, now. Eat it.' She took a bite obediently. He started the car and took the Memphis road. Again, the bitten sandwich in her hand, she ceased chewing and opened her mouth in that round, hopeless expression of a child; again his hand left the wheel and gripped the back of her neck and she sat motionless, gazing straight at him, her mouth open and the half-chewed mass of bread and meat lying upon her tongue.

They reached Memphis in mid-afternoon. At the foot of the bluff below Main Street Popeye turned into a narrow street of smoke-grimed frame houses with tiers of wooden galleries, set a little back in grassless plots, with now and then a forlorn and hardy tree of some shabby species gaunt, lopbranched magnolias, a stunted elm or a locust in greyish, cadaverous bloom — interspersed by rear ends of garages; a scrap-heap in a vacant lot; a low-doored cavern of an equivocal appearance where an oilcloth-covered counter and a row of backless stools, a metal coffee-urn and a fat man in a dirty apron with a toothpick in his mouth, stood for an instant out of the gloom with an effect as of a sinister and meaningless photograph poorly made. From the bluff, beyond a line of office buildings terraced sharply against the sunfilled sky, came a sound of traffic – motor horns, trolleys – passing high overhead on the river breeze; at the end of the street a trolley materialized in the narrow gap with an effect as of magic and vanished with a stupendous clatter. On a second-storey gallery a young negress in her underclothes smoked a cigarette sullenly, her arms on the balustrade.

Popeye drew up before one of the dingy three-storey houses, the entrance of which was hidden by a dingy lattice cubicle leaning a little awry. In the grimy grassplot before it two of those small, woolly, white, worm-like dogs, one with a pink, the other a blue, ribbon about its neck, moved about with an air of sluggish and obscene paradox. In the sunlight their coats looked as though they had been cleaned with gasoline.

Later Temple could hear them outside her door, whimpering and scuffing, or, rushing thickly in when the negro maid opened the door, climbing and sprawling on to the bed and into Miss Reba's lap with wheezy, flatulent sounds, billowing into the rich pneumasis of her breast and tonguing along the metal tankard which she waved in one ringed hand as she talked.

'Anybody in Memphis can tell you who Reba Rivers is. Ask any man on the street, cop or not. I've had some of the biggest men in Memphis right here in this house, bankers, lawyers, doctors – all of them. I've had two police captains drinking beer in my dining-room and the commissioner himself upstairs with one of my girls. They got drunk and crashed the door·in on him and found him buck-nekkid, dancing the highland fling. A man fifty years old, seven foot tall, with a head like a peanut. He was a fine fellow. He knew me. They all know Reba Rivers. Spent their money here like water, they have. They know me. I ain't never double-crossed nobody, honey.' She drank beer, breathing thickly into the tankard, the other hand, ringed with yellow diamonds as large as gravel, lost among the lush billows of her breast.

Her slightest movement appeared to be accomplished by an expenditure of breath out of all proportion to any pleasure the movement could afford her. Almost as soon as they entered the house she began to tell Temple about her asthma, toiling up the stairs in front of them, planting her feet heavily in worsted bedroom slippers, a wooden rosary in one hand and the tankard in the other. She had just returned from church, in a black silk gown and a hat savagely flowered; the lower half of the tankard was still frosted with inner chill. She moved heavily from big thigh to thigh, the two-dogs moiling underfoot, talking steadily back across her shoulder in a harsh, expiring, maternal voice.

'Popeye knew better than to bring you anywhere else but to my house. I been after him for, how many years I been after you to get you a girl, honey? What I say, a young fellow can't no more live without a girl than . . .' panting, she fell to cursing the dogs under her feet, stopping to shove them aside. 'Get back down there,' she said, shaking the rosary at them. They snarled at her in vicious falsetto, baring their teeth, and she leaned against the wall in a thin aroma of beer, her hand to her breast, her mouth open, her eyes fixed in a glare of sad terror of all breathing as she sought breath, the tankard a squat soft gleam like dull silver lifted in the gloom.

The narrow stairwell turned back upon itself in a succession of niggard reaches. The light, falling through a thickly-curtained door at the front and through a shuttered window at the rear of each stage, had a weary quality. A spent quality; defunctive, exhausted – a protracted weariness like a vitiated backwater beyond sunlight and the vivid noises of sunlight and day. There was a defunctive odour of irregular food, vaguely alcoholic, and Temple even in her ignorance seemed to be surrounded by a ghostly promiscuity of intimate garments, of discreet whispers, of flesh stale and oft-assailed and impregnable beyond each silent door which they passed. Behind her, about hers and Miss Reba's feet, the two dogs scrabbled in nappy gleams, their claws clicking on the metal strips which bound the carpet to the stairs.

Later, lying in bed, a towel wrapped about her naked loins, she could hear them sniffing and whining outside the door. Her coat and hat hung on nails on the door, her dress and stockings lay upon a chair, and it seemed to her that she could hear the rhythmic splash-splash of the washingboard somewhere, and she flung herself again in an agony for concealment as she had when they took her knickers off.

'Now, now,' Miss Reba said. 'I bled for four days, myself. It ain't nothing. Doctor Quinn'll stop it in two minutes, and Minnie'll have them all washed and pressed and you won't never know it. That blood'll be worth a thousand dollars to you, honey.' She lifted the tankard, the flowers on her hat rigidly moribund, nodding in macabre wassail. 'Us poor girls,' she said. The drawn shades, cracked into a myriad patterns like old skin, blew faintly on the bright air, breathing into the room on waning surges the sound of sabbath traffic, festive, steady, evanescent. Temple lay motionless in the bed, her legs straight and close, in covers to her chin and her face small and wan, framed in the rich sprawl of her hair. Miss Reba lowered the tankard, gasping for breath. In her hoarse, fainting voice she began to tell Temple how lucky she was.

'Every girl in the district has been trying to get him, honey. There's one, a little married woman slips down here sometimes, she offered Minnie twenty-five dollars just to get him into the room, that's all. But do you think he'd so much as look at one of them? Girls that have took in a hundred dollars a night. No, sir. Spend his money like water, but do you think he'd look at one of them except to dance with her? I always knowed it wasn't going to be none of these here common whores he'd take. I'd tell them, I'd say, the one of yez that gets him'll wear diamonds, I says, but it ain't going to be none of you common whores, and now Minnie'll have them washed and pressed until you won't know it.'

'I can't wear it again,' Temple whispered. 'I can't.'

'No more you'll have to if you don't want. You can give them to Minnie, though I don't know what she'll do with them except maybe –' At the door the dogs began to whimper louder. Feet approached. The door opened. A negro maid entered, carrying a tray bearing a quart bottle of beer and a glass of gin, the dogs surging in around her feet. 'And tomorrow the stores'll be open and me and you'll go shopping, like he said for us to. Like I said, the girl that gets him'll wear diamonds: you just see if I wasn't –' she turned, mountainous, the tankard lifted, as the two dogs scrambled on to the bed and then on to her lap, snapping viciously at one another. From their curled shapeless faces bead-like eyes blared with choleric ferocity, their mouths gaped pinkly upon needle-like teeth. 'Reba' Miss Reba said, 'get down! You, Mr Binford!' flinging them down, their teeth clicking about her hands. 'You just bite me, you – Did you get Miss – What's your name, honey? I didn't quite catch it.'

'Temple,' Temple whispered.

'I mean, your first name, honey. We don't stand on no ceremony here.'

'That's it. Temple. Temple Drake.'

'You got a boy's name, ain't you? – Miss Temple's things washed, Minnie?'

'Yessum,' the maid said. 'Hit's dryin now 'hind the stove.' She came with the tray, shoving the dogs gingerly aside while they clicked their teeth at her ankles.

'You wash it out good?'

'I had a time with it,' Minnie said. 'Seem like the most hardest blood of all to get –' With a convulsive movement Temple flopped over, ducking her head beneath the covers. She felt Miss Reba's hand.

'Now, now. Now, now. Here, take your drink. This one's on me. I ain't going to let no girl of Popeye's –'

'I don't want any more,' Temple said.

'Now, now,' Miss Reba said. 'Drink it and you'll feel better.' She lifted Temple's head. Temple clutched the covers to her throat. Miss Reba held the glass to her lips. She gulped it, writhed down again, clutching the covers about her, her eyes wide and black above the covers. 'I bet you got that towel disarranged,' Miss Reba said, putting her hand on the covers.

'No,' Temple whispered. 'It's all right. It's still there.' She shrank, cringing; they could see the cringing of her legs beneath the covers.

'Did you get Dr Quinn, Minnie?' Miss Reba said.

'Yessum.' Minnie was filling the tankard from the bottle, a dull frosting pacing the rise of liquor within the metal. 'He say he don't make no Sunday afternoon calls.'

'Did you tell him who wanted him? Did you tell him Miss Reba wanted him?'

'Yessum. He say he don't –'

'You go back and tell that suh – You tell him I'll – No; wait.' She rose heavily. 'Sending a message like that back to me, that can put him in jail three times over.' She waddled towards the door, the dogs crowding about the felt slippers. The maid followed and closed the door. Temple could hear Miss Reba cursing the dogs as she descended the stairs with terrific slowness. The sounds died away.

The shades blew steadily in the windows, with faint rasping sounds. Temple began to hear a clock. It sat on the mantel above a grate filled with fluted green paper. The clock was of flowered china, supported by four china nymphs. It had only one hand, scrolled and gilded, half-way between ten and eleven, lending to the otherwise blank face a quality of unequivocal assertion, as though it had nothing whatever to do with time.

Temple rose from the bed. Holding the towel about her she stole towards the door, her ears acute, her eyes a little blind with the strain of listening. It was twilight; in a dim mirror, a pellucid oblong of dusk set on end, she had a glimpse of herself like a thin ghost, a pale shadow moving in the uttermost profundity of shadow. She reached the door. At once she began to hear a hundred conflicting sounds in a single converging threat and she clawed furiously at the door until she found the bolt, dropping the towel to drive it home. Then she caught up the towel, her face averted, and ran back and sprang into the bed and clawed the covers to her chin and lay there, listening to the secret whisper of her blood.

They knocked at the door for some time before she made any sound. 'It's the doctor, honey,' Miss Reba panted harshly. 'Come on, now. Be a good girl.'

'I can't,' Temple said, her voice faint and small. 'I'm in bed.'

'Come on, now. He wants to fix you up.' She panted harshly. 'My God, if I could just get one full breath again. I ain't had a full breath since . . .' Low down beyond the door Temple could hear the dogs. 'Honey.'

She rose from the bed, holding the towel about her. She went to the door, silently.

'Honey,' Miss Reba said.

'Wait,' Temple said. 'Let me get back to the bed before – Let me get –'

'There's a good girl,' Miss Reba said. 'I knowed she was going to be good.'

'Count ten, now,' Temple said. 'Will you count ten, now?' she said against the wood. She slipped the bolt soundlessly, then she turned and sped back to the bed, her naked feet in pattering diminuendo.

The doctor was a fattish man with thin, curly hair. He wore horn-rimmed glasses which lent to his eyes no distortion at all, as though they were of clear glass and worn for decorum's sake. Temple watched him across the covers, holding them to her throat. 'Make them go out,' she whispered; 'if they'll just go out.'

'Now, now,' Miss Reba said, 'he's going to fix you up.'

Temple clung to the covers.

'If the little lady will just let . . .' the doctor said. His hair evaporated finely from his brow. His mouth nipped in at the corners, his lips full and wet and red. Behind the glasses his eyes looked like little bicycle wheels at dizzy speed; a metallic hazel. He put out a thick, white hand bearing a masonic ring, haired over with fine reddish fuzz to the second knuckle-joints. Cold air slipped down her body, below her thighs; her eyes were closed. Lying on her back, her legs close together, she began to cry, hopelessly and passively, like a child in a dentist's waiting-room.

'Now, now,' Miss Reba said, 'take another sup of gin, honey. It'll make you feel better.'

In the window the cracked shade, yawning now and then with a faint rasp against the frame, let twilight into the room in fainting surges. From beneath the shade the smoke-coloured twilight emerged in slow puffs like signal smoke from a blanket, thickening in the room. The china figures which supported the clock gleamed in hushed smooth flexions: knee, elbow, flank, arm and breast in attitudes of voluptuous lassitude. The glass face, become mirror-like, appeared to hold all reluctant light, holding in its tranquil depths a quiet gesture of moribund time, one-armed like a veteran from the wars. Half-past ten o'clock. Temple lay in the bed, looking at the clock, thinking about half-past ten o'clock.

She wore a too-large gown of cerise crêpe, black against the linen. Her hair was a black sprawl, combed out now; her face, throat and arms outside the covers were grey. After the others left the room she lay for a time, head and all beneath the covers. She lay so until she heard the door shut and the descending feet, the doctor's light, unceasing voice and Miss Reba's laboured breath grow twilight-coloured in the dingy hall and die away. Then she sprang from the bed and ran to the door and shot the bolt and ran back and hurled the covers over her head again, lying in a tight knot until the air was exhausted.

A final saffron-coloured light lay upon the ceiling and the upper walls, tinged already with purple by the serrated palisade of Main Street high against the western sky. She watched it fade as the successive yawns of the shade consumed it. She watched the final light condense into the clock face, and the dial change from a round orifice in the darkness to a disc suspended in nothingness, the original chaos, and change in turn to a crystal ball holding in its still and cryptic depths the ordered chaos of the intricate and shadowy world upon whose scarred flanks the old wounds whirl onward at dizzy speed into darkness lurking with new disasters.

She was thinking about half-past ten o'clock. The hour for dressing for a dance, if you were popular enough not to have to be on time. The air would be steamy with recent baths, and perhaps powder in the light like chaff in barn-lofts, and they looking at one another, comparing, talking whether you could do more damage if you could just walk out on the floor like you were now. Some wouldn't, mostly ones with short legs. Some of them were all right, but they just wouldn't. They wouldn't say why. The worst one of all said boys thought all girls were ugly except when they were dressed. She said the Snake had been seeing Eve for several days and never noticed her until Adam made her put on a fig leaf. How do you know? they said, and she said because the Snake was there before Adam, because he was the first one thrown out of heaven; he was there all the time. But that wasn't what they meant and they said, How do you know? and Temple thought of her kind of backed up against the dressing-table and the rest of them in a circle around her with their combed hair and their shoulders smelling of scented soap and the light powder in the air and their eyes like knives until you could almost watch her flesh where the eyes were touching it, and her eyes in her ugly face courageous and frightened and daring, and they all saying, How do you know? until she told them and held up her hand and swore she had. That was when the youngest one turned and ran out of the room. She locked herself in the bath and they could hear her being sick.

She thought about half-past ten o'clock in the morning. Sunday morning, and the couples strolling towards church. She remembered it was still Sunday, the same Sunday, looking at the fading peaceful gesture of the clock. Maybe it was half-past ten this morning, that half-past ten o'clock. Then I'm not here, she thought. This is not me. Then I'm at school. I have a date tonight with ... thinking of the student with whom she had the date. But she couldn't remember who it would be. She kept the dates written down in her Latin 'pony', so she didn't have to bother about who it was. She'd just dress, and after a while somebody would call for her. So I better get up and dress, she said, looking at the clock.

She rose and crossed the room quietly. She watched the clock face, but although she could see a warped turmoil of faint light and shadow in geometric miniature swinging across it, she could not see herself. It's this nightie, she thought, looking at her arms, her breast rising out of a dissolving pall beneath which her toes peeped in pale, fleet intervals as she walked. She drew the bolt quietly and returned to the bed and lay with her head cradled in her arms.

There was still a little light in the room. She found that she was hearing her watch; had been hearing it for some time. She discovered that the house was full of noises, seeping into the room muffled and indistinguishable, as though from a distance. A bell rang faintly and shrilly somewhere; someone mounted the stairs in a swishing garment. The feet went on past the door and mounted another stair and ceased. She listened to the watch. A car started beneath the window with a grind of gears; again the faint bell rang, shrill and prolonged. She found that the faint light yet in the room was from a street lamp. Then she realized that it was night and that the darkness beyond was full of the sound of the city.

She heard the two dogs come up the stairs in a furious scrabble. The noise passed the door and stopped, became utterly still; so still that she could almost see them crouching there in the dark against the wall, watching the stairs. One of them was named Mister something, Temple thought, waiting to hear Miss Reba's feet on the stairs. But it was not Miss Reba; they came too steadily and too lightly. The door opened; the dogs surged in in two shapeless blurs and scuttled under the bed and crouched, whimpering. 'You, dawgs!' Minnie's voice said. 'You make me spill this.' The light came on. Minnie carried a tray. 'I got you some supper,' she said. 'Where them dawgs gone to?'

'Under the bed,' Temple said. 'I don't want any.'

Minnie came and set the tray on the bed and looked down at Temple, her pleasant face knowing and placid. 'You want me to –' she said, extending her hand. Temple turned her face quickly away. She heard Minnie kneel, cajoling the dogs, the dogs snarling back at her with whimpering, asthmatic snarls and clicking teeth. 'Come outen there, now,' Minnie said. 'They know fo Miss Reba do when she fixing to get drunk. You, Mr Binford!'

Temple raised her head. 'Mr Binford?'

'He the one with the blue ribbon,' Minnie said. Stooping, she flapped her arm at the dogs. They were backed against the wall at the head of the bed, snapping and snarling at her in mad terror. 'Mr Binford was Miss Reba's man. Was landlord here eleven years until he die bout two years ago. Next day Miss Reba get these dawgs, name one Mr Binford and other Miss Reba. Whenever she go to the cemetery she start drinking like this evening, then they both got to run. But Mr Binford ketch it sho nough. Last time she throw him outen upstair window and go down and empty Mr Binford's clothes closet and throw everything out in the street except what he buried in.'

'Oh,' Temple said. 'No wonder they're scared. Let them stay under there. They won't bother me.'

'Reckon I have to. Mr Binford ain't going to leave this room, not if he know it.' She stood again, looking at Temple. 'Eat that supper,' she said. 'You feel better. I done slip you a drink of gin, too.'

'I don't want any,' Temple said, turning her face away. She heard Minnie leave the room. The door closed quietly. Under the bed the dogs crouched against the wall in that rigid and furious terror.

The light hung from the centre of the ceiling, beneath a fluted shade of rose-coloured paper browned where the bulb bulged it. The floor was covered by a figured maroon-tinted carpet tacked down in strips; the olive-tinted walls bore two framed lithographs. From the two windows curtains of machine lace hung, dust-coloured, like strips of lightly congealed dust set on end. The whole room had an air of musty stodginess, decorum; in the wavy mirror of a cheap varnished dresser, as in a stagnant pool, there seemed to linger spent ghosts of voluptuous gestures and dead lusts. In the corner, upon a faded scarred strip of oilcloth tacked over the carpet, sat a wash-stand bearing a flowered bowl and pitcher and a row of towels; in the corner behind it sat a slop jar dressed also in fluted rose-coloured paper.

Beneath the bed the dogs made no sound. Temple moved slightly; the dry complaint of mattress and springs died into the terrific silence in which they crouched. She thought of them, woolly, shapeless; savage, petulant, spoiled, the flatulent monotony of their sheltered lives snatched up without warning by an incomprehensible moment of terror and fear of bodily annihilation at the very hands which symbolized by ordinary the licensed tranquillity of their lives.

The house was full of sounds. Indistinguishable, remote, they came in to her with a quality of awakening, resurgence, as though the house itself had been asleep, rousing itself with dark; she heard something which might have been a burst of laughter in a shrill woman voice. Steamy odours from the tray drifted across her face. She turned her head and looked at it, at the covered and uncovered dishes of thick china. In the midst of them sat the glass of pale gin, a pack of cigarettes and a box of matches. She rose on her elbow, catching up the slipping gown. She lifted the covers upon a thick steak, potatoes, green peas; rolls; an anonymous pinkish mass which some sense – elimination, perhaps – identified as a sweet. She drew the slipping gown up again, thinking about them eating down at school in a bright uproar of voices and clattering forks; of her father and brothers at the supper table at home; thinking about the borrowed gown and Miss Reba saying that they would go shopping tomorrow. And I've just got two dollars, she thought.

When she looked at the food she found that she was not hungry at all, didn't even want to look at it. She lifted the glass and gulped it empty, her face wry, and set it down and turned her face hurriedly from the tray, fumbling for the cigarettes. When she went to strike the match she looked at the tray again and took up a strip of potato gingerly in her fingers and ate it. She ate another, the unlighted cigarette in her other hand. Then she put the cigarette down and took up the knife and fork and began to eat, pausing from time to time to draw the gown up on to her shoulder.

When she finished eating she lit the cigarette. She heard the bell again, then another in a slightly different key. Across a shrill rush of a woman's voice a door banged. Two people mounted the stairs and passed the door; she heard Miss Reba's voice booming from somewhere and listened to her toiling slowly up the stairs. Temple watched the door until it opened and Miss Reba stood in it, the tankard in her hand. She now wore a bulging house dress and a widow's bonnet with a veil. She entered on the flowered felt slippers. Beneath the bed the two dogs made a stifled concerted sound of utter despair.

The dress, unfastened in the back, hung lumpily about Miss Reba's shoulders. One ringed hand lay on her breast, the other held the tankard high. Her open mouth, studded with gold fillings, gaped upon the harsh labour of her breathing.

'Oh God oh God,' she said. The dogs surged out from beneath the bed and hurled themselves towards the door in a mad scramble. As they rushed past her she turned and flung the tankard at them. It struck the door jamb, splashing up the wall, and rebounded with a forlorn clatter. She drew her breath whistling, clutching her breast. She came to the bed and looked down at Temple through the veil. 'We was happy as two doves,' she wailed, choking, her rings smouldering in hot glints within her billowing breast. 'Then he had to go and die on me.' She drew her breath whistling, her mouth gaped, shaping the hidden agony of her thwarted lungs, her eyes pale and round with stricken bafflement, protuberant. 'As two doves,' she roared in a harsh, choking voice.

Again time had overtaken a dead gesture behind the clock crystal: Temple's watch on the table beside the bed said half-past ten. For two hours she had lain undisturbed, listening. She could distinguish voices now from below stairs. She had been hearing them for some time, lying in the room's musty isolation. Later a mechanical piano began to play. Now and then she heard automobile brakes in the street beneath the window; once two voices quarrelling bitterly came up and beneath the shade.

She heard two people – a man and a woman – mount the stairs and enter the room next hers. Then she heard Miss Reba toil up the stairs and pass her door, and lying in the bed, her eyes wide and still, she heard Miss Reba hammering at the next door with the metal tankard and shouting in to the wood. Beyond the door the man and woman were utterly quiet, so quiet that Temple thought of the dogs again, thought of them crouching against the wall under the bed in that rigid fury of terror and despair. She listened to Miss Reba's voice shouting hoarsely into the blank wood. It died away into terrific gasping, then it rose again in the gross and virile cursing of a man. Beyond the wall the man and woman made no sound. Temple lay staring at the wall beyond which Miss Reba's voice rose again as she hammered at the door with the tankard.

Temple neither saw nor heard her door when it opened. She just happened to look towards it after how long she did not know, and saw Popeye standing there, his hat slanted across his face. Still without making any sound he entered and shut the door and shot the bolt and came towards the bed. As slowly she began to shrink into the bed, drawing the covers up to her chin, watching him across the covers. He came and looked down at her. She writhed slowly in a cringing movement, cringing upon herself in as complete an isolation as though she were bound to a church steeple. She grinned at him, her mouth warped over the rigid, placative porcelain of her grimace.

When he put his hand on her she began to whimper. 'No, no,' she whispered, 'he said I can't now he said . . .' He jerked the covers back and flung them aside. She lay motionless, her palms lifted, her flesh beneath the envelope of her loins cringing rearward in furious disintegration like frightened people in a crowd. When he advanced his hand again she thought he was going to strike her. Watching his face, she saw it beginning to twitch and jerk like that of a child about to cry, and she heard him begin to make a whimpering sound. He gripped the top of the gown. She caught his wrists and began to toss from side to side, opening her mouth to scream. His hand clapped over her mouth, and gripping his wrist, the saliva drooling between his fingers, her body thrashing furiously from thigh to thigh, she saw him crouching beside the bed, his face wrung above his absent chin, his bluish lips protruding as though he were blowing upon hot soup, making a high whinnying sound like a horse. Beyond the wall Miss Reba filled the hall, the house, with a harsh choking uproar of obscene cursing.

Chapter Nineteen

'But that girl,' Horace said. 'She was all right. You know she was all right when you left the house. When you saw her in the car with him. He was just giving her a lift to town. She was all right. You know she was all right.'

The woman sat on the edge of the bed, looking down at the child. It lay beneath the faded, clean blanket, its hands upflung beside its head, as though it had died in the presence of an unbearable agony which had not had time to touch it. Its eyes were half open, the balls rolled back into the skull so that only the white showed, in colour like weak milk. Its face was still damp with perspiration, but its breathing was easier. It no longer breathed in those weak, whistling gasps as it had when Horace entered the room. On a chair beside the bed sat a tumbler half full of faintly discoloured water, with a spoon in it. Through the open window came the myriad noises of the square – cars, wagons, footsteps on the pavement beneath – and through it Horace could see the court-house, with men pitching dollars back and forth between holes in the bare earth beneath the locust and water oaks.

The woman brooded above the child. 'Nobody wanted her out there. Lee has told them and told them they must not bring women out there, and I told her before it got dark they were not her kind of people and to get away from there. It was that fellow that brought her. He was out there on the porch with them, still drinking, because when he came in to supper he couldn't hardly walk, even. He hadn't even tried to wash the blood off of his face. Little shirt-tail boys that think because Lee breaks the law, they can come out there and treat our house like a . . . Grown people are bad, but at least they take buying whisky like buying anything else; it's the ones like him, the ones that are too young to realize that people don't break the law just for a holiday.' Horace could see her clenched hands writhing in her lap. 'God, if I had my way, I'd hang every man that makes it or buys it or drinks it, every one of them.

'But why must it have been me, us? What had I ever done to her, to her kind? I told her to get away from there. I told her not to stay there until dark. But that fellow that brought her was getting drunk again, and him and Van picking at each other. If she'd just stopped running around where they had to look at her. She wouldn't stay anywhere. She'd just dash out one door, and in a minute she'd come running in from the other direction. And if he'd just let Van alone, because Van had to go back on the truck at midnight, and so Popeye would have made him behave. And Saturday night too, and them sitting up all night drinking anyway, and I had gone through it and gone through it and I'd tell Lee to let's get away, that he was getting nowhere, and he would have these spells like last night, and no doctor, no telephone. And then she had to come out there, after I had slaved for him, slaved for him.' Motionless, her head bent and her hands still in her lap, she had that spent immobility of a chimney rising above the ruin of a house in the aftermath of a cyclone.

'Standing there in the corner behind the bed, with that raincoat on. She was that scared, when they brought the fellow in, all bloody again. They laid him on the bed and Van hit him again and Lee caught Van's arm, and her standing there with her eyes like the holes in one of these masks. The raincoat was hanging on the wall, and she had it on, over her coat. Her dress was all folded up on the bed. They threw the fellow right on top of it, blood and all, and I said, "God, are you drunk too?" But Lee just looked at me and I saw that his nose was white already, like it gets when he's drunk.

There wasn't any lock on the door, but I thought that pretty soon they'd have to go and see about the truck and then I could do something. Then Lee made me go out too, and he took the lamp out, so I had to wait until they went back to the porch before I could go back. I stood just inside the door. The fellow was snoring, in the bed there, breathing hard, with his nose and mouth all battered up again, and I could hear them on the porch. Then they would be outdoors, around the house and at the back too I could hear them. Then they got quiet.

'I stood there, against the wall. He would snore and choke and catch his breath and moan, sort of, and I would think about that girl lying there in the dark, with her eyes open, listening to them, and me having to stand there, waiting for them to go away so I could do something. I told her to go away. I said "What fault is it of mine if you're not married? I don't want you here a bit more than you want to be here." I said "I've lived my life without any help from people of your sort; what right have you got to look to me for help?" Because I've done everything for him. I've been in the dirt for him. I've put everything behind me and all I asked was to be let alone.

'Then I heard the door open. I could tell Lee by the way he breathes. He went to the bed and said "I want the raincoat. Sit up and take it off" and I could hear the shucks rattling while he took it off of her, then he went out. He just got the raincoat and went out. It was Van's coat.

'And I have walked around that house so much at night, with those men there, men living off of Lee's risk, men that wouldn't lift a finger for him if he got caught, until I could tell any of them by the way they breathed, and I could tell Popeye by the smell of that stuff on his hair. Tommy was following him. He came in the door behind Popeye and looked at me and I could see his eyes, like a cat. Then his eyes went away and I could feel him sort of squatting against me, and we could hear Popeye over where the bed was and that fellow snoring and snoring.

'I could just hear little faint sounds, from the shucks, so I knew it was all right yet, and in a minute Popeye came on back, and Tommy followed him out, creeping along behind him, and I stood there until I heard them go down to the truck. Then I went to the bed. When I touched her she began to fight. I was trying to put my hand over her mouth so she couldn't make a noise, but she didn't anyway. She just lay there, thrashing about, rolling her head from one side to the other, holding to the coat. ' "You fool!" I says "It's me – the woman." '

'But that girl,' Horace said. 'She was all right. When you were coming back to the house the next morning after the baby's bottle, you saw her and knew she was all right.' The room gave on to the square. Through the window he could see the young men pitching dollars in the court-house yard, and the wagons passing or tethered about the hitching chains, and he could hear the footsteps and voices of people on the slow and unhurried pavement below the window; the people buying comfortable things to take home and eat at quiet tables. 'You know she was all right.'

That night Horace went out to his sister's, in a hired car; he did not telephone. He found Miss Jenny in her room. 'Well,' she said. 'Narcissa will –'

'I don't want to see her,' Horace said. 'Her nice, well-bred young man. Her Virginia gentleman. I know why he didn't come back.'

'Who? Gowan?'

'Yes; Gowan. And, by the Lord, he'd better not come back. By God, when I think that I had the opportunity –'

'What? What did he do?'

'He carried a little fool girl out there with him that day and got drunk and ran off and left her. That's what he did. If it hadn't been for that woman – And when I think of people like that walking the earth with impunity just because he has a balloon-tailed suit and went through the astonishing experience of having attended Virginia . . . On any train or in any hotel, on the street; anywhere, mind you –'

'Oh,' Miss Jenny said. 'I didn't understand at first who you meant. Well,' she said. 'You remember that last time he was here, just after you came? the day he wouldn't stay for supper and went to Oxford?'

'Yes. And when I think how I could have –'

'He asked Narcissa to marry him. She told him that one child was enough for her.'

'I said she has no heart. She cannot be satisfied with less than insult.'

'So he got mad and said he would go to Oxford, where there was a woman he was reasonably confident he would not appear ridiculous to: something like that. Well.' She looked at him, her neck bowed to see across her spectacles. 'I'll declare, a male parent is a funny thing, but just let a man have a hand in the affairs of a female that's no kin to him ... What is it that makes a man think that the female flesh he marries or begets might misbehave, but all he didn't marry or get is bound to?'

'Yes,' Horace said, 'and thank God she isn't my flesh and blood. I can reconcile myself to her having to be exposed to a scoundrel now and then, but to think that at any moment she may become involved with a fool.'

'Well, what are you going to do about it? Start some kind of roach campaign?'

'I'm going to do what she said; I'm going to have a law passed making it obligatory upon everyone to shoot any man less than fifty years old that makes, buys, sells, or thinks whisky ... scoundrel I can face, but to think of her being exposed to any fool ...'

He returned to town. The night was warm, the darkness filled with the sound of new-fledged cicadas. He was using a bed, one chair, a bureau on which he had spread a towel and upon which lay his brushes, his watch, his pipe and tobacco pouch, and, propped against a book, a photograph of his stepdaughter, Little Belle. Upon the glazed surface a highlight lay. He shifted the photograph until the face came clear. He stood before it, looking at the sweet, inscrutable face which looked in turn at something just beyond his shoulder, out of the dead cardboard. He was thinking of the grape arbour in Kinston, of summer twilight and the murmur of voices darkening into silence as he approached, who meant them, her, no harm; who meant her less than harm, good God; darkening into the pale whisper of her white dress, of the delicate and urgent mammalian whisper of that curious small flesh which he had not begot and in which appeared to be vatted delicately some seething sympathy with the blossoming grape.

He moved, suddenly. As of its own accord the photograph had shifted, slipping a little from its precarious balancing against the book. The image blurred into the highlight, like something familiar seen beneath disturbed though clear water; he looked at the familiar image with a kind of quiet horror and despair, at a face suddenly older in sin than he would ever be, a face more blurred than sweet, at eyes more secret than soft. In reaching for it, he knocked it flat; whereupon once more the face mused tenderly behind the rigid travesty of the painted mouth, contemplating something beyond his shoulder. He lay in bed, dressed, with the light burning, until he heard the court-house clock strike three. Then he left the house, putting his watch and his tobacco pouch into his pocket.

The railroad station was three-quarters of a mile away. The waiting-room was lit by a single weak bulb. It was empty save for a man in overalls asleep on a bench, his head on his folded coat, snoring, and a woman in a calico dress, in a dingy shawl and a new hat trimmed with rigid and moribund flowers set square and awkward on her head. Her head was bent; she may have been asleep; her hands crossed on a paper-wrapped parcel upon her lap, a straw suitcase at her feet. It was then that Horace found that he had forgot his pipe.

The train came, finding him tramping back and forth along the cinder-packed right-of-way. The man and woman got on, the man carrying his rumpled coat, the woman the parcel and the suitcase. He followed them into the day coach filled with snoring, with bodies sprawled half into the aisle as though in the aftermath of a sudden and violent destruction, with dropped heads, open-mouthed, their throats turned profoundly upwards as though waiting the stroke of knives.

He dozed. The train clicked on, stopped, jolted. He waked and dozed again. Someone shook him out of sleep into a primrose dawn, among unshaven puffy faces washed lightly over as though with the paling ultimate stain of a holocaust, blinking at one another with dead eyes into which personality returned in secret opaque waves. He got off, had breakfast, and took another accommodation, entering a car where a child wailed hopelessly, crunching peanut-shells under his feet as he moved up the car in a stale ammoniac odour until he found a seat beside a man. A moment later the man leaned forward and spat tobacco juice between his knees. Horace rose quickly and went forward into the smoking-car. It was full too, the door between it and the jim crow car swinging open. Standing in the aisle he could look forward into a diminishing corridor of green plush seat-backs topped by hatted cannonballs swaying in unison, while gusts of talk and laughter blew back and kept in steady motion the blue acrid air in which white men sat, spitting into the aisle.

He changed again. The waiting crowd was composed half of young men in collegiate clothes with small cryptic badges on their shirts and vests, and two girls with painted small faces and scant bright dresses like identical artificial flowers surrounded each by bright and restless bees. When the train came they pushed gaily forward, talking and laughing, shouldering aside older people with gay rudeness, clashing and slamming seats back and settling themselves, turning their faces up out of laughter, their cold faces still toothed with it, as three middle-aged women moved down the car, looking tentatively left and right at the filled seats.

The two girls sat together, removing a fawn and a blue hat, lifting slender hands and preening not-quite-formless fingers about their close heads seen between the sprawled elbows and the leaning heads of two youths hanging over the back of the seat and surrounded by coloured hat-bands at various heights where the owners sat on the seat arms or stood in the aisle; and presently the conductor's cap as he thrust among them with plaintive, fretful cries, like a bird.

'Tickets. Tickets, please,' he chanted. For an instant they held him there, invisible save for his cap. Then two young men slipped swiftly back and into the seat behind Horace. He could hear them breathing. Forward the conductor's punch clicked twice. He came on back. 'Tickets,' he chanted. 'Tickets.' He took Horace's and stopped where the youths sat.

'You already got mine,' one said. 'Up there.'

'Where's your check?' the conductor said.

'You never gave us any. You got our tickets, though. Mine was number –' He repeated a number glibly, in a frank, pleasant tone. 'Did you notice the number of yours, Shack?'

The second one repeated a number in a frank, pleasant tone. 'Sure you got ours. Look and see.' He began to whistle between his teeth, a broken dance rhythm, unmusical.

'Do you eat at Gordon hall?' the other said.

'No. I have natural halitosis.' The conductor went on. The whistle reached crescendo, clapped off by his hands on his knees, ejaculating duh-duh-duh. Then he just squalled, meaningless, vertiginous; to Horace it was like sitting before a series of printed pages turned in furious snatches, leaving a series of cryptic, headless and tailless evocations on the mind.

'She's travelled a thousand miles without a ticket.'

'Marge too.'

'Beth too.'

'Duh-duh-duh.'

'Marge too.'

'I'm going to punch mine Friday night.'

'Eeeeyow.'

'Do you like liver?'

'I can't reach that far.'

'Eeeeeyow.'

They whistled, clapping their heels on the floor to furious crescendo, saying duh-duh-duh. The first jolted the seat back against Horace's head. He rose. 'Come on,' he said. 'He's done gone.' Again the seat jarred into Horace and he watched them return and join the group that blocked the aisle, saw one of them lay his bold, rough hand flat upon one of the bright, soft faces uptilted to them. Beyond the group a countrywoman with an infant in her arms stood braced against a seat. From time to time she looked back at the blocked aisle and the empty seats beyond.

At Oxford he descended into a throng of them at the station, hatless, in bright dresses, now and then with books in their hands and surrounded still by swarms of coloured shirts. Impassable, swinging hands with their escorts, objects of casual and puppyish pawings, they dawdled up the hill towards the college, swinging their little hips, looking at Horace with cold, blank eyes as he stepped off the walk in order to pass them.

At the top of the hill three paths diverged through a broad grove beyond which, in green vistas, buildings in red brick or grey stone gleamed, and where a clear soprano bell began to ring. The procession became three streams, thinning rapidly upon the dawdling couples, swinging hands, strolling in erratic surges, lurching into one another with puppyish squeals, with the random intense purposelessness of children.

The broader path led to the post office. He entered and waited until the window was clear.

'I'm trying to find a young lady, Miss Temple Drake. I probably just missed her, didn't I?'

'She's not here any longer,' the clerk said. 'She quit school about two weeks ago.' He was young: a dull, smooth face behind horn glasses, the hair meticulous. After a time Horace heard himself asking quietly:

'You don't know where she went?'

The clerk looked at him. He leaned, lowering his voice: 'Are you another detective?'

'Yes,' Horace said, 'yes. No matter. It doesn't matter.' Then he was walking quietly down the steps, into the sunlight again. He stood there while on both sides of him they passed in a steady stream of little coloured dresses, bare-armed, with close bright heads, with that identical cool, innocent, unabashed expression which he knew well in their eyes, above the savage identical paint upon their mouths; like music moving, like honey poured in sunlight, pagan and evanescent and serene, thinly evocative of all lost days and outpaced delights, in the sun. Bright, trembling with heat, it lay in open glades of mirage-like glimpses of stone or brick: columns without tops, towers apparently floating above a green cloud in slow ruin against the south-west wind, sinister, imponderable, bland; and he standing there listening to the sweet cloistral bell, thinking Now what? What now? and answering himself : Why, nothing. Nothing. It's finished.

He returned to the station an hour before the train was due, a filled but unlighted cob pipe in his hand. In the lavatory he saw, scrawled on the foul, stained wall, her pencilled name. Temple Drake. He read it quietly, his head bent, slowly fingering the unlighted pipe.

A half-hour before the train came they began to gather, strolling down the hill and gathering along the platform with thin, bright, raucous laughter, their blonde legs monotonous, their bodies moving continually inside their scant garments with that awkward and voluptuous purposelessness of the young.

The return train carried a pullman. He went on through the day coach and entered it. There was only one other occupant: a man in the centre of the car, next the window, bareheaded, leaning back, his elbow on the window-sill and an unlighted cigar in his ringed hand. When the train drew away, passing the sleek crowns in increasing reverse, the other passenger rose and went forward towards the day coach. He carried an overcoat on his arm, and a soiled, light-coloured felt hat. With the corner of his eye Horace saw his hand fumbling at his breast pocket, and he remarked the severe trim of hair across the man's vast, soft, white neck. Like with a guillotine, Horace thought, watching the man sidle past the porter in the aisle and vanish, passing out of his sight and his mind in the act of flinging the hat on to his head. The train sped on, swaying on the curves, flashing past an occasional house, through cuts and across valleys where young cotton wheeled slowly in fanlike rows.

The train checked speed; a jerk came back, and four whistle-blasts. The man in the soiled hat entered, taking a cigar from his breast pocket. He came down the aisle swiftly, looking at Horace. He slowed, the cigar in his fingers. The train jolted again. The man flung his hand out and caught the back of the seat facing Horace.

'Ain't this Judge Benbow?' he said. Horace looked up into a vast, puffy face without any mark of age or thought whatever – a majestic sweep of flesh on either side of a small blunt nose, like looking out over a mesa, yet withal some indefinable quality of delicate paradox, as though the Creator had completed his joke by lighting the munificent expenditure of putty with something originally intended for some weak, acquisitive creature like a squirrel or a rat. 'Don't I address Judge Benbow?' he said, offering his hand. 'I'm Senator Snopes, Cla'ence Snopes.'

'Oh,' Horace said, 'yes. Thanks,' he said, 'but I'm afraid you anticipate a little. Hope, rather.'

The other waved the cigar, the other hand, palm-up, the third finger discoloured faintly at the base of a huge ring, in Horace's face. Horace shook it and freed his hand. 'I thought I recognized you when you got on at Oxford,' Snopes said, 'but I – May I set down?' he said, already shoving at Horace's knee with his leg. He flung the overcoat – a shoddy blue garment with a greasy velvet collar – on the seat and sat down as the train stopped. 'Yes, sir, I'm always glad to see any of the boys, any time . . .' He leaned across Horace and peered out the window at a small dingy station with its cryptic bulletin board chalked over, an express truck bearing a wire chicken coop containing two forlorn fowls, at three or four men in overalls gone restfully against the wall, chewing. "Course you ain't in my country no longer, but what I say a man's friends is his friends, whichever way they vote. Because a friend is a friend, and whether he can do anything for me or not . . .' He leaned back, the unlighted cigar in his fingers. 'You ain't come all the way up from the big town, then.'

'No,' Horace said.

'Any time you're in Jackson, I'll be glad to accommodate you as if you was still in my county. Don't no man stay so busy he ain't got time for his old friends, what I say. Let's see, you're in Kinston, now, ain't you? I know your senators. Fine men, both of them, but I just cain't call their names.'

'I really couldn't say, myself,' Horace said. The train started. Snopes leaned into the aisle, looking back. His light grey suit had been pressed but not cleaned. 'Well,' he said. He rose and took up the overcoat. 'Any time you're in the city . . . You going to Jefferson, I reckon?'

'Yes,' Horace said.

'I'll see you again, then.'

'Why not ride back here?' Horace said. 'You'll find it more comfortable.'

'I'm going up and have a smoke,' Snopes said, waving the cigar. 'I'll see you again.'

'You can smoke here. There aren't any ladies.'

'Sure,' Snopes said. 'I'll see you at Holly Springs.' He went on back towards the day coach and passed out of sight with the cigar in his mouth. Horace remembered him ten years ago as a hulking, dull youth, son of a restaurant-owner, member of a family which had been moving from the Frenchman's Bend neighbourhood into Jefferson for the past twenty years, in sections; a family of enough ramifications to have elected him to the legislature without recourse to a public polling.

He sat quite still, the cold pipe in his hand. He rose and went forward through the day coach, then into the smoker. Snopes was in the aisle, his thigh draped over the ann of a seat where four men sat, using the unlighted cigar to gesture with. Horace caught his eye and beckoned from the vestibule. A moment later Snopes joined him, the overcoat on his arm.

'How are things going at the capital?' Horace said.

Snopes began to speak in his harsh, assertive voice. There emerged gradually a picture of stupid chicanery and petty corruption for stupid and petty ends, conducted principally in hotel rooms into which bellboys whisked with bulging jackets upon discreet flicks of skirts in swift closet doors. 'Any time you're in town,' he said. 'I always like to show the boys around. Ask anybody in town; they'll tell you if it's there, Cla'ence Snopes'll know where it is. You got a pretty tough case up home there, what I hear.'

'Can't tell yet,' Horace said. He said: 'I stopped off at Oxford today, at the university, speaking to some of my stepdaughter's friends. One of her best friends is no longer in school there. A young lady from Jackson named Temple Drake.'

Snopes was watching him with thick, small, opaque eyes. 'Oh yes; Judge Drake's gal,' he said. 'The one that ran away.'

'Ran away?' Horace said. 'Ran back home, did she? What was the trouble? Fail in her work?'

'I don't know. When it come out in the paper, folks thought she'd run off with some fellow. One of them companionate marriages.'

'But when she turned up at home, they knew it wasn't that, I reckon. Well, well, Belle'll be surprised. What's she doing now?

Running around Jackson, I suppose?'

'She ain't there.'

'Not?' Horace said. He could feel the other watching him. 'Where is she?'

'Her paw sent her up north somewhere, with an aunt. Michigan. It was in the papers couple days later.'

'Oh,' Horace said. He still held the cold pipe, and he discovered his hand searching his pocket for a match. He drew a deep breath. 'That Jackson paper's a pretty good paper. It's considered the most reliable paper in the state, isn't it?'

'Sure,' Snopes said. 'You was at Oxford trying to locate her?'

'No, no. I just happened to meet a friend of my daughter who told me she had left school. Well, I'll see you at Holly Springs.'

'Sure,' Snopes said. Horace returned to the pullman and sat down and lit the pipe.

When the train slowed for Holly Springs he went to the vestibule, then he stepped quickly back into the car. Snopes emerged from the day coach as the porter opened the door and swung down the step, stool in hand. Snopes descended. He took something from his breast pocket and gave it to the porter. 'Here, George,' he said, 'have a cigar.'

Horace descended. Snopes went on, the soiled hat towering half a head above any other. Horace looked at the porter.

'He gave it to you did he?'

The porter chucked the cigar on his palm. He put it in his pocket.

'What're you going to do with it?' Horace said.

'I wouldn't give it to nobody I know,' the porter said.

'Does he do this very often?'

'Three-four times a year. Seems like I always git him, too . . . Thank' suh.'

Horace saw Snopes enter the waiting-room; the soiled hat, the vast neck, passed again out of his mind. He filled the pipe again.

From a block away he heard the Memphis-bound train come in. It was at the platform when he reached the station. Beside the open vestibule Snopes stood, talking with two youths in new straw hats, with something vaguely mentorial about his thick shoulders and his gestures. The train whistled. The two youths got on. Horace stepped back around the corner of the station.

When his train came he saw Snopes get on ahead of him and enter the smoker, Horace knocked out his pipe and entered the day coach and found a seat at the rear, facing backwards.

Chapter Twenty

As Horace was leaving the station at Jefferson a townward-bound car slowed beside him. It was the taxi which he used to go out to his sister's. 'I'll give you a ride, this time,' the driver said.

'Much obliged,' Horace said. He got in. When the car entered the square, the court-house clock said only twenty minutes past eight, yet there was no light in the hotel room window. 'Maybe the child's asleep,' Horace said. He said: 'If you'll just drop me at the hotel –' Then he found that the driver was watching him, with a kind of discreet curiosity.

'You been out of town today,' the driver said.

'Yes,' Horace said. 'What is it? What happened here today?'

'She ain't staying at the hotel any more. I heard Mrs Walker taken her in at the jail.'

'Oh,' Horace said. 'I'll get out at the hotel.'

The lobby was empty. After a moment the proprietor appeared: a tight, iron-grey man with a toothpick, his vest open upon a neat paunch. The woman was not there. 'It's these church ladies,' he said. He lowered his voice, the toothpick in his fingers. 'They come in this morning. A committee of them. You know how it is, I reckon.'

'You mean to say you let the Baptist church dictate who your guests shall be?'

'It's them ladies. You know how it is, once they get set on a thing. A man might just as well give up and do like they say. Of course, with me –'

'By God, if there was a man –'

'Shhhhhh,' the proprietor said. 'You know how it is when them –'

'But of course there wasn't a man who would – And you call yourself one, that'll let –'

'I got a certain position to keep up myself,' the proprietor said in a placative tone. 'If you come right down to it.' He stepped

back a little, against the desk. 'I reckon I can say who'll stay in
my house and who won't,' he said. 'And I know some more folks
around here that better do the same thing. Not a mile off, neither.
I ain't beholden to no man. Not to you, noways.'

'Where is she now? or did they drive her out of town?'

'That ain't my affair, where folks go after they check out,' the
proprietor said, turning his back. He said: 'I reckon somebody
took her in, though.'

'Yes,' Horace said. 'Christians. Christians.' He turned towards
the door. The proprietor called him. He turned. The other was
taking a paper down from a pigeon-hole. Horace returned to the
desk. The paper lay on the desk. The proprietor leaned with his
hands on the desk, the toothpick tilted in his mouth.

'She said you'd pay it,' he said.

He paid the bill, counting the money down with shaking hands.
He entered the jail yard and went to the door and knocked. After
a while a lank, slattern woman came with a lamp, holding a man's
coat across her breast. She peered at him and said before he
could speak:

'You're lookin' fer Miz Goodwin, I reckon.'

'Yes. How did – Did –'

'You're the lawyer. I've seed you befo'. She's hyer. Sleepin'
now.'

'Thanks,' Horace said. 'Thanks. I knew that someone – I didn't
believe that –'

'I reckon I kin always find a bed fer a woman and child,' the
woman said. 'I don't keer whut Ed says. Was you wantin' her
special? She's sleepin' now.'

'No, no; I just wanted to –'

The woman watched him across the lamp. ''Tain't no need
botherin' her, then. You kin come around in the mawnin' and
git her a boa'din-place.'Tain't no hurry.'

On the next afternoon Horace went out to his sister's, again
in a hired car. He told her what had happened. 'I'll have to take
her home now.'

'Not into my house,' Narcissa said.

He looked at her. Then he began to fill his pipe slowly and
carefully. 'It's not a matter of choice, my dear. You must see
that.'

'Not in my house,' Narcissa said. 'I thought we settled that.'

He struck the match and lit the pipe and put the match carefully into the fireplace. 'Do you realize that she has been practically turned into the streets? That –'

'That shouldn't be a hardship. She ought to be used to that.'

He looked at her. He put the pipe in his mouth and smoked it to a careful coal, watching his hand tremble upon the stem. 'Listen. By tomorrow they will probably ask her to leave town. Just because she happens not to be married to the man whose child she carries about these sanctified streets. But who told them? That's what I want to know. I know that nobody in Jefferson knew it except –'

'You were the first I heard tell it,' Miss Jenny said. 'But Narcissa, why –'

'Not in my house,' Narcissa said.

'Well,' Horace said. He drew the pipe to an even coal. 'That settles it, of course,' he said, in a dry, light voice.

She rose. 'Will you stay here tonight?'

'What? No. No. I'll – I told her I'd come for her at the jail and . . .' He sucked at his pipe. 'Well, I don't suppose it matters. I hope it doesn't.'

She was still paused, turning. 'Will you stay or not?'

'I could even tell her I had a puncture,' Horace said. 'Time's not such a bad thing after all. Use it right, and you can stretch anything out, like a rubber band, until it busts somewhere, and there you are, with all tragedy and despair in two little knots between thumb and finger of each hand.'

'Will you stay, or won't you stay, Horace?' Narcissa said.

'I think I'll stay,' Horace said.

He was in bed. He had been lying in the dark for about an hour, when the door of the room opened, felt rather than seen or heard. It was his sister. He rose to his elbow. She took shape vaguely, approaching the bed. She came and looked down at him. 'How much longer are you going to keep this up?' she said.

'Just until morning,' he said. 'I'm going back to town. You need not see me again.'

She stood beside the bed, motionless. After a moment her cold unbending voice came down to him: 'You know what I mean.'

'I promise not to bring her into your house again. You can send Isom in to hide in the canna bed.' She said nothing. 'Surely you don't object to my living there, do you?'

'I don't care where you live. The question is, where I live. I live here, in this town. I'll have to stay here. But you're a man. It doesn't matter to you. You can go away.'

'Oh,' he said. He lay quite still. She stood above him, motionless. They spoke quietly, as though they were discussing wallpaper, food.

'Don't you see, this is my home, where I must spend the rest of my life. Where I was born. I don't care where else you go nor what you do. I don't care how many women you have nor who they are. But I cannot have my brother mixed up with a woman people are talking about. I don't expect you to have consideration for me; I ask you to have consideration for our father and mother. Take her to Memphis. They say you refused to let the man have bond to get out of jail; take her on to Memphis. You can think of a lie to tell him about that, too.'

Oh. So you think that, do you?'

'I don't think anything about it. I don't care. That's what people in town think. So it doesn't matter whether it's true or not. What I do mind is, every day you force me to have to tell lies for you. Go away from here, Horace. Anybody but you would realize it's a case of cold-blooded murder.'

'And over her, of course. I suppose they say that too, out of their odorous and omnipotent sanctity. Do they say yet that it was I killed him?'

'I don't see that it makes any difference who did it. The question is, are you going to stay mixed up with it? When people already believe you and she are slipping into my house at night.' Her cold, unbending voice shaped the words in the darkness above him. Through the window, upon the blowing darkness, came the drowsy dissonance of cicada and cricket.

'Do you believe that?' he said.

'It doesn't matter what I believe. Go on away, Horace. I ask it.'

'And leave her – them, flat?'

'Hire a lawyer, if he still insists he's innocent. I'll pay for it. You can get a better criminal lawyer than you are. She won't know it. She won't even care. Can't you see that she is just leading you on to get him out of jail for nothing? Don't you know that woman has got money hidden away somewhere? You're going back into town tomorrow, are you?' She turned, began to dissolve into the blackness. 'You won't leave before breakfast.'

The next morning at breakfast, his sister said: 'Who will be the lawyer on the other side of the case?'

'District Attorney. Why?'

She rang the bell and sent for fresh bread. Horace watched her. 'Why do you ask that?' Then he said: 'Damn little squirt.' He was talking about the District Attorney, who had also been raised in Jefferson and who had gone to the town school with them. 'I believe he was at the bottom of that business night before last. The hotel. Getting her turned out of the hotel for public effect, political capital. By God, if I knew that, believed that he had done that just to get elected to Congress . . .'

After Horace left, Narcissa went up to Miss Jenny's room. 'Who is the District Attorney?' she said.

'You've known him all your life,' Miss Jenny said. 'You even elected him. Eustace Graham. What do you want to know for? Are you looking around for a substitute for Gowan Stevens?'

'I just wondered,' Narcissa said.

'Fiddlesticks,' Miss Jenny said. 'You don't wonder. You just do things and then stop until the next time to do something comes around.'

Horace met Snopes emerging from the barber-shop, his jowls grey with powder, moving in an effluvium of pomade. In the bosom of his shirt, beneath his bow-tie, he wore an imitation ruby stud which matched his ring. The tie was of blue polka-dots; the very white spots on it appeared dirty when seen close; the whole man with his shaved neck and pressed clothes and gleaming shoes emanated somehow the idea that he had been dry-cleaned rather than washed.

'Well, Judge,' he said, 'I hear you're having some trouble gettin' a boarding-place for that client of yourn. Like I always say' – he leaned, his voice lowered, his mud-coloured eyes roving aside – 'the church ain't got no place in politics, and women ain't got no place in neither one, let alone the law. Let them stay at home and they'll find plenty to do without upsetting a man's law-suit. And besides, a man ain't no more than human, and what he does ain't nobody's business but his. What you done with her?'

'She's at the jail,' Horace said. He spoke shortly, making to pass on. The other blocked his way with an effect of clumsy accident.

'You got them all stirred up, anyhow. Folks is saying you wouldn't git Goodwin no bond, so he'd have to stay –' again Horace made to pass on. 'Half the trouble in this world is caused by women, I always say. Like that girl gittin' her paw all stirred up, running off, like she done. I reckon he done the right thing sending her clean outen the State.'

'Yes,' Horace said in a dry, furious voice.

'I'm mighty glad to hear your case is going all right. Between you and me, I'd like to see a good lawyer make a monkey outen that District Attorney. Give a fellow like that a little county office and he gits too big for his pants right away. Well, glad to've saw you. I got some business up town for a day or two. I don't reckon you'll be going up that-a-way?'

'What?' Horace said. 'Up where?'

'Memphis. Anything I can do for you?'

'No,' Horace said. He went on. For a short distance he could not see at all. He tramped steadily, the muscles beside his jaws beginning to ache, passing people who spoke to him, unawares.

Chapter Twenty-one

As the train neared Memphis Virgil Snopes ceased talking and began to grow quieter and quieter, while on the contrary his companion, eating from a paraffin-paper package of popcorn and molasses, grew livelier and livelier with a quality something like intoxication, seeming not to notice the inverse state of his friend. He was still talking away when, carrying their new, imitation leather suitcases, their new hats slanted above their shaven necks, they descended at the station. In the waiting-room Fonzo said:

'Well, what're we going to do first?' Virgil said nothing. Someone jostled them; Fonzo caught at his hat. 'What we going to do?' he said. Then he looked at Virgil, at his face. 'What's the matter?'

'Ain't nothing the matter,' Virgil said.

'Well, what're we going to do? You been here before. I ain't.'

'I reckon we better kind of look around,' Virgil said.

Fonzo was watching him, his blue eyes like china. 'What's the matter with you? All the time on the train you was talking about how many times you been to Memphis. I bet you ain't never bu –'

Someone jostled them, thrust them apart; a stream of people

began to flow between them. Clutching his suitcase and hat Fonzo fought his way back to his friend.

'I have, too,' Virgil said, looking glassily about.

'Well, what we going to do then? It won't be open till eight o'clock in the morning.'

'What you in such a rush for, then?'

'Well, I don't aim to stay here all night ... What did you do when you was here before?'

'Went to the hotel,' Virgil said.

'Which one? They got more than one here. You reckon all these folks could stay in one hotel? Which one was it?'

Virgil's eyes were also a pale, false blue. He looked glassily about. 'The Gayoso Hotel,' he said.

'Well, let's go to it,' Fonzo said. They moved towards the exit. A man shouted 'taxi' at them; a redcap tried to take Fonzo's bag. 'Look out,' he said, drawing it back. On the street more cabmen barked at them.

'So this is Memphis,' Fonzo said. 'Which way is it, now?' He had no answer. He looked around and saw Virgil in the act of turning away from a cabman. 'What you?'

'Up this way,' Virgil said. 'It ain't far.'

It was a mile and a half. From time to time they swapped hands with the bags. 'So this is Memphis,' Fonzo said. 'Where have I been all my life?' When they entered the Gayoso a porter offered to take the bags. They brushed past him and entered, walking gingerly on the tile floor. Virgil stopped.

'Come on,' Fonzo said.

'Wait,' Virgil said.

'Thought you was here before,' Fonzo said.

'I was. This hyer place is too high. They'll want a dollar a day here.'

'What we going to do, then?'

'Let's kind of look around.'

They returned to the street. It was five o'clock. They went on, looking about, carrying the suitcases. They came to another hotel. Looking in they saw marble, brass cuspidors, hurrying bellboys, people sitting among potted plants.

'That un'll be just as bad,' Virgil said.

'What we going to do, then? We cain't walk around all night.'

'Let's git off this hyer street,' Virgil said. They left Main Street. At the next corner Virgil turned again. 'Let's look down this-a-way. Git away from all that 'ere plate glass and monkey niggers.

That's what you have to pay for in them places.'

'Why? It's already bought when we got there. How come we have to pay for it?'

'Suppose somebody broke it while we was there. Suppose they couldn't ketch who done it. Do you reckon they'd let us out withouten we paid our share?'

At five-thirty they entered a narrow dingy street of frame houses and junk yards. Presently they came to a three-storey house in a small grassless yard. Before the entrance a latticework false entry leaned. On the steps sat a big woman in a mother hubbard, watching two fluffy white dogs which moved about the yard.

'Let's try that un,' Fonzo said.

'That ain't no hotel. Where's ere sign?'

'Why ain't it?' Fonzo said. "Course it is. Who ever heard of anybody just living in a three-storey house?'

'We can't go in this-a-way,' Virgil said. 'This hyer's the back. Don't you see that privy?' jerking his head towards the lattice.

'Well, let's go around to the front, then,' Fonzo said. 'Come on.'

They went around the block. The opposite side was filled by a row of automobile sales-rooms. They stood in the middle of the block, their suitcases in their right hands.

'I don't believe you was ever here before, noways,' Fonzo said.

'Let's go back. That must a been the front.'

'With the privy built on to the front door?' Fonzo said. 'We can ask that lady.'

'Who can? I ain't.'

'Let's go back and see, anyway.'

They returned. The woman and the dogs were gone.

'Now you done it,' Fonzo said. 'Ain't you?'

'Let's wait a while. Maybe she'll come back.'

'It's almost seven o'clock,' Fonzo said.

They set the bags down beside the fence. The lights had come on, quivering high in the serried windows against the tall serene western sky.

'I can smell ham, too,' Fonzo said.

A cab drew up. A plump blonde woman got out, followed by a man. They watched them go up the walk and enter the lattice. Fonzo sucked his breath across his teeth. 'Durned if they didn't,' he whispered.

'Maybe it's her husband,' Virgil said.

Fonzo picked up his bag. 'Come on.'

'Wait,' Virgil said. 'Give them a little time.'

They waited. The man came out and got in the cab and went away.

'Cain't be her husband,' Fonzo said. 'I wouldn't a never left. Come on.' He entered the gate.

'Wait,' Virgil said.

'You can,' Fonzo said. Virgil took his bag and followed. He stopped while Fonzo opened the lattice gingerly and peered in. 'Aw, hell,' he said. He entered. There was another door, with curtained glass. Fonzo knocked.

'Why din't you push that ere button?' Virgil said. 'Don't you know city folks don't answer no knock?'

'All right,' Fonzo said. He rang the bell. The door opened. It was the woman in the mother hubbard; they could hear the dogs behind her.

'Got ere extra room?' Fonzo said.

Miss Reba looked at them, at their new hats and the suitcases. 'Who sent you here?' she said.

'Didn't nobody. We just picked it out.' Miss Reba looked at him. 'Them hotels is too high.'

Miss Reba breathed harshly. 'What you boys doing?'

'We come hyer on business,' Fonzo said. 'We aim to stay a good spell.'

'If it ain't too high,' Virgil said.

Miss Reba looked at him. 'Where you from, honey?'

They told her, and their names. 'We aim to be hyer a month or more, if it suits us.'

'Why, I reckon so,' she said after a while. She looked at them. 'I can let you have a room, but I'll have to charge you extra whenever you do business in it. I got my living to make like everybody else.'

'We ain't,' Fonzo said. 'We'll do our business at the college.'

'What college?' Miss Reba said.

'The barber's college,' Fonzo said.

'Look here,' Miss Reba said, 'you little whipper-snapper.' Then she began to laugh, her hand at her breast. They watched her soberly while she laughed in harsh gasps. 'Lord, Lord,' she said. 'Come in here.'

The room was at the top of the house, at the back. Miss Reba showed them the bath. When she put her hand on the door a woman's voice said, 'Just a minute, dearie,' and the door opened and she passed them, in a kimono. They watched her go up the hall, rocked a little to their young foundations by the trail of scent which she left. Fonzo nudged Virgil surreptitiously. In their room again he said:

'That was another one. She's got two daughters. Hold me, big boy; I'm heading for the hen-house.'

They didn't go to sleep for some time that first night, what with the strange bed and room and the voices. They could hear the city, evocative and strange, imminent and remote; threat and promise both – a deep, steady sound upon which invisible lights glittered and wavered: coloured coiling shapes of splendour in which already women were beginning to move in suave attitudes of new delights and strange nostalgic promises. Fonzo thought of himself surrounded by tier upon tier of drawn shades, rose-coloured, beyond which, in a murmur of silk, in panting whispers, the apotheosis of his youth assumed a thousand avatars. Maybe it'll begin tomorrow, he thought; maybe by tomorrow night . . . A crack of light came over the top of the shade and sprawled in a spreading fan upon the ceiling. Beneath the window he could hear a voice, a woman's, then a man's: they blended, murmured; a door closed. Someone came up the stairs in swishing garments, on the swift hard heels of a woman.

He began to hear sounds in the house: voices, laughter; a mechanical piano began to play. 'Hear them?' he whispered.

'She's got a big family, I reckon,' Virgil said, his voice already dull with sleep.

'Family, hell,' Fonzo said. 'It's a party. Wish I was to it.'

On the third day as they were leaving the house in the morning, Miss Reba met them at the door. She wanted to use their room in the afternoons while they were absent. There was to be a detectives' convention in town and business would look up some, she said. 'Your things'll be all right. I'll have Minnie lock everything up beforehand. Ain't nobody going to steal nothing from you in my house.'

'What business you reckon she's in?' Fonzo said when they reached the street.

'Don't know,' Virgil said.

'Wish I worked for her, anyway,' Fonzo said. 'With all them women in kimonos and such running around.'

'Wouldn't do you no good,' Virgil said. 'They're all married. Ain't you heard them?'

The next afternoon when they returned from the school they

found a woman's undergarment under the washstand . . . Fonzo picked it up. 'She's a dressmaker,' he said.

'Reckon so,' Virgil said. 'Look and see if they taken anything of yourn.'

The house appeared to be filled with people who did not sleep at night at all. They could hear them at all hours, running up and down the stairs, and always Fonzo would be conscious of women, of female flesh. It got to where he seemed to lie in his celibate bed surrounded by women, and he would lie beside the steadily snoring Virgil, his ears strained for the murmurs, the whispers of silk that came through the walls and the floor, that seemed to be as much a part of both as the planks and the plaster, thinking that he had been in Memphis ten days, yet the extent of his acquaintance was a few of his fellow pupils at the school. After Virgil was asleep he would rise and unlock the door and leave it ajar, but nothing happened.

On the twelfth day he told Virgil they were going visiting, with one of the barber-students.

'Where?' Virgil said.

'That's all right. You come on. I done found out something. And when I think I been here two weeks without knowing about it –'

'What's it going to cost?' Virgil said.

'When'd you ever have any fun for nothing?' Fonzo said. 'Come on.'

'I'll go,' Virgil said. 'But I ain't going to promise to spend nothing.'

'You wait and say that when we get there,' Fonzo said.

The barber took them to a brothel. When they came out, Fonzo said, 'And to think I been here two weeks without never knowing about that house.'

'I wisht you hadn't never learned,' Virgil said. 'It cost three dollars.'

'Wasn't it worth it?' Fonzo said.

'Ain't nothing worth three dollars you cain't tote off with you,' Virgil said.

When they reached home Fonzo stopped. 'We got to sneak in, now,' he said. 'If she was to find out where we been and what we been doing, she might not let us stay in the house with them ladies no more.'

'That's so,' Virgil said. 'Durn you. Hyer you done made me

spend three dollars, and now you fixing to git us both throwed out.'

'You do like I do,' Fonzo said. 'That's all you got to do. Don't say nothing.'

Minnie let them in. The piano was going full blast. Miss Reba appeared in a door, with a tin cup in her hand. 'Well, well,' she said, 'you boys been out mighty late tonight.'

'Yessum,' Fonzo said, prodding Virgil towards the stairs. 'We been to a prayer-meeting.'

In bed, in the dark, they could still hear the piano.

'You made me spend three dollars,' Virgil said.

'Aw, shut up,' Fonzo said. 'When I think I been here for two whole weeks almost . . .'

The next afternoon they came home through the dusk, with the lights winking on, beginning to flare and gleam, and the women on their twinkling blonde legs meeting men and getting into automobiles and such.

'How about that three dollars now?' Fonzo said.

'I reckon we better not go over night,' Virgil said. 'It'll cost too much.'

'That's right,' Fonzo said. 'Somebody might see us and tell her.'

They waited two nights. 'Now it'll be six dollars,' Virgil said.

'Don't come, then,' Fonzo said.

When they returned home Fonzo said: 'Try to act like something, this time. She near about caught us before on account of the way you acted.'

'What if she does?' Virgil said in a sullen voice. 'She cain't eat us.'

They stood outside the lattice, whispering.

'How you know she cain't?' Fonzo said.

'She don't want to, then.'

'How you know she don't want to?'

'Maybe she don't,' Virgil said Fonzo opened the lattice door. 'I can't eat that six dollars, noways,' Virgjl said. 'Wisht I could.'

Minnie let them in. She said: 'Somebody huntin' you all.' They waited in the hall.

'We done caught now,' Virgil said. 'I told you about throwing that money away.'

'Aw, shut up,' Fonzo said.

A man emerged from a door, a big man with his hat cocked

over one ear, his arm about a blonde woman in a red dress. 'There's Cla'ence,' Virgil said.

In their room Clarence said: 'How'd you get into this place?'

'Just found it,' Virgil said. They told him about it. He sat on the bed, in his soiled hat, a cigar in his fingers.

'Where you been tonight?' he said. They didn't answer. They looked at him with blank, watchful faces. 'Come on. I know. Where was it?' They told him.

'Cost me three dollars, too,' Virgil said.

'I'll be durned if you ain't the biggest fool this side of Jackson,' Clarence said. 'Come on here.' They followed sheepishly. He led them from the house and for three or four blocks. They crossed a street of negro stores and theatres and turned into a narrow, dark street and stopped at a house with red shades in the lighted windows. Clarence rang the bell. They could hear music inside, and shrill voices, and feet. They were admitted into a bare hallway where two shabby negro men argued with a drunk white man in greasy overalls. Through an open door they saw a room filled with coffee-coloured women in bright dresses, with ornate hair and golden smiles.

'Them's niggers,' Virgil said.

''Course they're niggers,' Clarence said. 'But see this?' he waved a banknote in his cousin's face. 'This stuff is colour-blind.'

Chapter Twenty-two

On the third day of his search, Horace found a domicile for the woman and child. It was in the ramshackle house of an old half-crazed white woman who was believed to manufacture spells for negroes. It was on the edge of town, set in a tiny plot of ground choked and massed with waist-high herbage in an unbroken jungle across the front. At the back a path had been trodden from the broken gate to the door. All night a dim light burned in the crazy depths of the house and at almost any hour of the twenty-four a wagon or a buggy might be seen tethered in the lane behind it and a negro entering or leaving the back door.

The house had been entered once by officers searching for whisky. They found nothing save a few dried bunches of weeds, and a collection of dirty bottles containing liquid of which they could say nothing surely save that it was not alcoholic, while the old woman, held by two men, her lank greyish hair shaken before the glittering collapse of her face, screamed invective at them in her cracked voice. In a lean-to shed room containing a bed and a barrel of anonymous refuse and trash in which mice rattled all night long, the woman found a home.

'You'll be all right here,' Horace said. 'You can always get me by telephone, at –' giving her the name of a neighbour. 'No: wait; tomorrow I'll have the telephone put back in. Then you can –'

'Yes,' the woman said. 'I reckon you better not be coming out here.'

'Why? Do you think that would – that I'd care a damn what –'

'You have to live here.'

'I'm damned if I do. I've already let too many women run my affairs for me as it is, and if these uxorious . . .' But he knew he was just talking. He knew that she knew it too, out of that feminine reserve of unflagging suspicion of all people's actions which seems at first to be mere affinity for evil but which is in reality practical wisdom.

'I guess I'll find you if there's any need,' she said. 'There's not anything else I could do.'

'By God,' Horace said, 'don't you let them . . . Bitches,' he said; 'bitches.'

The next day he had the telephone installed. He did not see his sister for a week; she had no way of learning that he had a phone, yet when, a week before the opening of Court, the telephone shrilled into the quiet where he sat reading one evening, he thought it was Narcissa until, across a remote blaring of victrola or radio music, a man's voice spoke in a guarded, tomb-like tone.

'This is Snopes,' it said. 'How're you, Judge?'

'What?' Horace said. 'Who is it?'

'Senator Snopes, Cla'ence Snopes.' The victrola blared, faint, far away; he could see the man, the soiled hat, the thick shoulders, leaning above the instrument – in a drugstore or a restaurant – whispering into it behind a soft, huge, ringed hand, the telephone toylike in the other.

'Oh,' Horace said. 'Yes? What is it?'

'I got a little piece of information that might interest you.'

'Information that would interest me?'

'I reckon so. That would interest a couple of parties.' Against Horace's ear the radio or the victrola performed a reedy arpeggio of saxophones. Obscene, facile, they seemed to be quarrelling with one another like two dexterous monkeys in a cage. He could hear the gross breathing of the man at the other end of the wire.

'All right,' he said. 'What do you know that would interest me?'

'I'll let you judge that.'

'All right. I'll be down town in the morning. You can find me somewhere.' Then he said immediately: 'Hello!' The man sounded as though he were breathing in Horace's ear: a placid, gross sound, suddenly portentous somehow. 'Hello!' Horace said.

'It evidently don't interest you, then. I reckon I'll dicker with the other party and not trouble you no more. Good-bye.'

'No; wait,' Horace said. 'Hello! Hello!'

'Yeuh?'

'I'll come down tonight. I'll be there in about fifteen –'

'"Tain't no need of that,' Snopes said. 'I got my car. I'll drive up there.'

He walked down to the gate. There was a moon tonight. Within the black-and-silver tunnel of cedars fireflies drifted in fatuous pinpricks. The cedars were black and pointed on the sky like a paper silhouette; the sloping lawn had a faint sheen, a patina like silver. Somewhere a whippoorwill called, reiterant, tremulous, plaintful above the insects. Three cars passed. The fourth slowed and swung towards the gate. Horace stepped into the light. Behind the wheel Snopes loomed bulkily, giving the impression of having been inserted into the car before the top was put on. He extended his hand.

'How're you tonight, Judge? Didn't know you was living in town again until I tried to call you out at Mrs Sartoris's.'

'Well, thanks,' Horace said. He freed his hand. 'What's this you've got hold of?'

Snopes creased himself across the wheel and peered out beneath the top, towards the house.

'We'll talk here,' Horace said. 'Save you having to turn around.'

'It ain't very private here,' Snopes said. 'But that's for you to say.' Huge and thick he loomed, hunched, his featureless face moonlike itself in the refraction of the moon. Horace could feel Snopes watching him, with that sense of portent which had come over the wire; a quality calculating and cunning and pregnant. It seemed to him that he watched his mind flicking this way and that, striking always that vast, soft, inert bulk, as though it were caught in an avalanche of cottonseed-hulls.

'Let's go to the house,' Horace said. Snopes opened the door. 'Go on,' Horace said, 'I'll walk up.' Snopes drove on. He was getting out of the car when Horace overtook him. 'Well, what is it?' Horace said.

Again Snopes looked at the house. 'Keeping batch, are you?' he said. Horace said nothing. 'Like I always say, every married man ought to have a little place of his own, where he can git off to himself without it being nobody's business what he does. 'Course a man owes something to his wife, but what they don't know cain't hurt them, does it? Long's he does that, I cain't see where she's got ere kick coming. Ain't that what you say?'

'She's not here,' Horace said, 'if that's what you're hinting at. What did you want to see me about?'

Again he felt Snopes watching him, the unabashed stare calculating and completely unbelieving. 'Well, I always say, can't nobody tend to a man's private business but himself. I ain't blaming you. But when you know me better, you'll know I ain't loose-mouthed. I been around. I been there . . . Have a cigar?' His big hand flicked to his breast and offered two cigars.

'No, thanks.'

Snopes lit a cigar, his face coming out of the match like a pie set on edge.

'What did you want to see me about?' Horace said.

Snopes puffed the cigar. 'Couple days ago I come on to a piece of information which will be of value to you, if I ain't mistook.'

'Oh. Of value. What value?'

'I'll leave that to you. I got another party I could dicker with, but being as me and you was fellow-townsmen and all that.'

Here and there Horace's mind flicked and darted. Snopes's family originated somewhere near Frenchman's Bend and still lived there. He knew of the devious means by which information passed from man to man of that illiterate race which populated that section of the county. But surely it can't be something he'd try to sell to the State, he thought. Even he is not that big a fool.

'You'd better tell me what it is, then,' he said.

He could feel Snopes watching him. 'You remember one day you got on the train at Oxford, where you'd been on some bus –'

'Yes,' Horace said.

Snopes puffed the cigar to an even coal, carefully, at some length. He raised his hand and drew it across the back of his neck. 'You recall speaking to me about a girl.'

'Yes. Then what?'

'That's for you to say.'

He could smell the honeysuckle as it bore up the silver slope, and he heard the whippoorwill, liquid, plaintful, reiterant. 'You mean, you know where she is?' Snopes said nothing. 'And that for a price you'll tell?' Snopes said nothing. Horace shut his hands and put them in his pockets, shut against his flanks. 'What makes you think that information will interest me?'

'That's for you to judge. I ain't conducting no murder case. I wasn't down there at Oxford looking for her. Of course, if it don't, I'll dicker with the other party. I just give you the chance.'

Horace turned towards the steps. He moved gingerly, like an old man. 'Let's sit down,' he said. Snopes followed and sat on the step. They sat in the moonlight. 'You know where she is?'

'I seen her.' Again he drew his hand across the back of his neck. 'Yes, sir. If she ain't – hasn't been there, you can git your money back. I cain't say no fairer, can I?'

'And what's your price?' Horace said. Snopes puffed the cigar to a careful coal. 'Go on,' Horace said. 'I'm not going to haggle.' Snopes told him. 'All right,' Horace said. 'I'll pay it.' He drew his knees up and set his elbows on them and laid his hands to his face. 'Where is – Wait. Are you a Baptist, by any chance?'

'My folks is. I'm putty liberal, myself. I ain't hidebound in no sense, as you'll find when you know me better.'

'All right,' Horace said from behind his hands. 'Where is she?'

'I'll trust you,' Snopes said. 'She's in a Memphis 'ho-'house.'

Chapter Twenty-three

As Horace entered Miss Reba's gate and approached the lattice door, someone called his name from behind him. It was evening; the windows in the weathered, scaling wall were close pale squares. He paused and looked back. Around an adjacent corner Snopes's head peeped, turkey-like. He stepped into view. He looked up at the house, then both ways along the street. He came along the fence and entered the gate with a wary air.

'Well, Judge,' he said. 'Boys will be boys, won't they?' He didn't offer to shake hands. Instead he bulked above Horace with that air somehow assured and alert at the same time, glancing over his shoulder at the street. 'Like I say, it never done no man no harm to git out now and then and —'

'What is it now?' Horace said. 'What do you want with me?'

'Now, now, Judge. I ain't going to tell this at home. Git that idea clean out of your mind. If us boys started telling what we know, cain't none of us git off a train at Jefferson again, hey?'

'You know as well as I do what I'm doing here. What do you want with me?'

'Sure; sure,' Snopes said. 'I know how a feller feels, married and all and not being sho where his wife is at.' Between jerky glances over his shoulder he winked at Horace. 'Make your mind easy. It's the same with me as if the grave knowed it. Only I hate to see a good —' Horace had gone on towards the door. 'Judge,' Snopes said in a penetrant undertone. Horace turned. 'Don't stay.'

'Don't stay?'

'See her and then leave. It's a sucker place. Place for farmboys. Higher'n Monte Carlo. I'll wait out hyer and I'll show you a place where —' Horace went on and entered the lattice. Two hours later, as he sat talking to Miss Reba in her room while beyond the door feet and now and then voices came and went in the hall and on the stair, Minnie entered with a torn scrap of paper and brought it to Horace.

'What's that?' Miss Reba said.

'That big pie-face-ted man left it fer him,' Minnie said. 'He say fer you to come on down there.'

'Did you let him in?' Miss Reba said.

'Nome. He never tried to git in.'

'I guess not,' Miss Reba said. She grunted. 'Do you know him?' she said to Horace.

'Yes. I can't seem to help myself,' Horace said. He opened the paper. Torn from a handbill, it bore an address in pencil in a neat, flowing hand.

'He turned up here about two weeks ago,' Miss Reba said. 'Come in looking for two boys and sat around the dining-room blowing his head off and feeling the girls' behinds, but if he ever spent a cent I don't know it. Did he ever give you an order, Minnie?'

'Nome,' Minnie said.

'And a couple of nights later he was here again. Didn't spend nuttin, didn't do nuttin but talk, and I says to him "Look here, mister, folks what uses this waiting-room has got to get on the train now and then". So next time he brought a half-pint of whisky with him. I don't mind that, from a good customer. But when a fellow like him comes here three times, pinching my girls and bringing one half-pint of whisky and ordering four coca-colas . . . Just a cheap, vulgar man, honey. So I told Minnie not to let him in any more, and here one afternoon I ain't no more than laid down for a nap when – I never did find out what he done to Minnie to get in. I know he never give her nuttin. How did he do it, Minnie? He must a showed you something you never seen before. Didn't he?'

Minnie tossed her head. 'He ain't got nothing I wantin to see. I done seed too many now fer my own good.' Minnie's husband had quit her. He didn't approve of Minnie's business. He was a cook in a restaurant and he took all the clothes and jewellery the white ladies had given Minnie and went off with a waitress in the restaurant.

'He kept on asking and hinting around about that girl,' Miss Reba said, 'and me telling him to go ask Popeye if he wanted to know right bad. Not telling him nuttin except to get out and stay out, see; so this day it's about two in the afternoon and I'm asleep and Minnie let's him in and he asks her who's here and she tells him ain't nobody, and he goes on upstairs. And Minnie says about that time Popeye comes in. She says she don't know what to do. She's scared not to let him in, and she says she knows if she does and he spatters that big bastard all over the upstairs floor, she knows I'll fire her and her husband just quit her and all.

'So Popeye goes on upstairs on them cat feet of his and comes on your friend on his knees, peeping through the keyhole. Minnie says Popeye stood behind him for about a minute, with his hat cocked over one eye. She says he took out a cigarette and struck a match on his thumb-nail without no noise and lit it and then she says he reached over and held the match to the back of your friend's neck, and Minnie says she stood there half-way up the stairs and watched them: that fellow kneeling there with his face like a pie took out of the oven too soon and Popeye squirting smoke through his nose and kind of jerking his head at him. Then she come on down and in about ten seconds here he comes down the stairs with both hands on top of his head, going wump-wump-wump inside like one of these here big dray-horses, and he pawed at the door for about a minute, moaning to himself like the wind in a chimney, Minnie says, until she opened the door and let him out. And that's the last time he's even rung this bell until tonight . . . Let me see that.' Horace gave her the paper. 'That's a nigger whore-house,' she said. 'The lous — Minnie, tell him his friend ain't here. Tell him I don't know where he went.'

Minnie went out. Miss Reba said:

'I've had all sorts of men in my house, but I got to draw the line somewhere. I had lawyers, too. I had the biggest lawyer in Memphis back there in my dining-room, treating my girls. A millionaire. He weighed two hundred and eighty pounds and he had his own special bed made and sent down here. It's upstairs right this minute. But all in the way of my business, not theirs. I ain't going to have none of my girls pestered by lawyers without good reason.'

'And you don't consider this good reason? That a man is being tried for his life for something he didn't do? You may be guilty right now of harbouring a fugitive from justice.'

'Then let them come take him. I got nuttin to do with it. I had too many police in this house to be scared of them.' She raised the tankard and drank and drew the back of her hand across her mouth. 'I ain't going to have nuttin to do with nuttin I don't know about. What Popeye done outside is his business. When he starts killing folks in my house, then I'll take a hand.'

'Have you any children?' She looked at him. 'I don't mean to pry into your affairs,' he said. 'I was just thinking about that woman. She'll be on the streets again, and God only knows what will become of that baby.'

'Yes,' Miss Reba said. 'I'm supporting four, in a Arkansaw home now. Not mine, though.' She lifted the tankard and looked into it, oscillating it gently. She set it down again. 'It better not been born at all,' she said. 'None of them had.' She rose and came towards him, moving heavily, and stood above him with her harsh breath. She put her hand on his head and tilted his face up. 'You ain't lying to me, are you?' she said, her eyes piercing and intent and sad. 'No you ain't.' She released him. 'Wait here a minute. I'll see.' She went out. He heard her speak to Minnie in the hall, then he heard her toil up the stairs.

He sat quietly as she left him. The room contained a wooden bed, a painted screen, three over-stuffed chairs, a wall safe. The dressing-table was littered with toilet articles tied in pink satin bows. The mantel supported a wax lily beneath a glass bell; above it, draped in black, the photograph of a meek-looking man with an enormous moustache. On the walls hung a few lithographs of spurious Greek scenes, and one picture done in tatting. Horace rose and went to the door. Minnie sat in a chair in the dim hall.

'Minnie,' he said, 'I've got to have a drink. A big one.'

He had just finished it when Minnie entered again. 'She say fer you to come on up,' she said.

He mounted the stairs. Miss Reba waited at the top. She led the way up the hall and opened a door into a dark room. 'You'll have to talk to her in the dark,' she said. 'She won't have no light.' Light from the hall fell through the door and across the bed. 'This ain't hers,' Miss Reba said. 'Wouldn't even see you in her room at all. I reckon you better humour her until you find out what you want.' They entered. The light fell across the bed, upon a motionless curving ridge of bedclothing, the general tone of the bed unbroken. She'll smother, Horace thought. 'Honey,' Miss Reba said. The ridge did not move. 'Here he is, honey. Long as you're all covered up, let's have some light. Then we can close the door.' She turned the light on.

'She'll smother,' Horace said.

'She'll come out in a minute,' Miss Reba said. 'Go on. Tell her what you want. I better stay. But don't mind me. I couldn't a stayed in my business without learning to be deaf and dumb a long time before this. And if I'd ever a had any curiosity, I'd have worn it out long ago in this house. Here's a chair.' She turned, but Horace anticipated her and drew up two chairs. He sat down beside the bed and, talking at the top of the unstirring ridge, he told her what he wanted.

'I just want to know what really happened. You won't commit yourself. I know that you didn't do it. I'll promise before you tell me a thing that you won't have to testify in Court unless they are going to hang him without it. I know how you feel. I wouldn't bother you if the man's life were not at stake.'

The ridge did not move.

'They're going to hang him for something he never done,' Miss Reba said. 'And she won't have nuttin, nobody. And you with diamonds, and her with that poor little kid. You seen it, didn't you?'

The ridge did not move.

'I know how you feel,' Horace said. 'You can use a different name, wear clothes nobody will recognize you in, glasses.'

'They ain't going to catch Popeye, honey,' Miss Reba said. 'Smart as he is. You don't know his name, noway, and if you have to go and tell them in the court, I'll send him word after you leave and he'll go somewheres and send for you. You and him don't want to stay here in Memphis. The lawyer'll take care of you and you won't have to tell nuttin you –' The ridge moved. Temple flung the covers back and sat up. Her head was tousled, her face puffed, two spots of rouge on her cheekbones and her mouth painted into a savage cupid's bow. She stared for an instant at Horace with black antagonism, then she looked away.

'I want a drink,' she said, pulling up the shoulder of her gown.

'Lie down,' Miss Reba said. 'You'll catch cold.'

'I want another drink,' Temple said.

'Lie down and cover up your nekkidness, anyway,' Miss Reba said, rising. 'You already had three since supper.'

Temple dragged the gown up again. She looked at Horace. 'You give me a drink, then.'

'Come on, honey,' Miss Reba said, trying to push her down. 'Lie down and get covered up and tell him about that business. I'll get you a drink in a minute.'

'Let me alone,' Temple said, writhing free. Miss Reba drew the covers about her shoulders. 'Give me a cigarette, then. Have you got one?' she asked Horace.

'I'll get you one in a minute,' Miss Reba said. 'Will you do what he wants you to?'

'What?' Temple said. She looked at Horace with her black, belligerent stare.

'You needn't tell me where your – he –' Horace said.

'Don't think I'm afraid to tell,' Temple said. 'I'll tell it anywhere. Don't think I'm afraid. I want a drink.'

'You tell him, and I'll get you one,' Miss Reba said.

Sitting up in the bed, the covers about her shoulders, Temple told him of the night she had spent in the ruined house, from the time she entered the room and tried to wedge the door with the chair, until the woman came to the bed and led her out. That was the only part of the whole experience which appeared to have left any impression on her at all: the night which she had spent in comparative inviolation. Now and then Horace would attempt to get her on ahead to the crime itself, but she would elude him and return to herself sitting on the bed, listening to the men on the porch, or lying in the dark while they entered the room and came to the bed and stood there above her.

'Yes; that,' she would say. 'It just happened. I don't know. I had been scared so long that I guess I had just gotten used to being. So I just sat there in those cotton-seeds and watched him. I thought it was the rat at first. There were two of them there. One was in one corner looking at me and the other was in the other corner. I don't know what they lived on, because there wasn't anything there but corn-cobs and cotton-seeds. Maybe they went to the house to eat. But there wasn't any in the house. I never did hear one in the house. I thought it might have been a rat when I first heard them, but you can feel people in a dark room: did you know that? You don't have to see them. You can feel them like you can in a car when they begin to look for a good place to stop – you know: park for a while.' She went on like that, in one of those bright, chatty monologues which women can carry on when they realize that they have the centre of the stage; suddenly Horace realized that she was recounting the experience with actual pride, a sort of naïve and impersonal vanity, as though she were making it up, looking from him to Miss Reba with quick, darting glances like a dog driving two cattle along a lane.

'And so whenever I breathed I'd hear those shucks. I don't see how anybody ever sleeps on a bed like that. But maybe you get used to it. Or maybe they're tired at night. Because when I breathed I could hear them, even when I was just sitting on the bed. I didn't see how it could be just breathing, so I'd sit as still

as I could, but I could still hear them. That's because breathing
goes down. You think it goes up, but it doesn't. It goes down
you, and I'd hear them getting drunk on the porch. I got to
thinking I could see where their heads were leaning back against
the wall and I'd say Now this one's drinking out of the jug. Now
that one's drinking. Like the mashed-in place on the pillow after
you got up, you know.

'That was when I got to thinking a funny thing. You know how
you do when you're scared. I was looking at my legs and I'd try
to make like I was a boy. I was thinking about if I just was a boy
and then I tried to make myself into one by thinking. You know
how you do things like that. Like when you know one problem
in class and when they came to that you look at him and think
right hard, Call on me. Call on me. Call on me. I'd think about
what they tell children, about kissing your elbow, and I tried to.
I actually did. I was that scared, and I'd wonder if I could tell
when it happened. I mean, before I looked, and I'd think I had
and how I'd go out and show them – you know. I'd strike a match
and say Look. See? Let me alone, now. And then I could go back
to bed. I'd think how I could go to bed and go to sleep then,
because I was sleepy. I was so sleepy I simply couldn't hardly hold
my eyes open.

'So I'd hold my eyes tight shut and say Now I am. I am now.
I'd look at my legs and I'd think about how much I had done for
them. I'd think about how many dances I had taken them to –
crazy, like that. Because I thought how much I'd done for them,
and now they'd gotten me into this. So I'd think about praying
to be changed into a boy and I would pray and then I'd sit right
still and wait. Then I'd think maybe I couldn't tell it and I'd get
ready to look. Then I'd think maybe it was too soon to look; that
if I looked too soon I'd spoil it and then it wouldn't, sure enough.
So I'd count. I said to count fifty at first, then I thought it as still
too soon, and I'd say to count fifty more. Then I'd think if I
didn't look at the right time, it would be too late.

'Then I thought about fastening myself up some way. There
was a girl went abroad one summer that told me about a kind of
iron belt in a museum a king or something used to lock the queen
up in when he had to go away, and I thought if I just had that.
That was why I got the raincoat and put it on. The canteen was
hanging by it and I got it too and put it in the –'

'Canteen?' Horace said. 'Why did you do that?'

'I don't know why I took it. I was just scared to leave it there,

I guess. But I was thinking if I just had that French thing. I was thinking maybe it would have long sharp spikes on it and he wouldn't know it until too late and I'd jab it into him. I'd jab it all the way through him and I'd think about the blood running on me and how I'd say I guess that'll teach you! I guess you'll let me alone now! I'd say. I didn't know it was going to be just the other way . . . I want a drink.'

'I'll get you one in a minute,' Miss Reba said. 'Go on and tell him.'

'Oh,, yes; this was something else funny I did.' She told about lying in the darkness with Gowan snoring beside her, listening to the shucks and hearing the darkness full of movement, feeling Popeye approaching. She could hear the blood in her veins, and the little muscles at the corners of her eyes cracking faintly wider and wider, and she could feel her nostrils going alternately cool and warm. Then he was standing over and she was saying Come on. Touch me. Touch me! You're a coward if you don't. Coward! Coward!

'I wanted to go to sleep, you see. And he just kept on standing there. I thought if he'd just go on and get it over with, I could go to sleep. So I'd say You're a coward if you don't! You're a coward if you don't! and I could feel my mouth getting fixed to scream, and that little hot ball inside you that screams. Then it touched me, that nasty little cold hand, fiddling around inside the coat where I was naked. It was like alive ice and my skin started jumping away from it like those little flying-fish in front of a boat. It was like my skin knew which way it was going to go before it started moving, and my skin would keep on jerking just ahead of it like there wouldn't be anything there when the hand got there.

'Then it got down to where my insides begin, and I hadn't eaten since yesterday at dinner and my insides started bubbling and going on and the shucks began to make so much noise it was like laughing. I'd think they were laughing at me because all the time his hand was going inside the top of my knickers and I hadn't changed into a boy yet.

'That was the funny thing, because I wasn't breathing then. I hadn't breathed in a long time. So I thought I was dead. Then I did a funny thing. I could see myself in the coffin. I looked sweet – you know: all in white. I had on a veil like a bride, and I was crying because I was dead or looked sweet or something. No: it was because they had put shucks in the coffin. I was crying because they had put shucks in the coffin where I was dead, but all the time I could feel my nose going cold and hot and cold and hot, and I could see all the people sitting around the coffin, saying Don't she look sweet. Don't she look sweet.

'But I kept on saying Coward! Coward! Touch me, coward! I got mad, because he was so long doing it. I'd talk to him. I'd say Do you think I'm going to lie here all night, just waiting on you? I'd say. Let me tell you what I'll do, I'd say. And I'd lie there with the shucks laughing at me and me jerking away in front of his hand and I'd think what I'd say to him, I'd talk to him like the teacher does in school, and then I was a teacher in school and it was a little black thing like a nigger boy, kind of, and I was the teacher. Because I'd say How old am I? and I'd say I'm forty-five years old. I had iron-grey hair and spectacles and I was all big up here like women get. I had on a grey tailored suit, and I never could wear grey. And I was telling it what I'd do, and it kind of drawing up like it could already see the switch.

'Then I said That won't do. I ought to be a man. So I was an old man, with a long white beard, and then the little black man got littler and littler and I was saying Now. You see now. I'm a man now. Then I thought about being a man, and as soon as I thought it, it happened. It made a kind of plopping sound, like blowing a little rubber tube wrongside outward. It felt cold, like the inside of your mouth when you hold it open. I could feel it, and I lay right still to keep from laughing about how surprised he was going to be. I could feel the jerking going on inside my knickers ahead of his hand and me lying there trying not to laugh about how surprised and mad he was going to be in about a minute. Then all of a sudden I went to sleep. I couldn't even stay awake until his hand got there. I just went to sleep. I couldn't even feel myself jerking in front of his hand, but I could hear the shucks. I didn't wake up until that woman came and took me down to the crib.'

As he was leaving the house Miss Reba said: 'I wish you'd get her down there and not let her come back. I'd find her folks myself, if I knowed how to go about it. But you know how . . . She'll be dead, or in the asylum in a year, way him and her go on up there in that room. There's something funny about it that I ain't found out about yet. Maybe it's her. She wasn't born for this kind of life. You have to be born for this like you have to be born a butcher or a barber, I guess. Wouldn't anybody be either of them just for money or fun.'

Better for her if she were dead tonight, Horace thought, walking on. For me, too. He thought of her, Popeye, the woman, the child, Goodwin, all put into a single chamber, bare, lethal, immediate and profound: a single blotting instant between the indignation and the surprise. And I too, thinking how that were the only solution. Removed, cauterized out of the old and tragic flank of the world. And I, too, now that we're all isolated; thinking of a gentle dark wind blowing in the long corridors of sleep; of lying beneath a low cosy roof under the long sound of the rain: the evil, the injustice, the tears. In an alley-mouth two figures stood, face to face, not touching; the man speaking in a low tone unprintable epithet after epithet in a caressing whisper, the woman motionless before him as though in a musing swoon of voluptuous ecstasy. Perhaps it is upon the instant that we realize, admit, that there is a logical pattern to evil, that we die, he thought, thinking of the expression he had once seen in the eyes of a dead child, and of other dead: the cooling indignation, the shocked despair fading, leaving two empty globes in which the motionless world lurked profoundly in miniature.

He did not even return to his hotel. He went to the station. He could get a train at midnight. He had a cup of coffee and wished immediately that he had not, for it lay in a hot ball on his stomach. Three hours later, when he got off at Jefferson, it was still there, unassimilated. He walked to town and crossed the deserted square. He thought of the other morning when he had crossed it. It was as though there had not been any elapsed time between: the same gesture of the lighted clock-face, the same vulture-like shadows in the doorways; it might be the same morning and he had merely crossed the square, about-faced and was returning; all between a dream filled with all the nightmare shapes it had taken him forty-three years to invent, concentrated in a hot, hard lump in his stomach. Suddenly he was walking fast, the coffee jolting like a hot, heavy rock inside him.

He walked quietly up the drive, beginning to smell the honeysuckle from the fence. The house was dark, still, as though it were marooned in space by the ebb of all time. The insects had fallen to a low monotonous pitch, everywhere, nowhere, spent, as though the sound were the chemical agony of a world left stark and dying above the tide-edge of the fluid in which it lived and breathed. The moon stood overhead, but without light; the earth lay beneath, without darkness. He opened the door and felt his way into the room and to the light. The voice of the night

– insects, whatever it was – had followed him into the house; he knew suddenly that it was the friction of the earth on its axis, approaching that moment when it must decide to turn on or to remain forever still: a motionless ball in cooling space, across which a thick smell of honeysuckle writhed like cold smoke.

He found the light and turned it on. The photograph sat on the dresser. He took it up, holding it in his hands. Enclosed by the narrow imprint of the missing frame Little Belle's face dreamed with that quality of sweet chiaroscuro. Communicated to the cardboard by some quality of the light or perhaps by some infinitesimal movement of his hands, his own breathing, the face appeared to breathe in his palms in a shallow bath of highlight, beneath the slow, smoke-like tongues of invisible honeysuckle. Almost palpable enough to be seen, the scent filled the room and the small face seemed to swoon in a voluptuous languor, blurring still more, fading, leaving upon his eye a soft and fading aftermath of invitation and voluptuous promise and secret affirmation like a scent itself.

Then he knew what that sensation in his stomach meant. He put the photograph down hurriedly and went to the bathroom. He opened the door running and fumbled at the light. But he had not time to find it and he gave over and plunged forward and struck the lavatory and leaned upon his braced arms while the shucks set up a terrific uproar beneath her thighs. Lying with her head lifted slightly, her chin depressed like a figure lifted down from a crucifix, she watched something black and furious go roaring out of her pale body. She was bound naked on her back on a flat car moving at speed through a black tunnel, the blackness streaming in rigid threads overhead, a roar of iron wheels in her ears. The car shot bodily from the tunnel in a long upward slant, the darkness overhead now shredded with parallel attenuations of living fire, towards a crescendo like a held breath, an interval in which she would swing faintly and lazily in nothingness filled with pale, myriad points of light. Far beneath her she could hear the faint, furious uproar of the shucks.

Chapter Twenty-four

The first time Temple went to the head of the stairs Minnie's eyeballs rolled out of the dusky light beside Miss Reba's door. Leaning once more within her bolted door Temple heard Miss Reba toil up the stairs and knock. Temple leaned silently against the door while Miss Reba panted and wheezed beyond it with a mixture of blandishment and threat. She made no sound. After a while Miss Reba went back down the stairs.

Temple turned from the door and stood in the centre of the room, beating her hands silently together, her eyes black in her livid face. She wore a street dress, a hat. She removed the hat and hurled it into a corner and went and flung herself face down upon the bed. The bed had not been made. The table beside it was littered with cigarette stubs, the adjacent floor strewn with ashes. The pillow-slip on that side was spotted with brown holes. Often in the night she would wake to smell tobacco and to see the single ruby eye where Popeye's mouth would be.

It was mid-morning. A thin bar of sunlight fell beneath the drawn shade of the south window, lying upon the sill and then upon the floor in a narrow band. The house was utterly quiet, with that quality as of spent breathing which it had in mid-morning. Now and then a car passed in the street beneath.

Temple turned over on the bed. When she did so she saw one of Popeye's innumerable black suits lying across a chair. She lay looking at it for a while, then she rose and snatched the garments up and hurled them into the corner where the hat was. In another corner was a closet improvised by a print curtain. It contained dresses of all sorts and all new. She ripped them down in furious wads and flung them after the suit, and a row of hats from a shelf. Another of Popeye's suits hung there also. She flung it down. Behind it hanging from a nail, was an automatic pistol in a holster of oiled silk. She took it down gingerly and removed the pistol and stood with it in her hand. After a moment she went to the bed and hid it beneath the pillow.

The dressing-table was cluttered with toilet-things – brushes and mirrors, also new; with flasks and jars of delicate and bizarre shapes, bearing French labels. One by one she gathered them up and hurled them into the corner in thuds and splintering crashes. Among them lay a platinum bag: a delicate webbing of metal upon the smug orange gleam of banknotes. This followed the other things into the corner and she returned to the bed and lay again on her face in a slow thickening of expensive scent.

At noon Minnie tapped at the door. 'Here yo' dinner.' Temple didn't move, 'I ghy leave it here by the door. You can git it when you wants it.' Her feet went away. Temple did not move.

Slowly the bar of sunlight shifted across the floor; the western side of the window-frame was now in shadow. Temple sat up, her head turned aside as though she were listening, fingering with deft habitude at her hair. She rose quietly and went to the door and listened again. Then she opened it. The tray sat on the floor. She stepped over it and went to the stairs and peered over the rail. After a while she made Minnie out, sitting in a chair in the hall.

'Minnie,' she said. Minnie's head jerked up; again her eyes rolled whitely. 'Bring me a drink,' Temple said. She returned to her room. She waited fifteen minutes. She banged the door and was tramping furiously down the stairs when Minnie appeared in the hall.

'Yessum,' Minnie said, 'Miss Reba say – We ain't got no –' Miss Reba's door opened. Without looking up at Temple she spoke to Minnie. Minnie lifted her voice again. 'Yessum; all right. I bring it up in just a minute.'

'You'd better,' Temple said. She returned and stood just inside the door until she heard Minnie mount the stairs. Temple opened the door, holding it just ajar.

'Ain't you going to eat no dinner?' Minnie said, thrusting at the door with her knee. Temple held it to.

'Where is it?'she said.

'I ain't straightened your room this mawnin',' Minnie said.

'Give it here,' Temple said, reaching her hand through the crack. She took the glass from the tray.

'You better make that un last,' Minnie said. 'Miss Reba say you ain't ghy git no more . . . What you want to treat him this-a-way, fer? Way he spend his money on you, you ought to be ashamed. He a right pretty little man, even if he ain't no John Gilbert, and

way he spendin' his money –' Temple shut the door and shot the
bolt. She drank the gin and drew a chair up to the bed and lit a
cigarette and sat down with her feet on the bed. After a while
she moved the chair to the window and lifted the shade a little
so she could see the street beneath. She lit another cigarette.

At five o'clock she saw Miss Reba emerge, in the black silk and
flowered hat, and go down the street. She sprang up and dug the
hat from the mass of clothes in the corner and put it on. At the
door she turned and went back to the corner and exhumed the
platinum purse and descended the stairs. Minnie was in the hall.

'I'll give you ten dollars,' Temple said. 'I won't be gone ten
minutes.'

'I cain't do it, Miss Temple. Hit be worth my job if Miss Reba
find it out, and my th'oat too, if Mist Popeye do.'

'I swear I'll be back in ten minutes. I swear I will. Twenty
dollars.' She put the bill in Minnie's hand.

'You better come back,' Minnie said, opening the door. 'If you
ain't back here in ten minutes, I ain't going to be, neither.'

Temple opened the lattice and peered out. The street was
empty save for a taxi at the kerb across the way, and a man in a
cap standing in a door beyond it. She went down the street,
walking swiftly. At the corner a cab overtook her, slowing, the
driver looking at her interrogatively. She turned into the drug-
store at the corner and went back to the telephone booth. Then
she returned to the house. As she turned the corner she met the
man in the cap who had been leaning in the door. She entered
the lattice. Minnie opened the door.

'Thank goodness,' Minnie said. 'When that cab over there
started up, I got ready to pack up too. If you ain't ghy say nothing
about it, I git you a drink.'

When Minnie fetched the gin Temple started to drink it. Her
hand was trembling and there was a sort of elation in her face as
she stood again just inside the door, listening, the glass in her
hand. I'll need it later, she said. I'll need more than that. She
covered the glass with a saucer and hid it carefully. Then she
dug into the mass of garments in the corner and found a dancing-
frock and shook it out and hung it back in the closet. She looked
at the other things a moment, but she returned to the bed and
lay down again. At once she rose and drew the chair up and sat
down, her feet on the unmade bed. While daylight died slowly
in the room she sat smoking cigarette after cigarette, listening to
every sound on the stairs.

At half-past six Minnie brought her supper up. On the tray was another glass of gin. 'Miss Reba sent this un,' she said. 'She say, how you feelin'?'

'Tell her, all right,' Temple said. 'I'm goin' to have a bath and then go to bed, tell her.'

When Minnie was gone Temple poured the two drinks into a tumbler and gloated over it, the glass shaking in her hands. She set it carefully away and covered it and ate her supper from the bed. When she finished she lit a cigarette. Her movements were jerky; she smoked swiftly, moving about the room. She stood for a moment at the window, the shade lifted aside, then she dropped it and turned into the room again, spying herself in the mirror. She turned before it, studying herself, puffing at the cigarette.

She snapped it behind her, towards the fireplace, and went to the mirror and combed her hair. She ripped the curtain aside and took the dress down and laid it on the bed and returned and drew out a drawer in the dresser and took a garment out. She paused with the garment in her hand, then she replaced it and closed the drawer and caught up the frock swiftly and hung it back in the closet. A moment later she found herself walking up and down the room, another cigarette burning in her hand, without any recollection of having lit it. She flung it away and went to the table and looked at her watch and propped it against the pack of cigarettes so she could see it from the bed, and lay down. When she did so she felt the pistol through the pillow. She slipped it out and looked at it, then she slid it under her flank and lay motionless, her legs straight, her hands behind her head, her eyes focusing into black pinheads at every sound on the stairs.

At nine she rose. She picked up the pistol again; after a moment she thrust it beneath the mattress and undressed, and in a spurious Chinese robe splotched with gold dragons and jade and scarlet flowers she left the room. When she returned her hair curled damply about her face. She went to the washstand and took up the tumbler, holding it in her hands, but she set it down again.

She dressed, retrieving the bottles and jars from the corner. Her motions before the glass were furious yet painstaking. She went to the washstand and took up the glass, but again she paused and went to the corner and got her coat and put it on and put the platinum bag in the pocket and leaned once more to the mirror. Then she went and took up the glass and gulped the gin and left the room, walking swiftly.

A single light burned in the hall. It was empty. She could hear voices in Miss Reba's room, but the lower hall was deserted. She descended swiftly and silently and gained the door. She believed that it would be at the door that they would stop her and she thought of the pistol with acute regret, almost pausing, knowing that she would use it without any compunction whatever, with a kind of pleasure. She sprang to the door and pawed at the bolt, her head turned over her shoulder.

It opened. She sprang out and out the lattice door and ran down the walk and out the gate. As she did so a car, moving slowly along the kerb, stopped opposite her. Popeye sat at the wheel. Without any apparent movement from him the door swung open. He made no movement, spoke no word. He just sat there, the straw hat slanted a little aside.

'I won't!' Temple said. 'I won't!'

He made no movement, no sound. She came to the car.

'I won't, I tell you!' Then she cried wildly: 'You're scared of him! You're scared to!'

'I'm giving him his chance,' he said. 'Will you go back in that house, or will you get in this car?'

'You're scared to!'

'I'm giving him his chance,' he said, in his cold, soft voice. 'Come on. Make up your mind.'

She leaned forward, putting her hand on his arm. 'Popeye,' she said; 'daddy.' His arm felt frail, no larger than a child's, dead and hard and light as a stick.

'I don't care which you do,' he said. 'But do it. Come on.'

She leaned towards him, her hand on his arm. Then she got into the car. 'You won't do it. You're afraid to. He's a better man than you are.'

He reached across and shut the door. 'Where?' he said. 'Grotto?'

'He's a better man than you are!' Temple said shrilly. 'You're not even a man! He knows it. Who does know it if he don't?' The car was in motion. She began to shriek at him. 'You, a man, a bold bad man, when you can't even – When you had to bring a real man in to – And you hanging over the bed, moaning and slobbering like a – You couldn't fool me but once, could you? No wonder I bled and bluh –' his hand came over her mouth, hard, his nails going into her flesh. With the other hand he drove the car at reckless speed. When they passed beneath lights she could see him watching her as she struggled, tugging at his hand, whipping her head this way and that.

She ceased struggling, but she continued to twist her head

from side to side, tugging at his hand. One finger, ringed with a thick ring, held her lips apart, his finger-tips digging into her cheek. With the other hand he whipped the car in and out of traffic, bearing down upon other cars until they slewed aside with brakes squealing, shooting recklessly across intersections. Once a policeman shouted at them, but he did not even look around.

Temple began to whimper, moaning behind his hand, drooling upon his fingers. The ring was like a dentist's instrument; she could not close her lips to regurgitate. When he removed it she could feel the imprint of his fingers cold on her jaw. She lifted her hand to it.

'You hurt my mouth,' she whimpered. They were approaching the outskirts of the city, the speedometer at fifty miles. His hat slanted above his delicate hooked profile. She nursed her jaw. The houses gave way to broad, dark subdivisions out of which realtors' signs loomed abrupt and ghostly, with a quality of forlorn assurance. Between them low, far lights hung in the cool empty darkness blowing with fireflies. She began to cry quietly, feeling the cooling double drink of gin inside her. 'You hurt my mouth,' she said in a voice small and faint with self-pity. She nursed her jaw with experimental fingers, pressing harder and harder until she found a twinge. 'You'll be sorry for this,' she said in a muffled voice. 'When I tell Red. Don't you wish you were Red? Don't you? Don't you wish you could do what he can do? Don't you wish he was the one watching us instead of you?'

They turned into the Grotto, passing along a closely curtained wall from which a sultry burst of music came. She sprang out while he was locking the car and ran on up the steps. 'I gave you your chance,' she said. 'You brought me here. I didn't ask you to come.'

She went to the washroom. In the mirror she examined her face. 'Shucks,' she said, 'it didn't leave a mark, even'; drawing the flesh this way and that. 'Little runt,' she said, peering at her reflection. She added a phrase, glibly obscene, with a detached parrotlike effect. She painted her mouth again. Another woman entered. They examined one another's clothes with brief, covert, cold, embracing glances.

Popeye was standing at the door to the dance-hall, a cigarette in his fingers.

'I gave you your chance,' Temple said. 'You didn't have to come.'

'I don't take chances,' he said.

'You took one,' Temple said. 'Are you sorry? Huh?'

'Go on,' he said, his hand on her back. She was in the act of stepping over the sill when she turned and looked at him, their eyes almost on a level; then her hand flicked towards his armpit. He caught her wrist; the other hand flicked towards him. He caught that one too in his soft, cold hand. They looked eye to eye, her mouth open and the rouge spots darkening slowly on her face.

'I gave you your chance back there in town,' he said. 'You took it.'

Behind her the music beat, sultry, evocative; filled with movement of feet, the voluptuous hysteria of muscles warming the scent of flesh, of the blood. 'Oh, God; oh, God,' she said, her lips scarce moving. 'I'll go. I'll go back.'

'You took it,' he said. 'Go on.'

In his grasp her hands made tentative plucking motions at his coat just out of reach of her finger-tips. Slowly he was turning her towards the door, her head reverted. 'You just dare!' she cried. 'You just –' His hand closed upon the back of her neck, his fingers like steel, yet cold and light as aluminium. She could hear the vertebrae grating faintly together and his voice, cold and still.

'Will you?'

She nodded her head. Then they were dancing. She could still feel his hand at her neck. Across his shoulder she looked swiftly about the room, her gaze flicking from face to face among the dancers. Beyond a low arch, in another room, a group stood about the crap-table. She leaned this way and that, trying to see the faces of the group.

Then she saw the four men. They were sitting at a table near the door. One of them was chewing gum; the whole lower part of his face seemed to be cropped with teeth of an unbelievable whiteness and size. When she saw them she swung Popeye around with his back to them, working the two of them towards the door again. Once more her harried gaze flew from face to face in the crowd.

When she looked again two of the men had risen. They approached. She dragged Popeye into their path, still keeping his back turned to them. The men paused and essayed to go around her; again she backed Popeye into their path. She was trying to say something to him, but her mouth felt cold. It was like trying to pick up a pin with the fingers numb. Suddenly she felt herself lifted bodily aside, Popeye's small arms light and rigid as aluminium. She stumbled back against the wall and watched the two men leave the room. 'I'll go back,' she said. 'I'll go back.' She began to laugh shrilly.

'Shut it,' Popeye said. 'Are you going to shut it?'

'Get me a drink,' she said. She felt his hand; her legs felt cold too as if they were not hers. They were sitting at a table. Two tables away the man was still chewing, his elbows on the table. The fourth man sat on his spine, smoking, his coat buttoned across his chest.

She watched hands: a brown one in a white sleeve, a soiled white one beneath a dirty cuff, setting bottles on the table. She had a glass in her hand. She drank, gulping; with the glass in her hand she saw Red standing in the door, in a grey suit and a spotted bow-tie. He looked like a college boy, and he looked about the room until he saw her. He looked at the back of Popeye's head, then at her as she sat with the glass in her hand. The two men at the other table had not moved. She could see the faint, steady movement of the one's ears as he chewed. The music started.

She held Popeye's back towards Red. He was still watching her, almost a head taller than anybody else. 'Come on,' she said in Popeye's ear. 'If you're going to dance, dance.'

She had another drink. They danced again. Red had disappeared. When the music ceased she had another drink. It did no good. It merely lay hot and hard inside her. 'Come on,' she said, 'don't quit.' But he wouldn't get up, and she stood over him, her muscles flinching and jerking with exhaustion and terror. She began to jeer at him. 'Call yourself a man, a bold, bad man, and let a girl dance you off your feet.' Then her face drained, became small and haggard and sincere; she spoke like a child, with sober despair. 'Popeye.' He sat with his hands on the table, finicking with a cigarette, the second glass with its melting ice before him. She put her hand on his shoulder. 'Daddy,' she said. Moving to shield them from the room, her hand stole towards his armpit, touching the butt of the flat pistol. It lay rigid in the light, dead vice of his arm and side. 'Give it to me,' she whispered. 'Daddy. Daddy.' She leaned her thigh against his shoulder, caressing his arm with her flank. 'Give it to me, Daddy,' she whispered. Suddenly her hand began to steal down his body in a swift, covert movement; then it snapped away in a movement of revulsion. 'I forgot,' she whispered; 'I didn't mean . . . I didn't . . .'

One of the men at the other table hissed once through his teeth. 'Sit down,' Popeye said. She sat down. She filled her glass, watching her hands perform the action. Then she was watching the corner of the grey coat. He's got a broken button, she thought stupidly. Popeye had not moved.

'Dance this?' Red said.

His head was bent but he was not looking at her. He was turned a little, facing the two men at the other table. Still Popeye did not move. He shredded delicately the end of the cigarette, pinching the tobacco off. Then he put it into his mouth.

'I'm not dancing,' Temple said through her cold lips.

'Not?' Red said. He said, in a level tone, without moving: 'How's the boy?'

'Fine,' Popeye said. Temple watched him scrape a match, saw the flame distorted through glass. 'You've had enough,' Popeye said. His hand took the glass from her lips. She watched him empty it into the ice bowl. The music started again. She sat looking quietly about the room. A voice began to buzz faintly at her hearing, then Popeye was gripping her wrist, shaking it, and she found that her mouth was open and that she must have been making a noise of some sort with it. 'Shut it, now,' he said. 'You can have one more.' He poured the drink into the glass.

'I haven't felt it at all,' she said. He gave her the glass. She drank. When she set the glass down she realized that she was drunk. She believed that she had been drunk for some time. She thought that perhaps she had passed out and that it had already happened. She could hear herself saying I hope it has. I hope it has. Then she believed it had and she was overcome by a sense of bereavement and of physical desire. She thought, It will never be again, and she sat in a floating swoon of agonized sorrow and erotic longing, thinking of Red's body, watching her hand holding the empty bottle over the glass.

'You've drunk it all,' Popeye said. 'Get up, now. Dance it off.' They danced again. She moved stiffly and languidly, her eyes open but unseeing; her body following the music without hearing the tune for a time. Then she became aware that the orchestra was playing the same tune as when Red was asking her to dance. If that were so then it couldn't have happened yet. She felt a wild surge of relief. It was not too late: Red was still alive; she felt long shuddering waves of physical desire going over her, draining the colour from her mouth, drawing her eyeballs back into her skull in a shuddering swoon.

They were at the crap-table. She could hear herself shouting to the dice. She was rolling them, winning; the counters were piling up in front of her as Popeye drew them in, coaching her, correcting her in his soft, querulous voice. He stood beside her, shorter than she.

He had the cup himself. She stood beside him cunningly, feeling the desire going over her in wave after wave, involved with the music and with the smell of her own flesh. She became quiet. By infinitesimal inches she moved aside until someone slipped into her place. Then she was walking swiftly and carefully across the floor towards the door, the dancers, the music swirling slowly about her in a bright myriad wave. The table where the two men had sat was empty, but she did not even glance at it. She entered the corridor. A waiter met her.

'Room,' she said. 'Hurry.'

The room contained a table and four chairs. The waiter turned on the light and stood in the door. She jerked her hand at him; he went out. She leaned against the table on her braced arms, watching the door, until Red entered.

He came towards her. She did not move. Her eyes began to grow darker and darker, lifting into her skull above a half-moon of white, without focus with the blank rigidity of a statue's eyes. She began to say Ah-ah-ah-ah in an expiring voice, her body arching slowly backwards as though faced by an exquisite torture. When he touched her she sprang like a bow, hurling herself upon him, her mouth gaped and ugly like that of a dying fish as she writhed her loins against him.

He dragged his face free by main strength. With her hips grinding against him, her mouth gaping in straining protrusion, bloodless, she began to speak. 'Let's hurry. Anywhere. I've quit him. I told him so. It's not my fault. Is it my fault? You don't need your hat and I don't either. He came here to kill you but I said I gave him his chance. It wasn't my fault. And now it'll just be us. Without him there watching. Come on. What're you waiting for?' She strained her mouth towards him, dragging his head down, making a whimpering moan. He held his face free. 'I told him I was. I said if you bring me here. I gave you your chance I said. And now he's got them there to bump you off. But you're not afraid. Are you?'

'Did you know that when you telephoned me?' he said.

'What? He said I wasn't to see you again. He said he'd kill you. But he had me followed when I telephoned. I saw him. But you're

not afraid. He's not even a man, but you are. You're a man.
You're a man.' She began to grind against him, dragging at his
head, murmuring to him in parrot-like underworld epithet, the
saliva running pale over her bloodless lips. 'Are you afraid?'

'Of that dopey bastard?' Lifting her bodily he turned so that
he faced the door, and slipped his right hand free. She did not
seem to be aware that he had moved.

'Please. Please. Please. Please. Don't make me wait. I'm burning
up.'

'All right. You go on back. You wait till I give you the sign.
Will you go on back?'

'I can't wait. You've got to. I'm on fire, I tell you.' She clung
to him. Together they blundered across the room towards the
door, he holding her clear of his right side; she in a voluptuous
swoon, unaware that they were moving, straining at him as
though she were trying to touch him with all of her body-surface
at once. He freed himself and thrust her into the passage.

'Go,' he said. 'I'll be there in a minute.'

'You won't be long? I'm on fire. I'm dying, I tell you.'

'No. Not long. Go on, now.'

The music was playing. She moved up the corridor, staggering
a little. She thought that she was leaning against the wall, when
she found that she was dancing again; then that she was dancing
with two men at once; then she found that she was not dancing
but that she was moving towards the door between the man with
the chewing-gum and the one with the buttoned coat. She tried
to stop, but they had her under the arms; she opened her mouth
to scream, taking one last despairing look about the swirling
room.

'Yell,' the man with the buttoned coat said. 'Just try it once.'

Red was at the crap-table. She saw his head turned, the cup in
his lifted hand. With it he made her a short, cheery salute. He
watched her disappear through the door, between the two men.
Then he looked briefly about the room. His face was bold and
calm, but there were two white lines at the base of his nostrils
and his forehead was damp. He rattled the cup and threw the
dice steadily.

'Eleven,' the dealer said.

'Let it lay,' Red said. 'I'll pass a million times tonight.'

They helped Temple into the car. The man in the buttoned
coat took the wheel. Where the drive joined the lane that led to
the highroad a long touring car was parked. When they passed

it Temple saw, leaning to a cupped match, Popeye's delicate
hooked profile beneath the slanted hat as he lit the cigarette.
The match flipped outwards like a dying star in miniature, sucked
with the profile into darkness by the rush of their passing.

Chapter Twenty-five

The tables had been moved to one end of the dance floor. On
each one was a black table-cloth. The curtains were still drawn;
a thick, salmon-coloured light fell through them. Just beneath
the orchestra platform the coffin sat. It was an expensive one:
black, with silver fittings, the trestles hidden by a mass of flowers.
In wreaths and crosses and other shapes of ceremonial mortality,
the mass appeared to break in a symbolical wave over the bier
and on upon the platform and the piano, the scent of them thickly
oppressive.

The proprietor of the place moved about among the tables,
speaking to the arrivals as they entered and found seats. The
negro waiters, in black shirts beneath their starched jackets, were
already moving in and out with glasses and bottles of ginger ale.
They moved with swaggering and decorous repression; already
the scene was vivid, with a hushed, macabre air a little febrile.

The archway to the dice-room was draped in black. A black
pall lay upon the crap-table, upon which the overflow of floral
shapes was beginning to accumulate. People entered steadily, the
men in dark suits of decorous restraint, others in the light, bright
shades of spring, increasing the atmosphere of macabre paradox.
The women – the younger ones – wore bright colours also, in
hats and scarves; the older ones in sober grey and black and navy
blue, and glittering with diamonds: matronly figures resembling
housewives on a Sunday afternoon excursion.

The room began to hum with shrill, hushed talk. The waiters
moved here and there with high, precarious trays, their white
jackets and black shirts resembling photograph negatives. The
proprietor went from table to table with his bald head, a huge

diamond in his black cravat, followed by the bouncer, a thick, muscle-bound, bullet-headed man who appeared to be on the point of bursting out of his dinner-jacket through the rear, like a cocoon.

In a private dining-room, on a table draped in black, sat a huge bowl of punch floating with ice and sliced fruit. Beside it leaned a fat man in a shapeless greenish suit, from the sleeves of which dirty cuffs fell upon hands rimmed with black nails. The soiled collar was wilted about his neck in limp folds, knotted by a greasy black tie with an imitation ruby stud. His face gleamed with moisture and he adjured the throng about the bowl in a harsh voice:

'Come on, folks. It's on Gene. It don't cost you nothing. Step up and drink. There wasn't never a better boy walked than him.' They drank and fell back, replaced by others with extended cups. From time to time a waiter entered with ice and fruit and dumped them into the bowl; from a suitcase under the table Gene drew fresh bottles and decanted them into the bowl; then, proprietorial, adjurant, sweating, he resumed his harsh monologue, mopping his face on his sleeve. 'Come on, folks. It's all on Gene. I ain't nothing but a bootlegger, but he never had a better friend than me. Step up and drink, folks. There's more where that come from.'

From the dance hall came a strain of music. The people entered and found seats. On the platform was the orchestra from a downtown hotel, in dinner coats. The proprietor and a second man were conferring with the leader.

'Let them play jazz,' the second man said. 'Never nobody liked dancing no better than Red.'

'No, no,' the proprietor said. 'Time Gene gets them all ginned up on free whisky, they'll start dancing. It'll look bad.'

'How about the Blue Danube?' the leader said.

'No, no; don't play no blues, I tell you,' the Proprietor said. 'There's a dead man in that bier.'

'That's not blues,' the leader said.

'What is it?' the second man said.

'A waltz. Strauss.'

'A wop?' the second man said. 'Like hell. Red was an American. You may not be, but he was. Don't you know anything American? Play I Can't Give You Anything But Love. He always liked that.'

'And get them all to dancing?' the proprietor said. He glanced back at the tables, where the women were beginning to talk a little shrilly. 'You better start off with Nearer, My God, To Thee,' he said, 'and sober them up some. I told Gene it was risky about that punch, starting it so soon. My suggestion was to wait until we started back to town. But I might have knowed somebody'd have to turn it into a carnival. Better start off solemn and keep it up until I give you the sign.'

'Red wouldn't like it solemn,' the second man said. 'And you know it.'

'Let him go somewheres else, then,' the proprietor said. 'I just done this as an accommodation. I ain't running no funeral parlour.'

The orchestra played Nearer, My God, To Thee. The audience grew quiet. A woman in a red dress came in the door unsteadily. 'Whoopee,' she said, 'so long, Red. He'll be in hell before I could even reach Little Rock.'

'Shhhhhhhh!' voices said. She fell into a seat. Gene came to the door and stood there until the music stopped.

'Come on, folks,' he shouted, jerking his arms in a fat, sweeping gesture, 'come and get it. It's on Gene. I don't want a dry throat or eye in this place in ten minutes.' Those at the rear moved towards the door. The proprietor sprang to his feet and jerked his hand at the orchestra. The cornetist rose and played In That Haven of Rest in solo, but the crowd at the back of the room continued to dwindle through the door where Gene stood waving his arm. Two middle-aged woman were weeping quietly beneath flowered hats.

They surged and clamoured about the diminishing bowl. From the dance hall came the rich blare of the cornet. Two soiled young men worked their way towards the table, shouting 'Gangway. Gangway' monotonously, carrying suitcases. They opened them and set bottles on the table, while Gene, frankly weeping now, opened them and decanted them into the bowl. 'Come up, folks. I couldn't a loved him no better if he'd a been my own son,' he shouted hoarsely, dragging his sleeve across his face.

A waiter edged up to the table with a bowl of ice and fruit and went to put them into the punch-bowl. 'What the hell you doing?' Gene said, 'putting that slop in there? Get to hell away from here.'

'Ra-a-a-a-y-y-y-y!' they shouted, clashing their cups, drowning all save the pantomime as Gene knocked the bowl of fruit from the waiter's hand and fell again to dumping raw liquor into the bowl, sploshing it into and upon the extended hands and cups.

The two youths opened bottles furiously.

As though swept there upon a brassy blare of music the proprietor appeared in the door, his face harried, waving his arms. 'Come on, folks,' he shouted, 'let's finish the musical programme. It's costing us money.'

'Hell with it,' they shouted.

'Costing who money?'

'Who cares?'

'Costing who money?'

'Who begrudges it? I'll pay it. By God, I'll buy him two funerals.'

'Folks! Folks!' the proprietor shouted. 'Don't you realize there's a bier in that room?'

'Costing who money?'

'Beer?' Gene said. 'Beer?' he said in a broken voice. 'Is anybody here trying to insult me by –'

'He begrudges Red the money.'

'Who does?'

'Joe does, the cheap son of a bitch.'

'Is somebody here trying to insult me –'

'Let's move the funeral, then. This is not the only place in town.'

'Let's move Joe.'

'Put the son of a bitch in a coffin. Let's have two funerals.'

'Beer! Beer? Is somebody –'

'Put the son of a bitch in a coffin. See how he likes it.'

'Put the son of a bitch in a coffin,' the woman in red shrieked. They rushed towards the door, where the proprietor stood waving his hands above his head, his voice shrieking out of the uproar before he turned and fled.

In the main room a male quartet engaged from a vaudeville house was singing. They were singing mother songs in close harmony; they sang Sonny Boy. The weeping was general among the older women. Waiters were now carrying cups of punch in to them and they sat holding the cups in their fat, ringed hands, crying.

The orchestra played again. The woman in red staggered into the room. 'Come on, Joe,' she shouted, 'open the game. Get that damn stiff out of here and open the game.' A man tried to hold her; she turned upon him with a burst of filthy language and went on to the shrouded crap-table and hurled a wreath to the floor. The proprietor rushed towards her, followed by the bouncer. The proprietor grasped the woman as she lifted another

floral piece. The man who had tried to hold her intervened, the
woman cursing shrilly and striking at both of them impartially
with the wreath. The bouncer caught the man's arm; he whirled
and struck at the bouncer, who knocked him half-way across the
room. Three more men entered. The fourth rose from the floor
and all four of them rushed at the bouncer.

He felled the first and whirled and sprang with unbelievable
celerity, into the main room. The orchestra was playing. It was
immediately drowned in a sudden pandemonium of chairs and
screams. The bouncer whirled again and met the rush of the four
men. They mingled; a second man flew out and skittered along
the floor on his back; the bouncer sprang free. Then he whirled
and rushed them and in a whirling plunge they bore down upon
the bier and crashed into it. The orchestra had ceased and were
now climbing on to their chairs, with their instruments. The
floral offerings flew; the coffin teetered. 'Catch it!' a voice
shouted. They sprang forward, but the coffin crashed heavily to
the floor, coming open. The corpse tumbled slowly and sedately
out and came to rest with its face in the centre of a wreath.

'Play something!' the proprietor bawled, waving his arms; 'play!
Play!'

When they raised the corpse the wreath came too, attached to
him by a hidden end of a wire driven into his cheek. He had
worn a cap which, tumbling off, exposed a small blue hole in the
centre of his forehead. It had been neatly plugged with wax and
was painted, but the wax had been jarred out and lost. They
couldn't find it, but by unfastening the snap in the peak, they
could draw the cap down to his eyes.

As the cortège neared the downtown section more cars joined
in. The hearse was followed by six Packard touring cars with the
tops back, driven by liveried chauffeurs and filled with flowers.
They looked exactly alike and were of the type rented by the
hour by the better-class agencies. Next came a nondescript line
of taxis, roadsters, sedans, which increased as the procession
moved slowly through the restricted district where faces peered
from beneath lowered shades, towards the main artery that led
back out of town, towards the cemetery.

On the avenue the hearse increased its speed, the procession
stretching out at swift intervals. Presently the private cars and
the cabs began to drop out. At each intersection they would turn
this way or that, until at last only the hearse and the six Packards

were left, each carrying no occupant save the liveried driver. The street was broad and now infrequent, with a white line down the centre that diminished on ahead into the smooth asphalt emptiness. Soon the hearse was making forty miles an hour and then forty-five and then fifty.

One of the cabs drew up at Miss Reba's door. She got out, followed by a thin woman in sober, severe clothes and gold nose-glasses, and a short plump woman in a plumed hat, her face hidden by a handkerchief, and a small bullet-headed boy of five or six. The woman with the handkerchief continued to sob in snuffy gasps as they went up the walk and entered the lattice. Beyond the house door the dogs set up a falsetto uproar. When Minnie opened the door they surged about Miss Reba's feet. She kicked them aside. Again they assailed her with snapping eagerness; again she flung them back against the wall in muted thuds.

'Come in, come in,' she said, her hand to her breast. Once inside the house the woman with the handkerchief began to weep aloud.

'Didn't he look sweet?' she wailed. 'Didn't he look sweet?'

'Now, now,' Miss Reba said, leading the way to her room, 'come in and have some beer. You'll feel better. Minnie!' They entered the room with the decorated dresser, the safe, the screen, the draped portrait. 'Sit down, sit down,' she panted, shoving the chairs forward. She lowered herself into one and stooped terrifically towards her feet.

'Uncle Bud, honey,' the weeping woman said, dabbing at her eyes, 'come and unlace Miss Reba's shoes.'

The boy knelt and removed Miss Reba's shoes. 'And if you'll just reach me them house-slippers under the bed there, honey,' Miss Reba said. The boy fetched the slippers. Minnie entered, followed by the dogs. They rushed at Miss Reba and began to worry the shoes she had just removed.

'Scat!' the boy said, striking at one of them with his hand. The dog's head snapped around, its teeth clicking, its half-hidden eyes bright and malevolent. The boy recoiled. 'You bite me, you thon bitch,' he said.

'Uncle Bud' the fat woman said, her round face, rigid in fatty folds and streaked with tears, turned upon the boy in shocked surprise, the plumes nodding precariously above it. Uncle Bud's head was quite round, his nose bridged with freckles like splotches of huge summer rain on a sidewalk. The other woman sat primly erect, in gold nose-glasses on a gold chain and neat iron-grey hair. She looked like a school-teacher. 'The very idea!' the fat woman said. 'How in the world he can learn such words on an Arkansaw farm, I don't know.'

'They'll learn meanness anywhere,' Miss Reba said. Minnie leaned down a tray bearing three frosted tankards. Uncle Bud watched with round cornflower eyes as they took one each. The fat woman began to cry again.

'He looked so sweet!' she wailed.

'We all got to suffer it,' Miss Reba said. 'Well, may it be a long day,' lifting her tankard. They drank, bowing formally to one another. The fat woman dried her eyes; the two guests wiped their lips with prim decorum. The thin one coughed delicately aside, behind her hand.

'Such good beer,' she said.

'Ain't it?' the fat one said. 'I always say it's the greatest pleasure I have to call on Miss Reba.'

They began to talk politely, in decorous half-completed sentences, with little gasps of agreement. The boy had moved aimlessly to the window, peering beneath the lifted shade.

'How long's he going to be with you, Miss Myrtle?' Miss Reba said.

'Just till Sat'dy,' the fat woman said. 'Then he'll go back home. It makes a right nice little change for him, with me for a week or two. And I enjoy having him.'

'Children are such a comfort to a body,' the thin one said.

'Yes,' Miss Myrtle said. 'Is them two nice young fellows still with you, Miss Reba?'

'Yes,' Miss Reba said. 'I think I got to get shut of them, though. I ain't specially tender-hearted, but after all it ain't no use in helping young folks to learn this world's meanness until they have to. I already had to stop the girls running around the house without no clothes on, and they don't like it.'

They drank again, decorously, handling the tankards delicately, save Miss Reba who grasped hers as though it were a weapon, her other hand lost in her breast. She set her tankard down empty. 'I get so dry, seems like,' she said. 'Won't you ladies have another?' They murmured, ceremoniously. 'Minnie!' Miss Reba shouted.

Minnie came and filled the tankards again. 'Reely, I'm right ashamed,' Miss Myrtle said. 'But Miss Reba has such good beer. And then we've all had a kind of upsetting afternoon.'

'I'm just surprised it wasn't upset no more,' Miss Reba said. 'Giving away all that free liquor like Gene done.'

'It must have cost a good piece of jack,' the thin woman said.

'I believe you,' Miss Reba said. 'And who got anything out of it? Tell me that. Except the privilege of having his place hell-full of folks not spending a cent.' She had set her tankard on the table beside her chair. Suddenly she turned her head sharply and looked at it. Uncle Bud was now behind her chair, leaning against the table. 'You ain't been into my beer, have you, boy?' she said.

'You, Uncle Bud,' Miss Myrtle said. 'Ain't you ashamed? I declare, it's getting so I don't dare take him nowhere. I never see such a boy for snitching beer in my life. You come out here and play, now. Come on.'

'Yessum,' Uncle Bud said. He moved, in no particular direction. Miss Reba drank and set the tankard back on the table and rose.

'Since we all been kind of tore up,' she said, 'maybe I can prevail on you ladies to have a little sup of gin?'

'No; reely,' Miss Myrtle said.

'Miss Reba's the perfect hostess,' the thin one said. 'How many times you heard me say that, Miss Myrtle?'

'I wouldn't undertake to say, dearie,' Miss Myrtle said.

Miss Reba vanished behind the screen.

'Did you ever see it so warm for June, Miss Lorraine?' Miss Myrtle said.

'I never did,' the thin woman said. Miss Myrtle's face began to crinkle again. Setting her tankard down she began to fumble for her handkerchief.

'It just comes over me like this,' she said, 'and them singing that Sonny Boy and all. He looked so sweet,' she wailed.

'Now, now,' Miss Lorraine said. 'Drink a little beer. You'll feel better. Miss Myrtle's took again,' she said, raising her voice.

'I got too tender a heart,' Miss Myrtle said. She snuffled behind the handkerchief, groping for her tankard. She groped for a moment, then it touched her hand. She looked quickly up. 'You, Uncle Bud!' she said. 'Didn't I tell you to come out from behind there and play? Would you believe it? The other afternoon when we left here I was so mortified I didn't know what to do. I was ashamed to be seen on the street with a drunk boy like you.'

Miss Reba emerged from behind the screen with three glasses of gin. 'This'll put some heart into us,' she said. 'We're setting here like three old sick cats.' They bowed formally and drank, patting their lips. Then they began to talk. They were all talking at once, again in half-completed sentences but without pauses for agreement or affirmation.

'It's us girls,' Miss Myrtle said. 'Men just can't seem to take us and leave us for what we are. They make us what we are, then they expect us to be different. Expect us not to never look at another man, while they come and go as they please.'

'A woman that wants to fool with more than one man at a time is a fool,' Miss Reba said. 'They're all trouble, and why do you want to double your trouble? And the woman that can't stay true to a good man when she gets him, a free-hearted spender that never give her a hour's uneasiness or a hard word . . .' looking at them, her eyes began to fill with a sad, unutterable expression, of baffled and patient despair.

'Now, now,' Miss Myrtle said. She leaned forward and patted Miss Reba's huge hand. Miss Lorraine made a faint clucking sound with her tongue. 'You'll get yourself started.'

'He was such a good man,' Miss Reba said. 'We was like two doves. For eleven years we was like two doves.'

'Now, dearie; now, dearie,' Miss Myrtle said.

'It's when it comes over me like this,' Miss Reba said. 'Seeing that boy laying there under them flowers.'

'He never had no more than Mr Binford had,' Miss Myrtle said. 'Now, now. Drink a little beer.'

Miss Reba brushed her sleeve across her eyes. She drank some beer.

'He ought to known better than to take a chance with Popeye's girl,' Miss Lorraine said.

'Men don't never learn better than that, dearie,' Miss Myrtle said. 'Where you reckon they went, Miss Reba?'

'I don't know and I don't care,' Miss Reba said. 'And how soon they catch him and burn him for killing that boy, I don't care neither. I don't care none.'

'He goes all the way to Pensacola every summer to see his mother,' Miss Myrtle said. 'A man that'll do that can't be all bad.'

'I don't know how bad you like them, then,' Miss Reba said. 'Me trying to run a respectable house, that's been running a shooting-gallery for twenty years, and him trying to turn it into a peep-show.'

'It's us poor girls,' Miss Myrtle said, 'causes all the trouble and gets all the suffering.'

'I heard two years ago he wasn't no good that way,' Miss Lorraine said.

'I knew it all the time,' Miss Reba said. 'A young man spending his money like water on girls and not never going to bed with one. It's against nature. All girls thought it was because he had a little woman out in town somewhere, but I says mark my words, there's something funny about him. There's a funny business somewhere.'

'He was a free spender, all right,' Miss Lorraine said.

'The clothes and jewellery that girl bought, it was a shame,' Miss Reba said. 'There was a Chinse robe she paid a hundred dollars for – imported, it was – and perfume at ten dollars an ounce; next morning when I went up there, they was all wadded in the corner and the perfume and rouge busted all over them like a cyclone. That's what she'd do when she got mad at him, when he'd beat her. After he shut her up and wouldn't let her leave the house. Having the front of my house watched like it was a . . .' She raised the tankard from the table to her lips. Then she halted it, blinking. 'Where's my –'

'Uncle Bud!' Miss Myrtle said. She grasped the boy by the arm and snatched him out from behind Miss Reba's chair and shook him, his round head bobbing on his shoulders with an expression of equable idiocy. 'Ain't you ashamed? Ain't you *ashamed*? Why can't you stay out of these ladies' beer? I'm a good mind to take that dollar back and make you buy Miss Reba a can of beer, I am for a fact. Now, you go over there by that window and stay there, you hear?'

'Nonsense,' Miss Reba said. 'There wasn't much left. You ladies are about ready too, ain't you? Minnie!'

Miss Lorraine touched her mouth with her handkerchief. Behind her glasses her eyes rolled aside in a veiled, secret look. She laid the other hand to her flat spinster's breast.

'We forgot about your heart, honey,' Miss Myrtle said. 'Don't you reckon you better take gin this time?'

'Reely, I –' Miss Lorraine said.

'Yes; do,' Miss Reba said. She rose heavily and fetched three more glasses of gin from behind the screen. Minnie entered and refilled the tankards. They drank, patting their lips.

'That's what was going on, was it?' Miss Lorraine said.

'First I knowed was when Minnie told me there was something funny going on,' Miss Reba said. 'How he wasn't here hardly at all, gone about every other night, and that when he was here, there wasn't no signs at all the next morning when she cleaned up. She'd hear them quarrelling, and she said it was her wanting to get out and he wouldn't let her. With all them clothes he was buying her, mind, he didn't want her to leave the house, and she'd get mad and lock the door and wouldn't even let him in.'

'Maybe he went off and got fixed up with one of these glands, these monkey glands, and it quit on him,' Miss Myrtle said.

'Then one morning he come in with Red and took him up there. They stayed about an hour and left, and Popeye didn't show up again until next morning. Then him and Red come back and stayed up there about an hour. When they left, Minnie come and told me what was going on, so next day I waited for them. I called him in here and I says "Look here, you son of a buh . . ." ' She ceased. For an instant the three of them sat motionless, a little forward. Then slowly their heads turned and they looked at the boy leaning against the table.

'Uncle Bud, honey,' Miss Myrtle said, 'don't you want to go and play in the yard with Reba and Mr Binford?'

'Yessum,' the boy said. He went towards the door. They watched him until the door closed upon him. Miss Lorraine drew her chair up; they leaned together.

'And that's what they was doing?' Miss Myrtle said.

'I says "I been running a house for twenty years, but this is the first time I ever had anything like this going on in it. If you want to turn a stud in to your girl," I says "go somewhere else to do it. I ain't going to have my house turned into no French joint".'

'The son of a bitch,' Miss Lorraine said.

'He'd ought to've had sense enough to got a old ugly man,' Miss Myrtle said. 'Tempting us poor girls like that.'

'Men always expects us to resist temptation,' Miss Lorraine said. She was sitting upright like a school-teacher. 'The lousy son of a bitch.'

'Except what they offers themselves,' Miss Reba said. 'Then watch them . . . Every morning for four days that was going on, then they didn't come back. For a week Popeye didn't show up at all, and that girl wild as a young mare. I thought he was out of town on business maybe, until Minnie told me he wasn't and that he gave her five dollars a day not to let that girl out of the house nor use the telephone. And me trying to get word to him to come and take her out of my house because I didn't want nuttin' like that going on in it. Yes, sir, Minnie said the two of them would be nekkid as two snakes, and Popeye hanging over the foot of the bed without even his hat took off, making a kind of whinnying sound.'

'Maybe he was cheering for them,' Miss Lorraine said. 'The lousy son of a bitch.'

Feet came up the hall; they could hear Minnie's voice lifted in adjuration. The door opened. She entered, holding Uncle Bud erect by one hand. Limp-kneed he dangled, his face fixed in an expression of glassy idiocy. 'Miss Reba,' Minnie said, 'this boy done broke in the icebox and drunk a whole bottle of beer. You, boy!' she said, shaking him, 'stan' up!' Limply he dangled, his face rigid in a slobbering grin. Then upon it came an expression of concern, consternation; Minnie swung him sharply away from her as he began to vomit.

Chapter Twenty-six

When the sun rose, Horace had not been to bed nor even undressed. He was just finishing a letter to his wife, addressed to her at her father's in Kentucky, asking for a divorce. He sat at the table, looking down at the single page written neatly and illegibly over, feeling quiet and empty for the first time since he had found Popeye watching him across the spring four weeks ago. While he was sitting there he began to smell coffee from somewhere. 'I'll finish this business and then I'll go to Europe. I am sick. I am too old for this. I was born too old for it, and so I am sick to death for quiet.'

He shaved and made coffee and drank a cup and ate some bread. When he passed the hotel, the bus which met the morning train was at the kerb, with the drummers getting into it. Clarence Snopes was one of them, carrying a tan suitcase.

'Going down to Jackson for a couple of days on a little business,' he said. 'Too bad I missed you last night. I come on back in a car. I reckon you was settled for the night, maybe?' He looked down at Horace, vast, pasty, his intention unmistakable. 'I could have took you to a place most folks don't know about. Where a man can do just whatever he is big enough to do. But there'll be another time, since I done got to know you better.' He lowered

his voice a little, moving a little aside. 'Don't you be uneasy. I
ain't a talker. When I'm here, in Jefferson, I'm one fellow; what
I am up town with a bunch of good sports ain't nobody's business
but mine and theirn. Ain't that right?'

Later in the morning, from a distance he saw his sister on the
street ahead of him turn and disappear into a door. He tried to
find her by looking into all the stores within the radius of where
she must have turned, and asking the clerks. She was in none of
them. The only place he did not investigate was a stairway that
mounted between two stores, to a corridor of offices on the first
floor, one of which was that of the District Attorney, Eustace
Graham.

Graham had a club foot, which had elected him to the office
he now held. He worked his way into and through the State
University; as a youth the town remembered him as driving
wagons and trucks for grocery stores. During his first year at the
University he made a name for himself by his industry. He waited
on table in the commons and he had the government contract
for carrying the mail to and from the local post office at the
arrival of each train, hobbling along with the sack over his
shoulder: a pleasant, open-faced young man with a word for
everyone and a certain alert rapacity about the eyes. During his
second year he let his mail contract lapse and he resigned from
his job in the commons; he also had a new suit. People were glad
that he had saved through his industry to where he could give
all his time to his studies. He was in the law school then, and the
law professors groomed him like a race-horse. He graduated well,
though without distinction. 'Because he was handicapped at the
start,' the professors said. 'If he had had the same start that the
others had . . . He will go far,' they said.

It was not until he had left school that they learned that he
had been playing poker for three years in the office of a livery
stable, behind drawn shades. When, two year's out of school he
got elected to the State legislature, they began to tell an anecdote
of his school days.

It was in the poker game in the livery stable office. The bet
came to Graham. He looked across the table at the owner of the
stable, who was his only remaining opponent.

'How much have you got there, Mr Harris?' he said.

'Forty-two dollars, Eustace,' the proprietor said. Eustace shoved
some chips into the pot. 'How much is that?' the proprietor said.

'Forty-two dollars, Mr Harris.'

'Hmmm,' the proprietor said. He examined his hand. 'How many cards did you draw, Eustace?'

'Three, Mr Harris.'

'Hmmm. Who dealt the cards, Eustace?'

'I did, Mr Harris.'

'I pass, Eustace.'

He had been District Attorney but a short time, yet already he had let it be known that he would announce for Congress on his record of convictions, so when he found himself facing Narcissa across the desk in his dingy office, his expression was like that when he had put the forty-two dollars into the pot.

'I only wish it were your brother,' he said. 'I hate to see a brother-in-arms, you might say, with a bad case.' She was watching him with a blank, enveloping look. 'After all, we've got to protect society, even when it does seem that society does not need protection.'

'Are you sure he can't win?' she said.

'Well, the first principle of law is, God alone knows what the jury will do. Of course, you can't expect –'

'But you don't think he will.'

'Naturally, I –'

'You have good reason to think he can't. I suppose you know things about it that he doesn't.'

He looked at her briefly. Then he picked up a pen from his desk and began to scrape at the point with a papercutter. 'This is purely confidential. I am violating my oath of office. I won't have to tell you that. But it may save you worry to know that he hasn't a chance in the world. I know what the disappointment will be to him, but that can't be helped. We happen to know that the man is guilty. So if there's any way you know of to get your brother out of the case, I'd advise you to do it. A losing lawyer is like a losing anything else, ball-player or merchant or doctor: his business is to –'

'So the quicker he loses, the better it would be, wouldn't it?' she said. 'If they hung the man and got it over with.' His hands became perfectly still. He did not look up. She said, her tone cold and level: 'I have reasons for wanting Horace out of this case. The sooner the better. Three nights ago that Snopes, the one in the legislature, telephoned out home, trying to find him. The next day he went to Memphis. I don't know what for. You'll have to find that out yourself. I just want Horace out of this business as soon as possible.'

She rose and moved towards the door. He hobbled over to open it; again she put that cold, still, unfathomable gaze upon him as though he were a dog or a cow and she waited for it to get out of her path. Then she was gone. He closed the door and struck a clumsy clog-step, snapping his fingers just as the door opened again; he snapped his hands towards his tie and looked at her in the door, holding it open.

'What day do you think it will be over with?' she said.

'Why, I cuh – Court opens the twentieth,' he said. 'It will be the first case. Say . . . two days. Or three at the most, with your kind assistance. And I need not assure you that this will be held in strictest confidence between us . . .' He moved towards her, but her blank calculating gaze was like a wall, surrounding him.

'That will be the twenty-fourth.' Then she was looking at him again. 'Thank you,' she said, and closed the door.

That night she wrote Belle that Horace would be home on the twenty-fourth. She telephoned Horace and asked for Belle's address.

'Why?' Horace said.

'I'm going to write her a letter,' she said, her voice tranquil, without threat. Dammit, Horace thought, holding the dead wire in his hand, How can I be expected to combat people who will not even employ subterfuge. But soon he forgot it, forgot that she had called. He did not see her again before the trial opened.

Two days before it opened Snopes emerged from a dentist's office and stood at the kerb, spitting. He took a gold-wrapped cigar from his pocket and removed the foil and put the cigar gingerly between his teeth. He had a black eye, and the bridge of his nose was bound in soiled adhesive tape. 'Got hit by a car in Jackson,' he told them in the barber-shop. 'But don't think I never made the bastard pay,' he said, showing a sheaf of yellow bills. He put them into a notecase and stowed it away. 'I'm an American,' he said. 'I don't brag about it, because I was born one. And I been a decent Baptist all my life, too. Oh, I ain't no preacher and I ain't no old maid; I been around with the boys now and then, but I reckon I ain't no worse than lots of folks that pretends to sing loud in church. But the lowest, cheapest thing on this earth ain't a nigger: it's a jew. We need laws against them. Drastic laws. When a durn low-life jew can come to a free country like this and just because he's got a law degree, it's time to put a stop to things. A jew is the lowest thing on this creation.

And the lowest kind of jew is a jew lawyer. And the lowest kind of jew lawyer is a Memphis jew lawyer. When a jew lawyer can hold up an American, a white man, and not give him but ten dollars for something that two Americans, Americans, southron gentlemen; a judge living in the capital of the State of Mississippi and a lawyer that's going to be as big a man as his pa some day, and a judge too; when they give him ten times as much for the same thing than the low-life jew, we need a law. I been a liberal spender all my life; whatever I had has always been my friends' too. But when a durn, stinking, low-life jew will refuse to pay an American one tenth of what another American, and a judge at that? –'

'Why did you sell it to him, then?' the barber said.

'What?' Snopes said. The barber was looking at him.

'What was you trying to sell to that car when it run over you?' the barber said.

'Have a cigar,' Snopes said.

Chapter Twenty-seven

The trial was set for the twentieth of June. A week after his Memphis visit, Horace telephoned Miss Reba. 'Just to know if she's still there,' he said. 'So I can reach her if I need to.'

'She's here,' Miss Reba said. 'But this reaching. I don't like it. I don't want no cops around here unless they are on my business.'

'It'll be only a bailiff,' Horace said. 'Someone to hand a paper into her own hand.'

'Let the postman do it, then,' Miss Reba said. 'He comes here anyway. In a uniform too. He don't look no worse in it than a full-blowed cop, neither. Let him do it.'

'I won't bother you,' Horace said. 'I won't make you any trouble.'

'I know you ain't,' Miss Reba said. Her voice was thin, harsh over the wire. 'I ain't going to let you. Minnie's done took a crying spell tonight, over that bastard that left her, and me and

Miss Myrtle was sitting here, and we got started crying too. Me and Minnie and Miss Myrtle. We drunk up a whole new bottle of gin. I can't afford that. So don't you be sending no jay cops up here with no letters for nobody. You telephone me and I'll turn them both out on the street and you can have them arrested there.'

On the night of the nineteenth he telephoned her again. He had some trouble in getting in touch with her.

'They're gone,' she said. 'Both of them. Don't you read no papers?'

'What papers?' Horace said. 'Hello. Hello!'

'They ain't here no more, I said,' Miss Reba said. 'I don't know nuttin about them and I don't want to know nuttin except who's going to pay me a week's room rent on –'

'But can't you find where she went to? I may need her.'

'I don't know nuttin and I don't want to know nuttin,' Miss Reba said. He heard the receiver click. Yet the disconnection was not made at once. He heard the receiver thud on to the table where the telephone sat, and he could hear Miss Reba shouting for Minnie: 'Minnie. Minnie!' Then some hand lifted the receiver and set it on to the hook; the wire clicked in his ear. After a while a detached Delsarte-ish voice said: 'Pine Bluff dizzent . . . Enkyew!'

The trial opened the next day. On the table lay the sparse objects which the District Attorney was offering: the bullet from Tommy's skull, a stoneware jug containing corn whisky.

'I will call Mrs Goodwin to the stand,' Horace said. He did not look back. He could feel Goodwin's eyes on his back as he helped the woman into the chair. She was sworn, the child lying on her lap. She repeated the story as she had told it to him on the day after the child was ill. Twice Goodwin tried to interrupt and was silenced by the Court. Horace would not look at him.

The woman finished her story. She sat erect in the chair, in her neat, worn grey dress and hat with the darned veil, the purple ornament on her shoulder. The child lay on her lap, its eyes closed in that drugged immobility. For a while her hand hovered about its face performing those needless maternal actions as though unawares.

Horace went and sat down. Then only did he look at Goodwin. But the other sat quietly now, his arms folded and his head bent a little, but Horace could see that his nostrils were waxy white with rage against his dark face. He leaned towards him and whispered, but Goodwin did not move.

The District Attorney now faced the woman.

'Mrs Goodwin,' he said, 'what was the date of your marriage to Mr Goodwin?'

'I object!' Horace said, on his feet.

'Can the prosecution show how this question is relevant?' the Court said.

'I waive, your Honour,' the District Attorney said, glancing at the jury.

When court adjourned for the day Goodwin said bitterly: 'Well, you've said you would kill me some day, but I didn't think you meant it. I didn't think that you –'

'Don't be a fool,' Horace said. 'Don't you see your case is won? That they are reduced to trying to impugn the character of your witness?' But when they left the jail he found the woman still watching him from some deep reserve of foreboding. 'You mustn't worry at all, I tell you. You may know more about making whisky or love than I do, but I know more about criminal procedure than you, remember.'

'You don't think I made a mistake?'

'I know you didn't. Don't you see how that explodes their case? The best they can hope for now is a hung jury. And the chances of that are not one in fifty. I tell you, he'll walk out of that jail tomorrow a free man.'

'Then I guess it's time to think about paying you.'

'Yes,' Horace said, 'all right. I'll come out tonight.'

'Tonight?'

'Yes. He may call you back to the stand tomorrow. We'd better prepare for it, anyway.'

At eight o'clock he entered the mad woman's yard. A single light burned in the crazy depths of the house, like a firefly caught in a brier patch, but the woman did not appear when he called. He went to the door and knocked. A shrill voice shouted something; he waited a moment. He was about to knock again when he heard the voice again, shrill and wild and faint, as though from a distance, like a reedy pipe buried by an avalanche. He circled the house in the rank, waist-high weeds. The kitchen door was open. The lamp was there, dim in a smutty chimney, filling the room a jumble of looming shapes rank with old foul female flesh not with light but with shadow. White eyeballs rolled in a high, tight bullet head in brown gleams above a torn singlet strapped into overalls. Beyond the negro the mad woman turned in an open cupboard, brushing her lank hair back with her forearm.

'Your bitch has gone to jail,' she said. 'Go on with her.'

'Jail?' Horace said.

'That's what I said. Where the good folks live. When you get a husband, keep him in jail where he can't bother you.' She turned to the negro, a small flask in her hand. 'Come on, dearie. Give me a dollar for it. You got plenty money.'

Horace returned to town, to the jail. They admitted him. He mounted the stairs; the jailer locked a door behind him.

The woman admitted him to the cell. The child lay on the cot. Goodwin sat beside it, his arms crossed, his legs extended in the attitude of a man in the last stage of physical exhaustion.

'Why are you sitting there, in front of that slit?' Horace said. 'Why not get into the corner, and we'll put the mattress over you.'

'You come to see it done, did you?' Goodwin said. 'Well, that's no more than right. It's your job. You promised I wouldn't hang, didn't you?'

'You've got an hour yet,' Horace said. 'The Memphis train doesn't get here until eight-thirty. He's surely got better sense than to come here in that canary-coloured car.' He turned to the woman. 'But you. I thought better of you. I know that he and I are fools, but I expected better of you.'

'You're doing her a favour,' Goodwin said. 'She might have hung on with me until she was too old to hustle a good man. If you'll just promise to get the kid a newspaper grift when he's old enough to make change, I'll be easy in my mind.'

The woman had returned to the cot. She lifted the child on to her lap. Horace went to her. He said: 'You come on, now. Nothing's going to happen. He'll be all right here. He knows it. You've got to go home and get some sleep, because you'll both be leaving here tomorrow. Come, now.'

'I reckon I better stay,' she said.

'Damn it, don't you know that putting yourself in the position for disaster is the surest way in the world to bring it about? Hasn't your own experience shown you that? Lee knows it. Lee, make her stop this.'

'Go on, Ruby,' Goodwin said. 'Go home and go to bed.'

'I reckon I better stay,' she said.

Horace stood over them. The woman mused above the child,

her face bent and her whole body motionless. Goodwin leaned
back against the wall, his brown wrists folded into the faded
sleeves of his shirt. 'You're a man now,' Horace said. 'Aren't
you? I wish that jury could see you now, locked up in a concrete
cell, scaring women and children with fifth-grade ghost stories.
They'd know you never had the guts to kill anybody.'

'You better go on and go to bed yourself,' Goodwin said. 'We
could sleep here, if there wasn't so much noise going on.'

'No; that's too sensible for us to do,' Horace said. He left the
cell. The jailer unlocked the door for him and he quitted the
building. In ten minutes he returned, with a parcel. Goodwin
had not moved. The woman watched him open the package. It
contained a bottle of milk, a box of candy, a box of cigars. He
gave Goodwin one of the cigars and took one himself. 'You
brought his bottle, didn't you?'

The woman produced the bottle from a bundle beneath the
cot. 'It's got some in it,' she said. She filled it from the bottle.
Horace lit his and Goodwin's cigars. When he looked again the
bottle was gone.

'Not time to feed him yet?' he said.

'I'm warming it,' the woman said.

'Oh,' Horace said. He tilted the chair against the wall, across
the cell from the cot.

'Here's room on the bed,' the woman said. 'It's softer. Some.'

'Not enough to change, though,' Horace said.

'Look here,' Goodwin said, 'you go on home. No use in you
doing this.'

'We've got a little work to do,' Horace said. 'That lawyer'll call
her again in the morning. That's his only chance: to invalidate
her testimony someway. You might try to get some sleep while
we go over it.'

'All right,' Goodwin said.

Horace began to drill the woman, tramping back and forth
upon the narrow floor. Goodwin finished his cigar and sat motionless again, his arms folded and his head bent. The clock above
the square struck nine and then ten. The child whimpered,
stirred. The woman stopped and changed it and took the bottle
from beneath her flank and fed it. Then she leaned forward
carefully and looked into Goodwin's face. 'He's asleep,' she
whispered.

'Shall we lay him down?' Horace whispered.

'No. Let him stay there.' Moving quietly she laid the child on

the cot and moved herself to the other end of it. Horace carried
the chair over beside her. They spoke in whispers.

The clock struck eleven. Still Horace drilled her, going over
and over the imaginary scene. At last he said: 'I think that's all.
Can you remember it, now? If he should ask you anything you
can't answer in the exact words you've learned tonight, just say
nothing for a moment. I'll attend to the rest. Can you remember,
now?'

'Yes,' she whispered. He reached across and took the box of
candy from the cot and opened it, the glazed paper crackling
faintly. She took a piece. Goodwin had not moved. She looked
at him, then at the narrow slit of window.

'Stop that,' Horace whispered. 'He couldn't reach him through
that window with a hat-pin, let alone a bullet. Don't you know
that?'

'Yes,' she said. She held the bon-bon in her hand. She was not
looking at him. 'I know what you're thinking,' she whispered.

'What?'

'When you got to the house and I wasn't there. I know what
you're thinking.' Horace watched her, her averted face. 'You
said tonight was the time to start paying you.'

For a while longer he looked at her. 'Ah,' he said. 'O tempora!
O mores! O hell! Can you stupid mammals never believe that any
man, every man – You thought that was what I was coming for?
You thought that if I had intended to, I'd have waited this long?'

She looked at him briefly. 'It wouldn't have done you any good
if you hadn't waited.'

'What? Oh. Well. But you would have tonight?'

'I thought that was what –'

'You would now, then?' She looked around at Goodwin. He
was snoring a little. 'Oh, I don't mean right this minute,' he
whispered. 'But you'll pay on demand.'

'I thought that was what you meant. I told you we didn't have
– If that ain't enough pay, I don't know that I blame you.'

'It's not that. You know it's not that. But can't you see that
perhaps a man might do something just because he knew it was
right, necessary to the harmony of things that it be done?'

The woman turned the bon-bon slowly in her hand. 'I thought
you were mad about him.'

'Lee?'

'No. Him.' She touched the child. 'Because I'd have to bring
him with us.'

'You mean, with him at the foot of the bed, maybe? perhaps you holding him by the leg all the time, so he wouldn't fall off?'

She looked at him, her eyes grave and blank and contemplative. Outside the clock struck twelve.

'Good God,' he whispered. 'What kind of men have you known?'

'I got him out of jail once that way. Out of Leavenworth, too. When they knew he was guilty.'

'You did?' Horace said. 'Here. Take another piece. That one's about worn out.' She looked down at her chocolate-stained fingers and the shapeless bon-bon. She dropped it behind the cot. Horace extended his handkerchief.

'It'll soil it,' she said. 'Wait.' She wiped her fingers on the child's discarded garment and sat again, her hands clasped in her lap. Goodwin was snoring regularly. 'When he went to the Philippines he left me in San Francisco. I got a job and I lived in a hall room, cooking over a gas-jet, because I told him I would. I didn't know how long he'd be gone, but I promised him I would and he knew I would. When he killed that other soldier over that nigger woman, I didn't even know it. I didn't get a letter from him for five months. It was just when I happened to see an old newspaper I was spreading on a closet shelf in the place where I worked that I saw the regiment was coming home, and when I looked at the calendar it was that day. I'd been good all that time. I'd had good chances; every day I had them with the men coming in the restaurant.

'They wouldn't let me off to go and meet the ship, so I had to quit. Then they wouldn't let me see him, wouldn't even let me on the ship. I stood there while they came marching off it, watching for him and asking the ones that passed if they knew where he was and them kidding me if I had a date that night, telling me they never heard of him or that he was dead or he had run off to Japan with the colonel's wife. I tried to get on the ship again, but they wouldn't let me. So that night I dressed up and went to the cabarets until I found one of them and let him pick me up, and he told me. It was like I had died. I sat there with the music playing and all, and that drunk soldier pawing at me, and me wondering why I didn't let go, go on with him, get drunk and never sober up again and me thinking And this is the sort of animal I wasted a year over. I guess that was why I didn't.

'Anyway, I didn't. I went back to my room and the next day I started looking for him. I kept on, with them telling me lies and

trying to make me, until I found he was in Leavenworth. I didn't
have enough money for a ticket, so I had to get another job.
It took two months to get enough money. Then I went to
Leavenworth. I got another job as a waitress, in Childs', nightsh-
ifts, so I could see Lee every other Sunday afternoon. We decided
to get a lawyer. We didn't know that a lawyer couldn't do anything
for a federal prisoner. The lawyer didn't tell me, and I hadn't
told Lee how I was getting the lawyer. He thought I had saved
some money. I lived with the lawyer two months before I found
it out.

'Then the war came and they let Lee out and sent him to
France. I went to New York and got a job in a munitions plant.
I stayed straight too, with the cities full of soldiers with money
to spend, and even the little ratty girls wearing silk. But I stayed
straight. Then he came home. I was at the ship to meet him. He
got off under arrest and they sent him back to Leavenworth for
killing that soldier three years ago. Then I got a lawyer to get a
Congressman to get him out. I gave him all the money I had
saved too. So when Lee got out, we had nothing. He said we'd
get married, but we couldn't afford it. And when I told him
about the lawyer, he beat me.'

Again she dropped a shapeless piece of candy behind the cot
and wiped her hands on the garment. She chose another piece
from the box and ate it. Chewing, she looked at Horace, turning
upon him a blank, musing gaze for an unhurried moment.
Through the slotted window the darkness came chill and dead.

Goodwin ceased snoring. He stirred and sat up.

'What time is it?' he said.

'What?' Horace said. He looked at his watch. 'Half-past two.'

'He must have had a puncture,' Goodwin said.

Towards dawn Horace himself slept, sitting in the chair. When
he waked a narrow rosy pencil of sunlight fell level through the
window. Goodwin and the woman were talking quietly on the
cot. Goodwin looked at him bleakly.

'Morning,' he said.

'I hope you slept off that nightmare of yours,' Horace said.

'If I did, it's the last one I'll have. They say you don't dream
there.'

'You've certainly done enough not to miss it,' Horace said. 'I
suppose you'll believe us, after this.'

'Believe, hell,' Goodwin said, who had sat so quiet, so contained
with his saturnine face negligent in his overalls and blue shirt;

'do you think for one minute that man is going to let me walk out of that door and up the street and into that court-house after yesterday? What sort of men have you lived with all your life? In a nursery? I wouldn't do that, myself.'

'If he does, he has sprung his own trap,' Horace said.

'What good will that do me? Let me tell –'

'Lee,' the woman said.

'– you something: the next time you want to play dice with a man's neck –'

'Lee,' she said. She was stroking her hand slowly on his head, back and forth. She began to smooth his hair into a part, patting his collarless shirt smooth. Horace watched them.

'Would you like to stay here today?' he said quietly. 'I can fix it.'

'No,' Goodwin said. 'I'm sick of it. I'm going to get it over with. Just tell that goddamned deputy not to walk too close to me. You and her better go and eat breakfast.'

'I'm not hungry,' the woman said.

'You go on like I told you,' Goodwin said.

'Lee.'

'Come,' Horace said. 'You can come back afterwards.'

Outside, in the fresh morning, he began to breathe deeply. 'Fill your lungs,' he said. ' A night in that place would give anyone the jimjams. The idea of three grown people ... My Lord, sometimes I believe that we are all children, except children themselves. But today will be the last. By noon he'll walk out of there a free man: do you realize that?'

They walked on in the fresh sunlight, beneath the high, soft sky. High against the blue fat little clouds blew up from the south-west, and the cool steady breeze shivered and twinkled in the locusts where the blooms had long since fallen.

'I don't know how you'll get paid,' she said.

'Forget it. I've been paid. You won't understand it, but my soul has served an apprenticeship that has lasted for forty-three years. Forty-three years. Half again as long as you have lived. So you see that folly, as well as poverty, cares for its own.'

'And you know that he – that –'

'Stop it, now. We dreamed that away, too. God is foolish at times, but at least He's a gentleman. Don't you know that?'

'I always thought of Him as a man,' the woman said.

The bell was already ringing when Horace crossed the square towards the court-house. Already the square was filled with wagons and cars and the overalls and khaki thronged slowly beneath the Gothic entrance of the building. Overhead the clock was striking nine as he mounted the stairs.

The broad double doors at the head of the cramped stair were open. From beyond them came a steady preliminary stir of people settling themselves. Above the seat-backs Horace could see their heads – bald heads, grey heads, shaggy heads and heads trimmed to recent feather-edge above sun-baked necks, oiled heads above urban collars and here and there a sun-bonnet or a flowered hat.

The hum of their voices and movements came back upon the steady draught which blew through the door. The air entered the open windows and blew over the heads and back to Horace in the door, laden with smells of tobacco and stale sweat and the earth and with that unmistakable odour of court-rooms; that musty odour of spent lusts and greeds and bickerings and bitterness, and withal a certain clumsy stability in lieu of anything better. The windows gave upon balconies close under the arched porticoes. The breeze drew through them, bearing the chirp and coo of sparrows and pigeons that nested in the eaves, and now and then the sound of a motor-horn from the square below, rising out of and sinking back into a hollow rumble of feet in the corridor below and on the stairs.

The Bench was empty. At one side, at the long table, he could see Goodwin's black head and gaunt brown face, and the woman's grey hat. At the other end of the table sat a man picking his teeth. His skull was capped closely by tightly-curled black hair thinning upon a bald spot. He had a long, pale nose. He wore a tan palm beach suit; upon the table near him lay a smart leather brief-case and a straw hat with a red-and-tan band, and he gazed lazily out a window above the ranked heads, picking his teeth. Horace stopped just within the door. 'It's a lawyer,' he said. 'A jew lawyer from Memphis.' Then he was looking at the backs of the heads about the table, where the witnesses and such would be. 'I know what I'll find before I find it,' he said. 'She will have on a black hat.'

He walked up the aisle. From beyond the balcony window where the sound of the bell seemed to be and where beneath the eaves the guttural pigeons crooned, the voice of the bailiff came:

'The honourable Circuit Court of Yoknapatawpha county is now open according to law . . .'

Temple had on a black hat. The clerk called her name twice before she moved and took the stand. After a while Horace realized that he was being spoken to, a little testily, by the Court.

'Is this your witness, Mr Benbow?'

'It is, your Honour.'

'You wish her sworn and recorded?'

'I do, your Honour.'

Beyond the window, beneath the unhurried pigeons, the bailiff's voice still droned, reiterant, importunate, and detached, though the sound of the bell had ceased.

Chapter Twenty-eight

The District Attorney faced the jury. 'I offer as evidence this object which was found at the scene of the crime.' He held in his hand a corn-cob. It appeared to have been dipped in dark brownish paint. 'The reason this was not offered sooner is that its bearing on the case was not made clear until the testimony of the defendant's wife, which I have just caused to be read aloud to you gentlemen from the record.

'You have just heard the testmony of the chemist and the gynaecologist – who is, as you gentlemen know, an authority on the most sacred affairs of that most sacred thing in life: womanhood – who says that this is no longer a matter for the hangman, but for a bonfire of gasoline –'

'I object!' Horace said 'The prosecution is attempting to sway –'

'Sustained,' the Court said. 'Strike out the phrase beginning "who says that", mister clerk. You may instruct the jury to disregard it, Mr Benbow. Keep to the matter in hand, Mr District Attorney.'

The District Attorney bowed. He turned to the witness stand, where Temple sat. From beneath her black hat her hair escaped in tight red curls like clots of resin. The hat bore a rhinestone ornament. Upon her black satin lap lay a platinum bag. Her pale tan coat was open upon a shoulder knot of purple. Her hands lay motionless, palm-up on her lap. Her long blonde legs slanted, lax-ankled, her two motionless slippers with their glittering buckles lay on their sides as though empty. Above the ranked intent faces, white and pallid as the floating bellies of dead fish, she sat in an attitude at once detached and cringing, her gaze fixed on something at the back of the room. Her face was quite pale, the two spots of rouge like paper discs pasted on her cheekbones, her mouth painted into a savage and perfect bow, also like something both symbolical and cryptic cut carefully from purple paper and pasted there.

The District Attorney stood before her.

'What is your name?' She did not answer. She moved her head slightly, as though he had obstructed her view, gazing at something in the back of the room. 'What is your name?' he repeated, moving also, into the line of her vision again. Her mouth moved. 'Louder,' he said, 'Speak out. No one will hurt you. Let these good men, these fathers and husbands, hear what you have to say and right your wrong for you.'

The Court glanced at Horace, his eyebrows raised. But Horace made no move. He sat with his head bent a little, his hands clutched in his lap.

'Temple Drake,' Temple said.

'Your age?'

'Eighteen.'

'Where is your home?'

'Memphis,' she said in a scarce distinguishable voice.

'Speak a little louder. These men will not hurt you. They are here to right the wrong you have suffered. Where did you live before you went to Memphis?'

'In Jackson.'

'Have you relations there?'

'Yes.'

'Come. Tell these good men –'

'My father.'

'Your mother is dead?'

'Yes.'

'Have you any sisters?'

'No.'

'You are your father's only daughter?'

Again the Court looked at Horace; again he made no move.

'Yes.'

'Where have you been living since May twelfth of this year?'

Her head moved faintly, as though she would see beyond him.
He moved into her line of vision, holding her eyes. She stared at
him again, giving her parrot-like answers.

'Did your father know you were there?'

'No.'

'Where did he think you were?'

'He thought I was in school.'

'You were in hiding, then, because something had happened
to you and you dared not –'

'I object!' Horace said. 'The question is lead –'

'Sustained,' the Court said. 'I have been on the point of warning
you for some time, Mr Attorney, but defendant would not take
exception, for some reason.'

The District Attorney bowed towards the Bench. He turned
to the witness and held her eyes again.

'Where were you on Sunday morning, May twelfth?'

'I was in the crib.'

The room sighed, its collective breath hissing in the musty
silence. Some newcomers entered, but they stopped at the rear
of the room in a clump and stood there. Temple's head had
moved again. The District Attorney caught her gaze and held it.
He half turned and pointed at Goodwin.

'Did you ever see that man before?' She gazed at the District
Attorney, her face quite rigid, empty. From a short distance her
eyes, the two spots of rouge and her mouth, were like five
meaningless objects in a small heart-shaped dish. 'Look where I
am pointing.'

'Yes.'

'Where did you see him?'

'In the crib.'

'What were you doing in the crib?'

'I was hiding.'

'Who were you hiding from?'

'From him.'

'That man there? Look where I am pointing.' ·

'Yes.'

'But he found you?'

'Yes.

'Was anyone else there?'

'Tommy was. He said –'

'Was he inside the crib or outside?'

'He was outside by the door. He was watching. He said he wouldn't let —'

'Just a minute. Did you ask him not to let anyone in?'

'Yes.'

'And he locked the door on the outside?'

'Yes.'

'But Goodwin came in.'

'Yes.'

'Did he have anything in his hand?'

'He had the pistol.'

'Did Tommy try to stop him?'

'Yes. He said he —'

'Wait. What did he do to Tommy?'

She gazed at him.

'He had the pistol in his hand. What did he do then?'

'He shot him.' The District Attorney stepped aside. At once the girl's gaze went to the back of the room and became fixed there. The District Attorney returned, stepped into her line of vision. She moved her head; he caught her gaze and held it and lifted the stained corn-cob before her eyes. The room sighed, a long hissing breath.

'Did you ever see this before?'

'Yes.'

The District Attorney turned away. 'Your honour and gentlemen, you have listened to this horrible, this unbelievable, story which this young girl has told; you have seen the evidence and heard the doctor's testimony: I shall no longer subject this ruined, defenceless child to the agony of —' He ceased; the heads turned as one and watched a man come stalking up the aisle towards the Bench. He walked steadily, paced and followed by a slow gaping of the small white faces, a slow hissing of collars. He had neat white hair and a clipped moustache like a bar of hammered silver against his dark skin. His eyes were pouched a little. A small paunch was buttoned snugly into his immaculate linen suit. He carried a panama hat in one hand and a slender black stick in the other. He walked steadily up the aisle in a slow expulsion of silence like a prolonged sigh, looking to neither side. He passed the witness stand without a glance at the witness, who still gazed at something in the back of the room, walking right through her line of vision like a runner crossing a tape, and stopped before the bar above which the Court had half risen, his arms on the desk.

'Your Honour,' the old man said, 'is the Court done with this witness?'

'Yes, sir, Judge,' the Court said; 'yes, sir. Defendant, do you waive –'

The old man turned slowly, erect above the held breaths, the little white faces, and looked down at the six people at the counsel table. Behind him the witness had not moved. She sat in her attitude of childish immobility, gazing like a drugged person above the faces, towards the rear of the room. The old man turned to her and extended his hand. She did not move. The room expelled its breath, sucked it quickly in and held it again. The old man touched her arm. She turned her head towards him, her eyes blank and all pupil above the three savage spots of rouge. She put her hand in his and rose, the platinum bag slipping from her lap to the floor with a thin clash, gazing again at the back of the room. With the toe of his small gleaming shoe the old man flipped the bag into the corner where the jury-box joined the Bench, where a spitoon sat, and steadied the girl down from the dais. The room breathed again as they moved on down the aisle.

Half-way down the aisle the girl stopped again, slender in her smart open coat, her blank face rigid, then she moved on, her hand in the old man's. They returned down the aisle, the old man erect beside her, looking to neither side, paced by that slow whisper of collars. Again the girl stopped. She began to cringe back, her body arching slowly, her arm tautening in the old man's grasp. He bent towards her, speaking; she moved again, in that shrinking and rapt abasement. Four younger men were standing stiffly erect near the exit. They stood like soldiers, staring straight ahead until the old man and the girl reached them. Then they moved and surrounded the other two, and in a close body the girl hidden among them, they moved towards the door. Here they stopped again; the girl could be seen shrunk against the wall just inside the door, her body arched again. She appeared to be clinging there, then the five bodies hid her again and again in a close body the group passed through the door and disappeared. The room breathed: a buzzing sound like a wind getting up. It moved forward with a slow increasing rush, on above the long table where the prisoner and the woman with the child and Horace and the District Attorney and the Memphis lawyer sat, and across the jury and against the Bench in a long sigh. The Memphis lawyer was sitting on his spine, gazing dreamily out the window. The child made a fretful sound, whimpering.

'Hush,' the woman said. 'Shhhhhhhh.'

Chapter Twenty-nine

The jury was out eight minutes. When Horace left the court-house it was getting towards dusk. The tethered wagons were taking out, some of them to face twelve and sixteen miles of country road. Narcissa was waiting for him in the car. He emerged among the overalls, slowly; he got into the car stiffly, like an old man, with a drawn face. 'Do you want to go home?' Narcissa said.

'Yes,' Horace said.

'I mean, to the house, or out home?'

'Yes,' Horace said.

She was driving the car. The engine was running. She looked at him, in a new dark dress with a severe white collar, a dark hat.

'Which one?'

'Home,' he said. 'I don't care. Just home.'

They passed the jail. Standing along the fence were the loafers, the countrymen, the blackguard boys and youths who had fol-lowed Goodwin and the deputy from the courthouse. Beside the gate the woman stood, in the grey hat with the veil, carrying the child in her arms. 'Standing where he can see it through the window,' Horace said. 'I smell ham, too. Maybe he'll be eating ham before we get home.' Then he began to cry, sitting in the car beside his sister. She drove steadily, not fast. Soon they had left the town and the stout rows of young cotton swung at either hand in parallel and diminishing retrograde. There was still a little snow of locust blooms on the mounting drive. 'It does last,' Horace said. 'Spring does. You'd almost think there was some purpose to it.'

He stayed to supper. He ate a lot. 'I'll go and see about your room,' his sister said, quite gently.

'All right,' Horace said. 'It's nice of you.' She went out. Miss Jenny's wheel-chair sat on a platform slotted for the wheels. 'It's nice of her,' Horace said. 'I think I'll go outside and smoke my pipe.'

'Since when have you quit smoking it in here?' Miss Jenny said.

'Yes,' Horace said. 'It was nice of her.' He walked across the porch. 'I intended to stop here,' Horace said. He watched himself cross the porch and then tread the diffident snow of the last locusts; he turned out of the iron gates, on to the gravel. After about a mile a car slowed and offered him a ride. 'I'm just walking before supper,' he said; 'I'll turn back soon.' After another mile he could see the lights of town. It was a faint glare, low and close. It got stronger as he approached. Before he reached town he began to hear the sound, the voices. Then he saw the people, a shifting mass filling the street, and the bleak, shallow yard above which the square and slotted bulk of the jail loomed. In the yard, beneath the barred window, a man in his shirt sleeves faced the crowd, hoarse, gesticulant. The barred window was empty.

Horace went on towards the square. The sheriff was among the drummers before the hotel, standing along the kerb. He was a fat man, with a broad, dull face which belied the expression of concern about his eyes. 'They won't do anything,' he said. 'There is too much talk. Noise. And too early. When a mob means business, it don't take that much time and talk. And it don't go about its business where every man can see it.'

The crowd stayed in the street until late. It was quite orderly, though. It was as though most of them had come to see, to look at the jail and the barred window, or to listen to the man in shirt sleeves. After a while he talked himself out. Then they began to move away, back to the square and some of them homeward, until there was left only a small group beneath the arc light at the entrance to the square, among whom were two temporary deputies, and the night marshal in a broad pale hat, a flash-light, a time clock, and a pistol. 'Git on home now' he said. 'Show's over. You boys done had your fun. Git on home to bed, now.'

The drummers sat a little while longer along the kerb before the hotel, Horace among them; the southbound train ran at one o'clock. 'They're going to let him get away with it, are they?' a drummer said. 'With that corn-cob? What kind of folks have you got here? What does it take to make you folks mad?'

'He wouldn't a never got to trial, in my town,' a second said.

'To jail, even,' a third said. 'Who was she?'

'College girl. Good looker. Didn't you see her?'

'I saw her. She was some baby. Jeez. I wouldn't have used no cob.'

Then the square was quiet. The clock struck eleven; the drummers went in and the negro porter came and turned the chairs back into the wall. 'You waiting for the train?' he said to Horace.

'Yes. Have you got a report on it yet?'

It's on time. But that's two hours yet. You could lay down in the Sample Room, if you want.'

'Can I?' Horace said.

'I'll show you,' the negro said. The Sample Room was where the drummers showed their wares. It contained a sofa. Horace turned off the light and lay down on the sofa. He could see the trees about the court-house, and one wing of the building rising above the quiet and empty square. But people were not asleep. He could feel the wakefulness, the people awake about the town. 'I could not have gone to sleep, anyway,' he said to himself.

He heard the clock strike twelve. Then – it might have been thirty minutes or maybe longer than that – he heard someone pass under the window, running. The runner's feet sounded louder than a horse, echoing across the empty square, the peaceful hours given to sleeping. It was not a sound Horace heard now; it was something in the air which the soumd of the running feet died into.

When he went down the corridor towards the stairs he did not know he was running until he heard beyond a door a voice say, 'Fire! it's a . . .' Then he had passed it. 'I scared him,' Horace said. 'He's just from Saint Louis, maybe, and he's not used to this.' He ran out of the hotel, on to the street. Ahead of him the proprietor had just run, ludicrous; a broad man with his trousers clutched before him and his braces dangling beneath his night-shirt, a tousled fringe of hair standing wildly about his bald head; three other men passed the hotel running. They appeared to come from nowhere, to emerge in midstride out of nothingness, fully dressed in the middle of the street, running.

'It is a fire,' Horace said. He could see the glare; against it the jail loomed in stark and savage silhouette.

'It's in that vacant lot,' the proprietor said, clutching his trousers. 'I can't go because there ain't anybody on the desk . . .'

Horace ran. Ahead of him he saw other figures running, turning into the alley beside the jail; then he heard the sound of the fire; the furious sound of gasoline. He turned into the alley. He could see the blaze, in the centre of a vacant lot where on

market days wagons were tethered. Against the flames black
figures showed, antic; he could hear panting shouts; through a
fleeting gap he saw a man turn and run, a mass of flames, still
carrying a five-gallon coal-oil can which exploded with a rocket-
like glare while he carried it, running.

He ran into the throng, into the circle which had formed about
a blazing mass in the middle of the lot. From one side of the
circle came the screams of the man about whom the coal-oil can
had exploded, but from the central mass of fire there came no
sound at all. It was now indistinguishable, the flames whirling in
long and thunderous plumes from a white-hot mass out of which
there defined themselves faintly the ends of a few posts and
planks. Horace ran among them; they were holding him, but he
did not know it; they were talking, but he could not hear the
voices.

'It's his lawyer.'

'Here's the man that defended him. That tried to get him
clear.'

'Put him in, too. There's enough left to burn a lawyer.'

'Do to the lawyer what he did to him. What he did to her. Only
we never used a cob. We made him wish we had used a cob.'

Horace couldn't hear them. He couldn't hear the man who
had got burned screaming. He couldn't hear the fire, though it
still swirled upward unabated, as though it were living upon itself,
and soundless: a voice of fury like in a dream, roaring silently
out of a peaceful void.

Chapter Thirty

The trains at Kinston were met by an old man who drove a seven-
passenger car. He was thin, with grey eyes and a grey moustache
with waxed ends. In the old days, before the town boomed
suddenly into a lumber town, he was a planter, a landholder, son
of one of the first settlers. He lost his property through greed
and gullibility, and he began to drive a hack back and forth

between town and the trains, with his waxed moustache, in a top-hat and a worn Prince Albert coat, telling the drummers how he used to lead Kinston society; now he drove it.

After the horse era passed, he bought a car, still meeting the trains. He still wore his waxed moustache, though the top-hat was replaced by a cap, the frock-coat by a suit of grey striped with red made by Jews in the New York tenement district. 'Here you are,' he said, when Horace descended from the train. 'Put your bag into the car,' he said. He got in himself. Horace got into the front seat beside him. 'You are one train late,' he said.

'Late?' Horace said.

'She got in this morning. I took her home. Your wife.'

'Oh,' Horace said. 'She's home?'

The other started the car and backed and turned. It was a good, powerful car, moving easily. 'When did you expect her? . . .' They went on. 'I see where they burned that fellow over at Jefferson. I guess you saw it.'

'Yes,' Horace said. 'Yes. I heard about it.'

'Served him right,' the driver said. 'We got to protect our girls. Might need them ourselves.'

They turned, following a street. There was a corner, beneath an arc light. 'I'll get out here,' Horace said.

'I'll take you on to the door,' the driver said.

'I'll get out here,' Horace said. 'Save you having to turn.'

'Suit yourself,' the driver said. 'You're paying for it, anyway.'

Horace got out and lifted out his suitcase; the driver did not offer to touch it. The car went on. Horace picked up the suitcase, the one which had stayed in the closet at his sister's home for ten years and which he had brought into town with him on the morning when she had asked him the name of the District Attorney.

His house was new, on a fairish piece of lawn, the trees, the poplars and maples which he had set out, still new. Before he reached the house, he saw the rose-coloured shade at his wife's windows. He entered the house from the back and came to her door and looked into the room. She was reading in bed, a broad magazine with a coloured back. The lamp had a rose-coloured shade. On the table sat an open box of chocolates.

'I came back,' Horace said.

She looked at him across the magazine.

'Did you lock the back door?' she said.

'Yes, I knew she would be,' Horace said. 'Have you tonight . . .'

'Have I what?'

'Little Belle. Did you telephone . . .'

'What for? She's at that house party. Why shouldn't she be? Why should she have to disrupt her plans, refuse an invitation?'

'Yes,' Horace said. 'I knew she would be. Did you . . .'

'I talked to her night before last. Go lock the back door.'

'Yes,' Horace said. 'She's all right. Of course she is. I'll just . . .' The telephone sat on a table in the dark hall. The number was on a rural line; it took some time. Horace sat beside the telephone. He had left the door at the end of the hall open. Through it the light airs of the summer night drew, vague, disturbing. 'Night is hard on old people,' he said quietly, holding the receiver. 'Summer nights are hard on them. Something should be done about it. A law.'

From her room Belle called his name, in the voice of a reclining person. 'I called her night before last. Why must you bother her?'

'I know,' Horace said. 'I won't be long at it.'

He held the receiver, looking at the door through which the vague, troubling wind came, He began to say something out of a book he had read: 'Less oft is peace. Less oft is peace,' he said.

The wire answered. 'Hello! Hello! Belle?' Horace said.

'Yes?' her voice came back thin and faint. 'What is it? Is anything wrong?'

'No, no,' Horace said. 'I just wanted to tell you hello and good night.'

'Tell what? What is it? Who is speaking?' Horace held the receiver, sitting in the dark hall.

'It's me, Horace. Horace. I just wanted to –'

Over the thin wire there came a scuffling sound; he could hear Little Belle breathe. Then a voice said, a masculine voice: 'Hello, Horace; I want you to meet a –'

'Hush!' Little Belle's voice said, thin and faint; again Horace heard them scuffling; a breathless interval. 'Stop it!' Little Belle's voice said. 'It's Horace! I live with him!' Horace held the receiver to his ear. Little Belle's voice was breathless, controlled, cool, discreet, detached. 'Hello. Horace. Is Mamma all right?'

'Yes. We're all right. I just wanted to tell you . . .'

'Oh. Good night.'

'Good night. Are you having a good time?'

'Yes. Yes. I'll write tomorrow. Didn't Mamma get my letter today?'

'I don't know. I just –'

'Maybe I forgot to mail it. I won't forget tomorrow, though. I'll write tomorrow. Was that all you wanted?'

'Yes. Just wanted to tell you . . .'

He put the receiver back; he heard the wire die. The light from his wife's room fell across the hall. 'Lock the back door,' she said.

Chapter Thirty-one

While on his way to Pensacola to visit his mother, Popeye was arrested in Birmingham for the murder of a policeman in a small Alabama town on June 17 of that year. He was arrested in August. It was on the night of June 17 that Temple had passed him sitting in the parked car beside the road-house on the night when Red had been killed.

Each summer Popeye went to see his mother. She thought he was a night clerk in a Memphis hotel.

His mother was the daughter of a boarding-house keeper. His father had been a professional strike-breaker hired by the street railway company to break a strike in 1900. His mother at that time was working in a department store down-town. For three nights she rode home on the car beside the motorman's seat on which Popeye's father rode. One night the strike-breaker got off at her corner with her and walked to her home.

'Won't you get fired?' she said.

'By who?' the strike-breaker said. They walked along together. He was well-dressed. 'Them others would take me that quick. They know it, too.'

'Who would take you?'

'The strikers. I don't care a damn who is running the car, see. I'll ride with one as soon as another. Sooner, if I could make this route every night at this time.'

She walked beside him. 'You don't mean that,' she said.

'Sure I do.' He took her arm.

'I guess you'd just as soon be married to one as another, the same way.'

'Who told you that?' he said. 'Have them bastards been talking about me?'

A month later she told him that they would have to be married.

'How do you mean, have to?' he said.

'I don't dare to tell them. I would have to go away. I don't dare.'

'Well, don't get upset. I'd just as lief. I have to pass here every night anyway.'

They were married. He would pass the corner at night. He would ring the foot-bell. Sometimes he would come home. He would give her money. Her mother liked him; he would come roaring into the house at dinner-time on Sunday, calling the other clients, even the old ones, by their first names. Then one day he didn't come back; he didn't ring the foot-bell when the trolley passed. The strike was over by then. She had a Christmas card from him; a picture, with a bell and an embossed wreath in gilt, from a Georgia town. It said: 'The boys trying to fix it up here. But these folks awful slow. Will maybe move on until we strike a good town ha ha.' The word, strike, was underscored.

Three weeks after her marriage, she had begun to ail. She was pregnant then. She did not go to a doctor, because an old negro woman told her what was wrong. Popeye was born on the Christmas Day on which the card was received. At first they thought he was blind. Then they found that he was not blind, though he did not learn to walk and talk until he was about four years old. In the meantime, the second husband of her mother, an undersized, snuffy man with a mild, rich moustache, who pottered about the house – he fixed all the broken steps and leaky drains and such – left home one afternoon with a cheque signed in blank to pay a twelve-dollar butcher's bill. He never came back. He drew from the bank his wife's fourteen-hundred-dollar savings account, and disappeared.

The daughter was still working down-town, while her mother tended the child. One afternoon one of the clients returned and found his room on fire. He put it out; a week later he found a smudge in his waste-basket. The grandmother was tending the child. She carried it about with her. One evening she was not in sight. The whole household turned out. A neighbour turned in a fire alarm and the firemen found the grandmother in the attic, stamping out a fire in a handful of excelsior in the centre of the floor, the child asleep in a discarded mattress near by.

'Them bastards are trying to get him,' the old woman said. 'They set the house on fire.' The next day, all the clients left.

The young woman quit her job. She stayed at home all the time. 'You ought to get out and get some air,' the grandmother said.

'I get enough air,' the daughter said.

'You could go out and buy the groceries,' the mother said. 'You could buy them cheaper.'

'We get them cheap enough.'

She would watch all the fires; she would not have a match in the house. She kept a few hidden behind a brick in the outside wall. Popeye was three years old then. He looked about one, though he could eat pretty well. A doctor had told his mother to feed him eggs cooked in olive-oil. One afternoon the grocer's boy, entering the area-way on a bicycle, skidded and fell. Something leaked from the package. 'It ain't eggs,' the boy said. 'See?' It was a bottle of olive-oil. 'You ought to buy that oil in cans, anyway,' the boy said. 'He can't tell no difference in it. I'll bring you another one. And you want to have that gate fixed. Do you want I should break my neck on it?'

He had not returned by six o'clock. It was summer. There was no fire, not a match in the house. 'I'll be back in five minutes,' the daughter said.

She left the house. The grandmother watched her disappear. Then she wrapped the child up in a light blanket and left the house. The street was a side street, just off a main street where there were markets, where the rich people in limousines stopped on the way home to shop. When she reached the corner, a car was just drawing in to the kerb. A woman got out and entered a store, leaving a negro driver behind the wheel. She went to the car.

'I want a half a dollar,' she said.

The negro looked at her. 'A which?'

'A half a dollar. The boy busted the bottle.'

'Oh,' the negro said. He reached in his pocket. 'How am I going to keep it straight, with you collecting out here? Did she send you for the money out here?'

'I want a half a dollar. He busted the bottle.'

'I reckon I better go in, then,' the negro said. 'Seem like to me you folks would see that folks got what they buy, folks that had been trading here long as we is.'

'It's a half a dollar,' the woman said. He gave her a half-dollar and entered the store. The woman watched him. Then she laid the child on the seat of the car, and followed the negro. It was a self-serve place, where the customers moved slowly along a railing in single file. The negro was next to the white woman who had left the car. The grandmother watched the woman pass back to the negro a loose handful of bottles of sauce and catsup. 'That'll be a dollar and a quarter,' she said. The negro gave her the money. She took it and passed them and crossed the room. There was a bottle of imported Italian olive-oil, with a price tag. 'I got twenty-eight cents more,' she said. She moved on, watching the price tags, until she found one that said twenty-eight cents. It was seven bars of bath soap. With the two parcels she left the store. There was a policeman at the corner. 'I'm out of matches,' she said.

The policeman dug into his pocket. 'Why didn't you buy some while you were there?' he said.

'I just forgot it. You know how it is, shopping with a child.'

'Where is the child?' the policeman said.

'I traded it in,' the woman said.

'You ought to be in vaudeville,' the policeman said. 'How many matches do you want? I ain't got but one or two.'

'Just one,' the woman said. 'I never do light a fire with but one.'

'You ought to be in vaudeville,' the policeman said. 'You'd bring down the house.'

'I am,' the woman said. 'I bring down the house.'

'What house?' He looked at her. 'The poor-house?'

'I'll bring it down,' the woman said. 'You watch the papers tomorrow. I hope they get my name right.'

'What's your paper? Calvin Coolidge?'

'No, sir. That's my boy.'

'Oh. That's why you had so much trouble shopping, is it? You ought to be in vaudeville . . . Will two matches be enough?'

They had had three alarms from that address, so they didn't hurry. The first to arrive was the daughter. The door was locked, and when the firemen came and chopped it down, the house was already gutted. The grandmother was leaning out an upstairs window through which the smoke already curled. 'Them bastards,' she said. 'They thought they would get him. But I told them I would show them. I told them so.'

The mother thought that Popeye had perished also. They

held her, shrieking, while the shouting face of the grandmother vanished into the smoke, and the shell of the house caved in; that was where the woman and the policeman carrying the child, found her: a young woman with a wild face, her mouth open, looking at the child with a vague air, scouring her loose hair slowly upwards from her temples with both hands. She never wholly recovered. What with the hard work and the lack of fresh air, diversion, and the disease, the legacy which her brief husband had left her, she was not in any condition to stand shock, and there were times when she still believed that the child had perished, even though she held it in her arms crooning above it.

Popeye might well have been dead. He had no hair at all until he was five years old, by which time he was already a kind of day pupil at an institution: an undersized, weak child with a stomach so delicate that the slightest deviation from a strict regimen fixed for him by the doctor would throw him into convulsions. 'Alcohol would kill him like strychnine,' the doctor said. 'And he will never be a man, properly speaking. With care, he will live some time longer. But he will never be any older than he is now.' He was talking to the woman who had found Popeye in her car that day when his grandmother burned the house down and at whose instigation Popeye was under the doctor's care. She would fetch him to her home in afternoons and for holidays, where he would play by himself. She decided to have a children's party for him. She told him about it, bought him a new suit. When the afternoon of the party came and the guests began to arrive, Popeye could not be found. Finally a servant found a bathroom door locked. They called the child, but got no answer. They sent for a locksmith, but in the meantime the woman, frightened, had the door broken in with an axe. The bathroom was empty. The window was open. It gave on to a lower roof, from which a drainpipe descended to the ground. But Popeye was gone. On the floor lay a wicker cage in which two lovebirds lived; beside it lay the birds themselves, and the bloody scissors with which he had cut them up alive.

Three months later, at the instigation of a neighbour of his mother, Popeye was arrested and sent to a home for incorrigible children. He had cut up a half-grown kitten the same way.

His mother was an invalid. The woman who had tried to befriend the child supporting her, letting her do needlework and such. After Popeye was out – he was let out after five years, his behaviour having been impeccable, as being cured – he would write to her two or three times a year, from Mobile and then New Orleans and then Memphis. Each summer he would return home to see her, prosperous, quiet, thin, black, and uncommunicative in his narrow black suits. He told her that his business was being night clerk in hotels; that, following his profession, he would move from town to town, as a doctor or lawyer might.

While he was on his way home that summer they arrested him for killing a man in one town and at an hour when he was in another town killing somebody else – that man who made money and had nothing he could do with it, spend it for, since he knew that alcohol would kill him like poison, who had no friends and had never known a woman and knew he could never – and he said, 'For Christ's sake,' looking about the cell in the jail of the town where the policeman had been killed, his free hand (the other was handcuffed to the officer who had brought him from Birmingham) finicking a cigarette from his coat.

'Let him send for his lawyer,' they said, 'and get that off his chest. You want to wire?'

'Nah,' he said, his cold, soft eyes touching briefly the cot, the high small window, the grated door through which the light fell. They removed the handcuff; Popeye's hand appeared to flick a small flame out of thin air. He lit the cigarette and snapped the match towards the door. 'What do I want with a lawyer? I never was in – What's the name of this dump?'

They told him. 'You forgot, have you?'

'He won't forget it no more,' another said.

'Expect he'll remember his lawyer's name by morning,' the first said.

They left him smoking on the cot. He heard doors clash. Now and then he heard voices from the other cells; somewhere down the corridor a negro was singing. Popeye lay on the cot, his feet crossed in small, gleaming black shoes. 'For Christ's sake,' he said.

The next morning the judge asked him if he wanted a lawyer.

'What for?' he said. 'I told them last night I never was here before in my life. I don't like your town well enough to bring a stranger here for nothing.'

The judge and the bailiff conferred aside.

'You'd better get your lawyer,' the judge said.

'All right,' Popeye said. He turned and spoke generally into the room: 'Any of you ginneys want a one-day job?'

The judge rapped on the table. Popeye turned back, his tight shoulders lifted in a faint shrug, his hand moving towards the pocket where he carried his cigarettes. The judge appointed him counsel, a young man just out of law school.

'And I won't bother about being sprung,' Popeye said. 'Get it over with all at once.'

'You wouldn't get any bail from me, anyway,' the judge told him.

'Yeuh?' Popeye said. 'All right, Jack,' he told his lawyer, 'get going. I'm due in Pensacola right now.'

'Take the prisoner back to jail,' the judge said.

His lawyer had an ugly, eager, earnest face. He rattled on with a kind of gaunt enthusiasm while Popeye lay on the cot, smoking, his hat over his eyes, motionless as a basking snake save for the periodical movement of the hand that held the cigarette. At last he said: 'Here. I ain't the judge. Tell him all this.'

'But I've got –'

'Sure. Tell it to them. I don't know nothing about it. I wasn't even there. Get out and walk it off.'

The trial lasted one day. While a fellow-policeman, a cigar-clerk, a telephone girl testified, while his own lawyer rebutted in a gaunt mixture of uncouth enthusiasm and earnest ill-judgement, Popeye lounged in his chair, looking out the window above the jury's heads. Now and then he yawned; his hand moved to the pocket where his cigarettes lay, then refrained and rested idle against the black cloth of his suit, in the waxy lifelessness of shape and size like the hand of a doll.

The jury was out eight minutes. They stood and looked at him and said he was guilty. Motionless, his position unchanged, he looked back at them in a slow silence for several moments. 'Well, for Christ's sake,' he said.

The judge rapped sharply with his gavel; the officer touched his arm.

'I'll appeal,' the lawyer babbled, plunging along beside him. 'I'll fight them through every court –'

'Sure,' Popeye said, lying on the cot and lighting a cigarette; 'but not in here. Beat it, now. Go take a pill.'

The District Attorney was already making his plans for the appeal. 'It was too easy,' he said. 'He took it – Did you see how he took it? like he might be listening to a song he was too lazy to either like or dislike, and the Court telling him on what day they were going to break his neck. Probably got a Memphis lawyer already there outside the Supreme Court door now, waiting for a wire. I know them. It's them thugs like that that have made justice a laughing-stock, until even when we get a conviction, everybody knows it won't hold.'

Popeye sent for the turnkey and gave him a hundred-dollar bill. He wanted a shaving-kit and cigarettes. 'Keep the change and let me know when it's smoked up,' he said.

'I reckon you won't be smoking with me much longer,' the turnkey said. 'You'll get a good lawyer, this time.'

'Don't forget that lotion,' Popeye said. 'Ed Pinaud.' He called it 'Py-nawd.'

It had been a grey summer, a little cool. Little daylight ever reached the cell, and a light burned in the corridor all the time, falling into the cell in a broad pale mosaic, reaching the cot where his feet lay. The turnkey gave him a chair. He used it for a table; upon it the dollar watch lay, and a carton of cigarettes and a cracked soup bowl of stubs, and he lay on the cot, smoking and contemplating his feet while day after day passed. The gleam of his shoes grew duller, and his clothes needed pressing, because he lay in them all the time, since it was cool in the stone cell.

One day the turnkey said: 'There's folks here says that deppity invited killing. He done two-three means things folks knows about.' Popeye smoked, his hat over his face. The turnkey said: 'They might not sent your telegram. You want me to send another one for you?' Leaning against the grating he could see Popeye's feet, his thin, black legs motionless, merging into the delicate bulk of his prone body and the hat slanted across his averted face, the cigarette in one small hand. His feet were in shadow, in the shadow of the turnkey's body where it blotted out the grating. After a while the turnkey went away quietly.

When he had six days left the turnkey offered to bring him magazines, a deck of cards.

'What for?' Popeye said. For the first time he looked at the turnkey, his head lifted, in his smooth, pallid face his eyes round and soft as those prehensile tips on a child's toy arrows. Then he lay back again. After that each morning the turnkey thrust a rolled newspaper through the door. They fell to the floor and lay there, accumulating, unrolling and flattening slowly of their own weight in diurnal progression.

When he had three days left a Memphis lawyer arrived. Unbidden, he rushed up to the cell. All that morning the turnkey heard his voice raised in pleading and anger and expostulation; by noon he was hoarse, his voice not much louder than a whisper.

'Are you just going to lie here and let –'

'I'm all right,' Popeye said. 'I didn't send for you. Keep your nose out.'

'Do you want to hang? Is that it? Are you trying to commit suicide? Are you so tired of dragging down jack that . . . You, the smartest –'

'I told you once. I've got enough on you.'

'You, to have it hung on you by a small-time J.P.! When I go back to Memphis and tell them, they won't believe it.'

'Don't tell them, then.' He lay for a time while the lawyer looked at him in baffled and raging unbelief. 'Them durn hicks,' Popeye said. 'Jesus Christ . . . Beat it, now,' he said. 'I told you. I'm all right.'

On the night before, a minister came in.

'Will you let me pray with you?' he said.

'Sure,' Popeye said; 'go ahead. Don't mind me.'

The minister knelt beside the cot where Popeye lay smoking. After a while the minister heard him rise and cross the floor, then return to the cot. When he rose Popeye was lying on the cot, smoking. The minister looked behind him, where he had heard Popeye moving and saw twelve marks at spaced intervals along the base of the wall, as though marked there with burned matches. Two of the spaces were filled with cigarette stubs laid in neat rows. In the third space were two stubs. Before he departed he watched Popeye rise and go there and crush out two more stubs and lay them carefully beside the others.

Just after five o'clock the minister returned. All the spaces were filled save the twelfth one. It was three-quarters complete. Popeye was lying on the cot. 'Ready to go?' he said.

'Not yet,' the minister said. 'Try to pray,' he said. 'Try.'

'Sure,' Popeye said; 'go ahead.' The minister knelt again. He heard Popeye rise once and cross the floor and then return.

At five-thirty the turnkey came. 'I brought –' he said. He held his closed fist dumbly through the grating. 'Here's your change from that hundred you never – I brought . . . It's forty-eight dollars,' he said. 'Wait; I'll count it again; I don't know exactly, but I can give you a list – them tickets . . .'

'Keep it,' Popeye said, without moving. 'Buy yourself a hoop.'

They came for him at six. The minister went with him, his hand under Popeye's elbow, and he stood beneath the scaffold praying, while they adjusted the rope, dragging it over Popeye's sleek, oiled head, breaking his hair loose. His hands were tied, so he began to jerk his head, flipping his hair back each time it fell forward again, while the minister prayed, the others motionless at their posts with bowed heads.

Popeye began to jerk his neck forward in little jerks. 'Psssst!' he said, the sound cutting sharp into the drone of the minister's voice; 'pssssst!' The sheriff looked at him,; he quit jerking his neck and stood rigid, as though he had an egg balanced on his head. 'Fix my hair, Jack,' he said.

'Sure,' the sheriff said. 'I'll fix it for you'; springing the trap.

It had been a grey day, a grey summer, a grey year. On the street old men wore overcoats, and in the Luxembourg Gardens as Temple and her father passed the women sat knitting in shawls and even the men playing croquet played in coats and capes, and in the sad gloom of the chestnut trees the dry click of balls, the random shouts of children, had that quality of autumn, gallant and evanescent and forlorn. From beyond the circle with its spurious Greek balustrade, clotted with movement, filled with a grey light of the same colour and texture as the water which the fountain played into the pool, came a steady crash of music. They went on, passed the pool where the children and an old man in a shabby brown overcoat sailed toy boats, and entered the trees again and found seats. Immediately an old woman came with decrepit promptitude and collected four sous.

In the pavilion a band in the horizon blue of the army played Massenet and Scriabine, and Berlioz like a thin coating of tortured Tschaikovsky on a slice of stale bread, while the twilight dissolved in wet gleams from the branches, on to the pavilion and the sombre toadstools of umbrellas. Rich and resonant the brasses crashed and died in the thick green twilight, rolling over them in rich sad waves. Temple yawned behind her hand, then she took out a compact and opened it upon a face in miniature sullen and discontented and sad. Beside her her father sat, his hands crossed on the head of his stick, the rigid bar of his moustache beaded with moisture like frosted silver. She closed the compact and from beneath her smart new hat she seemed to follow with her eyes the waves of music, to dissolve into the dying brasses, across the pool and the opposite semicircle of trees where at sombre intervals the dead tranquil queens in stained marble mused, and on into the sky lying prone and vanquished in the embrace of the season of rain and death.

INTRUDER IN THE DUST

Chapter One

It was just noon that Sunday morning when the sheriff reached the jail with Lucas Beauchamp though the whole town (the whole county too for that matter) had known since the night before that Lucas had killed a white man.

He was there, waiting. He was the first one, standing lounging trying to look occupied or at least innocent, under the shed in front of the closed blacksmith's shop across the street from the jail where his uncle would be less likely to see him if or rather when he crossed the Square towards the post office for the eleven o'clock mail.

Because he knew Lucas Beauchamp too – as well that is as any white person knew him. Better than any maybe unless it was Carothers Edmonds on whose place Lucas lived seventeen miles from town, because he had eaten a meal in Lucas' house. It was in the early winter four years ago; he had been only twelve then and it had happened this way: Edmonds was a friend of his uncle; they had been in school at the same time at the State University, where his uncle had gone after he came back from Harvard and Heidelberg to learn enough law to get himself chosen County Attorney, and the day before Edmonds had come in to town to see his uncle on some county business and had stayed the night with them and at supper that evening Edmonds had said to him:

'Come out home with me tomorrow and go rabbit hunting:' and then to his mother: 'I'll send him back in tomorrow afternoon. I'll send a boy along with him while he's out with his gun:' and then to him again: 'He's got a good dog.'

'He's got a boy,' his uncle said and Edmonds said:

'Does his boy run rabbits too? and his uncle said:

'We'll promise he wont interfere with yours.'

So the next morning he and Aleck Sander went home with Edmonds. It was cold that morning, the first winter cold-snap; the hedgerows were rimed and stiff with frost and the standing

water in the roadside drainage ditches was skimmed with ice and
even the edges of the running water in the Nine Mile branch
glinted fragile and scintillant like fairy glass and from the first
farmyard they passed and then again and again and again came
the windless tang of woodsmoke and they could see in the back
yards the black iron pots already steaming while women in the
sunbonnets still of summer or men's old felt hats and long men's
overcoats stoked wood under them and the men with crokersack
aprons tied with wire over their overalls whetted knives or already
moved about the pens where hogs grunted and squealed, not
quite startled, not alarmed but just alerted as though sensing
already even though only dimly their rich and immanent destiny;
by nightfall the whole land would be hung with their spectral
intact tallow coloured empty carcasses immobilized by the heels
in attitudes of frantic running as though full tilt at the centre of
the earth.

And he didn't know how it happened. The boy, one of
Edmonds' tenant's sons, older and larger than Aleck Sander who
in his turn was larger than he although they were the same age,
was waiting at the house with the dog – a true rabbit dog, some
hound, a good deal of hound, maybe mostly hound, redbone and
black-and-tan with maybe a little pointer somewhere once, a
potlicker, a nigger dog which it took but one glance to see had
an affinity a rapport with rabbits such as people said Negroes
had with mules – and Aleck Sander already had his tapstick –
one of the heavy nuts which bolt railroad rails together, driven
on to a short length of broomhandle – which Aleck Sander could
throw whirling end over end at a running rabbit pretty near as
accurately as he could shoot the shotgun – and Aleck Sander and
Edmonds' boy with tapsticks and he with the gun they went
down through the park and across a pasture to the creek where
Edmonds' boy knew the footlog was and he didn't know how it
happened, something a girl might have been expected and even
excused for doing but nobody else, half, way over the footlog
and not even thinking about it who had walked the top rail of a
fence many a time twice that far when all of a sudden the known
familiar sunny winter earth was upside down and flat on his face
and still holding the gun he was rushing not away from the earth
but away from the bright sky and he could remember still the
thin bright tinkle of the breaking ice and how he didn't even feel
the shock of the water but only of the air when he came up again.
He had dropped the gun too so he had to dive, submerge again

to find it, back out of the icy air in to the water which as yet felt neither, neither cold or not and where even his sodden garments – boots and thick pants and sweater and hunting coat – didn't even feel heavy but just slow, and found the gun and tried again for bottom then thrashed one-handed to the bank and treading water and clinging to a willow-branch he reached the gun up until someone took it; Edmonds' boy obviously since at that moment Aleck Sander rammed down at him the end of a long pole, almost a log whose first pass struck his feet out from under him and sent his head under again and almost broke his hold on the willow until a voice said:

'Get the pole out of his way so he can get out' – just a voice, not because it couldn't be anybody else but either Aleck Sander or Edmonds' boy but because it didn't matter whose: climbing out now with both hands among the willows, the skim ice crinkling and tinkling against his chest, his clothes like soft cold lead which he didn't move in but seemed rather to mount into like a poncho or a tarpaulin: up the bank until he saw two feet in gum boots which were neither Edmonds' boy's nor Aleck Sander's and then the legs, the overalls rising out of them and he climbed on and stood up and saw a Negro man with an axe on his shoulder, in a heavy sheeplined coat and a broad pale felt hat such as his grandfather had used to wear, looking at him and that was when he saw Lucas Beauchamp for the first time that he remembered or rather for the first time because you didn't forget Lucas Beauchamp; gasping, shaking and only now feeling the shock of the cold water, he looked up at the face which was just watching him without pity commiseration or anything else, not even surprise: just watching him, whose owner had made no effort whatever to help him up out of the creek, had in fact ordered Aleck Sander to desist with the pole which had been the one token towards help that anybody had made – a face which in his estimation might have been under fifty or even forty except for the hat and the eyes, and inside a Negro's skin but that was all even to a boy of twelve shaking with cold and still panting from shock and exertion because what looked out of it had no pigment at all, not even the white man's lack of it, not arrogant, not even scornful: just intractable and composed. Then Edmonds' boy said something to the man, speaking a name: something Mister Lucas: and then he knew who the man was, remembering the rest of the story which was a piece, a fragment of the country's chronicle which few if any knew better than his uncle: how the man was son of one of old Carothers McCaslin's, Edmonds' great grandfather's, slaves who had been not just old Carothers' slave but his son too: standing and shaking steadily now for what seemed to him another whole minute while the man stood looking at him with nothing whatever in his face. Then the man turned, speaking not even back over his shoulder, already walking, not even waiting to see if they heard, let alone were going to obey:

'Come on to my house.'

'I'll go back to Mr Edmonds',' he said. The man didn't look back. He didn't even answer.

'Tote his gun, Joe,' he said.

So he followed, with Edmonds' boy and Aleck Sander following him, in single file along the creek towards the bridge and the road. Soon he had stopped shaking; he was just cold and wet now and most of that would go if he just kept moving. They crossed the bridge. Ahead now was the gate where the drive went up through the park to Edmonds' house. It was almost a mile; he would probably be dry and warm both by the time he got there and he still believed he was going to turn in at the gate and even after he knew that he wasn't or anyway hadn't, already beyond it now, he was still telling himself the reason was that, although Edmonds was a bachelor and there were no women in the house, Edmonds himself might refuse to let him out of the house again until he could be returned to his mother, still telling himself this even after he knew than the true reason was that he could no more imagine himself contradicting the man striding on ahead of him than he could his grandfather, not from any fear of nor even the threat of reprisal but because like his grandfather the man striding ahead of him was simply incapable of conceiving himself by a child contradicted and defied.

So he didn't even check when they passed the gate, he didn't even look at it and now they were in no well-used tended lane leading to tenant or servant quarters and marked by walking feet but a savage gash half gully and half road mounting a hill with an air solitary independent and intractable too and then he saw the house, the cabin and remembered the rest of the story, the legend: how Edmonds' father had deeded to his Negro first cousin and his heirs in perpetuity the house and the ten acres of land it sat in – an oblong of earth set for ever in the middle of the two-thousand-acre plantation like a postage stamp in the centre of an envelope – the paintless wooden house, the paintless picket fence whose paintless latchless gate the man kneed open

still without stopping or once looking back and, he following and
Aleck Sander and Edmonds' boy following him, strode on into
the yard. It would have been grassless even in summer; he could
imagine it, completely bare, no weed no sprig of anything, the
dust each morning swept by some of Lucas' womenfolks with a
broom made of willow switches bound together, into an intricate
series of whorls and overlapping loops which as the day advanced
would be gradually and slowly defaced by the droppings and the
cryptic three-toed prints of chickens like (remembering it now at
sixteen) a terrain in miniature out of the age of the great lizards,
the four of them walking in what was less than walk because its
surface was dirt too yet more than path, the footpacked strip
running plumbline straight between two borders of tin cans and
empty bottles and shards of china and earthenware set into the
ground, up to the paintless steps and the paintless gallery along
whose edge sat more cans but larger – empty gallon buckets
which had once contained molasses or perhaps paint and wornout
water or milk pails and one five-gallon can for kerosene with its
top cut off and half of what had once been somebody's (Edmonds'
without doubt) kitchen hot water tank sliced longways like a
banana – out of which flowers had grown last summer and from
which the dead stalks and the dried and brittle tendrils still leaned
and drooped, and beyond this the house itself, grey and weathered
and not so much paintless as independent of and intractable to
paint so that the house was not only the one possible continuation
of the stern untended road but was its crown too as the carven
ailanthus leaves are the Greek column's capital.

Not did the man pause yet, up the steps and across the gallery
and opened the door and entered and he and then Edmonds' boy
and Aleck Sander followed: a hall dim even almost dark after the
bright outdoors and already he could smell that smell which he
had accepted without question all his life as being the smell always
of the places where people with any trace of Negro blood live as
he had that all people named Mallison are Methodists, then a
bedroom: a bare worn quite clean pantless rugless floor, in one
corner and spread with a bright patchwork quilt a vast shadowy
tester bed which had probably come out of old Carothers McCaslin's house, and a battered cheap Grand Rapids dresser and then
for the moment no more or at least little more; only later would
he notice – or remember that he had seen – the cluttered mantel
on which sat a kerosene lamp hand-painted with flowers and a
vase filled with spills of twisted newspaper and above the mantel

the coloured lithograph of a three-year-old calendar in which
Pocahontas in the quilled fringed buckskins of a Sioux or Chip-
pewa chief stood against a balustrade of Italian marble above a
garden of formal cypresses and shadowy in the corner opposite
the bed a chromo portrait of two people framed heavily in gold-
painted wood on a gold-painted easel. But he hadn't seen that at
all yet because that was behind him and all he now saw was the
fire – the clay-daubed fieldstone chimney in which a halfburned
backlog glowed and smouldered in the grey ashes and beside it
in a rocking chair something which he thought was a child until
he saw the face, and then he did pause long enough to look at
her because he was about to remember something else his uncle
had told him about or at least in regard to Lucas Beauchamp,
and looking at her he realized for the first time how old the man
actually was, must be – a tiny old almost doll-sized woman much
darker than the man, in a shawl and an apron, her head bound
in an immaculate white cloth on top of which sat a painted straw
hat bearing some kind of ornament. But he couldn't think what
it was his uncle had said or told him and then he forgot that he
had remembered even the having been told, sitting in the chair
himself now squarely before the hearth where Edmonds' boy was
building up the fire with split logs and pine slivers and Aleck
Sander squatting tugged off the wet boots and then his trousers
and standing he got out of the coat and sweater and his shirt,
both of them having to dodge around and past and under the
man who stood straddled on the hearth, his back to the fire in
the gum boots and the hat and only the sheepskin coat removed
and then the old woman was beside him again less tall then he
and Aleck Sander even at twelve, with another of the bright
patchwork quilts on her arm.
'Strip off,' the man said.
'No I –' he said.
'Strip off,' the man said. So he stripped off the wet unionsuit
too and then he was in the chair again in front of the now bright
and swirling fire, enveloped in the quilt like a cocoon, enclosed
completely now in that unmistakable odour of Negroes – that
smell which if it were not for something that was going to happen
to him within a space of time measurable now in minutes he
would have gone to his grave never once pondering speculating
if perhaps that smell were really not the odour of a race nor even
actually of poverty but perhaps of a condition: an idea: a belief:
an acceptance, a passive acceptance by them themselves of the

idea that being Negroes they were not supposed to have facilities to wash properly or often or even to wash bathe often even without the facilities to do it with; that in fact it was a little to be preferred that they did not. But the smell meant nothing now or yet; it was still an hour yet before the thing would happen and it would be four years more before he would realize the extent of its ramifications and what it had done to him and he would be a man grown before he would realize, admit that he had accepted it. So he just smelled it and then dismissed it because he was used to it, he had smelled it off and on all his life and would continue to: who had spent a good part of that life in Paralee's, Aleck Sander's mother's cabin in their back yard where he and Aleck Sander played in the bad weather when they were little and Paralee would cook whole meals for them halfway between two meals at the house and he and Aleck Sander would eat them together, the food tasting the same to each; he could not even imagine an existence from which the odour would be missing to return no more. He had smelled it for ever, he would smell it always; it was a part of his inescapable past, it was a rich part of his heritage as a Southerner; he didn't even have to dismiss it, he just no longer smelled it at all as the pipe smoker long since never did smell at all the cold pipereek which is as much a part of his clothing as their buttons and buttonholes, sitting drowsing a little even in the warm huddled rankness of the quilt, rousing a little when he heard Edmonds' boy and Aleck Sander get up from where they had been squatting against the wall and leave the room, but not much, sinking again into the quilt's warm reek while there stood over him still, back to the fire and hands clasped behind him and except for the clasped hands and the missing axe and the sheeplined coat exactly as when he had looked up out of the creek and seen him first, the man in the gum boots and the faded overalls of a Negro but with a heavy gold watch-chain looping across the bib of the overalls and shortly after they entered the room he had been conscious of the man turning and taking something from the cluttered mantel and putting it into his mouth and later he had seen what it was: a gold toothpick such as his own grandfather had used: and the hat was a worn handmade beaver such as his grandfather had paid thirty and forty dollars apiece for, not set but raked slightly above the face pigmented like a Negro's but with a nose high in the bridge and even hooked a little and what looked out through it or from behind it not black nor white either, not arrogant at all and not even scornful: just intolerant, inflexible, and composed.

Then Aleck Sander came back with his clothes, dried now and still almost hot from the stove and he dressed, stamping into his stiffened boots; Edmonds' boy squatting again against the wall was still eating something from his hand and he said: 'I'll have my dinner at Mr Edmonds'.'

The man neither protested nor acquiesced. He didn't stir; he was not even looking at him. He just said, inflexible and calm: 'She done already dished it up now:' and he went on past the old woman who stood aside from the door to let him pass, into the kitchen: an oilcloth-covered table set in the bright sunny square of a southern window where – he didn't know how he knew it since there were no signs, traces, soiled plates to show it – Edmonds' boy and Aleck Sander had already eaten, and sat down and ate in his turn of what obviously was to be Lucas' dinner – collard greens, a slice of sidemeat fried in flour, big flat pale heavy half-cooked biscuits, a glass of buttermilk: nigger food too, accepted and then dismissed also because it was exactly what he had expected, it was what Negroes ate, obviously because it was what they liked, what they chose; not (at twelve: he would be a man grown before he experienced his first amazed dubiety at this) that out of their long chronicle this was all they had had a chance to learn to like except the ones who ate out of white folks' kitchens but that they had elected this out of all eating because this was their palates and their metabolism; afterwards, ten minutes later and then for the next four years he would be trying to tell himself that it was the food which had thrown him off. But he would know better; his initial error, misjudgement had been there all the time, not even needing to be abetted by the smell of the house and the quilt in order to survive what had looked out (and not even at him: just looked out) from the man's face; rising at last and with the coin, the half-dollar already in his hand going back into the other room: when he saw for the first time because he happened to be facing it now the goldframed portrait-group on its gold easel and he went to it, stooping to peer at it in its shadowy corner where only the gold leaf gleamed, before he knew he was going to do it. It had been retouched obviously; from behind the round faintly prismatic glass dome as out of a seer's crystal ball there looked back at him again the calm intolerant face beneath the swaggering rake of the hat, a tieless starched collar clipped to a white starched shirt with a collarbutton shaped like a snake's head and almost as large, the watchchain looped now across a broadcloth vest inside a broadcloth coat and only the toothpick missing, and beside him the tiny doll-like woman in another painted straw hat and a shawl; that is it must have been the woman though it looked like nobody he had ever seen before and then he realized it was more than that: there was something ghastly, almost intolerably wrong about it or her: when she spoke and he looked up, the man still standing straddled before the fire and the woman sitting again in the rocking chair in its old place almost-in the corner and she was not looking at him now and he knew she had never looked at him since he re-entered yet she said:

'That's some more of Lucas' doings:' and he said,

'What?' and the man said,

'Molly dont like it because the man that made it took her headrag off:' and that was it, she had hair; it was like looking at an embalmed corpse through the hermetic glass lid of a coffin and he thought *Molly. Of course* because he remembered now what it was his uncle had told him about Lucas or about them. He said:

'Why did he take it off?'

'I told him to,' the man said. 'I didn't want no field nigger picture in the house:' and he walked towards them now, putting the fist holding the half-dollar back into his pocket and scooping the dime and the two nickels – all he had – into the palm with it, saying,

' You came from town. My uncle knows you – Lawyer Gavin Stevens.'

'I remember your mama too,' she said. 'She use to be Miss Maggie Dandridge.'

'That was my grandmother,' he said. 'My mother's name was Stevens too:' and extended the coins: and in the same second in which he knew she would have taken them he knew that only by that one irrevocable second was he for ever now too late, for ever beyond recall, standing with the slow hot blood as slow as minutes themselves up his neck and face, for ever with his dumb hand open and on it the four shameful fragments of milled and minted dross, until at last the man had something that at least did the office of pity.

'What's that for?' the man said, not even moving, not even tilting his face downwards to look at what was on his palm: for another etemity and only the hot dead moveless blood until at last it ran to rage so that at least he could bear the shame: and watched his palm turn over not flinging the coins but spurning them downwards ringing on to the bare floor, bouncing and one of the nickels even rolling away in a long swooping curve with a dry minute sound like the scurry of a small mouse: and then his voice:

'Pick it up!'

And still nothing, the man didn't move, hands clasped behind him, looking at nothing; only the rush of the hot dead heavy blood out of which the voice spoke, addressing nobody: 'Pick up his money:' and he heard and saw Aleck Sander and Edmonds' boy reach and scurry among the shadows near the floor. ' Give it to him,' the voice said: and saw Edmonds' boy drop his two coins into Aleck Sander's palm and felt Aleck Sander's hand fumble the four of them at his own dropped hand and then into it. 'Now go on and shoot your rabbit,' the voice said. 'And stay out of that creek'

Chapter Two

And they walked again in the bright cold (even though it was noon now and about as warm as it would ever get today probably), back across the creek bridge and (suddenly: looking around, they had gone almost a half-mile along the creek and he didn't even remember it) the dog put a rabbit into a brier patch beside a cottonfield and yapping hysterically hoicked it out again, the small frantic tawny-coloured blob looking one instant spherical and close-coupled as a croquet ball and the next one long as a snake, bursting out of the thicket ahead of the dog, the small white flare of its scut zigzagging across the skeletoned cottonrows like the sail of a toy boat on a windy pond while across the thicket Aleck Sander yelled:

'Shoot him! Shoot him!' then 'Whyn't you shoot him?' and then he turned without haste and walked steadily to the creek and drew the four coins from his pocket and threw them out into the water: and sleepless in bed that night he knew that the food had been not just the best Lucas had to offer but all he had to offer; he had gone out there this morning as the guest not of Edmonds but of old Carothers McCaslin's plantation and Lucas knew it when he didn't and so Lucas had beat him, stood straddled in front of the hearth and without even moving his clasped hands from behind his back had taken his own seventy cents and beat him with them, and writhing with impotent fury he was already thinking of the man whom he had never seen but once and that only twelve hours ago, as within the next year he was to learn every white man in that whole section of the country had been thinking about him for years: *We got to make him be a nigger first. He's got to admit he's a nigger. Then maybe we will accept him as he seems to intend to be accepted.* Because he began at once to learn a good deal more about Lucas. He didn't hear it: he learned it, all that anyone who knew that part of the country could tell him about the Negro who said 'ma'am' to women just as any white man did and who said 'sir' and 'mister' to you if you were white but who you know was thinking neither and he knew you knew it but who was not even waiting, daring you to make the next move, because he didn't even care. For instance, this.

It was a Saturday afternoon three years ago at the crossroads store four miles from Edmonds' place where at some time during Saturday afternoon every tenant and renter and freeholder white or black in the neighbourhood would at least pass and usually stop, quite often even to buy something, the saddled trace-galled mules and horses tied among the willows and birches and sycamores in the trampled mud below the spring and their riders overflowing the store itself out on to the dusty banquette in front, standing or squatting on their heels drinking bottled sodapop and spitting tobacco and rolling without hurry cigarettes and striking deliberate matches to smoked-out pipes; this day there were three youngish white men from the crew of a nearby sawmill, all a little drunk, one of whom had a reputation for brawling and violence, and Lucas came in in the worn black broadcloth suit which he wore to town and on Sundays and the worn fine hat and the heavy watch-chain and the toothpick, and something happened, the story didn't say or perhaps didn't even know what, perhaps the way Lucas walked, entered speaking to no one and went to the counter and made his purchase (it was a five-cent carton of gingersnaps) and turned and tore the end from carton and removed the toothpick and put it into his breast pocket and shook one of the gingersnaps into his palm and put it into to his mouth, or perhaps just nothing was enough, the white man on his feet suddenly saying something to Lucas, saying 'You goddamn biggity stiffnecked stinking burrheaded Edmonds sonofabitch:' and Lucas chewed the gingersnap and swallowed and the carton already tilted again over his other hand, turned his head quite slowly and looked at the white man a moment and then said:

'I aint a Edmonds. I dont belong to these new folks. I belongs to the old lot. I'm a McCaslin.'

'Keep on walking around here with that look on your face and what you'll be is crowbait,' the white man said. For another moment or at least a half one Lucas looked at the white man with a calm speculative detachment; slowly the carton in one of his hands tilted further until another gingersnap dropped into his other palm, then lifting the corner of his lip he sucked an upper tooth, quite loud in the abrupt silence but with no implication whatever of either derision or rebuttal or even disagreement, with no implication of anything at all but almost abstractedly, as a man eating gingersnaps in the middle of a hundred-mile solitude would – if he did – suck a tooth, and said:

'Yes, I heard that idea before, And I notices that the folks that brings it up aint even Edmondses:' whereupon the white man even as he sprang up reached blindly back where on the counter behind him lay a half-dozen plough singletrees and snatched one of them up and had already started on the downswing when the son of the store's proprietor, himself a youngish active man, came either around or over the counter and grasped the other so that the singletree merely flew harmlessly across the aisle and crashed against the cold stove; then another man was holding the man too.

'Get out of here, Lucas!' the proprietor's son said over his shoulder. But still Lucas didn't move, quite calm, not even scornful, not even contemptuous, not even very alert, the gaudy carton still poised in his left hand and the small cake in the right, just watching while the proprietor's son and his companion held the foaming and cursing white man. 'Get to hell out of here, you damn fool!' the proprietor's son shouted: and only then did Lucas move, without haste, turning without haste and going on towards the door, raising his right hand to his mouth so that as he went out the door they could see the steady thrust of his chewing.

Because there was the half-dollar. The actual sum was seventy cents of course and in four coins but he had long since during

that first few fractions of a second transposed translated them
into the one coin one integer in mass and weight out of all
proportion to its mere convertible value; there were times in fact
when, the capacity of his spirit for regret or perhaps just simple
writhing or whatever it was at last spent for a moment and even
quiescent, he would tell himself *At least I have the half-dollar, at
least I have something* because now not only his mistake and its
shame but its protagonist too – the man, the Negro, the room,
the moment, the day itself – had annealed vanished into the
round hard symbol of the coin and he would seem to see himself
lying watching regretless and even peaceful as day by day the
coin swelled to its gigantic maximum, to hang fixed at last for
ever in the black vault of his anguish like the last dead and
waneless moon and himself, his own puny shadow gesticulant and
tiny against it in frantic and vain eclipse: frantic and vain yet
indefatigable too because he would never stop, he could never
give up now who had debased not merely his manhood but his
whole race too; each afternoon after school and all day Saturday,
unless there was a ballgame or he went hunting or there was
something else he wanted or needed to do, he would go to his
uncle's office where he would answer the telephone or run
errands, all with some similitude of responsibility even if not
actually of necessity; at least it was an intimation of his willingness
to carry some of his own weight. He had begun it when he was
a child, when he could scarcely remember, out of that blind and
absolute attachment to his mother's only brother which he had
never tried to reason about, and he had done it ever since; later,
at fifteen and sixteen and seventeen he would think of the story
of the boy and his pet calf which he lifted over the pasture fence
each day; years passed and they were a grown man and a bull
still being lifted over the pasture fence each day.

He deserted his calf. It was less than three weeks to Christmas;
every afternoon after school and all day Saturday he was either
in the Square or where he could see it, watch it. It was cold for
another day or two, then it got warm, the wind softened then
the bright sun hazed over and it rained yet he still walked or
stood about the street where the store windows were already
filling with toys and Christmas goods and fireworks and coloured
lights and evergreen and tinsel or behind the steamy window of
the drugstore or barbershop watched the country faces, the two
packages – the four two-for-a-quarter cigars for Lucas and the
tumbler of snuff for his wife – in their bright Christmas paper in

his pocket, until at last he saw Edmonds and gave them to him to deliver Christmas morning. But that merely discharged (with doubled interest) the seventy cents; there still remained the dead monstrous heatless disc which hung nightly in the black abyss of the rage and impotence: *If he would just be a nigger first, just for one second, one little infinitesimal second:* so in February he began to save his money – the twenty-five cents his father gave him each week as allowance and the twenty-five cents his uncle paid him as office salary – until in May he had enough and with his mother helping him chose the flowered imitation silk dress and sent it by mail to Molly Beauchamp, care of Carothers Edmonds R.F.D. and at last he had something like ease because the rage was gone and all he could not forget was the grief and the shame; the disc still hung in the black vault but it was almost a year old now and so the vault itself was not so black with the disc paling and he could even sleep under it as even the insomniac dozes at last under his waning and glareless moon. Then it was September; school would begin in another week. He came home one afternoon and his mother was waiting for him.

'Here's something for you,' she said. It was a gallon bucket of fresh homemade sorghum molasses and he knew the answer at once long before she finished speaking: 'Somebody from Mr Edmonds' place sent it to you.'

'Lucas Beauchamp,' he said, cried almost. 'How long has he been gone? Why didn't he wait for me?'

'No,' his mother said. 'He didn't bring it himself. He sent it in. A white boy brought it on a mule.'

And that was all. They were right back where they had started; it was all to do over again; it was even worse this time because this time Lucas had commanded a white hand to pick up his money and give it back to him. Then he realized that he couldn't even start over again because to take the can of molasses back and fling it into Lucas' front door would only be the coins again for Lucas again to command somebody to pick up and return, not to mention the fact that he would have to ride a Shetland pony which he had outgrown and was ashamed of except that his mother wouldn't agree yet to let him have a full-sized horse or at least the kind of full-sized horse he wanted and that his uncle had promised him, seventeen miles in order to reach the door to fling it through. This would have to be all; whatever would or could set him free was beyond not merely his reach but even his ken; he could only wait for it if it came and do without it if it didn't.

And four years later he had been free almost eighteen months and he thought it was all: old Molly dead and her and Lucas' married daughter moved with her husband to Detroit and he heard now at last by chance remote and belated hearsay that Lucas was living alone in the house, solitary kindness and intractable, apparently not only without friends even in his own race but proud of it. He had seen him three times more, on the Square in town and not always on Saturday – in fact it would be a year from the last time before he would realize that he had never seen him in town on Saturday when all the other Negroes and most of the whites too from the country came in, nor even that the occasions when he did see him were almost exactly a year apart and that the reason he saw him then was not that Lucas' presence had happened to coincide with his own chance passage through the Square but that he had coincided with Lucas' annual and necessary visits – but on weekdays like the white men who were not farmers but planters, who wore neckties and vests like the merchants and doctors and lawyers themselves, as if he refused, declined to accept even that little of the pattern not only of Negro but of country Negro behaviour, and always in the worn brushed obviously once-expensive black broadcloth suit of the portrait-photograph on the gold easel and the raked fine hat and the boiled white shirt of his own grandfather's time and the tieless collar and the heavy watch-chain and the gold toothpick like the one his own grandfather had carried in his upper vest pocket: the first time in the second winter; he had spoken first though Lucas had remembered him at once; he thanked him for the molasses and Lucas had answered exactly as his grandfather himself might, only the words, the grammar any different:

'They turned out good this year. When I was making um I remembered how a boy's always got a sweet tooth for good molasses:' and went on, saying over his shoulder: 'Dont fall in no more creeks this winter:' and saw him twice more after that – the black suit, the hat, the watch-chain but the next time he didn't have the toothpick and this time Lucas looked straight at him, straight into his eyes from five feet away and passed him and he thought *He has forgotten me. He doesn't even remember me anymore* until almost the next year when his uncle told him that Molly, the old wife, had died a year ago. Nor did he bother, take time to wonder then how his uncle (obviously Edmonds had told him) happened to know about it because he was already counting rapidly backward; he said thought with a sense of vindication, easement, triumph almost: *She had just died then. That was why he didn't see me. That was why he didn't have the toothpick:* thinking with a kind of amazement: *He was grieving. You don't have to not be a nigger in order to grieve* and then he found that he was waiting, haunting the Square almost as he had done two years ago when he was watching for Edmonds to give him the two Christmas presents to deliver, through the next two then three then four months before it occurred to him that when he had seen Lucas in town it had always been only once each year in January or February and then for the first time he realized why: he had come in to pay the yearly taxes on his land. So it was late January, a bright cold afternoon. He stood on the bank corner in the thin sun and saw Lucas come out of the courthouse and cross the Square directly towards him, in the black suit and the tieless shirt and the fine old hat at its swaggering rake, walking so erect that the coat touched him only across the shoulders from which it hung and he could already see the cocked slanted glint of the gold toothpick and he could feel the muscles of his face, waiting and then Lucas looked up and once more looked straight into his eyes for perhaps a quarter of a minute and then away and came straight on and then even side-stepped a little in order to pass him and passed him and went on; nor did he look back either, standing at the kerb-edge in the thin cold sun thinking *He didn't even fail to remember me this time. He didn't even know me. He hasn't even bothered to forget me:* thinking in a sort of peace even: *It's over. That was all* because he was free, the man who for three years had obsessed his life waking and sleeping too had walked out of it. He would see him again of course; without doubt they would pass on the street in town like this once each year for the rest of Lucas' life but that would be all: the one no longer the man but only the ghost of him who had ordered the two Negro boys to pick up his money and give it back to him; the other only the memory of the child who had offered it and then flung it down, carrying into manhood only the fading tag end of that old once-frantic shame and anguish and need not for revenge, vengeance but simply for re-equalization, reaffirmation of his masculinity and his white blood. And someday the one would not even be any longer the ghost of the man who had ordered the coins picked up and to the other the shame and anguish would no longer be a thing remembered and recallable but merely a

breath a whisper like the bitter-sweet-sour taste of the sheep
sorrel eaten by the boy in his dead childhood, remembered only
in the instant of tasting and forgotten before it could be placed
and remembered; he could imagine them as old men meeting,
quite old, at some point in that agony of naked inanaesthetizable
nerve-ends which for the lack of a better word men call being
alive at which not only their elapsed years but the half-century
of discrepancy between them would be as indistinguishable and
uncountable as that many sand grains in a coal pile and he saying
to Lucas: *I was the boy who when you gave me half of your dinner tried
to pay you with some things which people in those days called seventy
cents' worth of money and so all I could think of to save my face was
to fling it on the floor? Don't you remember?* and Lucas: *Was that me?*
or vice versa, turned around and it was Lucas saying *I was the
man when you throwed your money on the floor and wouldn't pick it
up I had to have two niggers pick it up and hand it back to you? Dont
you remember?* and he this time: *Was that me?* Because it was over
now. He had turned the other cheek and it had been accepted.
He was free.

Then he came back through the Square late that Saturday
afternoon (there had been a ball game on the High School field)
and he heard that Lucas had killed Vinson Gowrie out at Fraser's
store; word had come for the sheriff about three o'clock and had
been relayed on by another party-line telephone down into the
opposite corner of the county where the sheriff had gone this
morning on business and where a messenger might quite possibly
find him some time between now and tomorrow's sunup: which
would make little difference since even if the sheriff had been in
his office he would probably be too late since Fraser's store was
in Beat Four and if Yoknapatawpha County was the wrong place
for a nigger to shoot a white man in the back then Beat Four was
the last place even in Yoknapatawpha County a nigger with any
judgement – or any other stranger of any colour – would have
chosen to shoot anybody least of all one named Gowrie before
or behind either; already the last car full of the young men and
some not so young whose business addresses not only on Saturday
afternoons but all week too were the poolhall and the barbershop
and some of whom even had some vague connection with cotton
or automobiles or land- and stock-sales, who bet on prizefights
and punchboards and national ballgames, had long since left the
Square to hurry the fifteen miles to park along the highway in
front of the constable's house where the constable had taken

Lucas and the story said had handcuffed him to a bedpost and was now sitting over him with a shotgun (and Edmonds too of course by now; even a fool country constable would have had sense enough to send for Edmonds only four miles away even before hollering for the sheriff) in case the Gowries and their connections decided not to wait until they had buried Vinson first; of course Edmonds would be there; if Edmonds had been in town today he would certainly have seen him at some time during the morning and before he went to the ballpark and since he had not obviously Edmonds had been at home, only four miles away; a messenger could have reached him and Edmonds himself could have been at the constable's house almost before the other messenger had memorized the sheriff's telephone and the message to give him and then rode to the nearest telephone where he could use either: which – Edmonds (again something nagged for a second's flash at his attention) and the constable – would be two while the Lord Himself would have to stop to count the Gowries and Ingrums and Workitts and if Edmonds was busy eating supper or reading the paper or counting his money or something the constable would be just one even with the shotgun: but then he was free, hardly even pausing really, walking on to the corner where he would turn for home and not until he saw how much of sun, how much was left of afternoon still in the street then turned back retracing his steps for several yards before he remembered why in the world he didn't cut straight across the now almost empty Square to the outside stairs leading up to the office.

Though of course there was really no reason to expect his uncle to be in the office this late on Saturday afternoon but once on the stairs he could at least throw that away, happening to be wearing rubber soles today though even then the wooden stairs creaked and rumbled unless you trod the inside edge close to the wall: thinking how he had never really appreciated rubber soles before, how nothing could match them for giving you time to make up your mind what you really wanted to do and then he could see the office door closed now although it was still too early for his uncle to have had the lights on but besides the door itself had that look which only locked doors have so even hard soles wouldn't have mattered, unlocking the door with his key then locking it with the thumb-latch behind him and crossed to the heavy swivel roller chair which had been his grandfather's before his uncle's and sat down behind the littered table which his uncle used in place of the rolltop desk of his grandfather's old time and across which the county's legal business had passed longer than he could remember, since in fact his memory was memory or anyway his, and so battered table and dogeared faded papers and the needs and passions they represented and the measured and bounded county too were all coeval and one, the last of the sun coming through the mullberry tree then the window behind him on to the table the stacked untidy papers the inkwell the tray of paperclips and fouled rusted penpoints and pipecleaners and the overturned corncob pipe in its spill of ash beside the stained unwashed coffeecup and saucer and the coloured mug from the Heidelberg *Stübe* filled with twisted spills of newspaper to light the pipes with like the vase sitting on Lucas' mantel that day and before he even knew he had thought of it he rose taking up the cup and saucer and crossed the room picking up the coffeepot and the kettle too in passing and in the lavatory emptied the grounds and rinsed the pot and cup and filled the kettle and set it and the pot the cup and saucer back on the shelf and returned to the chair and sat down again after really no absence at all, still in plenty of time to watch the table and all its familiar untidy clutter all fading towards one anonymity of night as the sunlight died: thinking remembering how his uncle had said that all man had was time, all that stood between him and the death he feared and abhorred was time yet he spent half of it inventing ways of getting the other half past: and suddenly he remembered from nowhere what it was that had been nagging at his attention: Edmonds was not at home nor even in Mississippi; he was in a hospital in New Orleans being operated on for gallstones, the heavy chair making a rumbling clatter on the wooden floor almost as loud as a wagon on a wooden bridge as he rose and then stood beside the table until the echo died away and there was only the sound of his breathing: because he was free: and then he moved: because his mother would know what time baseball games finished even if she couldn't have heard the yelling from across the edge of town and she would know that even he could use up only so much of twilight getting home, locking the door behind him then down the stairs again, the Square filled with dusk now and the first lights coming on in the drugstore (they had never been off in the barbershop and the poolhall since the bootblack and the porter unlocked the doors and swept out the hair and cigarette stubs at six o'clock this morning) and the mercantile ones too so that the rest of the county except Beat Four would have somewhere to wait until word could come in from Fraser's store that all was okeydoke again and they could unpark the trucks and cars and wagons and mules from the back streets and alleys and go home and go to bed: turning the corner this time and now the jail, looming, lightless except for the one crossbarred rectangle in the upper front wall where on ordinary nights the nigger crapshooters and whisky-peddlers and razor-throwers would be yelling down to their girls and women on the street below and where Lucas would have been these three hours now (very likely banging on the steel door for somebody to bring him his supper or perhaps having already had it and now merely to complain about its quality since without doubt he would consider that his right too along with the rest of his lodging and keep) except that people seemed to hold that the one sole end of the entire establishment of public office was to elect one man like Sheriff Hampton big enough or at least with sense and character enough to run the county and then fill the rest of the jobs with cousins and inlaws who had failed to make a living at everything else they ever tried. But then he was free and besides it was probably all over by now and even if it wasn't he knew what he was going to do and there was plenty of time yet for that, tomorrow would be time enough for that; all he would need to do tonight was to give Highboy about two extra cups of oats against tomorrow and at first he believed he was or at least in a moment was going to be ravenously hungry himself, sitting down at the familiar table in the familiar room among the bright linen and silver and the water glasses and the bowl of narcissus and gladioli and a few roses in it too and his uncle said,

'Your friend Beauchamp seems to have done it this time.'

'Yes,' he said. 'They're going to make a nigger out of him once in his life anyway.'

'Charles!' his mother said – eating rapidly, eating quite a lot and talking rapidly and quite a lot too about the ballgame and waiting to get hungry any minute any second now until suddenly he knew that even the last bite had been too much, still chewing at it to get it down to where it would swallow, already getting up.

'I'm going to the picture show,' he said.

'You haven't finished,' his mother said: then she said, 'The show doesn't begin for almost an hour yet:' and then not even just to his father and uncle but to all time all A.D. of Our Lord one thousand and nine hundred and thirty and forty and fifty: 'I dont want him to go to town tonight. I dont want –' and then at

last one wail one cry to the supreme: his father himself: out of
that nightraddled dragonregion of fears and terrors in which
women mothers anyway – seemed from choice almost to dwell:
'Charlie –' until his uncle put his napkin down and rose too and
said:

'Then here's your chance to wean him. I want him to do an
errand for me anyway:' and out: on the front gallery in the dark
cool and after a while his uncle said: 'Well? Go on.

'Aint you coming?' he said. Then he said, 'But why? Why?'

'Does that matter?' his uncle said, and then said what he had
already heard when he passed the barbershop going on two hours
ago now: 'Not now. Not to Lucas nor anybody else of his colour
out there.' But he had already thought of that himself not just
before his uncle said it but even before whoever it had been in
front of the barbershop two hours ago did, and for that matter
the rest of it too: 'In fact the true why is not what crisis he faced
beyond which life would be no longer bearable until he shot a
white man in the back but why of all white men he must pick a
Gowrie to shoot and out of all possible places Beat Four to do it
in – Go on. But don't be late. After all a man ought to be kind
even to his parents now and then.'

And sure enough one of the cars and for all he knew maybe
all of them had got back to the barbershop and the poolhall so
apparently Lucas was still chained and peaceful to the bedpost
and the constable sitting over him (it was probably a rocking
chair) with the cold shotgun and probably the constable's wife
had served their supper there and Lucas with a good appetite,
sharp set for his since he not only wouldn't have to pay for it but
you dont shoot somebody every day in the week: and at last it
seemed to be more or less authentic that the sheriff had finally
got the word and sent word back that he would return to town
late tonight and would fetch Lucas in early tomorrow morning
and he would have to do something, pass the time somehow until
the picture show was out so he might as well go to it and he
crossed the Square to the courthouse yard and sat down on a
bench in the dark cool empty solitude among the bitten shadows
the restless unwindy vernal leaves against the starry smore of
heaven where he could watch the lighted marquee in front of
the picture show and perhaps the sheriff was right; he seemed
able to establish enough contact with Gowries and Ingrums and
Workitts and McCallums to persuade them to vote for him every
eight years so maybe he knew approximately what they would do

under given situations or perhaps the people in the barbershop
were right and the Ingrums and Gowries and Workitts were
waiting not until they had buried Vinson tomorrow but simply
because it would be Sunday in three hours now and they didn't
want to have to hurry, bolt through the business in order to
finish it by midnight and not violate the Sabbath: then the first
of the crowd dribbled then flowed beneath the marquee blinking
into the light and even fumbling a little for a second or even a
minute or two yet, bringing back into the shabby earth a fading
remnant of the heart's celluloid and derring dream so he could
go home now, in fact he would have to: who knew by simple
instinct when picture shows were over just as she did when
ballgames were and though she would never really forgive him
for being able to button his own buttons and wash behind his
ears at least she accepted it and would not come after him herself
but merely send his father and by starting now ahead of the
picture show's dispersal he would have the empty street until he
got home, until he reached the corner of the yard in fact and his
uncle stepped out from beside the hedge, hatless, smoking one
of the cob pipes.

'Listen,' his uncle said. 'I talked to Hampton down at Peddlers
Field Old Town and he had already telephoned Squire Fraser
and Fraser himself went to Skipworth's house and saw Lucas
handcuffed to the bedpost and it's all right, everything's quiet
out there tonight and tomorrow morning Hampton will have
Lucas locked up in the jail –'

'I know,' he said. 'They wont lynch him until after midnight
tomorrow night, after they have buried Vinson and got rid of
Sunday:' walking on: 'It's all right with me. Lucas didn't have to
work this hard not to be a nigger just on my account.' Because
he was free: in bed: in the cool familiar room in the cool familiar
dark because he knew what he was going to do and he had
forgotten after all to tell Aleck Sander to give Highboy the extra
feed against tomorrow but in the morning would do just as well
because he was going to sleep tonight because he had something
about ten thousand times quicker than just sheep to count; in
fact he was going to go to sleep so fast he probably wouldn't have
time to count more than about ten of them: with rage, an almost
unbearable excruciation of outrage and fury: any white man to
shoot in the back but this one of all white men at all: youngest
of a family of six brothers one of whom had already served a
year in federal penitentiary for armed resistance as an army

deserter and another term at the state penal farm for making whisky, and a ramification of cousins and inlaws covering a whole corner of the county and whose total number probably even the old grandmothers and maiden aunts couldn't have stated offhand – a connection of brawlers and farmers and foxhunters and stock- and timber-traders who would not even be the last anywhere to let one of its number be killed by anyone but only among the last since it in its turn was integrated and interlocked and intermarried with other brawlers and foxhunters and whiskymakers not even into a simple clan or tribe but a race a species which before now had made their hill stronghold good against the county and the federal government too, which did not even simply inhabit nor had merely corrupted but had translated and transmogrified that whole region of lonely pine hills dotted meagrely with small titled farms and peripatetic sawmills and contraband whisky-kettles where peace officers from town didn't even go unless they were sent for and strange white men didn't wander far from the highway after dark and no Negro at any time – where as a local wit said once the only stranger ever to enter with impunity was God and He only by daylight and on Sunday – into a synonym for independence and violence: an idea with physical boundaries like a quarantine for plague so that solitary unique and alone out of all the county it was known to the rest of the county by the number of its survey coordinate – Beat Four – as in the middle twenties people knew where Cicero Illinois was and who lived there and what they did who neither knew nor cared what state Chicago was in: and since this was not enough choosing the one moment when the one man white or black – Edmonds – out of all Yoknapatawpha County or Mississippi or America or the world too for that matter who would have had any inclination let alone power and ability (and here he had to laugh even though he was just about to go to sleep, remembering how he had even thought at first that if Edmonds had been at home it would have made any difference anywhere, remembering the face the angle of the hat the figure straddled baronial as a duke or a squire or a congressman before the fire hands clasped behind it and not even looking down at them but just commanding two nigger boys to pick up the coins and give them back to him, not even needing to remember his uncle reminding him ever since he had got big enough to understand the words that no man could come between another man and his destiny because even his uncle for all Harvard and Heidelberg couldn't have pointed out the man with

enough temerity and delusion just to come between Lucas and
merely what he wanted to do) to try to stand between Lucas and
the violent fate he had courted was lying flat on his back in a
New Orleans operating room: yet that was what Lucas had had
to pick, that time that victim and that place: another Saturday
afternoon and the same store where he had already had trouble
with a white man at least once before: chose the first suitable
convenient Saturday afternoon and with an old single action Colt
pistol of a calibre and type not even made anymore which was
exactly the sort of pistol Lucas would own exactly as no other
still alive man in the county owned a gold toothpick lay in wait
at the store – the one sure place where sooner or later on Saturday
afternoon that whole end of the county would pass – until the
victim appeared and shot him and nobody knew why yet and as
far as he had discovered that afternoon or even when he finally
left the Square that night nobody had even wondered yet since
why didn't matter least of all to Lucas since he had apparently
been working for twenty or twenty-five years with indefatigable
and unflagging concentration towards this one crowning
moment; followed him into the woods about one good spit from
the store and shot him in the back within hearing distance of the
crowd around it and was still standing over the body the fired
pistol put neatly away into his hip pocket again when the first
ones reached the scene where he would without doubt have been
lynched immediately out of hand except for the same Doyle
Fraser who had saved him from the singletree seven years ago
and old Skipworth, the constable – a little driedup wizened
stonedeaf old man not much larger than a half-grown boy with
a big nickelplated pistol loose in one coat pocket and in the other
a guttapercha eartrumpet on a rawhide thong around his neck
like a foxhorn, who on this occasion anyway revealed an almost
gratuitous hardihood and courage, getting Lucas (who made no
resistance whatever, merely watching this too with that same
calm detached not even scornful interest) out of the crowd and
took him to his home and chained him to the bedpost until the
sheriff could come and get him and bring him in to town and
keep him while the Gowries and Workitts and Ingrums and the
rest of their guests and connections could get Vinson buried and
Sunday passed and so be fresh and untrammelled for the new
week and its duties and believe it or not even the night passed,
the tentative roosters at false dawn then the interval then the
loud fairy clangor of the birds and through the east window he

could see the trees against grey light and then the sun itself high
and furious above the trees glaring at him and it was already late,
this of course must happen to him too: but then he was free and
he would feel better after breakfast and he could always say he
was going to Sunday school but then he wouldn't have to say
anything by going out the back, strolling: across the back yard
and into the lot and across it and through the woods to the
railroad to the depot and then back to the Square then he thought
of a simpler way than that and then quit thinking about it at all,
through the front hall and across the front gallery and down the
walk to the street and it was here he would remember later
having first noticed that he had seen no Negro except Paralee
when she brought his breakfast; by ordinary at this hour on
Sunday morning he would have seen on almost every gallery
housemaids or cooks in their fresh Sunday aprons with brooms
or perhaps talking from gallery to gallery across the contiguous
yardspaces and the children too fresh and scrubbed for Sunday
school with clutched palmsweaty nickels though perhaps it was a
little too early for that or perhaps by mutual consent or even
interdiction there would be no Sunday school today, only church
and so at some mutual concorded moment say about half past
eleven all the air over Yoknapatawpha County would reverberate
soundlessly like heatshimmer with one concerted adjuration calm
the hearts of these bereaved and angry men vengeance is mine
saith the lord thou shalt not kill except that this was a little late
too, they should have mentioned this to Lucas yesterday, past the
jail the barred second storey window whose interstices on an
ordinary Sunday would have been thick with dark hands and
beyond them even a glint now and then of eyewhites in the
shadows and the mellow voices calling and laughing down to the
Negro girls and women passing or stopping along the street and
this was when he realized that except for Paralee he had seen no
Negro since yesterday afternoon though it would be tomorrow
before he would learn that the ones who lived in the Hollow and
Freedmantown hadn't come to work at all since Saturday night:
nor on the Square either, not even in the barbershop where
Sunday morning was the bootblack's best day shining shoes and
brushing clothes and running errands and drawing baths for the
bachelor truckdrivers and garage hands who lived in rented
rooms and the young men and the ones not so young who worked
hard all week in the poolhall and the sheriff really had finally got
back to town and had even torn himself away from his Sunday

to go for Lucas: listening: hearing the talk: a dozen of them who had hurried out to Fraser's store yesterday afternoon and returned empty-handed (and he gathered one car full had even gone back last night, yawning and lounging now and complaining of lack of sleep: and that to be added to Lucas' account too) and he had heard all this before too and had even thought of it himself before that:

'I wonder if Hampton took a shovel with him. That's all he's going to need.'

'They'll lend him a shovel out there.'

'Yes – if there's anything to bury. They have gasoline even in Beat Four.'

'I thought old Skipworth was going to take care of that.'

'Sure. But that's Beat Four. They'll do what Skipworth tells them as long as he's got the nigger. But he's going to turn him over to Hampton. That's when it'll happen. Hope Hampton might be sheriff in Yoknapatawpha County but he's just another man in Beat Four.'

'No. They wont do anything today. They're burying Vinson this afternoon and to burn a nigger right while the funeral's going on wouldn't be respectful to Vinson.'

'That's so. It'll probably be tonight.'

'On Sunday night?'

'Is that the Gowries' fault? Lucas ought to thought of that before he picked out Saturday to kill Vinson on.'

'I don't know about that. Hope Hampton's going to be a hard man to take a prisoner away from too.'

'A nigger murderer? Who in this county or state either is going to help him protect a nigger that shoots white men in the back?'

'Or the South either.'

'Yes. Or the South either.' He had heard it all before: outside again now: only his uncle might decide to come to town before time to go for the noon mail at the post-office and if his uncle didn't see him then he really could tell his mother he didn't know where he was and of course he thought first of the empty office but if he went there that's exactly where his uncle would come too: because – and he remembered again that he had forgot to give Highboy the extra feed this morning too but it was too late now and besides he was going to carry feed with him anyway – he knew exactly what he was going to do; the sheriff had left town about nine o'clock; the constable's house was fifteen miles away on a gravel road not too good but the sheriff should certainly go there and be back with Lucas by noon even if he stopped to make a few votes while there; long before that time he would go home and saddle Highboy and tie a sack of feed behind the saddle and turn him in a straight line in the opposite direction from Fraser's store and ride in that one undeviable direction for twelve hours which would be about midnight tonight and feed Highboy and rest him until daylight or even longer if he decided to and then ride the twelve hours back which would be eighteen actually or maybe even twenty-four or even thirty-six but at least all over finished done, no more fury and outrage to have to lie in bed with like trying to put yourself to sleep counting sheep and he turned the corner and went along the opposite side of the street and under the shed in front of the closed blacksmith shop, the heavy double wooden doors not locked with a hasp or latch but with a padlocked chain passed through an augerhole in each one so that the slack of the chain created an insag almost like an alcove; standing in it nobody could have seen him from either up the street or down it nor even passing along it (which would not be his mother anyway today) unless they stopped to look and now the bells began ringing in mellow unhurried discordant strophe and antistrophe from steeple to pigeonswirled steeple across the town, streets and Square one sudden decorous flow of men in their dark suits and women in silks and parasols and girls and young men two and two, flowing and decorous beneath that mellow uproar into that musical clamour: gone, Square and street empty again though still the bells rang on for a while yet, sky-dwellers, groundless denizens of the topless air too high too far insentient to the crawling earth then ceasing stroke by hasteless stroke from the subterrene shudder of organs and the cool frantic monotone of the settled pigeons. Two years ago his uncle had told him that there was nothing wrong with cursing; on the contrary it was not only useful but substituteless but like everything else valuable it was precious only because the supply was limited and if you wasted it on nothing on its urgent need you might find yourself bankrupt so he said *What the hell am I doing here* then answered himself the obvious answer: not to see Lucas, he had seen Lucas but so that Lucas could see him again if he so wished, to look back at him not just from the edge of mere uniqueless death but from the gasoline-roar of apotheosis. Because he was free. Lucas was no longer his responsibility, he was no longer Lucas' keeper; Lucas himself had discharged him.

Then suddenly the empty street was full of men. Yet there

were not many of them, not two dozen; some suddenly and quietly from nowhere. Yet they seemed to fill it, block it, render it suddenly interdict as though not that nobody could pass them, pass through it, use it as a street but that nobody would dare, would even approach near enough to essay the gambit as people stay well away from a sign saying High Voltage or Explosive. He knew, recognized them all; some of them he had even seen and listened to in the barbershop two hours ago – the young men or men under forty, bachelors, the homeless who had the Saturday and Sunday baths in the barbershop – truck-drivers and garage-hands, the oiler from the cotton gin, a sodajerker from the drugstore and the ones who could be seen all week long in or around the poolhall who did nothing at all that anyone knew, who owned automobiles and spent money nobody really knew exactly how they earned on weekends in Memphis or New Orleans brothels – the men who his uncle said were in every little Southern town, who never really led mobs nor even instigated them but were always the nucleus of them because of their mass availability. Then he saw the car; he recognized it too even in the distance without knowing or for that matter stopping to wonder how, himself moving out of his concealing doorway into the street and then across it to the edge of the crowd which made no sound but just stood there blocking the sidewalk beside the jail fence and overflowing into the street while the car came up not fast but quite deliberately, almost decorously as a car should move on Sunday morning, and drew in to the kerb in front of the jail and stopped. A deputy was driving it. He made no move to get out. Then the rear door opened and the sheriff emerged – a big, a tremendous man with no fat and little hard pale eyes in a cold almost bland pleasant face who without even glancing at them turned and held the door open. Then Lucas got out, slowly and stiffly, exactly like a man who has spent the night chained to a bedpost, fumbling a little and bumping or at least raking his head against the top of the door so that as he emerged his crushed hat tumbled from his head on to the pavement almost under his feet. And that was the first time he had ever seen Lucas without the hat on and in the same second he realized that with the possible exception of Edmonds they there in the street watching him were probably the only white people in the county who had ever seen him uncovered: watching as, still bent over as he had emerged from the car, Lucas began to reach stiffly for the hat. But already in one vast yet astonishingly supple stoop the sheriff had picked it up and handed it back to Lucas who still bent over seemed to fumble at the hat too. Yet almost at once the hat was creased back into its old shape and now Lucas was standing up, erect except for his head, his face as he brushed the hat back and forth against the sleeve of his forearm rapid and light and deft as you stroke a razor. Then his head, his face went back and up too and in a motion not quite sweeping he set the hat back on his head at the old angle which the hat itself seemed to assume as if he had flung it up, and erect now in the black suit crumpled too from whatever night he had spent (there was a long grimed smear down one entire side from shoulder to ankle as if he had been lying on an unswept floor a long time in one position without being able to change it) Lucas looked at them for the first time and he thought *Now. He will see me now* and then he thought *He saw me. And that's all* and then he thought *He hasn't seen anybody* because the face was not even looking at them but just towards them, arrogant and calm and with no more defiance in it than fear: detached, impersonal, almost musing, intractable and composed, the eyes blinking a little in the sunlight even after the sound, an indraw of breath went up from somewhere in the crowd and a single voice said:

'Knock it off again, Hope. Take his head too this time.'

'You boys get out of here,' the sheriff said. 'Go back to the barbershop:' turning, saying to Lucas: 'All right. Come on.' And that was all, the face for another moment looking not at them but just towards them, the sheriff already walking towards the jail door when Lucas turned at last to follow him and by hurrying a little he could even get Highboy saddled and be out of the lot before his mother began to send Aleck Sander to look for him to come and eat dinner. Then he saw Lucas stop and turn and he was wrong because Lucas even knew where he was in the crowd before he turned, looking straight at him before he got turned around even, speaking to him:

'You, young man,' Lucas said. 'Tell your uncle I wants to see him:' then turned again and walked on after the sheriff, still a little stiffly in the smeared black suit, the hat arrogant and pale in the sunlight, the voice in the crowd saying:

'Lawyer hell. He wont even need an undertaker when them Gowries get through with him tonight:' walking on past the sheriff who himself had stopped now and was looking back at them, saying in his mild cold bland heatless voice:

'I told you folks once to get out of here. I aint going to tell you again.'

Chapter Three

So if he had gone straight home from the barbershop this morning and saddled Highboy when he first thought of it he would be ten hours away by now, probably fifty miles.

There were no bells now. What people on the street now would have been going to the less formal more intimate evening prayer-meeting, walking decorously across the shadow-bitten darkness from streetlamp to streetlamp; so in keeping with the Sabbath's still suspension that he and his uncle would have been passing them steadily, recognizing them yards ahead without knowing or even pausing to speculate on when or how or why they had done so – not by silhouette nor even the voice needed: the presence, the aura perhaps; perhaps merely the juxtaposition: this living entity at this point at this moment on this day, as is all you need to recognize the people with, among whom you have lived all your life – stepping off the concrete on to the bordering grass to pass them, speaking (his uncle) to them by name, perhaps exchanging a phrase, a sentence then on, on to the concrete again.

But tonight the street was empty. The very houses themselves looked close and watchful and tense as though the people who lived in them, who on this soft May night (those who had not gone to church) would have been sitting on the dark galleries for a little while after supper in rocking chairs or porchswings, talking quietly among themselves or perhaps talking from gallery to gallery when the houses were close enough. But tonight they passed only one man and he was not walking but standing just inside the front gate to a small neat shoebox of a house built last year between two other houses already close enough together to hear one another's toilets flush (his uncle had explained that: 'When you were born and raised and lived all your life where you cant hear anything but owls at night and roosters at dawn and on damp days when sound carries your nearest neighbour chopping wood two miles away, you like to live where you can hear and smell people on either side of you every time they flush a drain or open a can of salmon or of soup.'), himself darker than shadow and certainly stiller – a countryman who had moved to town a year ago and now owned a small shabby side street grocery whose customers were mostly Negroes, whom they had not even seen until they were almost on him though he had already recognized them or at least his uncle some distance away and was waiting for them, already speaking to his uncle before they came abreast of him:

'Little early, aint you, Lawyer? Them Beat Four folks have got to milk and then chop wood to cook breakfast tomorrow with before they can eat supper and get in to town.'

'Maybe they'll decide to stay at home on a Sunday night,' his uncle said pleasantly, passing on: whereupon the man said almost exactly what the man in the barbershop had said this morning (and he remembered his uncle saying once how little of vocabulary man really needed to get comfortably and even efficiently through his life, how not only in the individual but within his whole type and race and kind a few simple clichés served his few simple passions and needs and lusts):

'Sho now. It aint their fault it's Sunday. That sonofabitch ought to thought of that before he taken to killing white men on a Saturday afternoon.' Then he called after them as they went on, raising his voice: 'My wife aint feeling good tonight, and besides I dont want to stand around up there just looking at the front of that jail. But tell um to holler if they need help.'

'I expect they know already they can depend on you, Mr Lilley,' his uncle said. They went on. 'You see?' his uncle said. 'He has nothing against what he calls niggers. If you ask him, he will probably tell you he likes them even better than some white folks he knows and he will believe it. They are probably constantly beating him out of a few cents here and there in his store and probably even picking up things – packages of chewing gum or bluing or a banana or a can of sardines or a pair of shoelaces or a bottle of hair-straightener – under their coats and aprons and he knows it; he probably even gives them things free of charge – the bones and spoiled meat out of his butcher's icebox and spoiled candy and lard. All he requires is that they act like niggers. Which is exactly what Lucas is doing: blew his top and murdered

a white man – which Mr Lilley is probably convinced all Negroes
want to do – and now the white people will take him out and
burn him, all regular and in order and themselves acting exactly
as he is convinced Lucas would wish them to act: like white folks;
both of them observing implicitly the rules: the nigger acting like
a nigger and the white folks acting like white folks and no real
hard feelings on either side (since Mr Lilley is not a Gowrie) once
the fury is over; in fact Mr Lilley would probably be one of the
first to contribute cash money towards Lucas' funeral and the
support of his widow and children if he had them. Which proves
again how no man can cause more grief than that one clinging
blindly to the vices of his ancestors.'

Now they could see the Square, empty too – the amphitheatric
lightless stores, the slender white pencil of the Confederate
monument against the mass of the courthouse looming in
columned upsoar to the dim quadruple face of the clock lighted
each by a single faint bulb with a quality as intransigent against
those four fixed mechanical shouts of adjuration and warning as
the glow of a firefly. Then the jail and at that moment, with a
flash and glare and wheel of lights and a roar of engine at once
puny against the vast night and the empty town yet insolent too,
a car rushed from nowhere and circled the Square; a voice, a
young man's voice squalled from it – no words, not even a shout:
a squall significant and meaningless – and the car rushed on
around the Square, completing the circle back to nowhere and
died away. They turned in at the jail.

It was of brick, square, proportioned, with four brick columns
in shallow basrelief across the front and even a brick cornice
under the eaves because it was old, built in a time when people
took time to build even jails with grace and care and he remembered how his uncle had said once that not courthouses nor
even churches but jails were the true records of a county's, a
community's history, since not only the cryptic forgotten initials
and words and even phrases cries of defiance and indictment
scratched into the walls but the very bricks and stones themselves
held, not in solution but in suspension, intact and biding and
potent and indestructible, the agonies and shames and griefs with
which hearts long since unmarked and unremembered dust had
strained and perhaps burst. Which was certainly true of this one
because it and one of the churches were the oldest buildings in
the town, the courthouse and everything else on or in the Square
having been burned to rubble by Federal occupation forces after

a battle in 1864. Because scratched into one of the panes of the fanlight beside the door was a young girl's single name, written by her own hand into the glass with a diamond in that same year and sometimes two or three times a year he would go up on to the gallery to look at it, it cryptic now in reverse, not for a sense of the past but to realize again the eternality, the deathlessness and changelessness of youth – the name of one of the daughters of the jailer of that time (and his uncle who had for everything an explanation not in facts but long since beyond dry statistics into something far more moving because it was truth: which moved the heart and had nothing whatever to do with what mere provable information said, had told him this too: how this part of Mississippi was new then, as a town a settlement a community less than fifty years old, and all the men who had come into it less long ago almost than even the oldest's lifetime were working together to secure it, doing the base jobs along with the splendid ones not for pay or politics but to shape a land for their posterity, so that a man could be the jailer then or the innkeeper or farrier or vegetable peddler yet still be what the lawyer and planter and doctor and parson called a gentleman) who stood at that window that afternoon and watched the battered remnant of a Confederate brigade retreat through the town, meeting suddenly across that space the eyes of the ragged unshaven lieutenant who led one of the broken companies, scratching into the glass not his name also, not only because a young girl of that time would never have done that but because she didn't know his name then, let alone that six months later he would be her husband.

In fact it still looked like a residence with its balustraded wooden gallery stretching across the front of the lower floor. But above that the brick wall was windowless except for the single tall crossbarred rectangle and he thought again of the Sunday nights which seemed now to belong to a time as dead as Nineveh when from suppertime until the jailer turned the lights out and yelled up the stairs for them to shut up, the dark limber hands would lie in the grimed interstices while the mellow untroubled repentless voices would shout down to the women in the aprons of cooks or nurses and the girls in their flash cheap clothes from the mail order houses or the other young men who had not been caught yet or had been caught and freed yesterday, gathered along the street. But not tonight and even the room behind it was dark though it was not yet eight o'clock and he could see, imagine them not huddled perhaps but certainly all together,

within elbow's touch whether they were actually touching or not
and certainly quiet, not laughing tonight nor talking either,
sitting in the dark and watching the top of the stairs because this
would not be the first time when to mobs of white men not only
all black cats were grey but they didn't always bother to count
them either.

And the front door was open, standing wide to the street which
he had never seen before even in summer although the ground
floor was the jailer's living quarters, and tilted in a chair against
the back wall so that he faced the door in full sight of the street,
was a man who was not the jailer nor even one of the sheriff's
deputies either. Because he had recognized him too: Will Legate,
who lived on a small farm two miles from town and was one of
the best woodsmen, the finest shot and the best deer-hunter in
the county, sitting in the tilted chair holding the coloured comic
section of today's Memphis paper, with leaning against the wall
beside him not the hand-worn rifle with which he had killed more
deer (and even running rabbits with it) than even he remembered
but a double barrelled shotgun, who apparently without even
lowering or moving the paper had already seen and recognized
them even before they turned in at the gate and was now watching
them steadily as they came up the walk and mounted the steps
and crossed the gallery and entered: at which moment the jailer
himself emerged from a door to the right – a snuffy untidy
potbellied man with a harried concerned outraged face, wearing
a heavy pistol holstered on to a cartridge belt around his waist
which looked as uncomfortable and out of place as a silk hat or
a fifth-century iron slavecollar, who shut the door behind him,
already crying at his uncle:

'He wont even shut and lock the front door! Just setting there
with that durn funny paper waiting for anybody that wants to to
walk right in!'

'I'm doing what Mr Hampton told me to,' Legate said in his
pleasant equable voice.

'Does Hampton think that funny paper's going to stop them
folks from Beat Four?' the jailer cried.

'I don't think he's worrying about Beat Four yet,' Legate said
still pleasantly and equably. 'This here's just for local consumption
now.'

His uncle glanced at Legate. 'It seems to have worked. We saw
the car – or one of them – make one trip around the Square as
we came up. I suppose it's been by here too.'

'Oh, once or twice,' Legate said. 'Maybe three times. I really aint paid much mind.'

'And I hope to hell it keeps on working,' the jailer said. 'Because you sure aint going to stop anybody with just that one britch-loader.'

'Sure,' Legate said. 'I don't expect to stop them. If enough folks get their minds made up and keep them made up, aint anything likely to stop them from what they think they want to do. But then, I got you and that pistol to help me.'

'Me?' the jailer cried. 'Me get in the way of them Gowries and Ingrums for seventy-five dollars a month? Just for one nigger? And if you aint a fool, you wont neither.'

'Oh I got to,' Legate said in his easy pleasant voice. 'I got to resist. Mr Hampton's paying me five dollars for it.' Then to his uncle: 'I reckon you want to see him.'

'Yes,' his uncle said. 'If it's all right with Mr Tubbs.'

The jailer stared at his uncle, irate and harried. 'So you got to get mixed up in it too. You can't let well enough alone neither.' He turned abruptly. 'Come on:' and led the way through the door beside which Legate's chair was tilted, into the back hall where the stairway rose to the upper floor, snapping on the light switch at the foot of the stairs and began to mount them, his uncle then he following while he watched the hunch and sag of the holster at the jailer's hip. Suddenly the jailer seemed about to stop; even his uncle thought so, stopping too but the jailer went on, speaking over his shoulder: 'Dont mind me. I'm going to do the best I can; I taken an oath of office too.' His voice rose a little, still calm, just louder: 'But dont think nobody's going to make me admit I like it. I got a wife and two children; what good am I going to be to them if I get myself killed protecting a goddamn stinking nigger?' His voice rose again; it was not calm now: 'And how am I going to live with myself if I let a passel of no-good sonabitches take a prisoner away from me?' Now he stopped and turned on the step above them, higher than both, his face once more harried and frantic, his voice frantic and outraged: 'Better for everybody if them folks had took him as soon as they laid hands on him yesterday –'

'But they didn't,' his uncle said. 'I dont think they will. And if they do, it wont really matter. They either will or they wont and if they dont it will be all right and if they do we will do the best we can, you and Mr Hampton and Legate and the rest of us,

what we have to do, what we can do. So we dont need to worry
about it. You see?'

'Yes,' the jailer said. Then he turned and went on, unsnapping
his keyring from his belt under the pistol belt, to the heavy door
which closed off the top of the stairs (It was one solid handhewn
piece over two inches thick, locked with a heavy modern padlock
in a handwrought iron bar through two iron slots which like the
heavy rosette-shaped hinges were handwrought too, hammered
out over a hundred years ago in the blacksmith shop across the
street where he had stood yesterday; one day last summer a
stranger, a city man, an architect who reminded him somehow
of his uncle, hatless and tieless, in tennis shoes and a pair of worn
flannel trousers and what was left of a case of champagne in a
convertible-top car which must have cost three thousand dollars,
driving not through town but into it, not hurting anyone but just
driving the car up on to the pavement and across it through a
plate glass window, quite drunk, quite cheerful, with less than
fifty cents in cash in his pocket but all sorts of identification cards
and a cheque folder whose stubs showed a balance in a New York
bank of over six thousand dollars, who insisted on being put in
jail even though the marshal and the owner of the window both
were just trying to persuade him to go to the hotel and sleep it
off so he could write a cheque for the window and the wall: until
the marshal finally put him in jail where he went to sleep at once
like a baby and the garage sent for the car and the next morning
the jailer telephoned the marshal at five o'clock to come and get
the man out because he had waked the whole household up
talking from his cell across to the niggers in the bullpen. So the
marshal came and made him leave and then he wanted to go out
with the street gang to work and they wouldn't let him do that
and his car was ready too but he still wouldn't leave, at the hotel
that night and two nights later his uncle even brought him to
supper, where he and his uncle talked for three hours about
Europe and Paris and Vienna and he and his mother listening
too though his father had excused himself: and still there two
days after that, still trying from his uncle and the mayor and the
board of aldermen and at last the board of supervisors themselves
to buy the whole door or if they wouldn't sell that, at least the
bar and slots and the hinges.) and unlocked it and swung it back.

But already they had passed out of the world of man, men:
people who worked and had homes and raised families and tried
to make a little more money than they perhaps deserved by fair

means of course or at least by legal, to spend a little on fun and still save something against old age. Because even as the oak door swung back there seemed to rush out and down at him the stale breath of all human degradation and shame – a smell of creosote and excrement and stale vomit and incorrigibility and defiance and repudiation like something palpable against the thrust and lift of their bodies as they mounted the last steps and into a passage which was actually a part of the main room, the bullpen, cut off from the rest of the room by a wall of wire mesh like a chicken run or a dog-kennel, inside which in tiered bunks against the farther wall lay five Negroes, motionless, their eyes closed but no sound of snoring, no sound of any sort, lying there immobile orderly and composed under the dusty glare of the single shadeless bulb as if they had been embalmed, the jailer stopping again, his own hands gripped into the mesh while he glared at the motionless shapes. 'Look at them,' the jailer said in that voice too loud, too thin, just under hysteria: 'Peaceful as lambs but aint a damned one of them asleep. And I dont blame them, with a mob of white men boiling in here at midnight with pistols and cans of gasoline – Come on,' he said and turned and went on. Just beyond there was a door in the mesh, not padlocked but just hooked with a hasp and staple such as you might see on a dog-kennel or a corn crib but the jailer passed it.

'You put him in the cell, did you?' his uncle said.

'Hampton's orders,' the jailer said over his shoulder. 'I dont know what the next white man that figgers he cant rest good until he kills somebody is going to think about it. I taken all the blankets off the cot though.'

'Maybe because he wont be here long enough to have to go to sleep?' his uncle said.

'Ha ha,' the jailer said in that strained high harsh voice without mirth: 'Ha ha ha ha:' and following behind his uncle he thought how of all human pursuits murder has the most deadly need of privacy; how man will go to almost any lengths to preserve the solitude in which he evacuates or makes love but he will go to any length for that in which he takes life, even to homicide, yet by no act can he more completely and irrevocably destroy it: a modern steel barred door this time with a built-in lock as large as a woman's handbag which the jailer unlocked with another key on the ring and then turned, the sound of his feet almost as rapid as running back down the corridor until the sound of the oak door at the head of the stairs cut them off, and beyond it the

cell lighted by another single dim dusty flyspecked bulb behind
a wire screen cupped to the ceiling, not much larger than a broom
closet and in fact just wide enough for the double bunk against
the wall, from both beds of which not just the blankets but the
mattresses too had been stripped, he and his uncle entering and
still all he saw yet was the first thing he had seen: the hat and
the black coat hanging neatly from a nail in the wall: and he
would remember afterwards how he thought in a gasp, a surge
of relief: *They've already got him. He's gone. It's too late. It's already
over now.* Because he didn't know what he had expected, except
that it was not this: a careful spread of newspaper covering neatly
the naked springs of the lower cot and another section as carefully
placed on the upper one so it would shield his eyes from the light
and Lucas himself lying on the spread papers, asleep, on his back,
his head pillowed on one of his shoes and his hands folded on his
breast, quite peacefully or as peacefully as old people sleep, his
mouth open and breathing in faint shallow jerky gasps; and he
stood in an almost unbearable surge not merely of outrage but
of rage, looking down at the face which for the first time,
defenceless at last for a moment, revealed its age, and the lax
gnarled old man's hands which only yesterday had sent a bullet
into the back of another human being, lying still and peaceful on
the bosom of the old-fashioned collarless boiled white shirt closed
at the neck with the oxidizing brass button shaped like an arrow
and almost as large as the head of a small snake, thinking: *He's
just a nigger after all for all his high nose and his stiff neck and his
gold watch-chain and refusing to mean mister to anybody even when he
says it. Only a nigger could kill a man, let alone shoot him in the back,
and then sleep like a baby as soon as he found something flat enough
to lie down on;* still looking at him when without moving otherwise
Lucas closed his mouth and his eyelids opened, the eyes staring
up for another second, then still without the head moving at all
the eyeballs turned until Lucas was looking straight at his uncle
but still not moving: just lying there looking at him.

'Well, old man,' his uncle said. 'You played hell at last.' Then
Lucas moved. He sat up stiffly and swung his legs stiffly over the
edge of the cot, picking one of them up by the knee between his
hands and swinging it around as you open or close a sagging gate,
groaning, grunting not just frankly and unabashed and aloud but
comfortably, as the old grunt and groan with some long familiar
minor stiffness so used and accustomed as to be no longer even
an ache and which if they were ever actually cured of it, they

would be bereft and lost; he listening and watching still in that rage and now amazement too at the murderer not merely in the shadow of the gallows but of a lynch-mob, not only taking time to groan over a stiffness in his back but doing it as if he had all the long rest of a natural life in which to be checked each time he moved by the old familiar catch.

'Looks like it,' Lucas said. 'That's why I sent for you. What you going to do with me?'

'Me?' his uncle said, 'Nothing. My name aint Gowrie. It aint even Beat Four.'

Moving stiffly again Lucas bent and peered about his feet, then he reached under the cot and drew out the other shoe and sat up again and began to turn creakily and stiffly to look behind him when his uncle reached and took the first shoe from the cot and dropped it beside the other. But Lucas didn't put them on. Instead he sat again, immobile, his hands on his knees, blinking. Then with one hand he made a gesture which completely dismissed Gowries, mob, vengeance, holocaust and all. 'I'll worry about that when they walks in here,' he said. 'I mean the law. Aint you the county lawyer?'

'Oh,' his uncle said. 'It's the District Attorney that'll hang you or send you to Parchman not me.'

Lucas was still blinking, not rapidly: just steadily. He watched him. And suddenly he realized that Lucas was not looking at his uncle at all and apparently had not been for three or four seconds.

'I see,' Lucas said. 'Then you can take my case.'

'Take your case? Defend you before the judge?'

'I'm gonter pay you,' Lucas said. 'You dont need to worry.'

'I dont defend murderers who shoot people in the back,' his uncle said.

Again Lucas made the gesture with one of the dark gnarled hands. 'Let's forget the trial. We aint come to it yet.' And now he saw that Lucas was watching his uncle, his head lowered so that he was watching his uncle upwards from beneath through the grizzled tufts of his eyebrows – a look shrewd secret and intent. Then Lucas said: 'I wants to hire somebody –' and stopped. And watching him, he thought remembered an old lady, dead now, a spinster, a neighbour who wore a dyed transformation and had always on a pantry shelf a big bowl of homemade teacakes for all the children on the street, who one summer (he couldn't have been over seven or eight then) taught all of them to play Five Hundred: sitting at the card table on her screened side

gallery on hot summer mornings and she would wet her fingers
and take a card from her hand and lay it on the table, her hand
not still poised over it of course but just lying nearby until the
next player revealed exposed by some movement or gesture of
triumph or exultation or maybe by just simple increased hard
breathing his intention to trump or overplay it, whereupon she
would say quickly: 'Wait. I picked up the wrong one' and take
up the card and put it back in to her hand and play another one.
That was exactly what Lucas had done. He had sat still before
but now he was absolutely immobile. He didn't even seem to be
breathing.

'Hire somebody?' his uncle said. 'You've got a lawyer. I had
already taken your case before I came in here. I'm going to tell
you what to do as soon as you have told me what happened.'

'No,' Lucas said. 'I wants to hire somebody. It dont have to be
a lawyer.'

Now it was his uncle who stared at Lucas. 'To do what?'

He watched them. Now it was no childhood's game of stakeless
Five Hundred. It was more like the poker games he had over-
looked. 'Are you or aint you going to take the job?' Lucas said.

'So you aint going to tell me what you want me to do until
after I have agreed to do it,' his uncle said. 'All right,' his uncle
said. 'Now I'm going to tell you what to do. Just exactly what
happened out there yesterday?'

'So you don't want the job,' Lucas said. 'You aint said yes or
no yet.'

'No!' his uncle said, harsh, too loud, catching himself but
already speaking again before he had brought his voice back
down to a sort of furious explicit calm: 'Because you aint got any
job to offer anybody. You're in jail, depending on the grace of
God to keep those damned Gowries from dragging you out of
here and hanging you to the first lamp post they come to. Why
they ever let you get to town in the first place I still dont
understand —'

'Nemmine that now,' Lucas. 'What I needs is —'

'Nemmine that!' his uncle said. 'Tell the Gowries to never mind
it when they bust in here tonight. Tell Beat Four to just forget
it —' He stopped; again with an effort you could almost see he
brought his voice back to that furious patience. He drew a deep
breath and expelled it. 'Now. Tell me exactly what happened
yesterday.'

For another moment Lucas didn't answer, sitting on the bunk, his hands on his knees, intractable and composed, no longer looking at his uncle, working his mouth faintly as if he were tasting something. He said: 'They was two folks, partners in a sawmill. Leastways they was buying the lumber as the sawmill cut it —'

'Who were they?' his uncle said.

'Vinson Gowrie was one of um.'

His uncle stared at Lucas for a long moment. But his voice was quite calm now. 'Lucas,' he said, 'has it ever occurred to you that if you just said mister to white people and said it like you meant it, you might not be sitting here now?'

'So I'm to commence now,' Lucas said. 'I can start off by saying mister to the folks that drags me out of here and builds a fire under me.'

'Nothing's going to happen to you — until you go before the judge,' his uncle said. 'Dont you know that even Beat Four dont take liberties with Mr Hampton — at least not here in town?'

'Shurf Hampton's home in bed now.'

'But Mr Will Legate's sitting down stairs with a shotgun.

'I aint 'quainted with no Will Legate.'

'The deer-hunter? The man that can hit a running rabbit with a thirty-thirty rifle?'

'Hah,' Lucas said. 'Them Gowries aint deer. They might be cattymounts and panthers but they aint deer.'

'All right,' his uncle said. 'Then I'll stay here if you'll feel better. Now. Go on. Vinson Gowrie and another man were buying lumber together. What other man?'

'Vinson Gowrie's the only one that's public yet.'

'And he got public by being shot in broad daylight in the back,' his uncle said. 'Well, that's one way to do it — All right,' his uncle said. 'Who was the other man?'

Lucas didn't answer. He didn't move; he might not even have heard, sitting peaceful and inattentive, not even really waiting: just sitting there while his uncle watched him. Then his uncle said:

'All right. What were they doing with it?'

'They was yarding it up as the mill cut it, gonter sell it all at once when the sawing was finished. Only the other man was hauling it away at night, coming in late after dark with a truck and picking up a load and hauling it over to Glasgow or Hollymount and selling it and putting the money in his pocket.'

'How do you know?'

'I seen um. Watched um.' Nor did he doubt this for a moment because he remembered Ephraim, Paralee's father before he died, an old man, a widower who would pass most of the day dozing and waking in a rocking chair on Paralee's gallery in summer and in front of the fire in winter and at night would walk the roads, not going anywhere, just moving, at times five and six miles from town before he would return at dawn to doze and wake all day in the chair again.

'All right,' his uncle said. 'Then what?'

'That's all,' Lucas said. 'He was just stealing a load of lumber every night or so.'

His uncle stared at Lucas for perhaps ten seconds. He said in a voice of calm, almost hushed amazement:, So you took your pistol and went to straighten it out. You, a nigger, took a pistol and went to rectify a wrong between two white men. What did you expect? What else did you expect?'

'Nemmine expecting,' Lucas said. 'I wants –'

'You went to the store,' his uncle said, 'only you happened to find Vinson Gowrie first and followed him into the woods and told him his partner was robbing him and naturally he cursed you and called you a liar whether it was true or not, naturally he would have to do that; may be he even knocked you down and walked on and you shot him in the back –'

'Never nobody knocked me down,' Lucas said.

'So much the worse,' his uncle said. 'So much the worse for you. It's not even self-defence. You just shot him in the back. And then you stood there over him with the fired pistol in your pocket and let the white folks come up and grab you. And if it hadn't been for that little shrunk-up rheumatic constable who had no business being there in the first place and in the second place had no business whatever, at the rate of a dollar a prisoner every time he delivered a subpoena or served a warrant, having guts enough to hold off that whole damn Beat Four for eighteen hours until Hope Hampton saw fit or remembered or got around to bringing you in to jail – holding off that whole countryside that you nor all the friends you could drum up in a hundred years –'

'I aint got friends,' Lucas said with stern and inflexible pride, and then something else though his uncle was already talking:

'You're damned right you haven't. And if you ever had that pistol shot would have blown them to kingdom come too – What?' his uncle said. 'What did you say?'

'I said I pays my own way,' Lucas said.

'I see,' his uncle said. 'You dont use friends; you pay cash. Yes. I see. Now you listen to me. You'll go before the grand jury tomorrow. They'll indict you. Then if you like I'll have Mr Hampton move you to Mottstown or even further away than that, until court convenes next month. Then you'll plead guilty; I'll persuade the District Attorney to let you do that because you're an old man and you never were in trouble before; I mean as far as the judge and the District Attorney will know since they dont live within fifty miles of Yoknapatawpha County. Then they wont hang you; they'll send you to the penitentiary; you probably wont live long enough to be paroled but at least the Gowries cant get to you there. Do you want me to stay in here with you tonight?'

'I reckon not,' Lucas said. 'They kept me up all last night and I'm gonter try to get some sleep. If you stay here you'll talk till morning.'

'Right,' his uncle said harshly, then to him: 'Come on:' already moving towards the door. Then his uncle stopped. 'Is there anything you want?'

'You might send me some tobacco,' Lucas said. 'If them Gowries leaves me time to smoke it.'

'Tomorrow,' his uncle said. 'I dont want to keep you awake tonight:' and went on, he following, his uncle letting him pass first through the door so that he stepped aside in his turn and stood looking back into the cell while his uncle came through the door and drew it after him, the heavy steel plunger crashing into its steel groove with a thick oily sound of irrefutable finality like that ultimate cosmolined doom itself when as his uncle said man's machines had at last effaced and obliterated him from the earth and, purposeless now to themselves with nothing left to destroy, closed the last carborundum-grooved door upon their own pro-genitorless apotheosis behind one clockless lock responsive only to the last stroke of eternity, his uncle going on, his feet ringing and echoing down the corridor and then the sharp rattle of his knuckles on the oak door while he and Lucas still looked at one another through the steel bars, Lucas standing too now in the middle of the floor beneath the light and looking at him with whatever it was in his face so that he thought for a second that Lucas had spoken aloud. But he hadn't, he was making no sound: just looking at him with that mute patient urgency until the jailer's feet thumped nearer and nearer on the stairs and the slotted bar on the door rasped back.

And the jailer locked the bar again and they passed Legate still with his funny paper in the tilted chair beside the shotgun facing the open door, then outside, down the walk to the gate and the street, following through the gate where his uncle had already turned towards home: stopping, thinking *a nigger a murderer who shoots white people in the back and aint even sorry.*

He said: 'I imagine I'll find Skeets McGowan loafing somewhere on the Square. He's got a key to the drugstore. I'll take Lucas some tobacco tonight.' His uncle stopped.

'It can wait till morning,' his uncle said.

'Yes,' he said, feeling his uncle watching him, not even wondering what he would do if his uncle said no, not even waiting really, just standing there.

'All right,' his uncle said. 'Dont be too long.' So he could have moved then. But still he didn't.

'I thought you said nothing would happen tonight.'

'I still dont think it will,' his uncle said. 'But you cant tell. People like the Gowries dont attach a great deal of importance to death or dying. But they do put a lot of stock in the dead and how they died – particularly their own. If you get the tobacco, let Tubbs carry it up to him and you come on home.'

So he didn't have to say even yes this time, his uncle turning first then he turned and walked towards the Square, walking on until the sound of his uncle's feet had ceased, then standing until his uncle's black silhouette had changed to the white gleam of his linen suit and then that faded beyond the last arclight and if he had gone on home and got Highboy as soon as he recognized the sheriff's car this morning that would be eight hours and almost forty miles, turning then and walking back towards the gate with Legate's eyes watching him, already recognizing him across the top of the funny paper even before he reached the gate and if he just went straight on now he could follow the lane behind the hedge and across into the lot and saddle Highboy and go out by the pasture gate and turn his back on Jefferson and nigger murderers and all and let Highboy go as fast as he wanted to go and as far as he wanted to go even when he had blown himself at last and agreed to walk, just so his tail was still turned to Jefferson and nigger murderers: through the gate and up the walk and across the gallery and again the jailer came quickly through the door at the right, his expression already giving way to the one of harried outrage.

'Again,' the jailer said. 'Dont you never get enough?'

'I forgot something,' he said.

'Let it wait till morning,' the jailer said.

'Let him get it now,' Legate said in his equable drawl. 'If he leaves it there till morning it might get trompled on.' So the jailer turned; again they mounted the stairs, again the jailer unlocked the bar across the oak door.

'Never mind the other one,' he said. 'I can attend to it through the bars:' and didn't wait, the door closed behind him, he heard the bar slide back into the slot but still all he had to do was just to rap on it, hearing the jailer's feet going away back down the stairs but even then all he had to do was just to yell loud and bang on the floor and Legate anyway would hear him, thinking *Maybe he will remind me of that goddamn plate of collards and sidemeat or maybe he'll even tell me I'm all he's got, all that's left and that will be enough* – walking fast, then the steel door and Lucas had not moved, still standing in the middle of the cell beneath the light, watching the door when he came up to it and stopped and said in a voice as harsh as his uncle's had ever been:

'All right. What do you want me to do?'

'Go out there and look at him,' Lucas said.

'Go out where and look at who?' he said. But he understood all right. It seemed to him that he had known all the time what it would be; he thought with a kind of relief *So that's all it is* even while his automatic voice was screeching with outraged disbelief: 'Me? *Me?*' It was like something you have dreaded and feared and dodged for years until it seemed like all your life, then despite everything it happened to you and all it was was just pain, all it did was hurt and so it was all over, all finished, all right.

'I'll pay you,' Lucas said.

So he wasn't listening, not even to his own voice in amazed incredulous outrage: 'Me go out there and dig up that grave?' He wasn't even thinking anymore *So this is what that plate of meat and greens is going to cost me.* Because he had already passed that long ago when that something – whatever it was – had held him here five minutes ago looking back across the vast, the almost insuperable chasm between him and the old Negro murderer and saw, heard Lucas saying something to him not because he was himself, Charles Mallison junior, nor because he had eaten the plate of greens and warmed himself at the fire, but because he alone of all the white people Lucas would have a chance to speak to between now and the moment when he might be dragged out of the cell and down the steps at the end of a rope, would hear the mute unhoping urgency of the eyes. He said:

'Come here,' Lucas did so, approaching, taking hold of two of the bars as a child stands inside a fence. Nor did he remember doing so but looking down he saw his own hands holding to two of the bars, the two pairs of hands, the black ones and the white ones, grasping the bars while they faced one another above them. 'All right,' he said. 'Why?'

'Go and look at him,' Lucas said. 'If it's too late when you get back, I'll sign you a paper now saying I owes you whatever you think it's worth.'

But still he wasn't listening; he knew it: only to himself: 'I'm to go seventeen miles out there in the dark –'

'Nine,' Lucas said. 'The Gowries buries at Caledonia Chapel. You takes the first right hand up into the hills just beyond the Nine-Mile branch bridge. You can be there in half an hour in your uncle's automobile.'

'– I'm to risk having the Gowries catch me digging up that grave. I aim to know why. I don't even know what I'll be looking for. Why?'

'My pistol is a fawty-one Colt,' Lucas said. Which it would be; the only thing he hadn't actually known was the calibre – that weapon workable and efficient and well cared for yet as archaic peculiar and unique as the gold toothpick, which had probably (without doubt) been old Carothers McCaslin's pride a half century ago.

'All right,' he said. 'Then what?'

'He wasn't shot with no fawty-one Colt.'

'What was he shot with?'

But Lucas didn't answer that, standing there on his side of the steel door, his hands light-clasped and motionless around the two bars, immobile save for the faint movement of his breathing. Nor had he expected Lucas to and he knew that Lucas would never answer that, say any more, any further to any white man, and he knew why, as he knew why Lucas had waited to tell him, a child, about the pistol when he would have told neither his uncle nor the sheriff who would have been the one to open the grave and look at the body; he was surprised that Lucas had come as near as he had to telling his uncle about it and he realized, appreciated again that quality in his uncle which brought people to tell him things they would tell nobody else, even tempting Negroes to tell him what their nature forbade them telling white men: remembering old Ephraim and his mother's ring that summer five years ago – a cheap thing with an imitation stone; two of them in fact, identical, which his mother and her room-mate at Sweetbriar Virginia had saved their allowances and bought and exchanged to wear until death as young girls will, and the room-mate grown and living in California with a daughter of her own at Sweetbriar now and she and his mother had not seen one another in years and possibly never would again yet his mother still kept the ring: then one day it disappeared; he remembered how he would wake at night and see lights burning downstairs and he would know she was still searching for it: and all this time old Ephraim was sitting in his home-made rocking chair on Paralee's front gallery until one day Ephraim told him that for half a dollar he would find the ring and he gave Ephraim the half dollar and that afternoon he left for a week at a Scout camp and returned and found his mother in the kitchen where she had spread newspapers on the table and emptied the stone crock she and Paralee kept the cornmeal in on to it and she and Paralee were combing through the meal with forks and for the first time in a week he remembered the ring and went back to Paralee's house and there was Ephraim sitting in the chair on the gallery and Ephraim said, 'Hit's under the hawg-trough at your pa's farm:' nor did Ephraim need to tell him how then because he had already remembered by then: Mrs Downs: an old white woman who lived alone in a small filthy shoebox of a house that smelled like a foxden on the edge of town in a settlement of Negro houses, in and out of which Negroes came and went steadily all day long and without doubt most of the night: who (this not from Paralee who seemed always to not know or at least to have no time at the moment to talk about it, but from Aleck Sander) didn't merely tell fortunes and cure hexes but found things: which was where the half dollar had gone and he believed at once and so implicitly that the ring was now found that he dismissed that phase at once and for ever and it was only the thing's secondary and corollary which moved his interest, saying to Ephraim: 'You've known all this week where it was and you didn't even tell them?' and Ephraim looked at him a while, rocking steadily and placidly and sucking at his cold ashfilled pipe with each rock like the sound of a small asthmatic cylinder: 'I mought have told your maw. But she would need help. So I waited for you. Young folks and womens, they aint cluttered. They can listen. But a middle-year man like your paw and your uncle, they cant listen. They aint got time. They're too busy with facks. In fact, you mought bear this in yo mind; someday you mought need it. If you ever needs to get anything done outside the common run, dont waste yo time on the menfolks; get the womens and children to working at it.' And he remembered his father's not rage so much as outrage, his almost furious repudiation, his transferrence of the whole thing into a realm of assailed embattled moral principle, and even his uncle who until now had had no more trouble than he believing things that all other grown people doubted for the sole reason that they were unreasonable, while his mother went serenely and stubbornly about her preparations to go out to the farm which she hadn't visited in over a year and even his father hadn't seen it since months before the ring was missing and even his uncle refused to drive the car so his father hired a man from the garage and he and his mother went out to the farm and with the help of the overseer found under the trough where the hogs were fed, the ring. Only this was no obscure valueless little ring exchanged twenty years ago between two young girls but the death by shameful violence of a man who would die not because he was a murderer but because his skin was black. Yet this was all Lucas was going to tell him and he knew it was all; he thought in a kind of raging fury: *Believe? Believe what?* because Lucas was not even asking him to believe anything; he was not even asking a favour, making no last desperate plea to his humanity and pity but was even going to pay him provided the price was not too high, to go alone seventeen miles (no, nine: he remembered at least that he had heard that now) in the dark and risk being caught violating the grave of a member of a clan of men already at the pitch to commit the absolute of furious and bloody outrage, without even telling him why. Yet he tried it again, as he knew Lucas not only knew he was going to but knew that he knew what answer he would get:

'What gun was he shot with, Lucas?' and got exactly what even Lucas knew he had expected:

'I'm gonter pay you,' Lucas said. 'Name yo price at anything in reason and I will pay it.'

He drew a long breath and expelled it while they faced each other through the bars, the bleared old man's eyes watching him, inscrutable and secret. They were not even urgent now and he thought peacefully *He's not only beat me, he never for one second had any doubt of it.* He said: 'All right. Just for me to look at him wouldn't do any good, even if I could tell you about the bullet.

So you see what that means. I've got to dig him up, get him out of that hole before the Gowries catch me, and in to town where Mr Hampton can send to Memphis for an expert that can tell about bullets.' He looked at Lucas, at the old man holding gently to the bars inside the cell and not even looking at him anymore. He drew a long breath again. 'But the main thing is to get him up out of the ground where somebody can look at him before the . . .' He looked at Lucas. 'I'll have to get out there and dig him up and get back to town before midnight or one o'clock and maybe even midnight will be too late. I dont see how I can do it. I cant do it.'

'I'll try to wait,' Lucas said.

Chapter Four

There was a weathered battered second-hand-looking pickup truck parked at the kerb in front of the house when he reached home. It was not well past eight o'clock; it was a good deal more than a possibility that there remained less than four hours for his uncle to go to the sheriff's house and convince him and then find a JP or whoever they would have to find and wake and then convince too to open the grave (in lieu of permission from the Gowries, which for any reason whatever, worst of all to save a nigger from being burned over a bonfire, the President of the United States himself let alone a country sheriff would never get) and then go out to Caledonia church and dig up the body and get back to town with it in time. Yet this of all nights would be one when a farmer whose stray cow or mule or hog had been impounded by a neighbour who insisted on collecting a dollar pound fee before he would release it, must come in to see his uncle, to sit for an hour in his uncle's study saying yes or no or I reckon not while his uncle talked about crops or politics, one of which his uncle knew nothing about and the other the farmer didn't, until the man would get around to telling what he came for.

But he couldn't stand on ceremony now. He had been walking pretty fast since he left the jail but he was trotting now, catacorner across the lawn, on to the gallery and across it into the hall past the library where his father would still be sitting under one reading lamp with the Memphis paper's Sunday crossword puzzle page and his mother under the other one with the new Book-of-the-Month book, and on back to what his mother used to try to call Gavin's study but which Paralee and Aleck Sander had long since renamed the office so that everyone now called it that. The door was closed; he could hear the murmur of the man's voice beyond it during the second in which without even stopping he rapped twice and at the same time opened the door and entered, already saying:

'Good evening, sir. Excuse me. Uncle Gavin –'

Because the voice was his uncle's; seated opposite his uncle beyond the desk, instead of a man with a shaved sunburned neck in neat tieless Sunday shirt and pants, was a woman in a plain cotton print dress and one of the round faintly dusty-looking black hats set squarely on the top of her head such as his grandmother had used to wear and then he recognized her even before he saw the watch – small gold in a hunting case suspended by a gold brooch on her flat bosom almost like and in almost exactly the same position as the heart sewn on the breast of the canvas fencing vest – because since his grandmother's death no other woman in his acquaintance wore or even owned one and in fact he should have recognized the pickup truck: Miss Habersham, whose name was now the oldest which remained in the county. There had been three once: Doctor Habersham and a tavern keeper named Holston and a Huguenot younger son named Grenier who had ridden horseback into the county before its boundaries had ever been surveyed and located and named, when Jefferson was a Chickasaw trading post with a Chickasaw word to designate it out of the trackless wilderness of canebrake and forest of that time but all gone now, vanished except the one even from the county's spoken recollection: Holston merely the name of the hotel on the Square and few in the county to know or care where the word came from, and the last of the blood of Louis Grenier the *elegante*, the *dilettante*, the Paris-educated architect who had practised a little of law but had spent most of his time as a planter and painter (and more amateur as a raiser of food and cotton than with canvas and brush) now warmed the bones of an equable cheerful middleaged man with the mind and

face of a child who lived in a half-shed half-den he built himself
of discarded boards and pieces of flattened stove-pipe and tin
cans on the bank of the river twenty miles away, who didn't know
his age and couldn't write even the Lonnie Grinnup which he
now called himself and didn't even know that the land he squatted
on was the last lost scrap of the thousands of acres which his
ancestor had been master of and only Miss Habersham remained:
a kindless spinster of seventy living in the columned colonial
house on the edge of town which had not been painted since her
father died and had neither water nor electricity in it, with two
Negro servants (and here again something nagged for an instant
at his mind his attention but already in the same second gone,
not even dismissed: just gone) in a cabin in the back yard, who
(the wife) did the cooking while Miss Habersham and the man
raised chickens and vegetables and peddled them about town
from the pickup truck. Until two years ago they had used a plump
aged white horse (it was said to be twenty years old when he first
remembered it, with a skin beneath the burnished white hairs as
clean and pink as a baby's) and a buggy. Then they had a good
season or something and Miss Habersham bought the pickup
truck second hand and every morning winter and summer they
would be seen about the streets from house to house, Miss
Habersham at the wheel in cotton stockings and the round black
hat which she had been wearing for at least forty years and the
clean print dresses which you could see in the Sears Roebuck
catalogues for two dollars and ninety-eight cents with the neat
small gold watch pinned to the flat unmammary front and the
shoes and the gloves which his mother said were made to her
measure in a New York shop and cost thirty and forty dollars a
pair for the one and fifteen and twenty for the other, while the
Negro man trotted his vast belly in and out of the houses with a
basket of bright greens or eggs in one hand and the plucked naked
carcass of a chicken in the other – recognized, remembered, even
(his attention) nagged at and already dismissed because there
wasn't time, saying rapidly:

'Good evening, Miss Habersham. Excuse me. I've got to speak
to Uncle Gavin:' then again to his uncle: 'Uncle Gavin –'

'So is Miss Habersham,' his uncle said quick and immediate, in
a tone a voice which in ordinary times he would have recognized
at once; at an ordinary time he might even have comprehended
the implication of what his uncle had said. But not now. He didn't
actually hear it. He wasn't listening. In fact he really didn't have

time to talk himself, saying rapid yet calm too, merely urgent and even that only to his uncle because he had already forgotten Miss Habersham, even her presence:

'I've got to speak to you:' and only then stopped not because he had finished, he hadn't even begun yet, but because for the first time he was hearing his uncle who hadn't even paused, sitting half sideways in the chair, one arm thrown over the back and the other hand holding the burning cob pipe on the table in front of him, still speaking in that voice like the idle flicking of a small limber switch:

'So you took it up to him yourself. Or maybe you didn't even bother with tobacco. And he told you a tale. I hope it was a good one.'

And that was all. He could go now, in fact should. For that matter he should never have stopped on his way through the hall or even come into the house at all but on around it where he could have called Aleck Sander on his way to the stable; Lucas had told him that thirty minutes ago in the jail when even he had come almost to the point and even under the very shadow of the Gowries had in the end known better than to try to tell his uncle or any other white man. Yet still he didn't move. He had forgotten Miss Habersham. He had dismissed her; he had said 'Excuse me' and so evanished her not only from the room but the moment too as the magician with one word or gesture disappears the palm tree or the rabbit or the bowl of roses and only they remained, the three of them: he at the door and still holding it, half in the room which he had never actually entered and shouldn't have come even that far and half already back out of it in the hall where he should never have wasted time passing to begin with, and his uncle half sprawled behind the table littered with papers too and another of the German beermugs filled with paper spills and probably a dozen of the corncob pipes in various stages of char, and half a mile away the old kinless friendless opinionated arrogant hardheaded intractable independent (insolent too) Negro man alone in the cell where the first familiar voice he would hear would probably be old one-armed Nub Gowrie's in the hall below saying, 'Git out of the way, Will Legate. We've come for that nigger,' while outside the quiet lamplit room the vast millrace of time roared not towards midnight but dragging midnight with it, not to hurl midnight into wreckage but to hurl the wreckage of midnight down upon them in one poised skyblotting yarn; and he knew now that the irrevocable moment

was not when he said 'All right' to Lucas through the steel door
of the cell but when he would step back into the hall and close
this one behind him. So he tried again, still calm, not even rapid
now, not even urgent: just specious explicit and reasonable;

'Suppose it wasn't his pistol that killed him.'

'Of course,' his uncle said. 'That's exactly what I would claim
myself if I were Lucas – or any other Negro murderer for that
matter or any ignorant white murderer either for the matter of
that. He probably even told you what he fired his pistol at. What
was it? a rabbit, or maybe a tin can or a mark on a tree just to
see if it really was loaded, really would go off. But let that pass.
Grant it for the moment: then what? What do you suggest? No;
what did Lucas tell you to do?'

And he even answered that: 'Couldn't Mr Hampton dig him
up and see?'

'On what grounds? Lucas was caught within two minutes after
the shot, standing over the body with a recently-fired pistol in
his pocket. He never denied having fired it; in fact he refused to
make any statement at all, even to me, his lawyer – the lawyer he
himself sent for. And how risk it? I'd just as soon go out there
and shoot another one of his sons as to tell Nub Gowrie I wanted
to dig his boy's body up out of the ground it had been consecrated
and prayed into. And if I went that far, I'd heap rather tell him
I just wanted to exhume it to dig the gold out of its teeth than
to tell him the reason was to save a nigger from being lynched.'

'But suppose –' he said.

'Listen to me,' his uncle said with a sort of weary yet indomitable
patience: 'Try to listen. Lucas is locked behind a proof steel door.
He's got the best protection Hampton or anybody else in this
county can possibly give him. As Will Legate said, there are
enough people in this county to pass him and Tubbs and even
that door if they really want to. But I dont believe there are that
many people in this county who really want to hang Lucas to a
telephone pole and set fire to him with gasoline.'

And now too. But he still tried. 'But just suppose –' he said
again and now he heard for the third time almost exactly what
he had heard twice in twelve hours, and he marvelled again at
the paucity, the really almost standardized meagreness not of
individual vocabularies but of Vocabulary itself, by means of
which even man can live in vast droves and herds even in concrete
warrens in comparative amity: even his uncle too:

'Suppose it then. Lucas should have thought of that before he

shot a white man in the back.' And it was only later that he would
realize his uncle was speaking to Miss Habersham too now; at the
moment he was neither rediscovering her presence in the room
nor even discovering it; he did not even remember that she had
already long since ceased to exist, turning, closing the door upon
the significantless speciosity of his uncle's voice: 'I've told him
what to do. If anything was going to happen, they would have
done it out there, at home, in their own back yard; they would
never have let Mr Hampton get to town with him. In fact, I still
dont understand why they did. But whether it was luck or
mismanagement or old Mr Gowrie is failing with age, the result
is good; he's all right now and I'm going to persuade him to
plead guilty to manslaughter; he's old and I think the District
Attorney will accept it. He'll go to the penitentiary and perhaps
in a few years if he lives –' and closed the door, who had heard
it all before and would no more, out of the room which he had
never completely entered anyway and shouldn't have stopped at
all, releasing the knob for the first time since he had put his hand
on it and thinking with the frantic niggling patience of a man in
a burning house trying to gather up a broken string of beads;
*Now I'll have to walk all the way back to the jail to ask Lucas where it
is:* realizing how Lucas probability doubts and everything else to
the contrary he actually had expected his uncle and the sheriff
would take charge and make the expedition, not because he
thought they would believe him but simply because he simply
could not conceive of himself and Aleck Sander being left with
it: until he remembered that Lucas had already taken care of
that too, foreseen that too; remembering not with relief but
rather with a new burst of rage and fury beyond even his own
concept of his capacity how Lucas had not only told him what he
wanted but exactly where it was and even how to get there and
only then as afterthought asked him if he would – hearing the
crackle of the paper on his father's lap beyond the library door
and smelling the cigar burning in the ashtray at his hand and
then he saw the blue wisp of its smoke float slowly out the open
door as his father must have picked it up in some synonymous
hiatus or throe and puffed it once: and (remembering) even by
what means to get out there and back and he thought of himself
opening the door again and saying to his uncle: *Forget Lucas. Just
lend me your car* and then walking into the library and saying to
his father who would have their car keys in his pocket until he
would remember when he undressed to leave them where his

mother could find them tomorrow: *Let me have the keys, Pop. I want to run out to the county and dig up a grave;* he even remembered Miss Habersham's pickup truck in front of the house (not Miss Habersham; he never thought of her again. He just remembered a motor vehicle sitting empty and apparently unwatched on the street not fifty yards away); the key might be, probably was, still in the switch and the Gowrie who caught him robbing his son's or brother's or cousin's grave might as well catch a car-thief too.

Because (quitting abandoning emerging from scattering with one sweep that confetti-swirl of raging facetiae) he realized that he had never doubted getting there and even getting the body up. He could see himself reaching the church, the graveyard without effort nor even any great elapse of time; he could see himself singlehanded even having the body up and out still with no effort, no pant and strain of muscles and lungs nor laceration of the shrinking sensibilities. It was only then that the whole wrecked and tumbling midnight which peer and pant though he would he couldn't see past and beyond, would come crashing down on him. So (moving: he had not stopped since the first second's fraction while he closed the office door) he flung himself bodily with one heave into a kind of deadly reasonableness of enraged calculation, a calm sagacious and desperate rationality not of pros and cons because there were no pros: the reason he was going out there was that somebody had to and nobody else would and the reason somebody had to was that not even Sheriff Hampton (vide Will Legate and the shotgun stationed in the lower hall of the jail like on a lighted stage where anybody approaching would have to see him or them before they even reached the gate) were completely convinced that the Gowries and their kin and friends would not try to take Lucas out of the jail tonight and so if they were all in town tonight trying to lynch Lucas there wouldn't be anybody hanging around out there to catch him digging up the grave and if that was a concrete fact then its obverse would be concrete too: if they were not in town after Lucas tonight then any one of the fifty or a hundred men and boys in the immediate connection by blood or just foxhunting and whiskeymaking and pine lumbertrading might stumble on him and Aleck Sander: and that too, that again: he must go on a horse for the same reason: that nobody else would except a sixteen-year-old boy who owned nothing to go on but a horse and he must even choose here: either to go alone on the horse in half the time and spend three times the time getting the body

up alone because alone he would not only have to do all the
digging but the watching and listening too, or take Aleck Sander
with him (he and Aleck Sander had travelled that way before on
Highboy for even more than ten miles – a big rawboned gelding
who had taken five bars even under a hundred and seventy-five
pounds and a good slow canter even with two up and a long
jolting driving trot as fast as the canter except that not even
Aleck Sander could stand it very long behind the saddle and then
a shuffling nameless halfrun halfwalk which he could hold for
miles under both of them, Aleck Sander behind him for the first
mile at the canter then trotting beside the horse holding to the
off stirrup for the next one) and so get the body up in a third of
the time at the risk of having Aleck Sander keeping Lucas
company when the Gowries came with the gasoline: and suddenly
he found himself escaped back into the confetti exactly as you
put off having to step finally into the cold water, thinking seeing
hearing himself trying to explain that to Lucas too:

We have to use the horse. We cant help it: and Lucas:
You could have axed him for the car: and he:
*He would have refused. Dont you understand? He wouldn't only
have refused, he would have locked me up where I couldn't even have
walked out there, let alone had a horse:* and Lucas:
*All right, all right. I aint criticizing you. After all, it aint you them
Gowries is fixing to set afire* – moving down the hall to the back
door: and he was wrong; not when he had said All right to Lucas
through the steel bars nor when he had stepped back into the
hall and closed the office door behind him, but here was the
irrevocable moment after which there would be no return; he
could stop here and never pass it, let the wreckage of midnight
crash harmless and impotent against these walls because they
were strong, they would endure; they were home, taller than
wreckage, stronger than fear – not even stopping, not even
curious to ask himself if perhaps he dared not stop, letting the
screen door quietly to behind him and down the steps into the
vast furious vortex of the soft May night and walking fast now
across the yard towards the dark cabin where Paralee and Aleck
Sander were no more asleep than all the other Negroes within a
mile of town would sleep tonight, not even in bed but sitting
quietly in the dark behind the closed doors and shuttered windows
waiting for what sound what murmur of fury and death to breathe
the spring dark: and stopped and whistled the signal he and Aleck
Sander had been using to one another ever since they learned to

whistle, counting off the seconds until the moment should come to repeat it, thinking how if he were Aleck Sander he wouldn't come out of the house to anybody's whistle tonight either when suddenly with no sound and certainly no light behind to reveal him by Aleck Sander stood out from the shadows, walking, already quite near in the moonless dark, a little taller than he though there was only a few months' difference between them: and came up, not even looking at him but past, over his head, towards the Square as if looking could make a lofting trajectory like a baseball, over the trees and the streets and the houses, to drop seeing into the Square – not the homes in the shady yards and the peaceful meals and the resting and the sleep which were the end and the reward, but the Square: the edifices created and ordained for trade and government and judgement and incarceration where strove and battled the passions of men for which the rest and the little death of sleep were the end and the escape and the reward.

'So they aint come for old Lucas yet,' Aleck Sander said.

'Is that what your people think about it too?' he said.

'And so would you,' Aleck Sander said. 'It's the ones like Lucas makes trouble for everybody.'

'Then maybe you better go to the office and sit with Uncle Gavin instead of coming with me.'

'Going where with you?' Aleck Sander said. And he told him, harsh and bald, in four words:

'Dig up Vinson Gowrie.' Aleck Sander didn't move, still looking past and over his head towards the Square. 'Lucas said it wasn't his gun that killed him.'

Still not moving Aleck Sander began to laugh, not loud and with no mirth: just laughing; he said exactly what his uncle had said hardly a minute ago: 'So would I,' Aleck Sander said. He said: 'Me? Go out there and dig that dead white man up? Is Mr Gavin already in the office or do I just sit there until he comes?'

'Lucas is going to pay you,' he said. 'He told me that even before he told me what it was.'

Aleck Sander laughed, without mirth or scorn or anything else: with no more in the sound of it than there is anything in the sound of breathing but just breathing. 'I aint rich,' he said. 'I dont need money.'

'At least you'll saddle Highboy while I hunt for a flashlight, wont you?' he said. 'You're not too proud about Lucas to do that, are you?'

'Certainly,' Aleck Sander said, turning.

'And get the pick and shovel. And the long tie-rope. I'll need that too.'

'Certainly,' Aleck Sander said. He paused, half turned. 'How you going to tote a pick and shovel both on Highboy when he dont even like to see a riding switch in your hand?'

'I dont know,' he said and Aleck Sander went on and he turned back towards the house and at first he thought it was his uncle coming rapidly around the house from the front, not because he believed that his uncle might have suspected and anticipated what he was about because he did not, his uncle had dismissed that too immediately and thoroughly not only from conception but from possibility too, but because he no longer remembered anyone else available for it to have been and even after he saw it was a woman he assumed it was his mother, even after he should have recognized the hat, right up to the instant when Miss Habersham called his name and his first impulse was to step quickly and quietly around the corner of the garage, from where he could reach the lot fence still unseen and climb it and go on to the stable and so go out the pasture gate without passing the house again at all, flashlight or not but it was already too late: calling his name: 'Charles:' in that tense urgent whisper then came rapidly up and stopped facing him, speaking in that tense rapid murmur:

'What did he tell you?' and now he knew what it was that had nudged at his attention back in his uncle's office when he had recognized her and then in the next second flashed away: old Molly, Lucas' wife, who had been the daughter of one of old Doctor Habersham's; Miss Habersham's grandfather's; slaves, she and Miss Habersham the same age, born in the same week and both suckled at Molly's mother's breast and grown up together almost inextricably like sisters, like twins, sleeping in the same room, the white girl in the bed, the Negro girl on a cot at the foot of it almost until Molly and Lucas married, and Miss Habersham had stood up in the Negro church as godmother to Molly's first child.

'He said it wasn't his pistol,' he said.

'So he didn't do it,' she said, rapid still and with something even more than urgency in her voice now.

'I dont know,' he said.

'Nonsense,' she said. 'If it wasn't his pistol –'

'I dont know,' he said.

'You must know. You saw him – talked to him –'

'I dont know,' he said. He said it calmy, quietly, with a kind of incredulous astonishment as though he had only now realized what he had promised, intended: 'I just dont know. I still dont know. I'm just going out there . . .' He stopped, his voice died. There was an instant a second in which he even remembered he should have been wishing he could recall it, the last unfinished sentence. Though it was probably already too late and she had already done herself what little finishing the sentence needed and at any moment now she would cry, protest, ejaculate and bring the whole house down on him. Then in the same second he stopped remembering it. She said:

'Of course': immediate murmurous and calm; he thought for another half of a second that she hadn't understood at all and then in the other half forgot that too, the two of them facing each other indistinguishable in the darkness across the tense and rapid murmur: and then he heard his own voice speaking in the same tone and pitch the two of them not conspiratorial exactly but rather like two people who have irrevocably accepted a gambit they are not at all certain they can cope with: only that they will resist it: 'We dont even know it wasn't his pistol. He just said it wasn't.'

'Yes.'

'He didn't say whose it was nor whether or not he fired it. He didn't even tell you he didn't fire it. He just said it wasn't his pistol.'

'Yes.'

'And your uncle told you there in his study that that's just exactly what he would say, all he could say.' He didn't answer that. It wasn't a question. Nor did she give him time. 'All right,' she said. 'Now what? To find out if it wasn't his pistol – find out whatever it was he meant? Go out there and what?'

He told her, as baldly as he had told Aleck Sander, explicit and succinct: 'Look at him:' not even pausing to think how here he should certainly have anticipated at least a gasp. 'Go out there and dig him up and bring him to town where somebody that knows bullet holes can look at the bullet hole in him –'

'Yes,' Miss Habersham said. 'Of course. Naturally he wouldn't tell your uncle. He's a Negro and your uncle's a man:' and now Miss Habersham in her turn repeating and paraphrasing and he thought how it was not really a paucity a meagreness of vocabulary, it was in the first place because the deliberate violent blotting out obliteration of a human life was itself so simple and so final that the verbiage which surrounded it enclosed it insulated it intact into the chronicle of man had of necessity to be simple and uncomplex too, repetitive, almost monotonous even; and in the second place, vaster than that, adumbrating that, because what Miss Habersham paraphrased was simple truth, not even fact and so there was not needed a great deal of diversification and originality to express it because truth was universal, it had to be universal to be truth and so there didn't need to be a great deal of it just to keep running something no bigger than one earth and so anybody could know truth; all they had to do was just to pause, just to stop, just to wait: 'Lucas knew it would take a child – or an old woman like me: someone not concerned with probability, with evidence. Men like your uncle and Mr Hampton have had to be men too long, busy too long – Yes?' she said. 'Bring him in to town where someone who knows can look at the bullet hole. And suppose they look at it and find out it was Lucas' pistol?' And he didn't answer that at all, nor had she waited again, saying, already turning: 'We'll need a pick and shovel. I've got a flashlight in the truck –'

'We?' he said.

She stopped; she said almost patiently: 'It's fifteen miles out there –'

'Ten,' he said.

'– a grave is six feet deep. It's after eight now and you may have only until midnight to get back to town in time –' and something else but he didn't even hear it. He wasn't even listening. He had said this himself to Lucas only fifteen minutes ago but it was only now that he understood what he himself had said. It was only after hearing someone else say it that he comprehended not the enormity of his intention but the simple inert unwieldy impossible physical vastness of what he faced; he said quietly, with hopeless indomitable amazement:

'We cant possibly do it.'

'No,' Miss Habersham said. 'Well?'

'Ma'am?' he said. 'What did you say?'

'I said you haven't even got a car.'

'We were going on the horse.'

Now she said, 'We?'

'Me and Aleck Sander.'

'Then we'll have three,' she said. 'Get your pick and shovel.

They'll begin to wonder in the house why they haven't heard my truck start.' She moved again.

'Yessum,' he said. 'Drive on down the lane to the pasture gate. We'll meet you there.'

He didn't wait either. He heard the truck start as he climbed the lot fence; presently he could see Highboy's blaze in the black yawn of the stable hallway; Aleck Sander jerked the buckled girth-strap home through the keeper as he came up. He unsnapped the tie-rope from the bit-ring before he remembered and snapped it back and untied the other end from the wall-ring and looped it and the reins up over Highboy's head and led him out of the hallway and got up.

'Here,' Aleck Sander said reaching up the pick and shovel but Highboy had already begun to dance even before he could have seen them as he always did even at a hedge switch and he set him back hard and steadied him as Aleck Sander said 'Stand still!' and gave Highboy a loud slap on the rump, passing up the pick and shovel and he steadied them across the saddle-bow and managed to hold Highboy back on his heels for another second, long enough to free his foot from the near stirrup for Aleck Sander to get his foot into it, Highboy moving then in a long almost buck-jump as Aleck Sander swung up behind and still trying to run until he steadied him again with one hand, the pick and shovel jouncing on the saddle, and turned him across the pasture towards the gate. 'Hand me them damn shovels and picks,' Aleck Sander said. 'Did you get the flashlight?'

'What do you care?' he said. Aleck Sander reached his spare hand around him and took the pick and shovel; again for a second Highboy could actually see them but this time he had both hands free for the snaffle and the curb too. 'You aint going anywhere to need a flashlight. You just said so.'

They had almost reached the gate. He could see the dark blob of the halted truck against the pale road beyond it: that is, he could believe he saw it because he knew it was there. But Aleck Sander actually saw it: who seemed able to see in the dark almost like an animal. Carrying the pick and shovel, Aleck Sander had no free hand, nevertheless he had one with which he reached suddenly again and caught the reins outside his own hands and jerked Highboy almost back to a squat and said in a hissing whisper: 'What's that?'

'It's Miss Eunice Habersham's truck,' he said. 'She's going with us. Turn him loose, confound it!' wrenching the reins from Aleck

Sander, who released them quickly enough now, saying,

'She's gonter take the truck:' and not even dropping the pick and shovel but flinging them clattering and clanging against the gate and slipping down himself and just in time because now Highboy stood erect on his hind feet until he struck him hard between the ears with the looped tie-rope.

'Open the gate,' he said.

'We wont need the horse,' Aleck Sander said. 'Unsaddle and bridle him here. We'll put um up when we get back.'

Which was what Miss Habersham said; through the gate now and Highboy still sidling and beating his hooves while Aleck Sander put the pick and shovel into the back of the truck as though he expected Aleck Sander to throw them at him this time, and Miss Habersham's voice from the dark cab of the truck:

'He sounds like a good horse. Has he got a four-footed gait too?'

'Yessum,' he said. 'Nome,' he said. 'I'll take the horse too. The nearest house is a mile from the church but somebody might still hear a car. We'll leave the truck at the bottom of the hill when we cross the branch.' Then he answered that too before she had time to say it: 'We'll need the horse to bring him back down to the truck.'

'Heh,' Aleck Sander said. It wasn't laughing. But then nobody thought it was. 'How do you reckon that horse is going to tote what you dug up when he dont even want to tote what you going to do the digging with?' But he had already thought of that too, remembering his grandfather telling of the old days when deer and bear and wild turkey could be hunted in Yoknapatawpha County within twelve miles of Jefferson, of the hunters: Major de Spain who had been his grandfather's cousin and old General Compson and Uncle Ike McCaslin, Carothers Edmonds' great-uncle, still alive at ninety, and Boon Hogganbeck whose mother's mother had been a Chickasaw woman and the Negro Sam Fathers whose father had been a Chickasaw chief, and Major de Spain's one-eyed hunting mule Alice who wasn't afraid even of the smell of bear and he thought how if you really were the sum of your ancestry it was too bad the ancestors who had evoluted him into a secret resurrector of country graveyards hadn't thought to equip him with a descendant of that unspookable one-eyed mule to transport his subjects on.

'I dont know,' he said.

'Maybe he'll learn by the time we get back to the truck,' Miss

Habersham said. 'Can Aleck Sander drive?'

'Yessum,' Aleck Sander said.

Highboy was still edgy; held down he would merely have lathered himself to no end so since it was cool tonight for the first mile he actually kept in sight of the truck's tail-light. Then he slowed, the light fled diminishing on and vanished beyond a curve and he settled Highboy into the shambling halfrun halfwalk which no show judge would ever pass but which covered ground; nine miles of it to be covered and he thought with a kind of ghastly amusement that at last he would have time to think, thinking how it was too late to think now, not one of the three of them dared think now, if they had done but one thing tonight it was at least to put all thought ratiocination contemplation forever behind them; five miles from town and he would cross (probably Miss Habersham and Aleck Sander in the truck already had) the invisible surveyor's line which was the boundary of Beat Four: the notorious, the fabulous almost and certainly least of all did any of them dare think now, thinking how it was never difficult for an outlander to do two things at once which Beat Four wouldn't like since Beat Four already in advance didn't like most of the things which people from town (and from most of the rest of the county too for that matter) did: but that it remained for them, a white youth of sixteen and a Negro one of the same and an old white spinster of seventy to elect and do at the same time the two things out of all man's vast reservoir of invention and capability that Beat Four would repudiate and retaliate on most violently: to violate the grave of one of its progeny in order to save a nigger murderer from its vengeance.

But at least they would have some warning (not speculating on who the warning could help since they who would be warned were already six and seven miles from the jail and still moving away from it as fast as he dared push the horse) because if Beat Four were coming in tonight he should begin to pass them soon (or they pass him) – the battered mud-stained cars, the empty trucks for hauling cattle and lumber, and the saddled horses and mules. Yet so far he had passed nothing whatever since he left town; the road lay pale and empty before and behind him too; the lightless houses and cabins squatted or loomed beside it, the dark land stretched away into the darkness strong with the smell of ploughed earth and now and then the heavy scent of flowering orchards lying across the road for him to ride through like stagnant skeins of smoke so maybe they were making better time than even he had hoped and before he could stop it he had thought *Maybe we can, maybe we will after all;* – before he could leap and spring and smother and blot it from thinking not because he couldn't really believe they possibly could and not because you dont dare think whole even to yourself the entirety of a dear hope or wish let alone a desperate one else you yourself have doomed it but because thinking it into words even only to himself was like the struck match which doesn't dispel the dark but only exposes its terror – one weak flash and glare revealing for a second the empty road's the dark and empty land's irrevocable immitigable negation.

Because – almost there now; Aleck Sander and Miss Habersham had already arrived probably a good thirty minutes ago and he took a second to hope Aleck Sander had had forethought enough to drive the truck off the road where anybody passing would not see it, then in the same second he knew that of course Aleck Sander had done that and it was not Aleck Sander he had ever doubted but himself for even for one second doubting Aleck Sander – he had not seen one Negro since leaving town, with whom at this hour on Sunday night in May the road should have been constant as beads almost – the men and young women and girls and even a few old men and women and even children before it got too late, but mostly the men the young bachelors who since last Monday at daylight had braced into the shearing earth the lurch and heave of ploughs behind straining and surging mules then at noon Saturday had washed and shaved and put on the clean Sunday shirts and pants and all Saturday night had walked the dusty roads and all day Sunday and all Sunday night would still walk them until barely time to reach home and change back into the overalls and the brogans and catch and gear up the mules and forty-eight hours even bedless save for the brief time there was a woman in it be back in the field again the plough's point set into the new furrow when Monday's sun rose: but not now, not tonight: where in town except for Paralee and Aleck Sander he had seen none either for twenty-four hours but he had expected that, they were acting exactly as Negroes and whites both would have expected Negroes to act at such a time; they were still there, they had not fled, you just didn't see them – a sense a feeling of their constant presence and nearness: black men and women and children breathing and waiting inside their barred and shuttered houses, not crouching cringing shrinking, not in anger and not quite in fear: just waiting, biding since theirs was an armament which the white man could not match nor – if he but knew it – even cope with: patience; just keeping out of sight and out of the way – but not here, no sense feeling here of a massed adjacence, a dark human presence biding and unseen; this land was a desert and a witness, this empty road its postulate (it would be some time yet before he would realize how far he had come: a provincial Mississippian, a child who when the sun set this same day had appeared to be – and even himself believed, provided he had thought about it at all – still a swaddled unwitting infant in the long tradition of his native land – or for that matter a witless foetus itself struggling – if he was aware that there had been any throes – blind and insentient and not even yet awaked in the simple painless convulsion of emergence) of the deliberate turning as with one back of the whole dark people on which the very economy of the land itself was founded, not in heat or anger nor even regret but in one irremediable invincible inflexible repudiation, upon not a racial outrage but a human shame.

Now he was there; Highboy tightened and even began to drive a little, even after nine miles, smelling water and now he could see distinguish the bridge or at least the gap of lighter darkness where the road spanned the impenetrable blackness of the willows banding the branch and then Aleck Sander stood out from the bridge rail; Highboy snorted at him then he recognized him too, without surprise, not even remembering how he had wondered once if Aleck Sander would have forethought to hide the truck, not even remembering that he had expected no less, not stopping, checking Highboy back to a walk across the bridge then giving him his head to turn from the road beyond the bridge and drop in stiff fore-legged jolts down towards the water invisible for a moment longer then he too could see the reflected wimpling where it caught the sky: until Highboy stopped and snorted again then heaved suddenly up and back, almost unseating him.

'He smell quicksand,' Aleck Sander said. 'Let him wait till he gets home, anyway. I'd rather be doing something else than what I am too.'

But he took Highboy a little further down the bank where he might get down to the water but again he only feinted at it so he pulled away and back on to the road and freed the stirrup for Aleck Sander, Highboy again already in motion when Aleck Sander swung up. 'Here,' Aleck Sander said but he had already swung Highboy off the gravel and into the narrow dirt road turning sharp towards the black loom of the ridge and beginning

almost at once its long slant up into the hills though even before
it began to rise the strong constant smell of pines was coming
down on them with no wind behind it yet firm and hard as a
hand almost, palpable against the moving body as water would
have been. The slant steepened under the horse and even carrying
double he essayed to run at it as was his habit at any slope,
gathering and surging out until he checked him sharply back and
even then he had to hold him hard-wristed in a strong lurching
uneven walk until the first level of the plateau flattened and even
as Aleck Sander said 'Here' again Miss Habersham stood out of
the obscurity at the roadside carrying the pick and shovel. Aleck
Sander slid down as Highboy stopped. He followed.

'Stay on,' Miss Habersham said. 'I've got the tools and the
flashlight.'

'It's a half mile yet,' he said. 'Up hill. This aint a sidesaddle
but maybe you could sit sideways. Where's the truck?' he said to
Aleck Sander.

'Behind them bushes,' Aleck Sander said. 'We aint holding a
parade. Leastways I aint.'

'No no,' Miss Habersham said. 'I can walk.'

'We'll save time,' he said. 'It must be after ten now. He's gentle.
That was just when Aleck Sander threw the pick and shovel –'

'Of course,' Miss Habersham said. She handed the tools to
Aleck Sander and approached the horse.

'I'm sorry it aint –' he said.

'Pah,' she said and took the reins from him and before he could
even brace his hand for her foot she put it in the stirrup and
went up as light and fast as either he or Aleck Sander could have
done, on to the horse astride so that he had just time to avert his
face, feeling her looking down in the darkness at his turned head.
'Pah,' she said again. 'I'm seventy years old. Besides, we'll worry
about my skirt after we are done with this:' – moving Highboy
herself before he had hardly time to take hold of the bit, back
into the road when Aleck Sander said:

'Hush.' They stopped, immobile in the long constant invisible
flow of pine. 'Mule coming down the hill,' Aleck Sander said.

He began to turn the horse at once. 'I dont hear anything,'
Miss Habersham said. 'Are you sure?'

'Yessum,' he said, turning Highboy back off the road:

'Aleck Sander's sure.' And standing at Highboy's head among
the trees and undergrowth, his other hand lying on the horse's
nostrils in case he decided to nicker at the other animal, he heard

it too – the horse or mule coming steadily down the road from the crest. It was unshod probably; actually the only sound he really heard was the creak of leather and he wondered (without doubting for one second that he had) how Aleck Sander had heard it at all the two minutes and more it had taken the animal to reach them. Then he could see it or that is where it was passing them – a blob, a movement, a darker shadow than shadow against the pale dirt of the road, going on down the hill, the soft steady shuffle and screak of leather dying away, then gone. But they waited a moment more.

'What was that he was toting on the saddle in front of him?' Aleck Sander said.

'I couldn't even see whether it was a man on it or not,' he said.

'I couldn't see anything,' Miss Habersham said. He led the horse back into the road. 'Suppose –' she said.

'Aleck Sander will hear it in time,' he said. So once more Highboy surged strong and steady at the steepening pitch, he carrying the shovel and clutching the leather under Miss Habersham's thin hard calf on one side and Aleck Sander with the pick on the other, mounting, really moving quite fast through the strong heady vivid living smell of the pines which did something to the lungs, the breathing as (he imagined: he had never tasted it. He could have – the sip from the communion cup didn't count because it was not only a sip but sour consecrated and sharp: the deathless blood of our Lord not to be tasted, moving not downwards towards the stomach but upwards and outwards into the Allknowledge between good and evil and the choice and the repudiation and the acceptance forever – at the table at Thanksgiving and Christmas but he had never wanted to) wine did to the stomach. They were quite high now, the ridged land opening and tumbling away invisible in the dark yet with the sense, the sensation of height and space; by day he could have seen them, ridge on pine-dense ridge rolling away to the east and the north in similitude of the actual mountains in Carolina and before that in Scotland where his ancestors had come from but he hadn't seen yet, his breath coming a little short now and he could not only hear but feel too the hard short blasts from Highboy's lungs as he was actually trying to run at this slope too even carrying a rider and dragging two, Miss Habersham steadying him, holding him down until they came out on to the true crest and Aleck Sander said once more 'Here' and Miss Habersham turned the horse out of the road because he could still see nothing until they were off the road and only then he distinguished the clearing not because it was a clearing but because in a thin distillation of starlight there stood, canted a little where the earth had sunk, the narrow slab of a marble headstone. And he could hardly see the church (weathered, unpainted, of wood and not much larger than a single room) at all even when he led Highboy around behind it and tied the reins to a sapling and unsnapped the tie-rope from the bit and went back to where Miss Habersham and Aleck Sander were waiting.

'It'll be the only fresh one,' he said. 'Lucas said there hasn't been a burying here since last winter.'

'Yes,' Miss Habersham said. 'The flowers too. Aleck Sander's already found it.' But to make sure (he thought quietly, he didn't know to whom: *I'm going to make a heap more mistakes but dont let this be one of them*) he hooded the flashlight in his wadded handkerchief so that one thin rapid pencil touched for a second the raw mound with its meagre scattering of wreaths and bouquets and even single blooms and then for another second the headstone adjacent to it, long enough to read the engraved name: *Amanda Workitt wife of N.B. Forrest Gowrie 1878-1926* then snapped it off and again the darkness came in and the strong scent of the pines and they stood for a moment beside the raw mound, doing nothing at all. 'I hate this,' Miss Habersham said.

'You aint the one,' Aleck Sander said. 'It's just a half a mile back to the truck. Down hill too.'

She moved; she was first. 'Move the flowers,' she said. 'Carefully. Can you see?'

'Yessum,' Aleck Sander said. 'Aint many. Looks like they throwed them at it too.'

'But we wont,' Miss Habersham said. 'Move them carefully.' And it must be nearing eleven now; they would not possibly have time; Aleck Sander was right: the thing to do was to go back to the truck and drive away, back to town and through town and on, not to stop, not even to have time to think for having to keep on driving, steering, keeping the truck going in order to keep on moving, never to come back; but then they had never had time, they had known that before they ever left Jefferson and he thought for an instant how if Aleck Sander really had meant it when he said he would not come and if he would have come alone in that case and then (quickly) he wouldn't think about that at all, Aleck Sander using the shovel for the first shift while he used the pick though the dirt was still so loose they didn't really need the pick (and if it hadn't been still loose they couldn't have done it at all even by daylight); two shovels would have done and faster too but it was too late for that now until suddenly Aleck Sander handed him the shovel and climbed out of the hole and vanished and (not even using the flashlight) with that same sense beyond sight and hearing both which had realized that what Highboy smelled at the branch was quicksand and which had discovered the horse or the mule coming down the hill a good minute before either he or Miss Habersham could begin to hear it, returned with a short light board so that both of them had shovels now and he could hear the *chuck!* and then the faint swish as Aleck Sander thrust the board into the dirt and then flung the load up and outwards, expelling his breath, saying 'Hah!' each time – a sound furious raging and restrained, going faster and faster until the ejaculation was almost as rapid as the beat of someone running: 'Hah! . . . Hah! . . . Hah!' so that he said over his shoulder:

'Take it easy. We're doing all right:' straightened his own back for a moment to mop his sweating face and seeing as always Miss Habersham in motionless silhouette on the sky above him in the straight cotton dress and the round hat on the exact top of her head such as few people had seen in fifty years and probably no one at any time looking up out of a halfway rifled grave: more than halfway because spading again he heard the sudden thud of wood on wood, then Aleck Sander said sharply:

'Go on. Get out of here and gimme room:' and flung the board up and out and took, jerked the shovel from his hands and he climbed out of the pit and even as he stooped groping Miss Habersham handed him the coiled tie-rope.

'The flashlight too,' he said and she handed him that and he stood too while the strong hard immobile flow of the pines bleached the sweat from his body until his wet shirt felt cold on his flesh and invisible below him in the pit the shovel rasped and scraped on wood, and stooping and hooding the light again he flashed it downwards upon the unpainted lid of the pine box and switched it off.

'All right,' he said. 'That's enough. Get out:' and Aleck Sander with the last shovel of dirt released the shovel too, flinging the whole thing arcing out of the pit like a javelin and followed it in one motion, and carrying the rope and the light he dropped into the pit and only then remembered he would need a hammer, crowbar – something to open the lid with and the only thing of

that nature would be what Miss Habersham might happen to
have in the truck a half-mile away and the walk back uphill,
stooping to feel, examine the catch or whatever it was to be
forced when he discovered that the lid was not fastened at all: so
that straddling it, balancing himself on one foot he managed to
open the lid up and back and prop it with one elbow while he
shook the rope out and found the end and snapped on the
flashlight and pointed it down and then said, 'Wait.' He said,
'Wait.' He was still saying 'Wait' when he finally heard Miss
Habersham speaking in a hissing whisper:

'Charles . . . Charles.'

'This aint Vinson Gowrie,' he said. 'This man's name is Montgomery. He's some kind of a shoestring timberbuyer from over in
Crossman County.'

Chapter Five

They had to fill the hole back up of course and besides he had
the horse. But even then it was a good while until daylight when
he left Highboy with Aleck Sander at the pasture gate and tried
remembered to tiptoe into the house but at once his mother her
hair loose and in her nightdress wailed from right beside the
front door: 'Where have you been?' then followed him to his
uncle's door and then while his uncle was putting some clothes
on: 'You? Digging up a grave?' and he with a sort of weary
indefatigable patience, just about worn out himself now from
riding and digging then turning around and undigging and then
riding again, somehow managing to stay that one jump ahead of
what he had really never hoped to beat anyway:

'Aleck Sander and Miss Habersham helped:' which if anything
seemed to be worse though she was still not loud: just amazed
and inexpugnable until his uncle came out fully dressed even to
his necktie but not shaved and said,

'Now Maggie, do you want to wake Charley?' then following
them back to the front door and this time she said – and he

thought again how you could never really beat them because of their fluidity which was not just a capacity for mobility but a willingness to abandon with the substanceless promptitude of wind or air itself not only position but principle too; you didn't have to marshal your forces because you already had them: superior artillery, weight, right justice and precedent and usage and everything else and made your attack and cleared the field, swept all before you – or so you thought until you discovered that the enemy had not retreated at all but had already abandoned the field and had not merely abandoned the field but had usurped your very battlecry in the process; you believed you had captured a citadel and instead found you had merely entered an untenable position and then found the unimpaired and even unmarked battle set up again in your unprotected and unsuspecting rear – she said:

'But he's got to sleep! He hasn't even been to bed!' so that he actually stopped until his uncle said, hissed at him:

'Come on. What's the matter with you? Dont you know she's tougher than you and me both just as old Habersham was tougher than you and Aleck Sander put together; you might have gone out there without her to drag you by the hand but Aleck Sander wouldn't and I'm still not so sure you would when you came right down to it.' So he moved on too beside his uncle towards where Miss Habersham sat in the truck behind his uncle's parked car (it had been in the garage at nine o'clock last night; later when he had time he would remember to ask his uncle just where his mother had sent him to look for him). 'I take that back,' his uncle said. 'Forget it. Out of the mouths of babes and sucklings and old ladies –' he paraphrased. 'Quite true, as a lot of truth often is, only a man just dont like to have it flung in his teeth at three o'clock in the morning. And dont even forget your mother, which of course you cant; she has already long since seen to that. Just remember that they can stand anything, accept any fact (it's only men who burk at facts) provided they dont have to face it; can assimilate it with their heads turned away and one hand extended behind them as the politician accepts the bribe. Look at her: who will spend a long contented happy life never abating one jot of her refusal to forgive you for being able to button your own pants.'

And still a good while until daylight when his uncle stopped the car at the sheriff's gate and led the way up the short walk and on to the rented gallery. (Since he couldn't succeed himself,

although now in his third term the elapsed time covering Sheriff
Hampton's tenure was actually almost twice as long as the twelve
years of his service. He was a countryman, a farmer and son of
farmers when he was first elected and now owned himself the
farm and house where he had been born, living in the rented
one in town during his term of office then returning to the farm
which was his actual home at each expiration, to live there until
he could run for – and be elected – sheriff again).

'I hope he's not a heavy sleeper,' Miss Habersham said. 'He
aint asleep,' his uncle said. 'He's cooking breakfast.'

'Cooking breakfast?' Miss Habersham said: and then he knew
that, for all her flat back and the hat which had never shifted
from the exact top of her head as though she kept it balanced
there not by any pins but simply by the rigid unflagging poise of
her neck as Negro women carry a whole family wash, she was
about worn out with strain and lack of sleep too.

'He's a country man,' his uncle said. 'Any food he eats after
daylight in the morning is dinner. Mrs Hampton's in Memphis
with their daughter waiting for the baby and the only woman
who'll cook a man's breakfast at half-past three a.m. is his wife.
No hired town cook's going to do it. She comes at a decent hour
about eight o'clock and washes the dishes.' His uncle didn't
knock. He started to open the door then stopped and looked
back past both of them to where Aleck Sander stood at the
bottom of the front steps. 'And dont you think you're going to
get out of it just because your mama dont vote,' he told Aleck
Sander. 'You come on too.'

Then his uncle opened the door and at once they smelled the
coffee and the frying hogmeat, walking on linoleum towards a
faint light at the rear of the hall then across a linoleum-floored
diningroom in rented Grand Rapids mission into the kitchen,
into the hard cheerful blast of a woodstove where the sheriff
stood over a sputtering skillet in his undershirt and pants and
socks, his braces dangling and his hair mussed and tousled with
sleep like that of a ten-year-old boy, a battercake turner in one
hand and a cuptowel in the other. The sheriff had already turned
his vast face towards the door before they entered it and he
watched the little hard pale eyes flick from his uncle to Miss
Habersham to himself and then to Aleck Sander and even then
it was not the eyes which widened so much for that second but
rather the little hard black pupils which had tightened in that
one flick to pinpoints. But the sheriff said nothing yet, just looking

INTRUDER IN THE DUST 667

at his uncle now and now even the little hard pupils seemed to expand again as when an expulsion of breath untightens the chest and while the three of them stood quietly and steadily watching the sheriff his uncle told it, rapid and condensed and succinct, from the moment in the jail last night when his uncle had realized that Lucas had started to tell – or rather ask – him something, to the one when he had entered his uncle's room ten minutes ago and waked him up, and stopped and again they watched the little hard eyes go flick, flick, slick, across their three faces then back to his uncle again, staring at his uncle for almost a quarter of a minute without even blinking. Then the sheriff said:

'You wouldn't come here at four o'clock in the morning with a tale like that if it wasn't so.'

'You aint listening just to two sixteen-year-old children,' his uncle said. 'I remind you that Miss Habersham was there.'

'You dont have to,' the sheriff said. 'I haven't forgot it. I dont think I ever will.' Then the sheriff turned. A gigantic man and in the fifties too, you wouldn't think he could move fast and he didn't really seem to yet he had taken another skillet from a nail in the wall behind the stove and was already turning towards the table (where for the first time he noticed, saw the side of smoked meat) before he seemed to have moved at all, picking up a butcher knife from beside the meat before his uncle could even begin to speak:

'Have we got time for that? You've got to drive sixty miles to Harrisburg to the District Attorney; you'll have to take Miss Habersham and these boys with you for witnesses to try and persuade him to originate a petition for the exhumation of Vinson Gowrie's body –'

The sheriff wiped the handle of the knife rapidly with the cuptowel. 'I thought you told me Vinson Gowrie aint in that grave.'

'Officially he is,' his uncle said. 'By the county records he is. And if you, living right here and knowing Miss Habersham and me all your political life, had to ask me twice, what do you think Jim Halladay is going to do? Then you've got to drive sixty miles back here with your witnesses and the petition and get Judge Maycox to issue an order –'

The sheriff dropped the cuptowel on to the table. 'Have I?' he said mildly, almost inattentively: so that his uncle stopped perfectly still watching him as the sheriff turned from the table, the knife in his hand.

'Oh,' his uncle said.

'I've thought of something else too,' the sheriff said. 'I'm surprised you aint. Or maybe you have.'

His uncle stared at the sheriff. Then Aleck Sander he was behind them all, not yet quite through the diningroom door into the kitchen – said in a voice as mild and impersonal as though he were reading off a slogan catchphrase advertising some object he didn't own and never expected to want:

'It mought not a been a mule. It mought have been a horse.'

'Maybe you've thought of it now,' the sheriff said.

'Oh,' his uncle said. He said: 'Yes.' But Miss Habersham was already talking. She had given Aleck Sander one quick hard look but now she was looking at the sheriff again as quick and as hard.

'So do I,' she said. 'And I think we deserve better than secrecy.'

'I do too, Miss Eunice,' the sheriff said. 'Except that the one that needs considering right now aint in this room.'

'Oh,' Miss Habersham said. She said 'Yes' too. She said, 'Of course:' already moving, meeting the sheriff halfway between the table and the door and taking the knife from him and going on to the table when he passed her and came on towards the door, his uncle then he then Aleck Sander moving out of the way as the sheriff went on into the diningroom and across it into the dark hall, shutting the door behind him: and then he was wondering why the sheriff hadn't finished dressing when he got up; a man who didn't mind or had to or anyway did get up at half-past three in the morning to cook himself some breakfast would hardly mind getting up five minutes earlier and have time to put his shirt and shoes on too then Miss Habersham spoke and he remembered her; a lady's presence of course was why he had gone to put on the shirt and shoes without even waiting to eat the breakfast and Miss Habersham spoke and he jerked, without moving heaved up out of sleep, having been asleep for seconds maybe even minutes on his feet as a horse sleeps but Miss Habersham was still only turning the side of meat on to its edge to cut the first slice. She said: 'Cant he telephone to Harrisburg and have the District Attorney telephone back to Judge Maycox?'

'That's what he doing now,' Aleck Sander said. 'Telephoning.'

'Maybe you'd better go to the hall where you can overhear good what he's saying,' his uncle told Aleck Sander. Then his uncle looked at Miss Habersham again; he too watched her slicing rapid slice after slice of the bacon as fast and even almost as a machine could have done it. 'Mr Hampton says we won't need any papers. We can attend to it ourselves without bothering Judge Maycox –'

Miss Habersham released the knife. She didn't lay it down, she just opened her hand and in the same motion picked up the cuptowel and was wiping her hands as she turned from the table, crossing the kitchen towards them faster, a good deal faster than even the sheriff had moved. 'Then what are we wasting time here for?' she said. 'For him to put on his necktie and coat?'

His uncle stepped quickly in front of her. 'We cant do anything in the dark,' he said. 'We must wait for daylight.'

'We didn't,' Miss Habersham said. Then she stopped; it was either that or walk over his uncle though his uncle didn't touch her, just standing between her and the door until she had to stop at least for the second for his uncle to get out of the way: and he looked at her too, straight, thin, almost shapeless in the straight cotton dress beneath the round exactitude of the hat and he thought *She's too old for this* and then corrected it: *No a woman a lady shouldn't have to do this* and then remembered last night when he had left the office and walked across the back yard and whistled for Aleck Sander and he knew he had believed – and he still believed it – that he would have gone alone even if Aleck Sander had stuck to his refusal but it was only after Miss Habersham came around the house and spoke to him that he knew he was going to go through with it and he remembered again what old Ephraim had told him after they found the ring under the hog trough: *If you got something outside the common run that's got to be done and cant wait, dont waste your time on the menfolks; the works on what your uncle calls the rules and the cases. Get the womens and the children at it; they works on the circumstances.* Then the hall door opened. He heard the sheriff cross the diningroom to the kitchen door. But the sheriff didn't enter the kitchen, stopping in the door, standing in it even after Miss Habersham said in a harsh, almost savage voice:

'Well?' and he hadn't put on his shoes nor even picked up the dangling galluses and he didn't seem to have heard Miss Habersham at all: just standing looming bulging in the door looking at Miss Habersham – not at the hat, not at her eyes nor even her face: just at her – as you might look at a string of letters in Russian or Chinese which someone you believed had just told you spelled your name, saying at last in a musing baffled voice:

'No:' then turning his head to look at him and saying, 'It aint you neither:' then turning his head further until he was looking at Aleck Sander while Aleck Sander slid his eyes up at the sheriff then slid them away again then slid them up again. 'You,' the sheriff said. 'You're the one. You went out there in the dark and helped dig up a dead man. Not only that, a dead white man that the rest of the white folks claimed another nigger had murdered. Why? Was it because Miss Habersham made you?'

'Never nobody made me,' Aleck Sander said. 'I didn't even know I was going. I had done already told Chick I didn't aim to. Only when we got to the truck everybody seemed to just take it for granted I wasn't going to do nothing else but go and before I knowed it I wasn't.'

'Mr Hampton,' Miss Habersham said. Now the sheriff looked at her. He even heard her now.

'Haven't you finished slicing that meat yet?' he said. 'Give me the knife then.' He took her by the arm, turning her back to the table. 'Aint you done enough rushing and stewing around tonight to last you a while? It'll be daylight in fifteen minutes and folks dont start lynchings in daylight. They might finish one by daylight if they had a little trouble or bad luck and got behind with it. But they dont start them by daylight because then they would have to see one another's faces. How many can eat more than two eggs?'

They left Aleck Sander with his breakfast at the kitchen table and carried theirs into the diningroom, he and his uncle and Miss Habersham carrying the platter of fried eggs and meat and the pan of biscuits baked last night and warmed again in the oven until they were almost like toast and the coffeepot in which the unstrained grounds and the water had been boiling together until the sheriff had thought to remove the pot from the hot part of the stove; four of them although the sheriff had set five places and they had barely sat down when the sheriff raised his head listening though he himself heard nothing, then rose and went into the dark hall and towards the rear of the house and then he heard the sound of the back door and presently the sheriff came back with Will Legate though minus the shotgun, and he turned his head enough to look out the window behind him and sure enough it was daylight.

The sheriff served the plates while his uncle and Legate passed theirs and the sheriff's cup to Miss Habersham at the coffeepot. Then at once he seemed to have been hearing for a long time the sheriff from a great distance saying '. . . boy . . . boy . . .' then 'Wake him up, Gavin. Let him eat his breakfast before he goes to sleep:' and he jerked, it was still only daylight, Miss Habersham was still pouring coffee into the same cup and he began to eat, chewing and even swallowing, rising and falling as though to the motion of the chewing along the deep soft bottomless mire of sleep; into then out of the voices buzzing of old finished things no longer concern of his: the sheriff's:

'Do you know Jake Montgomery, from over in Crossman County? Been in and out of town here for the last six months or so?' then Legate's:

'Sure. A kind of Jackleg timber buyer now. Used to run a place he called a restaurant just across the Tennessee line out of Memphis, though I never heard of nobody trying to buy nothing that had to be chewed in it, until a man went and got killed in it one night two-three years ago. They never did know just how much Jake did or didn't have to do with it but the Tennessee police run him back across the Mississippi line just on principle. Since then I reckon he's been laying around his pa's farm over beyond Glasgow. Maybe he's waiting until he figgers folks have forgot about that other business and he can set up again in another place on a highway with a hole under the floor big enough to hide a case of whisky in.'

'What was he doing around here?' the sheriff said: then Legate:

'Buying timber, aint he? Aint him and Vinson Gowrie . . .' Then Legate said with the barest inflection, '*Was?*' and then with no inflection at all: 'What is he doing?' and he this time, his own voice indifferent along the soft deep edge of sleep; too indifferent to bother if it were aloud or not:

'He aint doing anything now.'

But it was better afterwards, out of the stale warm house again into the air, the morning, the sun in one soft high level golden wash in the highest tips of the trees, gilding the motionless obese uprush of the town water tank in spiderlegged elongate against the blue, the four of them in his uncle's car once more while the sheriff stood leaned above the driver's window, dressed now even to a bright orange-and-yellow necktie, saying to his uncle:

'You run Miss Eunice home so she can get some sleep. I'll pick you up at your house in say an hour –'

Miss Habersham in the front seat with his uncle said 'Pah.' That was all. She didn't curse. She didn't need to. It was far more definite and final than just cursing. She leaned forward to look past his uncle at the sheriff. 'Get in your car and go to the jail or wherever you'll go to get somebody to do the digging this

time. We had to fill it up again because we knew you wouldn't
believe it even yet unless you saw it there yourself. Go on,' she
said. 'We'll meet you out there. Go on,' she said.

But the sheriff didn't move. He could hear him breathing, vast
subterrene and deliberate, like sighing almost. 'Of course I don't
know about you,' the sheriff said. 'A lady without nothing but a
couple thousand chickens to feed and nurse and water and a
vegetable farm hardly five acres big to run, might not have
nothing to do all day. But these boys anyway have got to go to
school. Leastways I never heard about any rule in the School
Board to give holidays for digging up corpses.'

And that even stopped her. But she didn't sit back yet. She still
leaned forward where she could look past his uncle at the sheriff
and he thought again *She's too old for this, to have to do this:* only
if she hadn't then he and Aleck Sander, what she and his uncle
and the sheriff all three and his mother and father and Paralee
too would have called children, would have had to do it – not
would have done it but would have had to do it to preserve not
even justice and decency but innocence: and he thought of man
who apparently had to kill man not for motive or reason but
simply for the sake the need the compulsion of having to kill
man, inventing creating his motive and reason afterward so that
he could still stand up among man as a rational creature: whoever
had had to kill Vinson Gowrie had then to dig him up dead and
slay another to put in his vacated grave so that whoever had to
kill him could rest; and Vinson Gowrie's kin and neighbours who
would have to kill Lucas or someone or anyone, it would not
really matter who, so that they could lie down and breathe quiet
and even grieve quiet and so rest. The sheriff's voice was mild,
almost gentle even: 'You go home. You and these boys have done
fine. Likely you saved a life. Now you go home and let us attend
to the rest of it. That won't be any place for a lady out there.'

But Miss Habersham was just stopped, nor even that for long:
'It wasn't for a man either last night.'

'Wait, Hope,' his uncle said. Then his uncle tumed to Miss
Habersham. 'Your job's in town here,' he said. 'Don't you know
that?' Now Miss Habersham watched his uncle. But she still hadn't
sat back in the seat, giving no ground to anyone yet; watching,
it was as though she had not at all exchanged one opponent for
another but without pause or falter had accepted them both,
asking no quarter, crying no odds. 'Will Legate's a farmer,' his
uncle said. 'Besides being up all night. He's got to go home and

see to his own business for a little while.'

'Hasn't Mr Hampton got other deputies?' Miss Habersham said. 'What are they for?'

'They're just men with guns,' his uncle said. 'Legate himself told Chick and me last night that if enough men made up their minds and kept them made up, they would pass him and Mr Tubbs both in time. But if a woman, a lady, a white lady . . .' His uncle stopped, ceased; they stared at each other; watching them he thought again of his uncle and Lucas in the cell last night (it was last night, of course; it seemed like years now); again except for the fact that his uncle and Miss Habersham were actually looking into each other's physical eyes instead of bending each upon the other that absolute concentration of all the senses in the sum of which mere clumsy fallible perception weighed little more than the ability to read Sanskrit would, he might have been watching the last two stayers in a poker-pot. '. . . just to sit there, in sight, where the first one that passes can have the word spread long before Beat Four can even get the truck cranked up to start to town . . . while we go out there and finish it for good, for ever –'

Miss Habersham leaned slowly back until her back came against the seat. She said: 'So I'm to sit there on that staircase with my skirts spread or maybe better with my back against the balustrade and one foot propped against the wall of Mrs Tubbs' kitchen while you men who never had time yesterday to ask that old nigger a few questions and so all he had last night was a boy, a child –' His uncle said nothing. The sheriff leaned above the window breathing vast subterranean sighs, not breathing hard but just as a big man seems to have to breathe. Miss Habersham said: 'Drive me home first. I've got some mending to do. I aint going to sit there all morning doing nothing so that Mrs Tubbs will think she has to talk to me. Drive me home first. I realized an hour ago what a rush and hurry you and Mr Hampton are in but you can spare the time for that. Aleck Sander can bring my truck to the jail on his way to school and leave it in front of the gate.'

'Yessum,' his uncle said.

Chapter Six

So they drove Miss Habersham home, out to the edge of town and through the shaggy untended cedar grove to the paintless columned portico where she got out and went into the house and apparently on through it without even stopping because at once they could hear her somewhere in the back yelling at someone – the old Negro man probably who was Molly's brother and Lucas' brother-in-law – in her strong voice strained and a little high from sleeplessness and fatigue, then she came out again carrying a big cardboard box full of what looked like unironed laundry and long limp webs and ropes of stockings and got back into the car and they drove back to the Square through the fresh quiet morning streets: the old big decaying wooden houses of Jefferson's long-ago foundation set like Miss Habersham's deep in shaggy untended lawns of old trees and rootbound scented and flowering shrubs whose very names most people under fifty no longer knew and which even when children lived in them seemed still to be spellbound by the shades of women, old women still spinsters and widows waiting even seventy-five years later for the slow telegraph to bring them news of Tennessee and Virginia and Pennsylvania battles, which no longer even faced the street but peered at it over the day-after-tomorrow shoulders of the neat small new one-storey houses designed in Florida and California set with matching garages in their neat plots of clipped grass and tedious flowerbeds, three and four of them now, a subdivision now in what twenty-five years ago had been considered a little small for one decent front lawn, where the prosperous young married couples lived with two children each and (as soon as they could afford it) an automobile each and the memberships in the country club and the bridge clubs and the junior rotary and chamber of commerce and the patented electric gadgets for cooking and freezing and cleaning and the neat trim coloured maids in frilled caps to run them and talk to one another over the telephone from house to house while the wives in sandals and pants and painted toenails puffed lipstick-stained cigarettes over shopping bags in the chain groceries and drugstores.

Or would have been and should have been; Sunday and they might have passed, accepted a day with no one to plug and unplug the humming sweepers and turn the buttons on the stoves as a day off a vacation or maybe an occasion like a baptizing or a picnic or a big funeral but this was Monday, a new day and a new week, rest and the need to fill time and conquer boredom was over, children fresh for school and husband and father for store or office or to stand around the Western Union desk where the hourly cotton reports came in; breakfast must be forward and the pandemoniac bustle of exodus yet still no Negro had they seen – the young ones with straightened hair and makeup in the bright trig tomorrow's clothes from the mailorder houses who would not even put on the Harper's Bazaar caps and aprons until they were inside the white kitchens and the older ones in the ankle-length homemade calico and gingham who wore the long plain homemade aprons all the time so that they were no longer a symbol but a garment, not even the men who should have been mowing the lawns and clipping the hedges; not even (crossing the Square now) the street department crews who should have been flushing the pavement with hoses and sweeping up the discarded Sunday papers and empty cigarette packs; across the Square and on to the jail where his uncle got out too and went up the walk with Miss Habersham and up the steps and through the still-open door where he could still see Legate's empty chair still propped against the wall and he heaved himself bodily again out of the long soft timeless rushing black of sleep to find as usual that no time had passed, his uncle still putting his hat back on and turning to come back down the walk to the car. Then they stopped at home, Aleck Sander already out of the car and gone around the side of the house and vanished and he said:

'No.'

'Yes,' his uncle said. 'You've got to go to school. Or better still, to bed and to sleep – Yes,' his uncle said suddenly: 'and Aleck Sander too. He must stay at home today too. Because this mustn't be talked about, not one word about it until we have finished it. You understand that.'

But he wasn't listening, he and his uncle were not even talking about the same thing, not even when he said 'No' again and his uncle out of the car and already turning towards the house stopped and looked back at him and then stood looking at him for a good long moment and then said:

'We are going at this a little hindpart-before, aint we? I'm the one who should be asking you if I can go.' Because he was thinking about his mother, not just remembered about her because he had done that as soon as they crossed the Square five minutes ago and the simplest thing would have been to get out of his uncle's car there and go and get in the sheriff's car and simply stay in it until they were ready to go back out to the church and he had probably thought about it at the time and would even have done it probably if he hadn't been so worn out and anticlimaxed and dull for sleep and he knew he couldn't cope with her this time even if he had been completely fresh; the very fact that he had already done it twice in eleven hours, once by secrecy and once by sheer surprise and rapidity of movement and of mass, but doomed him completer now to defeat and rout: musing on his uncle's naive and childlike rationalizing about school and bed when faced with that fluid and implacable attack, when once more his uncle read his mind, standing beside the car and looking down at him for another moment with compassion and no hope even though he was a bachelor of fifty thirty-five years free of woman's dominion, his uncle too knowing remembering how she would use the excuses of his education and his physical exhaustion only less quicker than she would have discarded them; who would listen no more to rational reasons for his staying at home than for – civic duty or simple justice or humanity or to save a life or even the peace of his own immortal soul – his going. His uncle said:

'All right. Come on. I'll talk to her.'

He moved, getting out; he said suddenly and quietly, in amazement not at despair of hope but at how much hopelessness you could really stand: 'You're just my uncle.'

'I'm worse than that,' his uncle said. 'I'm just a man.' Then his uncle read his mind again: 'All right. I'll try to talk to Paralee too. The same condition obtains there; motherhood doesn't seem to have any pigment in its skin.'

And his uncle too was probably thinking how you not only couldn't beat them, you couldn't even find the battlefield in time to admit defeat before they had moved it again; he remembered, it was two years ago now, he had finally made the high school football team or that is he had won or been chosen for one of the positions to make an out-of-town trip because the regular player had been injured in practice or fallen behind in his grades or maybe his mother either wouldn't let him go, something, he had forgotten exactly what because he had been too busy all that Thursday and Friday racking his brains in vain to think how to tell his mother he was going to Mottstown to play on the regular team; right up to the last minute when he had to tell her something and so did: badly: and weathered it since his father happened to be present (though he really hadn't calculated it that way – not that he wouldn't have if he hadn't been too worried and perplexed with a blending of anger and shame and shame at being angry and ashamed ((crying at her at one point: 'Is it the team's fault that I'm the only child you've got?')) to think of it) and left that Friday afternoon with the team feeling as he imagined a soldier might feel wrenching out of his mother's restraining arms to go fight a battle for some shameful cause; she would grieve for him of course if he fell and she would even look on his face again if he didn't but there would be always ineradicable between them the ancient green and perennial adumbration: so that all that Friday night trying to go to sleep in a strange bed and all the next forenoon too waiting for the game to start he thought better for the team if he had not come since he probably had too much on his mind to be worth anything to it: until the first whistle blew and on and afterwards until bottom-most beneath the piled mass of both teams, the ball clutched to his chest and his mouth and nostrils both full of the splashed dried whitewash marking the goal line he heard and recognized above all the others that one voice shrill triumphant and bloodthirsty and picked up at last and the wind thumped back into him he saw her foremost in the crowd not sitting in the grandstand but among the ones trotting and even running up and down the sideline following each play, then in the car that evening on the way back to Jefferson, himself in the front seat beside the hired driver and his mother and three of the other players in the back and her voice as proud and serene and pitiless as his own could have been: 'Does your arm still hurt?' – entering the hall and only then discovering that he had expected to find her still just inside the front door still in the loose hair and the nightdress and himself walking back even after three hours into the unbroken uninterrupted wail. But instead it was his father already roaring who came out of the diningroom and still at it even with his uncle yelling back almost into his face:

'Charley. Charley. Dammit, will you wait?' and only then his mother fully dressed, brisk busy and composed, coming up the hall from the back, the kitchen, saying to his father without even raising her voice:

'Charley. Go back and finish your breakfast. Paralee isn't feeling well this morning and she doesn't want to be all day getting dinner ready:' then to him – the fond constant familiar face which he had known all his life and therefore could neither have described it so that a stranger could recognize it nor recognize it himself from anyone's description but only brisk calm and even a little inattentive now, the wail a wail only because of the ancient used habit of its verbiage: 'You haven't washed your face:' nor even pausing to see if he followed, on up the stairs and into the bathroom, even turning on the tap and putting the soap into his hands and standing with the towel open and waiting, the familiar face wearing the familiar expression of amazement and protest and anxiety and invincible repudiation which it had worn all his life each time he had done anything removing him one more step from infancy, from childhood: when his uncle had given him the Shetland pony someone had taught to take eighteen- and twenty-four-inch jumps and when his father had given him the first actual powder-shooting gun and the afternoon when the groom delivered Highboy in the truck and he got up for the first time and Highboy stood on his hind legs and her scream and the groom's calm voice saying, 'Hit him hard over the head when he does that. You dont want him falling over backward on you' but the muscles merely falling into the old expression through inattention and long usage as her voice had merely chosen by inattention and usage the long-worn verbiage of wailing because there was something else in it now – the same thing which had been there in the car that afternoon when she said, 'Your arm doesn't hurt at all now does it?' and on the other afternoon when his father came home and found him jumping Highboy over the concrete watertrough in the lot, his mother leaning on the fence watching and his father's fury of relief and anger and his mother's calm voice this time: 'Why not? The trough isn't near as tall as that flimsy fence-thing you bought him that isn't even nailed together:' so that even dull for sleep he recognized it and turned his face and hands dripping and cried at her in amazed and incredulous outrage: 'You aint going too! You cant go!' then even dull for sleep realizing the fatuous naïveté of anyone using cant to her on any subject and so playing his last desperate card: 'If you go; then I wont! You hear me? I wont go!'

'Dry your face and comb your hair,' she said. 'Then come on down and drink your coffee.'

That too. Paralee was all right too apparently because his uncle was at the telephone in the hall when he entered the diningroom, his father already roaring again before he had even sat down:

'Dammit, why didn't you tell me last night? Dont you ever again –'

'Because you wouldn't have believed him either,' his uncle said coming in from the hall. 'You wouldn't have listened either. It took an old woman and two children for that, to believe truth for no other reason than that it was truth, told by an old man in a fix deserving pity and belief, to someone capable of the pity even when none of them really believed him. Which you didn't at first,' his uncle said to him. 'When did you really begin to believe him? When you opened the coffin, wasn't it? I want to know, you see. Maybe I'm not too old to learn either. When was it?'

'I dont know,' he said. Because he didn't know. It seemed to him that he had known all the time. Then it seemed to him that he had never really believed Lucas. Then it seemed to him that it had never happened at all, heaving himself once more with no movement up out of the long deep slough of sleep but at least to some elapse of time now, he had gained that much anyway, maybe enough to be safe on for a while like the tablets night truck drivers took not as big hardly as a shirt button yet in which were concentrated enough wakefulness to reach the next town because his mother was in the room now brisk and calm, setting the cup of coffee down in front of him in a way that if Paralee had done it she would have said that Paralee had slopped it at him: which, the coffee, was why neither his father nor his uncle had even looked at her, his father on the contrary exclaiming:

'Coffee? What the devil is this? I thought the agreement was when you finally consented for Gavin to buy that horse that he would neither ask for nor even accept a spoonful of coffee until he was eighteen years old:' and his mother not even listening, with the same hand and in the same manner half shoving and half popping the cream pitcher then the sugar bowl into his reach and already turning back towards the kitchen, her voice not really hurried and impatient: just brisk:

'Drink it now. We're already late:' and now they looked at her for the first time: dressed, even to her hat, with in the crook of her other arm the straw basket out of which she had darned his and his father's and his uncle's socks and stockings ever since he could remember, though his uncle at first saw only the hat and for a moment seemed to join him in the same horrified surprise he had felt in the bathroom.

'Maggie!' his uncle said. 'You cant! Charley —'

'I dont intend to,' his mother said, not even stopping. 'This time you men will have to do the digging. I'm going to the jail:' already in the kitchen now and only her voice coming back: 'I'm not going to let Miss Habersham sit there by herself with the whole county gawking at her. As soon as I help Paralee plan dinner we'll —' but not dying fading: ceasing, quitting: since she had dismissed them though his father still tried once more:

'He's got to go to school.'

But even his uncle didn't listen. 'You can drive Miss Eunice's truck, cant you?' his uncle said. 'There wont be a Negro school today for Aleck Sander to be going to so he can leave it at the jail. And even if there was I doubt if Paralee's going to let him cross the front yard inside the next week.' Then his uncle seemed even to have heard his father or at least decided to answer him: 'Nor any white school either for that matter if this boy hadn't listened to Lucas, which I wouldn't, and to Miss Habersham, which I didn't. Well?' his uncle said. 'Can you stay awake that long? You can get a nap once we are on the road.'

'Yes sir,' he said. So he drank the coffee which the soap and water and hard towelling had unfogged him enough to know he didn't like and didn't want but not enough for him to choose what simple thing to do about it: that is not drink it: tasting sipping then adding more sugar to it until each — coffee and sugar — ceased to be either and became a sickish quinine sweet amalgam of the worst of both until his uncle said:

'Dammit, stop that,' and got up and went to the kitchen and returned with a saucepan of heated milk and a soup bowl and dumped the coffee into the bowl and poured the hot milk into it and said, 'Go on. Forget about it. Just drink it.' So he did, from the bowl in both hands like water from a gourd, hardly tasting it and still his father flung a little back in his chair looking at him and talking, asking him just how scared Aleck Sander was and if he wasn't even scareder than Aleck Sander only his vanity wouldn't allow him to show it before a darky and to tell the truth now, neither of them would have touched the grave in the dark even enough to lift the flowers off of it if Miss Habersham hadn't driven them at it: his uncle interrupting:

'Aleck Sander even told you then that the grave had already been disturbed by someone in a hurry, didn't he?'

'Yes sir,' he said and his uncle said:

'Do you know what I'm thinking now?'

'No sir,' he said

'I'm being glad Aleck Sander couldn't completely penetrate darkness and call out the name of the man who came down the hill carrying something in front of him on the mule.' And he remembered that: the three of them all thinking it but not one of them saying it: just standing invisible to one another above the pit's invisible inky yawn.

'Fill it up,' Miss Habersham said. They did, the (five times now) loosened dirt going down much faster than it came up though it seemed for ever in the thin starlight filled with the constant sound of the windless pines like one vast abateless hum not of amazement but of attention, watching, curiosity; amoral, detached, not involved and missing nothing. 'put the flowers back,' Miss Habersham said.

'It'll take time,' he said.

'Put them back,' Miss Habersham said. So they did.

'I'll get the horse,' he said. 'You and Aleck Sander –'

'We'll all go,' Miss Habersham said. So they gathered up the tools and the rope (nor did they use the flashlight again) and Aleck Sander said 'Wait' and found by touch the board he had used for a shovel and carried that until he could push it back under the church and he untied Highboy and held the stirrup but Miss Habersham said, 'No. We'll lead him. Aleck Sander can walk exactly behind me and you walk exactly behind Aleck Sander and lead the horse.'

'We could go faster –' he said again and they couldn't see her face: only the thin straight shape, the shadow, the hat which on anyone else wouldn't even have looked like a hat but on her as on his grandmother looked exactly right, like exactly nothing else, her voice not loud, not much louder than breathing, as if she were not even moving her lips, not to anyone, just murmuring:

'It's the best I know to do. I dont know anything else to do.'

'Maybe we all ought to walk in the middle,' he said, loud, too loud, twice louder than he had intended or even thought; it should carry for miles especially over a whole countryside already hopelessly waked and alerted by the sleepless sibilant what Paralee probably and old Ephraim certainly and Lucas too would call 'miration' of the pines. She was looking at him now. He could feel it.

'I'll never be able to explain to your mother but Aleck Sander hasn't got any business here at all,' she said. 'You-all walk exactly behind me and let the horse come last:' and turned and went on though what good that would do he didn't know because in his understanding the very word 'ambush' meant 'from the flank, the side': back in single file that way down the hill to where Aleck Sander had driven the truck into the bushes: and he thought *If I were him this is where it would be* and so did she; she said, 'Wait.'

'How can you keep on standing in front of us if we dont stay together?' he said. And this time she didn't even say This is all I can think of to do but just stood there so that Aleck Sander walked past her and on into the bushes and started the truck and backed it out and swung it to point down the hill, the engine running but no lights yet and she said, 'Tie the reins up and let him go. Wont he come home?'

'I hope so,' he said. He got up.

'Then tie him to a tree,' she said. 'We will come back and get him as soon as we have seen your uncle and Mr Hampton –'

'Then we can all watch him ride down the road with maybe a horse or the mule in front of him too,' Aleck Sander said. He raced the engine then let it idle again. 'Come on, get in. He's either here watching us or he aint and if he aint we're all right and if he is he's done waited too late now when he let us get back to the truck.'

'Then you ride right behind the truck,' she said. 'We'll go slow –'

'Nome,' Aleck Sander said; he leaned out. 'Get started; we're going to have to wait for you anyway when we get to town.'

So – he needed no urging – he let Highboy down the hill, only holding his head up; the truck's light came on and it moved and once on the flat even in the short space to the highroad Highboy was already trying to run but he checked him back and up on to the highroad, the lights of the truck fanning up and out as it came down on to the flat then he slacked the curb, Highboy beginning to run, clashing the snaffle as always, thinking as always that one more champing regurg would get it forward enough to get his teeth on it, running now when the truck lights swung up on to the highroad too, his feet in eight hollow beats on the bridge and he leaned into the dark hard wind and let him go, the truck lights not even in sight during the full half-mile until he slowed him into the long reaching hard road-gait and almost a mile then before the truck overtook and then passed and the ruby tail-lamp drew on and away and then was gone but at least he was out of the pines, free of that looming down-watching sibilance uncaring and missing nothing saying to the whole circumambience: Look. Look: but then they were still saying it somewhere and they had certainly been saying it long enough for all Beat Four, Gowries and Ingrums and Workitts and Frasers and all to have heard it by this time so he wouldn't think about that and so he stopped thinking about it now, all in the same flash in which he had remembered it, swallowing the last swallow from the bowl and setting it down as his father more or less plunged up from the table, clattering his chairlegs back across the floor, saying:

'Maybe I better go to work. Somebody'll have to earn a little bread around here while the rest of you are playing cops and robbers:' and went out and apparently the coffee had done something to what he called his thinking processes or anyway the processes of what people called thinking because now he knew the why for his father too – the rage which was relief after the event which had to express itself some way and chose anger not because he would have forbidden him to go but because he had had no chance to, the pseudo-scornful humorous impugnment of his and Aleck Sander's courage which blinked not even as much at a rifled grave in the dark as it did at Miss Habersham's will – in fact the whole heavyhanded aspersion of the whole thing by reducing it to the terms of a kind of kindergarten witch-hunt: which was probably merely the masculine form of refusing also to believe that he was what his uncle called big enough to button his pants and so he dismissed his father, hearing his mother about to emerge from the kitchen and pushing his chair back and getting up himself when suddenly he was thinking how coffee was already a good deal more than he had known but nobody had warned him that it produced illusions like cocaine or opium: seeing watching his father's noise and uproar flick and vanish away like blown smoke or mist, not merely revealing but exposing the man who had begot him looking back at him from beyond the bridgeless abyss of that begetting not with just pride but with envy too; it was his uncle's abnegant and rhetorical self-lacerating which was the phony one and his father was gnawing the true bitter irremediable bone of all which was dismatchment with time, being born too soon or late to have been himself sixteen and gallop a horse ten miles in the dark to save an old nigger's insolent and friendless neck.

But at least he was awake. The coffee had accomplished that anyway. He still needed to doze only now he couldn't; the desire to sleep was there but it was wakefulness now he would have to combat and abate. It was after eight now; one of the county schoolbuses passed as he prepared to drive Miss Habersham's truck away from the kerb and the street would be full of children too fresh for Monday morning with books and paper bags of recesstime lunches and behind the schoolbus was a string of cars and trucks stained with country mud and dust so constant and unbroken that his uncle and his mother would already have reached the jail before he ever managed to cut into it because Monday was stock-auction day at the sales barns behind the Square and he could see them, the empty cars and trucks rank on dense rank along the courthouse kerb like shoats at a feed-trough and the men with their stock-trader walking-sticks not even stopping but gone straight across the Square and along the alley to the sales barns to chew tobacco and unighted cigars from pen to pen amid the ammonia-reek of manure and liniment and the bawling of calves and the stamp and sneeze of horses and mules and the secondhand wagons and plough gear and guns and harness and watches and only the women (what few of them that is since stock-sale day unlike Saturday was a man's time) remained about the Square and the stores so that the Square itself would be empty except for the parked cars and trucks until the men would come back for an hour at noon to meet them at the cafés and restaurants.

Whereupon this time he jerked himself, no reflex now, not even out of sleep but illusion, who had carried hypnosis right out of the house with him even into the bright strong sun of day, even driving the pickup truck which before last night he would not even have recognized yet which since last night had become as inexpugnable a part of his memory and experience and breathing as hiss of shovelled dirt or the scrape of a metal blade on a pine box would ever be, through a mirage-vacuum in which not simply last night had not happened but there had been no Saturday either, remembering now as if he had only this moment seen it that there had been no children in the schoolbus but only grown people and in the stream of cars and trucks following it and now following him where he had finally cut in, a few of which even on stock-auction Monday (on Saturday half of the flat open beds would have been jammed and packed with them, men women and children in the cheap meagre finery in which they came to town) should have carried Negroes, there had not been one dark face.

Nor one school-bound child on the street although he had heard without listening enough of his uncle at the telephone to know that the superintendent had called whether to have school today or not and his uncle had told him yes, and in sight of the Square now he could see already three more of the yellow buses supposed and intended to bring the county children in to school but which their owner-contractor-operators translated on Saturdays and holidays into pay-passenger transport and then the Square itself, the parked cars and trucks as always as should be but the Square itself anything but empty: no exodus of men towards the stock pens nor women into the stores so that as he drove the pickup into the kerb behind his uncle's car he could see already where visible and sense where not a moil and mass of movement, one dense pulse and hum filling the Square as when the crowd overflows the carnival midway or the football field, flowing into the street and already massed along the side opposite to the jail until the head of it had already passed the blacksmith's where he had stood yesterday trying to be invisible as if they were waiting for a parade to pass (and almost in the middle of the street so that the still unbroken stream of cars and trucks had to detour around them a clump of a dozen or so more like the group in a reviewing stand in whose centre in its turn he recognized the badged official cap of the town marshal who at this hour on this day would have been in front of the schoolhouse holding up traffic for children to cross the street and he did not have to remember that the marshal's name was Ingrum, a Beat Four Ingrum come to town as the apostate sons of Beat Four occasionally did to marry a town girl and become barbers and bailiffs and nightwatchmen as petty Germanic princelings would come down out of their Brandenburg hills to marry the heiresses to European thrones) – the men and the women and not one child, the weathered country faces and sunburned necks and backs of hands, the clean faded tieless earthcoloured shirts and pants and print cotton dresses thronging the Square and the street as though the stores themselves were closed and locked, not even staring yet at the blank front of the jail and the single barred window which had been empty and silent too for going on forty-eight hours now but just gathering, condensing, not

expectant nor in anticipation nor even attentive yet but merely
in that prelimary settling down like the before-curtain in a
theatre: and he thought that was it: holiday: which meant a day
for children yet here turned upside down: and suddenly he
realized that he had been completely wrong; it was not Saturday
which had never happened but only last night which to them had
not happened yet, that not only they didn't know about last night
but there was nobody, not even Hampton, who could have told
them because they would have refused to believe him; whereupon
something like a skim or a veil like that which crosses a chicken's
eye and which he had not even known was there went flick! from
his own and he saw them for the first time – the same weathered
still almost inattentive faces and the same faded clean cotton
shirts and pants and dresses but no crowd now waiting for the
curtain to rise on a stage's illusion but rather the one in the
courtroom waiting for the sheriff's officer to cry Oyez Oyez
Oyez: This honourable court; not even impatient because the
moment had not even come yet to sit in judgement not on Lucas
Beauchamp, they had already condemned him but on Beat Four,
come not to see what they called justice done nor even retribution
exacted but to see that Beat Four should not fail its white man's
high estate.

So that he had stopped the truck was out and had already
started to run when he stopped himself: something of dignity
something of pride remembering last night when he had instigated and in a way led and anyway accompanied the stroke which
not one of the responsible elders but had failed even to recognize
its value, let alone its need, and something of caution too remembering how his uncle had said almost nothing was enough to put
a mob in motion so perhaps even a child running towards the jail
would have been enough: then he remembered again the faces
myriad yet curiously identical in their lack of individual identity,
their complete relinquishment of individual identity into one We
not even impatient, not even hurryable, almost gala in its complete obliviousness of its own menace, not to be stampeded by a
hundred running children: and then in the same flash the obverse:
not to be halted or deflected by a hundred times a hundred of
them, and having realized its sheer hopelessness when it was still
only an intention and then its physical imponderability when it
entered accomplishment he now recognized the enormity of what
he had blindly meddled with and that his first instinctive impulse
– to run home and fling saddle and bridle on the horse and ride

as the crow flies into the last stagger of exhaustion and then sleep and then return after it was all over – had been the right one (who now simply because he happened not to be an orphan had not even that escape) because it seemed to him now that he was responsible for having brought in to the light and glare of day something shocking and shameful out of the whole white foundation of the county which he himself must partake of too since he too was bred of it, which otherwise might have flared and blazed merely out of Beat Four and then vanished back into its darkness or at least invisibility with the fading embers of Lucas' crucifixion.

But it was too late now, he couldn't even repudiate, relinquish, run: the jail door open and still opposite it now he could see Miss Habersham sitting in the chair Legate had sat in, the cardboard box on the floor at her feet and a garment of some sort across her lap; she was still wearing the hat and he could see the steady motion of her hand and elbow and it seemed to him he could even see the flash and flick of the needle in her hand though he knew he could not at this distance; but his uncle was in the way so he had to move further along the walk but at that moment his uncle turned and came out the door and recrossed the veranda and then he could see her too in the second chair beside Miss Habersham; a car drew up to the kerb behind him and stopped and now without haste she chose a sock from the basket and slipped the darningegg into it; she even had the needle already threaded stuck in the front of her dress and now he could distinguish the flash and glint of it and maybe that was because he knew so well the motion, the narrow familiar suppleness of the hand which he had watched all his life but at least no man could have disputed him that it was his sock.

'Who's that?' the sheriff said behind him. He turned. The sheriff sat behind the wheel of his car, his neck and shoulders bowed and hunched so he could peer out below the top of the window-frame. The engine was still running and he saw in the back of the car the handles of two shovels and the pick too which they would not need and on the back seat quiet and motionless save for the steady glint and blink of their eyewhites, two Negroes in blue jumpers and the soiled black-ringed convict pants which the street gangs wore.

'Who would it be?' his uncle said behind him too but he didn't turn this time nor did he even listen further because three men came suddenly out of the street and stopped beside the car and

as he watched five or six more came up and in another moment
the whole crowd would begin to flow across the street; already a
passing car had braked suddenly (and then the following one
behind it) at first to keep from running over them and then for
its occupants to lean out looking at the sheriff's car where the
first man to reach it had already stooped to peer into it, his brown
farmer's hands grasping the edge of the open window, his brown
weathered face thrust into the car curious divinant and abashless
while behind him his massed duplicates in their felt hats and
sweat-stained panamas listened.

'What you up to, Hope?' the man said. 'Dont you know the
Grand Jury'll get you, wasting county money this way? Aint you
heard about that new lynch law the Yankees passed? the folks
that lynches the nigger is supposed to dig the grave?'

'Maybe he's taking them shovels out there for Nub Gowrie and
them boys of his to practise with,' the second said.

'Then it's a good thing Hope's taking shovel hands too,' the
third said. 'If he's depending on anybody named Gowrie to dig
a hole or do anything else that might bring up a sweat, he'll sure
need them.'

'Or maybe they aint shovel hands,' the fourth said. 'Maybe it's
them the Gowries are going to practise on.' Yet even though
one guffawed they were not laughing, more than a dozen now
crowded around the car to take one quick allcomprehensive
glance into the back of it where the two Negroes sat immobile
as carved wood staring straight ahead at nothing and no movement even of breathing other than an infinitesimal widening and
closing of the whites around their eyeballs, then looking at the
sheriff again with almost exactly the expression he had seen on
the faces waiting for the spinning tapes behind a slotmachine's
glass to stop.

'I reckon that'll do,' the sheriff said. He thrust his head and
one vast arm out the window and with the arm pushed the nearest
ones back and away from the car as effortlessly as he would have
opened a curtain, raising his voice but not much: 'Willy.' The
marshal came up; he could already hear him:

'Gangway, boys. Lemme see what the high sheriff's got on his
mind this morning.'

'Why dont you get these folks out of the street so them cars
can get to town?' the sheriff said. 'Maybe they want to stand
around and look at the jail too.'

'You bet,' the marshal said. He turned, shoving his hands at the nearest ones, not touching them, as if he were putting into motion a herd of cattle. 'Now boys,' he said.

They didn't move, looking past the marshal still at the sheriff, not at all defiant, not really daring anyone: just tolerant, goodhumoured, debonair almost.

'Why, Sheriff,' a voice said, then another:

'It's a free street, aint it, Sheriff? You town folks wont mind us just standing on it long as we spend our money with you, will you?'

'But not to block off the other folks trying to get to town to spend a little,' the sheriff said. 'Move on now. Get them out of the street, Willy.'

'Come on, boys,' the marshal said. 'There's other folks besides you wants to get up where they can watch them bricks.' They moved then but still without haste, the marshal herding them back across the street like a woman driving a flock of hens across a pen, she to control merely direction not the speed and not too much of that, the fowls moving ahead of her flapping apron not recalcitrant, just unpredictable, fearless of her and not yet even alarmed; the halted car and the ones behind it moved too, slowly, dragging at creeping pace their loads of craned faces; he could hear the marshal shouting at the drivers: 'Get on. Get on. There's cars behind you –'

The sheriff was looking at his uncle again. 'Where's the other one?'

'The other what?' his uncle said.

'The other detective. The one that can see in the dark.'

'Aleck Sander,' his uncle said. 'You want him too?'

'No,' the sheriff said. 'I just missed him. I was just surprised to find one human in this county with taste and judgement enough to stay at home today. You ready? Let's get started.'

'Right,' his uncle said. The sheriff was notorious as a driver who used up a car a year as a heavy-handed sweeper wears out brooms: not by speed but by simple friction; now the car actually shot away from the kerb and almost before he could watch it, was gone. His uncle went to theirs and opened the door. 'Jump in,' his uncle said.

Then he said it; at least this much was simple: 'I'm not going.'

His uncle paused and now he saw watching him the quizzical saturnine face, the quizzical eyes which given a little time didn't miss much; had in fact as long as he had known them never missed anything until last night.

'Ah,' his uncle said. 'Miss Habersham is of course a lady but this other female is yours.'

'Look at them,' he said, not moving, barely moving his lips even. 'Across the street. On the Square too and nobody but Willy Ingrum and that damn cap –'

'Didn't you hear them talking to Hampton?' his uncle said.

'I heard them,' he said. 'They were not even laughing at their own jokes. They were laughing at him.'

'They were not even taunting him,' his uncle said. 'They were not even jeering at him. They were just watching him. Watching him and Beat Four, to see what would happen. These people just came to town to see what either or both of them are going to do.'

'No,' he said. 'More than that.'

'All right,' his uncle said, quite soberly too now. 'Granted. Then what?'

'Suppose –' But his uncle interrupted:

'Suppose Beat Four comes in and picked up your mother's and Miss Habersham's chairs and carries them out into the yard where they'll be out of the way? Lucas aint in that cell. He's in Mr Hampton's house, probably sitting in the kitchen right now eating his breakfast. What did you think Will Legate was doing coming in by the back door within fifteen minutes of when we got there and told Mr Hampton? Aleck Sander even heard him telephoning.'

'Then what's Mr Hampton in such a hurry for?' he said: and his uncle's voice was quite sober now: but just sober, that was all:

'Because the best way to stop having to suppose or deny either is for us to get out there and do what we have to do and get back here. Jump in the car.'

Chapter Seven

They never saw the sheriff's car again until they reached the church. Not for him was the reason sleep who in spite of the coffee might have expected that and in fact had. Up to the moment when at the wheel of the pickup he had got near enough to see the Square and then the mass of people lining the opposite side of the street in front of the jail he had expected that as soon as he and his uncle were on the road back to the church, coffee or no coffee he would not even be once more fighting sleep but on the contrary would relinquish and accept it and so in the nine miles of gravel and the one of climbing dirt regain at least a half-hour of the eight he had lost last night and – it seemed to him now – the three or four times that many he had spent trying to quit thinking about Lucas Beauchamp the night before.

And when they reached town a little before three this morning nobody could have persuaded him that by this time, almost nine o'clock, he would not have made back at least five and a half hours of sleep even if not the full six, remembering how he – and without doubt Miss Habersham and Aleck Sander too – had believed that as soon as they and his uncle entered the sheriff's house that would be all of it; they would enter the front door and lay into the sheriff's broad competent ordained palm as you drop your hat on the hall table in passing, the whole night's nightmare of doubt and indecision and sleeplessness and strain and fatigue and shock and amazement and (he admitted it) some of fear too. But it hadn't happened and he knew now that he had never really expected it to; the idea had ever entered their heads only because they had been worn out, spend not so much from sleeplessness and fatigue and strain as exhausted by shock and amazement and anticlimax; he had not even needed the massed faces watching the blank brick front of the jail nor the ones which had crossed the street and even blocked it while they crowded around the sheriff's car, to read and then dismiss its interior with that one mutual concordant glance comprehensive abashless trustless and undeniable as the busy parent pauses for an instant to check over and anticipate the intentions of a loved though not too reliable child. If he needed anything he certainly had that – the faces the voices not even taunting and not even jeering: just perspicuant jocular and without pity – poised under the first relaxation of succumbence like a pin in the mattress so he was as wide awake as his uncle even who had slept all night or at least most of it, free of town now and going fast now, passing within the first mile the last of the cars and trucks and then no more of them because all who would come to town today would by this time be inside that last rapidly contracting mile – the whole white part of the county taking advantage of the good weather and the good all weather roads which were their roads because their taxes and votes and the votes of their kin and connexions who could bring pressure on the congressmen who had the giving away of the funds had built them, to get quickly into the town which was theirs too since it existed only by their sufferance and support to contain their jail and their courthouse, to crowd and jam and block its streets too if they saw fit: patient biding and unpitying, neither to be hurried nor checked nor dispersed nor denied since theirs was the murdered and the murderer too; theirs the affronter and the principle affronted: the white man and the bereavement of his vacancy, theirs the right not just to mere justice but vengeance too to allot or withhold.

They were going quite fast now, faster than he could ever remember his uncle driving, out the long road where he had ridden last night on the horse but in daylight now, morning's bland ineffable May; now he could see the white bursts of dogwood in the hedgerows marking the old section-line surveys or standing like nuns in the cloistral patches and bands of greening woods and the pink and white of peach and pear and the pinkwhite of the first apple trees in the orchards which last night he had only smelled: and always beyond and around them the enduring land – the fields geometric with furrows where corn had been planted when the first doves began to call in late March and April, and cotton when the first whippoorwills cried at night around the beginning of May a week ago: but empty, vacant of any movement and any life – the farmhouses from which no smoke rose because breakfast was long over by now and no dinner to be cooked where none would be home to eat it, the paintless Negro cabins where on Monday mornings in the dust of the grassless treeless yards halfnaked children should have been crawling and scrabbling after broken cultivator wheels and wornout automobile tyres and empty snuffbottles and tin cans and in the backyards smoke-blackened iron pots should have been bubbling over wood fires beside the sagging fences of vegetable patches and chickenruns which by nightfall would be gaudy with drying overalls and aprons and towels and unionsuits: but not this morning, not now; the wheels and the giant-doughnuts of chewed rubber and the bottles and cans lying scattered and deserted in the dust since that moment Saturday afternoon when the first voice shouted from inside the house, and in the back yards the pots sitting empty and cold among last Monday's ashes among the empty clothes-lines and as the car flashed past the blank and vacant doors he would catch one faint gleam of fire on hearth and no more see but only sense among the shadows the still white roll of eyes; but most of all, the empty fields themselves in each of which on this day at this hour on the second Monday in May there should have been fixed in monotonous repetition the land's living symbol – a formal group of ritual almost mystic significance identical and monotonous as milestones tying the county-seat to the county's ultimate rim as milestones would: the beast the plough and the man integrated in one foundationed into the frozen wave of their furrow tremendous with effort yet at the same time vacant of progress, ponderable immovable and immobile like groups of wrestling statuary set against the land's immensity – until suddenly (they were eight miles from town; already the blue-green lift of the hills was in sight) he said with an incredulous an almost shocked amazement who except for Paralee and Aleck Sander and Lucas had not seen one in going on forty-eight hours:

'There's a nigger.'

'Yes,' his uncle said. 'Today is the ninth of May. This county's got half of a hundred and forty-two thousand acres to plant yet. Somebody's got to stay home and work:' – the car rushing boring up so that across the field's edge and the perhaps fifty yards separating them he and the Negro behind the plough looked eye to eye into each other's face before the Negro looked away – the face black and gleamed with sweat and passionate with effort, tense concentrated and composed, the car flashing past and on while he leaned first out the open window to look back then turned in the seat to see back through the rear window, watching them still in their rapid unblurred diminishment – the man and

the mule and the wooden plough which coupled them furious
and solitary, fixed and without progress in the earth, leaning
terrifically against nothing.

They could see the hills now; they were almost there the long
lift of the first pine ridge standing across half the horizon and
beyond it a sense a feel of others, the mass of them seeming not
so much to stand rush abruptly up out of the plateau as to hang
suspended over it as his uncle had told him the Scottish highlands
did except for this sharpness and colour; that was two years ago,
maybe three and his uncle had said, 'Which is why the people
who chose by preference to live on them on little patches which
wouldn't make eight bushels of corn or fifty pounds of lint cotton
an acre even if they were not too steep for a mule to pull a plough
across (but then they dont want to make the cotton anyway, only
the corn and not too much of that because it really doesn't take
a great deal of corn to run a still as big as one man and his sons
want to fool with) are people named Gowrie and McCallum and
Fraser and Ingrum that used to be Ingraham and Workitt that
used to be Urquhart only the one that brought it to America and
then Mississippi couldn't spell it either, who love brawling and
fear God and believe in Hell –' and it was as though his uncle
had read his mind, holding the speedometer needle at fifty-five
into the last mile of gravel (already the road was beginning to
slant down towards the willow-and-cypress bottom of the Nine-
Mile branch) speaking, that is volunteering to speak for the first
time since they left town:

'Gowrie and Fraser and Workitt and Ingrum. And in the valleys
along the rivers, the broad rich easy land where a man can raise
something he can sell openly in daylight, the people named
Little John and Greenleaf and Armstead and Millingham and
Bookwright –' and stopped, the car dropping on down the slope,
increasing speed by its own weight; now he could see the bridge
where Aleck Sander had waited for him in the dark and below
which Highboy had smelled quicksand.

'We turn off just beyond it,' he said.

'I know,' his uncle said. '– And the ones named Sambo they
live in both, they elect both because they can stand either because
they can stand anything.' The bridge was quite near now, the
white railing of the entrance yawned rushing at them. 'Not all
white people can endure slavery and apparently no man can stand
freedom (Which incidentally – the premise that man really wants
peace and freedom – is the trouble with our relations with Europe

right now, whose people not only dont know what peace is but – except for Anglo-Saxons – actively fear and distrust personal liberty; we are hoping without really any hope that our atom bomb will be enough to defend an idea as obsolete as Noah's Ark); with one mutual instantaneous accord he forces his liberty into the hands of the first demagogue who rises into view: lacking that he himself destroys and obliterates it from his sight and ken and even remembrance with the frantic unanimity of a neighbourhood stamping out a grass-fire. But the people named Sambo survived the one and who knows? they may even endure the other. – And who knows –'

Then a gleam of sand, a flash and glint of water; the white rail streamed past in one roar and rush and rattle of planking and they were across. *He'll have to slow down now* he thought but his uncle didn't, merely declutching, the car rolling on its own momentum which carried it still too fast through a slewing skidding turn into the dirt road and on for fifty yards bouncing among the ruts until the last of flat land died headlong into the first gentle slant, its momentum still carrying the car in high speed gear yet up the incline until then after he saw the tracks where Aleck Sander had driven the pickup off the road into the bushes and where he had stood ready with his hand poised over Highboy's nostrils while the horse or the mule, whichever it was, had come down the hill with the burden in front of the rider which even Aleck Sander with his eyes like an owl or mink or whatever else hunts at night, had failed to descry (and he remembered again not just his uncle at the table this morning but himself standing in the yard last night during that moment after Aleck Sander walked away and before he recognized Miss Habersham when he actually believed he was coming out alone to do what must be done and he told himself now as he had at the table: *I wont think about that*); almost there now, practically were there in fact: what remained of space intervened not even to be measured in miles.

Though that little at a crawl, the car whining in second gear now against the motionless uprush of the main ridge and the strong constant resinous downflow of the pines where the dogwood looked indeed like nuns now in the long green corridors, up and on to the last crest, the plateau and now he seemed to see his whole native land, his home – the dirt, the earth which had bred his bones and those of his fathers for six generations and was still shaping him into not just a man but a specific man,

not with just a man's passions and aspirations and beliefs but the
specific passions and hopes and convictions and ways of thinking
and acting of a specific kind and even race: and even more: even
among a kind and race specific and unique (according to the
lights of most, certainly of all of them who had thronged into
town this morning to stand across the street from the jail and
crowd up around the sheriff's car, damned unique) since it had
also integrated into him whatever it was that had compelled him
to stop and listen to a damned highnosed impudent Negro who
even if he wasn't a murderer had been about to get if not about
what he deserved at least exactly what he had spent the sixty-odd
years of his life asking for – unfolding beneath him like a map in
one slow soundless explosion: to the east ridge on green ridge
tumbling away towards Alabama and to the west and south the
checkered fields and the woods flowing on into the blue and
gauzed horizon beyond which lay at last like a cloud the long wall
of the levee and the great River itself flowing not merely from
the north but out of the North circumscribing and outland – the
umbilicus of America joining the soil which was his home to the
parent which three generations ago it had failed in blood to
repudiate; by turning his head he could see the faint stain of
smoke which was town ten miles away and merely by looking
ahead he could see the long reach of rich bottom land marked
off into the big holdings, the plantations (one of which was
Edmonds' where the present Edmonds and Lucas both had been
born, stemming from the same grandfather) along their own
little river (though even in his grandfather's memory steamboats
had navigated it) and then the dense line of river jungle itself:
and beyond that stretching away east and north and west not
merely to where the ultimate headlands frowned back to back
upon the waste of the two oceans and the long barrier of Canada
but to the uttermost rim of earth itself, the North: not north but
North; outland and circumscribing and not even a geographical
place but an emotional idea, a condition of which he had fed
from his mother's milk to be ever and constant on the alert not
at all to fear and not actually anymore to hate but just – a little
wearily sometimes and sometimes even with tongue in cheek –
to defy: who had brought from infancy with him a childhood's
picture which on the threshold of manhood had found no reason
or means to alter and which he had no reason to believe in his
old age would alter either: a curving semicircular wall not high
(anyone who really wanted to could have climbed it; he believed

that any boy already would) from the top of which with the whole
vast scope of their own rich teeming never-ravaged land of
glittering undefiled cities and unburned towns and unwasted
farms so long-secured and opulent you would think there was no
room left for curiosity, there looked down upon him and his
countless row on row of faces which resembled his face and spoke
the same language he spoke and at times even answered to the
same names he bore yet between whom and him and his there
was no longer any real kinship and soon there would not even
be any contact since the very mutual words they used would no
longer have the same significance and soon after that even this
would be gone because they would be too far asunder even to
hear one another: only the massed uncountable faces looking
down at him and his in fading amazement and outrage and
frustration and most curious of all, gullibility: a volitionless,
almost helpless capacity and eagerness to believe anything about
the South not even provided it be derogatory but merely bizarre
enough and strange enough: whereupon once more his uncle
spoke at complete one with him and again without surprise he
saw his thinking not be interrupted but merely swap one saddle
for another:

'It's because we alone in the United States (I'm not speaking of
Sambo right now; I'll get to him in a minute) are a homogeneous
people. I mean the only one of any size. The New Englander is
too of course back inland from the coastal spew of Europe which
this country quarantined unrootable into the rootless ephemeral
cities with factory and foundry and municipal paycheques as tight
and close as any police could have done it, but there are no longer
enough of him just as there are not of the Swiss who are not a
people so much as a neat clean small quite solvent business. So
we are not really resisting what the outland calls (and we too)
progress and enlightenment. We are defending not actually our
politics or beliefs or even our way of life, but simply our homogeneity from a federal government to which in simple desperation
the rest of this country has had to surrender voluntarily more
and more of its personal and private liberty in order to continue
to afford the United States. And of course we will continue to
defend it. We (I mean all of us: Beat Four will be unable to sleep
at night until it has cancelled Lucas Beauchamp ((or someone
else)) against Vinson Gowrie in the same colour of ink, and Beat
One and Two and Three and Five who on heatless principle
intend to see that Beat Four makes that cancellation) dont know

why it is valuable. We dont need to know. Only a few of us know
that only from homogeneity comes anything of a people or for a
people of durable and lasting value – the literature, the art, the
science, that minimum of government and police which is the
meaning of freedom and liberty, and perhaps most valuable of
all a national character worth anything in a crisis – that crisis we
shall face someday when we meet an enemy with as many men
as we have and as much material as we have and – who knows? –
who can even brag and boast as we brag and boast.

'That's why we must resist the North: not just to preserve
ourselves nor even the two of us as one to remain one nation
because that will be the inescapable by-product of what we will
preserve: which is the very thing that three generations ago we
lost a bloody war in our own back yards so that it remain intact:
the postulate that Sambo is a human being living in a free country
and hence must be free. That's what we are really defending: the
privilege of setting him free ourselves: which we will have to do
for the reason that nobody else can since going on a century ago
now the North tried it and have been admitting for seventy-five
years now that they failed. So it will have to be us. Soon now this
sort of thing wont even threaten anymore. It shouldn't now. It
should never have. Yet it did last Saturday and it probably will
again, perhaps once more, perhaps twice more. But then no
more, it will be finished; the shame will still be there of course
but then the whole chronicle of man's immortality is in the
suffering he had endured, his struggle towards the stars in the
stepping-stones of his expiations. Someday Lucas Beauchamp can
shoot a white man in the back with the same impunity to lynch-
rope or gasoline as a white man; in time he will vote anywhen
and anywhere a white man can and send his children to the same
school anywhere the white man's children go and travel anywhere
the white man travels as the white man does it. But it wont be
next Tuesday. Yet people in the North believe it can be compelled
even into next Monday by the simple ratification by votes of a
printed paragraph: who have forgotten that although a long
quarter-century ago Lucas Beauchamp's freedom was made an
article in our constitution and Lucas Beauchamp's master was
not merely beaten to his knees but trampled for ten years on his
face in the dust to make him swallow it, yet only three short
generations later they are faced once more with the necessity of
passing legislation to set Lucas Beauchamp free.

'And as for Lucas Beauchamp, Sambo, he's a homogeneous

man too, except that part of him which is trying to escape not even into the best of the white race but into the second best – the cheap shoddy dishonest music, the cheap flash baseless overvalued money, the glittering edifice of publicity foundationed on nothing like a cardhouse over an abyss and all the noisy muddle of political activity which used to be our minor national industry and is now our national amateur pastime – all the spurious uproar produced by men deliberately fostering and then getting rich on our national passion for the mediocre: who will even accept the best provided it is debased and befouled before being fed to us: who are the only people on earth who brag publicly of being second-rate, i.e., lowbrows. I dont mean that Sambo. I mean the rest of him who has a better homogeneity than we have and proved it by finding himself roots into the land where he had actually to displace white men to put them down: because he had patience even when he didn't have hope, the long view even when there was nothing to see at the end of it, not even just the will but the desire to endure because he loved the old few simple things which no one wanted to take from him: not an automobile nor flash clothes nor his picture in the paper but a little of music (his own), a hearth, not his child but any child, a God a heaven which a man may avail himself a little of at any time without having to wait to die, a little earth for his own sweat to fall on among his own green shoots and plants. We – he and us – should confederate: swap him the rest of the economic and political and cultural privileges which are his right, for the reversion of his capacity to wait and endure and survive. Then we would prevail; together we would dominate the United States; we would present a front not only impregnable but not even to be threatened by a mass of people who no longer have anything in common save a frantic greed for money and a basic fear of a failure of national character which they hide from one another behind a loud lipservice to a flag.'

Now they were there and not too long behind the sheriff. For though the car was already drawn off the road into the grove in front of the church, the sheriff was still standing beside it and one of the Negroes was just passing the pick backwards out of the car to the other prisoner who stood holding both the shovels. His uncle drew in beside it and stopped and now in daylight he could see the church, for the first time actually who had lived within ten miles of it all his life and must have passed it, seen it at least half that many times. Yet he could not remember ever having actually looked at it before – a plank steepleless box no longer than some of the one-room cabins hill people lived in, paintless too yet (curiously) not shabby and not even in neglect or disrepair because he could see where sections of raw new lumber and scraps and fragments of synthetic roofing had been patched and carpentered into the old walls and shingles with a savage almost insolent promptitude, not squatting nor crouching nor even sitting but standing among the trunks of the high strong constant shaggy pines, solitary but not forlorn, intractable and independent, asking nothing of any, making compromise with none and he remembered the tall slender spires which said Peace and the squatter utilitarian belfries which said Repent and he remembered one which even said Beware but this one said simply: Burn: and he and his uncle got out; the sheriff and the two Negroes carrying the tools were already inside the fence and he and his uncle followed, through the sagging gate in the low wire enclosure massed with honeysuckle and small odourless pink and white climbing roses and he saw the graveyard too for the first time, who had not only violated a grave in it but exploded one crime by exposing another – a fenced square of earth less large than garden plots he had seen and which by September would probably be choked and almost impenetrable and wellnigh invisible with sagegrass and ragweed and beggarlice, out of which stood without symmetry or order like bookmarks thrust at random into a ledger or toothpicks in a loaf and canted always slightly as if they had taken their own frozen perpendicular from the limber unresting never-quite-vertical pines, shingle-thin slabs of cheap grey granite of the same weathered colour as the paintless church as if they had been hacked out of its flank with axes (and carved mottoless with simple names and dates as though there had been nothing even their mourners remembered of them than that they had lived and they had died) and it had been neither decay nor time which had compelled back into the violated walls the raw new patching of unplaned paintless lumber but the simple exigencies of mortality and the doom of flesh.

He and his uncle threaded on among them to where the sheriff and the two Negroes already stood above the fresh raw mound which likewise he who had violated it now actually saw for the first time. But they hadn't begun to dig yet. Instead the sheriff had even turned, looking back at him until he and his uncle came up and stopped too.

'Now what?' his uncle said.

But the sheriff was speaking to him in the mild heavy voice: 'I reckon you and Miss Eunice and your secretary were mighty careful not to let anybody catch you at this business last night; weren't you?'

His uncle answered: 'This is hardly the thing you'd want an audience at, is it?'

But the sheriff was still looking at him. 'Then why didn't they put the flowers back?'

Then he saw them too – the artificial wreath, the tedious intricate contrivance of wire and thread and varnished leaves and embalmed blooms which someone had brought or sent out from the florist in town, and the three bunches of wilted garden and field flowers tied with cotton string, all of which Aleck Sander had said last night looked as if they had been thrown at or on to the grave and which he remembered Aleck Sander and himself moving aside out of the way and which he knew they had put back after they filled the hole back up; he could remember Miss Habersham telling them twice to put them back even after he himself had protested about the un-need or at least the waste of time; perhaps he could even remember Miss Habersham herself helping to put them back: or they perhaps he didn't remember them being put back at all but merely thought he did because they obviously hadn't been, lying now tossed and inextricable to one side and apparently either he or Aleck Sander had trodden on the wreath though it didn't really matter now, which was what his uncle was just saying:

'Never mind now. Let's get started. Even when we finish here and are on the way back to town we will still be only started.'

'All right, boys,' the sheriff said to the Negroes. 'Jump to it. Let's get out of here –' and there was no sound, he heard nothing to warn him, he just looked up and around as his uncle and the sheriff did and saw, coming not down the road but around from behind the church as though from among the high windy pines themselves, a man in a wide pale hat and a clean faded blue shirt whose empty left sleeve was folded neatly back and pinned cuff to shoulder with a safetypin, on a small trim claybank mare showing too much eye-white and followed by two younger men riding double on a big saddleless black mule with a rope-burn on its neck and followed in their turn (and keeping carefully clear of the mule's heels) by two gaunt Trigg foxhounds, coming at a rapid trot across the grove to the gate where the man stopped the mare and swung himself lightly and rapidly down with his

one hand and dropped the reins across the mare's neck and came
with that light wiry almost springy rapidity through the gate and
up to them – a short lean old man with eyes as pale as the sheriff's
and a red weathered face out of which jutted a nose like the
hooked beak of an eagle, already speaking in a high thin strong
uncracked voice:

'What's going on around here, Shurf?'

'I'm going to open this grave, Mr Gowrie,' the sheriff said.

'No, Shurf,' the other said, immediate, with no change whatever in the voice: not disputative, nothing: just a statement: 'Not
that grave.'

'Yes, Mr Gowrie,' the sheriff said. 'I'm going to open it.'
Without haste or fumbling, almost deliberate in fact, the old man
with his one hand unbuttoned two buttons on the front of his
shirt and thrust the hand inside, hunching his hip slightly around
to meet the hand and drew from inside the shirt a heavy nickelplated pistol and still with no haste but no pause either thrust
the pistol into his left armpit, clamping it butt-forward against
his body by the stub of the arm while his one hand buttoned the
shirt, then took the pistol once more into the single hand not
pointing it at anything, just holding it.

But long before this he had seen the sheriff already moving,
moving with really incredible speed not towards the old man but
around the end of the grave, already in motion even before the
two Negroes turned to run, so that when they whirled they
seemed to run full tilt into the sheriff as into a cliff, even seeming
to bounce back a little before the sheriff grasped them one in
each hand as if they were children and then in the next instant
seemed to be holding them both in one hand like two rag dolls,
turning his body so that he was between them and the little wiry
old man with the pistol, saying in that mild even lethargic voice:

'Stop it. Dont you know the worst thing that could happen to
a nigger would be dodging loose in a pair of convict pants around
out here today?'

'That's right, boys,' the old man said in his high inflectionless
voice. 'I aint going to hurt you. I'm talking to the Shurf here.
Not my boy's grave, Shurf.'

'Send them back to the car,' his uncle murmured rapidly. But
the sheriff didn't answer, still looking at the old man.

'Your boy aint in that grave, Mr Gowrie,' the sheriff said. And
watching he thought of all the things the old man might have
said – the surprise, the disbelief, the outrage perhaps, even the

thinking aloud: *How do you come to know my boy aint there?* – the rationalizing by reflective in which he might have paraphrased the sheriff speaking to his uncle six hours ago: *You wouldn't be telling me this if you didn't know it was so;* watching, even following the old man as he cut straight across all this and he thought suddenly with amazement: *Why, he's grieving:* thinking how he had seen grief twice now in two years where he had not expected it or anyway anticipated it, where in a sense a heart capable of breaking had no business being: once in an old nigger who had just happened to outlive his old nigger wife and now in a violent foulmouthed godless old man who had happened to lose one of the six lazy idle violent more or less lawless a good deal more than just more or less worthless sons, only one of whom had ever benefited his community and kind and that only by the last desperate resort of getting murdered out of it: hearing the high flat voice again immediate and strong and without interval, inflectionless, almost conversational:

'Why, I just hope you dont tell me the name of the fellow that proved my boy aint there, Shurf. I just hope you wont mention that:' – little hard pale eyes staring at little hard pale eyes, the sheriff's voice mild still, inscrutable now:

'No, Mr Gowrie. It aint empty:' and later, afterwards, he realized that this was when he believed he knew not perhaps why Lucas had ever reached town alive because the reason for that was obvious: there happened to be no Gowrie present at the moment but the dead one: but at least how the old man and two of his sons happened to ride out of the woods behind the church almost as soon as he and the sheriff and his uncle reached the grave, and certainly why almost forty-eight hours afterwards Lucas was still breathing. 'It's Jake Montgomery down there,' the sheriff said.

The old man turned, immediate, not hurriedly and even quickly but just easily as if his spare small fleshless frame offered neither resistance to the air nor weight to the motive muscles, and shouted towards the fence where the two younger men still sat the mule identical as two clothing store dummies and as immobile, not even having begun yet to descend until the old man shouted: 'Here, boys.'

'Never mind,' the sheriff said. 'We'll do it.' He turned to the two Negroes. 'All right. Get your shovels –'

'I told you,' his uncle murmured rapidly again. 'Send them back to the car.'

'That's right, Lawyer – Lawyer Stevens, aint it? the old man said. 'Get 'em away from here. This here's our business. We'll attend to it.'

'It's my business now, Mr Gowrie,' the sheriff said.

The old man raised the pistol, steadily and without haste, bending his elbow until it came level, his thumb curling up and over the hammer cocking it so that it came already cocked level or not quite, not quite pointing at anything somewhere about the height of the empty belt-loops on the sheriff's trousers. 'Get them out of here, Shurf,' the old man said.

'All right,' the sheriff said without moving. 'You boys go back to the car.'

'Further than that,' the old man said. 'Send 'em back to town.'

'They're prisoners, Mr Gowrie,' the sheriff said. 'I cant do that.' He didn't move. 'Go back and get in the car,' he told them. They moved then, walking not back towards the gate but directly across the enclosure, walking quite fast, lifting their feet and knees in the filthy barred trousers quite high, walking quite fast by the time they reached the opposite fence and half stepping half hopping over it and only then changing direction back towards the two cars so that until they reached the sheriff's car they would never be any nearer the two white men on the mule than when they had left the grave: and he looked at them now sitting the mule identical as two clothes pins on a line, the identical faces even weathered exactly alike, surly quick-tempered and calm, until the old man shouted again:

'All right, boys:' and they got down as one, at the same time even like a trained vaudeville team and again as one stepped with the same left leg over the fence, completely ignoring the gate: the Gowrie twins, identical even to the clothing and shoes except that one wore a khaki shirt and the other a sleeveless Jersey; about thirty, a head taller than their father and with their father's pale eyes and the nose too except that it was not the beak of an eagle but rather that of a hawk, coming up with no word, no glance even for any of them from the bleak composed humourless faces until the old man pointed with the pistol (he saw that the hammer was down now anyway) at the two shovels and said in his high voice which sounded almost cheerful even:

'Grab'em, boys. They belong to the county; if we bust one it aint anybody's business but the Grand Jury's:' the twins, facing each other now at opposite ends of the mound and working again in that complete almost choreographic unison: the next two youngest before the dead one, Vinson; fourth and fifth of the six sons – Forrest, the oldest who had not only wrenched himself free of his fiery tyrant of a father but had even got married and for twenty years now had been manager of a delta cotton plantation above Vicksburg; then Crawford, the second one who had been drafted on the second day of November 1918 and on the night of the tenth (with a bad luck in guessing which, his uncle said, should not happen to any man – a point of view in which in fact his federal captors themselves seemed to concur since his term in the Leavenworth prison had been only one year) had deserted and lived for almost eighteen months in a series of caves and tunnels in the hills within fifteen miles of the federal courthouse in Jefferson until he was captured at last after something very like a pitched battle (though luckily for him nobody was seriously hurt) during which he made good his cave for thirty-odd hours armed with (and, his uncle said, a certain consistency and fitness here: a deserter from the United States army defending his freedom from the United States government with a piece of armament captured from the enemy whom he had refused to fight) an automatic pistol which one of the McCallum boys had taken from a captured German officer and traded shortly after he got home for a brace of Gowrie foxhounds, and served his year and came home and the town next heard of him in Memphis where it was said he was (1) running liquor up from New Orleans, (2) acting as a special employer-bonded company officer during a strike, but anyway coming back to his father's home suddenly where nobody saw much of him until a few years back when the town began to hear of him as having more or less settled down, dealing in a little timber and cattle and even working a little land; and Bryan, the third one who was the actual force, power, cohering element, whatever you might call it, in or behind the family farm which fed them all; then the twins, Vardaman and Bilbo who spent their nights squatting in front of smouldering logs and stumps while the hounds ran foxes and their days sleeping flat on the naked planks of the front gallery until dark came and time to cast the hounds again; and the last one, Vinson, who even as a child had shown an aptitude for trading and for money so that now, though dead at only twenty-eight, he was not only said to own several small parcels of farmland about the county but was the first Gowrie who could sign his name to a cheque and have any bank honour it – the twins, kneedeep then waistdeep, working with a grim and sullen speed, robotlike and in absolute unison so that the two shovels even seemed to ring at the same instant on the plank box and even then seeming to communicate by no physical means as birds or animals do: no sound no gesture: simply one of them released his shovel in a continuation of the same stroke which flung the dirt and then himself flowed effortless up out of the pit and stood among the rest of them while his brother cleaned off what remained of dirt from the top of the coffin, then tossed his shovel up and out without even looking and – as he himself had done last night – kicked the last of the earth away from the edge of the lid and stood on one leg and grasped the lid and heaved it up and over and away until all of them standing along the rim of the grave could look down past him into the box.

It was empty. There was nothing in it at all until a thin trickle of dirt flowed down into it with a whispering pattering sound.

Chapter Eight

And he would remember it: the five of them standing at the edge of the pit above the empty coffin, then with another limber flowing motion like his twin's the second Gowrie came up out of the grave and stooped and with an air of rapt displeased even faintly outraged concern began to brush and thump the clay particles from the lower legs of his trousers, the first twin moving as the second stooped, going straight to him with a blind unhurried undeviable homing quality about him like the other of a piece of machinery, the other spindle say of a lathe, travelling on the same ineluctable shaft to its socket, and stooped too and began to brush and strike the dirt from the back of his brother's trousers; and this time almost a spadeful of dirt slid down across the out-slanted lid and rattled down into the empty box, almost loud enough or with mass and weight enough to produce a small hollow echo.

'Now he's got two of them,' his uncle said.

'Yes,' the sheriff said. 'Where?'

'Durn two of them,' old Gowrie said. 'Where's my boy, Shurf?'

'We're going to find him now, Mr Gowrie,' the sheriff said. 'And you were smart to bring them hounds. Put your pistol up and let your boys catch them dogs and hold them till we get straightened out here.'

'Never you mind the pistol nor the dogs neither,' old Gowrie said. 'They'll trail and they'll ketch anything that ever run or walked either. But my boy and that Jake Montgomery – if it was Jake Montgomery whoever it was found laying in my son's coffin – never walked away from here to leave no trail.'

The sheriff said, 'Hush now, Mr Gowrie.' The old man glared back up at the sheriff. He was not trembling, not eager, baffled, amazed, not anything. Watching him he thought of one of the cold lightblue tearshaped apparently heatless flames which balance themselves on even less than tiptoe over gasjets.

'All right,' the old man said. 'I'm hushed. And now you get started. You're the one that seems to know all about this, that sent me word out to my breakfast table at six o'clock this morning to meet you here. Now you get started.'

'That's what we're going to do,' the sheriff said. 'We're going to find out right now where to start.' He turned to his uncle, saying in the mild rational almost diffident voice: 'It's say around eleven o'clock at night. You got a mule or maybe it's a horse, anyway something that can walk and tote a double load, and a dead man across your saddle. And you aint got much time; that is, you aint got all of time. Of course it's around eleven o'clock, when most folks is in bed, and a Sunday night too when folks have got to get up early tomorrow to start a new week in the middle of cotton-planting time, and there aint any moon and even if folks might still be moving around you're in a lonely part of the country where the chances all are you wont meet nobody. But still you got a dead man with a bullet hole in his back and even at eleven o'clock day's going to come sooner or later. All right. What would you do?'

They looked, stared at one another, or that is his uncle stared – the too-thin bony eager face, the bright intent rapid eyes, and opposite the sheriff's vast sleepy face, the eyes not staring, apparently not even looking, blinking almost drowsily, the two of them cutting without speech across all that too: 'Of course,' his uncle said. 'Into the earth again. And not far, since as you said daylight comes sooner or later even when it's still just eleven o'clock. Especially when he still had time to come back and do it

all over again, alone, by himself, no hand but this on the shovel
– And think of that too: the need, the terrible need, not just to
have it all to do again but to have to do it again for the reason
he had; to think that he had done all he possibly could, all anyone
could have asked or expected him to do or even dreamed that
he would have to do; was as safe as he could hope to be – and
then to be drawn back by a sound, a noise or perhaps he blundered
by sheer chance on the parked truck or perhaps it was just his
luck, his good fortune, whatever god or djinn or genie looks after
murderers for a little while, keeps him secure and safe until the
other fates have had time to spin and knot the rope – anyway to
have to crawl, tie the mule or horse or whatever it was to a tree
and crawl on his belly back up here to lie (who knows? perhaps
just behind the fence yonder) and watch a meddling old woman
and two children who should have been two hours ago in bed
ten miles away, wreck the whole careful edifice of his furious
labour, undo the work not merely of his life but of his death
too . . .' His uncle stopped, and now he saw the bright almost
luminous eyes glaring down at him: 'And you. You couldn't have
had any idea Miss Habersham was coming with you until you got
home. And without her, you could have had no hope whatever
that Aleck Sander would come with you alone at all. So if you
ever really had any idea of coming out here along to dig this
grave up, dont even tell me –'

'Let that be now,' the sheriff said. 'All right. Somewhere in
the ground. And what sort of ground? What dirt digs easiest and
fastest for a man in a hurry and by himself even if he has a shovel?
What sort of dirt could you hope to hide a body in quick even if
you never had nothing but a pocket knife?'

'In sand,' his uncle said immediately, rapidly, almost indiffer-
ently, almost inattentively. 'In the bed of the branch. Didn't they
tell you at three o'clock this morning that they saw him going
there with it? What are we waiting for?'

'All right,' the sheriff said. 'Let's go then.' Then to him: 'Show
us exactly where –'

'Except that Aleck Sander said it might not have been a mule,'
he said.

'All right,' the sheriff said. 'Horse then. Show us exactly
where . . .'

He would remember it: watching the old man clap the pistol
again butt-forward into his armpit and clamp it there with the
stump of the arm while the one hand unbuttoned the shirt then

took the pistol from the armpit and thrust it back inside the shirt then buttoned the shirt again then turned even faster quicker than the two sons half his age, already in front of everybody when he hopped back over the fence and went to the mare and caught reins and pommel all in one hand, already swinging up: then the two cars dropping in second speed against gravity back down the steep pitch until he said 'Here' where the pickup's tracks slewed off the road into the bushes then back into the road again and his uncle stopped: and he watched the fierce old stump-armed man jump the buckskin mare up out of the road into the woods on the opposite side already falling away down towards the branch, then the two hounds flowing up the bank behind him and then the mule with the two identical wooden-faced sons on it: then he and his uncle were out of the car the sheriff's car bumper to bumper behind them, hearing the mare crashing on down towards the branch and then the old man's high flat voice shouting at the hounds:

'Hi! Hi! Hum on boy! At him, Ring!' and then his uncle:

'Handcuff them through the steering wheel:' and then the sheriff:

'No. We'll need the shovels:' and he had climbed the bank too, listening off and downwards towards the crashing and the shouts, then his uncle and the sheriff and the two Negroes carrying the shovels were beside him. Although the branch crossed almost at right angles the highway just beyond where the dirt road forked away, it was almost a quarter-mile from where they now stood or walked rather and although they could all hear old Gowrie still whooping at the dogs and the crashing of the mare and the mule too in the dense thicket below, the sheriff didn't go that way, bearing instead off along the hill almost parallel with the road for several minutes and only beginning to slant away from it when they came out into the sawgrass and laurel and willow-choked flat between the hill and the branch: and on across that, the sheriff in front until he stopped still looking down then turned his head and looked back at him, watching him as he and his uncle came up.

'Your secretary was right the first time,' the sheriff said. 'It was a mule.'

'Not a black one with a rope-burn,' his uncle said. 'Surely not that. Not even a murderer is that crassly and arrogantly extrovert.'

'Yes,' the sheriff said. 'That's why they're dangerous, why we

must destroy them or lock them up:' and looking down he saw
them too: the narrow delicate almost finicking mule-prints out
of all proportion to the animal's actual size, mashed pressed deep,
too deep for any one mule no matter how heavy carrying just
one man, into the damp muck, the tracks filled with water and
even as he watched a minute aquatic beast of some sort shot
across one of them leaving a tiny threadlike spurt of dissolving
mud; and standing in the trail, now that they had found it they
could see the actual path itself through the crushed shoulder-
high growth in suspension held like a furrow across a field or the
frozen wake of a boat, crossing the marsh arrow-straight until it
vanished into the jungle which bordered the branch. They followed it, walking in it, treading the two sets of prints not going
and returning but both going in the same direction, now and
then the print of the same hoof superposed on its previous one,
the sheriff still in the lead talking again, speaking aloud but
without looking back as though – he thought at first to no one:

'He wouldn't come back this way. The first time he didn't have
time. He went back straight up the hill that time, woods or not
and dark or not. That was when he heard whatever it was he
heard.' Then he knew who the sheriff was talking to: 'Maybe
your secretary was whistling up there or something. Being in a
graveyard that time of night.'

Then they stood on the bank of the branch itself – a broad
ditch a channel through which during the winter and spring rains
a torrent rushed but where now there flowed a thin current
scarcely an inch deep and never much over a yard wide from
pool to pool along the blanched sand – and even as his uncle said,
'Surely the fool –' the sheriff ten yards or so further along the
bank said:

'Here it is:' and they went to him and then he saw where the
mule had stood tied to a sapling and then the prints where the
man himself had thrashed on along the bank, his prints also
deeper than any man no matter how heavy should have made
and he thought of that too: the anguish, the desperation, the
urgency in the black dark and the briers and the dizzy irrevocable
fleeing on seconds, carrying a burden man was not intended to
carry: then he was hearing a snapping and thrashing of underbrush still further along the bank and then the mare and then
old Gowrie shouted and then another crash which would be the
mule coming up and then simple pandemonium: the old man
shouting and cursing and the yelping of the hounds and the

thudding sound a man's shoe makes against a dog's ribs: but they couldn't hurry anymore, thrashing and crashing their own way through the tearing clinging briars and vines until they could look down into the ditch and the low mound of fresh shaled earth into which the two hounds had been digging and old Gowrie still kicking at them and cursing, and then they were all down in the ditch except the two Negroes.

'Hold up, Mr Gowrie,' the sheriff said. 'That aint Vinson.' But the old man didn't seem to hear him. He didn't even seem aware that anyone else was there; he seemed even to have forgot why he was kicking the dogs: that he had merely set out to drive them back from the mound, still hobbling and hopping after them on one leg and the other poised and cocked to kick even after they had retreated from the mound and were merely trying to dodge past him and get out of the ditch into safety, still kicking at them and cursing after the sheriff caught him by his one arm and held him.

'Look at the dirt,' the sheriff said. 'Cant you see! He hardly took time to bury it. This was the second one, when he was in the hurry, when it was almost daylight and he had to get it hidden?' and they could all see now – the low hummock of fresh dirt lying close under the bank and in the bank above it the savage ragged marks of the shovel as if he had hacked at the bank with the edge of the blade like swinging an axe (and again: thinking: the desperation the urgency the frantic hand-to-hand combat with the massy intolerable inertia of the earth itself) until enough of it shaled off and down to hide what he had to hide.

This time they didn't need even the shovels. The body was barely covered; the dogs had already exposed it and he realized now the true magnitude of the urgency and desperation: the frantic and desperate bankrupt in time who had not even enough of it left to hide the evidence of his desperation and the reason for his urgency; it had been after two o'clock when he and Aleck Sander, even two of them working with furious speed, had got the grave filled back up again: so that by the time the murderer, not only alone but who had already moved six feet of dirt and then put it back once since the sun set yesterday, had the second body out and the grave filled for the second time it must have been daylight, later than daylight perhaps, the sun itself watching him while he rode for the second time down the hill and across to the branch; morning itself watching him while he tumbled the body beneath the bank's overhang then hacked furiously from it just enough dirt to hide the body temporarily from sight with something of that frantic desperation of the wife flinging her peignoir over the lover's forgotten glove – lying (the body) face down and only the back of the crushed skull visible until the old man stooped and with his one hand jerked it stiffly over on to its back.

'Yep,' old Gowrie said in the high brisk carrying voice: 'It's that Montgomery, damned if it aint:' and rose lean and fast as a tripped watch-spring yelling shouting at the hounds again: 'Hi boys! Find Vinson!' and then his uncle shouting too to make himself heard:

'Wait, Mr Gowrie. Wait:' then to the sheriff: 'He was a fool then just because he didn't have time, not because he is a fool. I just dont believe it twice –' looking around, his eyes darting. Then he stopped them on the twins. He said sharply: 'Where's the quicksand?'

'What?' one of the twins said.

'The quicksand,' his uncle said. 'The quicksand bed in the branch here. Where is it?'

'Quicksand?' old Gowrie said. 'Sonabitch, Lawyer. Put a man in quicksand? my boy in quicksand?'

'Shut up, Mr Gowrie,' the sheriff said. Then to the twin: 'Well? Where?'

But he answered first. He had been intending to for a second or so. Now he did: 'It's by the bridge:' then – he didn't know why: and then that didn't matter either – 'It wasn't Aleck Sander that time. It was Highboy.'

'*Under* the highway bridge,' the twin corrected. 'Where it's been all the time.'

'Oh,' the sheriff said. 'Which one was Highboy?' And he was about to answer that: then suddenly the old man seemed to have forgot about his mare too, whirling, already running before any of them moved and even before he himself moved, running for several strides against the purchaseless sand while they watched him, before he turned and with that same catlike agility he mounted the mare with, clawed himself one-handed up the steep bank and was thrashing and crashing on out of sight before anybody else except the two Negroes who had never quitted it were even up the bank.

'Jump,' the sheriff said to the twins: 'Catch him.' But they didn't. They thrashed and crashed on after him, one of the twins in front then the rest of them and the two Negroes pell-mell

through the briers and brush, on back along the branch and out
of the jungle into the cleared right-of-way below the road at the
bridge; he saw the sliding hoof-marks where Highboy had come
almost down to the water and then refused, the stream the water
crowded over against the opposite concrete revetment flowing in
a narrow band whose nearer edge faded without demarcation
into an expanse of wet sand as smooth and innocent and markless
of surface as so much milk; he stepped sprang over a long willow
pole lying above the bank-edge and coated for three or four feet
up its length with a thin patina of dried sand like when you thrust
a stick into a bucket or vat of paint and even as the sheriff shouted
to the twin in front 'Grab him, you!' he saw the old man jump
feet first off the bank and with no splash no disturbance of any
sort continue right on not through the bland surface but past it
as if he had jumped not into anything but past the edge of a cliff
or a window-sill and then stopping half-disappeared as suddenly
with no shock or jolt: just fixed and immobile as if his legs had
been cut off at the loins by one swing of a scythe, leaving his
trunk sitting upright on the bland depthless milklike sand.

'All right, boys!' old Gowrie cried, brisk and carrying: 'Here
he is. I'm standing on him.'

And one twin got the rope bridle from the mule and the leather
one and the saddle girth from the mare and using the shovels
like axes the Negroes hacked willow branches while the rest of
them dragged up other brush and poles and whatever else they
could reach or find or free and now both twins and the two
Negroes, their empty shoes sitting on the bank, were down in
the sand too and steadily there came down from the hills the
ceaseless strong murmur of the pines but no other sound yet
although he strained his ears listening in both directions along
the road, not for the dignity of death because death has no dignity
but at least for the decorum of it: some little at least of that
decorum which should be every man's helpless right until the
carrion he leaves can be hidden from the ridicule and the shame,
the body coming out now feet first, gallowsed up and out of the
inscrutable suck to the heave of the crude tackle then free of the
sand with a faint smacking plop like the sound of lips perhaps in
sleep and in the bland surface nothing: a faint wimple wrinkle
already fading then gone like the end of a faint secret fading
smlle, and then on the bank now while they stood about and over
it and he was listening harder than ever now with something of
the murderer's own frantic urgency both ways along the road

though there was still nothing: only hearing recognizing his own voice apparently long after everyone else had, watching the old man coated to the waist with the same thin patina of sand like the pole, looking down at the body, his face wrenched and his upper lip wrenched upward from the lifeless porcelain glare and the pink bloodless gums of his false teeth:

'Oh gee, Uncle Gavin, oh gee, Uncle Gavin, let's get him away from the road, at least let's get him back into the woods –'

'Steady,' his uncle said. 'They've all passed now. They're all in town now:' and still watching as the old man stooped and began to brush clumsily with his one hand at the sand clogged into the eyes and nostrils and mouth, the hand looking curious and stiff at this which had been shaped so supple and quick to violence: to the buttons on the shirt and the butt and hammer of the pistol: then the hand went back and began to fumble at the hip pocket but already his uncle had produced a handkerchief and extended it but that was too late too as kneeling now the old man jerked out the tail of his shirt and bending to bring it close, wiped the or at the dead face with it then bending tried to blow the wet sand from it as though he had forgotten the sand was still damp. Then the old man stood up again and said in the high flat carrying voice in which there was still no real inflection at all:

'Well, Shurf?'

'It wasn't Lucas Beauchamp, Mr Gowrie,' the sheriff said. 'Jake Montgomery was at Vinson's funeral yesterday. And while Vinson was being buried Lucas Beauchamp was locked up in my jail in town.'

'I aint talking about Jake Montgomery, Shurf,' old Gowrie said.

'Neither am I, Mr Gowrie,' the sheriff said. 'Because it wasn't Lucas Beauchamp's old forty-one Colt that killed Vinson either.'

And watching he thought *No! No! Don't say it! Don't ask.!* and for a while he believed the old man would not as he stood facing the sheriff but not looking at him now because his wrinkled eyelids had come down hiding his eyes but only in the way they do when somebody looks down at something at his feet so you couldn't really say whether the old man had closed them or was just looking down at what lay on the ground between him and the sheriff. But he was wrong; the eyelids went up again and again the old man's hard pale eyes were looking at the sheriff; again his voice to nine hundred men out of nine hundred and one would have sounded just cheerful:

'What was it killed Vinson, Shurf?'

'A German Luger automatic, Mr Gowrie,' the sheriff said. 'Like the one Buddy McCallum brought home from France in 1919 and traded that summer for a pair of fox hounds.'

And he thought how this was where the eyelids might even should have closed again but again he was wrong: only until the old man himself turned, quick and wiry, already in motion, already speaking peremptory and loud, not brookless of opposition or argument, simply incapable of conceiving either:

'All right, sons. Let's load our boy on the mule and take him home.'

Chapter Nine

And two o'clock that afternoon in his uncle's car just behind the truck (it was another pickup; they – the sheriff – had commandeered it, with a slatted cattle frame on the bed which one of the Gowrie twins had known would be standing in the deserted yard of the house two miles away which had the telephone too – and he remembered how he wondered what the truck was doing there, how they had got to town themselves who had left it and the Gowrie had turned the switch on with a table fork which by the Gowrie's direction he had found in the unlocked kitchen when his uncle went in to telephone the coroner and the Gowrie was driving it) blinking rapidly and steadily not against glare so much as something hot and gritty inside his eyelids like a dust of ground glass (which certainly could and even should have been dust after twenty-odd miles of sand and gravel roads in one morning except that no simple dust refused as this did to moisten at all with blinking) it seemed to him that he saw crowding the opposite side of the street facing the jail not just the county, not just Beat One and Two and Three and Five in their faded tieless khaki and denim and print cotton but the town too – not only the faces he had seen getting out of the Beat Four dusty cars in front of the barbershop and the poolhall Saturday afternoon and then in the barbershop Sunday morning and again here in the

street Sunday noon when the sheriff drove up with Lucas, but
the others who except for the doctors and lawyers and ministers
were not just the town but the Town: merchants and cotton-
buyers and automobile dealers and the younger men who were
the clerks in the stores and cotton offices and salesrooms and
mechanics in the garages and filling stations on the way back to
work from lunch – who without even waiting for the sheriff's car
to get close enough to be recognized had already turned and
begun to flow back towards the Square like the turn of a tide,
already in motion when the sheriff's car reached the jail, already
pouring back into the Square and converging in that one direction
across it when first the sheriff then the truck then his uncle
turned into the alley beyond the jail leading to the loading ramp
at the undertaker's back door where the coroner was waiting for
them: so that moving not only parallel with them beyond the
intervening block but already in advance, it would even reach
the undertaker's first; and then suddenly and before he could
even turn in the seat to look back he knew that it had even boiled
into the alley behind them and in a moment a second now it
would roar down on them, overtake and snatch them up in order:
his uncle's car then the truck then the sheriff's like three hencoops
and sweep them on and fling them at last in one inextricable
aborted now-worthless jumble on to the ramp at the coroner's
feet; still not moving yet it seemed to him that he was already
leaning out the window or maybe actually clinging to the fleeing
runningboard yelling back at them in a kind of unbearable
unbelieving outrage:

'You fools, don't you see you are too late, that you'll have to
start all over again now to find a new reason?' then turning in
the seat and looking back through the rear window for a second
or maybe two he actually saw it – not faces but a face, not a mass
nor even a mosaic of them but a Face: not even ravening nor
uninsatiate but just in motion, insensate, vacant of thought or
e⎽ en passion: an Expression significantless and without past like
the one which materializes suddenly after seconds or even minutes
of painful even frantic staring from the innocent juxtaposition
of trees and clouds and landscape in the soap-advertisement
puzzle-picture or on the severed head in the news photo of the
Balkan or Chinese atrocity: without dignity and not even evocative of horror: just neckless slack-muscled and asleep, hanging
suspended face to face with him just beyond the glass of the back
window yet in the same instant rushing and monstrous down at

him so that he actually started back and had even begun to think *In a second more it will* when flick! it was gone, not only the Face but the faces, the alley itself empty behind them: nobody and nothing in it at all and in the street beyond the vacant mouth less than a dozen people now standing looking up the alley after them who even as he looked turned also and began to move back towards the Square.

He hesitated only an instant. *They've all gone around to the front* he thought rapid and quite calm, having a little trouble (he noticed that the car was stopped now) getting his hand on to the door handle, remarking the sheriff's car and the truck both stopped too at the loading ramp where four or five men were lifting a stretcher up to the truck's open endgate and he even heard his uncle's voice behind him:

'Now we're going home and put you to bed before your mother has a doctor in to give us both a squirt with a needle:' then finding the handle and out of the car, stumbling a little but only once, then his heels although he was not running at all pounding too hard on the concrete, his leg-muscles cramped from the car or perhaps even charley-horsed from thrashing up and down branch bottoms not to mention a night spent digging and undigging graves but at least the jarring was clearing his head somewhat or maybe it was the wind of motion doing it; anyway if he was going to have delusions at least he would have a clear brain to look at them with: up the walkway between the undertaker's and the building next to it though already too late of course, the Face in one last rush and surge long since by now already across the Square and the pavement, in one last crash against then right on through the plate glass window trampling to flinders the little bronze-and-ebony membership plaque in the national funeraleers association and the single shabby stunted palm in its maroon earthenware pot and exploding to tatters the sunfaded purple curtain which was the last frail barrier shielding what was left of Jake Montgomery had of what was left of his share of human dignity.

Then out of the walkway on to the sidewalk, the Square, and stopped dead still for what seemed to him the first time since he and his uncle left the supper table and walked out of the house a week or a month or a year ago or whenever it had been that last Sunday night was. Because this time he didn't even need the flick. They were there of course nose-pressed to the glass but there were not even enough of them to block the pavement let

alone compound a Face; less than a dozen here too and some
most of them were even boys who should have been in school at
this hour – not one country face nor even one true man because
even the other four or five were the man-sized neither men nor
boys who were always there when old epileptic Uncle Hogeye
Mosby from the poorhouse fell foaming into the gutter or when
Willy Ingrum finally managed to shoot through the leg or loins
what some woman had telephoned him was a mad-dog: and
standing at the entrance to the walkway while his uncle came
pounding up it behind him, blinking painfully his painful moist-
ureless eyelids he watched why: the Square not empty yet because
there were too many of them but getting empty, the khaki and
denim and the printed cotton streaming into it and across it
towards the parked cars and trucks, clotting and crowding at the
doors while one by one they crawled and climbed into the seats
and beds and cabs; already starters were whining and engines
catching and racing and idling and gears scraping and grinding
while the passengers still hurried towards them and now not one
but five or six at once backed away from the kerb and turned
and straightened out with people still running towards them and
scrambling aboard and then he could no longer have kept count
of them even if he had ever tried, standing beside his uncle
watching them condense into four streams into the four main
streets leading out of town in the four directions, already going
fast even before they were out of the Square, the faces for one
last moment more looking not back but out, not at anything, just
out just once and that not for long and then no more, vanishing
rapidly in profile and seeming already to be travelling much
faster than the vehicle which bore them, already by their faces
out of town long before they had passed from view: and twice
more even from the car; his mother standing suddenly not
touching him, come obviously through the walkway too from the
jail right past where they were probably still hoicking Montgomery out of the truck but then his uncle had told him they could
stand anything provided they still retained always the right to
refuse to admit it was visible, saying to his uncle:
    'Where's the car?' then not even waiting to be answered,
turning back into the walkway ahead of them, walking slender
and erect and rigid with her back looking and her heels clicking
and popping on the concrete as they did at home when he and
Aleck Sander and his father and uncle all four had better walk
pretty light for a while, back past the ramp where only the

sheriff's empty car and the empty truck stood now and on to the alley where she was already holding open the door of the car when he and his uncle got there and saw them again crossing the mouth of the alley like across a stage – the cars and trucks, the faces in invincible profile not amazed not aghast but in a sort of irrevocable repudiation, shooting across the alley-mouth so constant and unbroken and so many of them it was like the high school senior class or maybe an itinerant one-night travelling troupe giving the Battle of San Juan Hill and you not only didn't hear you didn't even need to not listen to the muted confused backstage undersounds to the same as see the marching or charging troops as soon as they reached the wings break into a frantic stumbling run swapping coats and caps and fake bandages as they doubled back behind the rippling cheesecloth painted with battle and courage and death to fall in on their own rear and at heroic attention cross the footlights again.

'We'll take Miss Habersham home first,' he said.

'Get in,' his mother said and one turn to the left into the street behind the jail and he could still hear them and another turn to the left into the next cross street and there they were again fleeing across that proscenium too unbroken and breakless, the faces rigid in profile above the long tearing sound of cement and rubber and it had taken him two or three minutes in the pickup this morning to find a chance just to get into it and go the same way it was going; it would take his uncle five or ten to find a hole to get through it and go back to the jail.

'Go on,' his mother said. 'Make them let you in:' and he knew they were not going by the jail at all; he said:

'Miss Habersham –'·

'How do I do it?' his uncle said. 'just shut both eyes and mash hard with my right foot?' and perhaps did; they were in the stream too now turning with it towards home which was all right, he had never worried about getting into it but getting out of it again before that frantic pell-mell not of flight then if any liked that better so just call it evacuation swept them on into nightfall to spew them at last hours and miles away high and dry and battered and with the wind knocked out of them somewhere along the county's ultimate scarce-mapped perimeter to walk back in the dark: saying again:

'Miss Habersham –'

'She has her truck,' his uncle said. 'Don't you remember?' – who had been doing nothing else steadily for five minutes now,

even trying three times to say it: Miss Habersham in the truck
and her house not half a mile away and all holding her back was
she couldn't possibly get to it, the house on one side and the
truck on the other of that unpierceable barrier of rushing bum-
per-locked cars and trucks and so almost as interdict to an old
maiden lady in a second-hand vegetable-peddler's pickup as if it
were in Mongolia or the moon: sitting in the truck with the
engine running and the gears meshed and her foot on the
accelerator independent solitary and forlorn erect and slight
beneath the exact archaic even moribund hat waiting and watching and wanting only but nothing but to get through it so she
could put the darned clothes away and feed the chickens and eat
supper and get some rest too after going on thirty-six hours
which to seventy must have been worse than a hundred to sixteen,
watching and waiting that dizzying profiled blur for a while even
a good while but not for ever not too long because she was a
practical woman who hadn't taken long last night to decide that
the way to get a dead body up out of a grave was to go out to
the grave and dig it up and not long now to decide that the way
to get around an obstruction especially with the sun already
tumbling down the west was to go around it, the truck in motion
now running along parallel with the obstruction and in its direction, forlorn and solitary still yet independent still too and only
a little nervous, perhaps just realizing that she was already driving
a little faster than she was used and liked to, faster in fact than
she had ever driven before and even then not keeping abreast of
it but only beside it because it was going quite fast now: one
endless profiled whizz; and now she would know that when the
gap came perhaps she would not have the skill or strength or
speed or quickness of eye or maybe even the simple nerve: herself
going faster and faster and so intent trying to not miss the gap
with one eye and watch where she was going with the other that
she wouldn't realize until afterwards that she had made the turn
going not south but east now and not just her house diminishing
rapidly and squarely behind her but Jefferson too because they
or it was not moving in just one direction out of town but in all
of them on all the main roads leading away from the jail and the
undertaker's and Lucas Beauchamp and what was left of Vinson
Gowrie and Montgomery like the frantic scattering of waterbugs
on a stagnant pond when you drop a rock into it: so she would
be more desperate than ever now with all distance fleeing between
her and home and another night coming on, nerving herself for

any gap or crevice now, the battered pickup barely skimming the ground beside that impenetrable profiled blur drawing creeping closer and closer beside it when the inevitable happened: some failure of eye or tremor of hand or an involuntary flick of the eyelid on alertness's straining glare or maybe simple topography: a stone or clod in the path as inaccessible to indictment as God but anyway too close and then too late, the truck snatched up and into the torrent of ball-bearing rubber and refinanced pressed steel and hurled pell-mell on still gripping the useless steering wheel and pressing the gelded accelerator solitary and forlorn across the long peaceful creep of late afternoon, into the mauve windless dome of dusk, faster and faster now towards one last crescendo just this side of the county line where they would burst scattering into every crossroad and lane like rabbits or rats nearing at last their individual burrows, the truck slowing and then stopping a little crossways in the road perhaps where momentum had spewed it because she was safe now, in Crossman County and she could turn south again now along the edge of Yoknapatawpha turning on the lights now going as fast as she dared along the fringing unmarked country roads; full night now and in Mott County now she could even turn west at last watching her chance to turn north and make her dash, nine and ten o'clock along the markless roads fringing the imaginary line beyond which the distant frantic headlights flashed and darted plunging into their burrows and dens; Okatoba County soon and midnight and surely she could turn north then back into Yoknapatawpha, wan and spent solitary and indomitable among the crickets and treefrogs and lightningbugs and owls and whippoorwills and the hounds rushing bellowing out from under the sleeping houses and even at last a man in his nightshirt and unlaced shoes, carrying a lantern:

Where you trying to go, lady?

I'm trying to get to Jefferson.

Jefferson's behind you, lady. I know. I had to detour around an arrogant insufferable old nigger who got the whole county upset trying to pretend he murdered a white man: when suddenly he discovered that he was going to laugh, discovering it almost in time, not quite in time to prevent it but in time to begin to stop it pretty quick, really more surprised than anything else, until his mother said harshly:

'Blow the horn. Blow them out of the way' and he discovered that it was not laughing at all or anyway not just laughing, that

is the sound it was making was about the same as laughing but
there was more of it and it felt harder, seemed to be having more
trouble getting out and the harder it felt and sounded the less
and less he could seem to remember what he must have been
laughing at and his face was suddenly wet not with a flow but a
kind of burst and spring of water; anyway there he was, a hulking
lump the second largest of the three of them, more bigger than
his mother than his uncle was than he, going on seventeen years
old and almost a man yet because three in the car were so crowded
he couldn't help but feel a woman's shoulder against his and her
narrow hand on his knee sitting there like a spanked child before
he had even had warning enough to begin to stop it.

'They ran,' he said.

'Pull out, damn you,' his mother said. 'Go around them:' which
his uncle did, on the wrong side of the street and going almost
as fast as he had driven this morning on the way to the church
trying to keep in sight of the sheriff and it wasn't because his
mother had rationalized that since all of them were already in
town trying their best to get out of it there wouldn't be anybody
to be coming towards the Square on that side of the street so it
was simply just having one in the car with you even if she wasn't
driving it, that's all you needed to do: remembering them once
before in a car and his uncle driving and his uncle said then,

'All right, how do I do it, just shut both eyes and mash the
accelerator?' and his mother said.

'How many collisions did you ever see with women driving
both of them?' and his uncle said,

'All right, touché, maybe it's because one of them's car is still
in the shop where a man ran into it yesterday:' then he could no
longer see them but only hear the long tearing without beginning
or end and leaving no scar of tyres and pavement in friction like
the sound of raw silk and luckily the house was on the same
wrong side of the street too and carrying the sound into the yard
with him too and now he could do something about the laughing
by taking a moment to put his hand on whatever it was that
seemed to have got him started and bringing it out into the light
where even he could see it wasn't that funny; about ten thousand
miles of being funny enough to set his mother swearing; he said:

'They ran' and at once knew that was wrong, almost too late
even while he was standing right there looking at himself, walking
fast across the yard until he stopped and not jerked just pulled
his arm away and said, 'Look, I'm not crippled. I'm just tired.

I'm going up to my room and lie down a while:' and then to his uncle: 'I'll be all right then. Come up and call me in about fifteen minutes:' then stopped and turned again again to his uncle: 'I'll be ready in fifteen minutes:' and went on this time carrying it into the house with him and even in his room too he could still hear it even through the drawn shades and the red jumped behind his eyelids until he started up on to one elbow under his mother's hand too again to his uncle just beyond the footboard:

'Fifteen minutes. You wont go without me? You promise?'

'Sure,' his uncle said. 'I wont go without you. I'll just –'

'Will you please get to hell out of here, Gavin?' his mother said and then to him, 'Lie down' and he did and there it still was even through even against the hand, the narrow slim cool palm but too dry too rough and maybe even too cool, the dry hot gritty feel of his skull better than the feel of the hand on it because at least he was used to it by now; he had had it long enough; even rolling his head but about as much chance to escape that one frail narrow inevictable palm as to roll your forehead out from under a birthmark and it was not even a face now because their backs were towards him but the back of a head, the composite one back of one Head one fragile mushfilled bulb indefensible as an egg yet terrible in its concorded unanimity rushing not at him but away.

'They ran,' he said. 'They saved their consciences a good ten cents by not having to buy him a package of tobacco to show they had forgiven him.'

'Yes,' his mother said. 'Just let go:' which was like telling a man dangling with one hand over a cliff to just hold on: who wanted nothing right now but a chance to let go and relinquish into the nothing of sleep what little of nothing he still had who last night had wanted to go to sleep and could have but didn't have time and now wanted more than ever to go to sleep and had all the time in the world for the next fifteen minutes (or the next fifteen days or fifteen years as far as anybody knew because there was nothing anybody could do but hope Crawford Gowrie would decide to come in and hunt up the sheriff and say All right I did it because all they had was Lucas who said that Vinson Gowrie wasn't shot with a forty-one Colt or anyway his, Lucas' forty-one Colt and Buddy McCallum to say or not say Yes I swapped Crawford Gowrie a German pistol twenty-five years ago; not even Vinson Gowrie for somebody from the Memphis police to come and look at and say what bullet killed him because the sheriff had already let old Gowrie take him back home and wash the quicksand off and bury him again tomorrow: where this time Hampton and his uncle could go out there tomorrow night and dig him up) only he had forgotten how: or maybe that was it and he didn't dare relinquish into nothing what little he had left: which was nothing: no grief to be remembered nor pity nor even awareness of shame, no vindication of the deathless aspiration of man by man to man through the catharsis of pity and shame but instead only an old man for whom grief was not even a component of his own but merely a temporary phenomenon of his slain son jerking a strange corpse over on to its back not in appeasement to its one mute indicting cry not for pity not for vengeance but for justice but just to be sure he had the wrong one, crying cheery abashless and loud: 'Yep it's that damned Montgomery damned if it aint,' and a Face; who had no more expected Lucas to be swept out of his cell shoulder high on a tide of expiation and set for his moment of vindication and triumph on the base say of the Confederate monument (or maybe better on the balcony of the post office building beneath the pole where the national flag flew) than he had expected such for himself and Aleck Sander and Miss Habersham: who (himself) not only had not wanted that but could not have accepted it since it would have abrogated and made void the whole sum of what part he had done which had to be anonymous else it was valueless: who had wanted of course to leave his mark too on his time in man but only that, no more than that, some mark on his part in earth but humbly, waiting wanting humbly even, not really hoping even, nothing (which of course was everything) except his own one anonymous chance too to perform something passionate and brave and austere not just in but into man's enduring chronicle worthy of a place in it (who knew? perhaps adding even one anonymous jot to the austerity of the chronicle's brave passion) in gratitude for the gift of his time in it, wanting only that and not even with hope really, willing to accept the fact that he had missed it because he wasn't worthy, but certainly he hadn't expected this – not a life saved from death nor even a death saved from shame and indignity nor even the suspension of a sentence but merely the grudging pretermission of a date; not indignity shamed with its own shameful cancellation, not sublimation and humility with humility and pride remembered nor the pride of courage and passion nor of pity nor the pride and austerity and grief, but austerity itself debased by what it had gained, courage and passion befouled by

what they had had to cope with – a Face, the composite Face of
his native kind his native land, his people his blood his own with
whom it had been his joy and pride and hope to be found worthy
to present one united unbreakable front to the dark abyss the
night – a Face monstrous unravening omniverous and not even
uninsatiate, not frustrated nor even thwarted, not biding nor
waiting and not even needing to be patient since yesterday today
and tomorrow are Is: Indivisible: One (his uncle for this too,
anticipating this too two or three or four years ago as his uncle
had everything else which as he himself became more and more
a man he had found to be true: 'It's all *now* you see. Yesterday
wont be over until tomorrow and tomorrow began ten thousand
years ago. For every Southern boy fourteen years old, not once
but whenever he wants it, there is the instant when it's still not
yet two o'clock on that July afternoon in 1863, the brigades are
in position behind the rail fence, the guns are laid and ready in
the woods and the furled flags are already loosened to break out
and Pickett himself with his long oiled ringlets and his hat in one
hand probably and his sword in the other looking up the hill
waiting for Longstreet to give the word and it's all in the balance,
it hasn't happened yet, it hasn't even begun yet, it not only hasn't
begun yet but there is still time for it not to begin against that
position and those circumstances which made more men than
Garnett and Kemper and Armstead and Wilcox look grave yet
it's going to begin; we all know that; we have come too far with
too much at stake and that moment doesn't need even a fourteen-
year-old boy to think *This time. Maybe this time* with all this much
to lose and all this much to gain: Pennsylvania, Maryland, the
world, the golden dome of Washington itself to crown with
desperate and unbelievable victory the desperate gamble, the cast
made two years ago; or to anyone who ever sailed even a skiff
under a quilt sail, the moment in 1492 when somebody thought
This is it: the absolute edge of no return, to turn back now and
make home or sail irrevocably on and either find land or plunge
over the world's roaring rim. A small voice, a sound sensitive
lady poet of the time of my youth said *the scattered tea goes with
the leaves and every day a sunset dies:* a poet's extravagance which
as quite often mirrors truth but upside down and backward since
the mirror's unwitting manipulator busy in his preoccupation has
forgotten that the back of it is glass too: because if they only did,
instead of which yesterday's sunset and yesterday's tea both
are inextricable from the scattered indestructible uninfusable

grounds blown through the endless corridors of tomorrow, into the shoes we will have to walk in and even the sheets we will have (or try) to sleep between: because you escape nothing, you flee nothing; the pursuer is what is doing the running and tomorrow night is nothing but one long sleepless wrestle with yesterday's omissions and regrets.'): who had pretermitted not even a death nor even a death to Lucas but merely Lucas, Lucas in ten thousand Sambo-avatars to scurry unheeding and not even aware through that orifice like mice through the slot of a guillotine until at the One unheeding moment the unheeding unwitting uncaring chopper falls; tomorrow or at least tomorrow or at most tomorrow and perhaps this time to intervene where angels fear no white and black children sixteen and an old white spinster long on the way to eighty; who ran, fled not even to deny Lucas but just to keep from having to send up to him by the drugstore porter a can of tobacco not at all to say they were sorry but so they wouldn't have to say out loud that they were wrong: and spurned the cliff away in one long plunge up and up slowing into it already hearing it, only the most faintly oscillant now hearing it listening to it, not moving yet nor even opening his eyes as he lay for a moment longer listening to it, then opened them and then his uncle stood silhouetted against the light beyond the footboard in that utter that complete that absolute silence now with nothing in it now but the breathing of darkness and the tree-frogs and bugs: no fleeing nor repudiation nor for this moment more even urgency anywhere in the room or outside it either above or below or before or behind the tiny myriad beast-sounds and the vast systole and diastole of summer night.

'It's gone,' he said.

'Yes,' his uncle said. 'They're probably all in bed asleep by now. They got home to milk and even have time before dark to chop wood for tomorrow's breakfast too.'

Which made once though still he didn't move. 'They ran,' he said.

'No,' his uncle said. 'It was more than, that.'

'They ran,' he said. 'They reached the point where there was nothing left for them to do but admit that they were wrong. So they ran home.'

'At least they were moving,' his uncle said: which made twice: who hadn't even needed the first cue since not only the urgency the need the necessity to move again or rather not really to have stopped moving at all at that moment four or five or six hours or whatever it had been ago when he really believed he was going to lie down for only fifteen minutes (and which incidentally knew fifteen minutes whether he apparently did or not) hadn't come back, it had never been anywhere to come back from because it was still there, had been there all the time, never for one second even vacated even from behind the bizarre phantasmagoriae whose ragtag and bobends still befogged him, with or among which he had wasted nearer fifteen hours than fifteen minutes; it was still there or at least his unfinished part in it which was not even a minuscule but rather a minutecule of his uncle's and the sheriff's in the unfinishability of Lucas Beauchamp and Crawford Gowrie since as far as they knew before he lost track this morning neither of them knew what they were going to do next even before Hampton had disposed of what little of evidence they had by giving it back to old one-armed pistol Gowrie where even two children and an old woman couldn't get it back this time; the need not to finish anything but just to keep moving not even to remain where they were but just desperately to keep up with it like having to run on a treadmill not because you wanted to be where the treadmill was but simply not to be flung pell-mell still running frantically backwards off the whole stage out of sight, and not waiting static for the moment to flow back into him again and explode him up into motion but rather already in endless motion like the treadmill's endless band less than an inch's fraction above the ultimate point of his nose and chest where the first full breath would bring him into its snatching orbit, himself lying beneath it like a hobo trapped between the rails under a speeding train, safe only so long as he did not move.

So he moved; he said 'Time:' swinging his legs over: 'What time is it? I said fifteen minutes. You promised –'

'It's only nine-thirty,' his uncle said. 'Plenty of time for a shower and your supper too. They wont leave before we get there.'

'They?' he said: up on to his bare feet (he had not undressed except his shoes and socks) already reaching for his slippers. 'You've been back to town. Before we get there? We're not going with them?'

'No,' his uncle said. 'It'll take both of us to hold Miss Habersham back. She's going to meet us at the office. So move along now; she's probably already waiting for us.'

'Yes,' he said. But he was already unfastening his shirt and his belt and trousers too with the other hand, all ready to step in one motion out of both. And this time it was laughing. It was all right. You couldn't even hear it. 'So that was why,' he said. 'So their women wouldn't have to chop wood in the dark with half-awake children holding lanterns.'

'No,' his uncle said. 'They were not running from Lucas. They had forgotten about him –'

'That's exactly what I'm saying,' he said. 'They didn't even wait to send him a can of tobacco and say It's all right, old man, everybody makes mistakes and we wont hold this one against you.'

'Was that what you wanted?' his uncle said. 'The can of tobacco? That would have been enough? – Of course it wouldn't. Which is one reason why Lucas will ultimately get his can of tobacco; they will insist on it, they will have to. He will receive instalments on it for the rest of his life in this country whether he wants them or not and not just Lucas but *Lucas: Sambo* since what sets a man writhing sleepless in bed at night is not having injured his fellow so much as having been wrong; the mere injury (if he cannot justify it with what he calls logic) he can efface by destroying the victim and the witnesses but the mistake is his and that is one of his cats which he always prefers to choke to death with butter. So Lucas will get his tobacco. He wont want it of course and he'll try to resist it. But he'll get it and so we shall watch right here in Yoknapatawpha County the ancient oriental relationship between the saviour and the life he saved turned upside down: Lucas Beauchamp once the slave of any white man within range of whose notice he happened to come, now tyrant over the whole county's white conscience. And they – Beat One and Two and Three and Five – knew that too so why take time now to send him a ten-cent can of tobacco when they have got to spend the balance of their lives doing it? So they had dismissed him for the time. They were not running from him, they were running from Crawford Gowrie; they simply repudiated not even in horror but in absolute unanimity a shall-not and should-not which without any warning whatever turned into a *must*-not. *Thou shalt not kill* you see – no accusative, heatless: a simple moral precept; we have accepted it in the distant anonymity of our forefathers, had it so long, cherished it, fed it, kept the sound of it alive and the very words themselves unchanged, handled it so long that all the corners are now worn smoothly off; we can sleep right in the bed with it; we have even distilled our own antidotes for it as the foresighted housewife keeps a solution of mustard or handy eggwhites on the same shelf with the ratpoison; as familiar as grandpa's face, as unrecognizable as grandpa's face beneath the turban of an Indian prince, as abstract as grandpa's flatulence at the family supper-table; even when it breaks down and the spilled blood stands sharp and glaring in our faces we still have the precept, still intact, still true: *we shall not kill* and maybe next time we even wont. But *thou shall not kill thy mother's child.* It came right down into the street that time to walk in broad daylight at your elbow, didn't it?'

'So for a lot of Gowries and Workitts to burn Lucas Beauchamp to death with gasoline for something he didn't even do is one thing but for a Gowrie to murder his brother is another.'

'Yes,' his uncle said.

'You cant say that,' he said.

'Yes,' his uncle said. '*Thou shalt not kill* in precept and even when you do, precept still remains unblemished and scarless: *Thou shalt not kill* and who knows, perhaps next time maybe you wont. But *Gowrie must not kill Gowrie's brother:* no maybe about it, no next time to maybe not Gowrie kill Gowrie because there must be no first time. And not just for Gowrie but for all: Stevens and Mallison and Edmonds and McCaslin too; if we are not to hold to the belief that that point not just shall not but must not and *can*not come at which Gowrie or Ingrum or Stevens or Mallison may shed Gowrie or Ingrum or Stevens or Mallison blood, how hope ever to reach that one where *Thou shalt not kill at all* where Lucas Beauchamp's life will be secure not despite the fact that he is Lucas Beauchamp but because he is?'

'So they ran to keep from having to lynch Crawford Gowrie,' he said.

'They wouldn't have lynched Crawford Gowrie,' his uncle said. 'There were too many of them. Dont you remember, they packed the street in front of the jail and the Square too all morning while they still believed Lucas had shot Vinson Gowrie in the back without bothering him at all?'

'They were waiting for Beat Four to come in and do it.'

'Which is exactly what I am saying – granted for the moment that that's true. That part of Beat Four composed of Gowries and Workitts and the four or five others who wouldn't have given a Gowrie or Workitt either a chew of tobacco and who would have come along just to see the blood, is small enough to produce a mob. But not all of them together because there is a simple numerical point at which a mob cancels and abolishes itself, maybe because it has finally got too big for darkness, the cave it was spawned in is no longer big enough to conceal it from light and so at last whether it will or no it has to look at itself, or maybe because the amount of blood in one human body is no longer enough, as one peanut might titillate one elephant but not two or ten. Or maybe it's because man having passed into mob passes then into mass which abolishes mob by absorption, metabolism, then having got too large even for mass becomes man again conceptible of pity and justice and conscience even if only in the recollection of his long painful aspiration towards them, towards that something anyway of one serene universal light.'

'So man is always right,' he said.

'No,' his uncle said. 'He tries to be if they who use him for their own power and aggrandizement let him alone. Pity and justice and conscience too – that belief in more than the divinity of individual man (which we in America have debased into a national religion of the entrails in which man owes no duty to his soul because he has been absolved of soul to owe duty to and instead is static heir at birth to an inevictable quit-claim on a wife a car a radio and an old-age pension) but in the divinity of his continuity as Man; think how easy it would have been for them to attend to Cawford Gowrie: no mob moving fast in darkness watching constantly over its shoulder but one indivisible public opinion: that peanut vanishing beneath a whole concerted trampling herd with hardly one elephant to really know the peanut had even actually been there since the main reason for a mob is that the individual red hand which actually snapped the thread may Danish for ever into one inviolable confraternity of nameless-ness: where in this case that one would have had no more reason to lie awake at night afterwards than a paid hangman. They didn't want to destroy Crawford Gowrie. They repudiated him. If they had lynched him they would have taken only his life. What they really did was worse: they deprived him to the full extent of their capacity of his citizenship in man.'

He didn't move yet. 'You're a lawyer.' Then he said, 'They were not running from Crawford Gowrie or Lucas Beauchamp either. They were running from themselves. They ran home to hide their heads under the bedclothes from their own shame.'

'Exactly correct,' his uncle said. 'Haven't I been saying that all the time? There were too many of them. This time there were enough of them to be able to run from shame, to have found

unbearable the only alternative which would have been the mob's:
which (the mob) because of its smallness and what it believed was
its secretness and tightness and what it knew to be its absolute
lack of trust in one another, would have chosen the quick and
simple alternative of abolishing knowledge of the shame by
destroying the witness to it. So as you like to put it they ran.'

'Leaving you and Mr Hampton to clean up the vomit, which
even dogs dont do. Though of course Mr Hampton is a paid dog
and I reckon you might be called one too – Because dont forget
Jefferson either,' he said. 'They were clearing off out of sight
pretty fast too. Of course some of them couldn't because it was
still only the middle of the afternoon so they couldn't shut up
the stores and run home too yet; there still might be a chance to
sell each other a nickel's worth of something.'

'I said Stevens and Mallison too,' his uncle said.

'Not Stevens,' he said. 'And not Hampton either. Because
somebody had to finish it, somebody with a strong enough
stomach to mop a floor. The sheriff to catch (or try to or hope
to or whatever it is you are going to do) the murderer and a
lawyer to defend the lynchers.'

'Nobody lynched anybody to be defended from it,' his uncle
said.

'All right,' he said. 'Excuse them then.'

'Nor that either,' his uncle said. 'I'm defending Lucas Beauchamp. I'm defending Sambo from the North and East and West
– the outlanders who will fling him decades back not merely into
injustice but into grief and agony and violence too by forcing on
us laws based on the idea that man's injustice to man can be
abolished overnight by police. Sambo will suffer it of course;
there are not enough of him yet to do anything else. And he will
endure it, absorb it and survive because he is Sambo and has that
capacity; he will even beat us there because he has the capacity
to endure and survive but he will be thrown back decades and
what he survives to may not be worth having because by that
time divided we may have lost America.'

'But you're still excusing it.'

'No,' his uncle said. 'I only say that the injustice is ours, the
South's. We must expiate and abolish it ourselves, alone and
without help nor even (with thanks) advice. We owe that to Lucas
whether he wants it or not (and this Lucas anyway wont) not
because of his past since a man or a race either if he's any good
can survive his past without even needing to escape from it and

not because of the high quite often only too rhetorical rhetoric
of humanity but for the simple indubitable practical reason of
his future: that capacity to survive and absorb and endure and
still be steadfast.'

'All right,' he said again. 'You're still a lawyer and they still
ran. Maybe they intended for Lucas to clean it up since he came
from a race of floor-moppers. Lucas and Hampton and you since
Hampton ought to do something now and then for his money
and they even elected you to a salary too. Did they think to tell
you how to do it? what to use for bait to get Crawford Gowrie to
come in and say All right, boys, I pass. Deal them again. Or were
they too busy being – being . . .'

His uncle said quietly: 'Righteous?'

Now he completely stopped. But only for a second. He said,
'They ran,' calm and completely final, not even contemptuous,
flicking the shirt floating away behind him and at the same
moment dropping the trousers and stepping barefoot out of them
in nothing now but shorts. 'Besides, it's all right. I dreamed
through all that; I dreamed through them too, dreamed them
away too; let them stay in bed or milking their cows before dark
or chopping wood before dark or after or by lanterns or not
lanterns either. Because they were not the dream; I just passed
them to get to the dream –' talking quite fast now, a good deal
faster than he realized until it would be too late: 'It was something
. . . somebody . . . something about how maybe this was too much
to expect of us, too much for people just sixteen or going on
eighty or ninety or whatever she is to have to bear, and then
right off I was answering what you told me, you remember, about
the English boys not much older than me leading troops and
flying scout aeroplanes in France in 1918? how you said that by
1918 all British officers seemed to be either subalterns of seventeen or one-eyed or one-armed or one-legged colonels of twenty-
three?' – checking then or trying to because he had got the
warning at last quite sharp not as if he had heard suddenly in
advance the words he was going to say but as if he had discovered
suddenly not what he had already said but where it was going,
what the ones he had already spoken were going to compel him
to say in order bring them to a stop: but too late of course
like mashing suddenly on the brake pedal going downhill then
discovering to your horror that the brake rod had snapped:
'– only there was something else too – I was trying . . .' and he
stopped them at last feeling the hot hard blood burn all the way

up his neck into his face and nowhere even to look not because
he was standing there almost naked to begin with but because
no clothes nor expression nor talking either smoke-screened
anything from his uncle's bright grave eyes.

'Yes?' his uncle said. Then his uncle said, 'Yes. Some things
you must always be unable to bear. Some things you must never
stop refusing to bear. Injustice and outrage and dishonour and
shame. No matter how young you are or how old you have got.
Not for kudos and not for cash: your picture in the paper nor
money in the bank either. Just refuse to bear them. That it?'

'Who, me,' he said, moving now already crossing the room,
not even waiting for the slippers. 'I haven't been a Tenderfoot
scout since I was twelve years old.'

'Of course not,' his uncle said. 'But just regret it; don't be
ashamed.'

Chapter Ten

Perhaps eating had something to do with it, not even pausing
while he tried with no particular interest nor curiosity to compute
how many days since he had sat down to a table to eat and then
in the same chew as it were remembering that it had not been
one yet since even though already half asleep he had eaten a
good breakfast at the sheriff's at four this morning: remembering
how his uncle (sitting across the table drinking coffee) had said
that man didn't necessarily eat his way through the world but by
the act of eating and maybe only by that did he actually enter
the world, get himself into the world: not through it but into it,
burrowing into the world's teeming solidarity like a moth into
wool by the physical act of chewing and swallowing the substance
of its warp and woof and so making, translating into a part of
himself and his memory, the whole history of man or maybe even
relinquishing by mastication, abandoning, eating it into to be
annealed, the proud vainglorious minuscule which he called his
memory and his self and his I-Am into that vast teeming anony-

mous solidarity of the world from beneath which the ephemeral
rock would cool and spin away to dust not even remarked and
remembered since there was no yesterday and tomorrow didn't
even exist so maybe only an ascetic living in a cave on acorns and
spring water was really capable of vainglory and pride; maybe
you had to live in a cave on acorns and spring water in rapt
impregnable contemplation of your vainglory and righteousness
and pride in order to keep up to that high intolerant pitch of its
worship which brooked no compromise: eating steadily and quite
a lot too and at what even he knew by this time was too fast since
he had been hearing it for sixteen years and put his napkin down
and rose and one last wail from his mother (and he thought how
women couldn't really stand anything except tragedy and poverty
and physical pain; how this morning when he was where at sixteen
he had no business being and doing what even at twice sixteen
he had no business doing: chasing over the country with the
sheriff digging up murdered corpses out of a ditch: she had been
a hundred times less noisy than his father and a thousand times
more valuable, yet now when all he intended was to walk to town
with his uncle and sit for an hour or so in the same office in
which he had already spent a probably elapsed quarter of his life,
she had completely abolished Lucas Beauchamp and Crawford
Gowrie both and had gone back indefatigable to the day fifteen
years ago when she had first set out to persuade him he couldn't
button his pants):
   'But why cant Miss Habersham come here to wait?'
   'She can,' his uncle said. 'I'm sure she can find the house again.'
   'You know what I mean,' she said. 'Why dont you make her?
Sitting around a lawyer's office until twelve o'clock at night is no
place for a lady.'
   'Neither was digging up Jake Montgomery last night,' his uncle
said. 'But maybe this time we will break Lucas Beauchamp of
making this constant drain on her gentility. Come along, Chick:'
and so out of the house at last, not walking out of the house into
it because he had brought it out of the house with him, having
at some point between his room and the front door not acquired
it nor even simply entered it nor even actually regained it but
rather expiated his aberration from it, become once more worthy
to be received into it since it was his own or rather he was its and
so it must have been the eating, he and his uncle once more
walking the same street almost exactly as they had walked it not
twenty-two hours ago which had been empty then with a sort of

aghast recoiled consternation: because it was not empty at all now, deserted and empty of movement certainly running as vacant of life from street lamp to street lamp as a dead street through an abandoned city but not really abandoned not really withdrawn but only making way for them who could do it better, only making way for them who could do it right, not to interfere or get in the way or even offer suggestion or even permit (with thanks) advice to them who would do it right and in their own homely way since it was their own grief and their own shame and their own expiation, laughing again now but it was all right, thinking: *Because they always have me and Aleck Sander and Miss Habersham, not to mention Uncle Gavin and a sworn badge-wearing sheriff:* when suddenly he realized that that was a part of it too that fierce desire that they should be perfect because they were his and he was theirs, that furious intolerance of any one single jot or tittle less than absolute perfection – that furious almost instinctive leap and spring to defend them from anyone anywhere so that he might excoriate them himself without mercy since they were his own and he wanted no more save to stand with them unalterable and impregnable: one shame if shame must be, one expiation since expiation must surely be but above all one unalterable durable impregnable one: one people one heart one land: so that suddenly he said,

'Look –' and stopped but as always no more was needed:

'Yes?' his uncle said, then when he said no more: 'Ah, I see. It's not that they were right but that you were wrong.'

'I was worse,' he said. 'I was righteous.'

'It's all right to be righteous,' his uncle said. 'Maybe you were right and they were wrong. Just don't stop.'

'Dont stop what?' he said,

'Even bragging and boasting is all right too,' his uncle said. 'Just dont stop.'

'Dont stop what?' he said again. But he knew what now; he said.

'Aint it about time you stopped being a Tenderfoot scout too?'

'This is not Tenderfoot,' his uncle said. 'This is the third degree. What do you call it? –'

'Eagle scout,' he said.

'Eagle scout,' his uncle said. 'Tenderfoot is, Don't accept. Eagle scout is, Don't stop. You see? No, that's wrong. Don't bother to see. Don't even bother to not forget it. Just don't stop.'

'No,' he said. 'We don't need to worry about stopping now. It seems to me what we have to worry about now is where we're going and how.'

'Yes you do,' his uncle said. 'You told me yourself about fifteen minutes ago, dont you remember? About what Mr Hampton and Lucas were going to use for bait to fetch Crawford Gowrie in to where they could put Mr Hampton's hand on him? They're going to use Lucas –'

And he would remember: himself and his uncle standing beside the sheriff's car in the alley beside the jail watching Lucas and the sheriff emerge from the jail's side door and cross the dark yard towards them. It was quite dark in fact since the street light at the corner didn't reach this far nor any sound either; only a little after ten o'clock and on Monday night too yet the sky's dark bowl cupped as though in a vacuum like the old bride's bouquet under its glass bell the town, the Square which was more than dead: abandoned: because he had gone on to look at it, without stopping leaving his uncle standing at the corner of the alley who said after him:

'Where are you going?' but not even answering, walking the last silent and empty block, ringing his footfalls deliberate and unsecret into the hollow silence, unhurried and solitary but nothing at all of forlorn, instead with a sense a feeling not possessive but proprietary, viceregal, with humility still, himself not potent but at least the vessel of a potency like the actor looking from wings or perhaps empty balcony down upon the waiting stage vacant yet garnished and empty yet, nevertheless where in a moment now he will walk and posture in the last act's absolute cynosure, himself in himself nothing and maybe no world-beater of a play either but at least his to finish it, round it and put it away intact and unassailable, complete: and so on to into the dark and empty Square stopping as soon as he could perceive at effortless once that whole dark lifeless rectangle with but one light anywhere and that in the cafe which stayed open all night on account of the long-haul trucks whose (the cafe's) real purpose some said, the real reason for the grant of its licence by the town was to keep Willy Ingrum's nocturnal counterpart awake who although the town had walled him off a little cubby-hole of an office in an alley with a stove and a telephone he wouldn't stay there but used instead the cafe where there was somebody to talk to and he could be telephoned there of course but some people old ladies especially didn't like to page the policeman in an all-night jukejoint coffee stall so the office telephone had been connected to a big burglar alarm bell on the outside wall loud enough for the counterman or a truck driver in the cafe to hear it and tell him it was ringing, and the two lighted second-storey windows (and he thought that Miss Habersham really had persuaded his uncle to give her the key to the office and then he thought that that was wrong, his uncle had persuaded her to take the key since she would just as soon have sat in the parked truck until they came - and then added If she had waited because that was certainly wrong and what had really happened was that his uncle had locked her up in the office to give the sheriff and Lucas time to get out of town) but since the lights in a lawyer's office were liable to burn any time the lawyer or the janitor forgot to turn them off when they left and the cafe like the power plant was a public institution they didn't count and even the cafe was just lighted (he couldn't see into it from here but he could have heard and he thought how that, formally shutting off the jukebox for twelve hours had probably been the night marshal's first official act besides punching every hour the time clock on the wall at the bank's back door since the mad-dog scare last August) and he remembered the other the normal Monday nights when no loud fury of blood and revenge and racial and family solidarity had come roaring in from Beat Four (or Beat One or Two or Three or Five for that matter or for the matter of that from the purlieus of the urban Georgian porticoes themselves) to rattle and clash among the old bricks and the old trees and the Doric capitals and leave them for one night anyway stricken: ten o'clock on Monday night and although the first run of the film at the picture show would be forty or fifty minutes over now a few of the patrons who had come in late would still be passing homeward and all the young men sitting since that time drinking coca cola and playing nickels into the drugstore jukebox would certainly be, strolling timeless and in no haste since they were going nowhere since the May night itself was their destination and they carried that with them walking in it and (stock-auction day) even a few belated cars and trucks whose occupants had stayed in for the picture show too or to visit and take supper with kin or friends and now at last dispersing nightward sleepward tomorrow-ward about the dark mile-compassing land, remembering no longer ago than last night when he had thought it was empty too until he had had time to listen to it a moment and realized that it was not empty at all: a Sunday night but with more than Sunday night's quiet, the sort of quiet

in fact that no night had any business with and of all nights
Sunday night never, which had been Sunday night only because
they had already named the calendar when the sheriff brought
Lucas in to jail: an emptiness you could call emptiness provided
you called vacant and empty the silent and lifeless terrain in
front of a mobilized army or peaceful the vestibule to a powder
magazine or quiet the spillway under the locks of a dam – a sense
not of waiting but of incrementation, not of people – women and
old folks and children – but of men not so much grim as grave
and not so much tense as quiet, sitting quietly and not even
talking much in back rooms and not just the bath-cabinets and
johns behind the barbershop and the shed behind the poolhall
stacked with soft drink cases and littered with empty whisky
bottles but the stock-rooms of stores and garages and behind the
drawn shades of the offices themselves whose owners even the
proprietors of the stores and garages conceded to belong not to
a trade but a profession, not waiting for an event a moment in
time to come to them but for a moment in time when in almost
volitionless concord they themselves would create the event,
preside at and even serve an instant which was not even six
or twelve or fifteen hours belated but was instead simply the
continuation of the one when the bullet struck Vinson Gowrie
and there had been no time between and so for all purposes
Lucas was already dead since he had died then on the same
instant when he had forfeited his life and theirs was merely to
preside at his suttee, and now tonight to remember because
tomorrow it would be over, tomorrow of course the Square would
wake and stir, another day and it would fling off hangover,
another and it would even fling off shame so that on Saturday
the whole county with one pierceless unanimity of click and pulse
and hum would even deny that the moment had ever existed
when they could have been mistaken: so that he didn't even need
to remind himself in the absolute the utter the complete silence
that the town was not dead nor even abandoned but only withdrawn giving room to do what homely thing must be done in its
own homely way without help or interference or even (thank
you) advice: three amateurs, an old white spinster and a white
child and a black one to expose Lucas' wouldbe murderer, Lucas
himself and the county sheriff to catch him and so one last time:
remembering: his uncle while he still stood barefoot on the run
with both edges of the unbuttoned shirt arrested in his hands
thirty minutes ago and when they were mounting the last pitch

of hill towards the church eleven hours ago and on what must have been a thousand other times since he had got big enough to listen and to understand and to remember: – *to defend not Lucas not even the union of the United States but the United States from the outlanders North East and West who with the highest of motives and intentions (let us say) are essaying to divide it at a time when no people dare risk division by using federal laws and federal police to abolish Lucas' shameful condition, there may not be in any random one thousand Southerners one who really grieves or even is really concerned over that condition nevertheless neither is there always one who would himself lynch Lucas no matter what the occasion yet not one of that nine hundred ninety-nine plus that other first one making the thousand whole again would hesitate to repulse with force (and one would still be that lyncher) the outlander who came down here with force to intervene or punish him, you say (with sneer) You must know Sambo well to arrogate to yourself such calm assumption of his passivity and I reply I dont know him at all and in my opinion no white man does but I do know the Southern white man not only the nine hundred and ninety-nine but that one other too because he is our own too and more than that, that one other does not exist only in the South you will see allied not only North and East and West and Sambo against a handful of white men in the South but a paper alliance of theorists and fanatics and private and personal avengers plus a number of others under the assumption of enough physical miles to afford a principle against and possibly even out-numbered a concorded South which has drawn recruits whether it would or no from your own back-areas, not just your hinterland but the fine cities of your cultural pride your Chicagoes and Detroits and Los Angeleses and wherever else live ignorant people who fear the colour of any skin or shape of nose save their own and who will grasp this opportunity to vent on Sambo the whole sum of their ancestral horror and scorn and fear of Indian and Chinese and Mexican and Carib and Jew, you will force us the one out of that first random thousand and the nine hundred and ninety-nine out of the second who do begrieve Lucas' shameful condition and would improve it and have and are and will until (not tomorrow perhaps) that condition will be abolished to be not forgotten maybe but at least remembered with less of pain and bitterness since justice was relinquished to him by us rather than torn from us and forced on him both with bayonets, willynilly into alliance with them with whom we have no kinship whatever in defence of a principle which we ourselves begrieve and abhor, we are in the position of the German after 1933 who had no other alternative between being either a Nazi or a Jew or the present*

Russian (European too for that matter) who hasn't even that but must be either a Communist or dead, only we must do it and we alone without help or interference or even (thank you) advice since only we can if Lucas' equality is to be anything more than its own prisoner inside an impregnable barricade of the direct heirs of the victory of 1861-5 which probably did more than even John Brown to stalemate Lucas' freedom which still seems to be in check going on a hundred years after Lee surrendered and when you say Lucas must not wait for that tomorrow because that tomorrow will never come because you not only cant you wont then we can only repeat Then you shall not and say to you Come down here and look at us before you make up your mind and you reply No thanks the smell is bad enough from here and we say Surely you will at least look at the dog you plan to housebreak, a people divided at a time when history is still showing us that the ante-room to dissolution is division and you say At least we perish in the name of humanity and we reply When all is stricken but that nominative pronoun and that verb what price Lucas' humanity then and turned and ran the short dead empty block back to the corner where his uncle had gone on without waiting and then up the alley too to where the sheriff's car stood, the two of them watching the sheriff and Lucas cross the dark yard towards them the sheriff in front and Lucas about five feet behind walking not fast but just intently, neither furtive nor covert but exactly like two men simply busy not exactly late but with no time to dawdle, through the gate and across to the car where the sheriff opened the back door and said,

'Jump in,' and Lucas got in and the sheriff closed the door and opened the front one and crawled grunting into it, the whole car squatting on to its springs and rims when he let himself down into the seat and turned the switch and started the engine, his uncle standing at the window now holding the rim of it in both hands as though he thought or hoped suddenly on some second thought to hold the car motionless before it could begin to move, saying what he himself had been thinking off and on for thirty or forty minutes:

'Take somebody with you.'

'I am,' the sheriff said. 'Besides I thought we settled all this three times this afternoon.'

'That's still just one no matter how many times you count Lucas,' his uncle said.

'You let me have my pistol,' Lucas said, 'and wont nobody have to do no counting. I'll do it:' and he thought how many times the sheriff had probably told Lucas by now to shut up, which

may have been why the sheriff didn't say it now: except that
(suddenly) he did, turning slowly and heavily and grunting in the
seat to look back at Lucas, saying in the plaintive heavily-sighing
voice:

'After all the trouble you got into Saturday standing with that
pistol in your pocket in the same ten feet of air a Gowrie was
standing in, you want to take it in your hand and walk around
another one. Now I want you to hush and stay hushed. And when
we begin to get close to Whiteleaf bridge I want you to be laying
on the floor close up against the seat behind me and still hushed.
You hear me?'

'I hear you,' Lucas said. 'But if I just had my pistol –' but the
sheriff had already turned to his uncle:

'No matter how many times you count Crawford Gowrie he's
still just one too:' and then went on in the mild sighing reluctant
voice which nevertheless was already answering his uncle's
thoughts before even his uncle could speak it: 'Who would he
get?' and he thought of that too remembering the long tearing
rubber-from-cement sound of the frantic cars and trucks scattering pell-mell hurling themselves in aghast irrevocable repudiation in all directions towards the county's outmost unmapped
fastness except that little island in Beat Four known as Caledonia
Church, into sanctuary: the old the used the familiar, home where
the women and older girls and children could milk and chop
wood for tomorrow's breakfast while the little ones held lanterns
and the men and older sons after they had fed the mules against
tomorrow's ploughing would sit on the front gallery waiting for
supper into the twilight: the whippoorwills: night: sleep: and this
he could even see (provided that even a murderer's infatuation
could bring Crawford Gowrie ever again into the range and
radius of that nub arm which – since Crawford was a Gowrie too
– in agreement here with the sheriff he didn't believe – and he
knew now why Lucas had ever left Fraser's store alive Saturday
afternoon, let alone ever got out of the sheriff's car at the jail:
that the Gowries themselves had known he hadn't done it so
they were just marking time waiting for somebody else, maybe
Jefferson to drag him out into the street until he remembered –
a flash, something like shame – the blue shirt squatting and the
stiff awkward single hand trying to brush the wet sand from the
dead face and he knew that whatever the furious old man might
begin to think tomorrow he held nothing against Lucas then
because there was no room for anything but his son) – night, the

diningroom perhaps and again seven Gowrie men in the twenty-
year womanless house because Forrest had come up from Vicksburg for the funeral yesterday and was probably still there this
morning when the sheriff sent word out for old Gowrie to meet
him at the church, a lamp burning in the centre of the table
among the crusted sugarbowls and molasses jugs and ketchup
and salt and pepper in the same labelled containers they had
come off the store shelf in and the old man sitting at the head
of it his one arm lying on the table in front of him and the big
pistol under his hand pronouncing judgement sentence doom
and execution too on the Gowrie who had cancelled his own
Gowriehood with his brother's blood, then the dark road the
truck (not commandeered this time because Vinson had owned
one new and big and powerful convertible for either logs or
cattle) the same twin driving it probably and the body boomed
down on to the running gear like a log itself with the heavy
logchains, fast out of Caledonia out of Beat Four into the dark
silent waiting town fast still up the quiet street across the Square
to the sheriff's house and the body tumbled and flung on to the
sheriff's front gallery and perhaps the truck even waiting while
the other Gowrie twin rang the doorbell. 'Stop worrying about
Crawford,' the sheriff said. 'He aint got anything against me. He
votes for me. His trouble right now is having to kill extra folks
like Jake Montgomery when all he ever wanted was just to keep
Vinson from finding out he had been stealing lumber from
him and Uncle Sudley Workitt. Even if he jumps on to the
runningboard before I have time to keep up with what's going
on he'll still have to waste a minute or two trying to get the door
open so he can see exactly where Lucas is – provided by that time
Lucas is doing good and hard what I told him to do, which I sure
hope for his sake he is.'
    'I'm going to,' Lucas said. 'But if I just had my –'
    'Yes,' his uncle said in the harsh voice: 'Provided he's there.'
    The sheriff sighed. 'You sent the message.'
    'What message I could,' his uncle said. 'However I could.
A message making an assignation between a murderer and a
policeman, that whoever finally delivers it to the murderer wont
even know was intended for the murderer, that the murderer
himself will not only believe he wasn't intended to get it but that
it's true.'
    'Well,' the sheriff said, 'he'll either get it or he wont get it and
he'll either believe it or he wont believe it and he'll either be

waiting for us in Whiteleaf bottom or he wont and if he aint me and Lucas will go on to the highway and come back to town.' He raced the engine let it idle again; now he turned on the lights. 'But he may be there. I sent a message too.'

'All right,' his uncle said. 'Why is that, Mr Bones?'

'I got the mayor to excuse Willy Ingrum so he could go out and set up with Vinson again tonight and before Willy left I told him in confidence I was going to run Lucas over to Hollymount tonight through the old Whiteleaf cutoff so Lucas can testify tomorrow at Jake Montgomery's inquest and reminded Willy that they aint finished the Whiteleaf fill yet and cars have to cross it in low gear and told him to be sure not to mention it to anybody.'

'Oh,' his uncle said, not quite turning the door loose yet. 'No matter who might have claimed Jake Montgomery alive he belongs to Yoknapatawpha County now – But then,' he said briskly, turning the door loose now, 'we're after just a murderer, not a lawyer – All right,' he said. 'Why dont you get started?'

'Yes,' the sheriff said. 'You go on to your office and watch out for Miss Eunice. Willy may have passed her on the street too and if he did she might still beat us to Whiteleaf bridge in that pickup.'

Then into the Square this time to cross it catacornered to where the pickup stood nosed-in empty to the otherwise empty kerb and up the long muted groan and rumble of the stairway to the open office door and passing through it he thought without surprise how she was probably the only woman he knew who would have withdrawn the borrowed key from the lock as soon as she opened the strange door not to leave the key on the first flat surface she passed but to put it back into the reticule or pocket or whatever she had put it in when it was lent to her and she wouldn't be sitting in the chair behind the table either and wasn't, sitting instead bolt upright in the hat but another dress which looked exactly like the one she had worn last night and the same handbag on her lap with the eighteen-dollar gloves clasped on top of it and the flat-heeled thirty-dollar shoes planted side by side on the floor in front of the hardest straightest chair in the room, the one beside the door which nobody ever really sat in no matter how crowded the office and only moving to the easy chair behind the table after his uncle had spent a good two minutes insisting and finally explained it might be two or three hours yet because she had the gold brooch watch on her bosom open when they came in and seemed to think that by this time the sheriff should not only have been back with Crawford Gowrie but probably on the way to the penitentiary with him: then he in his usual chair beside the water cooler and finally his uncle even struck the match to the cob pipe still talking not just through the smoke but into it with it:

'– what happened because some of it we even know let alone what Lucas finally told us by watching himself like a hawk or an international spy to keep from telling us anything that would even explain him let alone save him, Vinson and Crawford were partners buying the timber from old man Sudley Workitt who was Mrs Gowrie's second or fourth cousin or uncle or something, that is they had agreed with old Sudley on a price by the board foot but to be paid him when the lumber was sold which was not to be until the last tree was cut and Crawford and Vinson had delivered it and got their money and then they would pay old Sudley his, hiring a mill and crew to fell and saw and stack it right there within a mile of old Sudley's house and not one stick to be moved until it was all cut. Only – except this part we dont really know yet until Hampton gets his hands on Crawford except it's got to be this way or what in the world were you all doing digging Jake Montgomery out of Vinson's grave? – and every time I think about this part of it and remember you three coming back down that hill to the exact spot where two of you heard him and one of you even saw riding past the man who already with one murdered corpse on the mule in front of him experienced such a sudden and urgent alteration of plan that when Hampton and I got there hardly six hours later there was nobody in the grave at all –'

'But he didn't,' Miss Habersham said.

'– What?' his uncle said. '. . . Where was I? Oh yes – only Lucas Beauchamp taking his walk one night heard something and went and looked or maybe he was actually passing and saw or maybe he already had the idea which was why he took the walk or that walk that night and saw a truck whether he recognized it or not being loaded in the dark with that lumber which the whole neighbourhood knew was not to be moved until the mill itself closed up and moved away which would be some time yet and Lucas watched and listened and maybe he even went over in to Crossman County to Glasgow and Hollymount until he knew for sure not only who was moving some of that lumber every night or so, not much at a time, just exactly not quite enough for anyone who was not there everyday to notice its absence (and the only people there everyday or even interested even to that extent were Crawford who represented himself and his brother and uncle who owned the trees and the resulting lumber and so could do what they liked with it, the one of which was running about the country all day long attending to his other hot irons and the other an old rheumatic man to begin with and half blind on top of that who couldn't have seen anything even if he could have got that far from his house – and the mill crew who were hired by the day and so wouldn't have cared even if they had known what was going on at night as long as they got their pay every Saturday) but what he was doing with it, maybe learning even as far as Jake Montgomery though Lucas' knowing about Jake made no difference except that by getting himself murdered and into Vinson's grave Jake probably saved Lucas' life. But even when Hope told me how he had finally got that much out of Lucas in his kitchen this morning when Will Legate brought him from the jail and we were driving you home it explained only part of it because I was still saying what I had been saying ever since you all woke me this morning and Chick told me what Lucas had told him about the pistol: But why Vinson? Why did Crawford have to kill Vinson in order to obliterate the witness to his thieving? not that it shouldn't have worked of course since Lucas really should have died as soon as the first white man came in sight of him standing over Vinson's body with the handle of that pistol hunching the back of his coat, but why do it this way, by the bizarre detour of fratricide? so now that we had something really heavy enough to talk to Lucas with I went straight to Hampton's house this afternoon into the kitchen and there was Hampton's cook sitting on one side of the table and Lucas on the other eating greens and cornbread not from a plate but out of the two-gallon pot itself and I said,

' "And you let him catch you – and I dont mean Crawford –" and he said,

' "No. I means Vinson too. Only it was too late then, the truck was done already loaded and pulling out fast without no lights burning or nothing and he said Whose truck is that? and I never said nothing."

' "All right," I said. "Then what?"

' "That's all," Lucas said. "Nothing."

' "Didn't he have a gun?"

' "I dont know," Lucas said. "He had a stick:" and I said,

' "All right. Go on:" and he said,

' "Nothing. He just stood there a minute with the stick drawed

back and said Tell me whose truck that was and I never said
nothing and he lowered the stick back down and turned and then
I never saw him no more."

'"So you took your pistol," I said and he said, "and went –"
and he said,

'"I never had to. He come to me, I mean Crawford this time,
at my house the next night and was going to pay me to tell him
whose truck that was, a heap of money, fifty dollars, he showed
it to me and I said I hadn't decided yet whose truck it was and
he said he would leave me the money anyhow while I decided
and I said I had already decided what I was going to do, I would
wait until tomorrow – that was Friday night – for some kind of
a evidence that Mr Workitt and Vinson had got their share of
that missing timber money."

'"Yes?" I said. "Then what?"'

'"Then I would go and tell Mr Workitt he better –"'

'"Say that again," I said. "Slow."'

'"Tell Mr Workitt he better count his boards." ' "And you, a
Negro, were going up to a white man and tell him his niece's
sons were stealing from him – and a Beat Four white man on top
of that. Dont you know what would have happened to you?"'

'"It never had no chance," he said. "Because it was the next
day – Sat-dy – I got the message –" and I should have known
then about the pistol because obviously Gowrie knew about it;
his message couldn't have been *have replaced stolen money, would
like your personal approval, bring your pistol and be sociable* –
something like that so I said,

'"But why the pistol?" and he said,

'"It was Sat-dy," and I said,

'"Yes, the ninth. But why the pistol?" and then I understood;
I said: "I see. You wear the pistol when you dress up on Saturday
just like old Carothers did before he gave it to you:" and he said,

'"Sold it to me," and I said,

'"All right, go on," and he said,

'"– got the message to meet him at the store only –" ' and now
his uncle struck the match again and puffed the pipe still talking,
talking through the pipe stem with the smoke as though you were
watching the words themselves: 'Only he never got to the store,
Crawford met him in the woods sitting on a stump beside the
path waiting for him almost before Lucas had left home good
and now it was Crawford about the pistol, right off before Lucas
could say good afternoon or were Vinson and Mr Workitt glad

to get the money or anything, saying "Even if it will still shoot you probably couldn't hit anything with it" and so you can probably finish it yourself; Lucas said how Crawford finally put up a half dollar that Lucas couldn't hit the stump from fifteen feet away and Lucas hit it and Crawford gave him the half dollar and they walked on the other two miles towards the store until Crawford told Lucas to wait there, that Mr Workitt was sending a signed receipt for his share of the missing lumber to the store and Crawford would go and fetch it back so Lucas could see it with his own eyes and I said,

‘ "And you didn't suspicion anything even then?" and he said,

‘ "No. He cussed me so natural." And at least you can finish that, no need to prove any quarrel between Vinson and Crawford nor rack your brains very deep to imagine what Crawford said and did to have Vinson waiting at the store and then send him in front along the path since no more than this will do it: "All right. I've got him. If he still wont tell whose truck that was we'll beat it out of him:" because that doesn't really matter either, enough that the next Lucas saw was Vinson coming down the path from the store in a good deal of a hurry Lucas said but probably what he meant was impatient, puzzled and annoyed both but probably mostly annoyed, probably doing exactly what Lucas was doing: waiting for the other to speak and explain that Vinson quit waiting first according to Lucas, still walking saying getting as far as "So you changed your mind –" when Lucas said he tripped over something and kind of bucked down on to his face and presently Lucas remembered that he had heard the shot and realized that what Vinson had tripped over was his brother Crawford, then the rest of them were there Lucas said before he even had time to hear them running through the woods and I said,

‘ "I reckon it looked to you right then that you were getting ready to trip pretty bad over Vinson, old Slipworth and Adam Fraser or not" but at least I didn't say But why didn't you explain then and so at least Lucas didn't have to say Explain what to who: and so he was all right – I dont mean Lucas of course, I mean Crawford, no mere child of misfortune he –’ and there it was again and this time he knew what it was, Miss Habersham had done something he didn't know what, no sound and she hadn't moved and it wasn't even that she had got any stiller but something had occurred, not something happened to her from the outside in but something from the inside outwards as though she not only hadn't been surprised by it but had decreed authorized it but she hadn't moved at all not even to take an extra breath and his uncle hadn't even noticed that much '– but rather chosen and elected peculiar and unique out of man by the gods themselves to prove not to themselves because they had never doubted it but to man by this his lowest common denominator that he has a soul, driven at last to murder his brother –'

'He put him in quicksand,' Miss Habersham said.

'Yes,' his uncle said. 'Ghastly wasn't it – by the simple mischance of an old Negro man's insomnambulism and then having got away with that by means of a plan a scheme so simple and watertight in its biological and geographical psychology as to be what Chick here would call a natural, then to be foiled here by the fact that four years ago a child whose presence in the world he was not even aware of fell into a creek in the presence of that same Negro insomnambulist because this part we dont really know either and with Jake Montgomery in his present condition we probably never will though that doesn't really matter either since the fact still remains, why else was he in Vinson's grave except that in buying the lumber from Crawford (we found that out by a telephone call to the lumber's ultimate consignee in Memphis this afternoon) Jake Montgomery knew where it came from too since knowing that would have been Jake's nature and character too and indeed a factor in his middleman's profit and so when Vinson Crawford's partner tripped suddenly on death in the woods behind Fraser's store Jake didn't need a crystal ball to read that either and so if this be surmise then make the most of it or give Mr Hampton and me a better and we'll swap, Jake knew about Buddy McCallum's old war trophy too and I like to think for Crawford's sake –' and there it was again and still no outward sign but this time his uncle saw or felt or sensed (or however it was) it too and stopped and even for a second seemed about to speak then in the next one forgot it apparently, talking again: '– that maybe Jake named the price of his silence and even collected it or an instalment on it perhaps intending all the time to convict Crawford of the murder, perhaps with his contacts all established to get still more money or perhaps he didn't like Crawford and wanted revenge or perhaps a purist he drew the line at murder and simply dug Vinson up to load him on the mule and take him in to the sheriff but anyway on the night after the funeral somebody with a conceivable reason for digging Vinson up dug him up, which must have been Jake, and somebody who not only didn't want Vinson dug up but had a conceivable reason to be watching the someone who would have had a conceivable reason for digging him up, knew that he had been dug up within in – you said it was about ten when you and Aleck Sander parked the truck and it got dark enough for digging up graves about seven that night so that leaves three hours – and that's what I mean about Crawford,' his uncle said and this time he noticed that his uncle had even stopped, expecting it and it came but still no sound no movement, the hat immobile and exact the neat precision of the clasped gloves and handbag on her lap the shoes planted and motionless side by side as if she had placed them into a chalked diagram on the floor: '– watching there in the weeds behind the fence seeing himself not merely betrayed out of the blackmail but all the agony and suspense to go through again not to intention the physical labour who since one man already knew that the body couldn't bear examination by trained policemen, could never know how many others might know or suspect so the body would have to come out of the grave now though at least he had help here whether the help knew it or not so he probably waited until Jake had the body out and was all ready to load it on to the mule (and we found that out too, it was the Gowrie's plough mule, the same one the twins were riding this morning; Jake borrowed it himself late that Sunday afternoon and when you guess which Gowrie he borrowed it from you'll be right: it was Crawford) and he wouldn't have risked the pistol now anyway anymore than he would have used it if he could, who would rather have paid Jake over again the amount of the blackmail for the privilege of using whatever it was he crushed Jake's skull with and put him into the coffin and filled the grave back up – and here it is again, the desperate the dreadful urgency, the loneliness the pariah-hood having not only the horror and repudiation of all man against him but having to struggle with the sheer inertia of earth and the terrible heedless rush of time but even beating all that coalition at last, the grave decent again even to the displaced flowers and the evidence of his original crime at last disposed and secure –' and it would have been againbut this time his uncle didn't pause '– then to straighten up at last and for the first time draw a full breath since the moment when Jake had approached him rubbing his thumb against the tips of the same fingers – and then to hear whatever it was that sent him plunging back up the hill then crawling creeping to lie once more panting but this time not merely in rage and terror but in almost incredulous disbelief that one single man could be subject to this much bad luck, watching you three not only undo his work for the second time but double it now since you not only exposed Jake Montgomery but you refilled the grave and even put the flowers back: who couldn't afford to let his brother Vinson be found in that grave but durst not let Jake Montgomery be found in it when (as he must have known) Hope Hampton got there tomorrow:' and stopped this time waiting for her to say it and she did:

'He put his brother in quicksand.'

'Ah,' his uncle said. 'That moment may come to anyone when simply nothing remains to be done with your brother or husband or uncle or cousin or mother-in-law except destroy them. But you don't put them in quicksand. Is that it?'

'He put him in quicksand,' she said with calm and implacable finality, not moving nor stirring except her lips to speak until then she raised her hand and opened the watch pinned to her bosom and looked at it.

'They haven't reached Whiteleaf bottom yet,' his uncle said. 'But dont worry, he'll be there, my message might have reached him but no man in this county can possibly escape hearing anything ever told Willy Ingrum under the pledge of secrecy, because there's nothing else he can do you see because murderers are gamblers and like the amateur gambler the amateur murderer believes first not in his luck but in long shots, that the long shot will win simply because it's a long shot but besides that, say he already knew he was lost and nothing Lucas could testify about Jake Montgomery or anyone else could harm him further and that his one last slim chance was to get out of the country, or say he knew even that was vain, knew for sure that he was running through the last few pence and pennies of what he could still call freedom, suppose he even knew for certain that tomorrow's sun would not even rise for him – what would you want to do first, one last act and statement of your deathless principles before you left your native land for good and maybe even the world for good if your name was Gowrie and your blood and thinking and acting had been Gowrie all your life and you knew or even only believed or even only hoped that at a certain moment in an automobile creeping in low gear through a lonely midnight creek bottom would be the cause and reason for all your agony and frustration and outrage and grief and shame and irreparable loss and that not even a white man but a nigger and you still had the pistol

with at least one of the old original ten German bullets in it —
But dont worry,' he said quickly: 'Dont worry about Mr Hampton.
He probably wont even draw his pistol, I aint certain in fact that
he has one because he had a way of carrying right along with
him into all situations maybe not peace, maybe not abatement of
the base emotions but at least a temporary stalemate of crude
and violent behaviour just by moving slow and breathing hard,
this happened two or three terms ago back in the twenties, a
Frenchman's Bend lady naming no names at feud with another
lady over something which began (we understood) over the matter
of a prize cake at a church supper bazaar, whose — the second
lady's — husband owned the still which had been supplying Frenchman's Bend with whisky for years bothering nobody until the
first lady made official demand on Mr Hampton to go out there
and destroy the still and arrest the operator and then in about a
week or ten days came in to town herself and told him that if he
didn't she was going to report him to the governor of the state
and the president in Washington so Hope went that time, she
had not only given him explicit directions but he said there was
a path to it kneedeep in places where it had been trodden for
years beneath the weight of stopper-full gallon jugs so that you
could have followed it even without the flashlight which he had
and sure enough there was the still in as nice a location as you
could want, cosy and sheltered yet accessible too with a fire
burning under the kettle and a Negro tending it who of course
didn't know who owned it nor ran it nor anything about it even
before he recognized Hampton's size and finally even saw his
badge: who Hope said offered him a drink first and then did
fetch him a gourd of branch water and then made him comfortable sitting against a tree, even chunking the fire up to dry his
wet feet while he waited for the owner to come back, quite
comfortable Hope said, the two of them there by the fire in the
darkness talking about one thing and another and the Negro
asking him from time to time if he wouldn't like another gourd
of water until Hampton said the mockingbird was making so
confounded much racket that finally he opened his eyes blinking
for a while in the sunlight until he got them focussed and there
the mockingbird was on a limb not three feet above his head and
before they loaded up the still to move it away somebody had
gone to the nearest house and fetched back a quilt to spread over
him and a pillow to put under his head and Hope said he noticed
the pillow even had a fresh slip on it when he took it and the

quilt to Varner's store to be returned with thanks to whoever owned them and came on back to town. And another time –'

'I'm not worrying,' Miss Habersham said.

'Of course not,' his uncle said. 'Because I know Hope Hampton –'

'Yes,' Miss Habersham said. 'I know Lucas Beauchamp.'

'Oh' his uncle said. Then he said, 'Yes.' Then he said, 'Of course.' Then he said, 'Let's ask Chick to plug in the kettle and we'll have some coffee while we wait, what do you think?'

'That will be nice,' Miss Habersham said.

Chapter Eleven

Finally he even got up and went to one of the front windows looking down into the Square because if Monday was stock-auction and trade day then Saturday was certainly radio and automobile day; on Monday they were mostly men and they drove in and parked the cars and trucks around the Square and went straight to the sales barns and stayed there until time to come back to the Square and eat dinner and then went back to the sales barns and stayed there until time to come and get in the cars and trucks and drive home before full dark. But not Saturday; they were men and women and children too then and the old people and the babies and the young couples to buy the licences for the weddings in the country churches tomorrow, come in to do a week's shopping for staples and delicacies like bananas and twenty-five-cent sardines and machine-made cakes and pies and clothes and stockings and feed and fertilizer and plough-gear: which didn't take long for any of them and no time at all for some of them so that some of the cars never really became permanently stationary at all and within an hour or so many of the others had joined them moving steadily processional and quite often in second gear because of their own density round and round the Square then out to the end of the tree-dense residential streets to turn and come back and circle round and round the Square again as if they had come all the way in from the distant circumambient settlements and crossroads stores and isolate farms for that one purpose of enjoying the populous coming and going and motion and recognizing one another and the zephyr-like smoothness of the paved streets and alleys themselves as well as looking at the neat new painted small houses among their minute neat yards and flowerbeds and garden ornaments which in the last few years had come to line them as dense as sardines or bananas; as a result of which the radios had to play louder than ever through their supercharged amplifiers to be heard above the mutter of exhausts and swish of tyres and the grind of gears and the constant horns, so that long before you even reached the Square you not only couldn't tell where one began and another left off but you didn't even have to try to distinguish what any of them were playing or trying to sell you.

But this one seemed to be even a Saturday among Saturdays so that presently his uncle had got up from behind the table and come to the other window too, which was why they happened to see Lucas before he reached the office though that was not yet; he was still standing (so he thought) alone at the window looking down into the Square thronged and jammed as he couldn't remember it before – the bright sunny almost hot air heavy with the smell of blooming locust from the courthouse yard, the sidewalks dense and massed and slow with people black and white come in to town today as if by concert to collect at compound and so discharge not merely from balance but from remembering too that other Saturday only seven days ago of which they had been despoiled by an old Negro man who had got himself into the position where they had had to believe he had murdered a white man – that Saturday and Sunday and Monday only a week past yet which might never have been since nothing of them remained: Vinson and his brother Crawford (in his suicide's grave and strangers would be asking for weeks yet what sort of jail and sheriff Yoknapatawpha County had, where a man locked in it for murder could still get hold of a Luger pistol even if it didn't have but one bullet in it and for that many weeks nobody in Yoknapatawpha County would still be able to tell him) side by side near their mother's headstone in Caledonia churchyard and Jake Montgomery over in Crossman County where somebody probably claimed him too for the same reason somebody did Crawford and Miss Habersham sitting in her own hall now

mending the stockings until time to feed the chickens and Aleck
Sander down there on the Square in a flash Saturday shirt and a
pair of zoot pants and a handful of peanuts or bananas too
and he standing at the window watching the dense unhurried
unhurryable throng and the busy almost ubiquitous flash and
gleam on Willy Ingrum's cap-badge but mostly and above all the
motion and the noise, the radios and the automobiles – the
jukeboxes in the drugstore and the poolhall and the cafe and the
bellowing amplifiers on the outside walls not only of the record-
and-sheetmusic store but the army-and-navy supply store and
both feed stores and (that they might falter) somebody standing
on a bench in the courthouse yard making a speech into another
one with a muzzle like a siege gun bolted to the top of an
automobile, not to mention the ones which would be running in
the apartments and the homes where the housewives and the
maids made up the beds and swept and prepared to cook dinner
so that nowhere inside the town's uttermost ultimate corporate
rim should man woman or child citizen or guest or stranger be
threatened with one second of silence; and the automobiles
because explicitly speaking he couldn't see the Square at all: only
the dense impenetrable mass of tops and hoods moving in double-
line at a snail's crawl around the Square in a sharp invisible aura
of carbon monoxide and blatting horns and a light intermittent
clashing of bumpers, creeping slowly one by one into the streets
leading away from the Square while the other opposite line crept
as slowly one by one into it; so dense and slow dowelled into one
interlocked mosaic so infinitesimal of movement as to be scarcely
worthy of the word that you could have crossed the Square
walking on them – or even out to the edge of town for that
matter or even on a horse for that matter, Highboy for instance
to whom the five- or six-foot jump from one top across the
intervening hood to the next top would have been nothing or
say the more or less motionless tops were laid with one smooth
continuous surface of planks like a bridge and not Highboy but
a gaited horse or a horse with one gait: a hard-driving rack seven
feet in the air like a bird and travelling fast as a hawk or an eagle:
with a feeling in the pit of his stomach as if a whole bottle of hot
sodapop had exploded in it thinking of the gallant the splendid
the really magnificent noise a horse would make racking in any
direction on a loose plank bridge two miles long when suddenly
his uncle at the other window said,

'The American really loves nothing but his automobile: not his wife his child nor his country nor even his bank-account first (in fact he doesn't really love that bank-account nearly as much as foreigners like to think because he will spend almost any or all of it for almost anything provided it is valueless enough) but his motor-car. Because the automobile has become our national sex symbol. We cannot really enjoy anything unless we can go up an alley for it. Yet our whole background and raising and training forbids the sub rosa and surreptitious. So we have to divorce our wife today in order to remove from our mistress the odium of mistress in order to divorce our wife tomorrow in order to remove from our mistress and so on. As a result of which the American woman has become cold and undersexed; she has projected her libido on to the automobile not only because its glitter and gadgets and mobility pander to her vanity and incapacity (because of the dress decreed upon her by the national retailers association) to walk but because it will not maul her and tousle her, get her all sweaty and disarranged. So in order to capture and master anything at all of her anymore the American man has got to make that car his own. Which is why let him live in a rented rathole though he must he will not only own one but renew it each year in pristine virginity, lending it to no one, letting no other hand ever know the last secret forever chaste forever wanton intimacy of its pedals and levers, having nowhere to go in it himself and even if he did he would not go where scratch or blemish might deface it, spending all Sunday morning washing and polishing and waxing it because in doing that he is caressing the body of the woman who has long since now denied him her bed.'

'That's not true,' he said.

'I am fifty-plus years old,' his uncle said. 'I spent the middle fifteen of them fumbling beneath skirts. My experience was that few of them were interested in love or sex either. They wanted to be married.'

'I still dont believe it,' he said.

'That's right,' his uncle said. 'Dont. And even when you are fifty and plus, still refuse to believe it.' And that was when they saw Lucas crossing the Square, probably at that same time – the cocked hat and the thin fierce glint of the tilted gold toothpick and he said,

'Where do you suppose it was all the time? I never did see it. Surely he had it with him that afternoon, a Saturday when he was not only wearing that black suit but he even had the pistol?

Surely he never left home without the toothpick too.'

'Didn't I tell you?' his uncle said. 'That was the first thing he did when Mr Hampton walked into Skipworth's house where Skipworth had Lucas handcuffed to the bedpost – gave Hampton the toothpick and told him to keep it until he called for it.'

'Oh,' he said. 'He's coming up here.'

'Yes,' his uncle said. 'To gloat. Oh,' he said quickly, 'he's a gentleman; he wont remind me to my face that I was wrong; he's just going to ask me how much he owes me as his lawyer.'

Then in his chair beside the water cooler and his uncle once more behind the table they heard the long airy rumble and creak of the stairs then Lucas' feet steadily though with no haste and Lucas came tieless and even collarless this time except for the button but with an old-time white waistcoat not soiled so much as stained under the black coat and the worn gold loop of the watchchain – the same face which he had seen for the first time when he climbed dripping up out of the icy creek that morning four years ago, unchanged, to which nothing had happened since not even age – in the act of putting the toothpick into one of the upper waistcoat pockets as he came through the door, saying generally,

'Gentle-men,' and then to him: 'Young man –' courteous and intractable, more than bland: downright cheerful almost, removing the raked swagger of the hat: 'You aint fell in no more creeks lately, have you?'

'That's right,' he said. 'I'm saving that until you get some more ice on yours.'

'You'll be welcome without waiting for a freeze,' Lucas said.

'Have a seat, Lucas,' his uncle said but he had already begun to, taking the same hard chair beside the door which nobody else but Miss Habersham had ever chosen, a little akimbo as though he were posing for a camera, the hat laid crownup back across his forearm, looking at both of them still and saying again,

'Gentle-men.'

'You didn't come here for me to tell you what to do so I'm going to tell you anyway,' his uncle said.

Lucas blinked rapidly once. He looked at his uncle. 'I cant say I did.' Then he said cheerily: 'But I'm always ready to listen to good advice.'

'Go and see Miss Habersham,' his uncle said.

Lucas looked at his uncle. He blinked twice this time. 'I aint much of a visiting man,' he said.

'You were not much of a hanging man either,' his uncle said. 'But you dont need me to tell you how close you came.'

'No,' Lucas said. 'I dont reckon I do. What do you want me to tell her?'

'You cant,' his uncle said. 'You dont know how to say thank you. I've got that fixed too. Take her some flowers.'

'Flowers?' Lucas said. 'I aint had no flowers to speak of since Molly died.'

'And that too,' his uncle said. 'I'll telephone home. My sister'll have a bunch ready. Chick'll drive you up in my car to get them and then take you out to Miss Habersham's gate.'

'Nemmine that,' Lucas said. 'Once I got the flowers I can walk.'

'And you can throw the flowers away too,' his uncle said. 'But I know you wont do one and I dont think you'll do the other in the car with Chick.'

'Well,' Lucas said. 'If wont nothing else satisfy you –' (And when he got back to town and finally found a place three blocks away to park the car and mounted the stairs again his uncle was striking the match holding it to the pipe and speaking through with into the smoke: 'You and Booker T. Washington, no that's wrong, you and Miss Habersham and Aleck Sander and Sheriff Hampton, and Booker T. Washington because he did only what everybody expected of him so there was no real reason why he should have while you all did not only what nobody expected you to but all Jefferson and Yoknapatawpha County would have risen in active concord for once to prevent you if they had known in time and even a year from now some (when and if they do at all) will remember with disapproval and distaste not that you were ghouls not that you defied your colour because they would have passed either singly but that you violated a white grave to save a nigger so you had every reason why you should have. Just dont stop:' and he:

'You dont think that just because it's Saturday afternoon again somebody is hiding behind Miss Habersham's jasmine bush with a pistol aimed at her waiting for Lucas to walk up to the front steps. Besides Lucas didn't have his pistol today and besides that Crawford Gowrie –' and his uncle:

'Why not, what's out yonder in the ground at Caledonia Church was Crawford Gowrie for only a second or two last Saturday and Lucas Beauchamp will be carrying his pigment into ten thousand situations a wiser man would have avoided and a lighter escaped ten thousand times after what was Lucas Beauchamp for a second or so last Saturday is in the ground at his Caledonia Church too, because that Yoknapatawpha County which would have stopped you and Aleck Sander and Miss Habersham last Sunday night are right actually, Lucas' life the breathing and eating and sleeping is of no importance just as yours and mine are not but his unchallengeable right to it in peace and security and in fact this earth would be much more comfortable with a good deal fewer Beauchamps and Stevenses and Mallisons of all colours in it if there were only some painless way to efface not the clumsy room-devouring carcasses which can be done but the memory which cannot – that inevictible immortal memory awareness of having once been alive which exists forever still ten thousand years afterwards in ten thousand recollections of injustice and suffering, too many of us not because of the room we take up but because we are willing to sell liberty short at any tawdry price for the sake of what we call our own which is a constitutional statutory licence to pursue each his private postulate of happiness and contentment regardless of grief and cost even to the crucifixon of someone whose nose or pigment we dont like and even these can be coped with provided that few of others who believe that a human life is valuable simply because it has a right to keep on breathing no matter what pigment its lungs distend or nose inhales the air and are willing to defend that right at any price, it doesn't take many three were enough last Sunday night even one can be enough and with enough ones willing to be more than grieved and shamed Lucas will no longer run the risk of needing without warning to be saved:' and he:

'Maybe not three the other night. One and two halves would be nearer right:' and his uncle:

'I said it's all right to be proud. It's all right even to boast. Just dont stop.') – and came to the table and laid the hat on it and took from the inside coat pocket a leather snap-purse patina-ed like old silver and almost as big as Miss Habersham's handbag and said,

'I believe you got a little bill against me.'

'What for?' his uncle said.

'For representing my case,' Lucas said. 'Name whatever your fee is within reason. I want to pay it.'

'Not me,' his uncle said. 'I didn't do anything.'

'I sent for you,' Lucas said. 'I authorized you. How much do I owe you?'

'Nothing,' his uncle said. 'Because I didn't believe you. That boy there is the reason you're walking around today.'

Now Lucas looked at him, holding the purse in one hand and the other hand poised to unsnap it – the same face to which it was not that nothing had happened but which had simply refused to accept it; now he opened the purse. 'All right. I'll pay him.'

'And I'll have you both arrested,' his uncle said, 'you for corrupting a minor and him for practising law without a licence.'

Lucas looked back to his uncle; he watched them staring at one another. Then once more Lucas blinked twice. 'All right,' he said. 'I'll pay the expenses then. Name your expenses at anything within reason and let's get this thing settled.'

'Expenses?' his uncle said. 'Yes, I had an expense sitting here last Tuesday trying to write down all the different things you finally told me in such a way that Mr Hampton could get enough sense out of it to discharge you from the jail and so the more I tried it the worse it got and the worse it got the worse I got until when I came to again my fountain pen was sticking up on its point in the floor down here like an arrow. Of course the paper belongs to the county but the fountain pen was mine and it cost me two dollars to have a new point put in it. You owe me two dollars.'

'Two dollars?' Lucas said. He blinked twice again. Then he blinked twice again. 'Just two dollars?' Now he just blinked once, then he did something with his breath: not a sigh, simply a discharge of it, putting his first two fingers into the purse: 'That dont sound like much to me but then I'm a farming man and you're a lawing man and whether you know your business or not I reckon it aint none of my red wagon as the music box says to try to learn you different:' and drew from the purse a worn bill crumpled into a ball not much larger than a shrivelled olive and opened it enough to read it then opened it out and laid it on the desk and from the purse took a half dollar and laid it on the desk then counted on to the desk from the purse one by one four dimes and two nickels and then counted them again with his forefinger, moving them one by one about half an inch, his lips moving under the moustache, the purse still open in the other hand, then he picked up two of the dimes and a nickel and put them into the hand holding the open purse and took from the purse a quarter and put it on the desk and looked down at the coins for a rapid second then put the two dimes and the nickel back on the desk and took up the half dollar and put it back into the purse.

'That aint but six bits,' his uncle said.

'Nemmine that,' Lucas said and took up the quarter and dropped it back into the purse and closed it and watching Lucas he realized that the purse had at least two different compartments and maybe more, a second almost elbow-deep section opening beneath Lucas' fingers and for a time Lucas stood looking down into it exactly as you would look down at your reflection in a well then took from that compartment a knotted soiled cloth tobacco sack bulging and solid looking which struck on the desk top with a dull thick chink.

'That makes it out,' he said. 'Four bits in pennies. I was aiming to take them to the bank but you can save me the trip. You want to count um?'

'Yes,' his uncle said. 'But you're the one paying the money. You're the one to count them.' 'It's fifty of them,' Lucas said.

'This is business,' his uncle said. So Lucas unknotted the sack and dumped the pennies out on the desk and counted them one by one moving each one with his forefinger into the first small mass of dimes and nickels, counting aloud, then snapped the purse shut and put it back inside his coat and with the other hand shoved the whole mass of coins and the crumpled bill across the table until the desk blotter stopped them and took a bandana handkerchief from the side pocket of the coat and wiped his hands and put the handkerchief back and stood again intractable and calm and not looking at either of them now while the fixed blaring of the radios and the blatting creep of the automobile horns and all the rest of the whole County's Saturday uproar came up on the bright afternoon.

'Now what?' his uncle said. 'What are you waiting for now?'

'My receipt,' Lucas said.

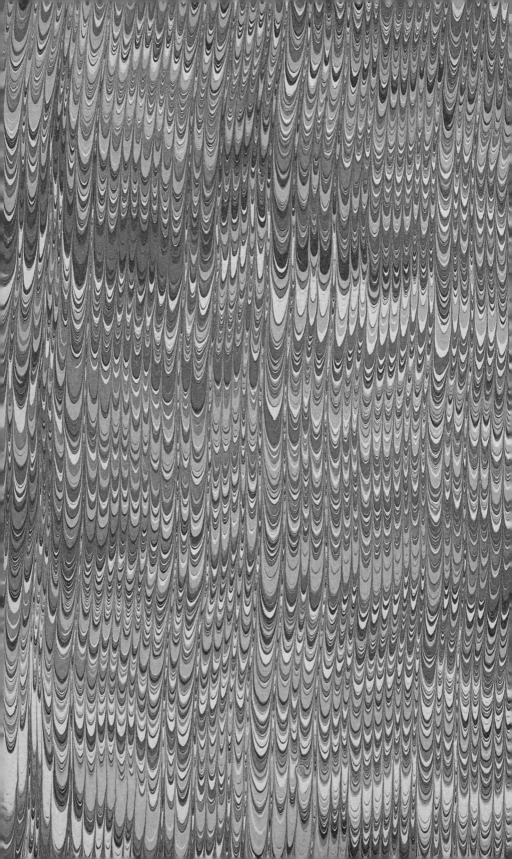